BASTET'S
LEGACY

BASTET'S LEGACY

JEMILLA MILLS-SMITH

iUniverse®

BASTET'S LEGACY

iUniverse books may be ordered through booksellers or by contacting:

iUniverse
1663 Liberty Drive
Bloomington, IN 47403
www.iuniverse.com
1-800-Authors (1-800-288-4677)

ISBN: 978-1-5320-9960-1 (sc)
ISBN: 978-1-6632-0415-8 (e)

Print information available on the last page.

iUniverse rev. date: 07/07/2020

"To all the girls with inner goddesses within them."

CHAPTER ONE

I've never been very good with authority. I wouldn't say that I'm the typical delinquent the media likes to stereotype me as, or a young adult with minimal motivation to apply themselves, or someone with little desire to contribute to society. I'm actually quite smart, if I do say so myself. I love learning new things; you could give me a book and I'd cherish it more than the newest iPhone that's out. I've been in more science fairs, spelling bees, and debate team competitions than I can count. It's no surprise but my favourite movie growing up was Akeelah and the Bee — It was the first time I saw someone like me on a screen. There isn't a book by James Baldwin or Shakespeare that I haven't read. All of my teachers in the past and present would be lying if they said I wasn't their smartest and most promising student. I've already gotten at least five promises for recommendation letters to top-level universities. I deeply consider education to be my passion. I just have never been good with authority.

We're expected to follow standardized rules and submit to authority because we're not yet the age that's allegedly good enough to make life-altering decisions. What's funny is that being 17 is only 365 days shy of the age that allows you to pay taxes, vote for representatives that have the power to effect change and, in most countries, buy alcohol. That's 365 days that we high school seniors have to prepare for adulthood, and make our own decisions. Yet, we're taught for the 4,745 days prior to do the exact opposite.

This is all a very roundabout way of explaining why I currently sit in the principal's office. My aunt Nellie is sitting beside me, looking sideways at me in a way you would only understand if you were black, and across from the very essence of authority personified: my principal.

"Jamila is an intelligent girl," says Mr. Williams, as he leans over his desk and clasps his hands; the go-to pose that aims to come off as benevolent. "She is one of the smartest students I've ever had the pleasure of knowing and her future is bright, but she has to discipline herself when working with others and respect her teachers and the faculty here."

I quickly avert my eyes, darting them around Mr. William's office. Pretty standard: framed diplomas and certificates from 'Insert Expensive Upper-Class Institution Here' hanging on the walls, several books displayed that allude to his intelligence and character, and photographs of family and notable individuals sitting on his polished-to-perfection wooden desk. Mahogany wood. The man's got class. The beige walls and interrogation-room-style lighting really captures the essence of administrative control our beloved principal prescribes to. The beige icing on the cake, his beige suit and groovy 70's tie. Seriously, this feels like an 80's teen movie. I feel like I should be skipping out on class, reacting rebelliously to my restrictive environment in a montage with some rock 'n' roll type of background music. A Breakfast Club remake — 2020 edition. All of this I've seen in his office before, but it's nice to see it again. Mr. Williams sits with a straight face, seriousness protruding from his muddy brown eyes — with crow's feet around them — which I don't think it's from smiling an awful lot.

"What exactly did she do this time?" asks my aunt, who is currently stewing with anger in her baby-blue scrubs and dad shoes. Her low bun is pulled back, rebellious strands escaping from their elastic confines, to frame a face that's concealing anger with rapt attention. This isn't the first time she's had to leave work to pick me up from school because of my behaviour.

Mr. Williams responds to Aunt Nellie, saying, "She called her history teacher an imbecile."

Aunt Nellie gives me the side-eye, immediately cutting her eye back towards Mr. Williams so he can continue. Now to the naked eye, you wouldn't assume much of this gesture but I know that means my ass is in trouble.

"Her teacher was discussing American society resulting from the end of slavery, and Jamila countered her lecture in a way that Ms. Boykin described as 'insulting and demeaning'," Mr. Williams continues. I roll my eyes. This was a passive-aggressive way of saying Ms. Boykin was offended that I argued against her in front of everyone.

"Why are we expected to raise our hands when we have a question, even when asking permission to use the bathroom?" I ask. "I find that incredibly humiliating, as if being a teenager isn't humiliating enough."

Aunt Nellie kicks my shin underneath the table, effectively shutting me up. It's not my fault Ms. Boykin can't handle a little educational debate. And it sure as hell ain't my fault that everybody laughed. I can't help the fact that I'm comedic gold.

Aunt Nellie goes in the best code-switching only she can master, "I apologize for my niece's behaviour, Mr. Williams. I've raised her to be a more respectful young woman, and I will definitely have a discussion with her about this." Mr. Williams looks content with this information. For now.

"As for you," Nellie continues, "I suggest employing staff that is knowledgeable about the curriculum they are teaching their students, *from every possible perspective.* For too long students have been getting a tunnel-vision view of history, and it's because of this that so few respectable educators, such as yourself, exist anymore. I understand that there's a difference in the motivations behind public schools compared to privatized, Catholic schools —"

"Mrs. Freeman," Mr. Williams interrupts.

"It's Ms., actually," Aunt Nellie says.

"Forgive me. Ms. Freeman, I assure you, that has nothing to do with the quality of the education given here. Public schools offer the same level of education to all of its students, just as Catholic schools do." Authoritative forms can be so hypocritical in nature, negating the entire purpose of this so-called path we're supposed to follow in life. This is where my undesire to submit to authority comes from.

"I should hope so, but after this recent incident, I'm starting to believe otherwise. After all, you wouldn't want your students walking away with a biased view of history, would you?"

Mr. William's expression drops, to what I can only assume is the visual representation of being stuck between a rock and a hard place. Nellie is kind of an expert in giving subtle back-handed compliments, and thank God it's for my benefit... this time. He quickly collects himself though. I gotta give props to him for that. Nellie's kind of a force to be reckoned with.

"Under no circumstances, ma'am. I will definitely discuss this with our staff. We pride ourselves on transparency, diversity and inclusion at Brimmer Hall High School. I will ensure that we continue to employ this value in our teaching."

"Thank you," responds Nellie. With that, she stands to shake his hand

and that is our cue to leave. We leave the principal's office, nodding to the secretary in farewell, and exit to the sound of phones ringing and staplers stapling. I briefly catch the tail-end of a conversation a student has with the reception, excusing himself for why he was watching porn in class. She doesn't look amused. As we walk down the school hallways that reeks of B.O., Victoria Secret perfume and Axe Body Spray, our shoes squeaking along the polished floors, Nellie and I walk in silence with the classes in progress. We open the main entrance doors and walk towards her beat-up '07 Buick parked at the curb. She comes around to my side to do the trick, the trick that actually gets the passenger's door open. She grabs the door handle, slams her hip into the door and pulls. Voila! Entrance to the blue beat-up chariot. We get in the car and Nellie takes a long deep sigh as if the weight of the world was on her shoulders. I mean it kind of is, having to deal with me. Raising me and my temperament, while being a full-time nurse isn't exactly the easiest undertaking. Nellie asks, "What exactly was it that Ms. Boykin said that sets you off?"

I take a deep breath and respond, "She said that after the end of slavery, enslaved African Americans were able to migrate to other cities and states, allowing them more freedom to create the culture that has influenced our society today."

"And what exactly was wrong with that?"

"Nothing, except that she totally disregarded Juneteenth, the day that slaves in the South were actually freed from enslavement. She made it seem like the decades of fighting for freedom and equality were seamless. And it was totally an American point-of-view. From the Canadian perspective it's a little different, and that gets written out of history so easily. I *politely* told her that, and further explained the oppression black people still had to face, the stigma placed around black culture she was alluding to and how it was further enforced. I even gave other examples of ways African Americans were placed in a different type of slavery. It was a discussion, not an argument. A dialogue about what we were talking about. Nothing more."

"Okay, but did you even let her finish?"

"I was going to, but then she started talking about all the degrees she earned that made her knowledgeable, allowing her to teach us in a compacted way so that students *like us* could understand or whatever."

"And that's when you called her an imbecile?"

"Not exactly." Nellie looks at me inquisitively as I continue, "I said only an imbecile would let her graduate thinking black people and the rest of the world were all *kumbaya*, and teach that nonsense to kids."

"Say word?"

"Deadass," I respond with a straight face. That gets Nellie laughing, her booming voice breaking through her throat. She reaches down to start the car, which always takes a few tries but eventually gets goin'.

"C'mon Tiffany Haddish, let's get some food," Nellie says, as the car finally purrs to life and we drive out of Brimmer Hall's parking lot.

I love Nellie's laugh. She's got this deep belly laugh. The kind that comes from deep in your gut and fills the room, which is surprising because she's such a tiny woman. If you ever hear it, you're blessed. Just hearing her laugh will make you smile, and Nellie isn't the type to throw you a pity laugh when your joke doesn't land. If she laughs, she LAUGHS. And I can always get her to laugh — maybe it's trying to get her to smile on days when life is a little harder to deal with, but I've mastered the art of cracking that smile. Sometimes just from acting a fool, even if she's laughing at my expense, I'm happy she's happy.

We continue to laugh at my stupid ass in Loni's Diner, a 24-hour Jamaican spot down the way from our house. Nellie and I have been coming here for as long as I can remember, and for every occasion. Whether it be me getting an A+ on a test or Nellie losing a patient at work that day. Loni's food just makes you feel good — the true epitome of soul food. Loni herself still works here, making food, throwing us a *'how you doin' baby girl?'* to check up on us, and running the place by herself for the past 40 years. She's the type of woman that kids like me can look up to when we second guess ourselves. Loni immigrated when she was not much older than me, starting from literally nothing, she bought this diner and made it a place for people around here to come for good food and community. She defied the odds that people put in place against her. They told her to *'put her money where her mouth is'* and she said *'I'd rather put my food there, 'cause Lord knows the money will follow.'* She always tells that story just like that whenever she's got us cornered. But to be honest, I don't mind hearing it over and over again. That may sound all sappy and stuff, the typical pull-yourself-up-by-your-bootstraps kind of immigrant story, but it's true. Loni is a real role model and the closest thing to family I could get without actually sharing blood.

I love Loni and her food, but I also love this diner. It's got that classic old-school vibe with the fluorescent lights, baby pink seats that your butt sinks into like memory foam, and the old jukebox that only plays music from before the 2000's. Thank God for that, because if it weren't for that jukebox I wouldn't know what quality music sounds like. The pink-orange-green walls hold framed pictures of famous people that have eaten here, her family that is doing big things and those who have passed away, old music memorabilia, and the first picture of young-Loni in front of her newly purchased diner. As far as Jamaican food places go, Loni really invested in the design part. Most places keep the same beige walls and boring tile, not even bothering to add more than a few chairs and tables. But usually the worse the design of the spot, the better the food tastes. Loni's diner is an exception, with her food mirroring the deliciousness of the decor. With the lingering smell of chicken and plantain that never quite goes away and the chatter of the neighbourhood, mixed with Bob Marley playing in the background telling me *everything's gonna be alright*, I feel more at home than ever.

Loni walks through the swinging doors wearing navy Capri jeans, a maroon t-shirt and orthopedic shoes. She throws Ray, one of her best employees, a quick nod and makes her way over to us with a fresh plate of cornbread with honey drizzled on top and cassava pudding on the side. Just the way I like it.

"Oh Loni we didn't order these," I say. "You don't have to keep making these for us all the time."

"Oh hush likkle girl," Ms. Loni responds in her Jamaican accent, continuing, "it's on the house." That's another thing I love about Loni, I don't even have to ask her to know she's gonna make my favourite for me, and she does it out of the kindness of her heart. That's just how she is.

Ms. Loni puts the plate on our table, putting her hand on my head in that doting-aunty type of way, and says "I made it just the way you like it, all soft and sticky on the inside. And the honey's fresh, and sweet just like you."

I smile back at her and kiss her on the cheek to give her thanks, even though nothing I do could ever show the gratitude I have for her affection. Nellie smiles at her too, but Loni sees right through her. You see, Loni has this way of getting to the issue that's irking you, even if you yourself didn't know there was something wrong. I remember one time I saw a drive-by shooting and I didn't even have to say anything, yet Loni knew that I had seen something traumatic. She knew just how to console me. Of course, honey-drizzled cornbread was a key factor but a long talk that explained to me why it happened and to be safe when these things happen again, because they will. And if it weren't for her, I, along with everyone else around here, wouldn't know how to live so happily. So even though now Nellie is smiling, Loni could see how tired she was.

"Oh baby," Ms. Loni says to Nellie, "why you gotta break your back like that every day? Workin' all'a dem double shifts ain't healthy for you baby. I can see the bags unda yuh eyes, you're dead tired. You got yuh self workin' like a donkey just to make ends meet, it's gonna kill you Nel. You gotta get some rest!"

"Ms. Loni I know that, but I gotta pay the bills. You know it's just me and J, and the money she makes at that little summer job ain't nothin' but groceries and savings for college." Loni looks at her sternly, in that one look delivering *"you know damn well that ain't no type of excuse,"* and Nellie looking back at her with exhaustion that replies *"that's just life I guess."* Loni abruptly turns on her toes and looks to me, turning on me in a way I wasn't expecting.

"And you. I know you and your moody ass ain't helpin' her either. I heard y'all talkin' about what happened at school today when you walked in." Loni leans over and smacks me upside the head hard before continuing in Patois, "Jamila Freeman, you ain't doin' nobody nuh favours by bein' a smart ass! Me nuh care 'bout your prissy teacha and whateva complex she ah aave, you respec' yuh teacher and all yuh elders. When yuh gaan from that school, she's still gonna be there teachin' other pickney, so talkin' back to her will only affect yuh."

I rub my head where she walloped me and respond, "I know I shouldn't have been rude like that alright, I know that. I promise I'll apologize to her tomorrow; but I swear, sometimes my teachers don't bother to think out of the box and teach us a little more than what the textbook says. What they teach us in class is so whitewashed. Honestly, I'm offended that the school board thinks that this excuse of a curriculum is gonna prepare us for the real world." Loni and Nellie look to each other and then at me with a wary gaze, knowing that I'm just getting started, preparing themselves for my lengthy monologue.

"Even S.T.E.M.," I continue. "I'm light years ahead of what I'm actually supposed to be learning in class."

"Whatcha call dat? What's S.T.E.M dem?"

"It's an acronym," I respond to Loni. "It stands for science, technology, engineering and mathematics." Loni nods her head in understanding before I continue.

"I don't act like a kiss-ass and show off my grades to the other kids in my class or anything, I'm not a jerk like that. But sometimes I think this is just a waste of my time."

Loni leans one hand on the table and her other hand on her hip and cocks it to the side, her go-to pose that comes with her sage advice. "School isn't just to teach you what's in the textbook, my girl. It's meant to teach yuh discipline, how to work with others, how to see things differently even if you don't agree or if you think it's wrong. Even if you think it's a waste of yuh time, it's teaching you stuff that you could neva learn without bein' around others. Silver an' gold may vanish away, but a good education will never decay."

I chuckle as I add another Jamaican proverb into my personal dictionary. Nellie smiles at Loni, I imagine also in appreciation of Loni and her maternal instinct, and places a peck on her hand. Loni smiles coyly and waves Nellie away, finicking with our plate and making it look pretty to hide her embarrassment from our loving attention.

Loni looks to me and throws me a wink before saying, "Stay sweet my girl." Nellie and I move to finish our meal as Loni pats my hand and walks to another table to see what's goin' on. The chatter gets louder as more people walk in the door, filling up the diner and bringing more life with conversations and laughter that mix with the jukebox playing in the background.

As we drive home, the itis kicks in real quick and I start to get drowsy from the late September heat. As I lean my head against the window, my eyes lazily scan the North York landscape. Dusk makes an entrance, deepening the bright sky from a bright yellow to a golden sunset. The radio plays in the background, playing Poetic Justice by Kendrick Lamar and Drake — one of my favourites — as we drive home. As we drive further from the safe haven of the diner, I see men on the street corner throwing dice on the ground. Some of them egging their boys on, and others bopping to the rap music playing from an Escalade. The music is so loud I can hear DaBaby from here. Apartment buildings, within walking distance from each other, share not only their location but also their resemblance. It holds people on its balconies, barely holding onto its skin as the outer surfaces peel from degradation. Apartment buildings turn into houses as we drive further down the road. There are houses in every shade of brown you could dream of, stacked close together like Lego. If you jumped from one rooftop to the other, I'm sure it wouldn't be any more than a quick step. There are women and their men chattering on their front porches, laughing, fighting, flirting, the usual. There are aunties and uncles, cousins and friends, relaying the events of their days, and gossiping without a care in the world. There are children playing double dutch and playground games on the sidewalk, and other kids scrolling on their phones and illuminating their faces with a fluorescent glow. That scene begins to change from domestic homes to businesses and stores as people let out the last of their customers, closing up shop as the workday comes to an end. I see the local barber Mr. James drawing the metal gate down on the shop while Mrs. James, his wife who runs the beauty salon attached next door, closes the shutters. While doing so, she waves to Reggie Min across the street, who's letting his last customer out before he closes Min's Convenience Store. Reggie's been working in his dad's shop since he got out of prison, so his dad can keep an eye on him and 'make an example' of him to his younger brothers. I don't think he's complaining though. All the girls 'round here drop in just to flirt with him, and he's not exactly resistant to the attention. Can't blame them though, he is fine as hell. If I had the time on my hands, I'd make a fool out of myself too with just a crack of a smile from him thrown my way. As we turn right on Jane Street, I see Ms. Dell swinging on her porch swing. Wearing a cotton nightgown and baby-pink rollers in her hair, her flip flops exposing her less-than-appealing toes, she nurses a glass of sorrel. A delicious, gingery red drink. She waves to our passing car and we pull into our driveway right next door. Her full name is Claudelle, but we call her Dell for short. All I want is my bed, but that means I'd have to get up. And this seat is feeling real comfortable right now.

"C'mon lazy, get up," Nellie says, reading my mind. I groan as I dramatically open the door, roll out of the car and thump up the steps to open the front door.

As we do, Ms. Dell yells from her porch, "Hey J! Hey Nellie, how you doin' down at Toronto General?"

"Oh, you know how it is Ms. Dell. Too many patients, not enough nurses, but we fightin' for shifts anyhow."

"I know that's right," Ms. Dell sympathizes, as she fans herself lazily. And she really does; Ms. Dell retired about a decade ago. But before that, she was one of the most respected nurses at Toronto General. She ran her ward like a general, and in the time she worked there, she cared for her patients like they were her family. Even though she's retired, she's never lost that caring demeanour, and she always wants to know the latest news on the block. It could be argued that she's more inquisitive than caring, but when it comes to Ms. Dell, you can't really separate the two.

We walk into the house, taking off our shoes and kicking them off by the door. We slide on our slippers before I make a beeline for the bathroom but Nellie and her damn high-school-track-legs beat me to it. She turns, looks at me and laughs demonically before slamming the door, and I groan in frustration. Now I'm gonna have to wait 20 minutes because she likes to take long-ass showers to 'oil her joints,' leaving me to get our lunches ready for the next day and wash the dishes from this morning. That's how it goes, one of the many routines we have to keep things going around here. Should I prepare tomorrow's lunch before I get to the shower? With Nel already in the shower, I have no choice.

As I walk through the living room into the kitchen, the beige carpet underneath my feet is hugging each toe as I take each step. I turn on the dim light and the ceiling fan that barely fulfills its purpose, springs into action. I walk to the sink and start washing the dishes, scraping the caked-on eggs from that morning off the pan and placing the freshly washed dishes in the dish drainer lying on the countertop. The white fridge that acts as an impromptu photo album, with pictures from my childhood and adolescence scattered all over, hums in the background. I open it to get our lunches ready for the next day. As I pull out everything needed to make a decent sandwich, a fly lazily moves along the floral curtain covering the tiny little window above the sink. It eventually moves to the screen door that opens to the little alley between ours and Ms. Dell's house. The humidity in the air settles to a point that it's almost as if I can smell it. The thickness of heat in the air settling into my skin and creating warning pinpricks of sweat in my armpits. I hear something rattling outside. Michael is probably emptying the trash.

Michael and I have been best friends from way back in the diaper days. We used to take baths together when we were toddlers, lost our baby teeth at the same time, had more sleepovers than I can remember, and have been sitting on the same cafeteria bench every day and clownin' on damn near everybody who walks by. He's the person I go to for everything and he has been my rock through the good times and the bad. I walk to the side door, watching him struggle to drag the trash bags in his hand. It's too good to resist. I mean, I'd be doing a disservice if I didn't take advantage of this moment.

I deepen my voice and yell, in my best impressions of Ms. Dell that I can muster, "Michael Jermaine Smith!" He quickly looks up and trips over the trash can, all the trash bags scattering everywhere. Priceless.

I bend over in laughter, hollering at the ease with which I can make him jump. He looks up and realizes it's me, his expression changing from fearful anticipation to annoyance.

"You a damn pain in my ass, you know that J? Why you gotta do me like that?"

"It's just too easy," I respond joyfully. I open the door and step out to help him pick up the bags as he collects himself. I may be a clown but I'm not a complete asshole.

"So what's your sentence?" I chuckle, assuming he's referring to my punishment for my less-than-admirable classroom behaviour.

"Nellie turned it back on him, I walked away scot-free," I respond.

"For real?" asks Michael.

"Yeah. She went all Becky on him and turned it around so I was the victim," I joke. Michael and I laugh as we each lean on our door frames. Michael's mawga frame, stretched out by his recent growth spurt, holds up his freshly-shaved head. His shoulders poke through his grey t-shirt as his hands rest in his front pockets. The porch light reflects off his dark skin, and bounce off the whites of his eyes. His smirking smile, stretched along his face to light up all of his features, causes me to smile in response.

Michael shakes his head, "You're always gettin' yourself in trouble J. Why you gotta be such a smart ass all the time?" Damn, if any more people keep saying I'm a smart ass, I might just start to believe them.

"You get yourself in any more trouble, and they ain't gonna care about your grades no more. Yo' ass is gonna end up expelled and strugglin' like Tahlia and them." He's referring to our peers who, like me, think school is a waste of time and who, unlike me, didn't think learning was important when they could just live off their sugar daddies.

"Why don't you stop worrying about me and mind your business? You know I'm not gonna do anything crazy."

"Yeah," he says, continuing with a small smile, "you're too much of a keener."

I look at him and kiss my teeth, but his goofy smile gets us both laughing again. We walk into my house, me resuming my post at the counter to pack our lunches and Michael opening the fridge to see what's good. He's been in this house so many times, it would be weird if he didn't make himself at home.

"You down to go to Loni's on free period tomorrow?" he asks, as he bends down to grab a Malt.

I respond, "I'm already making our lunches, maybe after though. We ridin' to school then?"

Michael nods in confirmation. That means we're gonna have to go past Blanco's boys, who always make a game of trying to steal our bikes. The guys who were throwing dice on the street corner earlier seem to always be there; sippin' Lean and Hennesy, catcalling at passing girls and ganging up on boys to show off their manpower. They always look like they're goofing off, yet they're the most feared gang around here, known for getting stuff done when it needs to be done.

Nellie walks in freshly showered, in her oversized University of Toronto t-shirt and baggy grey sweats. She sees Michael and without saying anything, bear-hugs him from behind and starts rocking him side to side. She knows he hates that.

"Oh, my baby!" Nellie exclaims, in an exaggerated way to really tick him off, "it's been so long! How's my Lil' Dumplin' doin'?"

Michael struggles to get out of her grip, groaning in indignation and looking ticked off. Not only is she hugging and kissing on him like a kid, but she's calling him by his childhood nickname: Lil' Dumplin'. What he hates even more is to be reminded of his chubby childhood frame, which funnily enough, happened because of his love for fried dumplings. The fact that he's so thin now is because his growth spurt came with a metabolism that sheds the fat like crazy. By the time summer was over, he had to get rid of all of his clothes because they were too big. But he kept eating dumplings like it was going out of style.

Nellie sees me snickering and says, "Oh, you think that's funny Jemima?"

I immediately stop laughing. I too am a victim of embarrassing childhood nicknames. All it took was for my gym teacher to call me Jemima. He said it was funny because it sounded like Jamila! Well it stuck. A little too well. Like maple syrup on pancakes. Ha.

"How's school?" Nellie asks Michael.

"It's aight," he responds. "My bio teacher's been bustin' my ass..." Nellie looks at him with a raised eyebrow. Michael quickly corrects himself, "Sorry, he's been on me about this project. We gotta find a natural remedy to an illness involving an organ he gave each of us, and the matching medicine that we'd use in the modern day. I don't know how I'm supposed to look up everything about a herb, or whatever, and then go look up a modern medicinal alternative. I'm not in A.P. Bio, it's just not my thing. Now if you give me a calculator, I could run laps around everybody."

Michael's insanely good at math. He's good at basically any subject that involves numbers, really. His dad was an accountant and his mother a physician, highly respected in our community, and the apple of Michael's and Ms. Dell's eyes. Before they passed away and Michael was raised by Ms. Dell, they had Michael doing college-level calculations by the age of eight. While my nose was stuck in a book, Michael was standing in front of a chalkboard, solving mathematical equations that I just started learning in senior year. I'm good with numbers too, don't get me wrong, but I couldn't hold a candle to him. It seems fated that the two biggest nerds in school just so happen to live next door to each other.

"Why don't you ask J for help," Nellie suggests to Michael. "She's got so many books about medicine and ancient medicinal remedies, I'm sure you'll ace that paper. Her momma..."

Nellie trails off and looks at me, knowing this is a touchy subject. My mother passed away shortly after Michael's parents died. Michael's parents died in a car crash. A drunk driver ran a red light, and Michael's parents met their untimely demise due to his idiocy. Michael's never been behind the wheel of any vehicle because of that and has been biking to school ever since. The only way he'll get in a car is if someone is driving him, allowing him the opportunity to become the perfect backseat driver. But even then, he's gripping his pants in anxious anticipation of something happening to him. His parents' death really hit him hard. The way he's handled it and how he still remains the sweetest, funniest and the most respectful guy I know, is admirable and honourable. I, on the other hand, completely shut down.

My mother and I were so inextricably linked that people used to call me 'Lil' Keba' because we were so similar, even from when I was a child. We had the same favourite foods, the same facial expressions, the same temperament, and the same love for history. She loved to use natural medicines, salves, oils and herbs for everything from a sore throat to detangling our hair. She was pretty earthy, but she still loved the modern world for all its new inventions and social changes. It's because of her that my love for history, technology and science is so strong, and why I love to learn. She always loved it when she caught me reading a book. For every book I read, she'd get me a milkshake at Loni's. Needless to say, I was a pretty chubby kid too.

My mother passed from an appendectomy gone wrong. Turns out she had a rare allergy to the anesthesia that was used and suffered from anaphylaxis during surgery. The whole thing was supposed to be a routine surgery. The surgeon caught the inflammation just in time and scheduled the surgery later that day. Mom had been feeling like something was going to happen for a week, and took digestive medicines to combat it. I don't know how she knew it was around her stomach area, but she knew. The day her actual appendix was inflamed, she knew that she had to get herself checked out. The doctor assured us he had done that type of surgery numerous times, and the incidence rate was very low, but my mother had a bad feeling about it. I learned to trust my mother's gut feeling from an early age. Her usually being right when such a feeling came on so strongly and she was so incredibly adamant about it that it worried Aunt Nellie and I. Especially since she knew that something was going to affect her physically for the past week before it actually happened. But I was at the age where I was taught to respect authority, and Nellie herself being a nurse in that hospital, trusted this doctor. So I sided with the surgeon because he assured us that everything would run smoothly, even though deep down I wanted to agree with my mother. I should have agreed with my mother. Maybe she'd still be here.

I continue for Nellie, swallowing the lump forming in my throat, "My mom loved this stuff, and has about as many books about it as the public library probably has. She left so many notes jotted in the margins, you'll have everything you'll need. Don't worry, I got you."

Michael smiles at me, knowing that it's tough for me to even talk about this. He walks over to me and places his hand on my head. Smiling, I do the same; our little version of a best friend handshake.

"You're gonna get an A on that assignment," I say, jokingly, "and every time you look at it, just remember it was my ass that helped you get it."

Michael kisses his teeth and pushes my head away, Nellie chuckles and walks over to the counter.

"Go on J, take a shower. I'll finish up. Michael baby, you want me to fix your lunch for you too?"

As Michael responds, him and Nellie settling into their own natural conversation, I head to the bathroom for my shower that's long overdue. I close the door and lean against it, looking at the bathroom in bliss. It's weird to love a bathroom, but I really love ours. Mom and Nellie both loved gardening and plants, so our house is scattered with foliage. Outside in our tiny little backyard is our garden, and here on randomly-placed shelves and from the ceiling hang potted Cacti, Spider Plants, Aloe Vera, Golden Pothos, and English Ivy. They all bloom and swing aimlessly, flourishing underneath the steam from Nellie's shower and the last rays of sunlight that stream from the tiny skylight in the ceiling. That's just a fancy way of saying there's a huge hole in the ceiling that we put glass in to make into a window. As the sun begins to set more and more, the room turns a pinky-orange, slicing through the thin white shower curtain and bouncing off the black and white checkered tile. Refracting off the water droplets that weigh down the leaves of the plants and shining into the mirror that I move towards. As I strip off my clothes, I stare into the mirror and assess the person that stands before me. Skin that's a cross between dark chocolate and coffee, shiny from the humidity in the air. A nose that's not too big, but big enough that I don't meet Instagram Baddies status. Plump lips with a heart shape. Kinky curly hair pulled into a bun to keep out of the way of my almond-shaped eyes, and eyebrows that, by their own volition, form into perfect arches that question everything. I rub my head where Michael's hand was, smiling to myself.

When I lost my mother, I went through a phase of not speaking. Not to Nellie, not to Michael, not to anyone. Her death hit me hard; but after the initial feeling of sadness, anger, confusion, and loss, I just felt empty. I couldn't fathom speaking when she no longer could, or of joking around because she wouldn't be here to hear it and laugh. So, I stopped talking because I felt like there was nothing important to say anymore. After a while I started to look in the mirror and hate what I saw; not because of the teasing in school, although there was plenty of that. But because I didn't see her hazel eyes, her slim nose, her caramel skin. My skin was darker, my hair kinkier, my body thicker. No matter how many voices directed to your ears offer loving affirmation of your beauty, the lack of voices can speak louder. The lack of seeing people that looked like me that were seen as beautiful, whether it be on my block, in books, or in the movies, were weighted with more importance than the opinions of those who knew my inner and outer self. I may have been Lil' Keba, but I didn't see any of her in me at that moment. She always told me how beautiful I was so there was always the affirmation of beauty, but I just wanted to be like my mom. I wanted to see her in me and I became so sad when I didn't see what I wanted, but I couldn't find the words to explain how I felt.

Until one day I went to the barbershop with Michael. Ms. Dell was taking him to get a fresh cut that day, and she thought getting me out of the house and around other people would be good for me. Silent as ever, I sat and watched as Michael sat in the barber's chair, and listened to the chatter around me. Men talking about their women, about getting pulled over yet again for a minor infraction, and countless other topics I soon tuned out. I turned my attention to the shop, with its evergreen walls enclosing us within a man-made jungle of fabricated foliage. Too-bright ceiling lights swinging overhead and a wood floor littered with woolly hair. Five barber stations — with Mr. James, Darnell Nichols, Big Tony, Junior Millwood, and Otto Smith standing at their posts — held mirrors with pictures of their families, hair products and supplies lying underneath. The lingering scent of shea butter and razor-bump cream permeated the air, and the radio blasted the latest song from an artist I can't recall. I was just about to zone out, but then Mr. James started talking, and his voice is the type that commands attention.

"You got to come here more often, boy. You don't take care of your hair right, people are gonna start to think less of you."

"It's just hair, Mr. James, it's not a big deal," fetus-Michael replied.

"Bite your tongue boy," scolded Mr. James, as his razor-wielding comrades shook their heads. "When you're black, your appearance matters twice as much as it does to anyone else. You wear clothes too baggy, walk too ghetto, talk in a way that makes you sound uneducated, they gon' call you a thug."

"What does that mean?" asked Michael.

"It's a word that's meant to make you feel bad for who you are. It makes black boys feel like they're bad compared to others 'cause they look a certain way. You can't let them have the one up on you, so you gotta give them less of a reason to pick on you."

"And I can do that through my hair?" asked Michael, as he looked at Mr. James through the mirror.

Mr. James looked back, and said, "Yes, boy. Your hair is important. It ties you to your ancestors, and it's the one thing that nobody else in the world got 'cept for your black brothers and sisters. There was a time when we didn't even have the choice to maintain our hair. Now that we have that right back, we got to make sure that we do it in the best way possible, to represent the best version of ourselves. That's the only way you gon' make it in this world boy; and a fresh cut, a new start, gets rid of all the bad that you went through and let you start anew. Best believe that."

As Mr. James bent Michael's head down, continuing his work, I thought about what he had just said. More than anything, I wanted to get rid of the sadness I felt, and feel like I could do better, be better, and start life over. I didn't know how I could do that, but at that moment I was looking for anything that could achieve that for me. And I thought I had just found it.

I walked over to Mr. James and asked, "Could you do me next?"

Mr. James, Michael, and Ms. Dell looked at me shell-shocked. Ms. Dell's mouth was wide open, Michael's eyes were as big as saucers, and Mr. Jame's eyebrows were raised so high I'm sure they would have flown off his forehead.

"You want me to shave your head, baby girl?" asked Mr. James in surprise. I simply nodded my head.

Mr. James looked at Ms. Dell for confirmation, eyes wide with not knowing what to do. I then looked at Ms. Dell, stance wide and with a firm look on my face. This is what I always did to get what I wanted, a foolproof move on my part. Ms. Dell could never resist that look, always saying that I looked like my momma reincarnated when I acted like that. She looked at me and immediately softened, nodding to Mr. James and giving him permission.

"Go ahead, Mark."

When it was finally my turn in the chair, my head bent down, I clearly remember seeing my hair falling to the floor and a scratchy feeling on the back of my head. I don't remember feeling like a weight was lifted off my shoulders, or anything like that, but when I looked in the mirror and saw my newly shaved head, I remember feeling lighter. When I turned around, Michael was looking at me with an expressionless face, something that's usually incapable of a nine-year-old.

Then suddenly, he walked over to me and placed his hand on my head. He rubbed it slowly and said, "Now you look like me, so we'll be better than best friends. We'll be family, starting a new life together."

I smiled, happy because I finally felt heard without having to say anything at all. I placed my hand on his head and there birthed the best friend handshake of our own making. We laughed at the goofiness of it all, as Mr. James and Ms. Dell chuckled at our childhood humour. I remember so distinctly never feeling closer to Michael, and ever since then, we've been tighter than Ms. Dell's weave.

I also remember the ass whooping I received when I got home. Nel wasn't exactly expecting to see a bald-headed version of her niece when she got home, and she let me hear it for a long time after that.

I rub my head and smile in the mirror, reminiscing about that memory and how I was changed after that. I remember how after that day I started talking more. Gradually, but eventually, I carried the conversation. Even threw in a couple of jokes that were partially humorous. I hop into the shower and turn the hot water on. I stand underneath the shower head as the hot water beats onto my face, burning away the events from today and washing my emotions down the drain. I hear the alley-door slam close, muffled underneath the water streaming around my ears, signaling that Michael's left to go home. After thoroughly scrubbing and cleaning, I walk freshly showered and toweled to my room.

In my own little island, the yellow-painted walls deepen into mustard as the sun sets its last gaze through my window. Setting more, the sun shines onto my twin-sized bed, the green duvet beckoning me to fall into its embrace and go to sleep. As I walk to my dresser I dart around the Novelfall. The one iconic part of my room is the numerous novels hanging from the ceiling from satin ribbons. My room is so small there wasn't any space for a bookshelf, but I kept racking up books and they had to be put somewhere. My mother's solution was a novel waterfall — a Novelfall she called it — that would allow me to *'take a walk through the works of the greatest literary artists of all time.'* Her ability to romanticize practically everything was astounding. But secretly, I do the same.

I dart around Ta-Nehisi Coates, J.K. Rowling, James Baldwin, and Stephen King to grab my pyjamas and then collapse onto my bed, scrolling through the electronic rectangle that ties me to civilization from the comfort of my own room. I scroll through my phone until I pull up the app I'm looking for. Another classmate posting a skin-revealing photo to exercise their feminist sexual freedom, ironically captioning it to allude to their superiority to other 'bitches.' Another guy from down the block postin' up in front of a Lambo, claiming that it's 'God's plan.' Everybody knows he still drives that '09 Honda Civic, but hey, who am I to out him. Scroll, scroll, scroll. Double tap, double tap, scroll, double tap. Is that an ad? It is, but it looks so natural it got me for a second. I switch to another app, scrolling through the hilarity of Black Twitter that manages to make me laugh every time. After a few minutes, I plug my phone into the charger and resolve to go to sleep. Unfortunately, my mind has other plans.

I go over the events of today, going back to the start of the whole incident and question my behaviour. Did I come off a little too strong? Was I too harsh? Should I have just let it slide? I have to be careful about these things. The last thing I need is to be labelled the angry black woman. That's a stereotype I'd prefer not to have attributed to me, along with many others. One stereotype can make or break the way people treat you, and the consequences of those actions. I wish my mom was here. She would know what to do. After I said what I said, the other kids in the class chuckled. Farah Muhammad whooped in jest, Lena Ramos exclaimed a "Damn!" underneath her hand, and Ms. Boykin just stood there, motionless in front of the class. Her face showed that she was clearly embarrassed, and taken aback by my comeback. And, despite her faults in the situation, I know that no one deserves that kind of humiliation from a bunch of kids. It wasn't right of me to ridicule her like that in front of the entire class — I should've had a conversation with her in private at least. It may not be the accountability Nellie was hoping for but hey, it's leaps and bounds compared to what I was feeling earlier.

Is my alarm set for 7:00 a.m.? I check my phone, pulling up the Clock app. Yes, it is. I have to make sure Nel is up at seven too or else she'll be late for work. I'll get all my school stuff ready tomorrow after I shower; I gotta remember my keys, I don't want to get locked out again. Dozens of thoughts continue to run concomitantly through my brain, racing with anticipation for the next day, while my body slowly sags into the mattress begging for sleep. I look at the clock. 10:45. I really have to fall asleep soon if I want to get enough sleep. It's so weird, falling asleep. You don't remember drifting off and you don't remember the last thought you had, no matter how hard you try. I wonder if I keep thinking the same thing I'll remember it the next morning. Keep thinking about the same thing. Keep thinking about the same —.

Leaves brush my face as I bolt by. Branches and rocks scratch my skin as I sprint. Twigs poke at my eyes as I run. I keep running, towards something that must be better than where I've been, or why else would I be running? All I see are lush green leaves that fly past me; all I hear are my feet slapping against the ground and the skin on the soles of my feet breaking as the rocky terrain rips through my epidermis. All I feel is fear. I'm scared. I'm scared. *I don't know where I am.*

"Hello?" I call out. Birds caw back to mock my call.

"HELLO?" I scream, with urgency. Silence answers my inquiry.

Where am I? I have to know. I need to know that I'm safer than where I've been. Where have I been? I can't remember. Why can't I remember?

I break through the thick foliage and enter an open space, where the leaves and trees have not encumbered the ground, allowing me room to check my surroundings. All I can see is green, and wildlife, and the unbeaten path. All I hear is my ragged breath as it tries to catch itself. All I feel is more fear.

I close my eyes, trying to slow my breathing and settle into my body. This is just a dream. I know this is just a dream. I've been through this before. I've dreamed this dream before. I know what to do. All I need to do is wake up and I'll be safe. Just wake up. Just — I open my eyes. Not to the safe scenery of my bedroom, but to the same lush landscape, rocky terrain, and silent night.

And a black cat. Staring right at me.

It's blacker than the night, its fur shiny and thick. Its eyes shine — brighter than gold. Its nose glistens, pinker than the flowers that surround us. It sits on its haunches, facing me, calmly wagging its tail back and forth. It continues to stare, as if in anticipation. I feel a wave of calm rush through me as it does so, and I feel a little peace knowing that there's a presence here with me. I don't know why but I don't feel an animalistic presence, but one that seems… human. Out of some deeper instinct, deep within me, I feel like this cat knows I'm scared. It knows I need guidance. It knows I need love. And I want it to give it to me. By all accounts, my lunacy would be ostracized if this were the real world, but because this is a dream I'll allow it. But even with what happens next, I question my own sanity.

"Daughter."

One word. That's all it says, one word. No, not it. She. It's a she. Clear as day it speaks, and in a female voice. But it's not the gender of its voice that shocks me — well, at least not as much — it's the fact the cat spoke to me at all! And, more audacious, I suddenly feel safer.

The cat turns and walks in the opposite direction. By some invisible force with persistent hands, I follow, knowing instinctively that she wants me to. As we continue to walk, the path becomes clearer and less foreboding. The foliage begins to pull back and I begin to see the trees more clearly. Spaces in the leaves above begin to pull back and I start to see more of the night sky, and all of its beautiful darkness. The cat begins to pick up speed, going from a lazy pace to a trot. I quicken my pace as my dark feline guide quickens to a full run. As I keep up, I begin to hear voices, coming from the direction that we now head towards. I stop for a moment, thinking that I'm for sure going crazy, but I hear it again. Female voices, all calling out to me.

Jamila. Daughter. Jamila.

I stay in shock, and my steps falter as I suddenly feel a surrounding presence increasing. But I collect myself and run faster, the sheer necessity to find the source of these voices driving me. I run faster still, now alongside the black — wait, panther?

The black cat's now a panther. Where did the cat go? When did that happen? Its foreboding shape, made evermore intimidating by its sure steps as it gallops fiercely and with increasing speed.

Unimportant compared to the voices, I continue to run as the voices get louder. Louder still, I feel an end to this journey in sight when I hear one voice louder than the others. More insistent in its meaning. More loving in its intention.

I hear a voice calling my name.

I hear my mother calling my name.

CHAPTER TWO

The dinging noise of my morning alarm wakes me, rousing me from my strange dream. I've had that dream so many times before, but it's never ended like that before. After my mom passed, I would have the same dream every night. Nel started taking me to a psychologist when the dreams were really keeping me from sleeping. I went for about a month, and her consensus was that my dreams were a reflection of my current emotional and mental state after the passing of my mother. She said that I felt lost, confused, and scared because I knew that my mother was not coming back, and my dreams were an unconscious portrayal of my emotions. Her prescription was to talk. At that time, I still wasn't really talking. I was only doing small talks in our sessions because I had to, and her diagnosis was to explain how I felt and to create a dialogue so I didn't feel trapped behind my feelings. I thought that made no sense: talk a little more and then I'd stop having nightmares? That didn't seem like it would make much of a difference. Turns out she was right. After my barbershop stunt, I started talking more and the dreams started happening less. I still had them every so often, whenever I really was thinking about my mother, but they were less frequent. The therapist gave me tips — tools she called them — to pull myself out of the dream and calm myself down. She said to breathe and to remind myself that this dream state is only in my head, and that the real world is safe and a good place most of the time. It just goes wrong sometimes and unfortunately, it went wrong when my mom died. Still, the dreams always ended the same. This time it was different. But today's no different — Tuesday still means school. Which means I still need to get ready like it's any other day.

After a brief contemplation of whether school was more valuable than sleep, I roll lazily out of bed, dropping to the floor and slouching against the bed frame. I sit for a second, collecting my last few moments of rest before I rise to start the day. I make my bed, tucking the duvet into the right corner that lies against the wall. I fluff up my pillows, making them look warm and welcoming for tonight when I'll fall into them. I head to the bathroom, opening the door to a room filled with fog. Nellie must've just gotten out of the shower not too long ago. I brush my teeth and wash my face. After taking a quick cold shower to wake up, I take off my shower cap and get to work on my hair. I wet my hair, apply some gel and pull my hair into a bun, tying a scarf on to lay down my edges. This is something most Caribbean girls can relate to; edges on fleek. After I put on a tank top and a pair of jeans, I head into the kitchen to find Nellie still in her pyjamas, already making my favourite breakfast: scrambled eggs with dumplings, bacon, and a side of Milo tea. The breakfast of champions.

"You sleep alright?" asks Nellie, sensing my presence. I walk over to where she's standing and get the plates and cups from the cupboard.

"Yeah, but I had the jungle dream again."

"The one where you're running around lost?" Nel asks, glancing at me.

I turn around and lean against the countertop, nodding, "Yeah, but it was different this time. It was so weird, there was this black cat that showed up out of nowhere and it spoke!"

Nellie halts what she was doing, then slowly continues to dump the eggs onto our plates. Without looking at me she asks, "A cat speaking? What did it say?"

"Just one word. 'Daughter,'" I reply flabbergasted, looking at Nellie who returns my look with an equal expression of surprise.

"Are you sure she said 'Daughter'?"

"Yeah, and then she —" I stop, realizing that I hadn't told Nel that the cat was a female. "Wait. How did you know that the cat was a she?"

Nellie looks away, seeming to search for an answer in the eggs. She spoons the eggs, shifts the tablecloth on the counter, looks everywhere but at me. She responds, "Oh, I just assumed. Most of the time animals in dreams take on a benevolent tone or assume the role of a caregiver that makes us feel safe. For many people, that means the animal will be female."

I look at her, questioning her sudden knowledge of the subconscious and her evasive demeanour. She looks at me, smiling with the corner of her lip cocked higher than the other, in her Nellie-way.

"Your mom was really into this stuff when she was pregnant with you.

She was always dreaming about being stranded in the middle of the ocean, with sharks and stuff threatening her. She even saw a beautiful fish that spoke and led her to safe land. She kept saying it had a childlike voice and insisted that it was the voice of her baby. Of you."

I look at Nellie, soaking in this new information.

"She never told me that before," I say, with a melancholic tone.

"She only ever told me. You were always so cynical about all the superstitions your mother and I believed in, maybe she thought you wouldn't take her seriously." I walk towards the table as she chuckles briefly, before continuing, "When you dream of fish, it means you're going to have a baby. She was sure that she was having a baby, even before she got the pregnancy test and ultrasound to confirm it. That's just how your mother was, she had a keen sixth sense."

I sit down as Nellie places my breakfast in front of me, and fills my mug with Milo. I sit motionless for a moment as the steam rises from the brim of the mug, wishing that it weren't true what Nellie said — that I would have brushed off my mother's dreams. Though, if I'm being honest with myself, I know that back then, and even now, I always thought all those Jamaican superstitions were just hocus pocus. I'm not too sure I would've taken her seriously, and it makes me sad that she knew this and didn't tell me something so important to her.

"You were saying something else before you lost your train of thought, that the cat did something else?"

I look up at her as she collects her food on her plate, trying to capture my train of thought out of the ether before I remember what I was going to say. "Oh yeah! I was saying that after she spoke, I followed her and she turned into a black panther. Then I started hearing all these voices, women's voices, calling out to me. And then…"

Nellie looks at me, "And then?"

"And then I heard mom. She said my name."

Nellie turns all the way around and walks to the table. She squats down and looks up into my face with love.

"Then it's simple, baby. You miss your momma."

I look away, knowing this to be true but not believing that that's all there was to the alternate ending of my dream. Nellie smiles at me and chucks my chin, bouncing back up to start eating her breakfast. I continue to stare into my plate, contemplating whether I was reading too much into it and it really was just as simple as me missing my mother. This is all making me lose my appetite and my will to continue the conversation.

"You know what Nel, I'm actually not that hungry. I think I'm just going to go to school," I say, as I stand and grab my backpack.

Nellie looks up at me, responding, "But this is your favourite breakfast. You gotta eat something J, you can't go to school hungry."

I quickly look to the counter where our lunch bags sit, grabbing mine with the apple that sits inside. I wave it in the air as a reply.

"This'll be good enough. Just put the plate in the microwave, I promise I'll finish it later." I quickly place a peck on Nel's cheek before I dash to the door.

"Love you, have a good day," I call out over my shoulder as I open the screen door. I quickly backtrack when I remember my scarf is still tied tight on my head. I pull the tie and throw it on the counter. As I turn around, I face Michael already waiting for me with his bike. Ready to roll.

"Took you long enough," he says as he lifts himself onto his seat. "C'mon, let's go. We might be able to sneak past Blanco's boys if you stop taking your sweet time."

I quickly lift myself onto my bike, placing my bag in the basket on my front handlebars, and catch up to him as we pedal down the street and head to school.

We pass Ms. Dell, resuming her post on the front porch swing. We wave to her as she wishes us a good day. We round the corner and smile to Mr. and Mrs. James as they arrive in front of their shops. We see Reggie and give him the nod as he opens up the store. The sun is hidden beneath the clouds, but it's still bright. The humidity in the air makes the heat settle into our skin, and I can already feel sweat pricking in my armpits. Hopefully, it doesn't stain my white tank top yellow. Michael and I swerve and crisscross, our butts hovering over our seats and pedaling lethargically. As we continue to pedal, we both see Blanco's boys at the same time, in the same spot as they were last night. They're smoking and talking about what I can only assume is 'grown folks business'. Michael and I look to each other, exchanging a game plan on how we're going to get past them without any trouble. Sometimes if we pedal fast enough and go different ways, we get around them. Sometimes we don't. Most times we don't. We both shrug hopefully, mutually agreeing to take a chance in the hopes that we'll get around them this time.

As we continue down the road, Blanco's boys catch sight of us and start moving towards us.

"Hey yo!" one of them yells. "What's goin' on wit' y'all?"

"We're good," Michael calls back, trying to end the conversation. "We're just trying to get to school."

Out of the group walks Ricky Brass, one of Blanco's main boys. He's known for getting results whenever Blanco has a problem, whether it be him not getting his money or someone trying to mess with his operations. Ricky Brass always brings something back for Blanco, usually by using his infamous brass knuckles that are known to cause damage. He's average height — about 5'10 or 5'11 — and average build. He's got a big nose and good teeth, but eyes that bug out like a fly. It's pretty unfortunate, especially since he's also known for being sensitive to women rejecting his advances. His toxic masculinity is like a character trait for him — without it, he wouldn't be Ricky Brass. He's the last person you want to offend, and it usually doesn't take much to set him off. And of course, who else would be heading directly towards us but him.

"School don't even start till nine anyhow," he says, as he walks towards us in an attempt to block our path. "Why don't y'all chill for a second, there ain't no hurry."

Michael and I begin to pick up speed, knowing that this could escalate quickly. Michael quickly responds, "No we're good, but thank you."

Ricky Brass gets in our path, grabbing Michael's handlebars and stopping him abruptly. He looks at Michael, trying to get him to look him in the eye — a test. Looking him in the eyes is the quickest way to set him off, so Michael continues to look down.

"Whatchu mean 'you're good'?" he asks, as he stares Michael down. "It's just a couple minutes, it ain't gon' kill you. I'm asking politely, and I could be a lot less kinder."

"Less kind," I correct.

Ricky Brass looks to me as if he just realized I was there and raise his eyebrows, questioning my audacity to correct him. Honestly, I'm questioning myself.

"Oh is that so?" he asks, directing his attention towards me. He lets go of Michael's bike and makes his way over to me; slowly, like a snake that's about to attack. He saunters over to my bike and looks me down — well, more like looks me in the eye. I've got pretty long legs. I've never been more inclined to piss my pants in my entire life, but I'll be damned if I let myself look weak.

"You think you smarter than me?" he asks.

"No —"

"Then why you correctin' me? Hmm?"

I struggle to find an answer that doesn't come off as pretentious, coming up with nothing. I quickly apologize, "I'm sorry. That was wrong of me, I didn't mean to demean your intelligence."

"So now you think you can make me feel a way, huh?" he responds, seeming angrier than before. I don't know how I offended him more by apologizing, all I know is that I just dug myself a deeper hole.

"No that's not it at all —" I fluster, trying to get myself out of this situation. Michael stands beside me in solidarity, not doing anything lest he gets in trouble, but not leaving me either. That's better than nothing.

"Damn right it's not." Ricky Brass continues, raising his voice, catching the attention of people passing by. Quickly realizing who we're interacting with, they quicken their pace and leave us in the dust. "Ain't no way you gon' make me feel some type of way, you ain't got that much power, baby girl."

He looks me up and down, assessing my slim-thick frame. He gets closer, right in my face, his sour breath that reeks of weed blowing into my face. He says, "You ain't all that, but you got a little somethin' I can work with… and your face ain't all that bad either — even though you dark as hell."

This causes me to look up. I've had issues with being dark-skinned and I may struggle with how I feel about myself because of it. Nevertheless, my mother and Nel always told me to never let anybody put me down because I was dark-skinned. He may be intimidating, but I'll be damned if I let him intimidate me into hating my skin.

"Clearly if I'm not too dark you can't peep me though, huh?" I fire back sarcastically — stunning Michael and — apparently, humouring Ricky Brass enough to put a smile on his face. "Couldn't miss that even if you tried. Those big-ass eyes you got give you 20/20 vision."

That wipes the smile off his face. He straightens up, looking like he's about to tear me to shreds. As I see the end clear as day in his dilated pupils, I send a silent prayer to the universe to make it end quickly. Suddenly, a voice from behind us that calls out his name changes his entire demeanour.

Blanco himself rises out of his black Escalade, his large frame causing the car to bounce up from the released weight of his body. He and his passenger slowly walk towards us, every step exuding an air of authority, swag, and power. His chains stay in place between his pecs, glistening on top of his all-black attire. His face offers no expression for me to go off of, all I can do is watch as I meet my maker.

Blanco looks at Ricky Brass and asks, "What's goin' on here?"

"Got a couple of lil' shits thinkin' they smarter than me. Just remindin' them of their place," Ricky responds, looking me dead in the eye. I see a desire to hurt me, and a desire to do something else to me. I'm not the only one who sees this either. Blanco looks from Ricky to me, an expression of recognition briefly passing over his face before it returns to its indomitable regularity.

"It's good you picked up on that. It's important to make sure everything runs the way it's s'posed to, and that we're shown the proper respect 'round here. But we don't intimidate little girls to do it."

Ricky looks to Blanco surprised, not expecting to hear this rebuke from him. Neither am I as I look to Blanco with surprise. Ricky quickly smiles nonchalantly, as if he wasn't just reprimanded for his behaviour.

"I wasn't intimidatin' them Blanco, I was just lettin' them know not to mess with us —"

"No, you were eyeing her. Your big-ass eyes were goin' all over her body, don't play me for no fool, Rick," Blanco says, looking down on Ricky. Ricky's eyes go wide, searching for a way out of the mess he made for himself.

"Yeah but I mean, look at her," Ricky flounders, pointing towards me, "I mean, how could I miss a body like that? It's damn near impossible —"

Blanco walks even closer to Ricky, their faces inches away from each other. Blanco's face goes expressionless, if it could get any more stoic than before. He looks Ricky in the eyes, unblinking.

"She's a little girl. We're men, we don't prey on girls like that. You can do whatever the hell you want with the hoes down at the club, but the last thing you gon' do is lower our credibility by running after tail that'll get you arrested."

Ricky's eyebrows quiver as the rest of Blanco's boys stand aside and watch the entire exchange; all of them looking to each other, questioning this public display of admonition. My breath staggers shallowly from witnessing Blanco's power firsthand, and Michael, unmoving in his natural response to danger, stands as still as a statue.

"We respect women, you understand?" Blanco states, more than asks, as he raises his eyebrow. Ricky breathes in deeply — in fear or in anger I couldn't tell you — and nods in agreement. Blanco looks to me, his face expressionless but his eyes offering a glimpse into a better version of the man in front of me. This doesn't excuse the behaviour he exhibits on a daily basis: he may have shown chivalry and saved our asses, but actions speak louder than words, and his actions on a day-to-day basis are less than admirable.

He walks up to us, looking at Michael briefly in acknowledgment of his presence, successfully ending his and Ricky's conversation. He looks at me for a moment longer — his face, again, expressionless — before turning on his heel.

"C'mon, I'll drive y'all to school. It's the least I can do for Ricky's behaviour makin' you late."

Michael and I look at each other in disbelief as Blanco walks away, presumably expecting us to follow him.

I quickly call out to him, "That's really not necessary. We wouldn't want to inconvenience you. Besides, we won't be too late."

Blanco turns around, eyebrow raised to challenge my sudden sprout of independence. He walks back towards us and says "Baby girl, I'm not askin'. It's just down the street, it really isn't an inconvenience to me. And the last thing I wanna be thinking about today is that I made Keba's little girl late for school."

This catches me off guard. I had no idea Blanco knew my mother on a first-name basis and I definitely did not think he knew that I was her daughter. My mouth gapes in disbelief, not knowing how to respond; unimportant regardless, as Blanco turns around — not expecting a reply I presume — and expects us once again to follow suit. I guess I'll have to process this later.

Michael and I pedal to the car and Blanco's driving buddy puts our bikes in the trunk. As we step into the backseat, I catch a glimpse of Ricky looking with disbelief, anger, and from what I can tell, jealousy. I throw him a quick smirk, taunting him further, before closing the door. Blanco drives off, one arm on the wheel and the other leisurely hanging out the window. We pull away with the distant sound of Ricky screaming an expletive.

After a minute of Blanco tapping his fingers on the steering wheel to OutKast exploding from the speakers, his driving associate bobbing his head to the rhythm, Michael and I find the courage to look to each other. Michael looks to me with wide eyes that ask, *'what the HELL is going on?'* My raised eyebrows and wide eyes respond, *'I don't know! Just keep it cool.'* Blanco looks into the rearview mirror to the backseat and turns the volume down on the radio.

"So, how's your aunty Nel doin'?" he asks. I look at him confused, wondering how he seemed to know me and my family so well and I only know him through his reputation.

"She's fine. Yeah, yeah, she's fine," I respond. I tell myself that simple response is all that I need to say, but my unwavering need to have my questions answered wins before I take a risk and continue. "How do you know her? And how'd you know my mother?"

He looks in my eyes through the mirror, emanating such a fierce emotion that I can't place, scaring me for some reason.

"Your aunty Nel, your Mom and I all went to school together. I was in the same grade as Nel, an' I knew your aunty through her. We used to do study group at Loni's back in the day — us and a couple of other kids in class."

Again conflicted by new information in the span of 12 hours, I sit back in disbelief as to why I'm just learning this now. Blanco went to school with my mother and my aunt? And they all knew each other? Actually, I'm not surprised that Blanco went to school with them — after all, he is around the same age; everybody knows he graduated high school and got his diploma at the local college before settling into his 'profession'. I'm more taken aback by the fact that he's on a first-name basis with the women I've known my entire life. Okay, maybe note-taking over 20 years ago isn't the most intimate medium on which a relationship is founded, but I think it's still enough to warrant mentioning.

"Your mother was somethin' else," he continues, his face going expressionless to almost reminiscent. "She used to help me with these cue cards she made an' used to quiz me whenever we had a test." He laughs, and smiles, "I was really bad at the science stuff, so she used to make little raps to help me remember. They were so corny, but I did actually remember it when we needed to study. And it made me laugh."

I sit back and look at Blanco, surprised at this sudden flow of fondness towards my mother.

"Your aunty on the other hand," he continues, shaking his head and whistling low, "she was on my ass all the time. She never wanted me 'round your mom, thinking I'd be a bad influence on her or something. Maybe she was right about that. I wasn't exactly a model student. But for all the attitude Nel threw my way, she still let me hang around and study with 'em. I gotta give respec' to her for that — not everyone can forget what they think about somebody and help them out. She a real one for that. She even helped me out a few times when I was causin' trouble in class. Said *'she didn't wanna be affiliated with a jackass,'*" he says with a laugh.

I smile knowingly, not surprised that a younger Nellie would say something like that. Michael chuckles with the same knowledge and then leans forward, about to do something that I'm definitely going to kill him for later.

"Sound just like J. She's always getting sent to the principal's office for being a smart ass in class," Michael says. I look at him with a death glare, delivering in it a promise that I'm going to cuss him out later. The smile wipes off his face and he leans back, knowing he's in big trouble.

"Oh really?" Blanco questions, looking back towards me in the rearview mirror with a small smile on his face. "You a troublemaker, baby girl?"

I look him in the eyes, a bold move that I didn't think I was capable of, and reply shortly, "It's Jamila. And no, I'm just not afraid to call things for what it is, regardless of where it comes from."

He looks at me, raising his eyebrows in surprise at my sudden bout of feistiness. He replies humorously, "My bad, *Jamila*. I see what your boy means — that attitude of yours must not sit well with everybody."

"That's not my problem," I fire back. Michael looks at me with an expression that tells me to stop talking, but he already knows once I get started there's no stopping me.

I continue, "It's not my job to get everyone to like me, only to not let people take advantage of me."

Blanco looks at me in the mirror, again with the same intense look that I cannot match or place, and holds my gaze until we arrive in front of Brimmer Hall. Michael and I unbuckle our seat belts as Blanco's companion jumps out to get our bikes from the trunk. We open our doors to step out, but I stop as Blanco says one last thing.

"Keep that grit in you baby girl," he says, looking forward with the same resigned expression. "It's what's gonna keep you goin' in life. Nobody wants their downfall to be 'cause they didn't stand up for themselves and speak their minds." I look at him, piqued by the seriousness of his tone.

"Thanks, I'll keep that in mind. And it's Jamila, not baby girl," I say, as I quickly hop out of the car. Blanco chuckles quietly before putting on his sunglasses. As soon as Michael shuts the door Blanco drives off, passing kids jumping out of the way. We grab our bikes off the ground and turn towards the school to the scene of dozens of classmates staring at us. Great.

As lunch period rolls around, I walk towards my locker, pushing my way through the throng of kids going the opposite direction. I grab my lunch, so that I can meet Michael outside at our bench. Our bench sits in front of the rear school doors to the parking lot, where all the kids meet for lunch and do all the usual teenage activities of our generation. As I place my books inside and grab my lunch, I see Ms. Boykin from the corner of my eye walking down the hall. Her straight-backed posture exudes an air of authority as she struts down the hall. Her tweed pants and a simple blouse that was ironed crisp to perfection, hangs on her skinny frame. Her head held high, sharp nose upturned surveys the hallway — she resembles a falcon gazing over her prey, ready to swoop down for the kill. Thinking about what Loni said last night, and my own revelations about my behaviour, I quickly make my way over to her.

"Ms. Boykin," I call out. She stops and sees me, a guarded expression on her face.

"Jamila. What can I help you with?"

I breathe in and say, "I wanted to apologize for my behaviour yesterday. Even if I didn't agree with your point, I shouldn't have said what I said in front of the class. Even if it were in private, I definitely could have reworded what I said in a more respectful way. It was rude and disrespectful, and I was out of line, and I just want to say I'm sorry."

Looking pleased with my apology, her face goes smug before feigning a look of benevolence. "I accept your apology," she says. I smile back, truly apologetic for my behaviour and glad that I was able to learn from it. It's hard to apologize and equally hard to accept an apology, and I'm glad that we were able to do both.

"I understand that you were just emotional," she continues. "It was a sensitive topic we were covering, and I know that it must be difficult to hear about your history and the implications of it. But you are a bright student, despite the odds, and I truly do appreciate your tenacious spirit, Jamila. It'll really help you out in the long run."

We were so close to avoiding a backhanded compliment. Despite the odds? What odds were those exactly? Give me a break, can this tired perception finally die? Am I supposed to be a degenerate delinquent just because I had a single mom and now I'm an orphan? My circumstances don't determine my actions, and she shouldn't put me in that narrow box. Then again, it could definitely be a lot worse so I'll just brush it off. I force a smile in farewell, walking towards the parking lot, glad that I learned from running my mouth. Even if the price I had to pay was to put up with covert racism in the process. As I open the door I see Michael already waiting for me at the bench, digging into Nel's sandwich while somehow simultaneously drinking out of a can. I swear his ability to wolf down extensive amounts of food and still stay skinny is both alarming and admirable.

I plop down beside him, looking at him eating in amazed disgust. "How the hell do you do that? That's gotta give you running belly."

"Nah," he replies, his tongue muffled by the food in his mouth. "It's all goin' in the same place anyhow, it doesn't ma'er if I eat i'all at the same time."

I return a look of disgust as I pull out my sandwich, crossing my legs and setting my sights on the lot. The small parking lot that's too small, overflows as the cars that couldn't find a parking space rest on the grass. Kids just finishing class run past us towards their friends, while some couples are making out and others are fighting. Other kids hop into cars and drive off to get their lunches or skip out on class. Kiara Davis walks past us, her oversized band tee barely covering her butt as she struts to her other half.

"That shirt couldn't get any shorter if she wore it as a belt," Michael says, his words still suppressed by his lunch. I cut my eye at him for his hypocrisy — he's always talking about people having the freedom to do what they want, but then judging them in the same breath. If Kiara Davis wants to show her ass to the world, then by all means, she should be allowed to. Then again, is it feminist if I say that she *should* show her ass? Ugh, feminism is complicated. Or at least the world thinks it is. I'm just going to mind my business.

To the right of the couple is a group of popular kids. One can deny that such social groups no longer exist but, let's be real: if you think the popular kids aren't a thing anymore, then it's probably because you are one of the popular kids. All known for being on the top tier of socializing and extroversion, they collectively glue their eyes to their phones while talking about the latest gossip. Around them are more kids in their respective social groups: the drama kids, rehearsing lines for the next play that no one actually plans on going to; the band kids playing their instruments to the tune of a song that seems to have a lot of squeaks; the emo kids taking a lighter to their jeans and then rubbing the fire away. I have to say, I've never understood the purpose of ruining a pair of jeans but hey, teenage angst is a killer.

"I apologized to Ms. Boykin," I tell Michael.

Michael looks to me with a look of surprise, a piece of lettuce hanging from the corner of his mouth. "Really? How'd that go?"

"She accepted my apology and then gave me a backhanded compliment. Said that 'despite the odds' I was an impressive student."

"So it went as expected then."

"Basically, yeah," I say laughing.

Michael, now finished scarfing down his lunch, crosses his legs at his ankles and leans back on his arms, joining me in watching our surroundings. His Vans, scrubbed clean every night with Mr. Clean magic eraser and a toothbrush, wave side to side as he unconsciously wags his feet. His waves, fresh from the durag he used last night, glistens in the sun that finally decided to make an appearance. His arms poke through his grey t-shirt while his boney knees poke through his denim jeans. His expression changes to one of longing, and I follow his gaze to see Taylor Stennett walking towards the group of popular kids, her glowing skin blinding me as the sun follows her every move.

"There goes the future Mrs. Michael Smith," I say jokingly.

"Shut it. Knowing you, your stank attitude is gonna jinx it."

Michael's had a crush on Taylor Stennett since the 5th grade; she's one of those girls who's nice to everyone and is genuinely a good person because she sees no benefit in being rude to people. The first time she ever spoke to us was in 5th grade when we were walking towards the locker rooms after playing baseball in gym class. Michael, aside from numbers, also has this affinity for hitting any ball that comes in his path. Whether it's with his foot, with his hand, or with a bat. He hit every single ball out of the park, or the tiny excuse for a park that was our playground, and apparently impressed her. She walked past us and all she had to say was "*Nice aim, Michael!*" and he was done for. For the past eight years, Taylor's been his one and only. In his mind of course. If he ever builds up the courage to actually go up and hold a conversation with her, that'll be the day pigs fly. With the fervour of a fanatic, Michael stares at her, creeping even *me* out.

"What are you trying to do, develop X-Ray vision? Stop staring at her! It's weird."

"I'm not staring at her."

"Your eyes are watering. Take a second to blink, she's not gonna disappear."

"She's so beautiful, she's like a walking dream. If I blink, I might wake up. I can't take that chance."

Shocked by his ability to make everything agonizingly corny, I roll my eyes and look at what's got him going so crazy. He's definitely not wrong about her being beautiful; inside and out, she's probably the most beautiful girl in school. With light brown eyes that always seem to shine and crinkle at the ends whenever her bright white smile graces our presence, she makes you feel happy whenever you talk to her. Her light brown skin glistens, and her brown hair falls in loose curls down to her shoulder blades. Thanks to her basketball prowess, her toned body puts my slim-thick body to shame. I'm not going to lie — while I prefer men, it would be impossible to not appreciate the sheer charm and beauty she has. It would make anyone love-struck, and Michael's one of the extreme cases.

"This may sound crazy — hear me out — but maybe if you actually *talk* to her then your dream could become a reality."

Michael looks to me as if I truly am crazy, and exclaims, "Are you mad? I can't speak to her; I can't get a single word out without stuttering."

"Yeah but she's nice, if you just talk to her I'm sure your nerves will die down."

Michael shakes his head fervently as if the sheer idea was out of the question. "I can't. I just can't. I can't talk to a girl like her; she's so perfect." I look to him quizzically, questioning his reasoning.

"But you can talk to me. What makes me so different?"

"Nah, you're not a girl. You're Jamila, that's completely different. You're a giant pain in my ass and that defies any societal constructs like gender."

I cut my eye at him, but I catch the smile tugging at his lips and we both burst into riotous laughter that scares a squirrel not too far from us. I look at Michael, his head thrown back from the force of his holler, giving me second-hand glee, when suddenly I get this feeling of sadness. My stomach drops as if I were on a roller coaster, and my bones begin to ache until they feel hollow. My smile slips off my face as I'm filled with dread and sadness. Michael is one of the most important people in my life and the constant catalyst for my smiling every day, and if I ever lost him I don't know how I'd bounce back. I don't know if I *would* bounce back. Michael shoves me on the shoulder, taking my drink to take a swig, bringing me back from my stupor.

Whoa, where did that come from?

The school bell rings to signal the end of the school day and everyone bounces from their seats. Our calculus teacher struggles to relay the homework for the day over the buzz of students already finished with anything academic-related. I write down what I can hear, being the model student that I am, and head to my locker. The same sinking feeling of sadness continues to settle in the bottom of my stomach, still present from lunch with Michael. I feel it in the pit of my stomach, while feeling that same ache settling into my bones, and it begins to give me a headache. I don't know why I'm feeling this way, but I just can't seem to shake it. I've felt like something is going to happen ever since lunch period, and I haven't been able to focus. I even answered a question with a mathematical equation when I wasn't paying attention, and I was in English class!

I walk in a daze until I reach our bikes outside the school, placing my bag in my bike's basket thoughtlessly and wait for Michael while I try to settle my nerves. I take a few breaths to try and clear my head, lifting my head towards the sky and closing my eyes as the hollowness in my bones continues to ache throughout my body. I open my eyes and see a throng of students exiting the school in anticipation for the afternoon. As I see Michael skip outside, his goofy grin plastered on his face, I try to assure myself that today is like any other day. Nothing bad is going to happen. Just breathe.

"Hey big head," Michael says, chucking my head to the side as he swings his legs onto his bike, placing his nerdy helmet on and buckling it. His bright yellow helmet, with all its anime stickers on it, is a crime against fashion.

Smiling to mask my anxiety, I respond, "You like to talk, but at least I don't have to worry about wearing a helmet that makes me look like a waste yute."

"Oh, you got jokes?"

"Lookin' like Tweety Bird with your baby ass."

"Swear down!" he exclaims, offended.

I start to ride off, taunting him over my shoulder, "Tawt, Tawt, goofy!"

"Ay!" he yells, rushing to catch up with me as I tease him and ride off to Loni's.

When we arrive, the diner is already starting to look busy — with students and part-timers finished with their day. Michael and I make a beeline for the counter, ready for our post-academic milkshakes. Banana Split for Michael, Vanilla Bean for me; it's our after-school ritual. As we plop down onto the plush stool seats, Ray, one of Loni's full-timers, welcomes us with a big grin that matches his big personality.

"How you kids doin'?" he bellows.

"Oh y' know. Homework. Teenage gossip. The sinking feeling of anxiety about the future mixed with the need for altruistic freedom. Just the usual," Michael says. Ray looks at him with a side-eye; annoyed by — but used to — Michael's sense of humour.

"That's just his way of saying everything's good," I say. "How are you doing?"

"Oh, you know how it is, sweet pea. Just tryn'a get by." He shakes his head in response to his situation. "I saw Louis Mackey today, the one who runs the auto shop down on Bellamy Rd., and we started talkin' 'bout the times man, and how it's gettin' harder to make ends meet. Low and behold he tells me he started drivin' for that company, the one that's takin' over cabs. It's like a taxi company but you call them on your phone through one of those apps."

"Uber? Or Lyft, maybe?" I suggest.

"Yeah, yeah, the second one. He started driving for 'em so he can get some more income. It's crazy man, everyone's strugglin' 'round here. Just the other day I was talking to Mrs. James about a wig for my lady, and —"

"Ray," Michael interrupts before he can settle into his story, "could we get our regulars, please?"

"Oh yeah. Yeah, of course." He starts to get our milkshakes going, pulling the milk and ingredients out of the fridge, adding a little commentary while we wait. "Anyways, I was talkin' to Mrs. James about that. She was sayin' how she's not gettin' a lot of girls in her shop 'cause not a lot of 'em can afford the lace front wigs no more. She said that's how she makes most of her money 'cept for them braids with the boxes." He uses a blender to mix everything together, adjusting his voice to bellow even louder so we can hear him over the noise. "She even said one of the girls that work down at the club tried to stiff her when she wanted one and tried to pay for the cheaper price 'cause she said '*it was all advertised as the same price online.*' Mrs. James don't even have a website. Talkin' about '*I'll pay you back, I'm good for it.*' Ha! Everybody know she ain't even one of the regulars down at the club, talkin' like she can put it on layaway or somethin'."

Ray pours our shakes into the old-school plastic glasses shaped like a cone 'till the top is bubbling with frothy bubbles. He places a maraschino cherry on the top of Michael's banana, and throws some chocolate shavings on top of my shake, before placing them in front of us. Glad to now have a delicious addition to our lengthy one-sided conversation, Michael and I start slurping from the candy-cane-striped straw. Like an old friend, I'm hit with the familiar, cinnamony taste of Loni's Vanilla Bean shake. Mixing the chocolate shavings until they, and the shake, become heterogeneous. I hum as I gulp it down, not learning from the countless consumptions of this liquid dessert that I should drink it slowly so that the taste can last longer. Once again, I can't be stopped.

Ray continues, "Mrs. James said '*If she wants good hair, then she needs good hair money. I can't give her the nice lace front if she ain't gonna pay me. That stuff's hard to come by, and all these girls 'round here wanna look pretty but they don't have the cash to back it up.*'"

"Ugh, as if lace front wigs are the only type of *good hair*," I start. "Everyone's always saying what 'good' hair is — as if different textures, colours, and lengths aren't *good* hair because it doesn't fit into the mould of a widely accepted standard. If I don't have loose curls that swing in the breeze, my hair suddenly isn't *good*? Good hair is whatever way your hair is healthy and maintained — that's it."

"I don't think she meant that other hair isn't *good* hair, she just meant that people want that hair because it's really pretty," Michael responds. "Aren't all the girls rockin' that lace front style now?"

"Yeah, they are. But their natural hair is just as pretty. It's nice to switch up your hair every once in a while, and some people have to give their hair a break. That's where wigs and weaves and extensions come in. When that's all you do because of what society portrays of looking glam, then you'll deceive yourself mentally into thinking that what you have isn't good enough. Then you start to have alopecia and start losing your hair, and then you rely on those wigs to feel pretty — as if you weren't already before."

"Dude, I really don't think it's that serious," Michael says exasperatedly.

"All you young'uns so loud about stuff that's not that important," Ray groans. Planting his feet and leaning backwards to crack his back, in his signature old-school fashion. He continues, "Back in my day, we would've gotten pulled over just for wearing our hair natural. And jobs? Forget about it. Ain't no way we'd even be able to get in the room to show 'em a resume. Even if we 'appened to make it that far, chances are 'Richard' or 'Edward' was gon' get the job 'fore we did. Specially if we got a name like 'Darnell,' or 'Tyrone', or somethin' like that. Y'all wanna focus on the little things when there are kids gettin' killed in the streets, and arrested for movin' reefer, when plenty of rich white kids are doin' the same thing in the rich neighbourhoods. Why don't y'all protest about the things that matter more?"

"Of course those things are important too, Ray," I say, turning to him. "It's a matter of life and death — and we do fight that fight. But if I don't fight for the right to the truth that my natural self is beautiful or important with the same vigour, then I'm gonna neglect myself. I'm not just black and I'm not just a woman — I'm a black woman. I don't get to choose between the two. I have to fight both fights with the same energy, or else I'm never going to get any sort of equality."

Michael looks away and nods his head slightly, absorbing my stance. Ray looks at me, leaning on the countertop.

"No one said you weren't beautiful or important, sweet pea."

"No one had to *say* anything, and that's just as powerful. Silence can speak just as loud as words can, especially when it's meant to suppress yours." I look to him, pleading with my eyes for him to hear and understand what I'm saying. I get that my generation is seen as this group of people who are sensitive to anything and everything. To an extent this is true, but we're also a generation of examples. We lead by example, the one that those before us, like Ray, have set. We can't just stop protesting because on surface-level it seems like everything's okay. There's always a sub-level catalyst that can affect progress. Even if a lot has been done, it's still not enough.

Ray looks to me, throwing his hands up to yield surrender, and bids us farewell as he walks to talk another customer's ear off. Michael looks at me, his trademark expression that offers nothing taking over his face.

"You good?" he asks.

"Yeah, I'm good."

"That got anything to do with what happened with Ricky today?"

I think about his query, about the validity of the possibility that Ricky's comments may have made me feel some type of way. He may have said that I don't have that type of effect, but there's no doubt that he certainly does.

"Maybe. I don't know. It's okay though, I'm good. Really. Don't worry about it."

Michael looks at me one last time, before rising from his seat and saying, "Alright." He walks to the cash register and pulls out his card to pay for our shakes. While he waits to tap his bank card, I slowly make my way outside when I'm hit once again with that sinking feeling in the pit of my stomach. There's no denying it this time, something is going to happen. The humidity in the air settles even more, making the sweat prick in my armpits once again — but the discomfort I'm feeling makes me feel even hotter. I blink my eyes to try and relieve the ache in my head when my vision starts to get — crisper. The colours of outside start to brighten, sharpen, deepen in their lustre, and my headache gets even worse from this change in scenery that I saw not even a second ago. What is happening?

Michael comes outside, in the middle of a phone conversation with someone.

"Yeah, yeah I have it. I'll bring it by. No, it's okay, I'll pay it — I have some cash on me. Okay, see you later. Bye." He puts his phone away and starts to put his helmet on, explaining, "My nana needs me to drop somethin' off for her at the library down by Downsview area, I gotta head there now."

"You're not ridin' home with me?" I ask.

"No, it's a book that she took out a month ago. I've been carrying it with me 'cause she didn't know when she'd be able to get down there, so I said I'd drop it off one of these days. She's had it all this time and totally forgot about it, so I gotta pay the late fee. I'm gonna swing by Min's Convenience on my way home too, you want anything?"

"No, no I'm good. Thanks, though."

Michael nods and starts to ride off, yelling, "Tawt, Tawt, goofy," over his shoulder.

As I smile and flip him off behind his back, I turn my gaze and spot a black cat on the street corner. Just like the one from my dream. Its fur is slick, glistening from the sunlight, and its pink nose shines against its nebulous coating. I can see the yellow of its eyes from here, resembling a gold coin. I'm used to seeing strays randomly about the neighbourhood, but the strong resemblance this cat has to the one in my dream makes me pause. Superstitions say that black cats are a sign of bad luck, especially when they crossed your path. But whenever I've seen a cat, I always get a good feeling. A feeling of home, or of finding a friend. When I see a black cat, however, it's like deja vu. I rarely see them, but I still feel like I've seen something — or will see something — that I've already seen before. It's like a warning. A warning of something to come.

The cat makes its way over to my side of the street, walking in a diagonal path that will inevitably cross mine. It moves lethargically, but with purpose — as if it's on the hunt. It stops mid-stride as it comes in front of me, and turns its head towards me. In that instant, I look into its eyes and I suddenly feel weightless. My head goes light and my vision disappears — but just for a second. Then suddenly, all I can see is Michael. It's like I'm watching a movie — or rather, like I'm in a movie. All I can see is Michael riding down the street on his bike. All I can see is Michael on his bike and a worker van approaching. Now all I can see is the worker van. And Michael's backpack lying on the street. And no Michael.

I look up in a panic, finding Michael riding to the stop sign at the end of the street. Without hesitation, I scream.

"MICHAEL!"

He turns around and stops, startled by my outburst. Not a second later, a car zooms past his face, where his body would have surely been if he hadn't stopped. Michael whips around, his shirt rustling from the blowback of the van speeding past him, and backs up from the curb. He stares in shock and fear after the car. No, not the car. The van. The *white* van.

I collapse onto my bike seat — scared, confused, relieved. How did I know that would happen? *The cat told you*, my thoughts whisper. No, that's crazy! There's no way that an *animal* could've warned me of danger without actually saying anything.

And yet, I am almost certain that this is true. Even if I don't want to admit it, I've always had a strong sixth sense like my mother, and am usually right when my premonitions cause me to proceed with caution. She used to say that it's our future selves travelling through time to make sure we don't make the same mistakes they did. I think that was just her way of explaining it to me as a kid so that I would understand. But some part of me took her words seriously; and now, as I remember this, I treat it with more weight than before. Ever since lunch today I've had that feeling, and when I looked into that cat's eyes…

I look around for the cat, only to find a side street empty, and no cat. It disappeared, vanished into thin air, but it was just here a second ago. Where could it have gone in that time? Instantly I knew without a doubt why I had been feeling the way I've been feeling all day. It was like I knew something bad was going to happen — something to Michael. It's like the cat was an omen: a sign of danger to come, its presence a prophetic message to confirm my gut feeling.

I look up at Michael, who turns around to look at me again, shock and fear on his face. I stand up, leaning on the bike's handlebars, and look at him — probing him from afar to make sure he's okay. He nods to me shakily in response, affirming that he is indeed alright and holds my gaze for a moment longer. Then, he looks both ways warily before crossing the street, riding off in the direction of the library.

I plop down onto my seat again, exhaling loudly and inhaling haggardly, continuing this cycle for a good few minutes. I look around me to the customary surroundings of my neighbourhood, my habitational peers undisturbed by my friend's near-death experience. At first I'm angry with my neighbours' callous complacency, but then rationality kicks in, and I calm down. The balance of indifference and compassion is an integral part of black survival: with lives threatened by death on a regular basis. Whether that be by drug abuse or a miscommunication between us and law enforcement, its a debilitating feat to offer aid and compassion for every threat to our lives when we each have to live our own. Michael didn't die; life goes on, and they have to keep going with theirs too. I breathe, taking in long breaths that I need to assuage my fear and anger, and set off for home.

I sit at the kitchen table in front of my homework, a mug of tea and a plate with bun and cheese beside me. I flow between algebraic equations and the events of today, my focus is indecisive to what's more important. Despite my desire to learn and avid ability to work, I also have a terrible attention span: a personality trait that is blocking my progress at the moment. I doodle in the margins of my notebook aimlessly, my hand creating long strokes and speeding in progress to shade in between lines. As I zone back in, I notice that underneath my pencil lies a black cat. Staring right at me. I put my textbook over my notebook to hide what's on my mind when Nellie walks in the door.

"You home?" she calls out.

"Yeah," I reply.

Nellie walks through the door with her blue scrubs still on, her hair pulled back into a low bun as she drops her backpack to the floor. As she kicks off her dad shoes, she looks to me.

"You took out the chicken, right?"

I forgot to take the chicken out of the fridge to defrost in the sink. Such a simple task, but somehow I seem to always forget until she walks through the door. Maybe the foreboding possibility of getting cussed out removes the mental block that caused me to forget the text she sent me not even an hour ago.

"Uh," I respond, smiling lazily to offset her annoyed face, "no, but we still have leftovers anyway so really I just saved us food that we can make tomorrow."

"Nah, you just forgot to take out the damn chicken again," Nellie says, cutting her eye at me before she walks to put her things away. I mouth a silent 'sorry', and start pulling out my history notebook, resolving to deal with my algebra homework another time. Ms. Boykin gave us a fairly vague task: research a specific event during the Civil Rights Movement and connect it to another event, in the present or events that occurred before the Civil Rights Movement, that correlate. With so much to work with, I don't know where to begin. There's the assassination of Martin Luther King Jr. that I could connect to the blatant killings of black activists by law enforcement today. I could also talk about the infamous actions of Rosa Parks, and connect it to the Me Too Movement. But then I would be disregarding the actions of Claudette Colvin who spearheaded the Montgomery Bus Boycott movement. Also, the facts of her premarital teen pregnancy could make it an even more difficult debate to bring to Ms.

Boykin, who isn't the most liberal of educators. But it would also make it easy to tie into the issues surrounding planned parenthood and women's rights surrounding their bodies, which allows me to kill 3 birds with one stone. And then I could connect it further to how black women aren't treated the same by the medical community and the ill-treatment of their bodies. Ugh, there's so much I could work with, it's kind of worrisome. Nellie walks in on me holding up my head with the palm of my hand, staring off into space, hoping that I will find the right answers.

"Ground control to Major Tom," Nellie says, as she regards me with amused curiosity. I smile and shrug to explain my zoned out expression.

"I'm just trying to figure out which angle I'm going to tackle this paper with. It's so vague that I could literally tackle dozens of different events and topics, but I want it to be a paper that actually…" I struggle with a proper description, "has something to say. And doesn't just get me brownie points to look good for a college application, y' know?"

"I get that. It's good that you want to actually make your paper matter. Most kids are worried about just passing and getting a good grade."

I nod in agreement and turn my attention back to my dilemma at hand while Nellie gets the leftovers out for dinner. After resolving to focus on the relation of the assassination of Martin Luther King, and the tensions between the black community and law enforcement today, I open my laptop and start to get to work. My thesis correlates the assassinations of black activists, specifically Martin Luther King and Black Lives Matter activists, to the tensions between the black community and law enforcement. There's so much research to back up my argument. Not to mention the news alone spewing new headlines every day that further corroborates my thesis, I'm pretty confident that it'll turn out to be a meaningful and insightful paper. My fingers speed up as I type faster, my keyboard assaulted by my fingers that are on a roll. After I've done some research and gotten myself several pages deep into my paper, I hear a commotion outside our driveway. Nellie must hear it too because she stops what she's doing and walks to the window. After a brief stop, she kisses her teeth and makes her way outside in her flip-flops. Confused, I get up to join her — crossing the kitchen and living room in four large strides. I stumble outside to find Nellie facing Ricky Brass and three of Blanco's boys. With Ricky Brass leaning on his car, and his associates dotting alongside him, Nel faces them all with a wide stance and her arms crossed.

"Well then you shoulda known better," Nel says, responding to a comment I must have missed.

"That little girl disrespected me, made me feel inferior, like she better than me or somethin'. I just came by to ensure that it won't happen again. Somebody must'a not told her to respect her elders, so I just came by to make sure she knows that."

"Don't worry, I got it."

Ricky leans off the car, walking slowly in his cobra-like way towards Nellie. "Obviously you ain't do a good job if she out here runnin' her mouth like that. I'm only doing you a favour — an attitude like that could get y'all in trouble."

"I've never had any problems so far. And thanks for paying me the favour," Nel responds shortly, "but I think I can take it from here."

"Just you? All by yourself?" Ricky stops in front of Nel, mimicking her wide stance and feigning a look of confused empathy. "Doesn't seem like you can protect yo'self all alone, let alone protect a lil' girl that doesn't know when to shut her trap."

Nellie uncrosses her arms and walks even closer to Ricky, looking the five or so inches up into his face yet somehow matching his height, and plants her feet.

"We've been doin' just fine. And I don't need to remind you that I can hold my own against the likes of you. Or do I need to educate you again?"

Ricky looks down at her with anger — his jaw clenched to the teeth-breaking point, but not before I catch a glimpse of embarrassed fear pass over his face. Confused as to what they are talking about, I walk down the steps to make my way over to Nellie, but she stops me.

"Stay on the porch, J," she says, without breaking her gaze from Ricky. "He's just leaving."

"Oh is that so?" He again feigns a look of confusion before continuing, "I don't remember saying that I was done."

"I don't see what else there is to it. You said what you came here to say, and we get the picture. Now get off my property before I call the police." Nellie puts her hands on her hips and whispers, "Or do I need to explain it to you in another way?"

Ricky inhales sharply and immediately moves back, backing away while looking at Nellie wide-eyed.

"C'mon, let's get outta here," he yells to his comrades. "This bitch is crazy."

Ricky quickly walks to the driver's side of his SUV and they all get in, their words muffled by the doors and glass, and speed off into the night. Nellie slowly turns around and exhales deep and slow, hobbling to the doorway as if all her energy has been drained.

"What was all that about?" I ask incredulously.

"He came here to tell me of the little conversation you guys had this morning," she replies nonchalantly. "And he wanted to make sure that we knew that no one should ever speak to him that way again."

She crosses the two front steps in one giant step, stopping in front of me and looking into my face. She's a little shorter than me, so even one step below me and I have to look down at her. Nellie isn't one to skirt around the issue, so she gives it to me straight.

"He wanted to remind us that we're no different from anybody else and how you spoke to him this morning wasn't gonna fly." She holds my chin, forcing me to look into her eyes that bore into mine with loving intensity. "He came here to bully us into submission, to make sure we don't cross him again. But what you said, although in your own *special* way, was completely valid. And you don't have to apologize for anything. Just try to be a little smarter about it — not everyone loves your biting personality."

I look at her with a small smile, grateful for her protection and love; but there is still a lingering question that rises above this feeling.

"I know that, but what were you talking about when you said you were going to tell him in another way?" I ask cautiously. "He seemed to get a little scared when you said that, and I didn't even know that you guys knew each other."

"Everybody knows Blanco and his boys, at least by reputation."

"Yeah, but when Blanco drove us to school —"

"He did WHAT?" Nellie exclaims, raising her eyebrows above wide eyes that now show a mixture of anger and surprise.

I continue trepidatiously, "He drove us to school. He said it was the least he could do after Ricky held us up." Nel fixes her mouth and looks at me with disappointment, ready to say something else.

I continue quickly, to reassure her, "Michael and I didn't want to and tried to say no but he insisted, and I didn't think we were in a position to refuse him. I barely got past the mess I made with Ricky, and I didn't want to make another."

Nellie looks at me with a side-eye but nods, annoyed but comprehending my reasoning. Doing a quiet exhale of relief, I do a silent "woo-hoo" to celebrate cruising past a potential Nellie-lecture. It may be a risk to continue with my query, but if I don't ask now I don't know if I'll ever get an answer.

"It was in the car that Blanco said that you guys actually knew each other. I knew you guys went to the same school, but I didn't know that you hung out together."

"That makes it seem like more than it actually was," Nellie says carelessly, walking into the house as I follow. "Your mom and I used to help him with his homework, along with a bunch of other kids. It was a study group really, nothing more than that."

As I shut the door and she kicks off her flip flops, I follow her into the kitchen to find her resuming her preparation for dinner. "That's still more than knowing him by just reputation," I press. "And it seemed like you know Ricky a little more than you're letting on by the way you were talking to each other. He looked *scared* when you warned him to leave us alone, and you're half his size."

Nel continues to put the now microwaved food onto our plates, continuing her task to an exasperating level of normalcy.

"He used to give everybody trouble back in the day. When he set his sights on your mother and me, I let him know that we were not to be messed with."

"How the hell did you do that?"

"That doesn't matter. What matters is that he knew better not to mess with you either. He knows you're my niece, and he should have known better. I just reminded him of that."

I look at her, dissatisfied with her answer, and frustrated with her indifferent treatment of the whole situation. Ricky has seriously hurt people — people much stronger and tougher than the two of us combined — including women who simply didn't want to be with him. There's only so much a sharp tongue can do before it comes to cut you yourself, and I don't understand how she can be so aloof about this and not fully answer my question. She seems to not notice my unease as she sets our food on the table and sits down, looking at me expectedly.

"C'mon now, let's stop talking about it. I've had a long day and haven't gotten a text from you all day. I'm jonesin' for some news! What's the tea? Is it hot? Go on, spill it."

Amused by her corniness and rudimentary knowledge of the latest slang, I smile and resolve to let it go as I sit down.

47

"It's just *spill the tea*, but yeah okay," I say laughing, ready to dig into some day old curry goat and greens. "It was pretty eventful. Just before lunch I saw Ms. Boykin and apologized for my behaviour."

Nel looks at me with surprise and says, "Oh really? How'd that go?"

"I mean, I am genuinely sorry for insulting her — I shouldn't have done that regardless of whether I agreed with her or not. So I said that, and then she goes —" I pinch my voice in my best Boykin impression before continuing, "'*despite your behaviour I really do value you and, despite the odds, your intelligence is going to carry you far in life.*'"

Nellie looks at me with a confused side-eye, and says, "Ew! Isn't that a back-handed compliment?"

"Yeah. Well, that's just Ms. Boykin."

Nellie shakes her head and smirks, forking her greens into the curry goat sauce.

"Yeah and then Michael and I were eating outside and he was ogling Taylor Stennett —"

"Again?"

"Yeah," I say laughing. "He kept giving me dumb reasons for why he couldn't just walk up to her and talk to her."

"And I bet it was a bunch of air pine and nuttin' drops."

I burst out laughing, Nellie following suit as we humour in Michael's inability to talk to women. Or rather, wom*an*. I sober up as I recount how the rest of the day went, trying to figure out how I'll explain it without sounding crazy.

"Then, after that, the rest of the day got... really weird. Michael and I were laughing and then I just started to feel so sad, like I was gonna lose him or something."

"Why? Did he say something?"

"No, I just felt like I was gonna lose him and I couldn't shake that feeling. We even got shakes at Loni's, and that sinking feeling was just... there. We had a conversation with Ray that wasn't exactly the best, but I don't think that has anything to do with it. And then when we were leaving and Michael and I went different ways —"

I stop. I'm hit again with the shock of the event before I find the breath to continue.

"He almost got hit by a truck at the stop sign."

Nellie drops her fork and straightens, looking at me with wide eyes.

"WHAT?" she shouts. "Is he alright? Is he hurt?"

"He is fine," I assure her, holding out my hand to calm her. "The van narrowly drove past him. But it was going so fast that if it had hit him, he would've really gotten hurt. I was so far back too — I hadn't moved from the diner doors, so I felt so helpless."

"Oh baby," Nellie consoles, reaching across the table to grab my hand. Rubbing her thumb along the curve between my right-hand thumb and forefinger, she calms me down. But tears still prick my eyes, making my vision hot.

"I was so scared Nel. All day I was feeling like something bad was gonna happen to Michael, and then something almost did! I just... I just —"

"Baby, of course, you were scared." Nellie looks into my now tear-filled eyes, speaking in her soothing voice that always calms my nerves. "Your best friend was almost injured in a way that really hits home, especially considering the way his parents passed. And even if you don't really believe it, our family has premonitions. We have this spiritual connection that just can't be explained. Our people all have a spiritual tether to this world that connects not only us to each other but to something greater than us. You can call it deja vu or whatever you like, but that feeling you were having was probably your sixth sense tellin' you something was gonna happen. But luckily enough it didn't. So don't stress yourself J, it's okay now. Alright?"

I look at Nellie, grateful for her settling me in the only way she can while wishing that I believed it.

"I know it didn't happen, but it could have. He could've been hit by that speeding van, and it would've kept going because the driver wouldn't have cared. Michael could've been hurt. He could've died!"

"I know baby girl, but that didn't happen —"

"Yes, but it could have," I insist. I look into her eyes, pleading for her to understand, "It could have happened just like that. I know it could have."

"Baby, how could you know that? It's very possible he could have been seriously hurt, but how could you know those other things would happen?"

"Because I felt it! I don't know how to explain it, okay, but the moment before he reached the stop sign," I explain, reaching out my left hand to visualize the scene, "I saw what could happen clear as day. I saw Michael — and then I didn't because of that van. He could've died if I didn't tell him to stop."

"You told him to stop?"

"Yeah. I yelled his name before he reached the stop sign, and he stopped just in time before the van drove by." Nellie looks as if she's going to praise me, but I continue, "But if I hadn't done that, and if it weren't for that cat, then he could've —"

"Wait, what cat? What are you talking about?"

"That's what's so weird about all of this," I say, perplexed — my train of thought changing rails. "I saw this black cat that started walking from across the street towards my side of the street, and then it looked at me. All of a sudden I saw what could've happened to Michael —"

Nellie suddenly tightens her grip on my hand, causing me to look up at her, with a new expression of seriousness on her face.

"What do you mean there was a black cat?"

I look at her confused and taken aback by her sudden firm tone. "Well... like I just said, there was a cat. There was a black cat across the street that was walking across, and then it looked at me and I just knew what would happen to Michael."

"Was the cat like the one in your dream?"

"Yeah," I drag out, puzzled by how she knew this.

Nellie suddenly lets go of my hand and collapses back into her chair, looking just above my head with a sombre and conflicted look on her face. I look at her, perplexed, and she continues to sit there — silently stewing in her thoughts.

"So you're telling me," she continues slowly, still looking in space above my head, "that you saw a black cat. This cat looked at you, and then you could clearly see that Michael was going to get hurt? You knew what would happen and everything?"

"Yes, I —"

"Explain to me exactly what it felt like."

I look at her confused, misunderstanding the importance of the black cat compared to Michael's near brush with death.

"I don't know, it felt like the feeling I had was building up all day — like there was pressure. Then when I saw the cat, it felt worse than it did all day; and when the cat looked at me, it was like... it was like a movie was playing in my mind. I felt weightless, and my vision disappeared for, like, a second. But then I saw what could've happened. Like I was seeing what was happening from a seat and I had no control. I just had to watch — kind of like that scene in Get Out, where the guy gets hypnotized and he's falling in the air and he sees what's going on but it's from far away, and he has no control over what's happening."

Nellie leans over to the side and rests her elbow on her knee, pinching the skin between her eyebrows and exhaling deeply. I put my hand on hers and bend my head down, assuming this was fatigue from her shift and her interaction with Ricky.

"Nel? You okay?"

"It's happening. Everything is happening so fast." She lifts her head and looks at me, with an air of fear. "You're gonna have to learn who you really are, now."

Nellie gets up and walks to the counter, grabbing her phone and dialling to call someone.

She mutters to herself underneath her breath, "I knew it was going to happen, but I didn't know it would escalate so quickly."

"Nellie, what are you talking about?" I ask, confused and a little apprehensive. Nellie opens her mouth to respond before the person she's calling picks up.

"Hey. It's me. It's happening. The dreams have changed, she's begun her transformation. Yeah, we're coming now."

Nellie places our plates in the fridge, grabbing her keys from the table.

"C'mon, let's go. We're going for a ride."

Confused, I rise from my chair and follow her into the foyer where she quickly puts her shoes on.

"Nel, what's going on? Where are we going?"

"I'll explain in the car, just get your things on quickly."

I stare at her for a moment, my face clearly expressing my unease with this entire situation, before putting my shoes on as well. Nellie walks over to my passenger door to help me open it, but I wave her away annoyed — I slam my hip into the door and pull it open. Nellie meekly backs away and walks wordlessly to the driver's side. Once we're in the car and Nellie starts pulling out of the driveway, I immediately turn to her.

"Alright, spill," I demand.

Nellie breathes in deeply before replying, "You know how ever since your mother passed, you've been having the same dream of being lost in the forest? It's always ended the same — you're lost in the middle of nowhere and you're freaking out because there's no one around to help you.

"Yeah," I reply.

"And then suddenly this morning that dream changes? Now there's a black cat, and it's leading you through the forest to safety, and you start hearing all these voices guiding you."

"Yeah," I reply apprehensively.

"And then today you've been having a feeling that something bad was going to happen. Then somehow, by sheer coincidence, there happens to be a black cat that clarifies that feeling for you to the point that you know exactly what would happen."

I stare at her, wondering what the end of her point is to all of this.

"It's no coincidence that you saw a black cat, J. That cat was sending a message. Leading you to safety, in a sense."

"What are you talking about Nel? That's crazy," I say.

"As crazy as you knowing exactly what would happen to Michael if you hadn't stopped him?"

I look at her with the realization that she is right. What she is saying is no crazier than what I was trying to explain to her earlier. I just can't wrap my head around her stressing the importance of *a cat*.

"I told you that our family is special; we have premonitions and a spiritual connection to this world and the people in it. All black women do, to be honest. But this spiritual connection also ties us to a world outside the realm of human reality."

"Nel, this is ridiculous. I was trying to tell you about something that really scared me today, and here you go bringing up this 'premonition' shit —"

"Watch your mouth, J," Nellie warns me.

"Look, I'm sorry, Nel, but you're not making any sense."

"Maybe not in the sphere of your everyday consciousness. But you have to step outside of what you think you know and try to listen to me."

I roll my eyes and look away before she continues with something that resonates with me.

"Who was it that said, '*There are more things in heaven and earth that are dreamt of in your philosophy*'?" She looks to me, fully aware that anything to do with Shakespeare will make me pay attention. I rely on the seen and the factual, proven by experimentation and repetition. What's been told, in the past and present, by those in power — without any proof of existence, is founded on pure fantasy — and not something I think can be taken seriously. But even those who believe in the rationality of fact also believe in the limitations it creates. Even the most perfectly calculated experiment will always have the hindrance of human error and can't be relied on fully.

"You can't discount what I'm saying just because it doesn't follow your rules of reasoning, Jamila. You know that your dreams, especially now that they've changed, mean something. And it's no coincidence that you saw a black cat in real life the same day you dreamed of one. The cat led you out of the confusion you had in the forest, and things started to clear as you neared safety. As soon as you saw the black cat in real life, what you had been feeling all day began to make sense and you weren't confused anymore. Both led you out of the forest, whether it was the physical one in your dream or the metaphorical one in your mind."

"Okay, fine." I relent, trying to come to terms with what she's telling me. "Let's say I take what you're saying seriously," I continue. "There's a spiritual connection that I have, and it allows me to have *'premonitions'* about the future?"

"Amongst other things," Nellie says mysteriously.

"Alright," I say slowly. "That still doesn't explain what a cat has to do with any of this. Or why we are driving late at night, to an undisclosed location I might add, for no reason."

"There is a reason, J. We'll be there soon, and I will explain as soon as we get there."

"No Nel, I need an explanation now. I may just be 17 but I still have the right to know these things. I deserve to know where I'm going."

Nellie exhales deeply and quickly slows into a lot, putting the car in park before turning to me. Nellie looks at me with love in her eyes but with an expression that implies I don't understand the gravity of the situation. Whatever this situation is.

"This spiritual connection that you have, I have as well. Your mother did too. It's in our blood. It's been in our family for generations, since before our ancestors were kidnapped from Africa and enslaved. It dates to the very first woman in our family. The woman who was the daughter of Bast."

Bast. That sounds familiar. I know that name.

"Bast? I've heard of that name. Isn't that Egyptian for something?"

"Yes, she's an Egyptian cat goddess," she says energetically. "She's the goddess of the home, of women's secrets, and fertility. She was also known for being a guide of the afterlife, and a helper to the dead. She was a fierce warrior, just as she was a protector, and many worshippers idolized her that way. But then history diminished her power and domesticized her into what you've probably seen her as today: a domestic house cat. Despite that, she's still worshiped and feared, just as equally as she is respected."

"Yeah, I know all that. I read a book on her in the public library when I went through my Ancient Egypt phase. I was obsessed with the mythology and the culture — I read dozens of books on it."

"I know you did," Nellie says smiling. "There were so many books piled around the house, your mother and I couldn't look anywhere without seeing one."

"I still don't understand how I'm connected to all of that. We're Jamaican, not Egyptian."

Nel leans forward, placing her elbow on the glove compartment, looking into my eyes before saying, "Our ancestors are the daughters of the goddess Bast. We are connected to her and have her spiritual abilities and powers. The very first woman in our family migrated to West Africa, and it was there that the daughters continued to grow. When we were enslaved, our ancestors were taken to Jamaica — and it was there our family grew."

I lean back and look at her with a blank stare. I cock my head to the side, eyebrows furrowed in disbelief. She leans back too, lips pursed and eyebrows raised in a silent reply — *yup, you heard me*, her expression says. I give my head a little shake — trying to simultaneously process and shake the cotton out of my ears because, let me tell you, they cannot believe what they're hearing. We're the daughters of this Egyptian cat goddess? That doesn't make any sense. I never believed Bast was actually real, and I definitely didn't think I come from a lineage of spiritual super-women. People aren't supposed to have superhuman abilities; we're all supposed to exist by the limitations of human biology. Some may be stronger, or faster, or have a higher IQ, but spiritual premonitions? Given to us by a cat goddess? That's a little far-fetched.

"It was our ancestors, it was our people, that created the medicines, treatments, and protections of pre-colonial Africa that the history books talk about. But the history books got it wrong — they usually do. When we were captured by the slave traders, many of our ancestors who survived were enslaved in different places. The ones that landed in Jamaica are our direct ancestors, and where your great-great-great-great grandmother used to live."

My mother used to tell me that my great-grandmother, three-times removed, was a slave for years, and that she escaped from slavery and got her freedom. Her mother apparently escaped from slavery too but my great-grandmother, thrice removed, was captured not too long after — and was a slave until she escaped. Then slavery was abolished in the 1850s and everyone was free. From chattel slavery that is. Her great-granddaughter immigrated to Canada in the 70s, and we've been in Toronto ever since.

"All this to say, Jamila, we have a power that many people don't have. People have called us witches and warriors, to try to label and define us. But we can't be defined by the laws of human understanding. We are the daughters of Bast, and that means a lot that simply cannot be explained. But I'm going to try as best as I can."

I look away as I try to process all this information — again. If what Nellie is saying is true which, let's be real, I'm really doubting, then everything I've based my beliefs on — the very foundation of my rational existence — has been unreliable. She's asking me to get rid of everything I believe to be true, and that's asking a lot. This can't be true — all of this would've had to have been documented one way or another, and surely history's academia would have relayed this history. Then again, centuries of history have been lost far more times than I could count on both hands, so maybe it's not really that big of a stretch. I look up to take in my surroundings and realize that I know where we are.

"Why are we at Loni's diner?"

CHAPTER THREE

Nellie and I walk up to Loni's diner entrance as I wonder how we're going to get in. It's past closing time and while Loni tends to stay late, all the lights are off and there's no one inside. Or so I thought — not a second later, a light at the back of the diner turns on and Loni walks towards us to open the door. Wearing a loose dress and a headwrap, her gold earrings bob as she moves swiftly.

"Come in, quick," Loni says. Nellie and I obey and scurry in as Loni quickly shuts the door behind us, taking a quick scan of the scene outside the diner before shutting the blinds and turning to us. Except for a lone car passing by, the streets remain deserted.

"Well. I imagine you must be feelin' all kinds of confused, huh baby girl?" I raise my eyebrows in agreement, and say, "Yeah, you could say that. What's going on, Loni? What's with all the secrecy?"

"Why don't we have a little bite to eat."

As I cut my eye in disagreement, Loni walks past us to the back and Nellie follows her, disappearing for a few minutes. I stand there looking at the tile, mouth pursed and eyes wide with disbelief that this is really happening — I mean really, what the hell? When Nellie returns, she slides into one of the booths and looks at me — expecting me to follow along. With no idea of what is happening, I do. I slide into the seat, all the while looking at her with a blank face that still conveys the impression that I am *not* okay with this. She returns my blank stare with her own, with the implicit expression that she couldn't care less — I'll just have to go with it. Black people have a way of saying a lot without having to say anything at all. I bounce my knee, looking around the diner — maybe expecting to discover something new, honestly I couldn't tell you. Loni then walks back through the traffic doors with a tray of cornbread and honey, and some tea in a teapot. Loni places the tray on the table and slides in beside Nellie, dishing the sweet treats onto tiny porcelain plates and serving them to us. She then pours the tea into porcelain cups adorned with tiny yellow daisies. After she's fulfilled her business owner role, she laces her fingers and rests her forearms on the table, looking at me with a small smile and exhaling through her nose deeply.

"You've had quite a day."

"Tuh! Who you tellin'?" She chuckles, but keeps her eyes serious. I continue cautiously, "You know about what happened? With Ricky and... everything else?"

"Yes, Nellie quickly filled me in. I've gotta say, that's one hell of a day you've had, my girl. From your dream this mawnin to a close-call with Michael. Then, come to find out, that close-call with Michael was because of who yuh are. Of what yuh are."

"What I am?"

"Yes. I assume Nellie's filled you in on a little bit of the history behind your... lineage?" Loni looks to Nellie for confirmation, which Nellie provides with a small nod. Loni turns back to me, looking deep into my eyes.

"You are a descendant of Bast, an' with that comes great power an' abilities that many people 'round the world only dream of having. What you went thru today wit' Michael was the beginnin' of your powers manifestin' within you, baby girl. You are beginnin' to evolve into your spiritual self, and it's gonna be a lot more eventful as you continue to grow."

"Wait, so everything Nel said — about our ancestors and the cat goddess — you're telling me is true?" I ask incredulously — not bothering to hide my judgy tone.

"Yes. But I imagine she wasn't able to tell yuh over 500 years of history in a five-minute car ride. Or that you're not alone." I look to Nellie. So there's more? Great.

"Loni is also a daughter of Bast," Nellie says. I stare at Nellie — mouth slightly open in disbelief, for a few moments long enough to make it creepy. She furrows her brow and looks at me, silently wondering if I've just gone comatose. I look to Loni, blinking profusely in confusion, as she nods in agreement. I involuntarily lean back as Loni leans further forward.

"I'm like you, baby girl. So is Nellie. So was your mother."

Okay, now *that* is a mic drop. My mother? A descendant of Bast? How could my mother not have told me this? For the short time my mother was in my life, she was a picture of perfect maternal affection and always showed me love that no other person could imitate. She told me everything — treating me like an actual person, and giving me the respect that came with it. She said she would never lie to me. How could she keep this secret from me?

"Mom lied to me?" I ask, voicing my thoughts aloud.

"She didn't lie to you J," says Nellie. "She just didn't tell you because you weren't ready yet."

"Ready for what? If this is so important, why wouldn't she tell me about this? The omission of the truth is no better than a lie."

"Jamila you have to understand, these abilities are not something to be taken lightly. It takes a lot of responsibility to manage them, let alone use them properly. You were a kid, and you weren't in the right state of mind to learn all of this. It would've been too early for you. You needed to live in the real world first so you could learn how to appreciate it when the rest of it came to light."

"Your aunt's right, baby girl," Loni says. "Everythin' that you can do is beyond what anybody is capable of; it's all in yuh blood, just as it's in mine. But it's a lot to handle — even for somebody grown — so it would've been too soon fi yuh motha to tell yuh about your powers at that age."

"How come I've never noticed these abilities before? You seem like a normal, working-class woman to me."

"Well, I'm not gonna advertise my powers to everybody now, am I? I had to keep it hidden, just as your aunty has."

I relent because she's right. I've never noticed Nel using or exhibiting any superhuman abilities, and my mother wasn't able to do anything out of the ordinary from what I can remember. Except, of course, put a smile on everybody's face. That's not something that everyone can do.

"We are descended from the women who migrated from Egypt," Loni continues, "the women who first had these abilities. We can do things beyond what normal humans are capable of doing — there's so much more we're capable of that defy the odds."

"What exactly?" I ask.

"Come," Loni says, before rising and walking once again towards the back room. I look to Nellie who returns my gaze with a reassuring smile before following Loni. With no other choice but to clarify the muddy waters of recent discovery, I follow as well. I walk through the back doors into the kitchen — past the steel tables that carry bowls, utensils, and cooking appliances on its back — and turn the corner past the stoves to a small brown door. Loni opens the door into darkness, before pulling a small string from the ceiling to dimly illuminate the small closet that lays before us.

Cluttered with janitorial equipment, perishable foods, and wooden shelves housing years of dust and cobwebs, this tiny closet makes me think that a person hasn't graced this space in a long time. But then I look down and see a space on the floor where no dust lies. Loni starts to move things to reveal a small square on the floor, from which a tiny ring protrudes on one side. Loni pulls the ring, disturbing several dust bunnies from their comfortable resting place in the corner, to reveal a small staircase leading lower down into the ground. With a sorry excuse for light that the bulb provides, my vision allows me about a metre into the obscure stairwell. Without delay, Loni descends into the stairwell as Nellie follows close behind. Hesitant to descend into darkness, Nellie looks up to me and reaches her hand out. Looking into Nellie's eyes, I know I can trust her so I grab her hand and follow.

I follow them into the stairwell, slowly tapping my foot along each step so as to not lose my balance, until we all reach the bottom. Dust bunnies tickle my nose as I breathe in the scent of sage and oil. Then, suddenly, light! Loni flips a switch to reveal a room of majestic wonder. Dark stoney walls hold shelves lined with herbs and liquids in glass jars of all shapes, colours, and sizes. Plants hanging from pots suspended from the ceiling cause us to duck in jagged patterns. The veins protrude from their evergreen skin — like the veins in the patches of walled dirt that expound earthy scents. Wooden tables border a path in the centre of the room, atop which lay books bound in leather and loose paper teasing me with fluid cursive writing. The lingering scent of jasmine and sage passes as the dust in the air continues to tickle my nose — accompanying that is the sound of rushing water flowing through the pipes overhead. The light that's been illuminating this magical scene are actually several twinkling bulbs scattered along the ceiling suspended by, to my surprise, nothing. Twinkling lights bobbing in the air, suspended by only the invisible particles of the air we breathe. Loni makes her way through the small path between the tables to a wall lined floor-to-ceiling with books. Nellie makes her way to shelves that house mysterious liquids, pastes, and herbs — a potion pantry of sorts. I stay behind as I take in my surroundings, at once amazed by the pure enchantment of this small space and astounded by the fact that it's beneath the diner of which I am a regular customer.

After Loni finds what she's looking for, she calls out to us, "Come, let me show you somethin'."

I walk towards her, Nellie putting down the bottle she was looking at and joining me, and stand on the other side of a wooden table to face Loni. She places a leather-bound book on the table — antique is the most appropriate description for its condition — and opens it to a page riddled with illustrations and cursive subtitles underneath. Loni points to a slender figure of a ferocious panther on the rustic page. Its skin is blacker than any black I've ever seen — its strong limbs jagged underneath its pelt, and its eyes staring into mine with a lifelike quality that — wait. Is it alive? I don't have much time to consider this before Loni opens the book to another page with a black panther on it.

"This is how Bast originally looked. Before she was made to look like an ordinary house cat, she was viewed as one of da fiercest goddesses in Egypt. She could communicate with the dead an' guide those to the afterlife, protect women against infertility an' sickness, an' avenge those who were wronged. She was a warrior for the people who were tortured and enslaved, an' freed many from their chains."

She turns the page to reveal a drawing of an African woman, with dark skin and white teeth, high cheekbones and carvings of moons indented into her skin.

"This is our African ancestor," Loni continues. "She was a Bastet, a descendant of Bast herself, and brought the bloodline to Africa. It was there that the daughters of Bast grew. She was one of the first Akan women of Ghana to protect the Asante people, and her daughters migrated all over West Africa, spreadin' the bloodline of Bast."

I know about the Asante women; I remember reading in a book that they were ferocious fighters that were also healers of sicknesses and diseases. They lived in the Western part of Africa, which was the most common place to sell and transport Africans to colonial slave traders. The Asante people would've been one of the first to experience slavery, and probably the first to die.

"Our ancestors were doctors and healers. They used local herbs and medicines, infusing it with the power of the bloodline, to cure sickness an' disease, and traded with other tribes to get what they couldn't grow demselves in their community. They often traded wit' other Bastets, keeping a line of communication goin' so that they always knew of new medicines, births of Bastets and when somethin' was threatenin' their people."

"You mean when there was a war, or slave traders capturing them?"

"Yes," Nellie replies. "They needed to always know of the danger that would soon come, so they could prepare for an attack to defend themselves, or to warn other tribes, where Bastets lived. But that wasn't the only threat. They had to know if there was a direct danger against their own lives because Bastets were being hunted."

"Hunted?"

Loni replies seriously, "Yes. Many slave traders, colonialists and missionaries, even other African tribes, said what we were doing was witchcraft. An abomination. We saved lives and protected even more, but those abilities weren't what humans were supposed to be able to do. Specially since so many of the colonialists dem were Christians, and what we did was Satanic to 'em. It was against their religions and contradicted everything they stood for. So they feared us, and this fear drove them to try an' exterminate us."

Loni flips a few more pages to reveal an illustration of carnage: women shot, women stabbed and lying in a pool of blood. Even women being skinned, burned at the stake, and beaten alive. My eyes are suddenly assaulted with the scene of complete and utter genocide.

"Many sought to kill us to try and get rid of our bloodline — even our children were murdered to kill off anyone who may later manifest powers."

"Oh my god," I lament, turning away to let my eyes rest from the darkness of that slaughter and yield to the darkness of my closed eyelids. I don't want to hear this, but I know that I need to. Just because it's not what I want to hear and it isn't pretty, doesn't mean that I can completely disregard my history. I can't believe that this is even my history to begin with, but it is. Being black comes with the same sad history, but I need to hear the other side to know *all* of who I am.

"Not all of them were killed though," Loni continues. "Some of us hid our powers an' cast protection spells on our houses, even entire cities, to keep hunters away. If we were captured, we protected entire slave ships — to keep the other captured Africans alive, and not make it suspicious that only we survived. Rumours spread, told by the foolish an' rich in power, that if you captured a Bastet and used her in some way, you'd be able to harness her abilities for their own gains. They would do this when they were enslaved, but many of us would rather have died than to let that happen. So, di white man dem would resort to using our families an' close ones against us, blackmailing us into submission."

Well, that sounds familiar — no matter where you look, it seems imperialism rears the same ugly head. Loni turns the page again to reveal a black woman dressed in finer clothes than field slaves were allowed to wear back then — holding a silver tray and standing beside a man in an expensive-looking armchair. Nellie walks over beside Loni as she continues, "Many of us were enslaved and forced to submit to their slave owners wishes if we wanted to protect our families and loved ones. They would seduce women for their masters by using perfumes that would put them in a drugged stupor — mostly slaves who were raped and wouldn't be able to prove it, or well-off women of society who were too esteemed to marry them otherwise. They'd prolong their lives with potions, protec' them against sickness an' disease, an' even kill their enemies. They were enslaved just as were other African people, but used in different types of ways."

I take all of this in as I look at the pages illustrated with different handwritings, scattered all over. This makes me wonder: how many people have written their stories in this book? How many have written our history in the countless books that surround us? How many have died to ensure that this history is told? Loni notices my trepidatious face and leans over the table, placing her hand atop my mine.

"You okay, baby?" she asks.

"Uh, yeah," I respond shakily. "It's just, y'know, a lot to take in. It would be stupid of me to not at least try to believe all of this, but this is all… so much. I feel like I have to do a factory reset on my brain and start over."

"I get that," Nellie says. "This is a lot to swallow, but you have to remember Jamila, that you aren't the first to go through all of this. It was a lot for me to take in when my powers started manifesting, and it sure took a lot out of your momma. We know how ludicrous all of this sounds, but don't think you're going through it blindly. You've got Loni and me. We're here for you baby."

I exhale deeply and smile at Nellie, appreciative of her loving kindness.

"So, I'm a Bastet?" I state, more than ask.

"Yes," Nellie and Loni say simultaneously.

"And we come from a long line of women who are descended from an Egyptian goddess."

"Yeah," Nellie says.

Loni replies, "That's right."

"And all these powers that they had, I'm going to have too?"

"Not exactly," Loni says. I look at her quizzically as she walks to the shelf to pull out another book. Laying it on the table, I come face to face with a black panther prowling behind a woman dressed in flowing dressings. The panther ferociously bares sharp teeth as it prowls across the cover of the book... beginning to *move*. Upon looking closer I realize that my eyes are not betraying me, and I truly do see the panther slowly slinking across the cover. It looks real, but I know it can't be more than magic playing tricks on me. Loni opens it to show, yet again, a black panther sitting beside an African woman — this time in red dressings.

"Every Bastet manifests their powers differently," Nellie says. "It wasn't always that way, but the years of rape by slave owners have... muddled our bloodline. Just as genetics gives you some traits from your mother and some from your father, Bastets soon had genetics from white men that eventually drowned out the supernatural traits of their Bastet mothers. Some of us weren't able to perform the same abilities and, eventually, some of us lost these powers altogether. Now it's just a whisper in some descendants. Women who have sleep paralysis or say they see ghosts in their sleep are actually connecting to their ability to speak to the afterlife, but it's just a little fuzzy. And what you would call deja vu is actually our ability to have premonitions, but it is very weak."

"Wait, are you saying we can see the future?"

"All Bastets were able to have premonitions, to predict when trouble was comin' for the people dem," Loni replies, "but many Bastets can't do that any more. We think you may be able to, after seeing what almost happened to Michael, but we can't be sure until your powers start manifestin' fully. Even though you are who you are, it might just be everyday deja vu creepin' up — and it may jus' be heightened because of your abilities. After all, I don't have that ability and neither does Nellie."

Nellie shakes her head in response. Loni points to the page to bring my attention to the panther and the woman again.

"Another ability that's long disappeared from our bloodline is our feline manifestation. Just as our goddess mother did, we were able to transform into the ferocious black panther. In times of trouble, our ancestors would change from their human form to their feline one and fight in battles — against other tribes or against slave owners who meant to enslave them, and to protect the tribe in defence."

"They turned into *black panthers*?"

"Yes," Loni replies. She sets to continue but I interrupt quickly, with a million questions sitting on the tip of my tongue.

"That's humanly impossible. People don't just turn into animals, let alone black panthers. The transformation of the human skeleton to that of a panther would be too much pain for a human to bear — we'd have a cardiac arrest from the pain alone. How long did this take? And wouldn't there be stories of women just suddenly turning into black panthers? That can't be true!"

"You thought everything else was impossible not too long ago, but you're startin' to believe it, aren't you?" Nellie asks. She shoots me a knowing look, in that one expression telling me to check myself. She's right — just an hour ago I thought all of this was insane, and now I'm starting to come to terms with the fact that what I thought to be true is really just a front for something bigger. Slowly, but surely.

"From what these books tell us, the transformation process hurts like hell," Nellie continues. She turns a few pages in the first book, looking for something specific and coming up with nothing. She then turns to the book with the lone panther on the cover and finds what she's looking for. She points to a page that shows an illustration similar to the 'Road to Homo Sapiens', but instead of an ape gradually transforming into a sapien, I see a black woman transforming into a black panther. Each figure is outlined, with the inner entrails exposed to show how the transformation from human to panther happens.

"It took centuries for humankind to evolve from the common ape, so imagine evolving from a human into a panther in a matter of seconds. It took years for the Bastet to control this transformation; lots of our ancestors couldn't control when they transformed and didn't know how to transform back. Some of them stayed in the feline state for so long that they weren't able to transform back into a human."

"Oh my God. They just stayed black panthers forever?"

"Yes, baby girl," Loni responds. She turns a few more pages to a white man, accompanied by several others, and brown men in traditional Egyptian attire, outside a cave. At the bottom of the page, it says '*Dig site of human and animal remains. Howard Carter. Cairo, Egypt. 1925.*'

"In the past, when archeologists went digging for remains in Egypt, they found panther remains in the fallen cities of villages. They assumed that they died from starvation, or were killed by other animals or the tribe. But as science advanced, they were able to see that the bones had human DNA. That by itself made no sense to them then — but to make it even more confusin', they discovered that the part that was human was always female. They couldn't explain it and so, ironically, they buried their findings. There were so many digs goin' on back then; everyone was crazy about Egypt and the mythology inna it, and they thought that the public wouldn't miss these, so they just focused on other sites and moved on."

"So there's nothing in the history books about this? Even if it didn't make any sense, this is a huge discovery to contribute to biology and science. Hell, Mythbusters would go crazy over this shit."

"Language," Nellie warns.

"Sorry," I reply.

"Can you tell me that you've ever read, or seen, anything 'bout a human-panther type-a hybrid?" Loni asks me incredulously. "Forget Bigfoot, or the Loch Ness Monsta. This would'a been too much for the public to handle. This was actual proof of something existin' that wasn't just human or animal, but both; the other myths were just that: a myth. This is somethin' they couldn't explain."

"Okay, I get that. I just can't believe that they were able to hide something this big."

"It isn't that far fetched," Nellie says. "You're always tellin' me how the history books leave stuff out or whitewash history, to make what actually happened look not so bad."

"Well, it's true!" I exclaim. "The education system brainwashes students into a postcard-pretty version of history that denies all the carnage, rape, and genocide that actually happened to Native people, African Americans, and countless others. I mean even Thanksgiving —"

"Uh-uh," Loni groans. "Don't get started, mi nuh wah hear anotha one of yuh rants. Come, step off yuh soapbox and get back to what we're talkin' about. Nellie, put dis bak pon da sumn deh, and grab mi di amulet."

Nellie obeys, placing the book back and grabbing a gold necklace with a dangling infinity symbol. Loni places it in the palm of her hand, the pendant sitting in the centre. As I look closer, I realize I've seen this necklace before.

"Wait, this is Mom's necklace! She used to wear it all the time, I'd never see her without it on. How did you get it?"

"After your momma died," Nellie replies, "we took it so that one day you could have it. Your mother always intended to give it to you when the time was right. Unfortunately, she didn't get that chance."

"In Egyptian mythology," Loni says, "Bast was said to be di mother of Ra, and so she was associated with the all-seeing eye. I cannot tell yuh for certain if this is true, but the eye can see beyond di limitations of time that humans aave created. This infinity symbol represents the all-seeing ability that Bastets wield, with our protective spirits an' ability to see into di future. This amulet helps us to focus so we can channel our abilities when we begin to manifest our powers. Three of our earliest ancestors made several, imbuing dem with the protective spirits they all possessed an' passed it down to the coming generations. This is one of the few that were made that still exist today. With this amulet, you will be able to control these abilities — when they happen, and how strong they are. Without it, you'll be flappin' like a sail in the wind; it'll surge through you and overpower you — and you may end up hurtin' yourself an' others. You'll need this, especially as your manifestations begin."

The entire time Loni was speaking, my eyes were transfixed onto the amulet. Its golden luminescence glisten underneath the twinkle of the lights and cast its shine to twinkle in my eyes. With an almost hypnotic effect, the amulet seems to cast a glow from its outer edges, pulsating and drawing my gaze ever closer. With her last sentence, however, my gaze shifts to Loni's eyes.

"Are my manifestations beginning to happen?" I ask.

"It appears that way, baby girl."

Nellie comes from the other side of the table to face me, leaning into her arm as she leans forward towards me.

"This is gonna be a lot, J. You need to know that goin' in. We're here for you every step of the way, but it's gonna be a mental and physical war that you never knew you enlisted for. This amulet will make things a little easier for you. Not *easy*, but easier."

I look into her eyes, searching for the truth in her words and coming up with love and protective instinct, and look again to the amulet within Loni's palm. I tentatively grab the amulet and place it in the palm of my hand, and feel a surge within my body. Like a gust of warm summer breeze, my entire body swells with — I don't know what. Power? Spirit? I guess I'll find out.

"Wear this around your neck," Loni says, "and do not take it off. It will help you to control your powers as they begin to reveal themselves and tap into your protective instinct as trouble comes near."

"That's convenient. Maybe this way I'll know when Blanco's boys are around."

"Yes, but there are worse dangers than the likes of dem eediats."

"Of course there is. This is Toronto. I can't turn a street corner without seeing something that I definitely shouldn't be seeing."

"You have more than that to be wary of, baby girl. There are still people in this world who wants to harm us, either for fear of our abilities or lustful control of them. We continue to be hunted and must be aware of coming Toubabs."

"Tou-*what*?"

"Yes, the Toubabs. The white men, and women, who enslaved the African people, and Bastets. The slave owners were called this by Africans they kidnapped, and as a sect of these slavers started hunting Bastets, it stuck. They still exist as a cult, calling themselves the Protectors of the Pure, and continue to kill and exploit us. They are stationed all over the world, but many are in the United States. Many of our people have been captured by the agents of this group, and countless more killed — either right away or from the torture of their capture."

"Wait, how can this be?" I ask. I don't wait for an answer, knowing right away the answer to my question. Our history books, though lacking severely in its authenticity, are ingrained with the blood inked by the pen of its authors. The same blood that was spilt by the very same hand as its writer, our history is a home for hate groups that aim to exterminate the people to whom are natives to this land, and the people who were taken from theirs to till it.

Nellie moves to answer my rhetorical question and says, "There are so many hate groups out there that want to harm people that are different — anyone that doesn't fit into their model of pure humanity. Bastet women tick a lot of the boxes that contradict their values and are the most hunted of all, though many don't know it. To know about this would mean that our history and our abilities were public knowledge, and that couldn't happen. The Toubabs knew that just as we did, so they hunted us in silence as we escaped underground."

"Are you saying that I'm being hunted? Like right now, as we speak? I haven't even done anything, and my powers haven't even shown up yet!"

"Yes I know, baby girl," Loni responds slowly. "But the Toubabs are always looking for us, even new Bastets that are — or will be — coming into their powers. You had a mark on your head from before you took your first steps, and must take many to keep you alive."

Keep me alive? This is all too much. I had no idea that my years were numbered before hearing all of this. Why do I have to be hunted? I've done nothing wrong. I don't even want to be a Bastet — who wants supernatural abilities anyways? This isn't a comic book — I don't need to save lives, I just need to live my own. I just want to be like everybody else: get good grades, graduate and go to a good school, have a boyfriend or two along the way, and live a normal, average, everyday life. Why do I need to be a saviour? Why do I need to be different from everybody else if it's only going to get me killed?

"No. No, this isn't what I want. I don't want to have to be scared and always be looking over my shoulder for someone trying to kill me. I want to live a normal life of a teenager. I want to go to school. I want to hang out with Michael. I want to eat at your diner — or I wanted to, before I knew that there was a witches lair down here."

"I know you want to go back to the way things were baby girl, but this is who you are. You don't get to live a normal life 'cause of the colour of your skin, an' you had to learn that just as you have to learn this. You're not like everybody else, you don't get to live the life others do. Just as you knew that your skin came with conditions before, so do your powers."

"No, I didn't sign up for this." I shake my head in denial of my situation, not wanting my fate to have been pre-written. Nellie moves towards me but I back away. I look into her eyes, conviction reflecting into mine that are filled with denial, and continue to shake my head.

"I don't want any of this."

I turn and speed walk, up to the stairs that groan in protest and out of the diner, and to the car. I bang my hip on the passenger door but it doesn't open. I growl in frustration, hitting my hip on the door one, two, three more times, before it finally opens and I swing the door open. I sit in my seat, breathing heavily — less from my sprint and more from the gravity of the situation. Of my situation. This is not what I thought was gonna happen when I woke up this morning. Silly me to expect a day of averageness: breakfast, school, lunch, more school, and post-school milkshakes. Sleep and Repeat. That is my everyday routine. Well, I certainly deviated from that routine, and it's shaken me up so much I feel every limb in my body as if I'm hyper-aware. I look at my arms, the lines on the palms of my hands, the veins in my wrists, even my fingernails, in the hopes that I won't find an indicator of this so-called 'power' that is manifesting within me. I didn't sign up for this. I didn't want any of this.

Nellie and Loni come to the doorway after a few minutes, looking at me every so often and exchanging words inside that are muffled by the door before finishing. Nellie walks to the car and leans into her seat with exhaustion; suddenly, it occurs to me how much this is taking out of Nellie. I seem to have forgotten that she's worked a full shift at the hospital and managed to take me on a late-night escapade while relaying centuries of history to a less-than-willing listener. She must be depleted of all her energy. My instinct to soothe her bubbles up from underneath my fear, but my juvenile disposition allows my fight or flight instinct to reign supreme, and I just stare at her. Way to go, Jamila. Nellie inhales deeply several times, her hands laying in the 10-and-2 position and her head bowed with eyes closed. She opens her eyes — wordlessly, she starts up the car and slowly pulls out of the parking lot — setting us homeward bound.

I plop into bed, my entire body exhaling exhaustion in preparation for a good night's rest. What a day it's been. I woke up from a weird dream, an unusual start to the day. I had to go about my day with an uncomfortable feeling in the pit of my stomach. Turns out that feeling in my stomach was the manifestation of an ability I have due to a centuries-long bloodline connected to an Egyptian goddess. And that ability helped me save my friend from dying a gruesome death. Did I miss anything? Oh yeah, and my aunt Nellie and Loni, the two closest women in my life after my mother, also have these powers. This must be how people feel when they find out family secrets. Except they don't have a bounty placed on their heads placed before they were even born. Okay, how am I not hyperventilating right now? How am I okay? This is all so wildly insane, but I mean stranger things have happened. Just look at the American President.

A knock raps on the door before Nellie enters my room, not bothering to wait for my reply before opening the door. She walks over to my bed and sits on the edge, cocking her head to the side and looking at me. Refusing to look at her, for fear that I'll burst into tears, I stare at the ceiling. The bubbling pattern of the white ceiling is just begging me to scrape it off. Man, that would be satisfying. So would escaping this conversation I'm about to be in.

"So," Nellie says.

"Yeah," I reply.

"That was somethin', huh?"

"You got that right." We sit in silence for a minute longer before Nellie continues.

"I know you don't want to accept this. I understand it's a lot to swallow at once. It's definitely not on the same playing field as college applications."

"It's not that I don't accept it," I counter, but then catch myself before continuing, "well, okay, I thought this was a bunch of hogwash at first but I came around eventually. This is our history. My history. It's who I am, whether I like it or not, and I have to come to terms with that."

"Yeah, well, knowing something and actually putting it into practice is not the same thing. You're scared, and you don't want this to be your reality. That's why you left. That's why you can't even look me in the eye."

This causes me to shift my gaze to her, forcing myself to hold it together and not tear up. She gives me a small smile, tenderly easing me into reality.

"I understand your fear, it's not irrational — but who you are is a beautiful thing. It's magic, baby. What you can do can cause a lot of damage, but it can also do a lot of good. Our history, though gory, is filled with pride, power, and passion. I can show you how to best control your abilities, and how to use them for good. The most damage you should do is in defence because, like it or not sweetie, you are in danger. Even if you cast away this part of yourself, you are still being watched. Accepting who you are will only help you to survive. To live. Loni and I want that for you, Mama, that's all."

I look away again, my eyes threatening to spill its salty contents, and turn to cuddle my pillow. I hear Nellie exhale behind me, then place her hand on my shoulder.

"Just let me know if you change your mind. I really hope you do." I hear Nellie make her way to the door and linger just inside the doorway before she bids me farewell, "Goodnight, J." She closes the door and as I turn over to watch her leave, my face brushes against something hard on my pillow. I look to find the amulet lying on my pillow, unclasped and ready to be clasped around my neck. I turn over again and my eyes, unable to hold back their brackish tides of water, as I cry myself to sleep.

I find myself yet again in the dark jungle. Leaves brush my face as the dirt pushes itself through my toes. Jagged stones cut through my skin as my haggard breath threatens to break through my chest. I'm running again. I'm always running away, but now I know what from. I'm running away from a danger that wishes to hurt me, to use me, to kill me. I must run away lest they get me. I must run away to freedom. I'm scared, but now I know why I am scared. Now I know that I have a reason to fear. But I'm lost. I'm still lost! I can't get out. How do I get out?

I break through to the clearing. The same clearing, open enough to grant me a 360-view of towering trees, evergreen foliage and fauna, and the surrounding wildlife.

"Hello?" I ask the trees. Silence answers with the echo of my cry.

"HELLO!" I scream to the sky. Her darkness answers in reply.

Once again I close my eyes and try to slow my breathing, struggling more to slow my fear that is running full-speed. I open my eyes to the sky to see the moon, its silvery shine lighting up the sky and the path. I look around, knowing how my last dream has changed, that I now have a feline companion to join me. I finally turn and see the black cat: its inklike fur still glistening, its golden eyes still piercing into my fear and inserting its protective spirit. Sitting in anticipation on its haunches, it waits for me. For what I do not know.

"Daughter," it says, its singular vocality a surprise despite my knowing of its arrival.

As I expected, it turns and starts walking down a path I hadn't seen before, expecting me to follow. But I hesitate. I know that she will lead me to safety and that I should trust her. Where she's leading me will definitely be better than where I've been — wherever that was — and it'll be better than wandering around lost in fear. But I hesitate.

As she walks further and further away, my fear begins to creep in once again with rapid speed. I can't stay here feeling like this; the fear is suffocating, and I know the more lost I get the more stifling the fear will be. But if I go with her, I may not know what will happen. I won't be the same. I'll be... I don't know what I'll be. Normal, everyday me is what I'm used to. It's what I'm good at. I've gotten by and survived this long by doing what I always do, and it's been working for me so far. Deviating from that would change everything, and not knowing what I'd actually be choosing over ordinary life makes it all the more daunting. The lack of knowledge is unchartered territory, ironically resembling where I currently stand, and it's not safe.

The cat stops and turns, sitting on its haunches again and looking at me. Wagging its tail lethargically, she waits in patience for my decision. I look into her golden benevolent eyes and feel as if they melt into my soul. My body relaxes with a feeling of warmth, the cat's liquid love melting into my bones, muscles, and ligaments to assuage my fears. In that instant, I know that wherever she is leading me offers more safety than where I stand. Routine is safe, its arms offer the comfort of security, but I now know that routine no longer awaits my reciprocated hug. No — instead I'll be embraced with a vice-like grip that intends to harm me. I know that I'm no longer safe, whether I continue to hide in the facade of routine refuge or follow my feline friend to terrain that, while uncharted, will allow me to defend myself from an unforeseen enemy. I can't hope that the fear will dissipate, I have to cast it away. And the only way I can do that is to cast away false security for my destiny. It'll be more of a safeguard against the dangers that threaten me simply for who I am.

I slowly walk towards the black cat that resumes walking into the jungle, onto the path that guides the way to discovery. She slowly picks up her pace, going from a walk to a trot, and from a trot to a run. I struggle to keep up with her — my face no longer scoured by passing branches and leaves, my feet no longer cut by jagged stones and terrain. Instead, the leaves seem to lift in passing, and the ground offers a cushion for my feet to beat along. As I begin to see where the path will clear, I turn to see, what was once the black cat, a black panther sprinting beside me. Staying within a speed that I can struggle to manage, I see its stretching limbs underneath its jet black pelt, its eyes glowing gold to illuminate our destination. As I come up beside the panther, I realize how odd it is that I'm able to keep up with this fast feline. I look at my feet, which blurs on the ground, and at the passing surroundings which look like a scene out of The Flash. I'm running. I'm running fast. Much faster than I've ever run before — and it's a trip. I begin to hear the voices calling to me again. Friendly voices. Friendly female voices. My feet beat along the path to the beat of my name being called, the surrounding night echoing Jamila.

Finally, I hear the one voice that towers above the rest. The voice that sung me to sleep, read me bedtime stories, and towards which I run ever faster now. My mother's voice, calling my name, gets louder as I get closer. Closer. Closer. Then, I arrive in a different clearing — a circle that's bordered with different foliage, fauna, trees, and the familiar night. The panther darts behind a large tree, creeping along the other side. The fear of losing sight of her causes me to start running, and I follow behind her. I pace behind her, following her around the trunk of the tree — but she's too fast. I struggle to keep up with her but she seems to always be just three steps ahead of me — until finally, I lose sight of her. Startled, I dart around the tree, going once, twice, three times around it — still, I don't see the panther. I begin to hyperventilate, grabbing frantically at the tree trunk as if she magically disappeared into the tree, scared once again of being lost and alone. I thump my forehead against the tree, the rough exterior unwelcoming to my skin — I breathe frantically. Then I hear my name.

"Jamila," my mother says.

I turn around and come face to face with my smiling mother. Dressed in all red — the thin fabric flowing over her slim frame, her brown skin glistening from the reflection of the moonlight and the whites of her eyes casting a different type of light. She looks at me, her eyes swimming with an emotion that I've wished for years that I could see again. At that moment, I feel everything that I've been feeling for the past decade: sadness, love, mourning, loss. I begin to tear up as she stares at me more, the intensity of her gaze holding me to my spot. She raises her arm and places her hand on my cheek, her light-touch heavy with love. My mouth, filled with cries, feels thick and heavy as my emotions overtake me. I open my mouth to call out her name when, suddenly, she places her hand on my forehead. Like a blow to the head, I fall back, my eyes closing from the impact.

I wake up in my bed, jumping up and breathing heavily. My skin is slick with sweat, and my bed sheet sticks to me all over. I fumble in the dark for a glass of water on my bedside table and gulp it down in 3 quick breaths. As I quench my thirst, I gasp again for air and struggle to calm down. This is the biggest change in my dream, even more than the previous night, and I grapple to figure out what this means. I begin to cry as the overwhelming nature of my situation — my dream, and my fight with who I am and who I want to be — culminates, to break down the dam holding back my tears.

It really couldn't get any clearer: I have to accept who I am and go under Nellie and Loni's wing. These dreams have been getting more intense, and more vivid as the days go by. I just saw my mother — and she touched me! Dreams can be pretty realistic, but this isn't like any dream I've had before. Especially since I know these dreams aren't just abnormal pictures in my brain — this is an actual connection between my mind and another reality. This isn't going to just go away. I'll always have to look over my shoulder if I try to deny and avoid my abilities — but if I let them help me, then at least I'll be prepared to defend myself when danger comes. I'm not really safe if I ignore my powers and my history because I'll be hunted no matter what. I pose a threat for simply being who I am already — a black woman. My powers just add fuel to that fire, but this is a fire that I have to keep raging or else I'll be extinguished. I cannot stifle my internal fire, I must let the flame burn eternal. But will that flame burn me in the process?

I rise from my bed as my alarm wails at 7:00, my body aching from lack of rest. I didn't fall back asleep after my dream, rather just tossed and turned and closed my eyes. But the image of my mother that I saw once my eyes closed, caused me to open them again. I roll from my bed onto the floor, prolonging the time before I have to take on the day. I lay on my back on the floor, staring up at the Novelfall as the books sway lazily from their satin ties. Staying there for a few minutes more, I finally get up to walk to my closet; since I go to public school, I don't have to wear a uniform. This means that I get to choose what I wear everyday — but today, I don't want to make that choice. I'd rather just go back to bed and not take on the day at all. Actually, you know what, I wish choosing an outfit was the hardest of all the choices I'll have to make today. I settle for my self-proclaimed uniform: a band tee, blue jeans, and some sneakers — setting the clothes on my bed and my shoes on the floor. I walk to the bathroom, looking at Nellie's room to see if she's awake and find an answer to my question after hearing the rustling of her preparing for the day as well. I won't greet her right away — I need just a little more time to come to terms with what I'm going to tell her.

I step into the shower, turning on the cold water in the hopes it will wake me up. Succumbing to my stubbornness, I turn it to a scalding hot temperature after just a minute. After I'm done, I step out onto the plush white bath mat and towel off before I brush my teeth. As I turn around and lean on the sink edge, I look up to the dangling plants that droop from the steam of my hot shower, bobbing in their hanging state. I stay in this tranquility a minute longer as the rising sun shines its light through the skylight, brightening the room to a more fairytale-like wonder. This gives me a little energy — the rays seeming to settle in my very bones, and the sun seems to shine even brighter as I wash out my mouth and get ready. After pulling my hair up into a bun and getting dressed, I walk to the kitchen and see Nellie already sitting at the table with a cup of coffee raised to her mouth. Her breakfast and mine are in their places on the table. She looks up to me as she does every day, with a small smirk ever present on her visage.

"Good morning," she says, as she sips from her mug and reads the daily news on her cell phone.

"Morning," I reply, sitting down to dig into my chocolate chip pancakes, drowning them in maple syrup. Last night really tired me out, so saying that I am hungry doesn't even begin to describe how ready I am to polish off this plate. But I need to do something first.

"I'll do it," I say. Nellie looks up from her phone, simultaneously dropping her mug, and looks at me.

"What?"

"I said I'll do it," I look at her, holding her gaze. "I'll accept my manifestation and do everything you and Loni say I need to do to control my powers. If they're coming, whether I like it or not, it's best I learn how to use them for good. So I'll do it."

With that, I end the conversation and dig into my pancakes. Enveloped with the task of stuffing my face, out of the corner of my eye, I see Nellie looking at me — smiling her small smile. Eventually, she continues to eat her breakfast and read the news, continuing our daily morning rituals that will likely be the only routine events that we'll ever do again.

CHAPTER FOUR

I met Michael outside and we biked to school — uninterrupted by locals, Blanco's boys, or a cult of hunters pursuing my body and soul. Nellie told me before I left to go to the diner after school — to do my homework, and that she'd meet me there after her shift. She said I needed to start my training right away, that we couldn't leave anything to chance and the sooner I learn what I can do, the better. I still hadn't told her about my dream from last night, the lump of fear and chocolate chip pancakes in my throat stopping any words from flowing — so I told myself that it could wait till tonight.

We arrive at Brimmer Hall in a normal, completely average way. We hop off our bikes and Michael fastens his to its lock. The school body rushes into school as 8:55 a.m. rolls in. We walk into school and to our lockers, which conveniently sit right across each other — the hallway, the only barrier to our conversation. I struggle to push past the throng of students who take up space in the hallway, Michael cutting his eyes at several couples making out against the lockers along the way. I've been a little quiet since this morning, which is quite unlike me, but I thought not so much that Michael would take notice. He, after all, likes to run his mouth just as much as I do; but he knows me better than I know myself, and must've taken notice of my change in character.

"Hey," he calls to me, opening his locker and getting his books for class. "You good? You've been off all morning. You've barely said a word and, usually, I can't get you to shut your trap." I smile mechanically, knowing that response is what's required after a joke, but I'm not feeling the emotion.

"Yeah, I'm good. Nellie and I had a talk at Loni's last night and it was some stuff that I didn't know about my mom."

"You were at Loni's last night? You went there again after we were there?"

I pause and wonder if I've said too much. After all, Nellie said that this was a centuries-old secret that has been kept under wraps, and I can only imagine that that must've been from everyone — even the friends closest to us.

I shrug nonchalantly and respond, "Yeah, I told her what almost happened to you and she took me out for some ice cream to cheer me up."

"Of course," he chuckles lowly, "I almost got mowed down and you were treated with an ice cream cone. I told Nana what happened to me, and she smacked me upside the head." He closes his locker door and makes his way over to me. Fixing his face and putting his hands on his hips, he impersonates Ms. Dell's voice, "*Michael Jermaine Smith. How dumb you gotta be to not see a van comin' your way? I done told you, time an' time again, to look both ways when crossin' the street. It ain't rocket science, pickney!*"

I laugh, this time sincerely, and close my locker before we head down the hallway. On Wednesdays, I have Advanced Bio first period and he has history, before the second period where we both have Art 3000. We stop in the middle of the hallway in front of our respective classroom doors and turn to each other. Stopping the flow of human traffic, students walk around us in a hurry to get to their classes. The couple that was preoccupied with each other's mouths not even a second ago, now throwing us dirty looks for being in their way. Michael kisses his teeth and cuts his eyes at them, annoyed with their audacious hypocrisy. A sophomore with his hands piled high with textbooks, even cusses us out before speed-walking away.

"That doesn't surprise me," I reply to Michael's story, "but that's just Ms. Dell's way of saying she's happy you're okay."

"Yeah. I just wish she would say it with less anger. Maybe even a smile if she's feelin' generous."

I smile amused before he continues, "So you were talkin' about your mom, huh? You okay?"

"Yeah," I reply. "It was just a lot to swallow, especially with what almost happened to you that day. Hearing something new, so long after she died..." I stop as my voice catches in my throat, suddenly overtaken with emotion. Michael puts his hand on my shoulder and looks me in the eye with empathy and understanding.

"I get it," he says, which I highly doubt. "You don't have to say anything else. I got you."

Even though Michael could have no idea what I'm talking about, he still knows that I was thrown from what Nellie told me, and whatever I'm going through, he was going to be there to support me. Regardless of what he knew, or didn't know, I couldn't ask for a better friend. I smile at him gratefully; returning my smile, we bump fists in farewell, him heading to the right and myself heading to the left.

As the bell rings to signal the end of the first period, I rise from my desk and rush to my locker, in order to make it to my next period within five minutes. Doors open down the hall as other classes come to an end, and students rush into the hallway to make it to their next classes. Kids calling out their friends names, saying "*Yo, fam*," and dapping in greeting. Others lazily move to their destinations — nowhere near ready to go to their next class. As I open my locker to put my books away, I see out of the corner of my eye the pictures taped to the inside of the door. There's the Polaroid of Nellie and I in Loni's diner after my first day of starting high school, taken by Loni herself. I know this because there's a smudge in the top right corner where her thumb was, and Loni isn't exactly a photography mogul. Below that is a picture of Michael and I when we were younger, swinging on Ms. Dell's porch swing. We were trying to see how high we could swing and were in the process of swinging it forward and almost breaking our necks. This didn't sit well with Ms. Dell, who is approaching us in the corner of the frame with her finger outstretched and her mouth wide, in what I can only assume was her mid-reprimand. Finally, at the bottom, is a picture of my mother. She's alone in this picture; her, Nellie and I went to the park that day for a picnic, as a celebration of me winning the spelling bee that year. She was picking flowers for us to put in a tiny little vase she brought, to add "Mother Nature's magic touch" to our picnic. In the picture, she's holding a handful of dandelions in her left hand that rests on her shoulder. Her left arm rests on top of her right arm that's crossed across her waist and holding onto her side. She's wearing a white floral sleeveless dress, with pink daisies printed all over and buttons going down the front of the bust. She's wearing the amulet, and her hair is loosely pulled back in a bun with strands framing her face. She's smiling, ever so carefree, and the sun shines on her as if it knew that she was shining from within herself. I remember that day so clearly — she smelled sweet and spicy, like honey and cinnamon. She smelled like home. She used to tell me that when I turned 18 she'd gift me that necklace; but after she died, I couldn't find it anywhere in her belongings. I was devastated to have lost something that reminded me of her, but I knew that even that necklace couldn't replace her. I had no idea it was something that could protect me and help me focus as my powers manifest. I guess there's a lot of things she didn't tell me. I stand there a moment longer, staring at that picture that I've ingrained in my memory with exacting clarity before I close my locker to make my way to Art 3000.

When I arrive in the room, I see Michael already sitting in our regular spot, hunching over a painting he's been working on for ages. The guy is a genius with numbers, but when it comes to art, his work is comparable to that of a kindergartener. The room attached to ours, where the band practices their songs every second period, echoes with saxophone squeaks and inconsistent beats from the drums. From the backroom to the left, where all the art supplies are stored, walks out our art teacher — Ms. Cortez. Besides Loni, Ms. Cortez is one of my favourite people ever. Ms. Cortez is pretty young, I don't think any older than 30, and I'm sure her beauty will stay with her for many years. She has light brown skin, brown eyes, and curly hair that she always keeps up in a bun with a single chopstick to hold it in place. Her daily uniform usually consists of an oversized button-up shirt of some kind, baggy blue jeans, and a pair of Vans — with a paint smudge on her cheek to accessorize. Not only is she laid back, but she's an expert at mingling her sweet personality with her sarcastic mentality. Her humour is pretty in line with mine and because of that, I took a liking to her almost instantly. I first met her sophomore year, when I was pulled aside by the principal because of a sketch I did for an art project where we had to show the hypocrisy of society. I did a drawing of Trayvon Martin raising his fist balled up while wearing a hoodie. The hoodie was made of words, both big and small, that contradicted each other: Threat, Child, Dangerous, Boy, Victim, Perpetrator, etc. I wanted to show that what was being said about him in the media, and what was being told about him by those closest to him, were so wildly different that one surely had to be false. His murder sparked in me the knowledge of how unjust the world is and I wanted to use my art project to showcase that. Mr. Williams said that, while a realistic likeness, it was too sensitive a subject to use and suggested I redo my project. Ms. Cortez, however, thought it was a perfect depiction of the contradiction between what's promised by the justice system, and what's actually received. She gave me an A. Ever since then, she's been my favourite teacher my whole academic life and is someone I look forward to seeing.

"Hey Jamila," Ms. Cortez greets me with a smile. "How are you doing today?"

"Oh you know," I reply, "just existing."

"Ah, so you're sticking it to the man?"

"Exactly," I say laughing. Ms. Cortez smiles as she walks to the front of the class, while I walk to Michael to interrupt his struggle.

"How's the painting comin' along?" I ask Michael.

"It's coming," he replies defensively.

"Okay, okay," I yield. "I gotta say, that's a pretty docile looking cat."

Michael shoots his head up to look at me with shocked disappointment. "It's supposed to be a dog!" he exclaims. He looks down at his failed attempt, his shoulders sagging in defeat. "Never mind," he says, throwing his brushes on the table and leaning back in his chair with a childlike disposition. I pat his shoulder in sympathy as he crosses his arms and pouts with his head bowed. Ms. Cortez claps loudly to get everyone's attention, signalling that class has officially begun.

"Alright everyone, how was everybody's weekend?" she asks, to which the class replies with a collective mumble. "Well," she says sarcastically, "don't hold back now. Any more excitement and I won't be able to control you." To this, the class laughs before she continues.

"For our next project, I want you to create something that speaks to you. Paint, draw, make a clay figurine, go crazy! For this project, I need a piece of work that has something meaningful to say, with a message that requires no words. It should be able to invoke a feeling so intense that words won't even describe it — and that can be whatever you want it to be. You have a complete creative license but please, for the love of God," she says, as she looks to Anthony Giuseppe, "no more images of scantily clad or naked women. I appreciate your support of sexual freedom and equality, but there's gotta be other ways you can show your support." Anthony laughs and gives one of his buddies a high five, while the girls around them roll their eyes and groan in disgust.

"This project is an in-class assignment and will be due at the end of the next class, so try and refrain from procrastination. For every day afterwards, I'll deduct a late mark of 5%. Have fun!"

With that, our classroom rises with activity. Michael makes a beeline for the watercolours — I tell you, I can't help but appreciate his persistence. His refusal to admit to his artistic inability to paint, while totally pathetic, is admirable. I, however, know my limitations — anything with a sharp point has my name written all over it, and I grab whatever I can get my hands on. As I sit down in front of my paper, I do so with an anticipation of an idea to pop up in my head. I've got pencil crayons, pastels, and two sharpened pencils. As Michael hunches over to begin painting, I once again stare at my paper and will something to inspire me. This is usually how things pop into my head when I'm at a loss — I just sit there and wait for the light bulb to switch on. That's not always the most effective tactic though — every grade I've gotten on a final exam is a testament to that. I still get A's, don't get it twisted, but it's definitely not as good as it could be if I knew the answer for sure. And with art, there is no *right* answer — needless to say, I'm getting by in this class with an 80% average. But as long as I see no B's, I'll be smiling like somebody said 'cheese.'

The drums from the band room, finally picking up a decent tune, plays in the background. As I continue to will inspiration to strike, the beat from the drums begin to get louder. Drowning out the chatter of the classroom, it becomes the one thing I can focus on and it seems to penetrate my very body. Entranced by the music, I begin to pick up a pencil and begin drawing — of what I do not know. The beating of the drum seems to drum in my ears, filling up all the sound that my ear cavity allows, and entering my body to beat in my bones. The beating continues as my hand draws lines, shades in spaces, and fills in details. I shade in the background to black, filling the space with stars to illuminate my muse, all the while in a trance. I feel a presence behind me, watching over my shoulder to see what I'm drawing, and that presence soon multiplies to multiple people watching me work. I won't pay attention — I'm too enthralled with what I'm doing to pay anyone or anything any mind. I somewhat notice Michael stopping his progress to watch me work. He drops his brushes once again — however, this time, I think in shock rather than frustration. The beat of the drum fills up my entire body — my very skeleton pulsing, the blood in my veins surging, my muscles and organs pounding with the internal pressure of the beat matching the drums. My hands work as an accessory to the beat — moving frantically and passionately as I continue to work on my piece — but I don't even know what that is. I'm drawing something — but I'm so entranced by the senses within my body that what's actually in front of me alludes me.

Suddenly, the musician stops drumming, and my body along with it. I blink my eyes, liberating myself from the trance that took hold of my body and take note of my surroundings. Students are all around me watching, with a look of surprise on their faces. Michael sits beside me, staring at me with a look of confusion and surprise on his face, while Ms. Cortez stands beside him with her head cocked to the side in wonder and amazement. Some other kids stand behind me, some looking at me and some looking at what lays before me. I turn to follow their gaze to the paper that was once blank, which now holds an image of my mother. She stands in front of a starry night, gazing at me mid-turn. She wears a flowing red dress that hangs from sleeveless straps; the bodice is sheer, fitted to her chest and waist, and draping strips of fabric along her arms. The skirt flows down to the ground, floating in the air in every which way from the gravity of her spin. Her bare feet, adorned with golden anklets, seem to levitate above the ground, and her hair defies gravity, looking like a sort of halo that crowns her head. She stares at me with an expression that I can't name, which seems insane seeing that I was the one who drew it. I look down at her hand which clutches, what I now realize, are silver chains. They trail the ground and differ in its dull clunkiness in comparison to the vivacity of my mother's presence. And she really does have a presence — and I have no idea how I drew that. The likeness is uncanny, and I'm floored at the sight of her for a moment. But only for a moment, because now I need to somehow explain the trance that overtook me.

"Wow, Jamila," Ms. Cortez exclaims, "this is amazing!" She walks over to stare over my shoulder, her eyes filled with amazement and her brows furrowed in confusion to this sudden burst of inspiration.

"Yeah, uh, thanks," I stutter.

"Damn J," Michael says, eyes still wide with amazement. "What the hell was that? You looked like you were under a spell or sumn."

"I don't know," I say truthfully. Because, in all honesty, I have no idea what just happened.

"The use of pastels really picks up on the complexity of the facial features," says Ms. Cortez. "And the pigment in the dress is so striking, it really becomes the centrepiece of the drawing. And the chains — the chains hint that she was once in captivity but now... now she's free. I can see that when I look at this — without a doubt. Unapologetic freedom. This is really beautiful, Jamila. Is this someone you know who inspired you?"

I sit there staring at the drawing, letting a few seconds pass by while I soak in the portrayal of my mother that captures all of who she was in one look.

"It's my mother," I say. Ms. Cortez blinks in surprise — she knows that my mother passed away when I was young, but never knew what she looked like. She looks at me for a moment with recognition and awareness, and smiles encouragingly.

"Well, she looks beautiful. If I looked that good in red, it would be the only colour in my closet." She smiles at me warmly and I smile back appreciatively, as she pats me on the shoulder.

"Alright people, move along — ain't nothing to see here. You all still have a project due by the end of tomorrow, so I suggest you scatter."

Everyone disperses and returns to their seats. Michael slaps me on the shoulder before returning to painting his project. I, finished with mine, continue to sit unmovingly and stare at my mother, who stares back at me with an expression of certainty. Of what she is certain, I don't know.

The school bell rings to signal the end of another school day, and not two minutes later the hall swells with students ready to start their extracurricular lives. I walk to my locker to get the necessary books and notebooks for homework that night, in a slight rush to get to Loni's. Michael walks up to his locker just as I shut mine, quickly dashing his textbooks to land haphazardly in his locker and grabbing a singular textbook: Advanced Geometry. Figures. Ha! Wow, I didn't even mean to make that pun.

"Where you headed after this?" Michael asks as I walk towards him.

"I'm goin' to Loni's."

"Oh dope, I'll come with you," he says, making his way over to follow me. "You can help me out with this Bio assignment."

I start to wonder for a second if bringing Michael with me is the wisest idea. Nellie said after her shift she would come to Loni's and I'd begin my training, and I'm to wait for her there until then. She never said how I could or couldn't pass the time until then. It should be fine — I mean,

I would just be doing my homework until she gets there anyway. And silently freaking out — but I can multitask.

"Okay, but I gotta get some work done too. I have a history assignment to work on, and still haven't finished my algebra homework from yesterday."

"Yeah, yeah, yeah, no problem."

We walk outside to our bikes. I place my backpack and phone into the bike basket — Michael once again strapping on his bright Tweety Bird helmet without remorse — and we set out for Loni's. The mid-afternoon settles into its hottest point — students who brought a light jacket this morning now having it tied around their waists as we ride past them. While we pedal, the sun beats down on our skin causing it to burn and glow simultaneously. Now that climate change is messing with the weather — thanks, Capitalism — it gets hotter later in the year, and we feel the heat of summer until a few weeks before Halloween comes. It's a little surreal, to be honest with you, and I wonder if *this* was the heat we were playing in when we were kids. How did we not die of heat stroke? When we get to Loni's, we ride up on the sidewalk and secure the bike locks to the bike racks. When we head inside, only a few people — it can't be more than five — are sitting in booths. One at the counter, a couple in booths, and a few by the jukebox — which blasts Yellowman from its speakers. We plop into a booth as Ray, one of Loni's full-timers, walks up to our table, rocking side to side as his steps shuffle underneath the weight of his extended belly.

"How y'all doin' today?" he asks, his voice booming.

"Good, Ray," I reply. "How are you?"

"Oh I'm good, but I just wanted to make sure y'all were alright. I heard what happened to you yesterday, Michael. You okay? That was a close call! Y'know, these worker vans outchea are driving like dey in di Fast and Furious or sumn. Can't seem to slow down even when pedestrians have the right ah way! This is just like a couple of weeks back when I was headin' to Food Basics down by Albion there —"

"Yeah, it was crazy," Michael interjects loudly, successfully cutting off a lengthy backstory. I look to him with a smirk, him returning it with an exhaustive knowing glance. "Luckily, Jamila was there and she stopped me before I got hurt."

Ray looks at me with raised eyebrows before congratulating me, "Well good on you, J! If it weren't for you, Michael here might'a ended up bein' a pancake! Which reminds me, y'all want some pancakes? Loni's got some batter leftover from this morning, and they're the buttermilk ones I know y'all like."

"Oh no, we're good Ray," I reply, as Michael and I pull out our books to begin working. "We'll just get our regular milkshakes."

"Could you also bring me some festivals, Ray?" Michael asks. Michael loves festival — the long, golden-yellow sweet fried dumpling. Unfortunately, it's usually in short supply in basically every Jamaican restaurant.

"Sorry kid, we nuh aave dat."

"For real? It seems like any place that says they got festival runs out before customers even get there. Do y'all just say you have it and then make, like, two? I swear I've never had any festival here — this feels like a bait and switch situation to me..."

"Nah, we make more than two," Ray replies, before leaning in and saying with a smiling face, "but I polish them off so likkle scrawny boys like you can't take 'em away from me. Keeps me curvy and beautiful!"

Ray pats his belly before bellowing a deep laugh. We chuckle as he writes down our order and walks away. Michael and I begin to settle in our homework mode as I dig into my algebra homework. Michael helps me with the questions that get me stuck while we await our milkshakes. Ray finally brings the milkshakes to us, and we slurp on them while continuing our homework. After a half-hour or so, I finally finish algebra and tuck it away — pulling out my laptop to continue my history paper as Michael struggles with research for his Bio assignment.

"You wouldn't happen to have memorized any of the info in your mom's books, would you?"

"No," I reply apologetically, "afraid not. I'll give them to you as soon as we get back, but what exactly are you stuck on?"

"Okay, one sec," he says, turning his laptop screen to me so that I can see his research. On his screen are so many open tabs that they look more like dots, and he settles on a diagram of the human body before scrolling down and pointing to a picture of the brain.

"Okay, so I decided to pick the visual cortex of the brain, and how some people who have illnesses like Parkinson's disease, would have an overactive visual cortex which makes them have hallucinations sometimes."

"Like schizophrenia?"

"Well, not actually. I thought the same thing," Michael responds, pointing his finger to the screen in his teacher-in-training way, before continuing, "but people with schizophrenia are more likely to have an overactive *auditory* cortex, so they end up hearing things. But it's kind of the same thing, because either way, both overactive cortices make you have a hallucination one way or another."

"Okay, so you have to find new and old medicine to help with this?"

"Yeah, but that's where I'm stuck! All the research I've done so far says that it could be psychoactive drugs that make this happen — but then, it could also just be from lack of sleep or stress. So there isn't really one medication that helps with this. When I try to find old medicine that helped with this, I get a lot of research saying that many cultures accepted this as normal and even encouraged it sometimes. They'd consider it communication with their ancestors, or the spirit world, and it would be a common ritual in their cultures. And even then, there are mentions of teas and psychoactive herbal mixtures that were used to strengthen this over-activeness. Or, they'd say they were crazy and lock them up — doing electroshock therapy until they were vegetables."

"Sweeping it under the rug," I say contemptuously, "like they do with everything else."

"Yeah, but that bit about talking to your ancestors?" Michael asks rhetorically, "That's a bit of a stretch for me."

"You think so?" I ask, my heart rate quickening. "Why?"

"I mean, c'mon," Michael says with humour. "Talking to the spirits? Seriously? People back then were probably using all these hallucinogenic drugs not realizing what they actually were, and jumped to the conclusion they were 'talking to the deities' when really it was just a reaction to the drug."

"Well, it might be true," I say sheepishly. "You never know, maybe those drugs removed blockers in the brain that kept them from fully communicating with…"

"What?" he asks incredulously. "*The ancestors?* In a spiritual place where they're watching over us and controlling how everything in the world works? C'mon, J. You can't actually believe that!"

"I don't know, man," I counter defensively. "Listen, I don't know everything. And for all intents and purposes, maybe those people back in the day knew something we aren't ready to accept."

"More like the other way around," he guffaws. "We've got the advanced science and technology to know better, J. Those people back then were probably just high on herb and needed something to make sense of the unknown. Now we know better. C'mon, man — I'm surprised you're even entertaining this. You — the person who rejects anything that hasn't been fact checked by data and science."

"It's not that I think that it's probably true," I reply, trying to backtrack. "I'm just saying that it's a possibility — all things are a possibility until they're proven to be wrong. Besides, thinking our ancestors are watching over us doesn't sound too bad, does it? Wouldn't you like to believe your parents are looking out for you, making sure you don't do anything too stupid? I sure hope my mom would be."

His face softens, and his eyes glaze with emotion. He nods slightly, mulling my words over.

"It would be nice to think that," he replies. "It would. But we're grown now, J. I'd love to think that they're watching over me but chances are they're just... gone. Into the ether."

"You really think that?"

"Yeah, I do," he says definitively. "Everything I do — whether that's talking to them when something big happens, or having a conversation with them when I visit their graves — it's all just to keep their memory alive. And to make me feel better about not having them here with me to see it all. But I don't actually think that they're in some other realm. I think that they're just... gone."

"Well... that makes sense," I reply. "But I want to hope that my mom isn't just gone. Her life was too bright to just be extinguished like that."

"I think so too, J," Michael replies. "But that's life. And death is part of the deal."

He shrugs, and I look at the table — nodding silently, taking everything in. I used to believe the same thing: I always respected the religions that people follow, but never personally felt connected to any one religion. Certain ideals, yeah, but not any one deity. But now that I know more and know that our ancestors are out there watching over us, I can't help but believe how the world works happened for a reason. It had to become this way by something more powerful than the Big Bang. The fact that I'm even thinking this is insane — not even a week ago I would look sideways at someone who thought these things. But now my eyes are starting to open.

"Anyways," Michael says, ending the conversation. "I'm just trying to find one type of medicine — old and new — that kind of did the same thing to *weaken*, not strengthen the overactive visual cortex, without harming them in some way. I'm just a little stuck."

"Yeah, I wish I could help you man," I reply apologetically. "If I had the books I'd know which one to give you, but I don't actually know the nitty-gritty of it; but I promise, I'll give you the books first thing when we get home."

"Okay, thanks J." Michael sits back into his seat, getting back into work as I settle back into my history paper.

I reread what I've already written, editing grammatical errors and sentences that I think can be reworded. So far, I've talked about the impact MLK had on the black community — not just in the United States but around the world. And, how his assassination was one of many activist deaths that happened during the Civil Rights Movement that left a mark on society. I left off introducing activism in the present political climate, talking mostly about Black Lives Matter. With so much that I could talk about here, I don't want to start going off a bunch of tangents and divert from my original thesis. I want the whole paper to flow, like a story, and not only finish the assignment but actually send a message.

I bring up another tab on my laptop that pulls up the increase in deaths of BLM activists from Ferguson, Missouri since the death of Michael Brown. After Trayvon Martin, Brown's death really showed me, like many other black teens, how we aren't treated the same as everybody else. It can be anything from walking late at night in a hoodie to a family reunion in the local park, to label us as a threat — and fighting for the right to live equally even more so. Activists have been dropping like flies fighting for the rights of black lives to be treated the same as everybody else's — similar to what Martin Luther King did in his career as an activist. I want to make sure it's clear that there's a connection between MLK's death and the deaths of these activists today. Furthermore, how they stem from the same thing and are affected by the same thing: law enforcement. I go back to my tab with my report, and get to typing:

MLK's death has been marked in the history books. Oftentimes, him being seen as a martyr in the fight for black lives — and that has not changed even today. BLM activists in Ferguson, like Baseem Masri and Darren Seals, have died in violent and mysterious circumstances that have largely been written off by law enforcement, and left the families and close loved ones of the victims with nothing but suspicions. Just as MLK's death was surrounded by scrutiny — with theories suggesting the involvement of law enforcement and/or hate groups in his death — the deaths of these BLM activists also suggest the work of white supremacy and/or law enforcement. The black community in America, and worldwide, as seen by the evidence, has had a generations-long battle with law enforcement—

I stop there, wondering if my wording is too forward or too one-sided. I reread my paragraph over again before continuing:

The black community, in all areas of the world, have had a generations-long relationship with law enforcement that is parasitic in nature: involving the unexplainable and grossly violent deaths of the former, and the profit, absolution and victimization of the latter.

I sit back in my chair, giving myself an imaginary pat on the back for my wording, before continuing again. I write a little bit more about the specifics of the deaths of the BLM activists in Ferguson and as I'm finishing the in-text citations, I see Loni come from the back. She sees me and makes her way to our table in her normal, Loni-esque fashion. Her orthopedic shoes stop right in front of our table. She rests her fists on her hips, gracing us with her smile that I've grown accustomed to over the years; however, this time I see her differently. This time I see her for who she really is.

"Hey, Michael, how you doin' baby?"

"Oh I'm good, Loni," Michael replies with a smile, slightly closing his laptop and leaning back into his seat. This allows us to see his bony shoulders fully, poking through the fabric of his striped shirt, much to Loni's detriment.

"Oh baby, yuh likkle scrawny frame wi bruk pah road if yuh continue wid weh yuh a eat. Ray," she yells to the back, catching his attention as he stands behind a pot on the stove that blows steam in front of his face. "Put a couple of the patties in the oven for Michael," she turns back to us and gives Michael a loving smile before adding, "on the house."

Michael smiles at Loni, "Thanks, Loni. You're the best."

Loni smiles and chucks Michael under the chin before turning her attention to me, her smile remaining on her face but her eyes changing from average politeness to knowingness.

"Hey J, how are you?"

"I'm good," I say nonchalantly.

"Had a late night last night, you feelin' alright?"

I see Michael look at me quizzically out of the corner of my eye. I ignore him and respond, "Yeah, I'm a little tired but I'm good. Ready to get to work."

Hearing this, Loni's smile deepens, her eyes sinking into her smile — content with my answer because she knows I'm ready for my training.

"Your aunty seh wi could get started soon as wi ready, an' she ah come join us afta she done her shift."

"Get started?" Michael asks curiously, looking from me, to Loni, and back to me. "Get started with what?"

"Oh, uh... me and Loni are gonna..." I struggle with a lie to cover up the truth.

"Mi aguh teach J how fi cook quality Jamaican food," Loni continues for me, saving my ass. "Her motha neva teach her how fi mek jerk chicken or curry goat, and Nellie always too busy to really sit down with har an' teach her. And she haffi learn how to cook propah when she leave her aunty an' live on her own."

I look to Michael and nod as if this is what I was going to say. My heart thuds in my chest as I try to go through with this lie. I've never really lied to Michael, only the occasional fib when he wanted to hang out and I was on my period or something. I analyze his face, which goes from quizzical curiosity to understanding.

"Oh cool, cool. Well, text me when you're home so I can come grab those books."

"Yeah, yeah, no, for sure," I reply quickly, grabbing my books and laptop and putting them in my bag. I jump up and follow Loni, who gives Michael a quick peck on the cheek before walking through the kitchen doors. We walk past Ray, who's putting patties on a plate — I assume to *finally* bring to Michael — and throws us a quick smile and wave. I return his smile as I follow Loni further into the back, back to the closet door hidden just behind the wall. I look behind me, worried that people will see our secret spot, but we can see everyone else — they can't see us. She opens the door and quickly shepherds me in. She closes the door, and I hear the switch of a door lock before she pulls the string on the bulb, giving her face new shadows as the highlights of her face are dimly illuminated by the weak light. She breathes in once, looking at me with an expressionless face, as I just stand there.

"You ready?" she asks me.

I breathe in shakily before responding, "As I'll ever be."

She motions for me to go in first — with my knowledge of what's down there, I don't hesitate like the last time to go down the stairs. I hear her follow behind me and as she closes the latch on the door, the light from above disappears and we are once again in darkness. I put my hands out in front of me to stabilize myself on the rickety steps until I feel myself land on firm ground. I walk a few steps forward to allow Loni some room behind me to land on the ground too. She must be used to coming down these steps in complete darkness, because I hear her walking quickly down the steps with no hesitation. She once again pulls a string, and the floating bulbs illuminate the magical space. I see the potion pantry, the tables pushed to the side of the room, and the numerous plants hanging from above and I feel the magic from last night — and a little bit of that same hysteria. The hopeless romantic in me — thanks, Mom — finds the whimsical-ness of this place stunning, and I feel the panic dissipate and begin sinking into a blissful stillness. Loni walks from behind me over to a small sink and washes her hands. I walk through the small path between the tables and take note of my surroundings again. The potion pantry, that I can look at with calmer nerves, holds herbs, liquids and pastes, in so many different bottle shapes and colours... but with no labels. How does Loni know the difference between them? I guess doing this as long as she has, she's developed a nose for what's what. I turn around and walk a little more, looking up to the floating bulbs and — by sheer desire — raise my hand to the ceiling to graze my fingers between them, and finding absolutely no string or anything that could be holding them up. I lower my hand and stare up in amazement before the scent of sage catches my attention and causes me to look around to find its source. I look to a table and find incense burning, a small string of smoke trailing from the stick. As I look slightly to the left, I see several books scattered on the same table. I walk towards the table to get a closer look and catch a glimpse of the black book with the panther on the cover from last night. Instantly, I remember the gravity of the situation — that I'm a descendant of a long line of powerful women that are being hunted to this day — and that my abilities are gonna be a mind trip. I back away and look everywhere: to the ceiling, to the ground, to the left, to the right. Anywhere that doesn't hold my new future. Loni finishes cleaning up and walks towards me; seeing that I'm fidgety, she approaches me slowly with her hand outstretched towards me and her face holding a look of worry.

"You okay, J?"

"Yeah, yeah," I reply shakily, bouncing from my left foot to my right. For Loni to not see how my fingers are trembling, I bring my hands behind my back and hold my left wrist with my right hand. She stands up a little straighter and drops her arm, looking at me with a set face and does a small nod. She walks away to a far corner of the room and bends over to grab a bin. As she rifles through it a little further, I keep shuffling my feet, looking down at the ground so I can calm down. As she makes her way back to me, I raise my head again and try my best to put up a strong front, and make it seem like I'm not completely freaking out. She stops in front of me and lowers the bin so it rests on her upper thighs. I look in and see containers of thick lotions, dark liquids, and some gels; I raise my eyes to look at her quizzically, and she returns my gaze with a humorous small smile.

"You seem like you need to relax for a little while." She walks towards me, hand outstretched towards my head. She looks to me with eyebrows raised, silently asking if it's alright — and I nod, giving her permission to touch my hair. She takes my hair out of its bun and feels through my hair, gently massaging my scalp. She clucks in disapproval, apparently not happy with what she's feeling, before she says, "Come, let me do yuh hair. It's so dry, you need to do a treatment. Come."

I look at her questioningly but does as she says, following her to the sink. She places a stool in front of it and motions for me to sit, and she moves to stand behind me as I do. She grabs a bottle with a dark fluid sloshing around inside and pulls out a comb with a pointy end. She begins to part my hair into four big sections and gets to work on one; parting it little by little, she squeezes the dark concoction onto my scalp and massages it in. Immediately I recognize the smell — the soothing scent of peppermint and aloe vera waft to my nose.

"Oh my gosh, that smells amazing," I revel.

Loni chuckles as she continues to massage, soon after parting my hair again. "The peppermint mek yuh scalp feel good, all tingly and cool to calm yuh nerves, and the lemongrass fi cleanse it. Your hair's dry baby girl, you need a pre-shampoo fi bring di oils in yuh scalp bak to normal."

She continues to part and oil my hair — at the end, massaging my entire scalp with firm but caressing fingers. I feel the muscles in my entire body relax in response to the soothing touch of her fingers, and my head flops backward involuntarily. Loni chuckles as she grabs a plastic shower cap and places it on my head. She pats me on the shoulder and motions for me to follow her to a table beside the sink. She pulls out a few bottles from the bin and places them on the table. She also grabs a bowl with different kinds of butter, vials of oils, and a mixing bowl with a whisk and spatula.

"While your hair is gettin' the treatment, we're going to make a hair butter for your hair," Loni says. "It'll moisturize it and make your curls look nice."

"Aren't we supposed to start my training?" I ask.

"How you expec' to conquer abilities with a plastic cap on your head and oil dripping down on your face? Tuh!" she clucks incredulously. I chuckle, gleefully knowing that she's making a joke out of all of this.

She smiles back before continuing, "Besides, it's obvious you need a minute before we get into the nitty-gritty of it all. This way we can kill two birds with one stone, 'cause Lord knows you haven't been takin' care ah yuh hair propah."

"Yeah, well, I've been busy," I mumble defensively. "It's only the beginning of the school year and I have so much work to do; not to mention schools to apply to, scholarships to apply for," my voice goes sarcastic as I add, "and the impending doom of an invisible hunter after powers I don't even know how to control yet."

Loni looks at me from the corner of her eye as she begins to pull out one of the butter and put it in the mixing bowl. "Yuh still need to mek time fi do yuh hair, Jamila. You can't just pull your hair up inna bun when you need to be quickie quickie — people will look down on yuh if your hair is messy. You gotta take care of it and make sure it's moisturized good and well maintained so it can be healthy. Your hair needs more love and you haffi give it, not just have your nose in a book all the time. And that doesn't mean focusing less on your studies! It just means havin' a balance. Your hair is just as important, J."

I relent and nod, as she finishes putting the different butters in a mixing bowl. She points to the original jars that they were in and describes them one by one.

"This is mango butter," she says as she points to a mason jar with a pale yellow lotion inside. "It's really moisturizing for your hair and it'll make your hair smell nice. This," she says as she points to a dark green jar with divots all around its surface, "is shea butter. It's got nutrients to moisturize your hair and scalp, and it'll keep if you put it in the fridge." She begins to bring the vials of oil in front of the mixing bowl and points out each one. "This is Vitamin E oil — it'll help with the breakage of your hair. This is tea tree oil, to help with the natural oils in yuh scalp — and it'll cleanse it too." She grabs the bowl and puts it on a stand with a hole in the center with which the bowl can sit comfortably. "I want you to add about four drops of each while I heat up the butta. Then add some Jamaican black castor oil and sweet almond oil too — a little more than the otha two oils."

"How are you going to do that? I don't see a burner —"

Before I can finish the sentence, a flame lights up beneath the bowl — out of nowhere. I stare in amazement, reactively taking a step back from the sudden flame that just appeared. Like magic. I look to her in surprise and she looks back at me with a small smile before walking away, as if this is completely normal. To her, I guess it is. I do a double-take, looking at her nonchalant figure walking away. I turn back and look at the flame again, passing my hand in the space between the bowl and the flame, and the flame and the table, and finding no source for this flame other than pure magic. I'm really amazed I haven't completely lost my mind yet. Getting back to the task at hand, I do as I'm told — squeezing four drops of vitamin E and tea tree oil into the bowl, adding a little more of the castor and sweet almond oils. Quickly the butters begin to melt — the solo flame from which the fire burns mystifying me — and after a couple of minutes, the butters become liquid.

"Hey Loni," I call out behind me, "I think the butters are finished melting." I turn around to look for her, seeing her stooped over a small indoor garden on the floor on the other side of the room. Bordered by a tiny green gate, potted plants dot the tiny square of earth, and welcome Loni into their space. She hacks at a potted plant and bends back up for me to see a stalk of aloe vera. She walks back over to me, holding a blade in one hand and a stalk of aloe vera in the other.

"Okay," she says breathlessly, throwing the aloe vera on the table. "I'm gonna put the bowl in the fridge and we'll leave it in there for an hour or so. While we do that, I'm gonna wash and condition your hair."

"What are we using the aloe vera for?"

"That's for after we wash your hair, we'll leave it for now. Come," she motions me to sit on the same stool and gently moves my head over the sink. I gaze up at her as she pulls out two bottles. One with a liquid that moves lazily in the bottle like molasses, and another that looks like cream. She begins to wet my hair, sectioning my hair and getting to work. After washing the first 3 sections, I look up at the woman I've known practically my entire life and wonder how I never knew this about her.

"I still can't believe I didn't know this about you," I say.

"Know what?"

"This," I say, as I raise my hands to gesture to the entire room. "Your abilities. This place. Everything."

"Is it really so hard to believe? This is a centuries-long secret that could mean the death of our people. People have been killed for a lot less — we can't risk the chance of putting ourselves an' our people in danger for anyone. Not even you, baby girl."

"Yeah, but you knew that I was a part of this lineage. You knew that eventually, one day, I would become like you. Surely you could've told me."

Loni stops massaging and leans on one side, looking down at me with her lips pursed. "Baby girl, you were a child. A baby. An' nuh matta how much yuh try, pickney caah keep a secret to save their lives."

I shrug and nod — if I had known about all of this, I probably would've blabbed and told everyone. I chuckle at the thought of telling Michael, which causes Loni to look at me curiously.

"What's so funny?" she asks.

"Oh, I was just thinking about how if I had known about all of this as a kid, I probably would've told Michael. And I love him, but he *really* can't keep a secret to save his life!"

Loni chuckles as she washes all the shampoo out of my hair and begins to condition each section.

"I remember I told him when I first got my period, like the next day or something, and he went and told Ms. Dell!"

"Ha," Loni hoots.

"It was so embarrassing! She came up to me the next day when we were gonna go biking for a bit, and she goes '*Oh baby, you growin' up! You ain't a baby no more — soon all the boys are gonna come knockin'.*' I didn't even know what she meant by that — I remember thinking, '*Boys are gonna visit me at home because of my period? Why?*'"

Loni rolls her eyes 'til I can see the whites of her eyes. She says, "Dell always being so cringey. She get on my nerves sometimes, always havin' to act so prim an' propah. I swear she shows the world one face, and shows me another. Me caah deal wid har sometimes, but she was dere fah mi when mi move to Canada, an' I aave to show har love fah dat."

"Was she your only friend when you moved here?"

"Friend is a bit of a stretch," she says slowly, causing me to chuckle. She smiles at me before continuing, "but she definitely helped me out. Before I left Jamaica I barely had anything, but I knew I had to leave or I'd rot there. I didn't live in a good neighbourhood and all my family was either dead or far away. I couldn't afford to get to them, and it was dangerous for young women in that part of town. So, mi did start think fi leave di island and go someweh I could aave a fresh start. The Civil Rights Movement was still sort'a happening in the States, and I thought Canada would be a safer option for me. That was naive, 'cause racism exists everywhere, an' you can never escape it."

"It's still a league better than in the States," I reply.

"You think that, but just 'cause someone isn't calling you the N-word to yuh face nuh mean they not sayin' it when yuh turn yuh back. Racism has many faces, and we often see the one that likes to come off like dey progressive an' all'a that. But dey really letting dey racist beliefs 'bout you flow underneath and control what they think of yuh — even if dey nuh realize it."

She's right. The racism we hear about that's explicit and causes outrage usually happens in the States, or countries that are still influenced by Eurocentrism. The racism here in Canada, though not so explicit and obvious, is still there. Don't get me wrong, there's still explicit racism here, but it's not as common as it is in the States. But sometimes, covert racism can be just as bad, especially when you let it build up inside. It festers until you explode, and can cause just as much damage as a slur can.

"Besides," Loni continues, "I would've dealt with it ten-fold if it meant I could escape being hunted." I move my head to look at her head-on, causing her to abruptly stop scrubbing so I don't splash water and conditioner everywhere.

"You were actually hunted?" I ask incredulously.

"Yes," she says somberly. "Your aunty and I weren't just saying that to scare you, J. This isn't the Boogeyman or sumn. There are real men out there, hiding in the dark like the animals they are, who want to use us. To kill us."

I settle back over the sink in bewilderment as Loni finishes conditioning the last section. "When I was 18," she says, "I started to hang with the wrong crowd. Selling drugs, guns and weapons, that sort of thing. And that connected me to some pretty rough people. After a while though, I started to think we could use our influence for good, an' I got my crew to start helpin' the community. We'd start smuggling food an' medicine for the people in our town who couldn't afford it. Or, we would use the money we did make from the drugs and weapons to pay school fees for

96

families that couldn't afford to send all their children dem to school, or pay for their uniforms. We still did bad stuff, but we used the money we made for good. Really, there was no other way. The banks seemed pitted against us, and nobody could get any money to save their lives that nuh aave a high-interest rate or a catch that would make it damn near impossible to pay back. An' dey liked to seh dem nah do dis, but di banks dem would reject more people from our neighbourhoods, and others like ours. An' we'd stay broke 'cause we naave no money, no education, an' often times no other way of getting out but to resort to gangs or selling ourselves."

I look at the ceiling — at a loss for words with what I'm hearing — as she detangles my hair.

"Eventually, the wrong people started to hear about this young woman," she gestures to herself before continuing, "who could do some pretty crazy things. Whenever the police dem ah come, me an' the people I rode with would always get out jus' in time. An' if the police happen to catch us, we'd always get out somehow. Rumours went around that one time when we were raided, I froze the police in place while we packed up all da money and supplies, and escaped to anotha house."

"You froze them?" I ask eagerly.

She chuckles at my eagerness and replies, "Yes, it's a part of my protective powers — I keep those who mean tuh cause me harm in their places so that I can escape to safety. It wasn't a rumour, it was true. The story spread so fast that there was nothing I could'a done to stop it — the story caught the attention of a wealthy man who lived in the nicer part of the island. A Toubab."

"Did he find you?"

"Yes, but I knew he was going to come for me. An ancestor came to me in my dream a few nights before and warned me of danger to come, with a devil who drained me of my powers chasing me as I ran. I knew this meant a Toubab was near; so, I immediately got all my things an' did all the necessary papers and fees to move to Canada. Just as I was about to leave he found me, but I had cast a protection spell on my home so he couldn't get in."

"A spell? Like a witch?"

Loni clucks and looks at me exasperated. "I hate that word," she says, annoyed. "It's like calling a woman a bitch, or a black person the N-word. It's a slur for our kind, and an insult."

"Sorry, sorry," I say apologetically.

"It's alright. But yes," she relents, "I cast protection on my house and was able to just escape through the back. But he saw me." Loni slows her combing and I look up to see a distant look on her face, her eyes clouded with memory. Her entire demeanor changes — her frame tensing up, her mouth slightly parted, and her forehead wrinkling in distress.

"He saw me and looked at me with the most... the most terrifying face. Like I was an animal that he wanted to hunt and kill for sport. I saw so much malice an' tyranny in that face, and to this day me neva figet it. And every day I lie in bed with fear, thinkin' that he'll come one day and finally find me again."

"But he won't, Loni," I console, the best I can. "That was so long ago. You've been living in Canada for decades and you haven't been caught —"

"Yet," she interjects. "I haven't been caught yet, J. I know yuh trynna mek me feel betta, but you have to remember that they neva stop. They neva stop hunting us; they see us as a virus, a plague on this Earth — even though it's really them that's doin' the damage."

"But you've had years to improve your powers. Everything gets better with time — remember you told me that when I saw that drive-by?"

"Yes," she smiles at me lovingly, "I do."

"Well, your powers have gotten better over time. You've had time to hone your skills and use them for good — and if they do come, then you'll be better prepared than when you were younger."

Loni looks at me smiling, with an expression I can't quite place — but, if I had to guess, gratitude of some sort.

"You're just like yuh motha you know that? For all the cynic that be in yuh, you still look at the bright side of things when someone you care about be hurtin'." She chucks my chin, causing me to smile which, in turn, causes her to smile wider.

"I love that you're still able to look on the bright side, but don't be naive. Neva forget that they neva stop. They want to use an' dispose of us until we're of no use to them no more. I don't want you to always be scared. I just want you to be smart, okay?"

I give her a small nod in understanding, and settle back over the sink. As she finishes detangling my hair, I think about how scared she must've been. I mean, she wasn't much older than me when that Toubab came for her, and she had to leave everything she knew and move to a country she knows nothing about. And to fear being found everyday? *Everyday*? For years — for decades! I don't know how she does it.

I look up at Loni, who hums aimlessly as she combs. Loni is a pillar in our neighbourhood. Everyone who knows her has a story about her, and it usually involves her helping us in some way. She's strong, and doesn't take crap from anybody. Not even when she was new to this country and knew nothing and no one — she wouldn't let anyone take advantage of her. And, she damn sure wasn't going to let anyone take her for granted. I admire her strength in so many ways, and how she can exude so much love even more. I guess it's not that crazy if she was able to handle all of this, especially when it's your life on the line — I guess you don't really have any choice.

She finishes combing and puts a plastic shower cap on my head, motioning for me to sit up as she washes off her hands. I dry off my face and stand up, so she can have some room to clean up. She walks over to me as she finishes cleaning up.

"Okay, while your hair is deep conditioning, we're gonna take this aloe vera and cut it up." I follow her to the table where we had just mixed the different butters. Loni cuts up the aloe vera into sections about 5 inches long. She cuts off the sides and then slices into the middle and cuts it out. After that, she pulls out a blender from underneath the table and puts the aloe vera in. She hands me the blade and places her hand on her cocked hip while leaning on the table.

"I want you to do that to the entire stalk and put it in the blender. Blend it up 'til it's a gel and there aren't any chunks in it. Call me over when you're done."

I start to do as I'm told as she walks away, slicing the sides of each section of aloe and cutting out the middle. After they're all in the blender, I make my way to press the button before stopping — thinking about the magic flame that I saw not too long ago.

"Wait," I say slowly, "are you gonna do something to make the blender turn on? Do you have like a spell that makes it turn on?"

Loni looks at me amused and walks to me. "Oh yeah," she says, looking me dead in the face as she bends down and grabs the plug. Waving it in front of my face, eyebrows raised and an amused look on her face. My face goes slack, annoyed as I realize her poking fun at me, as she jokes, "It's this magical thing called electricity, where I plug it into the wall an' di blenda start!"

"Funny," I say monotone. She hoots as she walks away, going to the potion pantry and pulling out vials and bottles. As she does whatever she's doing, I blend the aloe and stare off into space. My mind brings me to the events of yesterday, and the drawing I made in art class. It was so weird like I was in a trance or something. I don't even know how I drew it without really *knowing* what I was drawing. It's like my hands just knew where to go and what to do, and I ended up with a picture of my mother. A really good one too — the likeness is eerily accurate. And I don't know what it is, but ever since I had that dream about her, it's like I know that her soul — wherever it is — is watching over me and connecting to me. My drawing is exactly what I saw in my dream: the red dress, the ornate gold jewellery. That can't be a coincidence.

Suddenly, I feel a hand thump on my shoulder and I jump. Startled, I turn around and see Loni looking at me with a kind face.

"That's blended enough, J," she says softly. She gently takes my hands off the blender and holds them in her hands, caressing them and rubbing the spot between my thumbs and forefingers. I don't know how she knows that this calms me down, but she's doing a good job. She must've seen how spaced out I was — and while I do tend to daydream, she has a good nose for spotting when something is troubling me.

"I get it," she says matter-of-factly. "It's a lot. And if you ever need to talk about anythin', and I do mean *anything*," she emphasizes, looking intently into my eyes, "do not hesitate to call me. I'll always be here, baby girl."

I sigh deeply, grateful for her never-ending love that seems to just ooze out of her. She smiles warmly and pats my hand, holding on to them 'til we turn back to the table. She tells me to mix the aloe vera into the butter mixture we had refrigerated. After doing that, and mixing everything together, we now have a delicious butter concoction for my hair. She washes my conditioner out, adds a leave-in so my hair will be protected, and massages some more oil onto my scalp. Dangerously falling asleep under the sureness of her gentle fingers, she soon finishes and helps me twist my hair with the hair butter. She does the back and I do the front — and my shoulders burn as I hold my arms up to twist the crown section of my head. But I push through — it's kind of a requirement when you choose to go natural. Just feeling how moisturized my hair feels, lifts my spirit. Loni and I end up chatting and laughing about school, the diner, and our neighbourhood — just like old times. After all my twists — delightfully juicy and bouncy — are done, we clean up and walk over to a table piled high with books. Suddenly, the lights brighten and blink. Once, two times quickly, then three times slowly. Loni walks towards the stairs and opens the hatch. Confused, and a little scared, I back towards the wall as Loni walks down. When I hear a new set of footsteps come down the steps, I hug the wall — fearful of an intruder. No one else is supposed to know about this place, how would someone else know to come down here? The light from the closet above casts a shadow on the newcomer's face so I can't see who it is. After Loni closes the hatch and the light from above is gone, I see the woman I love the most in the world.

I exhale the breath I was holding in and walk towards Nellie, giving her a warm hug, and her reciprocating it while rocking me side to side.

"What took you so long?" I ask.

"I had to stay a little bit longer," Nellie replies. "One of my patients didn't have anyone to come to see him during visiting hours, and I just stayed to keep him company." I nod in comprehension as she grabs my cheeks, pushing them together towards my lips to give me chipmunk-face. I groan as she coos at me, effectively annoying me and humouring Loni who chuckles behind her. She thankfully releases my cheeks and caresses the sides of my head before pulling away. She looks at her now damp palms confused, dropping her hands and turning to look at Loni.

"You did her hair?"

"Yeah," Loni replies. "Just a little black girl magic therapy." I smile at her, and she smiles back warmly.

"You ready?" Nellie asks her.

Loni looks back to Nellie and nods silently. They both move to the other side of the table, facing me and settling into a serious stature. I match theirs, as I prepare myself for the beginning of what I know will be a long journey.

Loni pulls out a thick dark brown book, covered in what looks like vines and tree bark, and opens it to a page of Bast in a tomb.

"You may already know this, but Bast was a guide for the dead an' connected to the afterlife," Loni explains. "Over time, Bastets were able to hone this skill an' connec' to the dead. They would talk to the ancestors who had passed on, an' ask advice or guidance for those still livin'. An' for the people that were dyin', or death was soon comin' for them, she would guide them safely to the afterlife so they could rest in peace."

Loni turns a page to a woman in a half-asleep state, with a trail of smoke underneath her nose.

"If a connection couldn't be made to the afterlife," Nellie continues, "then the Bastets would calm their nerves with a sedative — usually in a tea or something they would smoke."

"The Bastets were gettin' high?" I ask surprised.

"It wasn't used the way it's used today, so get yuh mind out the gutta," Loni reprimands. I bow my head to hide my smile, and catch Nellie doing the same out of the corner of my eye. Loni annoyingly points to the next page, where a Bastet walks from a landscape with trees, flora and fauna, and wildlife — to one pitch black, the ground flowing with white smoke, signifying the transition from the world of living to that of the dead.

"Bastets were able to talk to our ancestors, as well as those of other people who needed our help. They would often do so when there was a threat and trouble was comin'. The sedative would sometimes be made of cannabis leaves, but this wasn't until our ancestors were enslaved in Jamaica. Before this, they would just be usin' peppermint and sage — breathin' it in to relax the nerves. Over time, as Bastets lost this ability, they leaned on the sedative more an' more to be able to talk to the afterlife. But then, we lost this ability altogether, an' only a few of us can actually connec' to the spirit world. Even if we can, it might only happen when we're in a resting state."

"Like if we're dreaming?" I ask.

"Yes, that was the most common," Loni responds. I think about my dream last night, and how I actually saw my mother. Was that the manifestation of my power connecting to the afterlife? Am I able to do that now — or is it just a coincidence?

"That dream you had a couple of nights ago was the beginning of your manifestation," Nellie says, answering my silent question. She leans on the table and continues, "The voices you heard were most likely our ancestors, guiding you to safety and watching over you. It's going to get a lot more intense as you embrace your powers more, so just make sure to let us know of any changes."

I nod, thinking about how my dream has changed so much already. I know I need to tell them, but something stops me from telling them. I will eventually — I know I have to — but I just need to process all of this first. Loni turns the page to a Bastet asleep, surrounded by what looks like a bunch of drums in the shape of an oval, and her in the middle. It's night time, with the moon and stars illuminated at the top of the page, and the bottom shaded a dark brown colour to show the ground on which she lays.

I recognize the shape the drums make after a few moments, and wonder if I'm seeing what I'm really seeing.

"Is that... is that the shape of an eye?"

"Yes," Loni says with a small smile. "The all-seein' eye is one of the symbols for the daughters of Bast, that helps us focus on our powers. This and the amulet that we gave you to wear," Loni pauses and Nellie pulls out the amulet that she had left on my pillow. She must've gone in when I was showering and grabbed it. Loni continues, "would protec' us from dangers — warning us an' allowin' us to tap into our premonition powers."

"This usually happens in a rest state too," Nellie finishes. "You could see something in a dream, or just be in a state of complete calm. Like if you were sitting and relaxing or something — and the eye would help you to see something that is going to happen. It doesn't have to always be something bad, either — it could be the birth of someone who will make history. Or, as simple as knowing what the weather will be like the next day. But, usually, our ancestors would see something in their rest state to prepare them for something to come. The most trained Bastets would be able to smell or hear something and take it as a sign, and not even need any visions at all. But then our bloodline lost this power, and now it shows up in spurts — and, usually, at the most random times."

"Like I said yesterday, you'd probably call it deja vu," Loni says, "and sometimes, that is just what it is. But other times it may be the abilities of someone who's a distant descendant of Bast, but they don't know how to tap into this powa and train it tuh truly use it to their advantage."

"Train it? Like a muscle?" I ask.

"Yes, exactly," Nellie says excitedly. She walks over to my side of the table, raising her arm and flexing to visualize, before continuing, "The more you work a muscle, exercising and strengthening it, the stronger you get. Our abilities work just the same — think of it like conditioning. We have to push it beyond our limits bit by bit, working them just past a point we haven't gone before, to make them stronger. The more you do that, the stronger your abilities get — and the better you can control them."

I look at the page, at the illustration of the Bastet in her dream state surrounded by the drums, before a question pops in my head. "Why is she surrounded by drums?"

"Our ancestors used the beat of the drums to focus on our senses," Loni says, "allowin' us to drown out all the distractions of the outside world. The Bastets from the past would dance to the beat and use this to channel their powers. Other Bastets, or women in the community who were trusted with the truth, would beat the drums. It would put the Bastet in a trance an' let her sink into an unconscious state — one where she still connec' to the real world, but also to the ethereal world."

I look at the page in astonishment. It sounds like how people put themselves in isolation tanks — to separate themselves from other senses and really tune in to their thoughts. In art class today, the band class beat the drums and I felt like it was all I could hear. It filled my entire body until I felt like my body itself was drumming from the inside. And then I drew that picture of my mom, without even realizing what I was doing or what I was drawing.

"Do you have to be wearing the amulet, or surrounded by drums in the shape of an eye, for you to have these premonitions?"

"No, the Bastets who tuned in to their abilities could train themselves and call on a premonition whenever they needed to," Loni responds. "But it usually helped to have the drums beating, so that di Bastets could concentrate."

I must've used one of my abilities without even realizing it, and I'm just starting to get them. I haven't even tried to use them yet. How is it that they're already so strong? Loni turns a few more pages until she lands on an illustration of a black woman with a mortar and pestle; several bowls and jars surrounding her and what looks like plants hanging from the ceiling.

Nellie starts, "Another ability of Bastets, one that exists strongly in most of us today and what many of us are able to control, are our healing powers. Our ancestors were able to heal sicknesses and carry many from the brink of death and bring them back to health."

"Is that why you went into nursing?" I ask in realization.

"Yes; many of us have gone into the medical field in some way. I did the modern version with nursing, but some Bastets use more traditional medicines even now — becoming herbalists, midwives and doulas. We have a knack for knowing which medicines to use to cure a sickness, and how much to give them for healing. And since Bast always protected the home — with women and children the life that was breathed into it, becoming a midwife just makes sense. You have a direct connection to the mother and the child at their most vulnerable moment, which makes it easier to protect them at their most exposed state. But with the power of our lineage, we are also able to heal the worst of sicknesses beyond what can be done with modern medicine. Bastets would cure the worst of it:

from organ failure to viruses that could only be cured with vaccines that science has just started to create."

"So we could heal beyond just traditional medicine?"

"Yes," Nellie says, turning the page to lines of what looks like prayers. "We're inherently protective spirits. We'd cast spells on homes to protect against sickness and disease, and evil spirits."

"Evil spirits? Like the Boogeyman?" I ask jokingly.

"Yuh love mek joke, but it ain't funny," Loni says seriously. I look to her and stop smiling, sobering up. "There are forces in dis world, capable of things beyond even what we are able to do, that threaten the peace that keeps humanity alive. Toubabs are one thing, but even they are limited to their human bodies. There are spiritual an' demonic forces out there that work in di background, workin' us like a puppeteer. It can be anythin' from sickness an' death to the genocide of an entire people. There's only so much we can do. Especially wit' so few of us left — we did do and we'll still do everythin' we can to protec' the community."

"And she didn't just protect women and children," Loni says. She pulls another book from underneath the mess; an olive green one with parchment-looking paper. She flips to a page of a village, with a woman looking over it from a high place. "Bastets would protec' the entire community, casting protection over di people dem — Bast was known for helping women an' children most. She'd also help them interpret dreams or things that be happenin' to dem, since they also had a spiritual connection that the men didn't have."

"Why did they have a spiritual connection?"

"Because they're more exposed to hormonal changes — and a change in hormones can affect our brain just as it can to our emotions," Nellie says calmly. "Women have this sixth sense already; sensing things that people don't, and knowing how people are feeling. Call it whatever you like, but we women can tap into a sense that increases our mental capacity, and that only gets stronger when we have children. Imagine a human being growing inside of you — your entire body changes. Your senses do too. And children carry this with them for a little while after birth — that's why you hear so many stories of children talking to ghosts," she raises her hands and air quotes, "or having *'imaginary friends'*."

I process what she's saying and realize that it makes sense. So many times I've heard of kids having imaginary friends, or seen YouTube videos of kids talking about people that lived decades ago as if they had actually *known* them. They wouldn't have known anything personal about these people *unless* they were talking to them. And women — I mean, I have to admit that there's just something about women that makes us inherently spiritual. I can always tell when someone's not acting like themselves, and I have this really weird ability to know if it's going to rain just by the way it smells outside. *From the day before.* So this does actually make sense — and I can't believe I'm even believing all of this, but I do.

"Now," Nellie says, walking over to fully face me. I turn to face her as she asks rhetorically, "what does this mean exactly? It doesn't mean that you'll have all of these abilities. I have a knack for healing, and no one can cast a protection spell like Loni," we both look to Loni who gives a small smile and a wink. I smile as Nellie continues, "but neither of us has the ability to have stronger premonitions. We've trained for years, each of us by ourselves and with each other — both Loni and I, and even your mother. But Loni and I were never able to master it, and your mother got close — but then, unfortunately, she passed."

Loni looks at me and says, "Your aunty's right. You might not have all these abilities, but from what we can see, your powers are manifestin'. With the dream you had an' that close-call with Michael, you may be manifestin' into your abilities to talk to the afterlife and aave premonitions. That vision you saw of Michael 'appened in broad daylight, with nothing to help you tap into your senses, so your powers are comin' strong."

"Okay, so what do we do?"

"Well, the only thing we can do is to help you control them," Nellie says, causing me to look at her. "They're only gonna get stronger with time, so we'll help you train your mind and your senses — tap into your body, and feel the ebb and flow of your powers running through you."

"This is a lot to take in at once, and we get that," Loni says. "We'll try to take it as slow as we can, but you caah figet there's a threat out there that will always be one step behind us. So, we haffi mek sure we stay three steps ahead — lest they catch us."

I nod slowly, remembering what Loni and I talked about before Nellie got here. She almost got caught herself, and I know she doesn't want that to happen to me. But I wonder if her fear is causing her to be a little overprotective.

"So where do we start then?" I ask.

"First things first," says Loni, as she leans over the table with her palm outstretched. I look down and see the amulet lying in her hand. I look back at her to see if she's looking at me intently. "This will help you to control your abilities betta — protectin' you and warnin' you when danger is coming. It only works if you wear it."

I look back at the golden amulet and nod. I take it and tie it around my neck as the pendant rests comfortably between the curves of my collarbone. Immediately, I feel the power emanating from where it lies on my chest, overwhelming me. I sway on my feet and grab the table. I've already experienced this once before when I held the amulet for the first time yesterday, but I'm still shocked by the power this necklace has. Nellie and Loni raise their hands to steady me and catch me if I should fall, but my swaying feet stay locked on solid ground. I take a few deep breaths and stand up straighter, causing Nellie to nod and lightly let out a relieved breath.

Loni straightens up as she continues, "We're going to have you focus on the power comin' from the amulet. We want you to focus on what happened to Michael to help you channel your premonition abilities."

"How am I supposed to tap into the amulet's power?" I ask. "I don't know what I'm doing. I don't even know how I did it the first time."

"That's why we're here, J," Nellie says calmly. "Just try to focus on what you feel from the amulet and drown out everything else. Then think about what happened to Michael. Where you were, what you felt, the way the sun was shining, what it smelt like — *anything* to help you focus on that day. Just try, Mama."

I silently nod and, despite all my doubts, try. I plant my feet firmly and roll my neck; I have no idea if this is going to help, but I'll do anything to relax. I roll my shoulders, sway my hips side to side a couple of times, and close my eyes. I take a few deep, slow breaths — the smell of plants and sage, and the nose-tickling feeling of dust particles teasing my nostrils — and try to focus on the amulet. It's powerful; it's like a wave of heat that's cool at the same time — like peppermint. The wave spreads through my chest, outward to the rest of my body. I focus on that, and feel the cool-heat spread down to my arms, into my belly and the pit of my stomach — before falling to my legs and pooling in my feet. It feels like liquid heat; igniting a fire within me while at the same time cooling me down. I feel light-headed, but at the same time, my head feels the heaviest it's ever felt — I've never felt this way before. I sway from the overwhelming power of the amulet. I feel a hand on my arm — not entirely sure if it's Loni's or Nellie's, steadying me and keeping me upright. Thankful for the presence, I continue to focus on the feeling until all I feel is the cool-heat in my entire body. I make myself think about what happened to Michael the other day. I remember it was hot — Michael had to take off his jacket and tie it around his waist when we biked to Loni's. I remember the feeling of frustration rise in me after the conversation with Ray in the diner. The taste of Vanilla Bean milkshake lingering on my tongue. The power from the pendant begins to burn, but not in a painful way. It's almost like the pendant is pushing more power into my chest and then pushing it back from within — pushing me to embrace my abilities. I struggle beneath the sureness of its power, but press on. I remember the feeling of imminent dread pooling in the pit of my stomach, and watching Michael bike away. I remember feeling that dread rising until it consumed my very body. Then I remember seeing the cat: the blackness of its fur, the luminescence of its eyes, the sureness of its slow pace. I remember it looking at me — no, looking *into* me. It looked into my very soul, and... I'm just realizing, as I continue to focus on this interaction, that it was as if the cat was pulling the feeling from the pit of my stomach through my body, up into my head, until it was right in front of my face. Like an out of body experience. Except instead of seeing something that was happening from an outside view, I was seeing something that hadn't yet happened — with stunning clarity.

Then I remember screaming Michael's name, and Michael stopping. And the heart-stopping feeling of seeing that van speeding by Michael.

I open my eyes, gasping for air. I start to struggle to bring air into my lungs, looking every which way for I don't know what, until I feel Nellie place her hands on either side of my head.

"It's okay, J," Loni assures. "It's alright girl, calm down!"

"Breathe Mama, just breathe," Nellie says. She firmly shakes my head once, effectively locking me into her gaze, piercing my wild eyes with her steady ones. Out of the corner of my eyes, I see her hands turn bright — an almost gold halo of light surrounding her fingers. I feel a calmness seep into my body from her hands — making its way from my head to my heart, slowing my breathing, and releasing the tense muscles. She breathes in and out slowly with wide eyes, imploring me to mimic her. Which I do, and I shakily breathe in and out until we both inhale and exhale at a smooth pace. We do this for a minute longer before I feel okay to stand alone; I nod once, giving the go-ahead for Nellie to let go of my head. She lets go of my head, only to place a hand on my back and one on my hand, which I rest on the edge of the table.

"What did you see? What did you feel," Loni presses gently.

"I — I felt a burn coming from the amulet — but it was cold at the same time. It was so weird, I've never felt anything like that before." I stop, struggling for breath. Nellie squeezes my hand, letting me know her presence supports me. After another moment, I continue. "I tried to remember that day. It was hot, really hot. And it was a normal day, except for, y'know, Ray's unwarranted commentary — but what else is new?"

Loni and Nellie chuckle at my lame attempt at a joke. It must've actually been funny though, or else Nellie wouldn't have laughed. She never laughs at lame jokes. Or, maybe she's throwing me a pity laugh because of the direness of the situation.

"Then I remember the cat," I continue.

"The black one — like the one in your dream," Nellie affirms.

"Yeah. I didn't realize it at the time, but I felt something in my actual body when I looked at it. Like it was pulling the bad feeling from inside me — the one I had been feeling all day — and showed it to me. Then I remember stopping Michael and he barely missed getting hit by the van."

Loni nods excitedly before saying, "That's good! That's good, J. You saw what was happenin', and that will help you when you get these feelings again."

I nod in comprehension, but still think about how overwhelming that just was; this is still a lot to handle all at once. And, I have to go from everything I've ever known and thought about the real world to tap into a part of myself that I would never have accepted. How am I just supposed to accept all of this so quickly without a little bit of time to freak out? Oh, so my ancestors smoked a joint and played the drums to talk to the dead? And they'd look up a woman's woo-ha when she's giving birth to make sure mommy and baby are all good? Oh! And Nellie has *glowing hands*? Cool. Awesome. Totally not freaking out! They must see the look in my eyes, as Loni goes from excitement to reserved calm.

"Okay, today was a good start. Why don't you both go home an' get some rest. Yuh doh wah tuh drain yuh self 'til yuh weak. And Nellie, I know you had a long day at the hospital. You need some rest too. Go home, I'll see you both tomorrow."

Nellie and I nod obediently and make our way to the stairs. Nellie grabs my backpack as we make our way up to the closet. Loni gives us a quick wave before closing the hatch behind us and staying downstairs. We walk out to the Buick and plop into our seats. Nellie looks to the floor and takes a few deep breaths, her hands in the 10-and-2 position on the wheel. The weight of my head pushes my head back on the headrest of the seat I close my eyes until I hear Nellie turn the key in the ignition, and I feel us pulling out of the parking lot to head home.

Nellie and I stand at the kitchen counter. She is cutting the tomatoes, lettuce, turkey, and cheese for our sandwiches, and myself taking the lightly-toasted bread and buttering the slices. Michael came by just a few minutes before to grab the books for his Bio assignment, and seeing the tension between us, he chose not to stay. We silently prepare our lunches for the next day, adding the small Tupperware of soup and fruit in our lunch bags: blackberries for her, diced cantaloupe for me. As Nellie cuts our sandwiches into diagonal pieces, I decide it's finally time to tell her about my dream.

"Nellie," I start warily.

"Yeah?"

"I have to tell you about my dream last night. It was like the one from the night before — it had changed, but more happened this time."

Nellie drops what she's doing, slowly turning to face me with her head cocked to the side and face fixed in wary confusion as she braces to hear what I have to say. "Okay…"

I take a deep breath as I start, "So, the cat showed up again. I hesitated this time, but I still followed it into the jungle. I was running beside it like last time, and I started hearing the voices again. It changed into the panther like before, but this time we came to a clearing and it disappeared. I was following it around the tree trunk it was circling, but I lost it. Then I turn around, and —"

"And?" Nellie pushes.

"Well, I saw Mom."

Nellie looks at me expressionless, before asking, "This happened last night?"

"Yeah."

"And you're just telling me this now?" I grimace, my teeth bared in sheepish apology as she looks at me stone-faced.

"I wanted to tell you earlier," I start, knowing that this would come up, "but I was overwhelmed! You and Loni were telling me so much at once, and I was just trying to process everything. I guess I just, I don't know, wanted to take things one step at a time. I thought I could tackle this later."

Nellie continues to look at me silently, before nodding slowly in understanding. She turns back towards the counter to finish packing our lunches, placing the Tupperware of soup, and baggies of our sandwiches and fruit in our lunch bags.

"So, what happened when you saw your mother?"

"Well, I was shocked. It was so real, like I was really seeing Mom right in front of me. She looked at me with so much love, and there were tears in her eyes. I swear, it was like she was really there and it was more than just a dream."

"That's because it *was* more than just a dream," Nellie says. I look to her, her meeting my gaze as she continues, "This proves what me and Loni had predicted — you have the ability to talk to the afterlife. We guessed it when you started hearing the voices, but you seeing your mom just confirms it."

I breathe shakily in astonishment, as I ask, "So... that really was my mother that I saw in my dream? It wasn't just a figment of my imagination?"

Nellie looks at me with a mixture of love and sadness, nodding to confirm my suspicion. So, I really saw my mother. I made contact with her last night and I didn't even realize it. Before I know it, my eyes begin to tear up. Nellie notices and her face saddens as she peers intently into my face.

"When your mother passed," she says sadly, "I tried so hard to connect with her. Loni helped me to calm my nerves, sedated me, and I pushed myself to look for her in my dreams. But I just couldn't do it." Nellie's eyes tear up, her voice wobbling as she continues, "I would've given anything to talk to her again, and it broke my heart. I wanted so badly to talk to her one last time, to ask her what to do. She was my baby sister but I looked up to her in so many ways." Nellie bows her head, turning back towards the counter. Her arms lean on the counter as she rocks back and forth — sobs settling in the back of her throat as she talks.

"I had you to take care of, and I was so scared I was going to mess up —"

"But you didn't Nel," I interrupt, grabbing her hands and caressing the space between her thumb and forefinger. She gives off a small, tear-filled chuckle as she realizes I'm trying to calm her down.

I continue, "Everything I am is because of Mom and you, and I wouldn't have been able to handle Mom's death if it weren't for you. You're so strong — every day you find the energy to get up, go to work, and help heal people. Then you have to come home and deal with my ass, and I know I'm no picnic."

Nellie lets out a short laugh; I smile, relieved that I was able to lift her spirits momentarily. I continue, "If Mom was here, I know that she would say that you're doing a great job. You're not her — but you are you, and I wouldn't want it any other way."

Nellie looks at me with a loving smile, filled with gratitude, and sighs. "Thank you, Mama." I smile back and let go of her hands; my face gets serious as I prepare myself to tell her about other recent events. She notices and the smile slips off her face.

"What else happened?" she states, more than asks.

"Today in art class, I had a kind of... episode."

"Episode? Did you have another premonition?"

"Maybe? I don't know." Nellie looks at me with confusion, head cocked to the side, as I explain. "We were given an assignment to draw something that means something to us. I sat down with everything I needed but I didn't really know what I was going to do. The band class was practicing next door, and then the drums started playing."

Nellie's brows raise in realization; she stands back, looking at me in understanding, as she says, "You had an episode." I nod warily in confirmation.

"I started drawing and I didn't even realize what I was drawing. I didn't even clock that I was drawing, to be honest. It was like I was in a trance; the beat from the drums sort of filled up my entire body and it was all I could hear or feel. I just kept drawing and when I was done, I looked down and I saw that I drew Mom."

"You drew your mother? Are you sure it was her?"

"Yes Nellie, I'm sure," I assure her. "It looked exactly like her, and I can draw and stuff but I've never done a likeness so close like that before. I shaded in the background so it looked like nighttime, and she was wearing a red dress and gold jewellery, and she was looking right at me. And that night when I had that jungle dream again and I saw her — she just touched my head and I instantly woke up." With this, Nellie's head shoots up and she looks at me.

"She touched you?"

"Yeah…"

"Are you absolutely sure?"

"Yeah, I'm absolutely sure, Nellie. Why does that matter?"

Nellie breathes in deeply, squeezing between her brows and closing her eyes to take a few breaths. After a few moments, she looks back to me with an expressionless face.

"I don't know for sure, I can only guess. I mean, Loni has more experience with interpretation than I do. But, if your mother was able to actually *touch you*, then you're getting closer and closer to the realm of the afterlife — and it may have been a warning. A premonition."

"But what was I foreseeing?"

"I don't know," she replies exasperatingly. She makes her way over to the kitchen table, plopping down into her seat with fatigue and heavily slouching back. "The Bastet priestesses in ancient Egypt usually wore red dresses, and Bastets that descended from her would wear red when they were performing a ritual or for ceremonies, and things like that. And if your mom touched your head, and actually made physical contact with you in the afterlife — then, I don't know for sure, but it could mean that your mother is telling you to prepare for something. She may have been placing protection over your spirit."

"But what am I preparing for —"

"I don't know, J. I don't know."

"You don't know? How could you not know?"

"I don't know the answer to everything, J. I told you, interpretation is Loni's specialty. I can do it a little bit and even then, I haven't mastered it yet —"

"Nellie, you told me to trust you," I say desperately. "All of these crazy things are happening to me: old-age, spiritual mumbo-jumbo shit that makes me a target —"

"Language!"

I ignore her as I continue, "And you said that you could help me. You *said* that I could trust you to control my abilities and train them so they don't consume me, and you're telling me that YOU DON'T KNOW? What can I do with that?"

"Keep on trusting me!" Nellie jumps up — heated from the emotion — and I take a step back, startled by her sudden outburst. She looks at me with pleading eyes, as she says, "Jamila, I was in the same boat as you. The only way I was able to get through was with Keba and Loni. If it weren't for them, I would be a wreck. I already was after our mom had just died."

Nellie and Mom's mother, my grandmother, died when they were in their teens. Mom was a junior in high school and Nellie was 18 and had just graduated. Her name was Belle Freeman. I only know her through pictures and stories since she died before I was born — and from what I've been told, she was amazing. And she was beautiful. She looks like a mix of Nellie and Mom — with dark brown skin and a slim frame. She had high cheekbones, almond-shaped eyes, and smooth skin. I always thought she looked like a queen. She never really smiled in her photos. Lots of Jamaicans don't, to be honest — preferring instead to serve face. And she always had this stoic face that gave off so much power. So much expression and vitality in a photo — and from what Mom and Nellie used to say about her, she did the same thing in life. She was a small woman, like Nellie, but she had this presence that made everyone look up to her. She was really young when she had Nellie and Mom, and had to take care of them by herself — working every day to keep a roof over their heads and food on the table. She died from a heart attack in her late 40s, a culmination of a life of hard work with no support — well, almost. Loni was there, helping my grandmother with Nellie and Mom whenever she needed. She had to send Mom and Nellie to live with an uncle in Canada until she got enough money for herself, but she never did. Before she died, their uncle would send money back to Belle when he could, but there was always something happening. Whether it was the crooked landlord asking her for more money, or the local gangs shaking her down for money when she was out late at night. Loni knew Belle from school days in Jamaica, and would give Nellie and Mom shifts at the diner so they could save and send money back to Belle. When she died, and Nellie became Mom's next of kin caregiver, she let Nellie and Mom stay at her house until they could afford a small one-bedroom apartment. Nellie worked her way through college and medical school, and helped Mom pay for a diploma — but if it weren't for Loni, they wouldn't have been able to achieve any of that. Loni was like a second mother to them, and was probably a seminal part of them learning their powers. I know from experience how hard it is to learn all of this without your mother. Don't get me wrong, Loni and Nellie are saints, but it's hard to do all of this underground without your mom. Your mother is that one person who can just bring you peace while pushing you to be better. Nellie does that for me — but without your mother, it's just different. I kind of forgot that Nellie had to go through that — and she's trying to help me as I go through it too, and I'm not exactly making it easy for her.

"Every Bastet is different," Nellie continues, "and we all experience our manifestations differently. So, we can't know for sure how best to train ourselves or one another, because history has affected our bloodline so much that what we *can* accomplish with our abilities is just too unpredictable. It took me forever to hone my abilities, while your mother was a natural. The one thing we had in common was that we had no idea what the hell we were doing, but we trusted in Loni to help us make sense of it all. You have to trust me — or at least try."

I stand there, taking in everything she's saying. Nellie went through what I'm going through now — albeit with her own trials and tribulations — and she had to trust that she'd get the help she needed. I have to at least try and trust she'll do the same for me.

"Okay," I say.

"Okay," she says.

CHAPTER FIVE

It's the next day, and the bell rings to signal the end of the first period. I make my way from AP Calculus and head to my locker. The sound of chattering teenagers makes its way to my ears as the rest of the student population exit their respective classrooms. I walk down the hallway — my pair of white Air Force One squeaking on the linoleum floor — as I make my way to my locker. The sunlight from outside streams in through the large windows, shining light on my side of lockers while the others are cast in shadow. Opening my locker and dropping my Calculus books in, I grab my history textbook and my history paper — safely stowed in a duo-tang folder — to hand in for my next class. Out of the corner of my eye I see Michael walking through the crowd, his boney frame more pronounced by his gangly walk — like his limbs are controlled by a puppeteer. He's wearing his new Nike's that he got for the start of the school year, and from here I can see not a smudge in sight. He keeps them clean with OCD-level attention — but then again, everybody does when they get fresh shoes right out of the box. Taylor Stennett walks out from a classroom right in front of him, and suddenly Michael turns into Boo-Boo the Fool. His eyes get wide and he stops, looking from left to right as he shuffles in place. I muffle a laugh as I see my friend turn into a complete moron, getting tongue-tied before he even says anything to her. An internal war rages behind his eyes before he finally walks forward, his gait changing in an attempt to look calm and collected, and he steps beside her.

"Hey, Taylor," he greets nonchalantly.

"Oh, hey, Michael," she says with a polite smile. She looks down, and with an impressed expression she says, "Nice Nike's, they're lookin' clean!"

For a brief second, Michael is the happiest I've ever seen him in our entire lives before he resumes his nonchalant composure — fixing his face to look casual and indifferent, and leaning back into his leg so he stands at an angle.

"Thanks, yours are pretty fresh too."

"Thanks," she says smiling, and with that, she's off to her next class. Michael's eyes get wide in disbelief as he stares after her, before he sees me on the side. He runs towards me, his limbs returning to their puppet-like disposition before he finally lands in front of me breathless — even though he dashed no more than one foot.

"Did you see that?" he asks incredulously. "DID YOU SEE THAT? She knew my name!"

"I know," I say amused. "It must be love." He cocks his upper lip in annoyance, clucking his tongue in reply.

"Shut up, you're not gonna ruin this for me, alright? She knew my name!" He looks at me with wide eyes, as if it's not clicking. "I didn't even think she remembered my face! But she remembered me and my name at the same time? Nah, nah, nah, I'm floatin' now."

"Okay, calm down Pennywise." The smile slips off his face as he cuts his eye at me. "It's just your name; you still have to have a conversation with her for her to actually have an opinion about you, my guy."

"And it'll happen —"

"*When*? We've known Taylor since elementary school and you've yet to hold a conversation with her that wasn't in your head," I say this as I poke his head, causing him to smack my hand away. I laugh as we walk down the hallway towards our classes, mine at the end of the hallway and his down the stairs and just a few rooms to the left.

"Alright, bet — I'm gonna talk to her today and I'm gonna make her *swoon*. Just you wait, we're gonna be talking about school and she's going to be wondering," he raises his voice to sound like a girl before continuing, "'*Oh! Who's this amazing, gorgeous, intellectually advanced guy that I've never noticed before? And why am I so attracted to him? Oh my!*' Just you wait! It's happenin'."

"Okay," I say doubtedly. "Well, when I see you moping down the hallways after school, I'll assume your plan didn't go as expected."

He rolls his eyes and pushes my head forward; kissing my teeth I try to do the same, but he speeds up and jogs down the stairs. I stand in front of my class and flip him off behind his back, and by some telepathic linkage, he does the same. I smile before heading into class.

"Okay, class. Welcome to another day of scholastic learning," Ms. Boykin says. The class mumbles in reply — rather unenthusiastically, but it's better than complete silence I guess.

"Today, we're going to continue with the African slave-trade — but instead of our regular note-taking, we're going to be watching the movie *Amistad*. It's a film adaptation of one of many instances where slaves attempted to take control of the ship. I'll get it all set up but as I do that, everyone hand in their history papers. They are due today — and I know you were hoping I would forget, but you're out of luck."

The class collectively groans as they get moving. Some students pull out their papers, some in folders like mine and others just bare paper, and some students stay where they are. I guess they either forget about the paper or, are working on an excuse for why they didn't do it. *My computer crashed. A shift at work ran long. My dog ate my homework.* Any of those are bound to be said. I grab my paper out of my backpack and wait to hand it in at the front of the class. As I'm waiting in the line, another student walks up to Ms. Boykin who's setting up the movie.

"Hey, Ms. Boykin," he starts. "My assignment is finished but I just haven't printed it yet. My computer crashed over the weekend and it's on Microsoft Word, but I'm getting my laptop fixed first thing tomorrow so I'll hand in my paper soon, I promise." I hide my smile as my suspicions are proven correct, and hand in my paper before heading to my seat. Ms. Boykin finishes her conversation with the other student before he sits down.

"Okay everyone, try and pay attention. No phones or laptops open please; I'm going to give you a sheet of paper and you just fill in the blanks." She starts handing out the papers before she goes to the back of the room. She turns the lights off before heading to the front and turning the movie on.

I've heard of this movie but never actually watched it. I wanted to watch it a year or two ago, but a student a year ahead of me told me they watched it in senior year and I thought I might as well wait to watch it in class. The movie begins, with the opening credits setting the stage. It starts how all slave movies usually start, with the story of a content African man, living the life they've always known: with their family, their village, and their land — and then they come in contact with one of the most powerful forces in the colonial era — Europe. Minutes pass and he's already been captured and held with many other countless slaves. The conditions they're kept in, while I'm aware of them, still makes my stomach curdle seeing them with such stunning imagery. The majesty that these people once enjoyed is dulled by the squalor they're subjected to. A juxtaposition of the highest order, with morality invisible to unjust treatment. After a few scenes, I see the main character — Sengbe — trying to talk to the man representing him in court, even though neither of them knows each other's language. The desperation with which he tries to communicate his situation, his life, makes my breath catch in my throat. The actual shackles latched on to his throat, and the chains he's kept in, makes my eyes tear. I begin to twitch and move around in my seat, which catches the attention of another student beside me.

"Hey," he whispers, "you good?"

I nod once, even though I'm sure my face says the exact opposite. I turn around and look at the clock and see that there's still ten minutes left in class. I turn back and exhale unsatisfied — I have to sit through this display of the worst part of my history for another ten minutes. Actually, now with what I've just learned, I'm not sure that this is the worst part of my history. Slavery is something that the majority of black people can say was a part of their family's history. If it wasn't, they were blessed to not come from a lineage of people who were enslaved, tortured, and deprived of their culture and country. But they don't have the added weight of coming from a lineage of superhuman women, and the dangers of that might be just as bad. I sometimes think about how lucky I am to live in the 21st century — with technology, societal progression, and globalism — but I also wonder how worth it all of that was. Were the centuries of slavery, genocide, and death worth all of that? Was the hunting, torture, and enslavement of the Bastet women worth me being here? As I'm watching this, I question it even more. I question if I'm being ungrateful to live here, now, and not 300 years ago.

Finally the movie pauses, and Ms. Boykin heads to the back of the room to turn the lights back on. As the shocking light causes us to close and squeeze our lids over our eyes, I breathe a sigh of relief that I can take a break from this display of carnage and inhumanity.

"Alright, we'll finish the rest of the movie for the next class. No homework today, but please finish the fill-in-the-blanks for the next class, and do be prepared with your textbooks for next class. Have a good lunch everyone."

With that, the room springs into action and rushes to get out of class;

I, however, stay in my seat for a moment longer. The same classmate who asked about me earlier stops, his backpack poised on one shoulder.

"You sure you're good?"

"Yeah," I reply breathy, "yeah I'm good, it's just a lot, you know."

"What's a lot?" he asks.

"Y'know, seeing all of that," I say, pointing to the screen that's paused on Sengbe's face. "It's a movie adaptation, but it's an adaptation of what *really* happened. Seeing it just makes it feel rawer. Like I'm forced to be confronted with this part of my past. This part of all of our pasts."

"It's not a part of my past," he says. "Yeah, the Europeans enslaved all of those people — and it was terrible — but I didn't do anything. And that was in the past, it happened so long ago, try not to let it bother you. You're here now, not in slavery and things are better than they were back then."

I look at him, stunned by his audacious ignorance — and by the fact that he looks back confused as if I'm the ignorant one. He doesn't wait for an answer and leaves the classroom while I sit there — still stunned. I blink in disbelief as I gather my books and phone, before Ms. Boykin notices that I'm still there.

"Jamila," she calls out to me. "I'll be looking forward to reading your interpretation of the assignment. It's a very sensitive, multifaceted topic to discuss, and I'm sure I won't be disappointed."

I reply with a small smile, before turning and leaving class to meet Michael at our lunch bench.

I sit at our lunch bench and look at my watch; it's been 10 minutes since the lunch period started, and Michael is usually here before I even get here. There are only 30 minutes for the lunch period, and I begin to wonder where he could be. The sun is hiding behind some clouds, and the air is muggy. The weather report called for thunderstorms later today, and I can already smell the rain in the air. It's still humid though, and I have to take off my jean jacket so I don't start to sweat too much. I sit on top of it and tie the sleeves around my waist, pulling out my striped t-shirt so it doesn't bunch underneath it and get wrinkly. I look up and, finally, I see him walk out from the east entrance; but instead of walking to our lunch bench, he keeps walking towards the parking lot. I look at him confused, and see that he looks nervous. Why does he look nervous? His gait is janky, short and dawdle, as if he's unsure of what he's going to do next. He keeps walking until I realize where he's going: the popular kids spot. More specifically, Taylor Stennett's car. He slows before he reaches her, his face clearly anxious to actually start a conversation, before he finally walks up to her. My eyes widen as I realize he's going to do it — he's going to actually start a conversation with her. Well, hallelujah. He's just within earshot so I can hear what they're saying, but just far away enough that it doesn't look like I'm eavesdropping — which is exactly what I'm doing.

"Hey Taylor," he says. She turns her head from the conversation she was having with Kiara Davis and Stephanie Williams, and smiles when she realizes it's Michael.

"Hey Michael, what's up?" she asks with a smile, as Kiara and Stephanie look at him with a mixture of confusion, humour, and nosiness.

"I just wanted to say that your English presentation was really great; I would have never thought to compare the patriotism in the book to the loyalty to basketball."

"What can I say, I'm a Raptors fan," she says laughing.

"Yeah," he replies with a small laugh, "who would'a thought that laying down one's life for your country would be so similar to faithfully following a play."

She laughs, genuinely, before he continues, "My friend is more into the English and literature stuff than I am; she could run circles around me when it comes to anything that doesn't involve numbers. You would like her."

I smile from the compliment from where I sit, as Taylor replies, "Oh yeah?"

"Yeah," he replies, "but you're not nearly as annoying as she is." With that, my smile drops. Asshole.

"Maybe you could show me how to write something that actually has something to say — you'd probably guarantee it make sense to me, and I could learn something."

"Oh, that's so sweet," she says. "But I could never work numbers like you can; I see you're always getting high 90s in Calc. You could teach me something too. I see numbers and my mind suddenly doesn't work, and I need a calculator to calculate 2+2."

Michael laughs, looking down and shuffling his feet, before replying, "Maybe we could hang out after school sometime, we could exchange notes and make sure it makes sense to each other."

"That sounds great," she says smiling before a thought comes across her face. "Actually, I have this extra ticket to the Raptors game tonight. My date did something stupid and got herself grounded," she cuts her eye at Kiara Davis, who replies with a childish eye-roll, before continuing, "so it's up for grabs."

Michael freezes, like a deer in the headlights, looking at Taylor with wide eyes.

"I mean, that is, of course, if you know how basketball works. I mean if my presentation was lost on you, are you gonna understand the game? You know that it works with two teams, right? There's a ball. It's round. They shoot it through a hoop, it's crazy! I don't know if you'll be able to keep up."

Michael laughs humourlessly, looking to the side with a small smirk — this makes him miss Taylor biting her lip and looking at him... like she likes him. Wait, is she *attracted* to him? Wild.

"Yeah. Yeah, I'd love that."

"Great! Well, give me your number and I'll text you the details."

Without any hesitation whatsoever, Michael whips out his phone so they can exchange numbers. They quickly bid each other farewell before Michael backs away, bumping into a few people and making Taylor giggle. As he turns around he spots me, his face gets toddler-level excited. He starts to run towards me before he second-guesses himself and speed-walks over instead.

"Holy crap. HOLY CRAP!" he exclaims, as he plops beside me. "Did you see that? Did you *see* that?"

"Yeah, I did. Heard it too. You finally grew a pair and spoke words to her, huh?"

"Oh don't make me blush; my nads will never be as big as yours."

I flip him off, which he returns with an air kiss, before continuing, "I cannot believe that I have a *date* with Taylor Stennet. Me. A Date!"

"I know — how audacious of you."

"This is crazy. I've been dreaming about this day for years, and I can't believe it's actually happening."

"Me either. Your first date with Taylor Stennett is a Raptors game?" He looks at me confused as I elaborate, "You know nothing about basketball. I'm sorry Michael, but you didn't even know how to pronounce Kawhi's name."

"Okay, yeah," he relents, "but what does that have to do with the actual game? You root for the team wearing the red and white, cheer when they shoot the ball in the hoop and boo when the other team shoots a ball in our hoop. Simple. What else am I missing?"

"An actual interest in the game."

He stops and thinks for a moment before replying, "I have a general interest in Taylor, who has a general interest in the game — so, through affiliation, I have a general interest in the game, and that'll have to do."

"Yeah, yeah, whatever." I roll my eyes as Michael chuckles, grabbing his lunch out of his bag.

"But for real though, I'm happy for you man. This is huge so you better not mess this up."

"I won't, I won't," he says, raising his hands in surrender. His face goes serious for a moment before he says, "But could you come over and help me pick out an outfit for tonight?"

I respond, my voice muffled behind my sandwich, "Sinth when did you care a'out your outfit?"

"Since I got a date with Taylor Stennett, bitch, that's when."

"Ay," I warn, my finger pointing at him, "don't call me a bitch. You may be my best friend but you're not my girl — you don't get that privilege."

"Oh come on, you already know I'm the baddest bitch out here," he replies, tossing his head to whip his imaginary tresses. Laughing with the food still in my mouth, struggling to swallow without choking as he flutters his lashes, and bows his head behind his shoulder coyly.

"Yeah sure, I'll help you out. But I've gotta do something at Loni's first, I'll probably be there around 7:30 ish."

"Damn, you're at Loni's again? Do you really not know how to cook at all?"

I reply quickly, "When have you ever seen me without a book in my hand? When exactly would I have any hands free to roll dumplings?" He laughs and nods his head in agreement. I'm both surprised and simultaneously unimpressed with how easy it's becoming to lie to my best friend, but I can't risk him finding out the truth — so lying it is.

"That's cool," he says. "The game doesn't start til 9:30, and I'm meeting her there. I'll pick out a couple of options and you can veto the ones that don't work."

"Alright, cool."

He nods before stuffing the entire sandwich in his mouth, not bothering to take a bite and, apparently, preferring to inhale the sandwich whole. I groan in disgust as I take a sip of my drink. He lets out a hoot of laughter, delighted by my disgust.

I unlock my bike from the bike rack and pull it from the space — holding it upright as I zip my water bottle and books into my backpack, stowing it safely in the basket. Michael walks up to the bike rack just as I hop onto my seat.

"See you at 7:30?"

"Yessir," I reply.

He smiles as I ride off, heading to Loni's. Several other students on bikes criss-cross and swerve on the street before heading to the bike lane. Others head to the public bus stop and wait for the bus, and others head back towards the east parking lot to their cars. I head west and, after looking back to see little to no cars, I bike in the middle of the street. It was raining after lunch but with the sun hiding behind the clouds, the smell of wet grass and concrete fills my nostrils. The air didn't cool down because of the rain, though, so the humidity remains — causing my t-shirt to stick underneath my armpits, to my lower back, and the space just below my breasts. I slow down to avoid working up too much of a sweat — to obviate going to Loni looking like a greaseball. I bike along and head towards Steeles Avenue, looking at the small businesses with blinking 'Open' signs, and the numerous hair stores, roti places and independently-owned jewellers that are dotted along every street. Finally, Loni's diner comes into view, and I bike a little bit faster so that I can seek the refuge of air conditioning. As I coast into the parking lot, a black Escalade that was driving on the street ahead of me slows before also pulling into the lot. It turns and drives towards me slowly — the tinted windshield hides the driver and its passengers, adding an ominous presence to this new visitor. I slowly walk my bike to the bike rack, looking to the car as nonchalantly as I can, as a precaution. As I bend over to fasten my bike with the lock, I hear the doors of the Escalade open and close before I hear a voice that I loathe to recognize.

"Hey slim-thick," Ricky Brass calls out.

I groan mentally, knowing that this encounter is not going to be good, before slowly turning around. Not only is Ricky Brass here, but two of

Blanco's boys are with him. And they're all walking towards me in the least welcoming way possible.

"I got into a lot of shit just for talking to you, and you were the one that disrespected me," he says, his face concealing anger but remaining as calm as possible.

"I never meant to get you in trouble," I say quietly, backing up and hugging the bike rack behind me. "But you should have never confronted us. I guess we both made a mistake."

His nostrils flare and his eyes widen in anger, his companions' faces setting to high-and-mighty airs and their legs widening into fighting stances. I don't know why they'd need to take a fighting stance when they're talking to a 17-year-old girl.

"Bitch," Ricky says, walking towards me in his cobra-like way, "you should know betta than to talk to grown folks that way. That mouth of yours is gonna get you in trouble, and don't think just cause you in school you smarter than me. You may be book smart, but the world has taught me shit you'd neva learn in no textbook. That shit would make you piss yo' self, and that's me bein' nice. Don't test me, bitch."

I start to quiver internally, terrified by the anger and dominance he regards me with. His eyes lower, wandering over my body and taking note of the sweat along my collarbone and chest. His eyes turn from hatred to lust, and he looks back to my face with so much disgusting desire my skin begins to crawl. He leans even closer, his sour breath once again wafting into my face as he whispers in my ear.

"Try me again, and I'll come an' use you however I want to. You run your mouth too much — keep doing that, and I'll have you usin' your mouth for somethin' else. Somethin' that might give me a reason to forgive your midnight-lookin' ass."

My entire body shakes, as my stomach drops to the floor. I don't handle threats well. I've never been good with confrontation, I only do it because it's better than being treated like a doormat — but I've never been threatened like this before. I don't know how to process this, and my entire body seems to shut down — frozen with fear. I hug myself even closer to the bike rack to get away from him, but he leans forward and grabs the bike rack, closing me in. The clink of his brass knuckles on the steel of the rack makes my nerves on edge, as he continues to look at me in silence. His breathing gets shallow, his stare gets longer; people walk past and slow, wondering what's happening but resolving to not get involved and continue with their day. One passerby does notice that this might not be the safest situation and calls out to us like the good Samaritan he is.

"Hey, y'all good?" he yells.

"Yeah, we good," Ricky calls back, without turning his head. He addresses to me, stating rather than asking, "We good, right slim-thick?"

I look at him as water stings my eyes, threatening to fall onto my cheeks. Being threatened by him is one thing, but being threatened with the intent of using me — for simply speaking my mind — instills a type of fear that I've heard of, and know exists, but have never experienced first-hand. I've heard so many stories of girls being harassed like this: stories in the news, on social media, even in my own family. It's nothing new to me but experiencing it is. Nellie once told me about a time when an uncle touched her and Mom when they were young. One of those uncles that aren't blood-related but are close enough family friends that they're considered family. Well, he had a moment alone with them, and used that time to exert the power he had — and she didn't remember it until years later. She had buried it so deep in her mind that she never wanted to remember it. Mom told me that her grandmother — Mumah Joy, who died long before I was born — was raped by her brother's best friend. She was forced to carry through with the pregnancy because her family was religious and any other option would've been blasphemous. But she lost the baby and had three miscarriages until she finally had my grandmother, Nana Belle. Nellie would say that black women's bodies are seen as brothels instead of temples. I used to think that sort of thing would never happen to me, and that I wouldn't be one of the many black girls who are only seen as objects. I guess I'm just unlucky. Suddenly, I see Loni out of the corner of my eye — walking towards us, sure in her purpose.

"What's going on here?" she asks, steel shooting from her voice.

Ricky looks at her, his face changing to one that almost resembles respect.

"Nothing Loni. I'm just having a little talk here with slim-thick about respecting people —"

"That's *Miss.* Loni to you," she says deadpan. He looks at her, slightly stunned by the force in her voice. "And she's the last person you should be talkin' to suh close. You naave no business with har, an' no business in front of my dina neitha."

"Now, Ms. Loni," he says, physically restraining himself out of respect,

"I know this is yo' diner, but she disrespected me. I have to let her know that I am not the one."

"Well then," she exclaims, walking in front of me and blocking his vision, "we seem to have something in common! Because *I* am not the one eitha. Now I'm gonna say dis once, an' me nah say it again — don't come 'round here talkin' to little girls that you don't have nuh business with. An' don't come on my property unless you fixin' for a meal. Cross me again, an' it'll be the last time I show you any mercy."

"Oh, this is mercy? I'm a regular paying customer, and this is terrible customer service."

"Tough. I don't mind losing a customa that disrespects my other regulars. You turn your back an' three more people who enjoy my service an' my food guh fi walk thru the door — and they'll have the good sense to treat other people in this space with respect an' human decency. With *manners*, not like they weren't raised right. Don't test me. Now get off'a mi property."

Ricky's face lights up in anger, his shoulders tensing and fists clenching — ready to lay his hands on her. But he must've been raised with some level of decency, because he backs away slowly before turning away, his compatriots giving us one final warning glare before following behind him. Loni takes me by my shoulders and turns me around, giving me my backpack and guiding me towards the door. As the doors slam behind us, I turn in time to see the Escalade speed out of the parking lot, ignoring the 60 km speed limit posted on the side street. We walk into the diner, a few people scattered around: listening to music, eating, and chatting with other customers. As we walk to the back, we see Ray — bending over to grab something at the counter. He glimpses us through the kitchen window.

"Hey J," he greets in his booming voice. "How you doin'?"

"We good, Ray," Loni replies for me, saving me from having to speak when my voice is still caught in my throat. "She just had a run-in with one'a Blanco's boys, just gonna calm her down a likkle."

Ray nods in apprehension, shaking his head as he turns around to greet a customer at the counter. Loni shepherds me to the back closet; I know that she turns on the light, opens the floor hatch, and guides me down the stairs — but honestly, I'm in a bit of a haze. I'm still struggling to process what just happened and I feel uncomfortable in my own skin. Like I want to just step out of my body and float away. Loni walks forward and grabs my backpack then places it by the leg of one of the tables. She looks at me for a moment before sighing and walking towards the mini kitchenette. I lethargically move towards the table, grabbing a chair and plopping down. I slump in the seat and stare at the floor, wanting to just be in my bed where I can curl into a ball, listen to some sad music and wet my pillow with tears. I can't bring myself to cry — maybe I'm still in shock — so I just sit there. Staring at the ground. Loni comes back with a teapot and two teacups on tiny plates — the nice ones that your grandmother would stow away in a transparent cabinet, teasing you because you were forbidden to touch them. I always did wonder why there were so many beautiful teacups put on display that would never be used. What the hell is the point of having nice china that you can't use anyway?

"Drink some tea," Loni says. "It'll calm yuh nerves a little bit."

I obey her and pour some for myself that fills three-quarters of the cup, dropping a couple of teaspoons of sugar in so it's sweet — just the way I like it. I blow a few times on the brim of the cup before taking a sip; it's a new flavour that I've never tasted before — like a mix of peppermint, cinnamon, and ginger. It's warm and welcoming so I continue to sip. Loni doesn't pour a cup for herself yet, but looks at me with questioning eyes.

"What happened?"

I look down into the cup, fumbling my fingers along the handle for a few moments before responding, "You saw what happened. He approached me and got all up in my face."

"Yeah, I know that much," she says. "But what *happened?*"

"Well… he, uh… he came up to me and said that if I don't watch my mouth he'd uh… he'd use my mouth for something else."

Loni takes a sharp breath, her nostrils flaring and head slightly shaking side to side. Her eyes close as she leans back into her chair, staying like that for a couple of seconds. She then opens her eyes and looks at me with an expressionless face.

"Men like him abuse the powa dey aave, threatenin' people into getting their way an' hurting those who don't give dem what they want. And then when we don't do what they want, they throw us aside and say we're crazy for getting hurt. He's weak. And he knows it, 'cause you're one'a the most dangerous thing that threatens his powa. You're a black woman with a brain who isn't afraid tuh use it, and knows her value."

"As opposed to what? A Neanderthal?" I joke half-heartedly.

"You know what I mean, pickney. You speak and powa flows off your tongue because your words mean something. Lots of us don't speak our minds an' end up losing the chance to really be happy or make a difference, or to change things. When you have something to say, you get a little stronga, and they get weak'a from not havin' a crutch to hold themselves up."

She leans forward and grabs my hand; I continue to look into my cup, but she shakes my hand once, causing me to look up into her face.

"Don't lose your voice, J. Ever. And don't let them intimidate yuh into suppressin' it eitha. It'll be the only thing that'll give you strength when everything else falls apart. You could learn to choose your words wisely from time tuh time," I smile at her joke, as she continues, "but you shouldn't stop using your words altogether. Because no one can say them like you can — and di world is a likkle bit betta because of it."

I nod silently, looking back into my cup and lifting it to my lips to take small sips. After a couple of minutes, I've finished the tea in my cup. We smile at each other silently, as we enjoy the comfortable silence. Gradually, I begin to feel light as a feather. My head feels weightless, yet heavy at the same time, and I feel calm. I was so wound up just a second ago, and now I feel as calm as a still lake. My eyes wander down to my cup, and a thought crosses my mind.

"What kind of tea is this?"

"It's a herbal tea," she says, as I raise my eyebrows in innocence.

"Oh," I say in realization.

"It helps to calm the nerves and settle a wired brain." I look up at her, her looking back at me with a deadpan face. My smile settles as I realize fully what she means.

"You drugged me!" I say surprised.

"I gave you a herbal sedative to calm you down; it's nothing more than that, don't stress yuh self."

She stands up and takes the teapot and cups to the sink; my head feels lighter than air, and my body feels as if I got a deep tissue massage. This feels good, but I didn't ask for this. My nerves spike and I feel this as cold sparks through the warm calm of my body.

"Loni, what the hell?" I say incredulously. "You just crossed so many moral boundaries! I didn't give you consent to sedate me."

"Just like you didn't give Ricky Brass consent to threaten you with sexual assault, and intimidate you. Tell me, which one do you prefer?"

I remain silent, without a response. Okay sure, being calmed down through a sedative is better than being sexually harassed. However, not willingly submitting to be sedated is still a red flag, and there is a fine line that is dangerously treading on right now. She washes the pot and teacups and dries her hands before she walks to the table on the other side of the room. She squats, struggling to pull out something large from beneath it which I won't bother to guess what it is. I'd much rather ride this roller coaster ride of bliss. I can already feel it beginning to wear off, but I'm trying to soak up the last dredgings of peace anyway. When she's once again beside me, I take account of a drum now in front of me — a beige top encased in a wooden frame, shaped like an hourglass and half my height. I stand up and look at it, remembering my episode in art class and the trance I was put in on accident.

"Nellie told me what 'appened to you in yuh art class the other day," she says. I look at her as she continues, "It sounds like you slipping into the Realm of Duality."

"What's that?" I ask lucidly.

"It's a place between this world and the spiritual world. It's not quite making a connection with the afterlife, but it puts you in a place where you can connec' with that world while still being connected to the physical world — a sort of in-between place."

"You think that's why I was in a trance?"

"I do. You told Nellie that the band in the room beside yours was playin' drums, an' then suddenly you were drawing this picture of your motha without realizin' you were doin' it. You transported yourself to the Realm of Duality without even realizin' it — or at least you were gettin' close to it. Remember I told you about how our ancestors would use the drums to drown out the outside world, an' help us tap into our senses?"

"Yeah, you said the Bastets would dance to the beat and sink into a state of unconsciousness."

"Yes," she exclaims, "that is so they could enter the Realm of Duality. That is the place that is safest for us. We can connec' to the realm of spirits and ask for guidance, or assist those passin' on, without going too far that we stretch our minds past redemption."

"What do you mean?"

"We can connec' to the afterlife, but it has its limits. If we stray too far away from the physical realm to connec' to the spiritual realm, the links we had to the physical world will begin to fray, until they tear completely." She looks around the room before she finds what she's looking for, going near the potion pantry and coming back with a small hemp rope.

"It's like your mind is a piece of rope. One end is connected to the spiritual world and the other is connected to the physical world. You're in the middle, in the Realm of Duality, safely." She begins to pull at one end of the rope roughly. "But the more you connec' to one realm, the less you become connected to the otha, until —"

She pulls until the middle of the rope begins to fray, tearing until it's connected by a small thread.

"Your mind begins to fray an' tear away from the world where your physical body remains. You aave to ensure that you stay firmly in the Realm of Duality..." The rope finally breaks apart, both ends falling limp in her hands.

"Or else you break from both realms, an' you're lost in the space between the two. Many people who are in a coma are in this space, but only Bastets — or people who are really in tune with their spiritual side — realize what this space is."

I look at the frayed ends, intimidated by a piece of rope and the convincing imagery used to communicate her point. She puts her hand on my shoulder, causing me to look up to her eyes.

"But we won't let you get there. You were lucky that you pulled out of the Realm of Duality 'fore you began to stray too far away from the physical realm — but you might not be so lucky again. Nellie and I will help you stay where you need to be, an' pull you out if it looks like you're strayin' too far. But you aave to exercise control. I'm tellin' you this now so you're prepared, 'cause it can be overwhelmin' once you're really in it."

I nod quickly, in understanding, as she continues, "You won't realize what you're doing in the physical world when you're makin' the connection to the spiritual realm. You may be drawing somethin', or writing somethin', or simply actin' something out that someone on the spiritual side is showin' you. You won't know what's 'appenin', but you still have to be aware of your body. Try your hardest to remember that you are skin and bone. Blood and flesh." She smacks my arms, my legs, then grabs my shoulders and shakes them firmly.

"This is your body," she affirms. "This is who you are. You may be a Bastet, but don't forget the second part of being superhuman, eh? You're still human, and you have limits and boundaries that you caah cross. Yuh hear me?"

"Yes, yes I understand," I say anxiously. She softens her face and looks at me with love, grabbing my hands in hers and squeezing as she shakes them several times.

"It's gonna be okay, baby girl. You're not goin' into this alone. You may be in the Realm of Duality by yourself, but you have us in the physical realm to support you, and your ancestors in the spiritual realm to guide you. You always aave support and love. Never forget that, eh?"

I nod — smiling to show my gratitude but still overwhelmed by everything being thrown at me all at once. She moves a chair to the middle of the aisle between the tables and guides me to sit down. She grabs the drum and puts it about a foot in front of me, standing behind it to face me and straightening her posture.

"This is a Djembe; it's an African drum that was used to help drown out the distractions of the physical realm to help connec' to the spiritual one. You're already calmed down a bit after the tea, so this shouldn't be too difficult; just don't allow yourself to sink too comfortably in the Realm of Duality. It'll only be that much easier to stray from the physical realm."

I nod shakily, straightening my posture in my seat. I shuffle my bum from side to side, roll my shoulders and neck, and look at Loni in fearful anticipation. She looks at me and smiles reassuringly, realizing my anxiety is mounting; she then leans forward on the Djembe.

"You've been through this before, so you have the advantage of at least knowing what might 'appen. And don't forget: you're not alone. Now, close your eyes."

I nod and do as she says, taking several shaky deep breaths until I feel myself regulating to a normal inhale-exhale pattern.

"I want you to think about things that bring you peace; whatever you do that calms your nerves, and mek you tranquil. Focus on that, an' nothin' else."

I close my eyes and breathe slowly. In and out. In and out. In... and out. The first thing that comes to mind is being with Nellie in the small garden in the backyard. We used to spend hours out there, just reading books and snacking on bun and cheese, and sipping iced tea to cool us down. We don't do that as much anymore since senior year started for me; I've been focusing more on school and, to be honest, less on Nellie. And she's been picking up more shifts to save for my college tuition, so it's more of a distant memory as the days go by. I hear Loni start to lightly tap on the drum, a slow tempo that I can barely hear yet I still take notice of. I think about Michael; just biking down the trail near the Lakeshore and joking around. He always makes me laugh, and I'm never more happy than when I'm laughing with him. The pounding of the drum begins to get louder and faster, more insistent in its purpose. I want to open my eyes and see what Loni is doing, but I keep them close so that I don't mess up the process. I think about Loni and the diner — about Ray and his lengthy monologues. And his milkshakes — God, I *love* his milkshakes. The smile on Loni's face as she would check on us, the warmth and camaraderie of the diner and its customers. The peace of the community.

Then I think about my mom. Just her face makes my heart pang with the pain of her loss, but I still remember our time together. Our picnics in the park in the summertime, our trips to the public library that would always result in me bringing home at least five books. Our cooking sessions with Nellie — which usually ended in Nellie just doing everything because Mom and I would always be messing around. And our dance parties. We used to have these spontaneous dance parties on the weekends when we were all cleaning the house. It's a thing in our house, in every Jamaican house I'm convinced, that when the music starts blasting first thing on a Saturday morning — it's time to do a deep cleaning of the house. Even if you tried to sleep in, somebody would bang through your door with a vacuum — a rude wake-up call to let you know that sleeping in wasn't an option. We all had our part, but then a certain song would play and Mom would be swept away by the music. We would dance until we were out of breath, and then dance some more. Nellie would dance with us too, but she was able to keep her feet on the ground while my mom and I had our heads up in the clouds. This meant she was also the one to clean the whole house while we fooled around. I smile, thinking about us dancing to Michael Jackson and somehow making a dance routine from nothing. I think about my chest hurting from laughing so hard when Michael and I would hang out — so much so that my throat would make that weird crackling sound that isn't really a sound but rather a feeling. I think about the tranquility of just being with Nellie, each of us reading our books and escaping into different worlds in each other's company. These thoughts become moving pictures in my brain, as I feel myself begin to get weightless. The pounding of the drum suddenly goes from being outside my head to inside my body; my very bones feel like they're thrumming from the inside out, and the reverberation from the drum pulses through my veins. It's like that episode in art class — but this time, I welcome the feeling, as I realize what it means.

My head feels heavy as I go from clearly seeing those moving pictures to seeing a ceiling. But it's not the ceiling of the basement — it's a generic beige ceiling, but I don't recognize it. After a moment I realize I'm not standing and looking up, but lying down horizontally. I feel the weight of my own body being pressed down from gravity, and feel my head pool with blood as I stare up. My eyes wander to the wall, then to the floor, then to the room. There's a big-screen TV and an iPhone plugged into a charger on top of a TV stand, and a plush leather chair near a table on the other side of the room. A window above the table shines light onto the floor — which is covered in stale looking carpet, littered with joint and cigarette butts and beer bottles. I realize that I'm on a bed. The sheets feel like cotton, and hot like I warmed them up with my body heat. It smells like musty carpet, with the lingering smell of burnt cigarettes and weed — and I don't know where I am. I've never been here before, so how did I get here?

I start to breathe rapidly, panicking from the unfamiliar environment and look around in vain — for what, I don't know. Suddenly I feel a weight on my body; I remember what Loni told me, about remembering that I have a physical body in the physical world, and to not let myself stray too far. It must be Loni's hand, to remind me that she is there for me. I close my eyes and breathe slowly, feeling the weight on my body and trying to isolate where it is. Okay, it's on my chest. I can feel it on my breasts — *I have breasts, and I wouldn't be able to notice that if I was in the spiritual world, so don't forget. The hand is* moving down, past my stomach, to my pelvis, and to my upper thighs. Confused, I stop slow breathing for a moment. Loni's hands wouldn't go down there. I open my eyes slowly to find myself in the same unfamiliar room. But now there's something else that's unfamiliar. I look up and see a man on top of me. The weight on my body was him pressing down on me, and I realize this slowly. Too slowly — because once I fully realize that there's an unfamiliar man on top of me, he begins to unzip my jeans. My heart begins racing as I fumble and try to push his hands away; but he's stronger, and I'm in the Realm of Duality and I have no idea what I'm doing. He grabs my hands and pins them down with his knees and goes back to hastily unzipping my jeans. I try to move my arms, but I feel like my body isn't responding and my arms stay where they are. I feel paralyzed and begin to panic because someone is going to force themselves on me. I know it, I just know it. I try to yell for help, but my tongue feels like cotton. It makes a muffled sound and nothing more. I look up at the man who is on top of me but I don't recognize him because I can't really see his face. I can see his body — the thickness of his arms, and the colour of his clothing — but I can't see his face. It's like having beer goggles on — the ones you wear in school when they teach you about vision impairment from drunk driving — and it's all a blur. So I can see his body but I can't identify him. I begin to sob. My tears being the one thing that seems to work in my body apparently — as he hastily yanks my pants down. I look at the ceiling, accepting that I'm going to be raped and I can't do anything about it. That's what this is. Rape. There's no nice word for it; no hush-hush word to soften it into something that isn't so harsh. So stark. It is what it is. Rape. And I'm about to see just what that is for myself. Then I look to the left, the sun streaming onto my face. I would much rather look into the light, even though I'm trapped in darkness. I look into the sunlight and start to see a figure materialize; I blink several times, wondering if my eyes are betraying me, and find the figure still forming until I can see a distinct body. As I keep blinking and my vision clears, I see that it's a woman's body. The sun shines on her so I can't see who it is, but she reaches her hand forward — palm outstretched towards me. In that instant, it doesn't matter to me who it is. It's a helping hand. I muster every bit of strength I have, pushing it from all the limbs in my body and forcing it to my left hand. I wrench it from underneath my captor's knees and just as he's about to pull my underwear down, I grab the helping hand. Once my fingers touch her fingers, and my hand rests firmly within her grasp, she tugs firmly and I'm pulled out from underneath him. I've been yanked away and I land firmly on the floor of Loni's basement, back safely in the protection of the diner. I start sobbing uncontrollably, rocking back and forth and struggling to breathe. I take notice that I am not the one rocking my body as I feel arms wrapped around my shoulders. I feel a cheek resting on my head, and I instantly start crying from relief that someone is comforting me.

"Shhhhhhhhh, Mama," Nellie says. "It's okay, it's alright. I'm here now. I'm here Mama, don't cry."

I ignore her plea and continue to sob, my throat closing and my breath haggardly escaping through stuffy nostrils. She continues to rock me back and forth, rubbing her fingers on my shoulders and grazing her cheek along my head. I don't know when she got here, but I'm glad she's here now. After rocking back and forth for a couple of minutes, I feel okay to sit up and open my eyes. Loni's squatting in front of us, her arms resting on her knees and her eyes looking at me with a mixture of concern and inquiry.

"You alright, baby girl?"

I breathe shakily, hiccuping wetly, before responding, "People who take drugs *wish* they could get an experience like that. Talk about an out-of-body experience."

Loni's face relaxes as she laughs, Nellie shaking her head and chuckling.

"If you're still able to crack a joke after that, then you're fine," Loni says smiling.

I return her smile with a small smile of my own, but it's still bordered with tears that lethargically drip down my face.

"Try not to cry too much, Mama," Nellie says. "You know you get headaches when you cry." I nod, trying to slow my breathing and wiping my tears away.

Loni's face regards mine, etched with concern as she cocks her head to the side and analyzes my face.

"You had a premonition," she says. I look at her, frozen in disbelief.

"How do you know that?"

"I can tell — you saw something that you've never seen before," she says, looking into my eyes as if searching for something. I nod slowly, my eyes still wide from disbelief.

"I was in a room I'd never seen before," I say quietly, confirming her suspicion. Nellie sits up, leaning back to look at me but keeping me embraced in her arms. I continue, "It was so clear though. I could see every detail: from the pattern on the ceiling to the fabric of the bedsheets I was lying on. I even remember the smell. But I'd never been there before."

Loni looks at me, nodding slightly but remaining silent so that I can continue. I look to the ground and stare into space, as the scene of my trance plays again in front of my eyes.

"I was on a bed and it took me a while to realize that I was being pinned down. There was a man on top of me, and I didn't recognize him. I could see his body — his clothes, his arms and legs, everything — but I couldn't see his face —"

"There was a man on top of you?" Nellie asks in surprise.

I nod silently as tears spring back into my eyes. Loni sighs and looks down, shaking her head as I continue, "He was... he was pinning my arms down with his knees and unzipping my pants. He was trying to... y'know."

"Yeah," Loni says. "We know."

"Yeah, well, I tried to move my arms to push him away, but it felt like I was paralyzed. It's like when people dream they're running, but they stay in the same spot and they can't move forward."

"Mm-hmm," Nellie says sadly, knowing what I mean.

"So I just laid there and cried, because I couldn't move — I couldn't stop him. Then I saw a woman on the other side of the room. I thought I was going crazy and just seeing things, but then I did see a woman's silhouette. But I couldn't see who it was because the light was shining on her back. She reached her hand out towards me, and when I grabbed it," I turn to look at Nellie as I say, "you pulled me out."

Nellie looks at me and nods as if what I said made sense to her. I look at her for a moment before I turn to Loni. "So that was a premonition I had?" I ask her.

She nods before bouncing up and shaking her legs to bring circulation back into them. "Yes. You could see the room as if you were actually in it, and see everything clearly — yet you'd never been in there before? It could be a dream in any otha situation, but not in this situation. It could only be a premonition, or someone from the spirit world showing you something. It could have been somethin' they experienced in their lives or a look into somethin' that is goin' to happen in the future."

"But it couldn't have been something that happened in their lives," I say in realization, as I recall the specifics of the dream. "I remember what the man was wearing. He was wearing a black t-shirt and jeans, and there was an iPhone on a table with a flat-screen TV. This was in this century — or it will be."

Nellie fully leans away now, taking her hands that were embracing me and grabbing me by the shoulders to face her.

"You're sure you saw all of that?"

"Yes, yes I'm sure! It has to be in the future — none of our ancestors would've lived in a time with that kind of technology, right?"

Nellie leans back and looks at Loni, Loni looking back and exchanging a conversation in worried looks. I look back and forth between them, trying to interpret their silent conversation, but fail.

"What does that mean? Why are you guys looking at each other like that? *Can I buy a vowel?*"

Nellie grabs my hands and looks at them, before looking up at me.

I look at her from the side of my eye and look to Loni who looks at me expressionlessly.

"Did I just have a premonition of... of my —"

"We don't know that," Loni says, hands raised to calm me down. "Premonitions are tricky; sometimes they don't involve us at all an' it's about people that are connected to us in some way. You may have seen what's going to 'appen to someone else that you're close with; the ancestors are just warnin' you that it is going to 'appen."

"But Loni," Nellie says cautiously, "every time a premonition has happened about someone else, Bastets were looking down and seeing the entire situation from the sidelines. Jamila saw it as if it was happening to her."

"Not all the time, Nellie," Loni replies. "It's different for everybody — sometimes they become the person who's going through it, and sometimes they watch from the sidelines."

I look back and forth between them as they have a separate conversation while I continue to panic.

"Yes but it's rare, Loni. More often than not, the Bastet would see it from another point of view. Even when Jamila saw what would've happened to Michael, she was seeing it from the sidelines."

Loni looks down for a moment, closing her eyes and nodding solemnly. When she opens her eyes, she looks at me apologetically. I look at her and shake my head in denial, my eyes beginning to tear again.

"No," I say. "No, no, no, no, please no. I don't want that to happen to me. Please, please, don't let that happen to me."

"Mama, look at me," Nellie pleads. I continue to shake my head vigorously, forcing her to shake my shoulders so I look at her. "*Look* at me. It's good that you saw what will happen, so when it does happen — and I'm sorry Mama, but it might — you'll at least be prepared. You know what the room looks like, so when you're there you can protect yourself. You do everything you can to make sure you're sober — and if there are other people there, make sure you scream. Maybe they can get you out of there. Did you see anyone else in the room?"

"No. No, I didn't see anyone else," I reply, my anxiety mounting.

"Okay," Nellie says calmly, "well, then it's more important than ever that you're prepared and able to control your abilities, so you can protect yourself."

I look to Loni, who nods encouragingly in agreement, and back to

Nellie who gives me a small smile. I nod, agreeing that preparing myself is the best way to go instead of freaking out about it. Nellie stands up, grabbing my arms, and gently guiding me to stand beside her. Loni and Nellie both face me, placing an arm on each of my shoulders, and leaning forward to place their foreheads on either side of my temples. I close my eyes as a comforting feeling of protection and love envelopes me.

"Lord," Loni prays, "please watch over yuh daughter Jamila. Protec' her in times of peril, an' give her strength as she discovers new parts of herself that will challenge her mentally, physically an' emotionally. In Jesus' name…"

"Amen," we say in unison. They lean back and stand straight. I look to Loni, smiling in surprise.

"I didn't know you were religious, Loni."

"Yes, my girl. I believe God gave us these abilities to use for good, just like he gave all of us his words to do good for others. It's just tossing the same coin to help those in need, just with two different sides."

I nod in understanding, but push, "But how can you believe in another deity when you say we were descended from an Egyptian cat goddess?"

She looks at me, taking a breath and a moment to collect her thoughts, before replying, "For me, it's like God sendin' a gift to the world to save it. I believe our powers an' abilities are a gift. Given to us by the first to eva use them centuries ago — to Bast. And, it's up to us to protec' those who are hurt, misunderstood and mistreated."

"It's up to you whether you want to believe," Nellie says. "I told you a long time ago that it's up to you what you choose to do with your beliefs. But, one thing is for sure — your abilities are a gift that if used right, can do a lot of good. And there's no religion in the world that says that doing good and helping others is a bad thing. It's up to you to choose when that time is. And when your gifts should be used."

I look at her, nodding in understanding and agreeing with her. Loni smiles at me before smacking my shoulders — hard — startling me.

"Well, I think that's enough trainin' for one day. We don't want to tire you out too much. But tomarro we're gonna dive into your abilities a likkle deepa; we need to take this more seriously if you're goin' to be prepared. But we don't wah fi drain yuh too much. Come upstairs, I'll make us some cornbread. With honey drizzled on it extra sweet, jus' how you like it."

I smile at her appreciatively before I remember that I have a previous engagement. I look at my watch before replying, "Thanks Loni, I really wish I could stay — trust me. But I promised Michael I'd help him with something and I have to be there in the next 20 minutes."

Loni raises her hands in surrender. "Okay. Okay, well I'll make a nice hot batch just for you tomarro. I'll see you after school."

I hug her quickly, grab my backpack, and head up the stairs. Nellie and I speed walk to the car, grab my bike, and put it in the back and rush — at a reasonable speed — out of the parking lot to head home.

"Okay, so here's what I'm thinking," Michael says, standing in front of me. I sit on his bed that's hidden underneath piles of textbooks, a calculator and laptop, notebooks, an open pencil case with its contents strewn everywhere, and several clothes that look as if they haven't been cleaned in weeks. His room, about the same size as mine, holds anime posters on its beige walls. The sunlight that sets outside shines the last of its rays from his tiny window above his desk, which is actually clean compared to the rest of his room. His floor, like his bed, is covered with clothes, underwear, and damn near everything else he owns. Luckily, Michael is one of few teenage boys that take smell very seriously, so his room smells like clean sheets and shea butter. I look around and find the culprit of the scent once I spot the open tub of shea butter lying on top of his dresser. I look back at him, his gangly-as-usual frame flopping everywhere as he presents to me in elated excitement.

"It's gonna be a little chilly tonight, and then it's always cold in the arena, so..." He pulls out a distressed grey hoodie and puts it over a pair of washed-out jeans with zippers all over the legs. I grimace and shake my head, and he looks at me defeated for a moment before holding his finger up.

"Okay, okay, that's not the only one. I was also thinking I could do this shirt," he pulls out a satin baby blue button-up shirt and then grabs a pair of beige slacks, "with these pants."

I look at him in disbelief; he returns my look with one of confusion. I swear, he's so smart but sometimes he can be such a dumb ass.

"You're taking her to a basketball game. Not to a trap house or the Ritz Carlton." He kisses his teeth in offence, but when have I ever cared whether I offended him or not? *Never.*

"Like you some stylist aficionado," he says defensively. "Always wearing a t-shirt and jeans — you ain't exactly drippin' in style neither."

"I know that, but at least I know what to wear to a ball game!"

"Oh yeah?" he asks incredulously. "And what's that?"

I raise my hands in exasperation, get up from the bed and go to his closet. After sifting through it for a few moments, I find what I'm looking for. I pull out a dark grey Henley shirt and dark-wash blue jeans. I throw them at his face and search the floor for the shoes to match. Finally, I spot his grey Under Armour sneakers and pull them from underneath a hoodie. After thinking about his grey Clarks for a moment, I start looking for them. He can at least have an option for what shoes he's going to wear.

He looks at the clothes and the shoes in my hands, before looking at me with a straight face. "This is just what you would wear if you were a dude."

"Correction, it's what I would wear *periodt*. This is a classic look — it's genderless, so anyone can wear it and look good. Including you." I raise the shoes for him to see both options, "Pick one."

He looks between the two, lays the shirt and pants on the bed, and looks at them for a few moments. He looks back at the shoes, back to the outfit, back to the shoes, cocks his hip, and looks back to the outfit.

"Oh my God, just *pick one!*"

"Okay, okay," he says, caving into my annoyance. He looks at the shoes again and points to the sneakers. I exhale gratefully, throwing the Clarks to the floor in annoyance and dashing the sneakers to his chest. I plop back onto the bed, leaning back and coming into contact with an action figure. I pick it up and shake my head. Wow. I may be skirting along the lines of nerd territory, but Michael did a full deep dive.

"Are you ever gonna clean your room?" I ask.

"Why would I need to do that?" Michael asks absent-mindedly, as he brushes his hair in front the wall mirror for the umpteenth time.

"Oh, I don't know," I raise the tiny Captain America into the air, "because you don't want to bring a girl in here and impale her with one of your dolls."

"They're action figures," he corrects.

"They're the representation of your immaturity. And it's embarrassing."

He kisses his teeth, cutting his eyes at me in the mirror. I stifle a laugh as he says, "What do I care if you see them? When was the last time I gave a rat's ass what you thought about my room?"

"I wasn't talking about me. I was talking about Taylor." He spins around, the speed almost knocking him off his own feet as he looks at me with wide eyes.

"What are you talking about?"

"Well, do you really think a girl will be into you if she's getting poked in the armpit by a doll? Sorry, *'action figure'*."

He laughs nervously, "You're saying that like she's gonna be in my room sometime soon."

"Well, isn't that the goal? I mean, I thought the general idea is that you date so that you're both comfortable enough with each other to... y'know... shake the bed."

"Dude! Chill," he says, flustered. I chuckle, amused by his embarrassment. "There's a lot of steps we have to take before we get to that point. I still have to go on the first date with her, first of all —"

"Yeah, yeah, that would be a good idea."

"Yeah, I'd like to think so," he says sarcastically. "But then we have to get to know each other, have our first kiss and cross all the bases, y'know. Then I have to meet her friends and get them to like me. Meeting her dad is probably going to be terrifying but it's better to get that out of the way as soon as possible and establish an image of a chivalrous guy and a gentleman and —"

"Whoa whoa whoa, slow down," I say, interrupting his incessant talking. "That's a hell of a lot of steps to cross. I had no idea you were so traditional," I say with amused surprise.

"Well, yeah. You get raised by a 65-year-old Trinidadian woman and you're bound to go the more traditional route." He puts his brush down and turns to face me, leaning against the wall. "I mean, I really want to *be* with her, y'know? I don't want to just smash and dash, I actually want to have a relationship with her. I want to take her out and pamper her, show her how much she means to me. I don't want it to just be physical." I give him the side-eye, which he returns with an eye roll.

"I mean, yeah, of course, I want to get physical. Eventually. But I just want to get to know her first. You look at me like that's crazy or something."

"No, no, no, I don't think it's crazy. Everyone wants different things; sometimes it's the traditional way and sometimes people just want the physical. Sometimes people don't want to conform to traditional expectations and do whatever feels natural. I guess we've never really

talked about it and — I don't know — I guess I didn't think you'd be so…
old school."

"You say that like there's a bad taste in your mouth," he says, smiling.
I laugh and think about it for a moment.

"Well I don't know, I guess it's just not what I really want to do."

"Really? You don't want to be pampered and taken out? I thought
most girls wanted guys to appreciate them."

"No, I do want my S/O to appreciate me — don't get me wrong. I
want to feel like I matter, but that doesn't mean that I have to be taken out
on dates and showered with gifts. Besides, I can do that myself." I think
about it for a second before continuing, "And I don't necessarily feel like
waiting for unconditional love the first time to have sex. If I'm sexually
attracted and feel mentally connected to my S/O, I'm not gonna wait 90
days to give it up. I wouldn't really be giving anything up but sharing my
sexual experience with someone who I feel is worthy to share it with. It
could take 90 days, more or less to figure that out. So, I never want to put
a time frame on anything. I don't know, maybe it's stupid."

"No, no, it's not stupid," Michael says seriously. "Hey, you thought that
me going the traditional route was unexpected, and just because you're a
girl doesn't mean that you want to do it that way either. You are who you
are and, to be honest, I'm not surprised at all."

"No?"

"Nah. You've always been the type to say what you want and get it,
and you work for it. I don't see why dating would be any different."

I smile, looking down at my legs that wobble from side to side. He
smiles too and looks to the side. A thought crosses his mind and his face
turns to one of confusion.

"Wow. I think this is the first serious conversation we've had in time."

"Well, there was that one in the diner with Ray," I remind him.

He chuckles, "Nah, Ray is too much. Any conversation with Ray I
just can't take seriously, so that doesn't count."

I laugh along with him, us doing that for a minute or two longer. He
pushes himself off the wall and peers at the clock on his desk. Suddenly,
he's a ball of energy and he's rushing around the room. He changes into
his outfit, not even caring if I'm there, and hastily puts on his shoes while
he sticks his wallet in his mouth.

"It's time for you to go. If I don't catch the next bus, I'm not gonna
meet Taylor in time."

"Okay, okay," I relent. I get up to grab my things, quickly putting my phone in my pocket, and putting my socks back on. I guess I must not be moving fast enough for him because he pushes me out of the room and out into the hallway.

"Hey, I'm moving!"

"Not fast enough!"

He pushes me from the hallway to the living room. Ms. Dell sits at the kitchen table to the right of us, sipping lemonade and snacking on Digestives — as always.

"Hey baby," Ms. Dell says to me. "How you doin'? I didn't see you come in."

"Oh, I'm —"

"She's good, Nana," Michael says for me, hastily grabbing a jacket and pushing me towards the door. "She's gotta go, though. I'm heading out now, I'll be back by midnight. I love you, see you later!"

"Wha... Okay, well be careful Michael. Remember, midnight. *Midnight.* Not a minute later, you hear me?" Ms. Dell yells, the sound hitting our backs as we lunge through the door.

"Jesus, Michael. Couldn't you give me a second to let my feet touch the ground?"

"Sorry, I have to get there on time. I'd do the same for you," he rushes down the stairs and runs down the street to catch the bus. "Wish me luck!"

"Don't mess it up," I yell back. I smile and shake my head as I head next door to my house. I open the door and the smell of chicken soup wafts into my face. As if pulled by a string, nose first, I head straight for the kitchen. I see Nellie stirring the thick, hearty soup in the big dutch pot. I run behind her and hug her around the waist, causing her to chuckle. She stirs and brings up cut up carrots, potatoes, celery, chicken drumsticks and, my personal favourite — dumplings. If there aren't any dumplings in your soup, get it away from me.

"I thought you'd want something warm and comforting after the day you've had," Nellie says.

"You guessed right."

Nellie chuckles as she picks up her phone and connects it to the small Bluetooth speaker in the living room. She plays her *Spirit Lifting* playlist and the soothing voice of Beres Hammond floats through the speaker. I move to the sink and start washing the dishes that she's finished with. Nellie joins me soon after putting the lid over the pot.

"So," she says after a few moments of me scrubbing and her rinsing and drying, "how you holdin' up?"

"Pretty good, all things considered. Remember that one time I had a panic attack over my Calculus final?"

"Yeah," she says amused.

"I think I'm handling it better than I handled that."

"Yeah," she laughs, "yeah, you are actually." She looks at me seriously, "But really though? How are you holding up?" She grabs the back of my neck and caresses it, soothing me and making me want to cry all at the same time. I exhale as the muscles in my neck relax, and untensing my shoulders that I didn't realize were tense to begin with.

"I mean," I pause, breathing in deeply so that I don't start crying, "it's a lot to take in. I mean, even though I've accepted all of this, and I do want to control my abilities, I'm a little shaken that I saw... what I saw."

"*Potentially*. We don't know for sure if it's going to happen to you, Mama."

"You said it yourself that if it's not going happen to me, then I would've seen it from an outside view. But I saw it as if it were actually happening to me," I look at her helplessly, dropping the dishes I was washing in the sink, "and I'm scared, Nel."

"Oh I know, Mama," she says, grabbing my hands and turning me towards her. "But you are strong. So much stronger than you know — than you give yourself credit for. You will get through this, and you will come out better and stronger than ever."

"It's a *'whatever doesn't kill you makes you stronger'* kind of thing, huh?"

"It's corny, but yeah. That's exactly what I'm saying." She looks into my eyes, smiling encouragingly, causing me to smile in response. She kisses my head and then my hands as the next song comes on. When Mary J. Blige's *'Real Love'* starts to play, she gasps and looks at me knowingly. I look at her and roll my eyes, not really in the mood but unable to resist 'our song.' Whenever this song comes on, Nel and I can't help but dance. It's one of those feel-good songs that makes you dance and you just can't help but be happy when you move to it.

She takes my hands and pulls me to the living room, walking backwards as she smiles at me. I reluctantly allow myself to be pulled along, unable to hold back my smile as I look at her goofy demeanor. She begins to shimmy her shoulders and her smile turns devious; I look at her uneasily, scared she's going to do that dance where she shakes her butt, chest, and arms all at the same time. It's incredibly embarrassing. She closes her eyes and fixes her mouth as if she smelled something bad — unfortunately, she thinks that's her 'Get It On' face. Pair that with the dance, and it makes me wonder how she and Mom are sisters because Mom actually had rhythm. I guess today is the day of premonitions because she bursts into the very dance I was hoping she wouldn't do, and with so much soul — I can't help but laugh at how into it she is. I stand there for a second and just watch her, mystified by the incredibly embarrassing way she shakes her butt and chest in one direction, and her arms every which way. Unable to resist her second-hand joy, I burst into dance too. Grinding my butt and shaking my head, I take my hair out of my bun and shake my hair until it obeys gravity and falls. I bop my shoulders and bend over, twerking my butt and wining on the air. Nellie does the 1-2 step, and I follow suit. We continue to dance for the entire song, and continue when Brandy and Monica's 'The Boy is Mine' comes on. Four songs later, we collapse onto the ground — the scratchy carpet itching my skin. We start to breathe heavily, struggling to catch our breaths as we laugh hysterically. Suddenly Nellie's face grimaces and she cups her waist. Sometimes when she dances too much, she gets this pain in her side and she has to walk it off. She stands up and arches her back, rubbing the spot that must be cramping. I stay on the floor and collect myself, wiping the sweat off my forehead with the back of my hand. Nellie walks to the kitchen and opens the fridge; her head ducks down as she looks for something, but kisses her teeth when she doesn't find what she's looking for.

"I forgot to buy more Island Sodas," she complains.

"Awwwwwwww," I groan.

"I know, I know." She reaches into her purse on the table and grabs her wallet. A smile bursts on my face, as she pulls out a five and holds it out to me.

"Bike down to Min's real quick and get two Kola Champagne and a Ginger Beer for me, okay?"

"Okay," I respond over my shoulder, as I shove the bill into my jeans pocket and grab my slip-on shoes. I put them on by the kitchen door and grab my bike from the alley between Michael's and my house. I bike slowly through and turn onto the street, waving at Ms. Dell through her front window. I bike lethargically, swerving between the spots of light the street lights cast on the pavement. No one is out at this hour, so I have the whole road to myself, except for the occasional car. The night is cooler, just as Michael predicted, and I regret not putting on a light jacket as the breeze pulls goosebumps up from beneath my skin. When I turn on Jane Street, I head through the small park across from Min's that I take as a shortcut. I hear a noise behind me, but ignore it and continue slowly. After a couple of seconds I hear it again, a glass bottle being kicked to the side, and I take more notice of it. I look behind me and don't see anyone; I turn back around and continue biking. The hairs on my arms stand on end and goosebumps rise on my body, my nerves triggered. That feeling in the pit of my stomach creeps up again, settling like a stone and making me uneasy. I feel a presence behind me, and start to speed up. The noise behind me changes to footsteps, and as I pedal faster the footsteps speed up. I pedal at a faster pace and the footsteps behind me begin to jog. My heart begins to race and I try to bike at full speed now, but two figures in front of me come from nowhere and block my path. As they get closer, I see that it's two of Blanco's boys — the ones that were with Ricky Brass earlier at Loni's diner. I stop and stand up with the bike between my legs — breathless from the brief sprint I tried to pull. They walk towards me, looking at me with vacancy in their eyes. I turn, struggling to inch the bike around, only to find Ricky Brass right behind me.

"Hey, slim-thick. It's kinda late for you to be out here, all by yo'self."

My heart starts pounding in my chest, but I will my face to remain indifferent. I shrug and say, "Yeah." My voice squeaks. I chastise myself for letting my nerves betray me making me an open-book. Why couldn't I be nonchalant instead of a total goober? "I'm just getting something at Min's real quick. Won't take too long."

"Oh, I don't think they are open; you know them Asians don't like black people. They ain't gonna open the door for you this late at night."

"The Min's are good people," I say defensively, his prejudice inciting anger within me. "They like me and have always been kind to me, I'm sure they won't turn me away."

I move to turn around but he grabs my handlebars, yanking them so I'm forced sideways between him and the two others.

"You still think you're smarter than me, huh?" he whispers angrily. "You a good for nothin', bitch. Don't you ever forget that." He inhales deeply, looking at the cleavage peeking through the neckline of my t-shirt. I try to move my shoulders, to hide my chest from his view, which only makes him notice it more.

"You can be good for one thing, though. Imma show you." Suddenly, he yanks my handlebars with one hand and grabs my arm with the other, throwing me to the ground. My foot, which was caught underneath one of the bike pedals, catches on the ground, and my face slams into the grass. I see stars for a few moments and struggle to push myself up, only for Ricky to pin me down with his knee. He turns me over and pins me down again, grabbing my face and forcing me to look up into his.

"You're gonna think twice next time you wanna run your mouth." He moves his knee and pins it onto my chest as he moves to unzip my pants. One of the other two guys steps forward, his face goes uneasy.

"Hey man, she's just a kid. Chill out, you shouldn't be doin' this." He grabs Ricky by the shoulder and tries to pull him up. Ricky looks at his friend, annoyed, and his nostrils flare. All of a sudden, the hand he was using to unzip my pants clenches into a fist and slams into his friend's face. His weight moves off my chest for a split second — just enough time for me to push his knee away and spring up off the ground. I sprint back the way I came, slowing only for a second to zip my pants back up. I'm running as fast as I can — but Ricky Brass, like my mother, was a track star when he was in high school, so he catches up to me easily. His arms grab me from behind and throw me to the ground again; I sit up, struggling to catch my breath, but Ricky comes up to me and punches me in the face. The shock lasts for not even a second before the pain settles into my cheek. I don't have much time to process it before he starts to punch my torso, laying down punch after punch and causing me the most pain I've ever experienced in my life. I try to crawl away but he slams his foot onto my ankle, keeping me there. I groan as a flash shoots through my vision — the pain from my ankle paralyzing me for a moment too long. He keeps punching me until I feel something crack underneath my torso. I scream in pain, as he continues to punch, then picking me up and slamming me into the ground. My head slams into the ground; the grass, sparse to begin with, does little to shield my head from the tough ground underneath, and my head begins to feel the hardness of the soil.

"Help," I scream out. "HELP!"

"Shut up, bitch!"

"Help me, PLEASE! Anyone, please HELP ME!"

Ricky continues to punch, the solidity of his brass knuckles creating fissures in my ribs. The pain becomes one endless wave of misery, and I begin to sob helplessly. I feel myself beginning to go unconscious, and I pass out as a stream of light passes over Ricky's face.

CHAPTER SIX

I hear muffled voices, their words blending with the ache that pangs through my forehead. A hollow pain sits between my brows, at the bridge of my nose, and extending upward into my head. It feels like my entire head is exploding from the inside out — the pain makes its way to my eyes, but I still force myself to open them. A bright light brings fireworks of blinding pain and causes me to close them again. I open them more slowly — blinking vigorously to allow my eyes to settle to what looks like a hospital room. Blurry bodies scurry outside the door of my room, coming in and out of view behind a blue curtain that's half drawn in front of the door. A table with a small vase holding an artificial plant sits in the corner. I look down to see myself — in a hospital gown, with tubes running from my arms to a machine that stands to my left. I slowly look to my right, my head heavy with pain and fatigue, and blurry figures begin to form into discernible bodies: one wears a white coat near the table, and the other two sit near my bed. Their voices start to get clearer and I notice the voice that rises above the rest is Nellie's. I blink a few more times and see one of the figures is Michael, wearing the outfit I picked out for him earlier, except more dishevelled. I groan as the brightness of the lights amplifies my headache, catching the attention of Nellie, Michael and, Mr. White Coat.

"Hey, Mama," Nellie says emotionally, her voice thick with tears. "Hey, can you hear my voice? Concentrate on my voice, sweetie."

"Nel, my head —"

"I know, I know baby. Just try to keep your eyes slightly closed. Okay? Try not to talk too much. Doctor, could you dim the lights a little, please?"

"Of course, Nellie," says Mr. White Coat. He goes to the wall by the door and pushes a switch down a few inches, dimming the lights. I sigh as the pain in my eyes alleviates a little. Only a little, though.

"Mama, what happened? Mr. Min heard screaming and ran outside; he called 9-1-1 and they got there just in time before there could be any... irreparable damage."

I look at her as tears spring to my eyes, making my headache even worse. God, I want to just remove my head off my body and put it on the table.

"He found me. They cornered me in the park and attacked me. I got away, but... he caught me and started to beat me up."

"Who, baby?" she asks emotionally.

I look at Mr. White Coat, who looks at me with feigned concern before I lean forward and whisper to Nellie, "Ricky Brass, and two of Blanco's boys."

Nellie's face drops, going from one full of emotion to one void of any — honestly, I think I prefer the former because the latter is freaking me out. She inches back slowly, nodding, and sits back in her seat. She takes my hand and rubs it aimlessly, staring off into space for a few moments. She's worrying me; there are dark circles underneath her eyes, and her hair is so messy that most of it escaped from the elastic tie around her bun. She wears the scrubs she had on before I left, and a thick knit cardigan that's tightly wrapped around her. She looks to Mr. White Coat, finally pulling herself out of her stupor.

"Can you tell us the diagnosis again, Dr. Aida?" she asks monotone.

"Of course, Nellie," he says. He turns on a switch on the wall and a harsh blue-white light shines through an X-ray of my torso. I squint more to adjust to the change in light but keep them open so I see all of my ribs, except with a new addition: three cracks running down the left side.

"Jamila has three cracked ribs. Luckily the force of the blows made clean cracks, so they will heal quickly. We'll give her pain medication for the next two weeks — and as long as she doesn't engage in any strenuous activity, the healing process should go by smoothly. She also has a sprained ankle and a severe concussion." Dr. Aida looks between me and Nellie, addressing both of us. "I want to perform an MRI as soon as possible; we need to rule out any severe damage to the brain that could cause a brain bleed, or create other serious consequences."

"Yes, yes, of course," Nellie affirms. She jumps up and guides him to the corner of the room, whispering medical jargon that I don't understand. Michael comes from where he was standing behind Nellie and takes her seat. He leans on the side of the bed and looks down at me with a smirk

— but I can see his red eyes and the wrinkled collar of his shirt. I know that he was a mess before I woke up, and he's trying to keep it together for me. Honestly, he's doing a pretty good job.

"Jesus, J. I leave you alone for one night and you go and get yourself beat up? I told you that you'd get in trouble for runnin' your mouth."

I laugh but then gasp in pain; he looks at me with a worried look, his face changing with rapid speed. I look at him and smile, "What can I say, I don't know when to stop."

"Damn straight." He smiles with me, but his eyes fill with sadness as he looks at me in bed. He looks from my face to my torso, to the bandage around my sprained ankle, and back up to me.

"Who did this to you?"

"Ricky Brass and his guys," I say.

He inhales sharply, nodding in apprehension. "Did they hurt you?"

"What'chu mean '*did they hurt you?*'" I ask incredulously, my voice quiet. "Of course they did, do you not see my bruised up body —"

"No, that's not what I mean." He stares into my eyes, and repeats, "Did they *hurt* you?"

I shake my head as I realize what he means, responding, "No. No they didn't get around to doing that."

He exhales deeply, sinking back into his seat. We stare at each other for a few minutes, while Nellie and Dr. Aida finish up their conversation. She turns and plasters a fake smile on her face, walking back towards us.

"Okay, Dr. Aida is going to run an MRI to make sure that it's nothing more than a concussion. It won't take long; it's late at night so no one will be using the machine right now. I'll be here waiting when it's over, okay?"

I nod even though I don't think I have any other choice — it's either do the MRI or possibly suffer a brain bleed. I'll take my chances with the MRI. Dr. Aida motions outside the door and two nurses walk in from the front desk, greeting me with polite smiles yet tired eyes. Nellie takes a clipboard out of Dr. Aida's hands and fills out so many forms I can't even begin to guess how many. She pulls out her purse and mine to provide identification, and fill in the blanks that she doesn't remember off the top of her head. After about ten minutes of that, Nellie finishes all the forms and gets the necessary receipts to submit to the insurance company. Dr. Aida then gives the go-ahead to get me ready for the scan. Michael steps back, letting the nurses do their thing, but stays close behind them keeping an eye on me —nervously lacing his fingers and leaning from foot-to-foot to contain his unease. The nurses flip something that makes a clicking noise and they push my bed, the wheels beneath slowly beginning to roll. The nurses roll me out of my hospital room, past the information desk and a set of double doors, to the elevator at the end of the hallway. They do this slowly, and I'm grateful — because any faster and the pain in my head would scream in protest. One of them pushes the elevator button and we remain still, waiting for the ding. Dr. Aida walks behind us, finished talking with Nellie — I presume mostly to calm her down rather than talking about the logistics of the scan — and waits for the elevator with us. The harsh lights overhead bring the pang of pain back between my brows, and I close my eyes to give them some relief. My head feels like hell, and I really can't wait to be drugged up and put to sleep. Finally, the doors open and I'm pushed into the elevator; we ride up two floors and I'm rolled onto the fifth floor. I loll my head, unable to fully move my neck due to the pain racking my body, to look at the nurses. The one on my right looks kind; crows feet around her eyes are a key indicator that she smiles a lot, which is a blessing when you have a job in this field. She wears white scrubs with a variety of fruits scattered all over it and a baby blue knit cardigan. Is it a requirement that all nurses own a knit cardigan? I think so. I loll my head to the other side as we turn a corner and my bed shifts left. The other nurse looks less happy, which doesn't affect her beauty at all. She's got beautiful black eyes and smooth skin. She looks Tamil, definitely South Asian; a couple strands of jet black hair escape her hijab, and I suddenly want to see her hair so badly. I bet she has jet black tresses down to her back — she probably does. She's so pretty — even without a smile she has this beautiful tranquility about her, that even I notice with all the pain I'm in. I wish I had natural beauty like that — beauty that just transcends conventions and just... *is*.

We pass a wall with a sign that indicates Room 512 and they roll me into the room, with a big machine in the middle. They roll down my blanket and help me sit up, guiding me to an upright position slowly so that my concussion doesn't obliterate my skull. They guide me to the flat table of the MRI machine and make sure that no metal is connected to or near me. Dr. Aida comes into my view and looks at me with his conditioned benevolence.

"This won't be long, okay Jamilia?"

"It's Jamila," I correct weakly. "It's pronounced Jam-ee-la."

"Oh," he says, eyes widening in guilt, "I'm so sorry."

"Don't worry about it, happens all the time," I say with a small smile.

He sighs in relief before continuing his spiel about the procedure, how long it should take, reminding me to hold my breath when he tells me to, and to remain absolutely still. He squeezes my shoulder once before he and the nurses leave the room. After a few minutes, I hear static and Dr. Aida's voice seeps through the intercom on the wall.

"Okay, ready Jamila?"

"As I'll ever be," I say weakly. A second passes and then the table beneath me jolts, startling me for a moment. It moves forward slowly — I remind myself to remain completely still, even though I couldn't move even if I wanted to. This pain is so excruciating, I fear if I move an inch my whole body will implode; I didn't know my head could handle so much pain without completely shutting down. The table stops moving, and a loud banging sound goes off every once in a while. I close my eyes and raise my eyebrows as this amplifies the pain — trying to alleviate it by breathing as low and slow as I possibly can. I lie there for what feels like a lifetime before, finally, the table jolts and moves back the way I came. I release a breath I hadn't realized I was holding, and pressure mounts between my brows. I squeeze my eyes, trying to release the tension at the upper bridge of my nose, but coming up unsuccessful.

That's how Dr. Aida finds me when he walks back into the room — with my face screwed up and my eyes squinted. He looks down at me and grimaces, his empathy genuine this time.

"I know — the pain is terrible. But the scan is over now; we'll get you back to your room and sedate you so you can sleep with a little less pain, okay?"

I nod as much as I can without my head hurting too much; he smiles and nods to the nurses, who begin to roll me back to my room. I follow the spaces between the overhead lights to give myself something to do, while also avoiding the harsh light as much as possible.

I look to Dr. Aida in the elevator and say quietly, "Dope me up with everything you got, that would be greatly appreciated." The nurses stifle a giggle while Dr. Aida looks down at me with a small smile. I like this guy, he seems like someone I can trust. I smile back, or at least I think I do. I can't tell the difference between a smile and a grimace at this point — I close my eyes and sigh. Once we're back in my room, Michael and Nellie spring up from their seats and look at me with the same feigned looks of happiness to appear as if they're not total wrecks.

"Please don't do that," I say.

"Don't do what, Mama?"

"That. That thing where you smile as if everything's okay even though it's a total disaster. I can see the bags under your eyes, Nellie. And don't act like you weren't a wreck before I woke up, Michael. I see your collar, I know you were wringing it and wrenching it back and forth. You always do that when you're scared."

Nellie and Michael look at each other, mouths gaped open as they try to come up with an excuse to disagree, but then give up — bowing their heads in defeat and nodding in agreement. The nurses secure my bed and attach all the tubes and needles back into my body so that I can be monitored overnight. The Tamil nurse works on the tubes attached to my arm and injects something into one of them. After fluffing up my pillow a little too much — yes, it was Ms. Crows Feet, God bless her — they leave the room.

"I want to keep you overnight to monitor you, and first thing in the morning we'll discuss your MRI scans together," Dr. Aida says. "We'll see if you need to stay any longer than tonight, but I don't think that will be necessary." He looks at me, placing his hand on my shoulder and saying with genuine concern, "Try to get some rest, okay? You had one hell of a night. Mrs. Burhindha gave you some morphine to ease the pain, and it might put you in a sedative state. So try to relax." I smile and give a small nod, which gets me a smirking smile in return. I really do like this guy. With that, Dr. Aida bids us farewell.

Sensing my discomfort, Nellie walks over silently and fluffs my pillow again, putting it back how I like it. I smile at her in gratitude, happy I have my own on-call nurse to help me out. Nellie smiles at me sadly and grabs my hand, rubbing the spot between my thumb and forefinger aimlessly. Immediately, tears spring to my eyes and, even though I'm in excruciating pain, I begin to sob uncontrollably. The weight of today finally becomes too much, and the dam that was holding my tears disintegrates as Nellie shows me love and affection. Nellie's eyes water too, and Michael's lip quivers as he holds back a sob in his throat. Nellie sits up from her chair and climbs into bed with me, facing me and continuing to caress the space between my fingers. Michael takes her seat and moves it to the other side of my bed, placing his hand on my arm and keeping it there for support. Nellie and I look at each other in silence for several minutes, and Michael's alright with just staying beside me to support me. The intercom in the hallway comes on to signal the end of visitation hours.

Nellie sighs sadly, taking her hand and placing it on my cheek. Wiping the tears that linger on my face, she leans in and whispers, "I'll be back first thing in the morning. Don't forget, you're never alone. You are a black woman with an immense reserve of strength within you, and come from a line of women who can do amazing things. Even without your abilities, your power would have no bounds. Never forget your power. Have a good sleep, Mama." She pats my face and sits up, summoning Michael to get his things. Michael comes around to the other side of the bed and stoops down, looking at me with that seriousness that I still find baffling that he's able to exude.

"Don't get your ass beat in the middle of the night or somethin'. Okay?"

I smile and nod slightly, causing him to smile sadly in return. He straightens up and slowly grabs his backpack, looking at me until he walks through the door and I can't see him anymore. Nellie grabs her purse and looks at me over her shoulder one last time, throwing me a smirk and a wink to give me strength, before she too walks through the door and closes it behind her. My head creates so much discomfort I wonder if I'll ever fall asleep, but finally I close my eyes and I'm slowly drifting off.

I think I was actually asleep for a good while, but now I'm in the jungle again. I'm running, my heart threatening to explode from my chest as I breathe ferociously. The pain in my head and fear from my assault is gone, but the fear of my situation returns all too familiar. I continue to run, ignoring the pain of the rocks ripping through my feet and the branches scratching my face until I reach the clearing.

"Where are you?" I call out, to the black cat I know is going to appear. Silence answers my question.

"HELLO? Please, I need you!" Crickets sing their song in reply.

I collapse to the ground, grabbing the ground and clawing at the dirt until it squeezes between my fingers — begging for someone, anyone, to come and help me. This is just like my assault — I was all alone, with only the darkness surrounding me. I can't live with another ordeal like that after just experiencing it. I begin to sob as I plead silently to the night for someone to come and save me when I hear a rustling in the leaves. I look up and see the black cat once again; I jump up and face it, looking at it with anticipation for it to turn around and lead me to the next clearing. But instead, it walks forward towards me, stopping directly in front of me and looking up into my face. Its eyes search mine, cocking its head one way and then turning it the other way. It looks like a cat's eyes, but it stares at me with such human-like emotion and I falter for a moment. I hadn't noticed this in my dreams before — the expression it's able to convey is not what a cat is usually able to do, and its human-like demeanour startles me. It stares at me for a moment longer — it just looks at me, giving no indication as to what it's thinking. Suddenly, it turns around and goes into the jungle — again expecting me to follow. And I do.

I jog behind the cat as it continues to quicken its pace, until I'm in a full sprint. I look at the cat fully, knowing that following it will be enough guidance, and I catch it transform from a domestic house cat to a ferocious black panther. Its limbs extend gracefully, its paws changing dramatically in size, and its snout widening over its mouth that struggles to conceal baring teeth. Its tiny shoulders extend until it pierces its jet black pelt from underneath, and its stomach widens as it leaps — step by step. Its eyes, the same brilliant radiance of gold, pierces the night and shines a light on the path towards the next clearing. Eventually, I start to hear the voices calling out to me.

Daughter. Jamila. Daughter.

I run faster towards the voices, my heart longing for the comfort that lies within them. I run, now knowing which direction I need to go, and I run with sureness towards my mother. Finally, I hear my mother's voice begin to tower above the rest, calling my name incessantly.

Jamila. Baby Girl. Jamila.

I run and burst through the foliage into the second clearing. I look around searching for her — into the trees, the leaves, the sky — but not finding her. The black panther circles around before plopping down a few feet away, licking its paws lazily. I look at it, expecting it to get up and disappear behind the tree — that's what happened in the last dream, just before my mother appeared. But it continues to clean itself, lethargically licking its paw and wagging its giant tail. I continue to look for her, going to the large tree trunk that I remember it disappeared behind and circling it one, two, three times, hoping to find her. But she's not there. I drop my head against the tree trunk, leaning against it in desperation when I hear a voice behind me.

"Well, that doesn't look too comfortable."

I spin around and see my mother standing before me, smiling. She's wearing a red gown with ornate gold jewellery — the red gown, from the drawing I made in art class. Her hair is curly and extends from her face — a braid bordering her forehead to pull the curls back from her face — so I can see the love in her eyes as I bound towards her in one mighty leap. I slam into her, surprised that I can feel her as if she was really there. As if I was really there. I begin to bawl, the relief from feeling her and seeing her after so long mounting until the dam completely obliterates. She hugs me sweetly and rocks me back and forth, humming a sweet tune I've never heard before and rubbing her hands on my back. I stand back and look at her through the tears in my eyes. She's so beautiful — she looks just how I remember her before she died, and she looks peaceful.

"Mom," I manage to say through my haggard gasps.

"Hi, Mama," she says sweetly, her baritone voice bringing even more tears to my eyes. "It's been a long time."

"Too long." She looks at me with smiling eyes as I continue, "I miss you so much. Oh God, I miss you. Things just aren't the same without you." I take in wet breaths as I struggle to speak through my sobs. "I love Nellie more than anything, and we've got a good thing going, but it's not the same without you there."

She places her hand on my cheek and cocks her head to the side, "I know, Mama. But that's life, right? It keeps hitting you and knocking you to the ground, but you've got to roll with the punches and push yourself back up."

I cry out and hug her again, fiercely and without any intention of letting go. I lean back up to look at her again, in disbelief that she's really right here in front of me, talking to me. A thought crosses my mind, and I look around to see the black panther but don't find it.

"Where'd the black panther go?"

Mom looks at me with a smile, "You haven't figured it out by now? C'mon, Mama. I know you're smarter than that. Think about it."

I look at her with my head cocked to the side and think back to what Loni said about our ancestors guiding us from our connection to the spiritual world, to help those in the living world. And our ancestor was an Egyptian cat goddess. Suddenly, realization hits. If there was a light bulb floating above my head, it would switch on right about now.

"You are the black panther," I say. She nods happily, glad that I've finally figured it out.

"But how come you're only showing yourself now when I've been running around lost for years?"

"You weren't ready, J. You were still mourning my death; seeing me would've been too much for you at the time. I needed the pain to dissipate a little bit so that you could handle it when you finally do see me again."

"Mom the pain never went away. It just got buried deep enough for me to get by."

"I know, Mama," she says apologetically. "But I still needed to give you time to settle into life without me. Plus, you didn't know about any of this yet. It wouldn't have been easy to try to explain it to you when you were so emotional, especially coming from me — your dead mother in a dream world."

A pang of pain thrums through my chest, but I nod as I accept the truth. But my mom was always able to see when something was wrong, and she looks me in the eyes firmly.

"You have to accept it, Mama. I'm gone, but I will always be with you. You've been blessed with the knowledge of your lineage — you know now that there's a long line of women who are watching over you. I'm just one of many, so don't be too sad that I'm not there anymore. Because I'm where I'm meant to be: watching over you, with the thousands of other Bastets doing the same thing."

My mouth wobbles but I won't cry again, because I know that she's right. Just thinking about her not being with us anymore makes my heart ache so much that I can't even imagine a worse pain. But, logically, I know that she isn't really gone. She never really died.

"So this whole time I was running around in the jungle and you couldn't help me out?" I ask monotonously.

She laughs heartily, her deep laughter making me smile and my heart swells with happiness. "I told you, Mama. I couldn't let you see me until you are ready. I was watching over you from afar, but I was always there. It's not my fault you have terrible depth perception." I kiss my teeth, cutting my eyes at her in annoyance.

"C'mon now. You know good and well that out of the two of us, I was the one with better direction. We'd go someplace and I'd remember how to get there forever. I had to tell you which bus to take to get to the movie theatre and you've been going there since you were a kid!"

She laughs, nodding her head in defeat. "You right. You right. But when it comes to the dream world, I think I've got a better sense of direction than you do." I laugh, taking her hands in mine and holding onto them tightly.

"I can't believe you're really here. It's taking everything in me to not totally debunk this and take it as a hallucination from the drugs."

"What drugs?" she asks.

"Oh," I say, realizing that I kind of dove in without any sort of explanation. "The drugs the nurses gave me at the hospital so I could rest." I pause, intending to continue — but she nods as if she totally understands. How could she know that though?

"Well believe it, Mama. You've gotta step outside what you believe, 'cause most of it is based on the seen and what people have been tellin' you for years. And what they know is only a small fraction of what's actually out there." She smiles, *causing me to smile in return. I look down and take in her dress, stepping back to look at her fully.*

"So, I guess this is the upgrade you get when you go to the afterlife, huh?"

She smiles amused before replying, "It's the traditional dressings of Bastet priestesses. They would wear red as a symbol of the cat goddess, and the gold jewellery — well, I don't know to be honest. But I'm not complaining. I look good, huh?"

I smile, not surprised at all that my mother brought her sense of humour with her to the afterlife. She smiles back at me and grabs my arm in hers, guiding us to the tree and sitting us down to lean against the trunk.

"So, tell me about what happened in the park," she says. I look at her with surprise, until I realize that ancestors in the spiritual realm probably have a see-all, know-all condition in their job description.

"Well, three of Blanco's boys jumped me and assaulted me. Ricky Brass tried to... to rape me, but I was able to get up from underneath him. I got away for a second, but he caught me again and attacked me. I actually can't feel it now, I guess because I'm in the spiritual realm with you, but I have: a concussion, a sprained ankle, and three broken ribs as my battle scars."

Mom sighs deeply, holding my hands silently and looking at me with concern.

"Do you know the other men that did this to you?"

"I only know Ricky Brass," as I say his name, her face darkens. "He was the one that was leading the other two. The one who started beef with me."

She looks at me for a few moments, her face changing to a level of darkness that I had never seen her convey when she was alive. It startles me more, especially knowing that she's dead.

"Jamila," she says, "what did Nellie and Loni tell you about Bast?"

"Well, they said she was a greatly feared goddess. She protected people against disease and sickness, especially women and children, helped with infertility, and connected to ancestors in the spiritual world and stuff."

"Yes, that's all true," she says nodding. "But she's also an avenger for those who were wronged by men. She punishes those who hurt women and children, and uses her vulnerability as a woman to draw them in — until they become her prey. It's like the cat and the mouse: the men see women as sexual objects, and she plays with them — using this against them — until she gets justice."

"Huh. Sounds like she and I would get along," I say.

Mom looks at me with a smile until it turns into sadness, exhaling deeply with great emotion. "Oh Mama," she says sadly. "I am so sorry this happened to you.

The one crappy thing about watching over you is that I can't really intervene. I can send you messages and signs for days, but taking action is kind of against the rules."

"It's okay," I reply sadly. "You couldn't have done anything — I should've defended myself. I have all this power and I don't even know how to use it."

"No," Mom warns seriously. "Don't do that. You're just coming into your abilities — everyone has trouble harnessing them at first. And that was a highly stressful situation, Jamila. Anyone in that situation wouldn't be able to react quickly, and it's a lot to handle when you're actually in it. You can't just pull them out of the air like a Superhero movie. It doesn't work that way. It takes time — all things do that help us to evolve. You can't blame yourself or wish that something different had happened, because then you're living in the past. You keep doing that and there's no way you'll grow into a better version of yourself. At least not in a healthy way."

I look at her with a pained face; I know that she's right, but I still can't believe this happened to me. I still can't believe that I didn't do more. I bow my head to hide my tears that, surprisingly, fall to wet my arms. As I'm sobbing and hugging her, I can feel the wetness of my tears, even through my sadness. Mom places her hand on my cheek and gently brings my face up so I look at her.

"You are a seventeen-year-old girl, who's been told a million things that you've had to break up and reconnect to the new pieces you're learning to fit into the real world. The one that really exists. This is a lot, and you can't expect yourself to just magically fall into all of this with grace. I didn't, and Nellie sure as hell didn't either."

"But you still did it, and you guys are so much stronger than I am. Hell, you guys moved to Canada when you were, what, not even seventeen? You had to leave everything behind and start all over in a place you guys didn't even know. I was born here and I have things way better than you guys did —"

"And you still have your own stuff to deal with," Mom says firmly. "You can't expect to get the same or better result out of something just because you start with a few more resources. Because just being you — a black girl — is going to set you back before you even start." She looks at me before sitting up straighter, putting her hands out and leaning towards me.

"Think of it this way," she explains to me. "It's like an experiment that always has a different outcome, regardless of the resources you started with. The dependent variable will always vary, even if the independent variable remains the same." Speaking to me in a language I understand, my mother translates to the language of nerds.

"Because times change," she continues, "cultures evolve, societies differ. You can't universalize your experiences, Jamila. Because your experiences are your own. They will never be like mine or Nellie's. Even if you think you've got it better than

we did, it doesn't mean that everything is gonna turn out better for you. But as long as you make the independent variable your mindset and not the life you were born into, then your life will depend on what you make of it. So go into things with a better mindset and no matter what happens, I promise *you things will get better."*

She grabs my hands and places them in her own, bringing them to her mouth and placing the most delicate kiss on them. She looks at me with a small smile, taking one of her hands and putting it on the side of my face.

"I love you to infinity," she says.

"And beyond," I finish. She smiles wider, suddenly taking her hand and placing it on my forehead. And everything goes black.

I wake up abruptly in my hospital bed — I look at the clock and see that it's 8:45 a.m. 15 more minutes until visitation hours again, which means 15 minutes and 11 seconds until I see Nellie. I can't believe I slept for so long, but I turn and see the morphine drip — drugs can do powerful things. My dream is still so vivid in my mind. It's changed so much, just like Loni said it would, and I have to make sure to let her and Nel know about seeing my mother when we're all together again. I can't believe I actually saw my mom and had a lucid conversation with her. It was like nothing's changed — she looked exactly like how she did before she died. I guess the perks of the afterlife is that you never really age. That's kind of the thing about immortality, no need for Botox.

I blink my eyes to settle them to the room, the drugs creating a haze that makes everything blurry. After a few moments my vision begins to clear and I look at my hospital room in the rising sun. The chairs that Nel and Michael were sitting on the night before, a pale blue colour, now borders the table with the vase in the middle — holding a pathetic excuse for a flower. But hey, any life in a building that constantly experiences death is better than nothing at all. The sun shines through the window on the wall where my bed is pushed against, shining its light onto the redness of the flower: a blood-red that stands out against the innocence of the pale colours. Quite a symbolic juxtaposition if I do say so myself. I turn my head, the pain dulled by the morphine, and look to the other side of my room. A tiny closet, with a few hangers and a small dresser within it, stands beside a door ajar to reveal the tiny bathroom. The light is off, but I can just make out a small counter and sink, with a toilet beside it. The tiny mirror above the sink reflects the small shower that stands behind the door, with a transparent shower curtain with — what looks like — rubber duckies scattered all over it. I close my eyes and turn my head to look at the ceiling. This ceiling doesn't have any pattern or any of that bubbly-looking texture that makes me just want to scrape it off. It's quite boring, to be honest, and I look away after just a minute.

I look at the tubes running from my arm to a machine to my left; it reads out my BPM, blood pressure, and other numbers that I'm not sure what they mean. The plastic baggie with the morphine vial attached to it drips lethargically into my veins - thankfully, because without it I would be in the fetal position right now. The clock finally strikes 9:00, and I count only seven seconds before I see Nellie and Michael walk past the information desk. Wow, she beats my guess by four seconds — she really outdid herself.

"Hey, Mama," Nel says lovingly, rushing to my side and hugging me. She does it a little too hard though, jabbing her shoulder into my throat. I make a gasping sound, causing her to jump back in worry.

"What, are you still in a lot of pain?"

"No, you just impaled my airway with your shoulder."

"Oh, sorry," she says embarrassed. Michael walks up behind her and throws me a smirk, but the bags under his eyes and wrinkled clothes are a dead giveaway.

"Did you get any sleep?" I ask him.

"Not really," he says truthfully. He never lies; I just wish I could do the same. "How 'bout you?"

"Oh, I had a wonderful slumber," I say happily. "Drugs really do something for the brain, really shuts it off, and makes it useless." Michael and Nellie chuckle, either relieved or annoyed that I still have my sense of humour and wits about me.

"I even had a dream," I say, looking at Nellie. She looks back at me with a knowing glance before I continue, "It may have been the drugs, but I feel like every dream has a message."

She looks at me, giving me a small nod that says she understands my subliminal message. She looks at me pointedly, telling me *"We'll talk about this later"*. Michael just looks at me and shrugs, before sitting at the table, legs open wide. Nellie turns around and notices, kissing her teeth and kicking one of his shins.

"Yuh caah act like you got manners? We don't need to see all'a that, close your legs." He sighs but obeys, closing his legs and crossing his foot over the other. Dr. Aida comes in a few minutes later, looking just as dishevelled as Michael but with the greys teasing his temples, looking even more haggard.

"Morning all," he greets us fatigued.

"Morning," we say in unison. He walks over to the projector and attaches an X-Ray to it; before turning on the light he takes a deep breath, head bowed, and finally flips the switch. On the screen is an image of a brain. I look to the top corner of the screen and see Freeman,Jamila etched in the corner, I take in that it's my cranium that's on display.

"The MRI scans from last night came in and I was looking at them for most of the night. Luckily there is no major damage that would give me a reason to believe that you'll have any problems beyond a minor concussion. So, we can rule out any brain bleeds or major damage to any of the hemispheres."

"Oh thank God," Nellie says relieved. Michael exhales deeply in relief as well, remaining silent so Dr. Aida can continue. His face contorts in confusion as he looks over the scan — and if my physician's face looks confused, then I have a reason to worry.

"Is there something else, Doc?" I ask. He looks at me as if he didn't realize I was there, as if he's seeing me for the first time, and my good mood starts to wane.

"Well, I was looking at your scans and I saw an anomaly. You have an incredibly overactive visual and auditory cortex. This is common in people who have Schizophrenia or Parkinson's disease, but you seem to be performing normally for your age."

"Wait," I say in confusion, taking a beat to process. "Normally? Are you saying I have Schizophrenia?"

Nellie follows up quickly, asking, "How is that possible? Jamila has shown no indicators of this for the past 17 years. She's been tested for neurological disorders by her school early on with those spelling and aptitude tests, just like all the other kids. She has good grades, a high IQ, a better memory than me and I have to memorize numbers all day every day —"

"I'm just telling you what I'm seeing, Nellie," Dr. Aida says tiredly. "This is better than serious physical damage, but it's pointing to all the signs of a neurological disorder."

Michael and I look at each other in surprise. This is what his Biology project is supposed to be about — we were talking about this in Loni's diner just a couple of days ago. How is it I have this anomaly?

"Is it possible that she's developing symptoms of these diseases because of her injuries?" Michael asks. Dr. Aida looks at him and shakes his head.

"No," he replies. "These injuries aren't serious enough to warrant a neurological disorder of this kind and aside from her injuries she incurred last night, Jamila is a healthy teenage girl. These anomalies look like they've been dormant for a while but were still present, and became more active recently — but more recently than last night. This doesn't seem to be hindering her mental abilities. If anything, this overactivity is increasing her mental efficiency, which is the opposite of what a neurological disease does. There's no reason to believe that she is, or will, develop Schizophrenia later on in life given her behaviour — but these scans suggest otherwise."

He looks at the scans, shaking his head in disbelief. "But the extent of this anomaly is mind-boggling. This level of overactivity, in *both* the audio and visual cortices, would mean that you are having hallucinations that would make it impossible to discern between reality — and what you're hearing and seeing that's just in your head."

I look to Nellie worried — who just looks at Dr. Aida normally and nods, even throwing in a couple *mm-hmm's* to come across normal. One of my abilities is to connect to the afterlife in the Realm of Duality, and I can have premonitions of things that haven't happened yet. I can see them, hear them, and feel them — as if they were really happening, in real-time. Is that the reason my brain looks that way? Did the scan actually pick up how my brain is able to do all of these things?

"Well Yousef," Nellie says, causing Dr. Aida to look towards her. "Jamila's brain is quite advanced. I mean, she's been doing college-level coursework since she was 12 and, I know you don't believe this sort of thing, but black people are very spiritual people. We have a dream and we interpret it, always giving it some kind of meaning." She laughs nonchalantly as she continues, "It's so crazy, but I swear we dream things that mean something. And our family is very superstitious — we've really tapped into our spiritual side, so I'm not surprised at all."

"Yes but Nellie, this level of activity is greater than any I've ever seen. I've had patients with Schizophrenia, and their scans don't show this level of activity. This level would indicate a hindrance to her neurological abilities, but it's enhancing them. Now I'm fairly certain that Jamila is not going to have or develop Schizophrenia, but I still would like to run a test to see if there are any markers for any potential neural disorders that could eventually develop."

"Yousef, is that really necessary?" Nellie asks. "You said it yourself there's no major brain damage besides the concussion, and if you have no reason to believe that it's going to cause any problems down the road then what's the problem?"

"It's just a precaution, Nellie." He turns to me, regarding me with the full weight of his attention. "This is just to make sure that there will be no problems for you down the line. You're a smart girl with a lot of promise, let's keep it that way and cover all the bases."

I look at him for a moment. I see only concern in his eyes, not that fake stuff that doctors throw at you to make you feel more comfortable. I really do respect this guy, and surely I can trust him. I look to Nellie who returns my glance. She looks at me normally, but her eyes convey worry.

"It's just one test," I say. "It can't hurt right?" She sighs and, for a brief moment, she looks disappointed. She nods and looks to Dr. Aida.

"Well, when can we do this then? How long will it take?"

"Well, we have to get everything in order. To make sure we're not keeping you overnight longer than necessary, we'll get it done tomorrow." He stops and motions his hand to wave someone in, and another white coat walks in. This man is tall — taller than Dr. Aida — with broad shoulders and a muscular physique. He has dark black hair shaved low to his head, with greys peppered at the temples. He's wearing a dark red button-up shirt, and black slacks with black shiny shoes. He has bright blue eyes that pierce mine as he smiles at me, his eyes somehow don't seem to smile — but instead keeping its voidness. He's handsome but something about his smile is off, it's not completely genuine somehow. But I was raised right, with some sense and manners, so I smile back politely.

"This is Dr. Churchill, a specialist in neurological defects. He'll be assisting me during your test tomorrow, and overseeing all of the results."

Nellie politely smiles to the doctor, but crosses her arms in a defensive position. I guess she doesn't entirely trust this new doctor either.

"Hello," Dr. Churchill says. "It's nice to meet all of you." He turns and walks to me, reaching out his hand to shake my hand. I take his hand and shake it with gumption, but his hand squeezes mine harder and makes me slightly wince in pain. What's with men always needing to break fingers when they shake hands? He takes his other hand and places it on top of mine, effectively trapping my hand in both of his.

"Jamila, Dr. Aida filled me in on your situation. I want you to know that we will do everything we can to get to the bottom of your scans. Oftentimes, blacks are susceptible to mental disabilities and deficiencies. It's very common that your people lack the mental capacities of other races, and Schizophrenia is very common among those with a family history of mental health issues. So these scans are not as surprising as Dr. Aida previously presumed."

My brows furrow at his wording: my people, blacks. What, is this guy from the 1940s? I look to Nellie and see her face screwed up, the corner of her lip snarled in disgust from Dr. Churchill's selective intelligence.

"That's a pretty old way of thinking, Dr. Churchill," Nellie says. Her words are polite, but her passive-aggressive tone and crossed arms show that this is just a professional way of saying, '*Watch yourself, old man*'.

She continues, "*Black people* — not blacks, black people — are susceptible to mental health issues just as others are. There's no definitive research that proves skin colour has a direct correlation to disorders like Schizophrenia. Besides, there's no history of any such disorder in our family either. Dr. Aida said himself that this is strange, given Jamila's performance: she's smart, intelligent, and functions better than most teenagers her age. She has no indication that she's mentally disabled, and I don't appreciate your implication that it's because she's black."

"My apologies, Ms. Freeman," Dr. Churchill says as he backs away; his eyes wide and hands up to calm Nellie down. A classic white dude move to de-escalate a completely average situation when he thinks he's in trouble with an *angry black woman*. He continues, "I didn't mean to imply that Jamila is mentally disabled because she's black. But as you know, African-Americans are more likely to have high blood pressure, heart conditions, and diabetes, and studies are being conducted into the susceptibility of this racial cohort to mental health disorders. I'm just explaining that there is a potential for this to be a cause — but it doesn't mean that it is for certain. Jamila is a fine girl, and from what Dr. Aida tells me, an intelligent young lady. I apologize for any confusion. Dr. Aida is right, these scans are out of the ordinary. If Jamila has been functioning normally, without exhibiting any signs of a mental disorder of any kind, and continues to excel — well, then the test will help clear any confusion and provide more answers."

Nellie raises her eyebrow, and does a small nod. She's not completely happy with his apology; probably because it wasn't really an apology. White people are exceptional at those, but she'll take what she can get for now. No need to be put in another situation where she's seen as the angry black woman just for defending me. Even with Dr. Churchill's particular brand of medical opinion, Dr. Aida's input is greatly appreciated — so I can handle Churchill's weird, holier-than-thou, pompous intelligence. He turns to me, trying his best to give me a reassuring smile but failing miserably. Man, this dude is handsome but he really can't smile warmly to save his life.

"You don't have to worry." He reaches in to shake my hand again, and out of politeness I reluctantly reach out and await the vice-like grip. He squeezes my hand again and places his hand atop mine, pressing a little deeper into our shake — a power move, something men do to assert themselves. Well, two can play at that game. I take my other hand and place it on top of his, looking into his eyes with as much strength that they can muster under the drugs.

"Thank you, Dr. Churchill," I reply. "I appreciate it. I trust Dr. Aida, and if he brought you here, then you must have as comparable advice as he does."

His smile falters, his eyes showing a flash of disdain — but it quickly returns to his face as he nods, trying to appear humble. He backs up to stand beside Dr. Aida, looking at me the entire time.

"We can wait till your lunch break to conduct the test, Nellie," Dr. Aida continues, "so that you can be in the room. She's still underage, and we need her parental guardian present to sign the paperwork. Now you know, Nellie, that you can't interfere in any way — you're a nurse here but you're her aunt when it comes to the legalities of guardianship. Any interference is a conflict of interest."

"Yes I know, Yousef," Nellie says. "I'll make sure to curb the backseat nursing."

"I trust you will," he says with a nervous laugh. I smile behind my hand. He must know Nellie as well as I do, and there's no chance in hell that she's going to keep her promise. "So around 1 p.m. tomorrow afternoon, that sounds alright?"

Nellie and I nod, and Dr. Aida happily nods in reply. He guides Nellie outside of the room, along with Dr. Churchill, talking about the test and what will happen. Michael rises from his seat and makes his way to my bedside, leaning on the armrest.

"Maybe this test will prove how much of a pain in my ass you are," he says.

"Do you really need a test to prove that?"

"Ha! You right, I *been* knowin' that from time." We both laugh, mine hindered by the drugs and the pain that still lingers.

"You never told me how your date with Taylor went," I say, in an effort to change the subject — and boy does it work.

"Oh man," he says, his eyes shining with happiness and a goofy smile rising to his face. I swear a glimmer sparkles in his eye, but maybe it's the morphine getting to me. I smile reflexively, his goofy smile never ceasing to put a smile on my face.

"It was amazing," he says romantically.

"Yeah?"

"Yeah," he says smiling. "It was Game 4, whatever that means — I think it's close to the finals or somethin'. We were pretty close to the court actually; we were right behind one of the nets and I think it was in the 100's or something. The Rap's ended up winning, and I'm not gonna lie, I actually got into the game. I even jumped up one time when the ref called a foul. Even I could see that it was bogus."

"Look at you: the ball fan. A week ago you didn't even know what a point guard was."

"I still don't know what that is. Is that like the basketball version of a quarterback or something?"

I laugh in disbelief, saying, "Never mind. Keep goin'."

"Okay. Well it was pretty cold, right, and I brought a jacket just in case but Taylor only had a thin long-sleeved shirt on. It was one of those with the low neck that scoops down so you can see the cleavage —"

"Yeah, I bet you noticed that."

"Shut up."

"Sorry."

"Anyways, that was all she had on. And we were waiting outside before the game for *time*, right, so I took off my jacket and put it on her and was like '*Here, keep yourself warm*'."

"How chivalrous," I say, faking a surprise.

"That's some gentleman-type shit. Anyways, we were talking about everything: the weather, school, what's happening in the States, damn near everything. When we started talking about the political stuff, she got super into it and she got so heated. I think she thought I was cool 'cause I was throwin' her damn near every big word I knew and I expressed how inhumane I thought all that stuff was."

"Wow. Using politics to impress a girl. That's next-level right there." He points at me excitedly, sitting on the corner of my bed and leaning in — causing me to smile bigger.

"I know! And when we got inside we had some time before the game, and we kept talking about random stuff and I was making her laugh so hard. Like people kept looking at us 'cause she was laughing so loud. And then she *held my hand.*"

"Whoa," I say, this time in genuine surprise. "Seriously? Wow, you must've lost your mind."

"I was internally screaming so hard." We laugh for a moment before his face goes deep in thoughts. "It was so amazing, J. I mean, I've been dreaming about being with Taylor since elementary school. I always used to imagine what it would be like to talk to her and be with her, and last night I thought I'd mess it up but I was just... myself. She's so funny, and in the weird quirky way that we are with each other but also different, and she showed herself fully — not trying to be cool or anything. She was genuinely just herself. And, low-key, I felt like she was humble to the point that she doesn't even know how beautiful and amazing she is. That makes me like her even more 'cause she really is just livin' life and not trying to front or anything. I felt so calm with her; low-key it felt like how I am with you, only better."

"Well, I'm happy for you man," I say smiling. "I'm glad you finally got a date with her. Do you think you'll go on another?"

"Well I got her number during half-time, but as soon as the game ended, I got a call from Nellie that you were in the hospital. I kind of ended things rushed 'cause all I was thinking about was getting to the hospital. She looked like she understood, but I wish I had ended the date better."

"Oh, I'm so sorry man," I say apologetically. "You finally get a date with Taylor and I mess it up."

"No, no, no," Michael says shaking his head, grabbing my hand. "It's not your fault, J. You know that I'd drop anything for you, even a date with the girl of my dreams. Don't go there dude, it's not your fault."

I nod, grateful for having such an amazing friend like him. Nellie, Dr. Churchill, and Dr. Aida finish talking and walk back into the room.

"Alright," Nellie says. "Michael I'm gonna drive you to school real quick before I start my shift, and if I have the time, I'll come and pick you up from school for Jamila's test tomorrow. If not I'll just shoot you a quick text, okay?"

"Awesome, thanks Nel."

"No problem, baby." She looks to me and says, "I'll see you after my shift, okay? Try and get some rest."

She goes to the table and reaches into her big tote bag. You know the ones — the ones from the bookstores that could hold your entire life in it. She pulls out my laptop and phone, the chargers, and a bag of extra buttery popcorn.

"You are a Godsend," I say in gratitude.

"You're damn right," she says matter-of-factly. "Now I hope you know that being in the hospital is the *only* reason you get out of schoolwork," I roll my eyes as she smiles jokingly, "so try and relax. Watch a movie or two, eat some popcorn and I'll see you later, okay?"

She places my things on the small table above my bed and kisses my forehead. I mouth a thank you as she grabs her things, walking with Michael past the information desk. Dr. Aida turns left to finish his rounds while Dr. Churchill follows.

After watching three Netflix movies and a bunch of videos on YouTube, I finally allow my eyes to rest a bit. I look at the clock and see it's been an hour since visitation hours have passed. Nellie must've gotten caught up with a patient and couldn't make it in time; that's okay though, I'll see her first thing tomorrow I'm sure. I slump my head back against the pillow and look at the ceiling. My phone vibrates and I pick it up to see a text from Michael.

'Still Alive?'
'Unfortunately, yes.'

I wait for him to reply, the bubbles appearing as he texts before he responds,

'Sorry I couldn't make it tonight. Nellie said she had to stay an extra two hours at the hospital, and my nana needed me to help her with the groceries when I got home.'
'It's cool, but are you still comin' tomorrow?'
'Yeah, yeah, no for sure. Nellie said she's still gonna drive me to school in the morning, and she'll let me know if she has time to get me for your test.'

'Okay, great. How was school?'

'It was aight. You're not missing much. Kiara's still dressing slutty and the popular kids are a living contradiction. The school is still a joke of an institution and the teachers feign benevolence like they're not confused about their own lives. So, all that normal stuff.'

'Glad to hear it,' I reply. 'Anything new with Taylor?'

'Oh yeah! She stopped me in the hallway before the second period and asked me if I wanted to go to Loni's for lunch tomorrow!'

'Dude, that's huge!'

'I know! I was doing everything to not burst into song right there, but I kept it cool.'

'You're so weird.'

'Yeah, well, you love me anyway.'

'LOL yeah, I do.'

'Wish you could be here to help me pick out another outfit.'

'I already know. That green t-shirt, 'cause it looks good on your skin, and the brown pants you got for your birthday. And your New Balances — that'll look sick.'

'Wow. You know when it comes to dressing yourself you're basic at best, but when it comes to other people you actually have a little competence.'

'STFU.'

'LOL. What've you been doing all day?'

'Just chillin'. I watched a couple of movies on Netflix and surfed YouTube for a while. Now Idk what to do.'

'Why don't you work on some homework? I know you're supposed to be relaxing, but you could get it out of the way since there's nothing else to do.'

'Or, I could just surf Black Twitter.'

'Or that, LOL.'

I close my messages and open Twitter, about to surf the hilarity that it is until Dr. Churchill walks into my room. He carries a clipboard in his hand with, from what I can see from my bed in the split second it turns towards my direction, my name and information on it. He wears the same dark red button-up shirt, black slacks, and black shoes. His bright blue eyes still look into mine with politeness — but they look dark somehow and the politeness looks even more strained — and not inviting.

"Hi Jamila, how are you doing?"

"Good," I say apprehensively. "Uh, what are you doing here Dr. Churchill? It's after visitation hours."

"Oh, I just came back to make sure you were comfortable, and to discuss the logistics of the test tomorrow with you. Dr. Aida will be busy tomorrow, so he's given your case over to me, and I'll share the results of the test with him afterwards."

"Oh, but Dr. Aida is my primary physician. He never said you'd be taking over. I thought he would've come by to tell me that. Or at least tell my aunt," I say.

"Well, Dr. Aida and I just discussed my transition into being the primary physician for your test fairly recently; I'll notify your aunt first thing tomorrow morning." He closes the door and sets his clipboard on the table, throwing me a smile that doesn't seem genuine. There's the routine smile he'd give me, all strained and not really reaching his entire face, but this one is different. This one is more… domineering. He asks, "Are you ready for the test?"

"Uh, I guess so," I say warily. "How long is it going to take?"

"Not long at all," he says, pulling the curtain closed so no one can see in through the door. He turns and his smile disappears, now replaced by a blank expression. Warning signs go off in my head as my stomach begins to sink. I have a really bad feeling about this guy, and I know that I shouldn't be alone in a room with him.

"Are you sure we shouldn't wait 'til my aunt and Dr. Aida are here tomorrow afternoon? Shouldn't there be another adult in the room — my legal guardian?"

"I had another look at your scans," he says ignoring me, "and they are quite exceptional. It's an anomaly unlike any I have ever seen, Jamila. You are quite the anomaly."

I look away, trying to look everywhere but into his eyes. He's really making me uncomfortable; his intensity is a little too much, and doctors aren't supposed to discuss results with minors. I respond, "Dr. Aida said it shouldn't be anything to worry about in terms of injuries or long term effects. It's just out of the ordinary to have this level of activity and function so effectively."

"Yes, you're right about that. It's *definitely* out of the ordinary." He walks up to my bed and leans on the armrest, leaning down until he's peering at my face like he's viewing an animal in a zoo. I lean back into the bed instinctively, but he doesn't back away.

"You are not ordinary. Extraordinary isn't quite the word, because that would imply that there's something good about it. No." He looks at me, his eyes suddenly lacing with venom. "Your anomaly is anything but good; it's a disgrace. You are a disgrace."

I look at him in disbelief, my eyes tearing up instinctively from his blatant hatred. I force myself to keep it together, but I'd be lying if I say this man isn't making me tremble with fear.

"What the hell?" I say incredulously. "How can you say that? You can't treat me like this — you're a doctor, you're supposed to be my physician and ensuring my health and safety. Not degrading me and making me uncomfortable — without any adults or guardians present might I add. Who do you think you are?" He moves and sits on the edge of the bed, leaning down closer to me as if we're casually hanging out; but it feels more like he's trapping me.

"The only one with the knowledge and intelligence to see what these scans mean — and to see you for who you are. For what you are."

My stomach sinks as he looks at me with an expressionless face; the way he said that makes me uneasy. For *what* I am? Why would he say that? He's a doctor, he's supposed to be a modern man, with progressive thoughts and ideals — not some weirdo racist with old-world tendencies.

"If I had known I was going to have a racist jerk as my doctor, I would've gone to another hospital," I say sarcastically.

"Funny," he says, with absolutely no humour in his voice. Although he does smirk which, to be honest, resembles more of a smile than that sorry excuse of a smile he was trying to pull earlier.

"I've been looking a long time for an anomaly like yours — someone with your strange defect. We all have. It's rare, and oftentimes it explains itself with the subject exhibiting some sort of neural defect later on in the future, and we're back to the drawing board. But you — your defect has been developing for years now, and you've been functioning above average. You have no signs of developing a neural defect later on in your life. If anything, your brain function is advancing at an exponential rate. And that — that is not ordinary."

I freeze, looking at him fully now.

"We?"

He smiles at me — but with danger now laced in his teeth. He leans forward even more until I notice something peeking out from underneath his collar. I look closer to see a gold necklace with a small pendant that holds what looks like a Swastika, except in between the spaces are little symbols. I can make out a crown in one space, and a gun in the other before he leans back a little and the necklace disappears. I look up at him and the same look of hatred and disgust remains on his face. I try to keep my face stoic — a poker face to ensure I give nothing away, including the fact that I am *freaking out.*

"You're a Toubab," I say in realization. He scoffs with a smirk, his eyes keeping the hatred within them. He leans back and fixes his arm cuffs; keeping an agonizingly calm demeanor about him that annoys the crap out of me.

"Your kind have been calling us that since you were in chains. I guess some things never change."

"Apparently. You still hunt us like it's the colonial era."

"And for good reason," he says. He thankfully stands back up and takes off his jacket. "Your people bring nothing but poverty and squalor to this world. All your kind do is kill and screw anything you lay your eyes on — creating more of you to lay waste to this world. If you don't do that, you use witchcraft. We use what good there is in people like you to help make this world better; if you're too far gone, there's no need for you."

"You talk about us as if we're a disease — pestilence or something. We're people. Humans. We deserve to be here and have every right to live life as you do, even though you're probably committing acts worse than I could imagine."

"I do what needs to be done," he says calmly, "and ensure that there is no anomaly that would threaten the progression of the human race." Folding his jacket and reaching into the front pocket, he takes a syringe out.

"What is that?" I ask warily.

"Just a sedative to put you to sleep — it'll be easier that way. Don't worry. It's not going to kill you. We still need you, to see what you can do."

He moves towards me swiftly, pointing the syringe towards my arm. I lean the other way abruptly and struggle to push him away, the monitor beside me beeping loudly as my heart rate escalates. He pushes me down easily with one hand and manages to get the needle in my vein, roughly pushing it in and injecting the transparent liquid. I yelp in pain — but he moves his hand to my mouth and keeps me down with his elbow, effectively cutting off my cries. I try to yell out for help, but his strong hand presses even harder onto my mouth and muffles my screams. I struggle with his meaty hands and the syringe, his fingers having a vice-like grip on my arm as I struggle to push him away. He quickly moves over me and turns the monitor off; as he leans over me, I flashback to Ricky Brass over me the night before. I was terrified, just as I am now, only this time the danger is worse. From within me, I feel a need to get this man away from me, and suddenly the haze from the drugs lifts and I sober up a little, feeling strength flow through my body.

I remember what Loni prayed over me last night. *'Protect her in times of peril,'* she said, *'and give her strength as she discovers new parts of herself that will challenge her mentally, physically, and emotionally.'* Give me strength. Strength.

I lift my hand with all the strength I have, then I feel a surge of power shoot through my arm, into my hand. I push his chest away from me with a mighty thrust that reverberates through his chest and pushes him across the room. He hits the opposite wall hard and falls to the floor limp, unconscious from the blow. I look at him in disbelief, frozen for a moment in shock. Holy crap! What did I just do? How did I do that? For a second I wonder if he's dead, but then I see the steady rise and fall of his slumped torso.

"I hope you feel that when you wake up," I say to his limp body, kissing my teeth.

I look at the clock and see that it's 8:24 p.m. If a nurse walks in to see an unconscious man they'll ask questions. And questions means trouble. Quickly, I pull the syringe and tubes out of my arm, grimacing in pain as I do it forcefully, and swing my legs to the side of the bed. The strength I had to push him away quickly disappears, and I'm reminded that I have three broken ribs as I gasp out from the sharp pain in my side. I wobble forward and grab the armrest to steady myself, clasping my other hand over my mouth to muffle my cry. I look to the curtain to see if a shadow moves to my door — a potential curious nurse or hospital employee. After a few moments of silence, I figure it's safe to start moving. I slowly stand up, testing my legs to see if they're stable enough — shaking the static out of my calves and feet so there's proper circulation. I take a few wobbly steps, my knees buckling — but I catch myself, and keep myself vertical. I grab my phone but leave my laptop and charger; I'm not strong enough to carry all of that and get out of here, and I can only assume Nellie will get it amidst the confusion in the morning. I make a move towards the door but then turn around, grabbing the man's white coat off the chair and his badge, sticking it in the front pocket of the coat. I rush to the bathroom, turning on the sink and wetting my hands. I smooth my hands on my hair and pull it back into a neater bun, closing the coat around my waist so it looks as if I could pass as a Toronto General doctor.

I make my way back to the door and peek through the curtain and look outside; there's one nurse at the information desk and it looks like the hallway is fairly deserted. The lights in the hall are dimmed, signalling the end of the night, and silence passes through the air. The phone rings and the nurse turns around in her chair to answer it. I take my chance and quietly slide the door open; I inch out of the room and run to the column beside the information desk, facing the elevator at the end of the hallway. I shake my head as my vision gets spotty and the pain from my ribs and sprained foot takes my breath away. Whatever he injected me with is already starting to set in, but I have to get out of here and try to get somewhere safe. I don't know if he's the only Toubab here, and I can't take any chances. I unlock my phone, turn it on mute and turn off the location. If he was able to find me with hospital records, I'm sure the Toubabs have the technology to find me with my phone location. Nellie's always telling me to keep it on, just so that she can know where I am at all times — but I'm going to assume this situation calls for a deviation from the rules. I look both ways — seeing a few people walking away from behind me and looking back in front of me to see a nurse standing at a cart, looking at a chart further down the hallway towards the elevator. If I wait then more people might appear, but if I go now, then someone might see a teen patient trying to pull a jailbreak situation. Weighing my options, with the time of the hour and the deserted nature of the floor, I take a shot and start walking towards the elevator.

I eye the nurse nervously as I try to make my wobbly steps seem steady. He's about my height, with thick hair and pockmarks along his cheekbones. He's young, maybe no older than 28 years old, and has kind eyes. Kind *tired* eyes. This is probably a long shift he's been working, and you can see the fatigue just exuding from him. Maybe I can work with that. As I near the nurse, I cross my arms across my chest to hide the hospital gown underneath the coat and fake a yawn. The nurse looks up and sees me, giving me an empathetic look.

"Burning the midnight oil?" he asks.

"Mm-hmm," I say tiredly, nodding in agreement. I keep my eyes closed and my hand in front of my mouth so he can't see my face. He throws me a sympathetic smile and looks back down to his clipboard. Once I'm safely behind him, I speed walk to the elevator; looking left to right from every room I pass to make sure no one walks out and sees me. I wince in pain as my pace quickens — but I need to get out of here. I finally make it to the elevator and press the button rapidly. I know that doesn't make it come faster, but I'm panicking and I very well might collapse in an unconscious heap any second and I'd rather do that somewhere else. The door dings open, and just before I step in, I spot a pair of sunglasses on a cart nearby. I snatch it quickly before stepping into the elevator and the doors close. I put the glasses on and press B for the basement. Getting out through the car park is probably better than the main floor, which could be crawling with Toubabs and other hospital employees that are going to try and stop me. I exhale deeply, and reflexively I start crying. God, I've gotten so teary lately — I didn't even cry this much when my mother died. I just felt empty without her because it was one less person in my life to make it better. But now it's my life that's being threatened, and I guess the gravity of the situation has opened the floodgates. My breath falters as snot runs down my nose, and I try to sniffle but that only makes the pain in my head worse. I groan in frustration and stomps my foot — immediately regretting it, I grab my ankle in pain and say a silent *'Ow'* in my head. I'm such a dumbass. The light indicates the basement is on the next floor. I roughly wipe the tears off my face and rub my nose with the sleeve of the coat. Ugh, I can still smell his cologne on the coat; even the fragrance smells obnoxious. *Rough and Repulsive Cologne — the cologne for pompous assholes.*

The doors open and I look left and right before stepping out; the garage is fairly empty, with only a few of the staff parking spots filled up. I see a door to my right that leads to a back room — I look in the small door window and see a group of employees. They're wearing dark blue jumpsuits with the burgundy logo of a garbage disposal company printed on the breast: sitting around a table, on break I guess, chatting and laughing. I slink back beside the door, ducking underneath the window so that they don't see me, and go to the other side and stand near a column. I take a few deep breaths — I'm not one for exercising except for the recreational biking every day, so this is like a marathon for me right now — especially with broken ribs and a sprained ankle. I look back to the break room and see a box with jumpsuits near the door: open and begging to be rifled through. The drugs kick in again and my vision fogs up for a minute. I lean forward and slap my head to clear the fog, forcing my limbs that move like molasses to move to the box. I grab a jumpsuit and, after seeing several work boots lined up to the side, grab a pair and quickly put them on behind the column. I check the phone wallet on the back of my phone and see my transit pass. I sigh in relief, pushing the sunglasses higher up on my nose and walk as nonchalantly as I possibly can towards the exit. I duck underneath the mechanical arm by the ticket stop and walk as fast as I can up the incline until I reach the street. Toronto General is in the heart of downtown — and even on a Thursday, the streets are busy at night. I duck my head and hunch my shoulders, putting my hands in my pockets and walking as nonchalantly as I can.

I make my way to the train station that's a few blocks away, speed through the stairs, and head to the Westbound platform. I tap my transit pass and almost walk into the doors before they actually swing open. A teenager dressed in double denim, hipster glasses, and a fedora looks at me strangely before he quickly looks away and goes about his night peacefully, clearly not wanting to provoke a conversation. The sound of a saxophone playing blares in my ears, creating an echo in my eardrum that amplifies the ache of my concussion. I bump into an Asian woman, raising my hands in silent apology, and stumble down the escalator to the platform. I thump against the wall and try my best to stand straighter because the last thing I need is people looking at me funny, and thinking I'm an addict. My head feeling heavier as I straighten, and the weight of my head carries my whole body forward until I'm right behind the yellow line.

"Yo," a bystander yells to my right, "be careful, eh? The train is gonna be here in a minute."

I turn my head towards the direction of the voice and nod lazily, shuffling my feet backwards and thumping into the wall again. Finally, the train comes, the wind from the speed of the train blowing on my face and sobering me up just a little bit. The doors open and I bound towards a corner seat; I collapse onto the less-than-plush red seat and lean my head against the window. I force myself to not fall asleep and open my eyes every so often. People come and go onto the train car: a businessman, a teenage girl, a homeless man asking for change. They all blur into one as time goes by. The drugs are strong — he didn't get a chance to inject much into me and yet I'm still struggling to stay awake. I close my eyes and re-open them with a jolt, seeing that we've already travelled several stops to Lansdowne station. I keep my eyes as open as they'll allow themselves to be, and read out the names of the stations as we arrive to keep myself conscious. Eventually, I make myself replay the incident in my head to keep myself awake and think back to the necklace he was wearing. It was a thin gold chain that held a rectangular-shaped pendant with the Swastika-looking symbol in the middle. The legs of the symbol were more curved than the ones the Neo-Nazis use, and there were four symbols in the spaces of the legs. I remember the crown in the upper right corner, and what looked like an older-looking gun in the bottom right corner. It was definitely a gun from before the 20th century, so this symbol must've been around for a long time. I can't remember what the other two symbols were, but I think one of the other symbols might've been a book. I might be reaching, I am under the influence of drugs after all and not a lot is making sense to me right now, but that's my best guess.

The overhead speaker announces that we've arrived at my subway station. I inch myself up — my head still on the window and grazing the glass as I push myself up — and stumble towards the door. I just make it out before the doors close, and I lean my head back and close my eyes, giving them rest from the bright lights overhead before heading towards the stairs. Using the hand rest, I take breaks to catch breath as I walk up the stairs since the escalator is out of order. I finally make it to the top and move in a haze outside. I look left and right trying to remember which way I go to get home. I finally settle on left and try to head home. I walk past an elderly woman on the sidewalk, pushing a cart filled with plastic bags, assorted foods, and perishables. I stumble further past a homeless man holding a sign that calls for the end of times and asks for any change we could give him. I keep walking until my steps turn into shuffles, my feet barely lifting off the ground until they start sliding forward. My back hunches forward, but the fabric of the jumpsuit refuses to stretch preventing me from slumping forward any further. I take in my surroundings and see several houses around me, all with lawns run down and bordering the main street, with large apartment complexes further down the road. I think I recognize one of the apartment complexes — it looks like the one that's only 10 minutes from my house, so I head in that direction. Suddenly my belly rumbles angrily and I know that she is no longer on my side. I see a side street and head towards it so that I can empty the contents of my stomach. I bend over and let it all come out, my headache pounding with persistence and the ache in my ribs pulsating as my stomach convulses. I rarely throw up because I almost never get sick, so I don't remember what it feels like to throw up. But I definitely remember that it doesn't feel good. I lean over and press my head against the cool concrete wall, my eyes closed and barely holding back tears. This is so sad. I know given my current situation that I should take it easy on myself, but this level of rock bottom is so pitiful.

I'm glad no one is around to see this — I can take solace in being at my lowest alone.

I collapse onto my knees and clutch the ground, feeling the haze pool from my head into my eyes, into my tongue that thickens underneath the stench of vomit until finally, I collapse onto my side. I press my face onto the cool pavement, ignoring the dirt that's most likely seeping into my pores, and close my eyes. Sweet sleep. What a concept.

CHAPTER SEVEN

───────── ∞ ─────────

I feel a throb behind the bridge of my nose and I wake up, opening my eyes abruptly. Man, I'm really getting tired of this headache — it's getting really old. My vision takes a moment to come into focus; black spots peppering my sight as I blink rapidly to fade them out of my vision. Eventually, my eyes focus on a hand holding a towel: a wet towel. A towel that pats my forehead lightly. It feels good — and I realize this at the same time I feel my head boiling as if it's on fire. Thank God for this damp towel. I follow the hand to a muscled arm, that is held by a ripped shoulder — it's amazing an arm like that can have such a light touch. The mystery man's ripped shoulder, overlaid with a black sleeve, hangs off a sturdy neck that holds a gold chain and a head. A head that I recognize.

"Well good morning, sunshine," says Blanco, looking down at me with a small smile. So small you wouldn't even be able to notice it at first glance. I look at him — I just look at him — and take in that he's towelling my head. Blanco is towelling my head. Blanco is towelling my head with an amused face and... whoa. What?

"Um…" I say, my voice croaking from dryness.

"I think the word you're lookin' for is *thank you*."

"That's an expression, not a word."

He closes his eyes and shakes his head in disbelief, saying, "Of course you'd correct my grammar, no matter what state you're in."

He moves outside my field of vision to reveal another man beside him who, I'm just realizing now, is icing my exposed ribs. I flinch and inch away, wincing from the pain but ignoring it nonetheless, because I don't know who this man is. He looks at me and raises his hands, assuring me that there's nothing to worry about, and slowly moves the ice back towards my torso. I slowly sink back to my original position — fairly easy since this leather couch melts into all the parts of my body — and allow him to ice my ribs. But I keep a wary eye on him. He hands me a glass of water from the coffee table, and I swiftly take it — gulping it down in one mighty inhale. I glance back towards Blanco, who is now across the room in the kitchen; he rinses out the towel and hangs it off the middle of the sink. He's in his usual uniform: all-black attire, with a gold chain hanging just below his collarbone. He turns and leans back on the sink, grabbing his wrist with his hand and looking at me expressionlessly. As always. Man, he and Michael have a knack with that; maybe they'd get along.

"So, what kind'a trouble you be in where you end up drugged up in an alleyway, in the middle of the night?" he asks monotone.

"It's a long story," I say tiredly.

"I like long stories." I look at him full-on, him returning my look with an unwavering deadpan one of his own. I appreciate that he helped me out but, honestly, I'm not entirely sure that I'm safer in his company.

"Look, I appreciate you bringing me here. Wherever we are…"

"You're at my place," he says matter-of-factly. I look at him surprised, then look around to take it all in. He leans against a sink that sits within a marble countertop, with cupboards hanging overtop. I look slightly to the left and see a wall dividing the kitchen from the hallway that leads to the front door. It's a fairly spacious condo, probably incredibly expensive given the new housing market, and looks even more spacious with the way the furniture is placed. He took advantage of the space — really feels like one open space where you can see everything. I'm laying on a couch: a beautiful dark brown leather one with mahogany cupholders on the sides, atop a fuzzy blanket. A glass table sits in front of me, with three books piled on top of each other and a wooden box beside it. There's also a bottle of Advil, a few rags and bloody cotton balls littered closer to the edge nearer to me. I guess I started bleeding after I collapsed. Beneath the couch, a plush rug lays atop the floor; across from me is also a glass table and a lone chair. It's a beautiful design — like the ones that you get from those flea markets that are only open on the weekends - and it perfectly fits with the decor of his place. Abstract paintings hang off the wall to my left, framed above and below each other to create a giant wall of abstract paintings. I had no idea Blanco was so well versed in art. I'm surprised to think this, but I think he and Ms. Cortez would get along — on the topic of art, of course. Anything else might be a bit of a stretch.

"Well, thank you for getting me off the streets, but," I start to get up, wincing from the pain but pushing through anyway, "I really should get back home." The man icing my ribs softly kisses his teeth in protest, but I push his hand away and slowly push myself up from the couch. I start to walk but my legs fail me, and I buckle towards the ground. Luckily, Blanco rushes over just in time to catch me.

"Whoa, whoa, whoa, you're not going anywhere for a while, baby girl," Blanco says, holding me upwards. "Whatever drugs are flowin' through you got you messed up bad, and I wanna get you home to Nellie too — believe you me — but you gotta rest a little. You got what looks like a concussion and got banged up pretty bad. You're safe here, aight? Just take a seat and rest for a little, and I promise I'll drive you to Nellie's soon."

I look at him with conviction even though my eyes begin to tear, exhausted from the past day's events, and desperate for someone to be there for me. Desperately, I ask, "You promise?"

He looks at me and his eyes soften, and he assures, "I promise."

I nod and walk back towards the couch, exhaling deeply and sinking into the couch while looking at Blanco. He walks and sits in the armchair to my left and leans on his knees, pressing his fingertips together as his elbows rest just above his knees.

"What the hell were you doing out there so late at night?" he asks — surprisingly upset. "A lil' girl like you shouldn't be out at this hour; there are crazy people outchea who won't care that you're a teenager. They'll hurt you and take advantage of you. Hell, it looks like they already did."

"What do you care?" I counter.

"I'm not a monster," he fires back, taking offense. "You're a good kid, anybody can see that. Even though you're a pain in the ass. You don't deserve to get hurt, but you shouldn't be putting yourself in that type of position by bein' out this late at night either."

"Yeah, well, I thought I was safe. I guess not."

"You can't just assume shit, baby girl. You're a young, beautiful girl, and that's reason enough for people to want to use you in whatever way they can."

"I told you," I start, annoyed, "my name is —"

"Jamila. Yeah, yeah I know," he says with a smile. "It's just a name, baby girl. No need to lose your mind over it."

"You're one to talk," I say sarcastically. "You out here making sure that everybody knows your name, maintaining your reputation by whatever means necessary. I thought you'd be the first to say that names matter."

He looks at me stone-faced, his mouth set tight. "Yeah, well, you right about that I guess. A name carries the weight of history and time, and it's up to us to live our lives to balance out the other side."

My eyes widen — stunned by the familiar phrase that I've heard countless times as a child. "My mother used to say that to me. Where did you hear that?"

He looks at the ground and smiles. "Where else? From your momma." I look at him with surprise, a small smile tugging at my lips.

"I remember I used to call her Keke, a lil' nickname just 'cause I was always givin' 'em to people. It wasn't a big deal to me, I mean it was the same amount of words as Keba. Keba, Keke, two syllables. Didn't make any difference to me. But she hated it," he says with a chuckle. The deepness of his laugh catches me off guard, but seeps into my limbs and warms my heart nonetheless.

"She used to say *'That's not my name, stop callin' me that Blanco,'*" he continues. "She was just like you — I guess you're a lot like your momma in that way. And I used to always be like *'What's it matter, it's just a name. It's not like I'm disrespectin' you or nothin.'* And she always used to say that. That names carry history and time, and it's up to us to live our lives to balance the past that history and time carry. I never really got it at the time but after a while, it started to make sense."

"Yeah," I say with a reminiscent smile, looking off into the distance. "Same for me. I started to think of it as a scale: all the past and history that comes with being who we are, of being black and — for me — being a girl, carries a lot of weight. And that can be a lot for us to handle; but if we live our lives right, happily and with love and stuff, then we can start to balance everything that came before us and start to balance the weight of the past."

I smile as I think of the first time my mother said this. It was while we were watching TV, some reality show I can't even remember, and she was talking about how she didn't know what her name meant. She said when she was in high school, she went to a library to go looking for the meaning of her name and came across mine — Jamila. It's African Arabic, it means beautiful. A few years later, when she was pregnant with me and was thinking of what to name me, that name popped in her head. She was just sitting there, she said, rubbing her belly and humming a tuneless tune — she said at that moment, she knew that name was meant for me. And so that's what she named me.

After a few moments, I snap back into reality and look at Blanco, who's looking at me with that same expression that I can't place. Actually, after seeing him again, I think I have an idea of what it could be. It looks like fondness. Or pride maybe? Now *that's* wild.

"I like that," he says. "That makes it make sense." He leans back and chuckles, and I smile in response to his. "She just used to say that Keba meant 'patience,' and her name mattered because she needed the patience to deal with me."

I burst into laughter, not at all surprised by my mother's tenacity, and Blanco follows suit and laughs along with me. The other man chuckles as he continues to ice my ribs. I completely forgot he was in the room, to be honest. Being with Blanco and talking about my mother, I actually forgot where I was for a moment and was just *in* the moment. It's crazy that he's able to make me just forget about everything and feel so comfortable after only talking to him once before, and knowing next to nothing about him except through infamy. Only three other people are able to do that: Nellie, Michael, and my mom. Well, she did. When she was still here.

I lightly tap the other man's hand and nod, saying, "Thank you, but I think I'm okay now." He nods and backs up, packing up the mess on the glass table and leaving through a door behind Blanco. Blanco still looks at me, but with a look of curiosity. Not like the one the Toubab gave me in the hospital, but one that still makes me a little frazzled.

"So you gonna answer my question?"

"Which question? You ask a lot of 'em, y'know?"

He smiles softly before continuing, "The first one. About why you were out in the middle of the night, beat up and unconscious. And I've seen enough people doped up to know you were hopped up on drugs. But you're the last person I'd ever think would be ridin' a high in an alley on this side of town, at this time of the night. And whatever you were on is hardcore shit that I ain't never seen before. So?"

I stop for a moment, thinking of a story to come up with that will seem plausible but will also not give away any of the truth. "Well, I was in the hospital. I got three broken ribs, a concussion, and a sprained ankle. The concussion was from banging my head on the ground when I fell from my bike, and the sprained ankle from falling down a flight of stairs at school."

"Shit," Blanco says, whistling low. "That must'a hurt."

"Yeah," I say, feigning a chuckle to pull off the lie. "It really did. I was supposed to stay overnight but —"

"But?" he asks, waiting for me to continue.

"But I had to leave. I accidentally took medication that I always use and it reacted badly with the medication the hospital gave me," I say, my stomach getting butterflies from the lie I'm trying to pass off as the truth.

"You took some meds that reacted with the meds the hospital gave you?" he says more than asks.

"Yeah."

"And that made you pass out in an alley, nowhere near the hospital? Why wouldn't the hospital help you? Why the hell are you all the way down here? They shouldn't have released you if you were strung out."

"Well, they didn't release me. I left."

"You left?" he says deadpan. My eyes dart above his head as I lose my cool beneath his scrutiny, but I force myself to meet his eyes again so it looks as if I'm being honest.

I nod as I say, "Yeah, the doctor said I would be released the next day, but I needed to see Nellie about something important."

"You still aren't supposed to be released 'til tomorrow. How important can it be for you to bust out the hospital when you're high as a kite and all battered up? You're still a minor, you need to have permission from an adult that's your legal guardian to do all'a that."

"It's really important," I say, with what I hope was conviction but probably came across as more pathetic. Please, please, *please* stop asking me questions. I'm not good with confrontation and, even worse, I'm not good with confrontation *from you.* He looks at me, not believing my story clearly but, thankfully, letting it go. He leans back and shakes his head in disbelief, but resolves to leave it alone.

"Well if it's that important for you to leave the hospital in the middle of the night like this, then I should probably get you to Nellie's soon as possible, huh?"

"Yeah," I say relieved. "Thank you."

"Yeah." He stands up and makes his way to the front door before he stops, turning on his toes to face me again with a questioning look.

"One more thing. Why were you in the hospital with broken ribs? The debate team jumpin' people nowadays?" I give a half-hearted laugh, which he clearly doesn't believe is genuine.

"No, uh," I say, stalling. I shuffle my feet as he awaits an answer. Just as I'm about to respond, someone walks out from the side door to our left. We both look to see my accuser, looking at me with a stunned face that barely conceals anger. Wearing a Bomber jacket, an olive-green longline tee and baggy jeans that I can tell are sagging below his butt, he looks like he normally does. But after attacking me, he's surrounded by this threatening aura that makes my bones quiver within me. The more I look at him, I realize that I can actually see an aura around him — the space around his body surrounded in red and black, shifting around him and flowing through him. I blink a few times to see if my eyes betray me, but the colours only come back stronger — and with a feeling. From here it's like a presence, an ominous one. It feels heavy and draining, and I'm not even that close to him. Did my abilities manifest themselves again after my attack? Loni did say that we are protective spirits — is this a part of that power? Blanco throws him a nod as I stare at Ricky with wide-eyes, my heartbeat rising.

"Wassup Blanco?" Ricky Brass asks. "What's goin' on here?"

"What's good man?" Blanco asks, throwing Ricky a quick dap. Ricky's eyes never leaving mine and Blanco clocks this, looking between the two of us.

"Jamila was just in a little trouble," he says, filling in the awkward silence. "I was helping her out. Imma take her home real quick, hold down the fort for me."

"Yeah, no for sure boss." He still looks at me, unblinking, "What kinda trouble was you in?"

I look at him in fear, trying to nonchalantly inch closer to Blanco to create some distance between us. "I just got a little hurt that's all, but I'm good now."

"Oh you got hurt?" he asks with fake incredulousness. "That's crazy. It's hard for young girls, y'know. Gotta be careful how you move outchea, or else somebody's gonna make an example of yuh."

My legs get weak in response to his threat as he continues to stare at me with his cobra-like eyes. Blanco looks between us and, out of a telepathic link to my fear, leans forward to hide me behind him and look at Ricky.

"She gets the picture, Ricky. I had a talk with her about it, and I didn't intimidate her into hearing what I had to say. So step off."

"Yeah, yeah for sure. I got you," Ricky replies, finally taking his eyes off me and looking at Blanco out of respect. He looks back towards me though, as he walks towards the kitchen and leans down into the fridge to grab a pitcher of a dark red drink. Blanco places his hand lightly on the small of my back and guides me towards the front door.

"Don't drink all of the sorrel, eh. Save some for me and stop bein' such a greed."

"Yeah, I got you," Ricky replies, keeping his eyes on me as he drinks slowly out of his cup. I look away and look at my feet, my heart racing as I wait for Blanco to open the door. Finally, he opens it and I bound into the hallway, sucking air between my teeth as the memory of my assault and the pain threatens to suffocate me. Blanco places his hand on the small of my back but I back away, trying to do so nonchalantly as if I'm just moving from the pain, and he backs off. Keeping his hand hovering above me, he politely shows me to the elevator and we ride down to the car park to his black chariot.

Blanco opens the car door for me and ever-so-gently eases me onto the seat. After closing my door and going to the driver's side, he wordlessly starts the car and pulls out of the lot. After we've pulled onto the street and head towards the direction of my house, I pull up the courage to sneak a glance at him who, not surprisingly, stares ahead with an expressionless face. I stare at him for a while, unbothered as to whether it's impolite or weird, and study the contours of his face. Objectively speaking, he's a very handsome man. He has a broad but sturdy nose, perfectly manicured eyebrows that men seem to just be born with, while I have to thread and tweeze mine into submission, and dark brown eyes within which his tiny storm lies. But there's a light within them — a small one, but one that exists nonetheless. I notice it when he smiles or laughs and, now that I think about it, when he looks at me with that odd expression. I also see it when he talks about my mom. How strange. He has those high cheekbones that connect him to his African lineage, and full lips that are sharply outlined with a manicured mustache and beard. Beard game on point — I gotta respect him for that.

"You gonna say sumn or you gonna just stare at me?" he asks, turning to look at me with a small smirk on his face. I turn my face away and blush, a smile of embarrassment creeping onto my face which turns hot from being ousted. I look back at him smiling, which he returns with his own that, strangely, makes me smile even harder.

"You know you have a nice smile?" I say. He looks at me slightly shocked, leaning back slightly in his seat, taken aback by my forwardness.

"That was random," he says.

"No, it wasn't," I say laughing. "You were smiling and I happened to see it and I happen to think it's nice. So I'm gonna compliment you seeing as the moment calls for it. You have a nice smile. Take the compliment."

He looks at me from the corner of his eye, a small smile on his lips that threatens to break through from the flattery. "Well, thank you," he says, nodding once in gratitude. I nod back in reply, and we turn our smiling faces to the road and ride in silence.

We pull into my driveway and have a split moment of bliss before the door swings open and Nellie comes outside. Well, we're in deep shit. She stands there for a moment, hands cocked on her hips and a wide stance that clearly does not take any bullshit, and just looks at us. She's still wearing her scrubs from today — or I guess yesterday, seeing as it's past midnight — with her fuzzy baby blue cardigan that's pulled tight across her body. I look at Blanco, who looks at me with raised eyebrows and an expression that already feels fatigued from the conversation we're about to have. I'm pretty sure I'm in deeper than he is though. We open our doors and step out, Nellie coming down the steps as we do, and I prepare myself for the onslaught. Out of the corner of my eye, I see Ms. Dell taking up her usual post on her porch swing, sipping her sweet tea and casting her bird's eye over us so that she has some tea to spill to the other church ladies on Sunday.

"Where the hell you been?" Nellie asks angrily, looking at me. "I get a call from the hospital sayin' you're missin' and you don't call me? Or text me? Or let me know that you're okay? Why the hell did you leave in the first place? You know you shouldn't have been goin' anywhere in your state!"

She looks at Blanco, her face changing to full-on anger. "And you," she says to him. "You betta have a damn good reason for why I see you pullin' up in my driveway with my niece. 'Cause I know there ain't no reason that would bring you two together and have you drivin' her home this late at night!"

Blanco starts, "Listen Nel, I can explain —"

"It's Nellie to you," she interrupts, giving him the death look that immediately shuts him up. "And it better be a damn good explanation. This girl has three broken ribs, a sprained ankle and a concussion, and she's in no condition to be goin' anywhere. She should be in a hospital, getting urgent care from medical professionals that know how to help her. Not some drug dealer that'll dope her up with a dutty syringe."

"I know that," he says exasperatedly. I shuffle my feet and look down at them, seeing Ms. Dell leaning in not-so-discreetly to listen in, in my periphery. "I found her unconscious in an alley, face down, and dressed in a raggedy jumpsuit. She was doped up on sumn," Nellie looks at him wide-eyed, lips sucked in anger, but Blanco quickly continues, "but it wasn't my stuff! Whatever she was on was some hardcore dope that I would never give to a drug addict let alone a little girl."

I start, "I'm not a little girl —"

"Be quiet," says Blanco and Nellie simultaneously, still looking at each other. I obey their command — they both have that steel in their voice that only a crazy person would think to counter at this moment.

"I was lucky to be gettin' gas at that time, otherwise she might'a been out there for God knows how long. I was just helpin' her out, Nellie. She looked more banged up than all those injuries you say she was in the hospital for, so whatever trouble she was in did a lot more damage."

Nellie looks at me with a confused look, her eyes brimming with anger, but concern for my well being as well. I walk towards her, my hands slightly raised to calm her down.

"I had to get out of the hospital, Nellie," I say. "It wasn't safe."

"Wasn't safe?" she asks incredulously. "It's the city hospital, and you were receiving top-level treatment for your injuries. How could it not be safe?"

"It's hard to explain, but you have to believe me — I *had* to leave," I say. Nellie looks away, not wanting to accept my excuse.

"Not everyone there had my best interest at heart. People with... more *traditional* methods of fixing people like me. Like us."

With that Nellie looks at me, her face expressionless but her eyes finally processing what I'm *really* saying. In so many words, she's understanding that a Toubab was in the hospital and that it wasn't safe for me there anymore. I return her look with one of my own, not trying to give too much away in my face, but exchanging a confirmation in my eyes that her suspicions are correct. Blanco looks between the both of us, eyebrows furrowed in confusion to the silent conversation we're having. Nellie clocks this and collects herself, brushing it off to not tip him off.

"I hear what you're saying, Jamila," Nellie says. "I still don't like that you didn't call or text me to let me know where you were," she looks at me, seriously meaning what she says, "but I understand why you left."

"You do?" Blanco asks confused.

"Yes. Jamila's a smart girl," Nellie says nonchalantly. "She knows when a situation is no longer safe, so I trust that if she had to leave the hospital in her state then it must've been for a good reason."

"Those are some pretty serious injuries there, Nel. She said she had something important to tell you, but it couldn't wait 'til morning? Or be said over the phone?"

"I guess not," she says firmly. He looks at her, still confused but aware that she remains unmoving. "Whatever she had to say must've been too important, and I trust her judgment. I don't like that she's coming home at this hour —"

"Or driven home by me," he interrupts, with a small smirk on his face. She looks at him, a small smile creeping on her face. Surprising.

"Yeah, well, that too," she says. They look at each other and smiles burst on their faces, and they share a small laugh. Now I stare at them in confusion — never in my wildest dreams did I think I'd ever see the day where Nellie and Blanco share a laugh.

"But I do appreciate it. Really," Nellie continues. "I'd rather it be you than a cop car — whether they were driving her home or telling me something worse. So thank you."

He shrugs, looking down and slightly shuffling his feet. This is so weird to me — seeing his embarrassment from the flattery. This huge rock of a man softening from a compliment is not only wild but really endearing. But also kind of scary — like, I don't know how to feel.

"Well," he says, looking at me, "I hope you get better. Whatever shit you were on was hardcore, and you're smarter than that to be on that stuff so I hope you learn from this. And don't go running from the hospital again and drugged out on the street."

I kiss my teeth and roll my eyes to the back of my eyelids, causing him to smile, but after a moment he places his hand on my shoulder and looks at me seriously. I look at him and nod, assuring him that I hear what he's saying. He nods back, satisfied by my compliance. He nods to Nellie in farewell. Nellie nods back, and he walks to his Escalade. As he pulls out of the driveway he lifts his hand in farewell, two of his fingers raised slightly higher than the others, and he drives off. I take a deep breath and turn around, to see Nellie once again standing with her hands on her hips. She shakes her head, looking at me disappointed, but pulls me in for a hug. I wince in pain, my body still racked with the consequences of my assault, and Nellie releases her grip a little bit — but only a little, still hugging me fiercely. She sways us side to side, keeping us there in silence for a moment. But that moment is swiftly interrupted by Ms. Dell's unwavering nosiness.

"Hey," she yells from her porch swing, leaning forward to the point she's almost over her stoop and onto ours, "y'all good?"

"Yeah Ms. Dell," Nellie responds exasperatedly, noticeable by me but apparently not by Ms. Dell, "we're good. We're gonna head in, have a good night."

"Aight, you too baby," Ms. Dell says, smiling at me lovingly. She may be a nosy church lady, but she's the most loving nosy church lady I've ever had the pleasure of knowing. I smile back at her as we go up our front steps, Nellie holding my elbow to help me up the steps and through the door. It smells like peppermint tea and cinnamon — she must've had so many cups of tea to try and calm down. We take off our shoes and walk towards the kitchen, Nellie placing me softly on the chair before walking over to the sink and leaning against it. She cocks her head back and takes several deep breaths, eyes closed as she collects her thoughts, remaining wordless. She opens the fridge and takes out the pitcher of water, and takes two glasses out of the cupboard, pouring the water in and walking back to the kitchen table where I sit. She places one in front of me and starts drinking hers. My body immediately senses the relief from a cold glass of water — the thirst is overwhelming and I gulp the water down in two mighty swigs. We sit there in silence for a few minutes, Nellie nursing her glass and me drinking the last of mine while I stare off into the distance. Finally Nellie takes a sharp breath and looks at me, moving her hands in a gesture that says '*Well? Go on with it then.*' I take a deep breath — never one to beat around the bush, I dive right into the thick of it.

"There was a Toubab at the hospital." Her face looks pained, as she closes her eyes and takes another deep breath. I continue, "It was Dr. Churchill." With this her head snaps up — her eyes widening and her body on full alert.

"What?" she cries in disbelief.

"Yeah, I know. He came in after visitation hours when everyone was gone — saying that he was taking over my case now and he'd be overseeing my test alone. He had my information and medical history and everything; he acted as he did with Dr. Aida, and then he just... changed,"

I continue. "His face went dark and he just became so hateful, like I was an abomination or something."

"What did he do? Was it just him and you alone, or were there other Toubabs?"

"It was just him, but I was already doped up from the sedative and I was in pain. I was right where he wanted me and I couldn't really do anything about it. He had a syringe in his coat pocket and he injected me with something —" my voice catches as a sob breaks through my throat and thickens my mouth with a cry. "He just held me down, and I tried to fight back but I was still in so much pain. I knew that it was wrong for him to be there, I had a feeling about it, but he said he was going to be taking over for Dr. Aida and I just —"

"Hey. Don't do that, Mama," Nellie says softly, grabbing my hand and stroking the space between my thumb and forefinger. "Don't blame yourself — you were in a vulnerable position, and there was no way of knowing that he was a Toubab."

"But I had a feeling about him..."

"Yes, that must've been your powers kicking in," she says, matter-of-factly. "Even I felt that his energy was off — a total pompous asshole, and that alone is enough to set off your powers. At least it gave you enough of a warning sign to not trust him. You have a sense when something is off-kilter, and there's nothing more off than a Toubab with a vendetta. But you're still coming into your powers, so you can't blame yourself for not trusting your senses fully. So cut yourself some slack."

"I can't, Nel. Whatever he injected me with was powerful, and he didn't even inject all of it in me. I was lucky to get the syringe out of my arm; but if he had injected all of it in my system, who knows if I would be here. Or if I'd even be alive."

"But you are here. And you are alive. There's no point in dwelling on the should'a-would'a-could'a, because it didn't happen. But it taught you to be more careful. These Toubabs are always watching, and they're everywhere — even where we least expect it — and we have to be vigilant. But this is all new for you, so don't put too much pressure on yourself, aight? Just let this be a lesson." She leans back and takes a breath, looking at me with kind eyes. I look back with a small smile, but my heart aches as the attack replays in my head.

"He hated me so much, Nellie. I mean racism and sexism, that type of hate has no rhyme or reason to it, but this was something different. Like my very existence was such an abomination to him. I could *feel* it in the way he looked at me. The way he spoke to me. It was terrifying."

"I know, Mama. That's why we have to always have our guard up and stay at least two steps ahead of them. If he found you in the hospital, then you're not safe anymore. He has access to your records — that has your blood type, your SIN Number, everything. The good news is that the test you were scheduled for isn't mandatory; Yousef might give me grief for it, but I'll just assure him that I'll monitor you. You were only supposed to stay for the night anyway, so first thing in the morning we'll go to the hospital and sign the release papers. But now he knows where we are, and if you're at school and he comes for you, then I can't help you."

My beating heart accelerates and my skin gets hot as fear sets in; Nellie notices and takes my hand, looking fiercely into my eyes. She slowly breathes in and out to get me to mimic her and, finally, I do. In and out. In and out. In... and out.

"So what do we do?" I finally ask, after I've calmed down somewhat.

"We have to make sure you're protected. We're all in danger now, but you especially."

"Why? Wouldn't you, or Loni, be more of a threat? You guys have more experience and more control of your powers. I barely know how to use mine."

"Exactly. If they capture you they could use your powers for their benefit, and the ways you use your powers greatly affect your personality. Think of it like a symbiotic relationship, where two variables are dependent on each other. Who you are as a person determines how you'll use your powers, but how you use your powers will affect the type of person you will become. It's all interconnected, and they know that. You are more of a threat *and* an asset to them because you're fresh. Raw, with more chances of them abusing your powers succeeding. That puts you at risk."

"So how do I protect myself then?" I ask, straightening in my chair.

"Keep practicing. You're gonna keep going to Loni's after school, every day, to hone your senses and tap into that part of your brain," she taps my forehead three times, "that you've been neglecting. It's time to fully sink into it, accept all of it — that's the only way you'll be able to really protect yourself. But we need to have some... insurance."

I look at her questioningly as she gets up and picks up her phone, dialing and waiting for the mystery person on the other line to pick up.

"Hey," she says as they answer, "we need your help. There was a

Toubab at the hospital; he drugged Jamila and she ran, but now they know where she is. Where we are. We have to make sure she's protected."

She looks at me as the tinny voice of the person — a woman, I realize, I can now make out on the other line — responds. She nods as she replies, "Alright, see you in a few." She hangs up and moves to sit back down, plopping in her seat and leaning back from the exhaustion of the day. I mimic her, leaning back and playing with the rim of the glass — my fingers circling the rim as the hand circles the clock as the seconds pass us by.

15 minutes later, Loni comes knocking on our door. Nellie lets her in and Loni takes off her orthopedic shoes by the door. Taking in her surroundings as she removes her light jacket, she catches sight of me in the kitchen. She's wearing a loose silky red shirt and black pants, with gold earrings dangling from her multiple piercings and gold rings on every single one of her fingers, reminding me of my drawing in art class. She holds a big bag, clearly filled inside with multiple contents. She gives me a small smile, her eyes filled with love and understanding, which immediately makes my throat thicken with sobs again. I speed-walk to her — well, more like speed-hobble with my sprained ankle — and hug her, her thick body welcoming me like a warm bed. She sways me side to side — I'm really lucky to be surrounded by women who are good at that — and Nellie looks at us with a small smile. When I pull away, Loni keeps her hands on my waist, causing me to wince. She takes note of it and starts assessing my injuries, lifting my fuzzy pyjama top that I had changed into to look at my ribs, and bending down to gently press on my sprained ankle underneath my fuzzy socks. She slowly rises back up, placing her palm on my forehead while her other hand cradles the base of my neck. She closes her eyes and breathes low and slow, a few moments passing by as we stand like this: I notice her lips move slightly, a silent chant passing her lips as she keeps her hands on my head. I feel a calm seep into me from where her hands touch me, rushing from my forehead and the base of my neck into my body. Like liquid love, whatever she chants releases a stillness into my bones that dulls the ache of my injuries, and they become tolerable. Wow, this is gonna be a lifesaver for menstrual cramps. She eventually releases me and looks at me, giving me a small nod. She looks around the house with

an expressionless face, taking note of our living space and what's visible from the front door, before looking at Nellie.

"Let's get to work," Loni says, and Nellie nods in reply. They move into action, Nellie going to the tiny room down the hall and to the left, that acts as an office and miniature library. Loni moves to the middle of the house - a space between the living room and the entrance to the kitchen where the carpet ends and the linoleum tile begins. She reaches into her big tote bag and pulls out one of the books from the diner basement — one with a mottled green cover that looks like moss, and opens it to the page she's looking for. Nellie comes back carrying a matchbook, wearing an oversized red silk button-up shirt, a white silk headscarf, a bunch of gold necklaces, and gold rings. With one necklace holding the infinity symbol spiraling on the top. I look at her questioningly as I wait for an explanation as to what's happening.

"I prayed this day would neva come," Loni says, her eyes quivering with fear but her face hard-set. "We aave to speed up your training so you can properly protec' yuhself, but we aave to cast a protection spell as well. On the day-to-day, you're eitha at school, at home, or at the dina. Maybe somewhere else. But with this Toubab in town, yuh aave to keep a low profile. Don't go anywhere except these three places, yuh ear? If you need to go someplace else you go with me, Nellie, or Michael. But you caah bring any unnecessary attention to yuhself, so you haffi mek sure yuh stick to the routine."

"Which is the exact opposite of what you guys have been telling me to do," I interject.

"Routine with your mind: yes. Routine with your schedule: no," Nellie counters. "If you so much as go to the mall, you might cross the path of a Toubab, and we can't take any chances. Until you harness your powers better, it's best to keep a low profile. Just for now, okay?"

"Okay," I obey, nodding seriously as the weight of the situation settles in.

"I've already cast a protection spell on the dina, an' I tested it to make sure it's safe. Now we haffi mek sure your home is too."

She grabs a wooden bowl out of her bag and walks to the kitchen, placing the bowl and the green book on the table. As we follow her, she pulls out a glass jar with powder inside, and two bottles: one an average-sized dark-blue bottle with a dark, thick liquid sloshing inside and the other a tall bottle shaped like a squash, with a thin, pale yellow liquid. It looks like pee, and I sincerely hope it isn't — and if it is, I hope it's not hers. Or wait, maybe it'd be better if it was. Then, she pulls out a box which — when she opens it — holds what looks like chopped up leaves, and sets them in front of the bowl in the shape of a semicircle.

"Okay," Loni says breathlessly. "We're going tuh mek the protection potion."

"A protection potion? What is this, Harry Potter?"

Loni kisses her teeth, ignoring me before continuing, "This will protec' your home an' everyone in it. So stop bein' a smart ass an' do as I say."

I raise my hands in defeat as she grabs the book, opening it to a page that reads a recipe for the protection potion in a different language. Lower down on the page are several translations until — 3rd from the bottom — reads the potion's translation in English. This book must be really old. To have this many translations, it must've been in the hands of several Bastets. I can only imagine the stories these pages would tell if they had the chance.

"Okay, I'll read out the ingredients an' how much to put in di bowl. Make sure to only do as much as I tell yuh, okay?" I nod as she stands more sure in her stance, and Nellie stands beside me to look over my shoulder, making sure that I don't mess up.

"Okay, take the powder and put three teaspoons into the bowl."

Nellie grabs a teaspoon from the cupboard and as I open the glass jar, the smell of the powder wafts into my nose and I feel like I'm going to collapse right there. It is the worst smell I've ever come across. Imagine the waste of the biggest animal in the world, combined with the sewage of every single country, with just a hint of onion. I gag, breathing through my mouth in the hopes of escaping the smell, but only feeling the lingering taste on my tongue. I screw up my nose as I quickly, but carefully, spoon the powder into the bowl three times. Nellie leans more over my shoulder, checking to make sure my measurements are accurate before leaning back, satisfied with my work.

"Now, take the dark blue bottle," I obey her, unscrewing the cap to reveal a dropper as she continues, "an' squeeze six drops of di liquid inna circle in di powder." I take the dropper and, holding my breath, carefully squeeze one-two-three-four-five... and six drops in a circle. As I do so I find, to my surprise, it disappears into the powder until not even a dark shadow remains as a clue to that it was there. I look back to Loni, who returns my look with a small smile.

"Now tek the box of chopped up Cherubim leaves —"

"Cherubim leaves? What's that?"

"It's what Bastets named this leaf. In the olden days, we would chop it up an' use the juices for healing sicknesses on the inside. And when we burned it, it would clear bad energy and spirits from the space — so we use it with these otha substances to protect a space an' all di people inna it. I think they called it that because they thought the leaves 'came from di saviour's tree.' Cherubim is another way to say angelic, so I guess they thought that was a good name for it. Now take it and grab a clump, about the size of a clementine, and sprinkle it ova the powder."

I carefully eye the leaves, pinching it and placing it in my other palm. It feels warm — and I wonder if it's because Loni was lugging it around in her bag, or if that's the leaves' protection powers at play. I sprinkle it over the powder in a zig-zag motion, and it stays on top as I await the next step.

"Now, take the glass bottle and pour the Ebani on top — again, in a circle. Nellie, can you grab a measuring cup for her please?" Nellie bends down beneath the sink, pulling out our glass measuring cup and handing it to me.

"I'm sorry. Did you say 'Ebani'?" Loni chuckles, while Nellie bows her head and smiles.

"Yes. I know what you're thinkin' — it looks like piss." I nod rapidly in agreement, as Nellie chuckles behind me. "But it's a concoction that a few Bastets cooked up centuries ago. With it, the love of all di Bastets that made it seeped inna it, an' it connects those who consume it in some way to their ancestors. Now luckily you don't have to drink it," I exhale thankfully, because even if it didn't look like pee, I'm not eager to drink it either. Loni continues, "But even spraying it on you would be a good idea. It'll allow the ancestors to keep a special eye on you — they already did before, but this'll put you at the top of the list. But for now, we'll just put it in the protection potion." I nod, and reluctantly open the bottle to find, to my surprise, the fresh smell of lemons rise to my nose. I breathe in deeper and smile, my shoulders relaxing a little bit.

"Measure about ⅓ of a cup and pour it into the bowl, and, this is very important, only in di very center of di mixture. Don't pour it inna big circle like you did before, mek sure it's only in the middle."

I nod, pouring the Ebani into the measuring cup until it reaches the dotted line that reads ⅓. I put the glass bottle down and pick up the measuring cup, positioning it low above the rim of the bowl and in the middle of the mixture. I hear Loni take a deep breath and, out of the corner of my eye, see Nellie dancing lightly on her feet. She always does that when she's nervous. I pour the liquid into the very center of the bowl, making sure to go slowly so that nothing splashes onto the sides, and my eyes widen as the mixture sinks towards the steady stream of the Liquid Love. The Cherubim leaves melt into the powder, and both sink towards the Liquid Love as it pools at the bottom of the bowl. Like a sinkhole, the bottom of the concoction turns up until it too sinks towards the stream. Suddenly, the granules of the powder and the leaves change their consistency and rise to form a sage-green coloured sludgy mixture.

I look into the bowl and try to make out how that just happened before my eyes — its thick consistency not giving anything away that it used to be a bunch of different ingredients. I reach in to try and touch it, but Loni slaps my hand away — quite hard, I might add.

"Do you just go sticking your fingers in things you've never seen before?" Loni asks incredulously.

"Ouch," I protest. "I just wanted to know how it feels…"

"It's a protection potion, not a face mask from Lush," Nellie answers sarcastically. "We burn it and the smoke releases into the air, protecting the house and everyone in it."

I nod, rubbing my hand where Loni slapped me, as she empties some of the mixture into a tinier wooden bowl. We walk back towards the space between the kitchen and the living room. I go back to my position on Loni's left. Loni turns her back to the door and places the book on her forearms while Nellie holds the bowl in the air; she grabs one of Loni's hands and gives the matchbook to me. As I take it from her with my right hand she grabs my left wrist, ties the silk scarf she was wearing around it, and holds the bowl closer to me.

"We're going to chant a protection spell and when I tell you, I want you to light the potion. When we're finished chanting you're gonna take the bowl, and walk through the entire house. Wave it in the air, gently but swiftly, and make sure you get every corner of the house — even the side alley near the kitchen, alright?"

I nod, ready to get started, as Loni looks to me.

"We all have to chant at the same time, so read off the page an' try your best to stay in sync. Nellie and I aave read it so many times we know it by heart so we'll be fine without it, but make sure you read it word for word."

I nod in obedience as Nellie and Loni change their gait: widening their stance and straightening their backs. I follow suit, mimicking their posture and keeping my head held high, but eyes on the page. With eyes open, not wide but not open normally, Loni and Nellie stare ahead. Not at each other, but at a space between each other, putting themselves in a trance. I start to do the same but remember that I have to be looking at the page so I look back down. Loni and Nellie intake breath deeply, and I take that as my cue to start reading.

> *Mothers of our mothers*
> *And the ancestors beyond*
> *Cast your light on this space*
> *Give us speed for the chase*
>
> *Protect this place from the spirits of evil*
> *The spirits that wish us harm and death*
> *Give us the strength to ward off the enemies*
> *Who chase us 'till our dying breath*
>
> *Protect our women who give life*
> *Who give support, solace, and love.*
> *Protect the children in which our legacy continues*
> *Whose strength comes from the ancestors above*

Nellie quickly looks at me and gives a quick nod, giving the signal to start lighting the potion. I light a match and hold it upside down, above the middle of the potion until it begins to smoke and catch fire. Entranced, I watch as a light green blaze sets fire on top of the entire potion, trailing a bright green smoke into the air. Nellie puts the bowl in my right hand and mimes for me to hold it up higher in the air so the smoke can trail upwards. I look at the smoke detector, worried that the alarm will set off, but then notice the light is off — no sirens of fire trucks will be plaguing us tonight. She grabs my left wrist again and we continue to chant:

> *Lay waste to our foes*
> *Bring justice and avenge your daughters*
> *Defend the wronged and persecuted*
> *In the name of Bast and the almighty Father*

Give us our freedom
So we may take back our lives
Give us the power
Over our senses to survive

With that, the chant is finished. Loni and Nellie come out of their trance and pull their gaze from the space between them, the apparent nothingness in which they were concentrating, and their bodies relax into their normal posture. Loni nods to me and mentally pushes me forward so that I can wave the smoke throughout the house. I move down the hallway, moving the burning bowl in my hand throughout the air, gently but swiftly. I'm surprised the heat doesn't seep into my palms as I hold the wooden bowl comfortably in my hands. I walk smoothly into the office/library — moving around the desk and bookshelves, careful to not come too close to the pots of plants scattered around. I catch a glimpse of a picture frame on Nellie's desk, of my mother and I when I was younger, mid-laugh and happy. A pang of sadness hits my chest, but I continue with my task swiftly. I leave the room and move down the hallway, going into Nellie's room, the bathroom, my room, and back down the hallway to the kitchen. I do a little circle in the center, sweeping an arc just above the pale-beige floor tile, and getting in the nooks and crannies before moving to the door for the alley. I wave the bowl in a little zig-zag in the air when I catch Michael in his house just across from me, making his way with a trash bag to the alley. I jolt and throw myself onto the floor below the window, muffling a groan as a pang of pain racks my body. I hear him open the trash bin and throw the bag in, hesitating for a moment outside. A second later I hear a click, and a few moments after that the scent of weed. We started experimenting with weed in middle school — even did edibles a few times when Nellie worked the night shift — but we haven't smoked in a while. The last few times we've done it was when we were stressed and needed a release and a good laugh. I guess he can only give himself the former right now. I hear him exhale deeply, and smoke a few more puffs before he moves to go back inside. I slowly rise back up and see his back as he walks away, his head down and feet shuffling. He looks so forlorn. I've never seen him like this — only a little upset if he doesn't get the grade he wants on a test, or if he's been thinking about his parents. This is different though. This is just like when his parents died, and this worries me. I look at him a moment longer, but then I remember that a centuries-old cult is hunting me at this moment and, even though I love and care about Michael, this is more of a priority right now.

I walk back into the living room where Nellie and Loni are talking in hushed tones; Nellie is kneeling on the floor by the coffee table, sorting out bowls of pastes and liquids, and Loni flips through the book, moving to sit in the armchair.

"Now that that's ova," Loni says, "we're going to cover you in a protective salve — it's a mix of the protection mixture we jus' made and other salves. You've already taken a shower, so we'll cover your entire body in it before we send you to bed. It'll dry ova'night and seep into your skin. You've been having more active dreams lately, connecting to our ancestors an' the Realm of Duality, so the salve may heighten that even more. But don't be scared — jus' ride it like a wave, and let it come naturally. If you resist an' hesitate to accept it fully it won't work, alright?"

I nod, Nellie nodding as she continues to mix the different pastes and liquids into the bigger brown-wooden bowl with the original potion. She grabs what looks like a basting brush, a dark brown one with beige bristles, and mixes it together until it has a thick-oily consistency. She hands it to Loni who takes it and then motions to me to lay down on the floor.

"Take off your pyjamas, but leave on your underwear," Loni instructs me. I do as she says, placing my pyjamas and fuzzy socks to the side but leaving my underwear on. I lie on the floor and look up at the ceiling, exhaling a slow breath to let out the tension of the past few hours. Loni and Nellie move above me, Nellie using the basting brush and dipping it in the bowl while Loni holds the bowl in one hand and cups the other slightly, scooping the salve onto her fingers. They bend down and begin to smooth it onto my skin, the salve cool to the touch but a tingling sensation bringing warmth just below my epidermis. Loni begins to pray:

> "God, grant her the serenity to accept the things she cannot change..."

Loni begins smoothing the salve onto my arms, massaging it into my neck and chest while Nellie works the basting brush onto my legs and feet. The tingly feeling starts in my feet and makes me feel as if I'm floating just above the ground, and it seeps like oil into the rest of my body as they continue to put the salve on my skin.

"The courage to change the things she can..."

As they both meet at my torso, massaging the salve into my stomach, I feel a rush of that hot-coolness making its way through my limbs. It feels like it's flowing on a line that runs from the soles of my feet to the crown of my head. It soothes my aches and pains, but at the same time feels like it's charging up my very heart. I get a tingly feeling in my fingers, and a power surging within me; I start breathing rapidly, the overwhelming and sudden feeling scaring me, but Nellie gives me a reassuring look and I calm myself down. Ride it out: that's what Loni said. She finishes the prayer:

"And the wisdom to know the difference."

With my entire body covered in this sticky goop I slowly stand up, being careful to not get any of the concoction on the carpet. Half-naked and, on instinct, with my arms and legs wide, I look at Loni and Nellie with a look that asks *'Now what?'* Despite the gravity of the situation, Nellie and Loni struggle to hide smiles until, unable to hold it any longer, they burst into uproarious laughter. I look at them in disbelief while they continue to laugh at my expense, Nellie bending over and stomping her foot and Loni arching her back and clutching her stomach as she hoots and hollers. I cock my hip and slowly blink, my face expressionless. I kiss my teeth and bend over to grab my pyjamas, delicately putting them on which causes them to laugh even harder. After I've got my clothes on, I cock my hip and cross my arms, waiting for them to finish laughing. Finally they stop laughing, wiping the tears from their eyes while I look at them unamused.

"Alright, alright," Nellie says, still stifling her laughter. "Now all that's left is for you to go to bed. Tomorrow morning, first thing, we're gonna go to the hospital and sign the release papers. I've got some old crutches stored somewhere you can use, but we'll see if you can get a new pair when we sign your release papers. Your medication should be available for pick-up right away, but if not I'll pick them up after work and bring them when I come to Loni's. You're going to go to school tomorrow as if nothing's changed, except for," she motions to my broken ribs, "that."

"Yeah. That."

"Try to leave out as little details as possible when people ask you about it; just say that you were assaulted, but that you managed to get away fairly unscathed. Michael cannot know anything about what happened after he left, so just be as vague as you possibly can."

"How am I supposed to do that?" I ask. "Michael knows me better than anyone — even if I leave out some of the truth, he'll know that I'm hiding something."

"Well then consid'a it practice for the big stuff," Loni replies, walking towards me. "Your powers, the abilities you're gonna manifest, they're not gonna be somethin' that you'll be able tuh hide so easily when they get stronga. But you haffi learn to omit the truth every once in a while, and you'll definitely need fi learn how to lie — unless yuh want random people findin' out you can talk to yuh ancestas an' see into di future."

She's right. It's not like I've never lied before. I mean, omitting the truth is basically what every teenager does — but something on this big of a scale? And to my best friend? Michael's my Day One: he's been there for me since the beginning, and we've supported each other through the good times and the bad. I can't imagine how I should hide something so big when it's such a big part of who I am. But it would keep him safe — he's already paranoid as is, I don't know what he'd be like if he knew about all of this — but keeping something like this from him seems like a betrayal of our friendship. Loni must hear my inner thoughts, because she walks even closer to me and looks me dead in the eye, unwavering and unmoving.

"He's betta off not knowing about this. The more he knows, the more danger he's in.

Toubabs don't care if he's a Bastet or not — just being affiliated with us puts him in danger. Just being a black boy puts him in danger as is, but this is even bigga. I know you love him, and you wouldn't want to put him more at risk. Besides, could you imagine if Michael knew? He'd spill the truth by the end of the day without even trying, and keeping a secret this big would only kill him."

She's right. I know she's right. I listen to her and nod; she gives me a small smile, and her shoulders relax. She turns and starts packing up the bowls of pastes and liquids into her tote bag, Nellie cleaning the tabletop with a damp rag she grabbed from the kitchen. I still don't like that I have to lie to Michael, especially when it's related to my assault — he'd only show concern for me. He already has. But I know that this is more than just a sexual assault. This is a witch hunt against me. He'd understand, but only the way a millennial could understand — and definitely not in the context of a centuries-old war between superhuman black women and bigoted racist ethnocentrists. With her bag slung over her shoulder, Loni faces Nellie and I before she bids us farewell.

"Remember, the dina is always safe. If you ever need to go someplace, the door is always open." She looks to Nellie, giving her a look that an elder gives to a young'un when it's time to listen. "You're one of the strongest women I know, Nel. But don't go tryin' fi carry everythin' on yuh back like it's you an' J against the world. You two are like family to me. You're like the daughters I neva had, and you always have me."

Nellie and I smile as she continues, "We're in this togetha. We're Bastets. We're black women. We've got the world stacked against us and we're expected to be able to handle it, but you need people with you to help hold yourself up against all'a that. That's what I'm here for — that's what we do for each otha. What no one else will do when the goin' gets tough. Remember that, an' neva forget that even if you haffi stand as one, you come as ten thousand."

I recognize who she's quoting, and say matter-of-factly, "Maya Angelou."

"Yes, a wise woman," Loni replies. "And there's never been anythin' more true than that when it comes to our people. Make that the motto you live by as you manifest yuh powers. You're never alone even if you by yuhself, because you stand with thousands upon thousands of Bastets standin' with you, supportin' you."

I smile as her reassuring words give me a boost. Loni and Nellie, and countless others have been through the thickest of the thick of it and they still stand strong. They shouldn't have to, because none of us should have to endure things like this, but going through it has made them able to enjoy life better because they can handle the worst of what's thrown their way. And in the process, appreciate every good thing that comes their way. Nellie's a registered nurse with a house, and it's not easy to do that when you're a single parent. Loni's an immigrant with her own business and enough cushion to live comfortably, after enduring discrimination of every sort and the constant threat of Toubabs looming in the shadows. And these women, these two figures that stand before me, are the best *livers* I've ever seen. Anyone can survive: going day-to-day, paying the bills and making ends meet, and getting the basics life has to offer. But to *live*? To actually enjoy life and all that it has to offer? That's something that takes a lot of courage. And what can be more courageous than choosing to live when the world tells you that you don't deserve to? When constant threats loom beneath the surface of the dark waters of life? Loni smiles deeply as she comes toward me, enveloping me in a light hug that seems to flow warmth from her body into mine. She turns her head slightly and brings her lips to my ear.

"Neva forget you aave the strength an' fight within you," she whispers, "even when you feel weak. All it takes is surrendering to the powas that be — the ones you already aave. Neva forget that, baby girl."

She pulls away and places her hand on my cheek, giving me a warm smile that causes me to smile back. She turns to Nellie and gives her an equally warm hug, swaying her side to side for a few moments before releasing her. She puts her shoes back on, gives us one final wave and leaves as Nellie closes the door behind her. Nellie pushes the lock and leans with her back on the door, closing her eyes for a moment and thumping her head against the door. After a moment longer she opens her eyes and looks at me, her face showing love mixed with exhaustion.

"Well, my dear," Nellie says. "You've had one hell of a night. I think it's time to turn in for the night."

I nod lethargically as she shuffles over, putting her hand on my shoulder and guiding me slowly to my room. She comes to my side and puts my arm over her shoulder, and we walk slowly down the hallway — me being careful and putting all my weight on my good foot. We dart around the Novelfall and I slide into my bed, collapsing into the soft mattress and pulling the cozy covers over me. It's hot tonight, but no matter how hot it is I have to have the bed covers over me. I've always had this subconscious belief that if I have the covers over me, then no dangers looming in the darkness — whether they be monsters under the bed or serial killers with a black girl fetish — will be able to get me. I never thought that a Toubab would be a danger that I wouldn't be able to protect myself from. And I highly doubt a duvet cover is going to be able to protect me from them. Nellie comes over and strokes my forehead, looking down at me with loving eyes.

"You're safe now, Mama. Tomorrow is unknown, but today you're at home and you're safe. Just try to remember that." I nod, my head heavy with sleep and body numbing the pain of yesterday. She takes a deep breath, readying herself to continue.

"But this salve is gonna put you in a part of the Realm of Duality that will make you more... open. You'll be fully connected to your spirit and the ancestors. Bastets have trouble keeping themselves together when they're just scratching the surface in the Realm, but you'll be fully open and vulnerable to the spirits and the rawness of your powers. You have to remember everything you've been told — you're here, in your bed, in your human body in the world of the living. Do not forget that. Remember this, and you'll be okay. Just be strong."

She continues to say something, but I'm so tired from the events of the day that I start to drift off. I feel her fingers caress my forehead as I slip into oblivion, darkness enveloping me within its warm grasp.

Blood. That's the first thing I notice. The first thing my senses allow me to recognize. The tinny scent of blood permeating the air. It's dark so I can't see where I am, but wherever it is, it feels cool. And it reeks of the smell of blood. I feel my body, the weight settling into itself and I feel the presence of myself. Slowly my eyes adjust to the darkness and I'm able to make out figures, and discern textures in the surrounding space where I am. Wherever that is. I feel where my arms are, and lift my hands to look at them. I blink some more as I realize something weighty on my arms, something darker than my skin, and see them covered in blood. My heart races as I look up, blinking to settle my eyes to the darkness, and I see a large shadow across the ground. As I keep blinking, a dull light shines from above and, as I look up, I realize that it's stars lighting up the sky. The moon, which was hiding behind dark clouds, starts to reveal itself. Bit by bit, as it pulls itself from behind the clouds and its light reveals the landscape from which darkness was concealing, I realize that the shadow across the ground are bodies. Human bodies. Lots of them.

The moon fully comes out, and I watch in horror as the light fully reveals a multitude of black bodies lying on the ground. Covered and drenched in their own blood. Blood dripping from their mouths, holes in their abdomens and heads, and gashes in their throats and chests. The ground becomes stained with red. I walk into the crowd of bodies and look at the faces, but I don't recognize these people. They're barely wearing any clothes, and the clothes they are wearing look like rags, and dated — from before the 1900s. Their blood stains their clothes as some of them, with eyes wide open, stare at me with vacant eyes while others with eyes shut peacefully, silently scream with mouths agape. I start to hyperventilate as I look further and see more black bodies. I back away as I breathe rapidly, bumping into a tree trunk. As I feel the trunk behind me — to grasp onto something, anything — I look into the surrounding green that borders the ground and realize that I recognize where I am. It's the clearing from my dream.

I don't understand. I thought the Realm of Duality was supposed to bring me closer to my ancestors. This is just carnage, and the only person here to witness it is me. I turn into the tree to escape the scene, closing my eyes and leaning my head against the rough layer of the tree. I breathe in deeply and hear a deep noise — I jolt up suddenly, startled by the noise, but assume that there's just phlegm in my chest. I clear my throat and try to breathe normally again, calming myself and keeping my cool amidst the genocide behind me, but then I hear the noise again. A deep, guttural growl that's coming from outside of my body. Actually, from the other side of the tree. The growling continues, getting louder and deeper, and starts to move. I inch closer to the tree, scared that I might have just found the culprit for this mass murder, and inch in the opposite direction of where the sound is coming from. As the growling crawls behind the tree towards my right, I — as silently as I can — tiptoe to the left. I breathe through my nose and will my nerves to calm down so that my shallow breaths won't be heard. After a few moments the growling stops, and whatever is on the other side of the tree seems to disappear. I know better though — watching a bunch of horror movies, where the girl who looks like me ends up dying first, tends to teach you a lesson. I stoop to my knees and continue to crawl to the left. I slowly do one lap around the tree, making sure to keep my eyes to the ground and ahead as far as I can see to keep a safe distance from this unknown danger. But after a second lap of not seeing anything, I resolve that whatever was following me around the tree is gone. I slowly rise from all fours onto my knees and turn back towards my right, but stop abruptly when I come face-to-face with a black panther.

My body and everything inside it freezes; my heart, my lungs. I just kneel there in shock, both startled and terrified to be in front of this ferocious animal. The panther sits in its pouncing position, ready to jump reflexively. My heart thuds in my chest as it leans forward ever so slowly, its teeth bared in an intimidating smile. Its teeth glow in the moonlight and its pink snout wrinkles as its mouth widens ever larger. I slowly lower to the ground onto my hands and knees, accepting that this is the end for me. I mean, I may have some superhuman abilities but I don't know what good they'll do in front of a predator that can kill me in a second. I avert my eyes and look down to the ground, bowing my head until it's underneath its shoulders, and submit to its power. I feel its whiskers tickle my neck, and its warm breath float onto my skin, causing me to close my eyes in fear and shiver. My shoulders hunch as I await the biting pain of its teeth on the back of my neck, and prepare myself for the violent shake of my body to break my neck. But then — nothing. I slowly open my eyes, wondering how I'm still alive, and dare to raise my head. I see it looking down at me with the same menacing smile, but only looking. I look at it, breathing slowly even as my heart beats faster than a hummingbird's wings, and bow my head again. I don't know why — a weight, or a feeling, or a push from some spiritual force, maybe — but I bow my head instinctively. I hear the panther move — but instead of swooping down to end my life, it lays its head atop mine. Slowly, it glides its head along mine, from the top of my head down towards the base, and down onto my neck until it sweeps to the side and pushes my head back up. As I raise my head, the panther's head is now below mine, and it stays there. Waiting. I wonder what, as I look down at this majestically dangerous creature that rests under me. I slowly lower my head onto its head, unsure if this is what I should do, starting at the top and making my way down to its neck, and then sweeping my chin off its neck and quickly sit back up onto my knees — a healthy distance away from its teeth. Slowly it rises and sits on its haunches, looking at me docile, and without menace. It raises its paw and licks it, like a domestic house cat, while I just stare in disbelief. Is this real? I mean, in terms of my past perception of reality — no — but even in my present understanding of the Realm of Duality and the world I now live in — I still don't know. I cautiously look past it, to the carnage that lays behind it and the bodies that lay waste to the Earth — but instead find nothing but luscious green land and the moonlight casting its light on the ground. My mouth gapes in disbelief. I look at the panther, to the space where the bodies once laid behind it, and back to the panther. I widen my eyes in questioning, expecting the panther to answer because I mean, c'mon, crazier things are happening in this dream right now.

I look at the landscape — the clearing where I spoke to my mother in my last dream. The large tree trunk I chased the panther around is the one I now lean on, with the same leaves, breaks in the foliage, and clearing in the trees that allow the moonlight to break through, jogging my memory. I look to the panther, and the thought pops into my head that this may be my mother. Maybe whatever hurt all those people back there is still out here, and she's protecting me. But if that was true, then why hasn't she transformed into her human form? Surely she would've done that by now. The panther rises back onto its legs, and I lean back reflexively. My body still clocks that this is a life-threatening animal, not a house cat, and I'm not too keen on ending up like those people that were back there. It comes towards me and gently prods my face with its snout, tickling my nose with its whiskers as its slobber spits onto my face. I inch my face away and screw up my nose in disgust, to shield myself from its slobber, but it continues to prod my face until I stand up. Even then it doesn't stop butting me with its nose, now prodding my bum until I start walking towards the clearing. Still aware of the threat this animal poses, I obey, my breathing haggard and arms slightly outstretched to not pose any threat to it. Once I'm somewhere in the middle, with the moonlight shining directly onto my head, it finally stops prodding me and goes back towards the tree to collapse and lay peacefully. I just look at it — wondering what the hell is going on — and it just returns my blank stare with one of its own.

Suddenly the moonlight gets brighter, and I look up into the sky — but its light is blinding. I shield my eyes with my hand, looking away as the moonlight shines like a flashlight. I squeeze my eyes shut, and feel a hollow pain start to creep into my bones. The ache begins to get stronger, and I groan and sink to the ground as it starts to pang throughout my whole body. I feel my bones underneath my skin as the pain becomes a presence within them, and then I feel my bones begin to change — sharply cracking from the position they once held and moving to a new one. I collapse onto my side and breathe shakily as the pain continues to ache through my body — staring at the leaves and the ground as the moonlight continues to blind me from above, and the smell of dirt wafts into my nostrils. I look at the panther helplessly, but it continues to lick its paws in peace. I close my eyes and beg, silently, for the pain to end. And then I beg loudly with screams, pleading for the night to grant me escape from this pain. Finally, the bones underneath my skin stop moving, and I'm left with a dull ache reverberating through my body. After a few minutes pass by, I feel strong enough to rise onto my hands and knees. What the hell was that? I look at the panther, who looks back at me with the same annoying blank stare. It rises onto its legs and trots over to me — I continue to breathe haggardly from the pain as I look at it, annoyed by how docile this damn cat is. It slows when it reaches me, circling once around me and then continuing into a break in the foliage. I catch the hint, and slowly rise onto my legs and unwillingly follow it. As I watch its tail and follow behind, I slowly realize that I'm at eye level with the cat — as in, I'm at the same level. But I'm standing on my legs — actually, I'm on my hands and knees. Why did I think I had stood up just a second ago? Before I can answer my own question, we arrive at a small little pond, the musty smell of moss permeating the air, and a small break in the trees allowing the moon to cast a small ray of light onto the water. The panther walks up to the water's edge and sits on its hind legs, turning its head towards me — waiting. I come up behind it, still wary to be following this dangerous creature but — ultimately — submitting to the unknown. I come up beside the panther and look at it, as it points its snout down into the reflection in the water. I follow its gaze and see its reflection — and the reflection of another panther right beside it. I spin around, looking for another panther — sure that I've found the killer of all those people — but only find the trees and the ground. I turn back and look fully into the water, confused as to where this second panther came from. But as I look closer, into the eyes of the animal, I see a reflection of a twinkle — a twinkle of humanity, one that I've seen countless times staring into my bathroom mirror. The twinkle I see in my own eyes.

The panther is me. What the hell???

CHAPTER EIGHT

I gasp for breath as I shoot up from bed — sweat slick on my neck, and an outline of my head darkening my pillow. What. The. Hell. What the *hell* was that? That was some Stephen King, Twilight-having, Lion King, thriller-movie-type shit. I swing my legs over to the side of the bed, and grab the glass of water on my nightstand — now lukewarm, thanks to the early-rising sun shining through my window — and take a mighty inhale of the refreshing drink in one gulp. My hand that's holding the glass with a vice-like grip, begins shaking, and I carefully place the glass back on the nightstand and wring my hands. I continue to struggle to catch my breath, leaning over and hunching my back, with my eyes closed. Loni and Nellie never mentioned anything about what I just saw — all the blood, death, and destruction. How was that a connection to the spirit world? I didn't see my mother, or any other ancestors — I wasn't enlightened or shown any signs. Only death. Unless that was the sign the ancestors were showing me. In that case, I think I'd prefer no sign at all.

I slowly rise from bed and stumble — all the blood rushes to my head, and I realize how lightheaded I am. I blink my eyes as spotty darkness clouds my vision, and lift my head and take slow, deep breaths. I open my eyes and try to take in my surroundings, bringing myself back to Earth. That's my closet to my right, with clothes hanging from their hangers and shoes that are strewn all over the floor. I turn my head to the left — there are my desk and cabinet, with the office chair and plush white carpet underneath, and books piled on top of the white tabletop. I look a little to the left of that to see my laptop on the ground, and my backpack and pencil case laying carelessly not too far beside it. Man, I really have to be better with my things. My dresser sits right beside my bed — with all my lotions, deodorant, hair products and trinkets strewn on the top, and the drawers barely keeping the contents within their confines. This is my room. This is reality. This is what'll bring me back to a state of calm when all the larger-than-life otherness makes everything fuzzy. I take another deep breath and feel my heart calm to a state of relative normality.

After I feel like I won't faint, I move again towards the door and I'm surprised to find my body aching. My dream ended with a surprise twist — I turned into a black panther, a depiction of the very thing I've been scared to embrace on this journey of learning about my true nature. Foregoing the obvious irony, I wonder why my body actually hurts. It was a dream after all — although realistic and spiritual in nature, it was all a dream. I chuckle, realizing that me quoting Biggie Smalls offers even a little bit of humour in this crazy situation. Honestly, I need a little humour right now. Still, I wonder if the pain from my feline transformation in my dream actually transferred over into the real world, and it's more than just sleeping in the wrong position. If so, that's some pretty impressive spiritual shit right there. Then I remember my attack from last night, and the broken ribs that remain broken. I'm so dumb, no wonder my body's aching. Unlike last night, I don't have the pleasure of morphine to numb the pain of my attack — I have to endure it until Nellie can pick up my medication. I shuffle to the door, walking in an old-lady fashion to offset my premature aches and pains and open the door. I gasp sharply as a wide-eyed Nellie startles me, causing me to brace my chest with my hand — as any old-lady ought to do.

"Sorry," she apologizes sheepishly, as I look at her annoyed. "Sorry, I didn't mean to scare you. I just wanted to see you first thing — see how you were doin', y'know?"

"Yeah," I say exasperatedly, "I figured." I walk past her to the bathroom, Nellie following quickly behind me.

"So, how was it?" she asks with restrained excitement. Her eyes wide — with a sparkle and shine in them — resembling that of a kid on Christmas, and it's so adorable I can't help but smile.

"How was what?" I retort, feigning ignorance.

"The dream! Your connection to the Realm," she inches herself further into the bathroom, coming right behind my shoulder as I bend over to wash my face. "What happened? Did you see your mother? Was there a sign you didn't understand? Maybe I could help you interpret it. Were you scared? I bet you were scared —"

"Nellie! Take a breath and slow down man, I can't understand you."

"Sorry," she says, as I continue to cleanse my face. "It's just, this is your first induced visit to the Realm, and it can be overwhelming. Me myself, I never had to go to the Realm — only by chance in my dreams — but I might be able to help you out with some of the confusing bits. Our ancestors aren't really known for being straightforward."

"Yeah," I scoff, my voice gurgling from the tap water. "Tell me about it." I fumble with eyes closed, reaching towards my right for a towel on the suspended wall rack, and towel my face.

I reach into the cabinet for toner and moisturizer as Nellie continues, "I couldn't sleep last night. All I could think was if you were okay, if you were scared or confused, and I just wanted to be there with you. Be there for you. I kept getting up to check on you but chickened out when I got to the door. I knew that even if I could've been there, this is something that you needed to do on your own."

I look to Nellie and give her a warm smile. "I appreciate that," I say. I think back to the dream, the horrifying scene I was plagued with, and I start to feel weak. It was all so draining — being in a place of pure fear, and not knowing what was going on. And being so exposed to a realm of reality, of consciousness, that I don't fully understand; subjecting myself to a spiritual vulnerability that boggles my concepts of reality and confounds my understanding of the duality. It's all just... a lot. I lethargically moisturize my face, and Nellie's attentive face goes from excitement to concern.

"Hey," she says softly, "you okay?"

"Yeah," I say, not too convincingly, "yeah I'm just, y'know, a little shook."

"Shooketh?" she asks amused.

"Yeah," I laugh half-heartedly. "Shooketh." She looks at me, her eyes filled with concern, but deciding regardless to not push me further.

"Okay," she relents. "Well, later today, after school, you're gonna tell Loni and I about what happened in that dream. Whatever it was, no matter if you felt or saw anything important, we still need to know what happened. That's the only way we'll be able to figure out how to protect you. But for now, we'll head to the hospital and sign your release papers."

I nod, my eyebrows scrunching together in worriment. Nellie gives me a small smirk, making a move to leave but, suddenly, slapping me on the butt and yelling over her shoulder, "Now brush your junjo teeth before I faint from whatever died in your mouth."

"Cho man, leave me alone," I reply annoyed, but smiling still — secretly grateful for her neverending teasing.

Our sneakers squeak on the linoleum floors as we walk to the receptionist desk. I look from left to right sharply, like a prey anticipating the descent of a predator, and stay close behind Nellie who, in comparison, was the perfect picture of calmness. A doctor with a white coat walks out from a room just ahead of us, and I grab Nellie's arm tightly, my breath stopping in my throat. As the doctor turns to greet a nurse to his left, I see it's an Asian man with a sweet smile, and that I have nothing to fear from him. Nellie turns her head slightly to the side, whispering with her mouth, "*It's alright*," and I shakily inhale and nod. We walk to the reception desk and come face to face with the same nurse from yesterday morning.

"Hey Nel," says the nurse, smiling to reveal the crow's feet around her eyes.

"Hey Rupal," replies Nellie warmly. "Doing the graveyard shift again?"

"Is there any other?" she replies jokingly, with a slight Indian accent. "I swear, you'd think these people never knew that I worked after dawn." She lets out a jolly laugh, Nellie joining her briefly before smiling.

"What can I do for you?" Rupal asks.

"It's so funny," Nellie says laughing, with a carefree smile on her face, probably to offset the fact that what she's about to say isn't really funny. "Jamila got herself all worked up and came home last night — getting on her sprained leg and taking the TTC in the middle of the night! This girl will be the death of me, man, but you have to forgive her. You see, she doesn't know about the release papers that needed to be signed, and guardian signatures being needed and all that stuff. I gave her hell last night, believe-you-me, ain't that right J?" She looks to me expectantly and I nod apologetically, playing along with Nellie's Oscar-winning performance.

"But she said she just needed to be home, to be around people who love her. After what happened to her, you can imagine why she'd think that."

"Oh, yes dear," Rupal says, softly bobbing her head in understanding, "I do. But she still shouldn't have left Nellie — it's against hospital protocol, and against the doctor's orders. If she took public transit then she would've been putting weight on her foot, which is exactly what Dr. Aida told her *not* to do. And that's just the minor injuries — I mean, Nellie, her ribs! That girl shouldn't even have been able to lift more than a few meters off her pillow with broken ribs like that, let alone get on the TTC and trek all the way to North York. And I'm surprised she was able to get there without fainting; those harsh lights in the stations are a lot for a person without a concussion to handle. I can only imagine her head hurting like hell."

"Trust me, I know Ru — but when this girl is on a mission, nothing gets in her way." She smiles and shrugs, as if my 'steel will' were out of her control. Nellie's charm is undeniable, and I can already see it beginning to loosen Rupal up.

"I have too much of a soft spot for you, Nel," Rupal says exasperatedly, with a small smile on her face as she reaches down below into a cabinet for, as I see when she sits back up, a stapled stack of papers.

"Here are the release forms. Dr. Aida is probably going to give you hell for this, but something tells me you'll be able to work your way out of it."

"Don't I always?" Nellie asks coyly. Rupal chuckles warmly, placing the form in front of Nellie and reaching in front of her for a blue pen. As Nellie begins reading the paper, Rupal starts reciting the script.

"She has to ice her ribs every night and keep her foot elevated whenever possible for the next two weeks. You can get a new set of crutches from Elaine after she's finished her break," she looks to me before continuing, "and make sure you use them." I nod, obeying her command, and she gives me a single nod, happy that I've listened to her.

"She already has her pain medication prescription written — it's attached to her chart, and you can get it from the pharmacy on the first floor. Cho should be working today, but if he's not, just tell whoever's working that Rupal sent you, and it's a rush order. You won't need a refill, but make sure when you pick it up to have your insurance and her health card ready — just so there isn't any trouble. Got it?"

"Got it," Nellie and I reply. Rupal gives a single nod again, content with our attentiveness, and starts typing — getting back to work on whatever she was working on before we interrupted her. Nellie flips through the form at a record pace — clearly familiar with this form already, and knowing where to sign and what to sign without even needing to more than skim the pages. I start to look elsewhere as she finishes signing the paper, looking at the passing doctors, nurses, and patients that bring life to the hospital — ironically, while challenging death. It's a real brain teaser. They rush through the hallways — some with file folders and tablets in their hands, others pulling gurneys and carts. Patients shamelessly exposing their untied hospital gowns, and others walking with their IV unit tagging along for the ride. I people watch — a favourite pastime of mine — and note the smell of the air. Antiseptic soap and that clinical smell. The one that all hospitals and doctors offices around the world have. A smell that doesn't really smell like anything else, but if you did smell it you would instantly know how to describe it as that clinical waiting room smell. I hate that smell — it always made me feel like I was in a place that was too clinical — too cold and unfeeling.

I look straight down the hallway, at nothing really, and notice a door towards the left end of the hallway opens. A man walks out in a white coat, and my breath stops cold in my throat. He stops to stand in the middle of the hallway, facing me and sending signals of threatening dominance from his presence to mine. He looks at me with a blank face — terrifying in its blankness of emotion, yet, somehow, being full of it as well. My heart starts pounding, and my legs turn to jelly — but I keep myself upright. He steps forward and slowly walks towards me, all the while looking at me with an unblinking stare. He holds a folder in his left hand — I notice this, strangely, because I realize that his arms aren't moving. Usually people move their arms when they walk; some with a gangly stride, and others swing their arms with purpose and grace. But his just doesn't move — completely still in his emptiness, he walks with no humanity. Just mechanic movement. A machine, more than a man. He comes closer towards us and I just stand there, frozen in place from fear. I can't believe he's here in broad daylight. He was unconscious when I left him — surely someone would've found him lying there, and called the authorities or something. But he's here — undeniably so. Nellie continues to fill out the form, unaware that a threat is looming closer and closer to us; and, frozen in my place, I can't seem to move to signal that I'm in distress. I just stand there, succumbing to the vice-like grip of uncertainty. But then Nellie stops writing and, with her head still down, looks up into an empty space. Her arms tensed — barely enough to notice, but I can since I'm so close to her. She knows the Toubab is here.

He walks up towards us, and Rupal greets him. "Good morning Dr. Churchill, how are you doing today?"

"Oh I'm well Ms. Dasminder, thank you," he replies monotonously. "I see you've found our little jailbreaker." With that Nellie looks up to regard our new visitor, looking at him with polite regard.

"Yes," Rupal says. "She took the TTC to her aunt's house in the middle of the night! Can you believe it? In her condition!"

"Yes," he replies, all the while looking at me with unblinking eyes. "That is quite the marvel. In your condition you shouldn't be able to move more than a few feet from your bed; although, I wouldn't recommend that either."

Nellie looks at me — she sees my distress and, quick as a whip, her maternal instinct kicks in. She discreetly moves in front of me, covering me from Churchill's view, and, finally, I can breathe. She looks up at him, her head not even coming up to his chin — but she manages to meet that distance with her strong stance.

"Yes it was quite the scare," Nellie says. "But given the circumstances I can't help but understand her motives — she just wanted to be safe."

"Well what could be safer than Toronto General?" Churchill asks, faking good-natured fun in his tone. God, he's such a douche. "She has medical professionals with sage advice and all the necessary medication and procedures to heal her of her condition."

"Yes," Nellie replies, "well, she also has me. Her injuries are fairly routine, and it's nothing a few pain pills and TLC can't fix — and that can be done from the comfort of her own home." Dr. Churchill looks at Nellie; he just looks at her. No smile, no anger, no giveaway as to what he's thinking. A true robot — showing no emotions whatsoever. He stands taller and straightens his head, looking down at Nellie over his bird-nose.

"Well, you are her legal guardian; you have complete licence over her medical care. However, I believe it to be in Jamila's best interest to go through with the test — to get to the bottom of her scans, and somehow explain her..." He looks at me behind Nellie, dead in the eyes as he finishes, "anomaly."

Nellie inches her head to the side to hide me once again, looking at Churchill with wide eyes and a fake smile. God, I love this woman and her passive-aggression. "I appreciate your concern, Dr. Churchill, but we will not be going through with the neural test. I've spoken with Dr. Aida — and as long as we closely monitor Jamila and her performance, and how she functions, then it should be good enough. If there are any red flags that give me a reason to worry, then I will contact Dr. Aida — her *primary physician*."

Churchill's nostrils flare, and his hands tighten on the beige folder he's holding. Rupal remains oblivious to this exchange, continuing to type and finish her tasks. She reaches down to grab something from the printer and effectively interrupts the tension — handing a prescription to Nellie.

"This is Jamila's pain medication prescription," Rupal says. "Try to get down there ASAP so you can see if Cho is there, and make sure she takes 2 pills a day six hours apart until they're finished."

Nellie continues to stare down Churchill as she takes the paper from Rupal gently. "Thank you, Rupal," she says. She folds it lethargically as she slightly cocks her head, her eyes never leaving Churchill's. He continues to look at her as well, his hand still tightly clutching the beige folder. Two foes in a stand-off, each the complete antithesis of each other. Nellie exudes power, dominance and emotion in her eyes as she stares Churchill down, while he looks at her with eyes void of emotion, his face empty of expression and life. Finally, he straightens and looks towards Rupal with a smile.

"Thank you, Rupal, I hope you have a lovely day." She smiles at him coyly, waving her hand at him to wave off his flattery, as he walks away. Again his arms don't move, and his mechanical movement pushes a final shudder through my body as he turns left down the hall. I release a breath I didn't know I had been holding, as Nellie turns to me with a tense look on her face. Her mouth is screwed tight and her nostrils flare, but her eyes remain calm. But I know she's anything but calm.

"That guy's an asshole," she says.

"Tuh!" I exclaim. "Tell me about it." I look past her shoulder after Churchill, not seeing him and instead being graced with a Churchill-less hallway. Nellie places her hand on the side of my face and makes me look at her — she looks at me with a supportive smile, and I exhale shakily and return it with my own.

"Stay here," she says. "I'm just going to see Elaine about that new set of crutches, okay?" I nod in reply — she nods once and turns, walking down the hallway and peeking into a room on her right. As she grabs my crutches, I lean on the counter and look at Rupal. She's a kind woman; she smells like she had just cooked something delicious, and her round spectacles don't hide her kind eyes. She sees me looking at her and smiles kindly — a very sweet response to realizing you're being watched.

"You in a lot of pain?" she asks.

"Well, it's definitely more than I've ever experienced before," I reply sarcastically. She chuckles as I continue, "But it's tolerable. I've never had any broken bones before. The worst injury I've had is when I got my wisdom teeth removed, and that's not even an injury!"

"Yeah, routine surgeries don't really fall in that category," she says jokingly.

I laugh as I reply, "No, but that's the most pain I've been in. I mean, I guess you could say cramps too, but that's a whole other type of pain that has its own category."

"Oh, tell me about it," she says. "The one good thing about menopause is that I don't have to deal with my uterus warping in on itself every month. 40 years was enough for me, thank you very much."

We laugh as we share a common plight: period cramps. Man, there really is no other pain like having your uterus contract in on itself and disintegrate its inside. Well, there's labour — but luckily, I won't have to experience that for a very long time. And even then it's only during the delivery; if I had to experience labour every month for the next 40 years, I would just remove my uterus. There's no point in even trying anymore — I'd just give up. I look and see Nellie walking with a shiny new pair of crutches, waving goodbye to a woman in the doorway of the room she just left.

"Alright," she says when she walks up to me. She plants the crutches firmly in front of me, a funny smile on her face. "Now you don't have to hop everywhere — use these crutches as much as possible, even on the stairs. And when you're in class, make sure to keep your foot elevated. Get an extra chair and put it in front of you, and if you can find a blanket in the lost and found, put that underneath your ankle to give it some cushion. Okay?"

"Okay," I reply, placing the crutches underneath my armpits. We wave goodbye to Rupal and head to the elevator.

"Okay," Nellie says, turning to me in the driver's seat as we stay parked in front of the school. "Here's what's going to happen. You're gonna go in there — everyone's gonna wonder why you're on crutches, that's just human nature. But the chances of someone asking you are slim — on the off-chance they do, you keep it short and sweet. You were attacked on your way home from the convenience store and have some injuries, and a sprained ankle from twisting it after trying to escape. No one needs to know more than that — the details will only raise more questions."

"And what do I tell Michael? He thinks that I should be taking a test to make sense of my scan results. What am I supposed to say when he asks why I'm not neck deep in a machine right now?"

"Do your best to avoid the subject," she replies. "Michael is smart, but he doesn't know everything — simply tell him that with my insistence, we cancelled the test until further notice. Yousef said himself that you were functioning properly, and Michael knows you better than anyone; if there were any serious cause to worry, then deciding to not take the test would be more of an issue. But you function well — better than a lot of kids your age — and he knows you well enough to know there's nothing to worry about. Just try to push that as much as you can."

I nod reluctantly. I'm worried — I never lie to Michael, and even when I do he can immediately call out my bullshit. How am I going to do this? I open the door, struggling to stand up from the low seat of the car — my ribs protest against my stomach crunching, and I silently groan. A couple of students walking up the steps turn to me upon hearing, and I nonchalantly smile to offset any curiosity. Nellie grabs my crutches from the backseat and walks over to me, helping me place them under my arms and guiding me up the steps to the front doors. We go at a snail's pace, my ribs outcrying with every step, and my ankle groaning from the pressure of my body weight. We finally stop in front of the double doors — Nellie and I look at each other, and we exhale slowly simultaneously. We chuckle at our tension, and I look through the doors into the empty hallway; class has already started, and I'm a little bit late. The emptiness of the hallway makes me shudder — the loneliness of such a vast space, that extends far past where my eyes can see. What symbolism.

"Hey," Nellie says, causing me to look at her. "You got this — just treat it as any normal day, and take it one step at a time."

"Literally," I say, looking down at my sprained ankle. She chuckles, and replies, "Yeah." Her face turns more serious as she places her hand on my shoulder, gripping it with a tender yet firm hand. I nod, understanding her support that emanates from her grip — she slides it behind my shoulder and gently pushes me towards the door, opening it for me so that I can enter freely. I crutch down the hallway, heading to my locker. The first period is already almost over, so I can put my books in my locker — I won't need them in history class, we still have to finish *Amistad*. I groan mentally, not at all enthused to have to sit in front of that gory display of my history — especially after narrowly escaping it not even 12 hours ago. I jump as the bell rings, signalling the end of the first period — not even a minute later, the hallway becomes congested with students ready to leave class. Just as I slam my locker doors, I catch sight of Michael coming down the stairs near the double doors. Gangly as ever, he walks down the hallway towards me. He doesn't see me right away and just walks with a pleasant small smile on his face, causing me to smile in return. Sometimes I forget to stop and just *be*; to appreciate all the gifts life gives me. And one of those gifts is Michael — I'm so lucky to have him as a friend. He's just so himself, and that's not something a lot of teens our age can say. He's funny, quirky, sarcastic, weird, and unapologetically himself. He's been there with me through my lowest lows and highest highs, and I'm glad to say I was there for him in those times too. As he notices me, his eyes widen in recognition and he smiles. Throwing me a quick nod, he quickens his pace — but, as he realizes that I'm not in the same condition I was in a couple of days ago, his pace slows and his face turns to one of confusion. I should be getting ready for my test right about now — and he's probably wondering why I'm not, and why I'm here. Ugh, here we go.

"Hey," he says slowly.

"Hey," I say happily, with a little too much enthusiasm. I fake a smile, leaning on my crutches like everything's normal. He eyes me up and down, his face still screwed in confusion.

"Uh, what are you doing here? Shouldn't you be getting ready for that test?"

"Oh yeah, that," I say, feigning nonchalance. "Nel actually decided not to go through with it. I mean, Dr. Aida said it wasn't absolutely necessary anyway, and if there's no indication in my behaviour that would suggest anything's wrong, then the test is just a precaution. And you know Nel — any reason to skip out on school isn't a good one, so she just cancelled it and said to take it easy. But I still have to go to school," I say laughing. Michael laughs with me, still unconvinced.

"Yeah, that sounds Nellie," he agrees. "But that other doctor — the stiff— was pretty adamant about you taking that test, and he is a specialist in over-active auditory and visual cortices. Which is crazy that he was even around to begin with right when Dr. Aida took that scan." I nod, secretly responding, "*Yes, it is odd. But it actually wasn't a coincidence at all — because he was deliberately looking for me, and posed as a doctor just so he could use me for my powers until I'm of no value to him.*" I don't say any of this, of course, and instead, shrug in reply.

"Dr. Aida was my primary physician and Nellie's my legal guardian — the test wasn't necessary so we just didn't do it. But what *is* necessary is this movie I have to finish watching in history class," I say, desperately trying to change the subject. "We're watching *Amistad* and it's making me so uncomfortable, but then everyone else is totally fine. We're so desensitized to this stuff that no one even reacts how they should to such a blatant violation of humanity."

"Yeah," Michael scoffs, walking over to his locker. I crutch behind him as he continues, "People think the length of time between events makes it long enough to not be affected by it — but they love to tout events as a crutch to rest their bigotry on." He and I look at my crutch and we both laugh, his pun not evading us. He grabs my backpack in one hand while he carries his books in his other, and walks with me in the direction of my history class. I smile in thanks, and he smiles back.

"Tell me about it," I continue. "9/11. The Holocaust. All terrible events that still affect millions of people to this day, but somehow slavery has to be accepted because it *'wasn't as bad as it seemed'* back then? Puh-lease!"

"Because those things happened to other people from others, but slavery was in our front yard — ugly and open for everyone to see, and that is what makes it hard for people to accept. The notion that their history is at fault for ours — such a claim is a threat to their self-image of goodness."

"Preach," I say. We arrive in front of the classroom door, and he hands me my backpack. "Aight, I'll see you at lunch period."

"Yeah," he agrees. "I'm actually gonna buy lunch today — it's pizza day in the caf." I hum in understanding as his face gets excited before he continues, "So I'll meet you by the line, okay?"

"Okay, cool," I respond. I throw him a quick dap and he goes back from whence he came, while I find my seat. I carefully maneuver myself between the close aisles of desks — I find my unassigned-assigned seat and place my backpack on the back of the chair. I look to the right corner of the room, where a bunch of spare chairs usually lie haphazardly, and spot a chair and, lucky for me, a small little pillow. The student government kids must've left it in here this morning after their weekly meeting. I place my crutches to the side of my desk and limp to the corner, grabbing a chair in one hand and the pillow in the other. I place it beside my desk and sit down, delicately placing my leg in the middle of the cushion, and apologizing silently to passing students for blocking their way. Ms. Boykin, who is always the first in class, sits at her desk looking over a stack of papers. She clucks in disapproval as she aggressively writes on a paper — I grimace, pitying the poor soul who has to receive that grade when it's time.

"Okay," she says, closing the duo-tang folder and stands up. "Today we're going to finish watching *Amistad*. I hope you still have your fill-in-the-blank sheets from the last class, as the majority of the back page will be from this last half of the movie." Several students, including myself, reach into our bags for the sheet in reply. She nods once and moves to the computer to resume the movie. As Joseph Cinque — the main character — pops up on the screen, that general feeling of discomfort thickens my throat, and pools to the pit of my stomach as Ms. Boykin turns off the light. The movie resumes, and I sink into my seat as I force myself to pay attention. I fill in the blanks as the movie plays on, and find myself faced with a generic story that seems to repeat like a broken record: black people fighting for their rights, being denied, and yet achieving it. Not through their own efforts however, as this would substantiate the validity of their actions. No — but rather by the 'heroic' efforts of white freedom fighters. I never really understood that — how they could be freedom fighters when they never had to fight for freedom. If anything, they were returning freedom that was stolen from the marginalized when they took it in the first place. Man, I thought gaslighting was a modern idea — but the damn thing's been happening since the dawn of imperialism.

The scene cuts to the 'slaves' working when, suddenly, my vision clouds. I blink my eyes to clear my vision, shaking my head to get rid of the worms that seep into my eyesight, but the room continues to blur. All I can see is the screen, and the movie playing out. Cinque is yelling, clearly upset, and his voice booms into my eardrums. The room around me seems to fog up, as if like a memory, and then warp — like the space is turning in on itself. I continue to look at the screen and the room around me sinks towards it, like a black hole pulling my surroundings in. Everyone around me is oblivious from what I can see. I'm still looking at the screen, but out of my periphery I can see everyone acting with a degree of normalcy, with no indication that they're aware of what I'm seeing. And then suddenly, I'm not in the room anymore. I'm no longer sitting — I'm standing on dirt ground, still in my shirt and jeans, looking down at my white sneakers as dirt scuffs up the soles. I'm standing normally, with no pain in my ankle, and the pain in my ribs is gone. I look up confused and scared, wondering where I am, when I see a man stopped down in front of me. He's hiding behind an embankment, peering over to look to what's ahead of us. A grand mansion that sits a ways away from us — with thick pillars holding up the numerous stories, and a wooden porch from which a man with his stance wide stands. The man looks over the scene before him, holding a gun at the plains of black slaves hunched over in servitude. My breath hitches in my throat as I watch the black people working in the burning sun — their excuse for clothing barely covering their skin, revealing the marks, lashes, and abrasions to show its ugly face to us. Some have baskets on their back, others in their hands, others having baskets and bags sitting beside them, as they hack at sugar cane with a ferocious strength. From here I can feel their fatigue, their weariness, their pain. And it makes me sick. I look to the man in front of me who is still stopped, clearly hiding — thinking that I'm more of an open target than him, I stoop down quickly and come behind him — giving us some space because I still don't know where I am or who this is.

"Hey," I whisper to him. He ignores me, and continues to look at the plantation with anger and fear.

"Hey," I say a bit louder, being careful not to be too loud to attract further attention, but he still doesn't hear me. I wave my hand to get his attention, waving it in front of his face even, but the man looks on. He can't see me. He can't hear me. He doesn't know that I'm here. His dark skin is shiny, slick with sweat and luminous underneath the sunlight — and I'm just now realizing how unforgiving this sunlight is, because it is hot. Like walking-on-the-sun level hot. The trees around us are thick and full — not evergreens or spruce like we have in Canada, but more tropical and bountiful. Everywhere is green, with flowers dotting the green with pink, yellow, and purple colours. I look back at him as he looks forward, his eyes yellow-ish rather than white, and the darkness of his eyes fierce in its intensity. His nose is broad and his cheekbones high, with muscles poised underneath his skin that are ready for any command he's yet to state.

"We aave to help dem," he says with a thick Jamaican accent.

"What?" I ask, confused.

He continues, "We caah jus' leave dem eere to die. Some ah dem won't even live 'til mawnin, we aave tuh do somethin!"

"And we will," replies a deep voice. I whirl around to find a woman come up beside him, her body turned towards him so I can't see her face. She stoops slightly behind him, placing her hand on his shoulder in a firm grip. She wears a white headwrap and barely any clothing — only her chest and her butt covered by a thin white fabric. It covers one shoulder and crosses over her chest and back, and a skirt covers her bottom halfway down her thighs, but the rest of her body exposes her shiny dark skin. Her feet are covered in a sort of sandal, and are weathered to the point of being unrecognizable. She has muscles that are so distinct not even a gym rat could get as taut as her — she also has scars all over her. On her arms, along her thighs, and as she comes closer to the man I can see her entire back covered in old and fresh scars. Her taut fingers pressed against the dirt as she leans forward, her other hand still on the man's shoulder. They both stoop down a little lower, making sure that they're not seen.

"We aave to be smart about dis," she continues. "If we go in now we'll get cut down by the oversee'a. We won't mek it back to di village, Quao."

"But if we go now we can at least save some ah dem — the ones closest to us. The white devil won't mek it to dem in time, and we can escape from di dogs wit' yuh by our side."

"It's a risk," she says, her deep voice booming with authority. "An unnecessary one. I'm not tekin' that chance. We come back at nightfall, and we'll aave more backup — and more chance of savin' more lives. Now come on Q, we aave to secure the food for di next fortnight."

She turns and stands up with her back stooped, walking back into the trees behind us while the man — Quao — stays a moment longer. He looks at the slaves, hacking under the burning sun and pushing through their fatigue, with a look of despair in his eyes. His mouth is fixed in anger, and his muscles are pulled tight from his restraint, but he finally turns around and follows the woman back into the trees. I never saw her face. Being alone, so close to a plantation scares me, and I quickly follow them back into the trees. I can hear them slicing through the leaves and I struggle to keep up, using my arms to sweep back large leaves and keep the woman's head in my eyesight. But the white headscarf begins to fade farther away from me, and my surroundings fog and warp in towards her and the man's body. Suddenly, I feel a push and I'm back in my seat — sitting in class with my leg elevated and my pencil in my hand, poised to fill in the next blank. I exhale sharply, looking right and left in confusion. A student beside me notices and scrunches her eyebrows, wondering why I'm freaking out. I pull myself together and duck my head down, pretending to fill in the blanks — she shrugs and goes back to her paper, ignoring me and my panic session. What the hell was that? Was that another episode? Another transition into the Realm of Duality? My first episode with Michael was during the day too, but that was a premonition — this looked like something that had already happened. And a very long time ago. The man and the mystery woman looked like they were on a mission, but I don't know why that mission was important for me to see. I look back to the screen to see *Amistad* playing once again — Cinque is on a boat, and text plays over his face. He regained his freedom and went back home — only to find his wife and child sold into slavery, and most of his village deserted. Finally the movie ends, with 20 minutes left in class to spare. Ms. Boykin walks to the back of the class and turns the lights on, all of us squinting our eyes from the harshness of the lights.

"Okay," she says, clapping her hands once. "I hope you all were paying attention because that sheet is worth 5%." She clasps her hands behind her back and walks slowly to her seat, looking at us as she continues, "Furthermore, you will have a paper that will discuss the events of the film and find specific ties to events in the Atlantic slave trade. Find specific time periods where rebellions, trends, and bans in the slave trade occurred, and relate it to Amistad." She stops, now beside me — she looks down at me, briefly glancing at my crutches before looking at me with a polite, yet forced, smile.

"I trust you all will be able to more than competently complete this assignment, and I look forward to any further insight you are able to provide." She leans closer to me, lowering her voice to speak only to me. "Please come see me when class is over." I nod hesitantly, as she quickly leans back up and continues walking to her desk.

"For the remainder of the class, you may get started on your next reading. It will be chapter eight, pages 325 to 342. Next class please come prepared for our discussion on Napoleon's early life, as this will be taken from the reading."

Kids reluctantly pull out their textbooks, while others towards the back of the class pull out their phones or talk in their groups. With no books with me, and with no one to text but Michael — who wouldn't answer anyway, because Advanced Calculus is his safe space and I wouldn't dare interrupt — I sit and doodle in the margins of my sheet. I draw the shape of an eye — no matter what, I can always draw a decent eye. I shade in the iris and the pupils, drawing in veins and lashes, and shading in the corner of the eye. After a few minutes I stop, satisfied with my work — and then, *blink.* I stare at the eye, doing a double take in disbelief — but then, *blink.*

I didn't imagine it. I'm not going crazy. Well, that's still left undetermined, but in this instance I'm not. The eye is *blinking* at me — no, it's a single eye, so actually, it's more like it's winking at me. I quickly look around me, wondering if anyone else saw this — but everyone is busy with their own thing, and I alone wonder if my eyes are starting to see things. What if there is some truth to Dr. Aida's scan? I mean, being a Bastet explains all of it; but what if the stress of all of this is getting to me? What if I am susceptible to those disorders he was talking about?

I shake my head and instead pull out my phone, going to some college websites and scrolling through the lists of undergraduate programs. With my love for school, I honestly want to learn as much as I can — but with Nellie alone, and my measly summer jobs, our savings are meager at best. Thanks to our provincial premier, government grants are few and far between, and loans are more readily available — which means more money that I'd have to pay back. I'm interested in the history program at Ryerson University, but the Environmental and Social Justice program at York is so appealing. I really want to pick a program that speaks to me, and nothing is more in line with my beliefs than achieving equality for all. The program at York is impressive — I'd be able to work in community organizations, environmental groups, even art agencies; but there's something about history that just makes me warm on the inside. I scroll through a few other programs before the bell rings, signalling the five-minute break in between class. Everyone gets up to leave but I take my time; staying behind to talk to Ms. Boykin. What a treat. I hop up and pack my things away, grabbing my crutches and awkwardly walking to Ms. Boykin's desk. She sits behind her desk with her hands clasped on top, her posture straight as an arrow, and her small smile fake as a reality show.

"Ms. Freeman, how are you doing?" she asks, looking to my sprained ankle. "That looks like a serious injury."

"Oh, yeah, I'm okay," I reply nonchalantly. "Just got into a little ruff-and-tough with some neighbours, no big deal."

"Ah," she says, a fleeting look of disapproval passing over her face. "Well, I called you back to discuss your report. Yours was one of the first I graded and, I have to say, I'm disappointed." I scrunch my eyebrows, confused.

"Disappointed? May I ask why?"

"Well, the purpose of the assignment was to relate *one* event from the Civil Rights Movement to a fairly recent event — instead, you related the assassination of MLK to the deaths of Ferguson activists and then went off on a tangent, relating it to the voices of black women in the feminist movement."

"Yeah," I say. "I —"

"Yes," she corrects quickly. I stop, slightly taken aback by her coldness.

"Sorry," I say, "*Yes*. I wanted to reveal the deaths of black women's voices in the feminist movement, and how their perspective is treated as a purely racial issue when actually it's a combination of the two. The two can't be separated, but people try to — to minimize the role that race plays, even though it plays a monumental role in the treatment of women of colour. I thought it was a good correlation to the MLK assassination — because his message, along with himself, was murdered in the name of a message that was considered more 'in line' with the general public. Even though it was really to mitigate the threat it posed to their message because it was a multifaceted perspective that would cloud the effect of theirs."

"Yes, I gathered that from your writing." She turns a page and clears her throat, reciting:

> The murder of the black female experience can be seen as similar to the murder of Martin Luther King Jr.: an assassination of a voice and perspective that threatens the 'right white' propaganda of a supposed 'American life.' It was a strategic choice — to mitigate the risks that a message like ours would pose, and was nothing more than a violation of human diversity and a stifling of multifaceted perspectives.

She looks back up at me, a disappointed look on her face. She says, "I appreciate your enthusiasm for the assignment, but my directions were very clear. This was added fluff that was unnecessarily brought to an assignment that, otherwise, would've gotten you an exceptional grade. But you went off on so many tangents it took away from the message that should've been told and was not what was required."

"I did do what was required," I counter hotly. "I related it to the Ferguson assassinations —"

"Which is another thing, Ms. Freeman," she interrupts. "The deaths of those activists in Ferguson are not confirmed as hate crimes. Ferguson is a place where a lot of crime occurs, and the deaths of those activists may have come at a strenuous time, but you cannot claim they were assassinations."

"Ms. Boykin," I say annoyed, "to think that would be naive."

"Excuse me," she says offended.

"*I said it would be naive to think that.* It was very clear that the tension in Ferguson was tightly wound — police were banging up against those activists like they were a terrorist threat, when all they were doing was protesting the death of Mike Brown. And then several activists suddenly turn up dead? With no witnesses and no indication that anyone in the neighbourhood would have any motive to kill them? It was a deliberate attempt to silence their activism — and that is exactly what happened with MLK. Everyone knew that it was because of his activism, but it was denied as a credible reason for the longest time. And it's still debated whether law enforcement was behind it — even though there's plenty of evidence that suggests they have motives and would have cause to assassinate him. So yes, Ms. Boykin, it *would* be naive to think that; because you would be willingly falling back into a safety net that likes to think activism doesn't put a target on your back. A target that law enforcement has been practicing on for decades. And that target reaches into more than just race — it pervades gender and sex, sexual orientation and every nook and cranny in between. So I genuinely do not think that I added an unnecessary element. If anything, I think I had the guts to shed light on something that kept getting swept under the rug."

Ms. Boykin fixes her mouth, clearly annoyed with me and trying to hold back any words that are most likely brewing in her mind. Ms. Boykin never really took much of a liking to me — every chance she gets she debates my stance in a report, and always talks to me so curtly and short. All my previous history teachers talked me up — saying how much effort I put in and how impressed they were of me, and I guess she got tired of hearing it. Maybe she thinks it was all talk — or maybe she wants to think that, and doesn't want my reputation that once preceded to be true. She takes a deep breath, clasping her hands once again.

"Be that as it may," she says tightly, "this class is not a soapbox for your ideas, Ms. Freeman. It is a place to learn history and do your assignments and tests to the best of your ability — and as your teacher, I believe your best is yet to come. You get a 70%."

I widen my eyes in disbelief, looking at her for a moment — searching for her justification, but only finding complete and utter nonsense. She looks down and closes the folder, organizing it amongst the other reports to end our conversation. I nod curtly, upset with the grade and her limited view, and quietly pick up my things and leave.

I crutch towards the cafeteria, showing an apologetic face to passing students for being in their way. Canadians really are too nice, eh? We're always apologizing, even if someone else bumped into us. And saying excuse me has become so ingrained in our vocabulary you'd swear it was permanently etched on the tips of our tongues. Take now for instance — I'm walking slower than everyone else, but for good reason. *I'm on crutches*. But we're also from the city of Toronto, and if you're not moving face-paced, you're not moving. So I apologize as students walk swiftly past me, rushing their way into the cafeteria line to take advantage of the pizza day before it becomes no-more-pizza day. I stand to the side of the door, readjusting the straps of my backpack on my shoulders while looking for Michael. If the boy loves anything more than festival it's pizza. He can't get enough of it; one time we ordered pizza and we got a half-and-half, and he ate half of my half! My side was normal pepperoni and cheese, and his was the works: olives, onions, peppers, anchovies, sardines and... pineapple. He thinks his love for pizza absolves him of his blasphemous act of putting pineapple on pizza, but it doesn't. We can argue about it until we're blue in the face — he thinks pineapple tastes great on pizza, and I think he's insane. If he wants to have soggy fruit on top of tomato sauce and cheese then that's his prerogative — but I'd prefer to have my sanity and taste buds. I look down the line of students, looking for a shaved head and a lanky frame. I see several teens in assorted attire, some texting and others talking to their friends, along with bored-looking servers aimlessly handing out the pizza with a look of vacancy in their eyes. To be fair, if I had to handle a bunch of rowdy teenagers on the most popular food day of the week I'd be a little detached too.

Finally, I see a bony shoulder poke out from the line towards the front. He's doing that thing where he shuffles from foot-to-foot — he must have to use the bathroom but didn't want to risk the chance of missing out on the goods. I pull out my phone to text him.

'👀.'

He turns around in the line, looking for a few moments in the crowd before spotting me by the doors. He smiles and throws me a quick head nod before turning back around — a few seconds pass before I see the bubbles pop up on my screen.

'Wassup?'
'You wasted no time getting in line 😒.'
'Nah man, I'm getting the works if it kills me.'
'LOL. I'll get us a table while you pay.'
'Okay, cool.'

I put my phone in my back pocket and crutch forward, looking for a table with a spot big enough for both of us. I would go to our spot, but Michael usually likes to go for seconds on pizza day so the closer to the line we are, the better. I finally find one on the other side of the caf, near the windows, and start to crutch over. When I'm about halfway there, I turn back to look to see how far Michael is in the line. He's now holding a red tray with a loaded pizza, soda, and some fries with ketchup all overtop. He must've gotten those for me — the cafeteria fries are one of the best things they serve, and ketchup squeezed all overtop is just how I like it. I smile and continue to the table, placing my backpack on the side where Michael will sit, and put my crutches to the side. A group of basketball kids sits a little ways away from me, jabbing each other and laughing about something I must've missed. They're pushing each other jokingly, laughing at each other falling over and taking delight in childish fun. I roll my eyes; if there's one thing that sucks about the basketball kids, is that they only care about one thing. Basketball. And parties, but mostly basketball. They loudly talk and laugh, some of the guys pushing and joking — getting in the way of some students trying to get by. They're all over the place, and don't have a care in the world how loud they're being — but the entire cafeteria is loud with conversations, so what's the hurt in having theirs too right? Across the room, Michael pays and makes his way over, holding the tray a ways away from him so he doesn't accidentally spill anything. When he's about halfway to the table, two of the basketball kids continue to push each other — trying to topple the other on the floor. When Michael is just passing them, one of them pushes the other so forcefully that he bumps into Michael. And he bumps into him hard. Michael's feet slip behind him as his entire body shoots forward — his face becomes shocked, and the tray slips from his hands. The guy that bumped into him shouts an expletive and rushes forward to try and catch him, and the kid that pushed him stands there in surprise. I shoot forward with my hand outstretched, my shock jumping to high gear as my friend is about to crash to the floor. A feeling surges through my body and a pulse reverberates through my arm; I feel the room beginning to slow, time moving like dripping molasses. Michael slows, dropping to the ground at a snail's pace, while the two basketball kids continue to look at him with regretful shock. I look to my hand, seeing a golden glow pulsing beneath my skin at the center of my palm. I turn it back and forth, and realize that I'm the only one moving at a normal speed. I'm doing this. I look back at Michael, that shocked look on his face slowly becoming more pronounced as he falls closer to the floor. The two basketball kids move in slow motion: one still reaching out to Michael to try and catch him, and the other slowly raising his fist to cover his mouth as he cusses. I move, hopping on my one good ankle at normal speed and bending down towards Michael. I grab his shoulders and turn him, angling him so that he's falling more on his butt than on his back. His eyebrows slowly inch up towards his hairline as his mouth widens in a shout. As the two basketball boys continue to move towards him, I grab the tray as it falls in midair — the fries that were bouncing upwards resume their position as I swoop the bowl right below it, and I catch the pizza that was toppling over the side and place it back on the tray. I place it in Michael's hands and make sure that he'll land safely on his bottom. I look around the room mystified — everything is slow, even the cafeteria servers on the other side of the room spooning macaroni and cheese at half speed.

The noise of the student body still fills my ears, but the tone is low and slow. Kids texting type the keypad at half-speed, and students laughing with their friends cock their head back in slow motion. I hop back to the table and stand back where I once was — if all of a sudden I'm in a different spot it might look suspicious, so I try to stand exactly where I was. I exhale shakily, waiting for the room to spring back into normal time; but time still goes on slowly. I cock my head confused — I stretch out my hand again, thinking maybe doing the same thing will make time go back to normal, but it continues to sludge on. The glow in my hand is gone, and I look at my normal pale-skinned palm. Still confused, I look left and right for an answer — I made this happen, now how do I undo it? I look at the clock on the wall near the doors — even the hands of the clock are rebelling time. Suddenly I think back to that eye I drew in class — it blinked at me, and

I was so shocked because drawings shouldn't be doing anything. Maybe that was a sign? Someone telling me ahead of time what to do when my powers kick in? It seems like a long shot, but I try it — what do I have to lose anyway? I look at the clock and wink — suddenly, a pulsating energy booms through the room with a flash of light, and the room resumes its regularly scheduled programming. Noisy chatter fills my ears once again, including the thud Michael makes as he plops onto the floor. He shouts in surprise before his face goes confused — he expected to land on his face, but instead he's comfortably sitting with his tray in his hand, with the food safely where it's supposed to be. The two basketball kids who were reaching for Michael suddenly stop, blinking and shaking their heads as they wonder what just happened. Some students who were watching us also look in confusion, cocking their heads to the side, wondering what just happened. I remember that I'm supposed to look confused like everyone else and spring into action, hopping towards Michael and putting on my best 'worried' face that I can muster.

"Oh my God, Michael! Are you okay?"

"Uh, yeah," he says, placing the tray beside him and looking at it confused — as if it would be able to answer his unspoken question. "Yeah I'm good. I just —"

"Those guys totally wiped you out," I say, trying to sound as worried as possible.

"Yeah," one of the basketball kids says, "sorry man. We were just messin' around and didn't mean to bump into you." He continues to look confused, his eyebrows scrunched together and forming a unibrow. "Good thing you landed on your ass though, and you still got your food."

Michael looks to the tray as he stands up, staring at it in further confusion. "Yeah. For real." He looks at me, his face confused. "What the hell just happened?"

"Those guys bumped into you and you fell over," I say matter-of-factly as if it should be obvious. Please, please, *please* don't cross-analyze the situation — I can barely lie to you, please don't make it harder than it already is.

"Yeah, yeah, I know that," he says. "But I was so sure I was gonna faceplant *hard* on the floor — and my food should'a been everywhere — but somehow I landed safely with the food in my hands?"

"Yeah," I say, trying to make my voice sound confused along with his. "That is weird — but maybe you turned over at the last second

233

without realizing. Honestly, it all happened so fast, I'm confused too." He nods slowly as he tries to make sense of my explanation. He still looks confused, and common sense is trying to undo my implausible excuse of an explanation in his brain, but he accepts it anyway. He shakes his head and chuckles, scratching the back of his head as he brushes it off.

"Yeah, it did happen out of nowhere, huh?" He goes to sit down, slowly sliding the tray onto the table and groaning into his seat. "But hey, at least I still have my pizza."

"Ha! Yeah, and my tasty fries," I say, reaching down and dramatically dropping a fry into my mouth, he chuckles at my silliness as I lower myself into my seat.

"I don't know how you eat fries like that — having the ketchup everywhere. It gets all over your fingers, doesn't that annoy you?"

I look at him incredulously, replying, "Says the guy who inhales his food and still manages to get it all over his face."

"You're not wrong," he says, shrugging his shoulders. I laugh as he digs into the fries, trying to find one not covered in ketchup and digging his fingers well into the pile to do so. I smack his hand in protest, but he just digs in deeper. Such a troll.

I sit in my last period of the day in chemistry class, watching our teacher present to us in class as we all take notes — some in notebooks, some on printouts of the slides, some on our laptops. I, however, sit immobile with my pen poised to take notes, but my mind not connecting with my hand. I stare at the screen but my mind is elsewhere, thinking about what happened in the cafeteria. Out of the corner of my eye I see an Indian kid by the window, leaning against the heater and watching the teacher with a bored look on his face. I look back to the screen and sink back into my thoughts. Loni and Nel told me that Bastets have protective powers — and Loni told me how she used them in Jamaica before she immigrated to Canada. She said that she used her powers to protect her crew when the police were near, and how they were always able to get out at the last minute before getting caught. She even used her powers to escape from the Toubab when he found her — maybe that's what I was doing. Michael was falling and he would've definitely hurt himself, and his food would've gone everywhere. I was in shock — people usually are when someone gets pushed over. I guess my shock triggered my powers and they kicked into full gear. It was all so sudden; the room went from being a rowdy cafeteria to moving like molasses. It even felt like the air around me was moving slowly, and I was slicing through it like a knife when I moved towards him. And the wink — what was that about? Is that how Loni did it? Did she literally slow time to escape?

"For next class," the teacher begins, interrupting my thoughts, "we're going to be discussing the majority of the next chapter, so please be sure to bring your textbooks!" Just as he finishes the bell rings, and students jump to action. Desperate to get to Loni's, I rush too, which is not like me at all. I spot the bored-looking student again — still in the same spot by the windows and not moving, watching all of us pack with an almost melancholic expression. Confused, but it's not my business; I look back to what I'm doing and finish collecting my things. Hopping on one foot and stuffing my books in my backpack, I quickly crutch out of the room and head down the stairs. I have to be careful since so many other rushing teenagers are thinking the same thing as me — the stairwell is crowded with rowdy kids, and I have to strategically maneuver myself down the steps without spraining my other ankle. Once safely on solid ground, I release the breath I was holding and crutch to my locker. I open my locker and quickly grab my history book, placing it in front of the chemistry book in my bag and slamming the locker closed. I feel a tap on my shoulder and turn around to see Michael, with his backpack already slung over his shoulder.

"You're in a hurry," he says amused. "I saw you crutching down that hallway like it was a race."

"Yeah," I say with a laugh, "I just really wanna get out of here. I want to get to Loni's to do some more… homework. And besides, I kinda just wanna get away from Brimmer Hall — Ms. Boykin gave me a stupid grade and I wanna be far away from this energy right now."

"Oh no, you didn't do well on the report?" he asks. We start walking down the hallway to the double doors, staying near to the lockers to not get in the way of students in a rush to get to their extracurricular activities.

"No, I did well on the report," I correct hotly. "She just gave me a grade that *she thought* was deserving. Trying to tell me I put more than what was necessary with my take on black feminism — when it actually supported my thesis and gave more weight to the topic."

"Oh," he says in realization. "I'm sorry, that sucks. Sometimes teachers just stick to their definition of what's right — even if it takes away from us actually *learning* stuff. But hey, maybe this is your origin story for when you're famous and have a bunch of Nobel Prizes."

"Maybe," I say laughing. We walk out the doors and towards the bike station — I'll have to stay back and call an Uber to go to Loni's since Nellie is still at the hospital working a double, but I still walk Michael to his bike.

"You wanna hang out after I get back from Loni's? The new season of Crazy Stuff finally came out, we can binge it 'til we're in denial about being tired."

"Oh really," he says excitedly. He clasps his helmet onto his head as his face goes apologetic, saying, "That sounds great but I can't — I'm meeting Taylor at the mall, we're gonna go see a movie."

"Really?" I ask, surprised and a little disappointed. "You guys really hit it off, huh?"

"Yeah," he says with a goofy smile. "I told her that you were in the hospital — and when she saw you today she totally understood. We talked it up a bit in between class — we ended up both being late to class 'cause we lost track of time." He sits on his bike seat and looks wistfully in the air — completely taken with the memory of their interaction. I've never seen him like this. I mean, he's been pining after Taylor for a while now, but this is different. They're actually having a connection, and it's going exactly the way he hoped it would. It's so cute… and a little weird.

"Anyways, there's this new sci-fi movie out that we both wanna see, and I have enough points to get us VIP tickets."

"Wow, luxury," I say sarcastically. He cuts his eye at me and I smile, chucking his shoulder to let him know I'm joking. "I'm just playin' — that sounds nice. Just the two of you in those nice, plush seats — you'll be closer together, and you guys can get comfortable."

"That's the goal," he says. "But we can watch the new season another time — maybe on the weekend, so Nellie and Nana can't get mad at us."

"Yeah, sure," I say with a smile. He smiles back and throws me a quick dap, backing out of the slot and turning onto the street. I look after him for a moment — I'm happy that he's finally getting his moment with Taylor, but I'd be lying if I didn't say I was a little disappointed I couldn't hang with him today. I know that I've had him to myself every day before now, but with everything that's been happening — with my new powers and the secrets I have to keep and the lies I have to tell because of it — I feel like I'm drifting away from him. He may not realize it yet because for him nothing's changed; everything's exactly the way it's always been, and we're still the two best friends from diaper days. But I know that that's not the case — I'm different. I've changed. And I just want something in my life to remain the same — to retain that feeling of normalcy. And our friendship, though still strong, is starting to shift with each of us entering new realms of reality. And I feel like it's all happening at once, at full speed. I try to shake this feeling out of me, reminding myself that Michael is still my best friend and always will be. This is just my anxiety getting to me — it's not like he's going to up and leave me forever. I need to get a grip, and release the one I'm trying to keep on our friendship. I pull out my phone and bring up the Uber app, clicking the Uber pool option to save a little money.

As I await the driver which is two minutes away, I people-watch the kids and faculty leaving the school. Some get into their cars, others walk to the bus stop to await the next bus, and some bike and walk to their respective locations. As I look down the street towards where I'll be heading, I spot a sleek black car parked on the other side. The windows are tinted which is strange, since it's illegal in this province, and the exhaust trailing from the back pipe tells me someone is inside. And they're just staying there, parked and unmoving. Discomfort rises within me and puts an unsettling feeling in my stomach — whoever this person is is completely invisible to the world around them, but has complete access to us. Like a fish in a tank, with these unknown watchers that annoying kid with braces tapping on the glass — except the tapping is general unease tapping away inside my anxious bones. What if this is the Toubab from last night? Has he found me? Did he contact his secret weirdo-sadistic cult and brings more along with him to capture me? The window begins to slowly wind down, and I can only make out darkness and the reflecting windshield on the other side. Finally I spot a car that matches the description on my app and crutch towards it, quickly opening the door and throwing my bag in. The driver sees me on my crutches and gets out of the car to help me, but I wave him down — politely, but urgently.

"No, no, don't worry. I'm fine," I say rushed with a smile.

"Okay," he says, with a slight Iranian accent. "Jamila, right?"

"That's me," I say as I plop onto the seat and close the door. As he slides into his seat and taps on his phone, I look back to the black car behind us. It rolls up its window, moves from its parked position and slowly crawls forward, driving down the same street we'll soon be heading down and turning right. I exhale shakily and slump against the seat.

"Alright then," he says while looking at the GPS. "Off to Loni's Diner."

CHAPTER NINE

I crutch towards the diner doors, trying to simultaneously rate the Uber driver on my phone. In front of the doors, I see a man on the other side trying to exit. Seeing me, he politely opens the door and stands to the side, ushering me in with a smile. I gratefully smile back and nod my head in thanks, walking to my favourite booth and plopping down onto the plush seat. The smell of milkshakes and oxtail greets my nose as I breathe in the ambiance in the air, and my nerves settle a little bit. Ray, talking up a customer near the jukebox, sees me as I sit down and waves to me. I wave back with a smile as he returns to his conversation — I chuckle, as the person he's talking to nods along with a pained look on his face. I know those ones.

I see Loni in the back, cooking up her next order in front of the window, and I watch her in silence. She's wearing a headwrap to keep her hair out of the way, and a thin long-sleeved shirt. Her chest is shiny from the steam of cooking, and her face glistens with sweat and that black-femme glow. This is her element — cooking food with love and integrity. She does it with such grace and tenderness, while at the same time being quick and efficient. I've watched her cook before from the front counter, while Michael and I have been sipping on milkshakes, and it's truly mesmerizing. The way she seasons the meat — letting the spices soak in, and rubbing the cut-up onions onto the meat and letting it sit in a pool of its own flavour — is done with a flick of the wrist, a grind of the palm, and the careful eye of a master. I love Nellie's cooking — nothing beats some good home cooking — but Loni's food is really top tier. It has this juiciness that coats your mouth, with a velvety mouthfeel that keeps you coming back for more. Pair that with her fruit punch and cornbread and you're set to sleep within an hour.

She must notice she's being watched because she looks up, and directly at me. I smile meekly and she smiles back, shaking her head with a small smile and chuckle. She looks down at what she's doing and continues for a few minutes longer before going to wash her hands. When she pops through the swinging doors, she towels her hands while greeting the other customers.

"Hey Jay, how's work goin'?" she says to a heavyset man in construction gear.

"Oh you know how it is, Loni — workin' hard 'til I'm sore and then doin' it all over again," he says.

"I hear that," she says, patting him on the shoulder. She nods and smiles to other customers, walking over to me and tucking the towel into her apron.

"How you doin', baby girl?" she asks me casually, but with a look that alludes to more query within her question.

"Good, all things considered," I reply, tapping the air thrice above my ribs. She nods and purses her lips before smiling and sliding into the seat beside me. She lightly scoots me with her bum, bumping my hip to get me to move over. I chuckle in confusion as I push myself against the wall, looking at her with amusement.

"Now that it's jus' us two, we can get a little more real wit' each otha," she says in a low tone. She leans back and looks me in my face with an expression of care, looking my body up and down to assess me. "Are you in a lot of pain?"

I exhale slowly, saying, "No. But it's definitely more than I've been in before — and, given the circumstances, it kind of makes the pain on the inside," resting my hand on my heart, "hurt a little deeper." She hums, nodding her head lightly. She looks at me more pointedly, clasping her hands in front of her.

"And what about after I left? Anythin' eventful happen?"

My breath hitches in my throat as everything that happened since Loni left our house last night rushes in at full speed. Would she be asking about the dream where I turned into a black panther? Or my run-in with the Toubab at the hospital? Or would it be the episode in school today where I slowed time? And let's not forget about the creepy stalker car that was in front of my school!

"Well, that's a fairly loaded question," I say with a heavy sigh. She raises an eyebrow and gives one single nod — this is definitely not a discussion to be having aboveground.

"Ay!" yells a customer behind us. Ray turns around, the customer looks to him and gestures to the TV hanging on the wall. "Turn that up."

Ray obeys, using the remote control to turn up the volume on the news. A manicured-to-perfection woman continues a news report, looking solemnly into the camera as she gives out the information.

"... late last night. A young man in his early twenties was shot multiple times outside the *Lucky Night* Stripclub in North York around 3 a.m., with a reported 34 casings littered on the ground. Ambulances arrived on the scene shortly after the shooting, but the victim was presumed dead at the scene."

"Damn," says the customer. "Another kid shot dead — this city is goin' to hell."

"Tell me about it," says Ray, as Loni shakes her head. "Seems every day there's another kid gettin' shot 'cause'a these damn gangs. How many more kids gotta die 'fore they realize this shit needs to stop!"

"Language," Loni warns.

"Yeah, yeah," he says, waving her off. "Fo' real though, if there's anythin' I can count on in the morning news, it's another shooting happenin' somewhere in this city."

"Yeah," says Loni, "and it just gives the police more reason to patrol the streets, and lock kids up in dem cages they call jails."

The news reporter continues, "Reports claim that police shot the suspect multiple times after several requests by police to lower his weapon, which they claim was a gun concealed on his person. Police have stated the suspect was irate and erratic, loudly spewing profanities and threatening the lives of the officers. Witnesses on the scene, however, claim the situation happened differently and escalated quickly."

"It was crazy," says an older woman, dressed in a loose t-shirt. Her name — Rashida Jenkins — is underwritten with the word Witness on the screen. "All these cops were pointin' guns at the kid and yellin' at him to put his hands on his head, an' you could hear the kid sayin' he was gonna put the gun on the ground. He was doin' it slowly too — even I could see it from across the street — 'cause I got good vision, always have since I was a kid y'know — and they shot him! A bunch of times, way too many than necessary; it was crazy. It was crazy!"

"Ontario police have yet to comment on the validity of these claims, and have released statements at 11 a.m. this morning on the matter of the case."

"Yeah," interrupts Loni, "and I bet they're gonna spin it to make the kid seem like a threat to dey lives. But nobody deserves to be shot 37 times — let alone a child." She shakes her head and rises from her seat, motioning with her head for me to follow her. I obey and slowly rise, awkwardly hopping on one foot to grab my things while grabbing my crutches. Loni thankfully grabs my bag and ushers me out of the booth towards the back door. As we leave the front, the voice of a police officer recounts the case from a press release earlier this morning.

"We entrust all our officers with the essential training to competently de-escalate a situation, and shooting is enforced under the direst of circumstances. As of this time, the officers on the scene are not suspended from the force and continue to cooperate with the proceedings of this case. Regardless of any situation, Toronto Police takes every case seriously, and we are committed to our motto. To Serve and Protect the citizens of this district."

His voice drowns out in the background underneath the chatter of the diner as we enter the back kitchen, walking to the isolated closet door.

"I'll be in the back doin' inventory, Ray," Loni yells over her shoulder as we squeeze through the tight space. I turn on the light as she closes and locks the door, then stooping down to pull the door open for me. I lift both crutches and grip them in one hand, using the floor as a hand rest as I hop down each step — Loni grips underneath my arm to help me, and once I'm too far down the steps to rely on the ground as a guide anymore, I lean back and use the steps behind me as support. I slide down each step slowly, the dusty residue that's been untouched for who knows how long now sticking to my palm. I finally land on the ground and straighten up, the tension in my lower back and abdomen releasing. Loni turns on the light and I'm graced with the welcoming warmth of the basement. I've really come to associate this place with a fond warmth in my heart, and it's hard to pinpoint just one thing. I limp forward, placing the crutches against one of the tables and walking towards a stool to sit. I look up at the lights — the twinkling, floating dots of light that scatter the ceiling. Maybe those lights are what make me feel so warm inside, the magic of illumination it grants makes it different from any ordinary set of lights — but then it wouldn't be the same without that smell of essential oils and sage that crowd my nostrils with every inhale. Dust too, but that's just a sacrifice you have to make when practicing your powers in secrecy. Oh, but then there's the potion pantry — I get up and walk over while Loni places my things in the corner and fiddles with some things on a table. I graze my fingers along the glass cupboard, looking in to see the various bottles and jars of pastes, powders, and liquids. I open the door and pick one up from the top shelf that catches my eye: a tall, translucent, electric blue bottle in the shape of a deformed wine bottle. I can make out a dark, sludgy liquid on the inside — but what catches my eye are the sparkles in the liquid — a dusting of gold peppered throughout the mixture. I open it and sniff, smelling a sickly sweet smell; almost like maple syrup. I turn it to and fro, lightly shaking the bottle to reveal the sparkle glowing — I shake harder, and the sparkles glow brighter. It's mesmerizing, and before long it's all I can notice. I get a warm feeling in my bones, warmer than the feeling that was already there, and I begin feeling weightless. Happy. Almost euphoric. The glowing sparkles pulse, clouding my vision with sparkles that make even my eyes feel warm and fuzzy. I giggle — this is *weird*. But it feels so good; like I'm floating on a cloud, and that cloud is made of cotton candy. And I'm eating it too because my mouth feels so cottony — sooooooooooooo cottony. I start giggling. I don't know what's so funny, but now that I've started I can't stop. This is all just so silly, so fuzzy, so — ha, ha, ha — wait. What was I saying? Or wait, was I speaking? Was I thinking out loud, or is my voice in my head just reaaaaaaaaaally loud right now? A brief interjection of common sense interrupts my jovial attitude, enough to give me a semi-coherent thought. Am I getting high?

"Eh-eh," Loni says, quickly snatching the bottle out of my hand and placing it in the pantry. She closes the door and looks at me with a cautious glance, warning, "What are you doing? *Are you mad?* This is not a toy, J. You caah mess around wit' these things — you don't even know what half of these things do."

"Well," I say, giggling, "you should tell me about them then — because I might just do something…" I pause, leaning forward. "Stupid! Ha."

Loni groans, shaking her head and ushering me back to the stool. "You already did pickney. You went and got yourself high."

"I did? Shh," I yell, smushing my fingers against her lips. "Don't tell Nellie." I keep giggling as Loni looks at me, her face annoyed and exasperated. The sparkles still glowing in my periphery and that warm fuzzy feeling seeps into my vision while the rest of my body sways from elation. Loni kisses her teeth in annoyance, rummaging on the shelf below

243

the cupboard and coming up with a small bowl and a bundle of what looks like short sticks.

"All those bottles in there and they don't even have any labels," I say lethargically. "How do you even know what those things do?"

"Years of practice," she says matter-of-factly. "And not bein' stupid enough to pick somethin' up when me nuh know what it is."

"Yeah, but what if you pick up one bottle thinking it's one thing aaaaaaaaaaand then next thing you know you take a sniff and your nose is *purple?*"

She looks at me, her eyebrow cocked as she asks, "Purple?"

"I like purple," I say with a childlike voice, giggling behind my hand and hunching over from laughing at my goofiness.

"Jesus be a fence," she says exasperatedly. "Goin' and stickin' your nose in whatchu don't undastan and now you high —"

"As a kite!" She looks at me annoyed, cutting her eye at me as she grabs a clear mason jar, filled with a yellowish-green powder, and sprinkles its contents into the bowl. She sticks the bundle in the center and grabs a match. Coming towards me, she sticks the bowl below my face — I jolt back confused, but almost stumble off the stool from the loss of my faculties. Loni catches me by the arm and sets me back upright, looking at me pointedly — I look back at her sheepishly, desperately trying to conceal a laugh that's threatening to burst from behind my lips. She flicks the match along the top of the table and she sets the bundle aflame where it meets the powder. It catches fire and releases a smoke that steadily snakes upward.

"Breathe it in," she commands. I do as she says; I know not to mess with Loni while sober, and even high I know to disobey her would be a mistake. I lean forward, swaying slightly but breathing in the smoke all the same. It doesn't have a smell other than that generic woody smoke scent — which I've always loved the smell of, so I breathe it in heartily. I continue to sway, a stupid grin plaster on my face as the gold sparkles shine in my eyes. But then they start to go away, and the warm fuzziness removes the film over my eyes and I regain clarity. It seeps out of my bones like water sliding off a duck's back, and I shoot up into a straighter position as lucidness returns to my consciousness.

"Whoa," I say.

"Yeah. YEAH," replies Loni. She smacks me upside the head, and I raise my hands to stop her from inflicting another blow. "*Don't stick your nose in whatchu don't understand.* This could'a been something that could cause a lot more damage besides a high, so if you want to test 'em *you ask.*"

"Yes ma'am," I reply sheepishly, standing up as she returns the bowl and its contents to the shelf.

"Why were you messin' around in the cabinet anyway?" she asks. "You couldn't wait?"

"I was just curious," I say sheepishly. "There's just so many bottles and jars in there y'know? They look so cool, they've been catching my attention."

"Mmm," she hums. "Well, if yuh gonna be thinkin' about them, might as well know what they do — before you end up unconscious on the floor." She opens the cabinet and reaches towards the top shelf for the same tall dark blue bottle, its sparkles shining bright as ever.

"This is the Drunken Fools potion. When you breathe in the scent, it makes the person feel as if they're drunk. Their senses go unda the influence of di potion and it makes them dizzy — affects di way they walk, how they move their arms, clouds their vision, all'a dat. But it's even more potent when you set it on fiyah. Our ancestors would often have a pot of dis brewin' somewhere in di area and if a threat — or a slave trader, or Toubab — was near, they'd light the potion on fiyah and the smoke would be raw and affect them easier."

"That's why I felt like I was high — I could literally see sparkles in my eyes."

"Yes, that's what the gold in the potion does; it clouds your vision and makes you feel all warm and fuzzy. If you're happy and feeling good, it distracts you from whateva yuh doin' — and if you're someone after a Bastet, it comes in handy to aave somethin' that'll disable dem long enough fah you to get away."

"Amazing," I say, my eyes fixated on the bottle in wonder. She chuckles, patting me on the shoulder dotingly.

"Yes, so let's not go huffing this for no reason, eh? It's only for emergencies." She puts it back in the cabinet, rearranging it so it stands behind shorter jars and bottles.

"Is that what you used to escape from that Toubab in Jamaica?"

"No," she says, turning around to look at me somberly. "No, I used a protection spell that allowed me to escape quickly."

"What kind of spell was that? Is it written down in that book you had from the other night?"

"No, it's not one that has to be spoken. One of our abilities as Bastets is to protec' those who are wronged, so we can create a way of escaping from a threat that may hurt us or those around us. When that Toubab found me, I used that power and it kept him from hurtin' me."

I think back to what happened today during lunch, looking at her with a cautious questioning face. "Did… you slow time?"

She cocks her head and looks at me, her face wary. "What would make you think that?"

"Well," I say cautiously, "I think I kind of did the same thing today at school."

She stands up straighter and comes closer to me, holding her hand out to punctuate her words as she says, "What do you mean you did it at school?"

"Today at lunch, Michael was walking towards me and a bunch of kids knocked him and sent him flying — and I panicked and shot my arm out to try and catch him and then… and then time just slowed." She looks at me with her eyebrows raised, a look of surprise etched on her face.

I continue, "I almost thought time stopped for a second, but then I saw everyone in the room still moving — they were just moving really slow."

"Are you serious?" she asks.

"Yes. It was so weird. I was the only one moving at normal speed, and everyone was moving at half-speed — *less* than half-speed. I moved to help Michael who was still falling but incredibly slow; I turned him around so he'd fall safely and made sure the tray was safely in his hands."

"That's amazing," she says with wonder. "I wasn't able to do that 'til years after my powers came in — an' even then, I couldn't control it for anotha year or two after that. How did you make everythin' go back to normal? You didn't even know you could do that — how did you make time resume itself?"

"That's what got me for a minute. I tried putting my hand out like I did when time first slowed down but nothing happened. But earlier in history class, we finished the film we were watching early and we had time before class ended. I was doodling on my paper and I drew an eye. *And it winked at me.*"

"Winked?"

"Yeah, winked. I thought maybe it was my mind playing tricks on me. From everything that's happened lately I haven't exactly been in the greatest state of mind, but when I was figuring out how to make time go back to normal I looked at the clock. I didn't know if it would work but I tried winking at the clock, and then all of a sudden everything went back to normal. Like nothing had changed."

"Hmm," she says, thinking. She walks over to the table and says, "Maybe that was a sign or a premonition that was tellin' you what you needed to know before it 'appened. Something similar 'appened to my granny when she was comin' into her powers to speak to the ancestors." She grabs a book and walks back over, placing it on the table and flipping through the pages. "My mother an' I were never able to do it, but she said before she started speaking to the ancestors an' going to the Realm of Duality more often, she got a sign in a dream that helped prepare her for when she started talkin' to those in the afterlife." She lands on a page with a lifelike sketch of an eye, with a clock in the center of its pupil. Underneath the eye is writing in pretty cursive, catching my eye and making the literary lover in me smile.

"One of the things Bastets can do is slow time — we use it to our advantage when we need to get away from someone hunting us or others. Egyptian myth says that Bast is related to the all-seeing eye which was this concept in their culture that was very important. For us, being able to see time for what it really is is our powa — everyone thinks time goes one way. Like a one way street, you can only move forward in a straight line and you caah go back. But time is not like a line. It curves — going forward and backward, fast-paced an' at half-speed, 'til you end up right where you started."

"Like an infinity symbol," I say in realization. She nods encouragingly in agreement.

"Exactly," she replies. "We aave this ability to actually see time an' manipulate it — it's like seein' the sun cast a shadow on the ground to let you know what time it is. We can see into anotha plane that shows us time an' how it moves, just like we can see things in this dimension."

"But wouldn't slowing time interrupt the flow of the timeline? That could have repercussions on the other side of the world that we don't even know about."

"You're still thinking of time like a straight line, J. Even if you drop a pebble inna river, it may cause a ripple but it won't interrupt the current of the river. Slowing time may change the speed of its flow but it won't change its trajectory — regardless of what you do, it will continue to curve until it winds up right where you started. Where *you* started — not everyone else, but you."

"Because I'm the point where the flow of time meets," I realize. "Because I interrupted the flow and it now flows through me."

She sits back with a satisfied smile on her face. "Exactly," she says. "You're a smart girl, J. You just aave to rememba that not everythin' is what it seems. You have to rewire your brain to think about everythin' you've learned from a new perspective. Even then, you're figurin' things out very quickly. Much quicker than me, or your motha or Nellie did, so keep doin' what you're doin'."

I slump on the stool, my mind processing everything I'm hearing. Now that she's explained it, it all makes sense, and the anxiety I had is slowly starting to dissolve away. I guess that all-seeing eye has some truth to it if we can see all of time. There's so little conclusive research on the concept of time — and I love sci-fi movies as much as the next person, but I find it hard to rely on a Hollywood film. Most of what I know about time is the generic stuff: the number of days in a year, daylight savings time, essential dates in history, that sort of thing. And even stuff like the grandfather paradox is college-level science information that I just read for fun. The grandfather paradox says that if you were to travel back in time and kill your grandfather, this would prevent one of your parents from being born and you would cease to exist. But the grandfather paradox is constrained by the realities of what we know so far — and almost no one knows about Bastets. If I can slow time to prevent something from happening, or protect someone, or change the events of time, then that would totally undercut most, if not all scientific research. Everything Einstein pledged his life to explain would just be the imaginative musings of a man who is looking at life through the eyes of a frog, while my ancestors have been looking at things from a bird's-eye view.

"This is crazy," I say, as Loni closes the book and puts it back. "This would negate everything that was proposed by modern science. Scientists have been studying the concept of science for *years*, and have theorized so many realities of the concept of time that have been relied on and trusted by the most respected in the field."

"And how many of these so-called '*respected scientists*' knew about Bastets?" she asks rhetorically. I shrug, nodding reluctantly along with her in agreement. She continues, "All ah dem scientists, proposin' these realities you're on about, were just proposin' *possibilities*. I read about

Einstein a few years back, jus' to see what the man had to say. The man was a genius, that's a given, but everythin' that he was known for was just a theory. I couldn't believe it when I was readin' an article an' I kept seeing the word theory poppin' up. Damn near the whole world remembers a man for his contributions when his contribution was just a bunch of theories. If he'd known a Bastet, he may aave gotten a few more things right."

I chuckle — I've thought so highly of Einstein. He's an icon — with his crazy white hair and major scientific research, he's an integral part of society and has influenced so much of what we know about science. So many scientists have: Edwin Hubble, Alexander Friedmann, Max Tegmark, and countless others. But science is what's known by man — what's studied and what's presumed based on what's been studied — and being a Bastet is a different world. A world of potions and powers, realms and ancestors, and that totally contradicts everything science values. It contradicts everything *I* value — or used to value at least.

"Now," she says walking back over to me, "let's talk about the Toubab." My breath hitches in my throat as his face pops back in my head; it's like just the mention of him brings unease and anxiety rushing back into my body.

"Tell me everything you can rememba about him — what he looks like, the way he smelled, the way his voice sounded, how tall he is, everythin'."

"Okay," I say, breathing shakily. "Well, he is tall — really tall and broad. I could tell he was muscular underneath what he was wearing, and he was wearing a dark red shirt and black pants. He has black hair with some greys at his temples, and really blue eyes." I pause, remembering his face. "He is handsome, but didn't seem... present."

"What do you mean?"

"He was like a robot. He didn't have any emotion, except disgust when he finally revealed who he was. He just seemed so cold, just a void of a person."

"Yes, that sounds about right," she says with melancholy. "When the Toubab found me, he seemed so cold. So empty. Even when he was hunting me, it felt like I was being chased by a machine more than a man."

"Yeah," I say thickly, "that's how it felt for me too." Loni looks at me and grabs my hand, squeezing it tenderly and smiling at me warmly. I try and smile back, but I don't really feel it's genuine.

"Tell me more. Nellie told me that he tried to drug you, but you knocked him out." I nod, taking a deep breath to gather myself.

"He had a syringe with him and injected some of whatever was in there into me, but the way he was holding me down felt just like how Ricky Brass did —"

"Ricky? What does that eediat have to do with this?"

"You don't know?" I ask her, surprised. "He and another two of Blanco's boys are who attacked me — but Ricky more than the other two. He held me down, trying to…" I mime with my hands how he held me down, my voice catching in my throat. Loni realizes and looks at me soberly.

"Ah, I see." She looks at me, her eyes wandering over my face. "Well, now we at least know that your first premonition was true — good thing it never fully happened."

"Yeah," I say thickly. "Well, when the Toubab was holding me down it felt like déjà vu. I panicked, I guess my body was reacting from what had happened with Ricky earlier and I went into shock. And then I just… shoved him against the wall."

"You were able to push him that hard in your condition?"

"That's the thing, I didn't just push him — it's like I could feel a power rushing through my arm and it pushed him across the room."

She looks at me surprised, her eyes wide. She turns around and walks forward, then stops — looking left, tapping her mouth with her finger and then looking right, stumbling forward as she tries to remember something. Suddenly she snaps her fingers and walks to the table in front of her and picks up the same book from before. She flips quickly through the pages as she walks back, landing on the page she's looking for and pointing to it excitedly.

"What you're sayin' is that you pushed the Toubab back with your powers?" she asks rhetorically.

"Yeah. Well, I mean that must be it, right? I was so weak from the attack, and even normally I never would've been able to push him across the room like that." She points at me as if I said what she was thinking, her eyes wide and a big grin stretched on her face.

"Then it must be your powers," she says breathlessly, placing the book in front of us. She looks back up at me as she explains, "Bastets used to be able to manifest their protective abilities into a literal force — we call

250

it a wave because they said it would feel like a wave flowin' through your body."

"Yeah! That's exactly how it felt. Like power was moving through my body, but it didn't boom or anything — it flowed through me."

"Like a wave," Loni says. "*The Wave.* Our ancestors used it with everythin', from protecting the village to helpin' push out a baby during childbirth. For centuries this power had been lost — with so many of us sold into slavery and raped, this power was drowned out of our genetics."

"So you and Nellie can't do this?"

"No," she replies, "and neither could your motha. For generations this power had been lost, and we just thought that Bastets would neva regain this power. It would be no different from our ability to transform into a black panther. We used to be able to, but we can't anymore."

I think about my dream from last night and how I turned into a black panther — Loni said that the salve would bring me deeper into the Realm of Duality. It definitely did. That transformation felt like it was really happening, and it hurt like hell. But if it felt so real… what if it was real? Was it a sign that I'm gaining that power?

Loni continues, "Maybe this is different though." She stands up and looks at me, full-on and with wonder. "Your other powers are coming in so strongly, and you're controlling them so quickly."

"Excuse me?" I ask incredulously. "When you transported me into the Realm with those drums I damn near had a panic attack."

"Well yeah, but you also had a vision of you eventually being attacked so that's understandable. Despite that, you're handling them so quickly — you're a smart girl, an' it's helping you to stay on top of all'a this. Half of my powers I couldn't fully control fah months after they manifested, an' even then I could only protec' myself an' others. But you," she walks with her hands outstretched towards me, hovering them beside my face. "You are different."

"Different," I say monotone. I chuckle humourlessly, shaking my head in disbelief. "Different? Yeah, I know that I'm different, Loni. During this whole process of discovering my powers, the one overarching concept that I keep realizing is that *I'm different.* I thought I was already different to begin with, but add superpowers and a lineage of superhuman ancestors to the mix and I got another thing coming, right?" I limp away, shaking my head annoyed.

"J, this is a good thing," Loni says warmly. "These powers mean they haven't been lost, an' it protects you even more from the Toubabs —"

"Oh! You mean the cult of sociopathic racists that've been hunting me from before I was born?" I ask sarcastically. "Yeah, that's another fun little tidbit. Being different is great — it means you're special, it means you're unique. You've got that *wow factor*. Most girls my age, when they hear they're different, it's because they've got a new outlook on life. Maybe they're destined to go to the Olympics or win a Nobel Peace Prize. But I'm different because I have powers most people aren't able to possess — and this puts a target on me. Because this aforementioned cult thinks I'm a sin. An aberration — when just last week I didn't know anything about this world. And now suddenly I'm at the center of it, thrown in the deep end without a life raft. It would be great to use these powers for good, but if I could trade that for *safety* — for the sweet boringness of normalcy — I would be more than willing right now."

Loni looks at me disappointed, cocking her hip and her head to the side. "Jamila, you knew goin' into this that this wasn't gonna be easy," she says. "The fact that you're manifesting these powers isn't just good because they've been lost for a long time — this'll mek you more prepared to protec' yourself. I know it doesn't seem fair, but more than anything this is a blessing. Not a curse."

"Well, it doesn't feel that way right now," I say curtly, struggling to keep my emotions at bay. I lean on the table with my head bent, breathing in and out slowly to calm myself down. I feel Loni's hand rest on my back before she firmly presses her finger up along my spine, forcing me to straighten up. I face her, looking at her face that's set in conviction.

"Life isn't a picnic, J. No matta what, you are gonna go through things in life that others neva have to deal wit'. That's just what comes with the skin," she says, pointing at my face. She then grabs me by the shoulders and looks fully in my face. "And this is no different," she says.

"I thought the most I'd have to deal with is the realities of being a black girl, but this… this is all so much more than I can deal with."

"You think so?" She looks at me curiously, shrugging, and turns around. "I don't think you give yourself enough credit." She plops down on the stool I was occupying and looks at me.

"Because the Jamila I know lost her motha at a young age, and she handled it. The Jamila I know kept gettin' told by the people at school that she was *beatin' the odds* but you handled it, and let 'em know that they were odd to doubt you in di first place. And the Jamila I know has been mastering her powers fasta then I've ever seen — listening to what we've been tellin' you and takin' everythin' in. You're processin', just like you do wit' everythin' else and yes, it may seem like too much to handle, but like everythin' else, you *will* handle it. You're different — that's just a fact. But your difference isn't a bad thing; it's what makes you able to handle your business. So when you're processin' all'a this, remamba that you were made different for a reason — you were made this way so you could take everythin' in on yuh own time, learning, an' usin' this knowledge to be betta. To be betta than any of us. I can already see it. So quit your whinin'."

She stands up and walks past me, going back to the potion pantry and opening the doors. I stand there flabbergasted, at a loss for words from Loni's reprimand/pep-talk. She reaches for the second shelf and pulls out a jar with dried leaves, a small bottle with a dropper, a bowl, and a pestle. She places them on the table and flips through the book, while I just stand there like a child unsure of what to do after being scolded.

"Well," she says to me, "are you going to just stand there with your lips flappin' like a fish outta wata, or are we gonna get to work?" I look at her wide-eyed, struggling to come up with a quick reply when I notice my lips flapping stupidly and stop myself.

"Let's handle our business," I say, walking up beside her. She smiles and looks down at the book, turning to a page with what looks like a recipe.

"This here is the protection for pregnancy spell. Many women had complicated pregnancies back in the day an' would often die during childbirth if the baby didn't — an' sometimes, it would be the both of dem. This mixture, when applied when this spell is spoken," she explains, pointing to the words on the page, "can help protec' the motha and the baby from any complications."

"They couldn't have protected them from everything, though," I say. "Without modern medicine, there were so many fetal deaths back then — thousands of women died during childbirth."

"Yes, but there's no record of Bastets even existin'. What makes you think there would be a record showing the rate of successful births when a Bastet was there?" She's got a point there.

"I'm not gonna read the specifics — last time I checked, neither of us knew anybody pregnant. But if the situation ever arises where you need to help the motha an' child during the birth, then this spell an' mixture will help to lessen any risks."

She begins to put the items back in the potion pantry as I ask, "Is that why a lot of Bastets were midwives? Or went into medicine in some way?"

"Yes," she says. "With modern medicine requirin' less need for midwives, Bastets started goin' to medical school to get in the hospital rooms — they still went to school to be midwives though, for the women who chose the traditional way. Bein' a nurse or doctor in the room got them close enough to ensure the motha would be protected."

"But how would they be able to rub the mixture on the mother with a bunch of people in the room? Including the mother — I don't think she'd be totally gung-ho about a random person rubbing green stuff on her belly." Loni chuckles, the sound deep and echoing from her chest.

"You saw for yourself how we can slow time in times of dire need. If the baby or the motha's life is in danger, then we as Bastets have the duty to help. If we can, we must."

That does make sense. If we're protectors of women and children, then being there at the moment when both are at their most vulnerable is vital. And what could be a better vantage point than being in the delivery room? Loni pulls out a tiny glass bottle in the shape of a clover, with a dark red liquid inside.

"This," she says, "is Liquid Love. It's Drunken Fools potion mixed with a potion that affects their hormones so they feel happiness an' affection for whoever's name the Bastet speaks."

"How does it do that?"

"It affects the serotonin, dopamine, and oxytocin in their bodies — elevating it to a level that keeps them on a peak for days at a time. Bastets would use the potion on men they wished would fall in love with them, or use it on women their slave owners lusted after. A spell, when spoken over this potion, would end with the names of the person that they're using it on an' the person that wants them to fall in love with them. It would make them so filled with affection — only feeling happiness and glee when around the person — that they would become literally drunk with love. It lasts for days but if reapplied, an' a new supply was constantly made, then that person could be in love for years an' be none the wiser that it wasn't their choice."

"So we made people fall in love against their own volition — women that had no choice? People that could've been in love with someone else?"

"You have to understand, our ancestors that were enslaved had to do what their masters said — not only because they were slaves, but because they couldn't risk their identity as a Bastet be outed. If a woman in high society, who would neva consider that man on their own, is who he truly desired, then he would command the Bastet to cast a love spell on her."

"But slave owners didn't just lust after women of high society — they raped slaves. Our ancestors." Loni looks at me with distress, her face pained.

"We tricked our own people into falling in love with men who were enslaving them. Kidnapping their children. Killing them and their families!"

"I don't like this history either, J," Loni says thickly. "It makes me sick to think that we would put our fellow women in that position — to get them to lie in the same bed as a monster. But if we didn't, our identity would've been revealed — we would've been hunted and killed by more than just the Toubabs. We would've been wiped out completely."

"Haven't we though?" I ask hopelessly.

"No," she says defiantly. "We most certainly have not — and with every generation we survive, our strength survives too — and only gets stronger. I told you that we protec' women an' children — well, even when we had to submit to our slave masters demands, we avenged the women we wronged." She flips a few pages over to a page coloured in red, with gold writing etched on the page. A drawing of a man sits on the opposite page, with a smile on his face and smoke surrounding his head.

"For the women that our ancestors were forced to cast this spell on, they remembered who they were. They never forgot how they were violated, an' always made sure that they were avenged. They would use that same potion and strengthen it, making the person so love-hungry that it would drive them insane. It's like in Romeo and Juliet, when the two didn't think of any otha option than tuh kill themselves when they thought they couldn't aave each otha. 'Cept instead of the man falling in love with the woman he took advantage of, our ancestors would mek them fall for us."

"We made our slave masters fall in love with us?" I ask confused.

"Yes, to lure them in. Our ancestors would compel the man to lust so strongly after us that we'd be all he'd think about. It would drive him so mad until we had him at his most vulnerable state. We toyed with them, like a cat playin' with a mouse until they couldn't take it anymore. The stronga the potion, the more infatuated they became — and the more they couldn't imagine life without us. They'd be consumed with love until they ended their lives because of it."

"That's... that's terrible," I say. She looks at me with her eyebrow raised, and I quickly move to explain myself. "Of course they were terrible people, the worst of the worst — they committed atrocities that I can't bear to imagine. But making them end their lives? That seems more like revenge than avenging. Who were we to decide whether they lived or died?"

"An' who were they to enslave us? Violate us an' kill us when we weren't of any use to dem anymore?" she asks hotly. "You make it seem like the playin' fields were fair. Sure, we had powers an' abilities beyond anyone's wildest dreams — and you think that would give us an unfair advantage. 'Cept they still owned us. Raped us. Used our powers against us an' others. And they killed us when we dared to defy them and fight for our freedom — a rebellion of the highest order."

She walks towards me, looking into my eyes intensely as she continues, "But we weren't the only ones there, J. We weren't the only ones raped, used, an' killed until we were empty. Those people we were avengin', even if they weren't Bastets like us, were still our people — and they didn't have powers an' abilities to defend themselves. Not against slavery or us, when we turned against them to survive. There's not a doubt in my mind that our ancestors did everythin' they could to not hurt their own people — but with the only otha option bein' death, sometimes turning against our people was the only way to keep a legacy alive to protect them in the long run. If someone is able to help anotha when they are unable to defend themselves, to bring them justice when others won't, then it is our responsibility to help them. To not do that would be to condemn them to the death of their will to live."

I look at her and nod, feeling the weight of her words. Who were we to get them to kill themselves? Who am I to question the validity of their actions? This is the 21st century, not the colonial slave era. I could never fully understand the gravity of that situation even if it were explained to me a thousand times over. To actually live life in a coffin built with the material of racism, sexism, and egotism, and nailed shut by our own inability to share our identities, is a life I could never comprehend. Who am I to assert my beliefs of what's right into their realities, when my beliefs of what's right don't have the full picture?

Loni leans on the table and closes her eyes, sighing deeply and shaking her head. "You have to be open, J," she says. "You're judging a life of women who made it so that you could be here. They suffered and survived the best way they could, and given the circumstances, they did a pretty damn good job."

"Yeah, well, I'm a Virgo — we tend to be pretty judgy."

"Miss me with that astrology crap," she says annoyed.

"Sorry," I say, a smile forming on my face to try and lighten the mood. Thankfully it works, and I see a small smile breaking the scowl on her face. She shakes her head and tries to hide her smile, facing the table fully and straightening her back.

"Enough chit-chat," she says seriously. "Let's get back to business."

For the rest of the night Loni shows me everything in the potion pantry — I know she's doing it for my benefit, but secretly I think she's enjoying herself too. She showed me a yellow paste that helps cure the common cold when you apply it on your nose, and a powder that makes you go blind when you blow it into someone's eyes. There was a cream that slowed aging by putting more collagen into your body, and an oil that made your whole body grow overnight. This is amazing, like a scene out of a movie or something. All these different potions that can do a bunch of things that people hope to get when puberty kicks in, or pay a doctor or surgeon thousands of dollars for. These potions have been curing illnesses and diseases for centuries before modern medicine had even created vaccinations — and even then, modern medicine hasn't even come close to making headway like my ancestors have.

Just as we're finishing up, the lights flicker. Once, two times fast, and three times slowly. Knowing this signal, I walk up the stairs and lift the hatch to see Nellie looking down at me. She smiles and leans down, easing herself onto the steps. I back down as she descends the steps and I see her fully — and she looks *tired*. Her topknot is less a knot and more a loose jumble of hair. Her frizzy hair extends from her hair and the nappy kitchen rebels against the hair tie. She walks weary; her steps heavy with exhaustion, and fatigue etched on her face.

"Long day?" I ask.

"Feels like forever," she says wearily. "And I have to go back — I only have an hour before I have to head back."

"No, you have to work a 12-hour shift?"

"Yeah. It was a wonder I was able to pull half shifts for so long. But more nurses are leaving and we're short-staffed. Not to mention we need the money — after all, you're going to be off to college soon, and that tuition isn't going to pay itself." She walks to one of the tables and puts her big bag on the table, plopping onto the stool and leaning in a slump.

"But we have money saved up, and I can get OSAP."

"That money won't cover more than two years of college — and with OSAP giving out more loans than grants, you'll be in debt up to your eyeballs for years, and I don't want you going through that. It would help to know how much tuition is going to be though — have you decided which school you're going to? And which program you are taking?"

"Not really," I say. "I'm in between Ryerson and York right now, but I can't decide if I want to do something in history or social and environmental justice. They're both around the same cost though, but I know I have to make a decision — the deadline for applications is in two months for both schools."

"You betta hop to it then," Loni says.

"I've been a little preoccupied lately," I say, throwing my hands up to gesture to the magical basement we're in.

"True," Loni admits. "But I know you — you love school more than anything. And to be honest, I always see you as someone doin' somethin' for di community. I know you love history an' everythin', but you've always been so passionate about things when it comes to somebody bein' wronged. Every time somethin' happens in the news or politics or anythin', your eyes light up. This is somethin' that fires you up, so that social justice program sounds like it'd be perfect fah you."

"Yeah, I know. I'll make a decision soon, I just need to process all of this for a little bit longer. Besides, I already have all my references and most recent grades in order, I just need to write a letter for each application explaining why I want to take that program. But I'll do that soon."

"Okay," Nellie says. "Well don't dawdle on that, alright?" I nod obediently, and she nods back. She gets up and walks slowly towards Loni with her hand bracing her lower back. Nellie's starting to worry me — she looks so run-down, she can't survive much longer working all these shifts with barely any break to rest.

"Nellie, are you sure you're okay? You look really tired."

"Yeah I'm fine, J. I'm just really tired."

"That's what you always say," I reply. "But it's really coded for something else." She chuckles and smiles at me, but even her grin is worn down with fatigue.

"Yeah, well, being perpetually tired is kind of the plight of any black woman, isn't it?"

"Tuh, you're preachin' to the choir," Loni says.

"But I'm good, J. Thanks for asking," she says with a smile. I smile back, grabbing her hand and squeezing it with love.

"Well, let's fill you in on what's been happenin'," Loni says to Nellie.

"Since I got here, Loni's just been teaching me a couple of things about the potion pantry —"

"The what?" Loni and Nellie ask.

"Oh," I say embarrassed. "That's just what I call the cupboard and shelves with all those potions — a potion pantry."

"Oh," Loni says with an impressed look on her face. "That's cute — don't know why I never thought of that before." I shrug, while Nellie chuckles. Loni continues, "But yes, that's what we've been doin' for the past while. I showed her a couple of spells and told her what everythin' does, but I don't think we need to teach her them seriously just yet."

"I agree," Nellie replies. "She has to get a handle on her powers."

"Well, I think she's doing pretty good with that right now." Loni looks at me with a knowing glance, making Nellie turn to look at me with a questioning one.

"I used my powers today — at lunch, when Michael was pushed over and almost fell."

"Did you have another premonition?"

"No — actually, I… I made time slow down."

Nellie raises her eyebrows until the wrinkles etch canyons within her forehead. She looks at me wide-eyed as she repeats, "You made time slow."

"Yeah." She looks at me, just looks at me, for a couple of seconds. She looks to Loni who just nods, then back to me with that same shocked look on her face.

"*You made time slow.*"

"Yes, Nellie. I think we all understand that," Loni says amused.

"How did you do it?" she asks me mystified.

"Well, Michael was pushed really hard — accidentally, but he was about to fall onto the floor and I knew he would've gotten hurt and our food would've been everywhere. I reached out to him and the next thing I know everyone was moving in slow motion."

"Unbelievable," she says. "And you didn't freak out? I know the first time I did that I was practically hyperventilating because I didn't know what I did or how I did it."

"Oh, I felt the same way — but I just figured I did it and, no matter how I did it, I had to help Michael. I made sure he landed safely and our food was safe —"

"Of course you did," Nellie says with a smirk.

"Well, I was hungry. And you always told me to never waste my food," I say. Nellie chucks my shoulder, trying to hide her smile. I continue, "But after I did that, I had no idea how to make everything go back to normal."

"But you figured out with that sign you received earlier," Loni says.

"What sign?" Nellie asks.

I reply, "Earlier in history class I was drawing an eye and it winked at me — and at that moment I saw the clock and thought I'd give it a shot. And when I winked, everything went back to normal."

"What made you think that winking would help?"

"Well the all-seeing eye keeps popping up everywhere," I say, motioning to the books piled up on the table. "And I might be going through a lot, but I didn't imagine that eye winking at me. So I figured why not, it could mean something — and it ended up making time go back to normal."

"An' not only that," Loni interjects, "but she was able to use her protective powers as The Wave, the night the Toubab cornered her in the hospital."

"What!" She looks at me, eyes wide with concern and inquiry.

"I freaked out when he was holding me down," I explain, "and I just wanted him off me. I was weak from the morphine and the drugs he had injected into me, but I wanted him so badly off me I just felt this strength within me and I pushed him away. But it was like a pulse shooting from my arm, and he shot across the room and slammed into the wall. It knocked him out cold, and that's how I was able to get away."

"J," Nellie says, "this is... this is amazing. Your powers are..."

"Coming in quickly, I know."

"And you're controlling them so... so —"

"So quickly. *I know*. It's been terrifying — but I'm just trying to go with the flow here and come out alive. I don't really have any other choice, right?"

Nellie looks at me for a moment, as if she's holding her breath, and then just starts laughing. She points her hands at me and then covers her mouth, shaking her head and looking at me with amazement.

"I can't believe you're picking this up so quickly," Nellie says.

"That's what I said," Loni says. She picks up some of the books as she continues, "She's learnin' everythin' fasta than you or yuh sista ever did — even fasta than I did. But she's quick as a whip. She just has to get ova her fears of her powers — I know she'll be just fine handlin' this once she does that."

"You're doin' amazing, sweetie," Nellie jokes. I laugh, rolling my eyes and following Loni as she finishes putting the books on the shelf.

"But seriously, I'm really proud of you, Mama. You getting that sign just shows how you're connecting with the Realm of Duality — and you're keeping your tether to the real world strong and intact, which is the safest place for you to be. And the fact that this power is kicking in so quickly helps not only you but eventually other people. God forbid you're in a situation where someone's in danger, you can slow the speed of time to help them. This'll prevent so many casualties, J. And if you can keep your connection to the Realm of Duality, these signs will keep coming in — and it'll only be a matter of time before you master your powers. The ones you have and the ones that are yet to show up."

"Yeah, that's another thing," I say slowly. Nellie and Loni both look at me, noticing the change in my voice. "Something else happened at school today. Right after I drew that eye, actually."

"What?" they both ask warily.

"We were watching the movie *Amistad* in history class, and there was a scene where the slaves were working. All of a sudden the room sort of just warped in on itself, and I was sucked in towards the screen and then — and then I was on a plantation."

"Can you describe it?" Loni asks, her tone becoming more serious.

"Yeah, it was hot. We were definitely in the tropics — there were palm trees everywhere, and a couple of flowers I now realize are from the islands, whatever island it was. I was in the bushes watching the slaves working. I know they were slaves because I could see the whip marks and chains on their bodies from where I was standing, and they were cutting down sugar cane. A white man was watching over them with a gun in his hands, so that must've been the overseer. There was a black man stooped in front of me hiding, and no one could see us — but when I tried to get his attention he couldn't hear me, he couldn't see me, he had no idea I was there. And I was practically yelling at him; or at least raising my voice as much as I could without getting the overseer's attention."

I move to sit down, as the memory of my vision comes back with clarity. Loni walks to the sink and fills a cup with water for me, handing it to me and letting me take a sip for a moment.

I continue, "When I was crouched behind him, someone else came up behind him — she couldn't see or hear me either, but I could tell she was a leader or something because he was listening to her. And no men were listening to black women like that, so I knew she had some pull. They were talking about rescuing some of the slaves — the man wanted to go in but the woman told him to wait, so they'd lose fewer people. She left, he stayed a little longer but then he left too, and they went into the trees."

"And what happened then?" Nellie asks.

"Well they seemed like a safer bet than staying where I was so I followed them into the trees, but they couldn't hear me and were moving so fast I couldn't keep up with them. And then everything warped in on itself and I was back in history class."

Nellie and Loni look at each other, an expression on their faces that I can't quite place — until a look of worry flashes across their eyes. Only for a split second, but long enough for me to notice.

"What?" I ask warily. Nellie looks down and takes a breath, looking at me calmly — which is what she does when she's about to give me some news that I won't want to hear.

"What you experienced was a vision, that's for sure — but it wasn't a premonition because if what you're saying is true, you went to the slavery era."

"An' if you saw into the past, then you were seein' through the eyes of one of your ancestors," Loni says.

"So what I saw... was in Jamaica then. If my ancestor was watching slaves tilling sugar cane, then it must've been when they were enslaved in Jamaica."

"Yes, I think it was," Loni says. "I'm surprised you're having so many visions this often. I didn't have more than a dream every few days when my powers first kicked in, but yours are 'appenin' multiple times inna day these days. But I don't know what that vision was supposed to be tellin' yuh. It takes years for even the most skilled Bastet to interpret signs inna vision — even when somethin' seems obvious it could be somethin' totally different, or have different layers that you wouldn't even think to look for. This could be your ancestors showing you somethin' you needed to see to help you with somethin' you're about to do."

"But what could that be?" I ask. "The only big things coming up for me are midterms and college applications."

"I don't know," she replies truthfully. "Maybe you have to help someone, or a group of people, from somethin' that's keepin' them in an unfair position. Maybe you have to fight to free someone from a terrible situation. I'm curious about this woman though — I want to know more about her. Did you get a good look at her? Is there anythin' else you can tell me about her?"

I think back to the woman, and can remember her clearly; she had this power that exuded from her so strongly I could almost feel it. "She was dark-skinned, probably from working out in the hot sun, and she was wearing a white headwrap and clothes that just covered her chest and her butt. She was strong — she had muscles that looked like they were carved into her. And she also had a lot of scars, all over her body. She looked so strong. So beautiful." Loni nods along as I describe how the woman looked, while Nellie stares at the ground with a perplexed look on her face.

"She might've been your ancestor — if she's as strong as you're sayin', then she probably survived long enough to aave kids. That's how you would've gotten here."

"But you said that I would've been looking *through* the eyes of my ancestor. So wouldn't that mean there was another person there? That I was looking through the eyes of a third person there?"

"But you said that they couldn't hear or see you — they had no idea you were even there. This is a memory, an' if there was a third person there then they would aave acknowledged that person."

"Your ancestor probably needed you to see her as well," Nellie says, "but didn't want you to see through her eyes. If you followed her through the trees and that's where the vision ended, it's because that's all that you were meant to see."

"So there's more that I need to see?"

"Probably, but not yet," Loni says. "Our ancestors are watching over you as your life plays out over time — and remember time isn't a straight line, it's curved. Everythin' that you do is constantly affectin' and bein' affected by things that have and haven't 'appened yet. If you saw more than you were ready to see, then somethin' might happen that isn't supposed to. Our ancestors are watchin' with eyes that see everythin', so trust that what's 'appenin' as it's 'appenin'— is what's meant to be, okay?"

I nod, saying, "Okay." Nellie gives a small smile before looking down at her watch, exhaling quietly. Her face gets even more exhausted from looking at the time, her break coming closer and closer to an end.

"You have to leave soon?" I ask her.

"Yeah, I can stay for another half hour and then I've got to leave."

"Well, you can't go back tuh work wit' an empty stomach," Loni says. She beckons her with her head, saying, "Come. I'll fix you somethin' to eat upstairs."

We obey and follow her, leaving my things down here so I can grab them later. When we're all above ground and the hatch is securely closed, Loni checks the kitchen to see if Ray is anywhere nearby — with the coast clear, we all quickly exit the closet and she locks the door behind us. Walking towards the front of the kitchen I see the diner busy, with Ray struggling to keep up with orders. He turns around and sees us, throwing his arms up in exasperation with an equally exasperated look on his face.

"Where the hell you been, Loni?" he asks annoyed. "I've been handlin' the floor alone for the past 30 minutes, and we're almost out of all the food — we needed a fresh batch 20 minutes ago."

"I'm sorry, Ray. Hush, hush, we'll get it done, don't worry." She quickly ties on her apron and puts on a hairnet, rubbing Ray's shoulder to calm him down. She turns to me and points. "J, you think you could help me out?"

"Of course, no worries."

"Aight, thank you, baby. Nellie just have a seat right there, I'll fix you a plate soon as I get the meat in the fryer."

"Oh don't worry about it Loni, really," she says. "I can just grab something to eat at the hospital, it'll be quick."

"Don't tell me that nonsense, Nellie," Loni replies. "You know good an' well you'll just pop back onto the floor and grab bites in between patients. Sit down an' rest child."

Nellie obeys reluctantly, but when she sits back down her face eases with relief. I wash my hands and step up to Loni, ready to help in any way I can.

"Ray, is the fryer all ready to go?"

"Been hot and ready for the past 10 minutes, Loni."

"Okay great." She turns to me and hands me an apron and a pair of clear gloves. "Baby girl, do me a favour and get all that chicken into the fryer — then tek the flour from up top the stove and put it on di counter so I can start gettin' the cornbread ready. You know what else I need for di ingredients?"

"I do, I'll get them all set up," I say, hopping into action. I put the gloves on and grab the tray with the chicken Loni was seasoning earlier. Walking to the fryer to my left, I grab some tongs and quickly place them in — the oil sizzles as the chicken meets the surface, and they start to get brown before I finish putting them all in. With that done, I grab the flour from the top shelf and dash it on the center counter. I grab the rest of the ingredients as Ray hobbles to each table and cashes out customers at the front counter. I grab eggs, vanilla extract, cornmeal, baking powder, brown sugar, and the trays. I dash them on the table and grab two big bowls and the electric mixer for Loni. I look to her and see her forking some greens, plantain, and fish onto a plate and hand it to Nellie, caressing her cheek as Nellie looks to her grateful. Nellie starts wolfing down her food as Loni starts walking to the front.

"Thanks, baby girl," she says to me. "Can you stock up the fridge in the front and make sure everythin' is clean on the floor?"

I nod and walk to the back, passing the closet and walking to the giant freezer to grab a box of drinks. I know that they're in here from the agonizingly hot summer of '08 — Michael and I were playing hide and seek with Ms. Dell, unbeknownst to her, and decided the walk-in freezer was the perfect place to hide. What we didn't know was that it locks from the outside unless you keep the door open with the wooden block near the door; which we happened to kick aside in pursuit of childlike glee. We ended up getting locked in for an hour and no one found us until Ray came to restock the fridge. We were popsicles by the time they found us — but quickly warmed up as Ms. Dell whooped us for our stupidity. I open the fridge and look for the drinks, my eyes skimming over the meat, fruits, and vegetables on the shelves. I finally spot the drinks in the bottom right corner — I grab an empty box off to the side and start filling it with different drinks, assuming we'll need a few of everything. I grab island sodas in pineapple, ginger beer, cream soda and kola champagne flavours, some fruit punches, some malts and Nutraments, and a couple bottles of water. I lift and immediately regret it, lowering it down to the ground — hell no. I may have powers, but I have limitations — there's only so much I can lift. I hunch down and grab the edge, dragging it out and closing the door. I hobble to the front and push through the doors, struggling to manoeuvre the box through the swinging doors. Finally, I make it behind the counter and start restocking the fridge. More customers walk through the door and the chatter in the diner gets louder, as the jukebox remains still and G98.7 plays over the loudspeaker. The radio host talks about Kanye's latest monologue while Ray goes from customer to customer at an impressive speed. Taking orders for one table while making milkshakes for customers at the counter, his loud voice along with the noise from the blender and the radio reverberates throughout the diner. Customers enter the booths just as quick as customers leave them, and the seats in front of the counter quickly become occupied by hungry customers ready for something tasty to end off the night. Finished restocking the fridge, I take the box and walk to the back. Nellie's finished eating, licking her fingers and sucking the fish bones dry, and starts packing her things to leave. She quickly pecks me on the cheek and squeezes Loni's shoulder in thanks.

"I'll see you in the morning, Mama," she says over her shoulder. "Get something to eat after Loni's less busy and make sure you eat a good breakfast!"

"Okay," I yell back, waving her goodbye and throwing Ray a quick wave. She speedwalks out of the diner and more customers walk in as she leaves through the door, a long line extending through the doors. I get worried as I look at the line of hungry customers, and back to the food that's currently cooking — doing the math, we're going to run out.

"Loni," I say lowering my voice, "I don't think there's going to be enough food for everyone."

"We saw that comin', J," she replies. "Half the time food runs out while dey wait in line and they still stick around for somethin'. Let's just get the food out as quick as we can 'til we run out. Let 'em know that we're out of oxtail, festival, and stew chicken. All we have left is jerk, fried, and the sides up on di menu there."

I nod and let out a shaky breath, putting on my best totally-not-freaking-out smile and walk through the double doors. Stepping up to the counter beside Ray, who is speeding through orders like a fiend, I project my voice and try to make it as peaceful as possible.

"Excuse me!" My voice squeaks painfully loud, and I silently cuss

266

for my throat betraying me. "For everyone who hasn't been helped, we are out of oxtail, festival, and stew chicken. We still have jerk chicken, fried chicken, and the other sides up on the menu. I'm so sorry for the inconvenience!"

Some people in the line groan, kiss their teeth, and roll their eyes in annoyance. Some actually leave, but others stay and look at the menu — deciding to take their chances on the food that's available. I start to head back to the kitchen, but Ray holds out his arm to motion me to stay.

"Baby girl, I need your help out on the floor. Loni will be good in the back, she's handled rushes before, but I need you to clean up the tables so other groups can sit down, aight?"

"Okay," I say breathlessly, looking behind the counter and finding a bucket with some cleaning supplies. While I grab a spray bottle and a rag, Ray continues to cash people out and get their drinks from the fridge.

"And while you're at it," he says, throwing a notebook and a pen towards me. "Take orders for the ones sittin' down."

I nod as I walk towards the first booth, with plates and napkins littered atop. You'd think with how often people come here they'd be a little more courteous and clean up after themselves. I quickly dash the napkins into a trash bin and stack the plates and cups in my arms. Walking butt-first into the back, I drop them in the sink and go back out. Out of the corner of my eye, I see Loni placing dinners in styrofoam boxes along the window ledge, and Ray reading out the order on the receipt and handing them to the customers. I head back to the same table and quickly wipe it down — not a moment later a family with two kids sit down and look up at me, ready to read out their order.

"I'll be right back, I'm just going to take the other tables orders first," I say apologetically. I move to the table beside them and see them almost finished with their meals.

"You guys doing okay?" I ask. I get a reply through "mmhmm's," emphatic nodding, and moaning through their food. I smile and breathe shakily, moving to the next table. Lo and behold I see Michael and Taylor, laughing over cups of water on either side of the table. They're leaning over the table and talking in hushed tones — they look like they're both sharing something just between them and, oddly, I feel like I'm encroaching on something that isn't my business.

"Hey," I say enthusiastically. They look up and realize it's me, Taylor looking at me with a sweet smile. I return her smile with a genuine one of my own — man, she's just so likeable.

"Hey J," Michael says, leaning backwards and smiling at me with that Michael smirk.

"Hey Jamila," Taylor says sweetly. "How are you?"

"Oh I'm good," I reply. "I'm just helping Loni out until it dies down a bit here. What about you guys? You saw that movie, right? How was it?"

"Oh it was great," Michael says. "There was this huge twist in the end where she found out that her mom she trusted with her life is who created the dystopian future that was keeping her from going outside."

"Wow, that's uh... that's crazy."

"I know right! But how are you doin'? You still cheesed about that grade Boykin gave you?" Taylor looks at me with a questioning glance, and I turn to her to fill her in.

"Ms. Boykin asked us to write a report that relates an event from the Civil Rights Movement to something that's happening right now or recently. And I did that, but she said I went overboard and did more than the assignment asked for and gave me a bullshit grade because of it."

"Aw man, that sounds like Boykin alright," she empathizes. "She was always on my ass last year about not using the right citations — and I get that, but we're going to be using APA in college anyways, and the *actual report* is what matters more. I just never understood how she always nitpicked about the little things."

"I know!" I exclaim. "You'd think that the content I'm actually writing would be what determines the grade, not if I put 'so and so' on the last page."

"Exactly," she says with a laugh. I laugh back as we share in the plight of learning from Ms. Boykin. She really is so likeable, I can already feel myself getting that feeling — you know the one. The one that creeps up on you, that makes being around someone easier and easier, until you're friends and you don't even know how or when that happened. Michael looks at us with a smile — I can tell he's happy we're getting along. His two favourite girls kicking it off, you really couldn't ask for anything better.

"Michael and I were just talking about what happened to him at lunch today — it was so weird, I saw the whole thing!" My skin spikes with goosebumps, as my body senses another lie that'll have to be told.

"I know right," trying to sound nonchalant — and actually succeeding. Wow, I'm worried how well I'm getting good at this. "One second he was falling and the next he was on the floor — he should try out for the football team, he can clearly take a hit."

"Yeah, but it was crazy how he was just... alright," she says amazed. "I thought his food would'a flown everywhere, but everything was totally fine. One of those guardian angel moments."

"Yeah," Michael chuckles, shaking his head — still in disbelief from the whole ordeal. I chuckle nervously and shrug, trying to shake the butterflies out of my stomach. Taylor looks at Michael with a look on her face — he's not catching it, too caught up in his own head, but I do. She's looking at him with fondness, the kind that develops when you really feel for someone. She likes him. She really likes him; I can see it in her eyes, she's into him. Wow, Michael's first girlfriend — I really need to catch up.

"Jamila!" Ray yells. I turn around shocked, and see him looking flustered and exasperated. "Are you dawdlin' or are you helpin'? Orders and tables, baby girl! Clear 'em and fix 'em up!"

"Okay, sorry!" I turn to Taylor and Michael, with a look of apology on my face. "Gotta go, but it was good to see you guys. Michael, I'll text you later."

He nods and resumes his conversation with Taylor, his body language and face a dead giveaway that he's in heaven. His smile is bigger, his eyes more attentive — those ears are big as ever, but I know that they're listening only to her. I'm happy for him. He's finally getting his moment with the girl of his dreams and, to my surprise, he's actually not screwing it up. I go to the next table and take their orders, quick as I can and being as polite as possible. I take a quick look out the window, to see if any more people are coming through the doors, and look to the street to see if any parked cars hold passengers ready for Loni's diner. On the other side of the street I see a few cars leaving, one driver holding a takeaway dinner in his hand until he drives off. When he does, I see a black car with the windows tinted. Tinted too dark to be legal, and this makes me pause for a moment. But the spike in volume snaps me back to reality and I get back to business. Seeding through tables, cleaning this one, checking on that one, bringing food to the next one, and on and on, until the sun sets and the chatter in the diner rises.

CHAPTER TEN

For the past month, I've been getting more and more familiar with my powers at Loni's every day after school. Other kids have basketball and after-school jobs for, y'know, normal after school stuff. Well, I have Bastet training. Nellie's been picking up more shifts at the hospital to put towards my college savings, so many days it's just Loni and I. She checks on me when she's home and makes sure I'm okay, but she can't be there hands-on with me like she really wants to. It's probably the most she's worked in such a short amount of time, and it's strange to not see her as often as I'm used to. I miss her and miss our quality time. But life comes at you fast, and things have to get done. On the plus side, Loni's been making me more dinners since Nellie's not home most nights — unfortunately, I can already see the effect taking hold on my waistline.

Michael's been getting closer and closer to Taylor, so luckily my lies haven't had to make an appearance as often as I thought. He does ask questions though, so I've been telling him that I'm doing SAT prep for a school in the States. Technically I was looking at an American school this past summer, so the lie wasn't that bad — and luckily, he didn't question it at all. Taylor and I have also been getting closer; we actually have a lot in common when you get rid of the whole popularity thing. We both love reading, hate mushrooms, and don't really understand Michael's fascination with Manga. We end up talking about one thing and then an hour later we've gone on a whole other tangent and wondered how we even got there. She's so much fun and has the same sense of humour as me. She's a lot more like me than I thought, and I don't know why I've waited so long to really get to know her. Her, Michael, and I have started hanging out in a trio together; usually after school or between breaks in class since she spends time with her other friends at lunch. But I think we've really got our own little thing going. She's my first girlfriend that I've ever had really, with Michael only knowing me to a certain extent. Michael's my day one, but there are some things that he couldn't understand because he could never experience what I have — but Taylor does, and gets it quick as a whip. Maybe not the whole superpower bit, but the rest she gets pretty clearly. We have so many of the same ideas and beliefs, and I'm ashamed to say I was surprised by her modern takes on things. I don't know why I thought she'd be the *I-cook-for-my-man-and-happily* type of girl, but from getting to know her over the past couple weeks I've come to realize that she is anything but that. And amidst all of the changes that I'm going through right now, getting closer to Taylor is the one that actually makes me excited.

The rest of the changes though? Yeah, those are coming in hot — and I'm barely keeping up with them without breaking down. Since my powers came in so quickly, Loni wants to make sure that I don't leave anything to chance and I have a good handle on them. More and more she's been transitioning me into the Realm of Duality, to condition me to hold a healthy balance between the spirit world and the real world. However, all I've been getting during these visits are little signs here and there that aren't related to me or my journey with my powers. In one premonition I saw a baby; nothing else, just a baby making noise and baby movements. But the noise it was making seemed wrong — non-human in a way, and it wasn't acting with that innocence most babies have. Loni told me babies are a sign of death in Jamaica — lo and behold, I overheard a classmate in biography class telling his friend his dog died the night before. I also dreamt of talking to Mr. Min about his son, and the very next day I was buying some snacks with Michael at the convenience store and we were having that exact conversation. I didn't realize it was happening at first until he said one line that I remembered from my vision, and standing there I knew what he was going to say just as he was saying it. The look on his face was priceless — Mr. Min is pretty superstitious himself, so I probably set off some sirens in his head that he needed to distance himself from me as fast as he could.

Loni's also been showing me how to work with the potions more lately — and I have to say, that's been my favourite part. Every day after school, while Loni's preparing for the evening rush, I do my homework and prepare for the next day of school. After that, we take ourselves to the basement. She first showed me how to use the spell with the Liquid Love;

I'll probably never use it, but it's one of the ones that piqued my interest the most. She said spraying it on someone can cause that unconditional love — but baking it into food would last longer because it would stay inside them, instead of just staying on their skin. So all those girls that used to make you pies and cookies? Hopefully, it wasn't a Bastet making you love crazy. When you're making the potion, you have to recite a spell to hyperactivate the dopamine, serotonin and oxytocin. The book Loni was reading from when I first opened the potion pantry is this thick, dark blue book. The pages are a dark cream colour, with black and gold writing and gold illustrations to show how the potion works. On the page that reads Liquid Love, a cartoonish-crude drawing of a man looks up at me in an infatuated stupor. A bottle in the shape of an upside down heart, looking a lot like the one Loni has, has a puff drawn from its head to underneath the man's nose. The spell is written in gold letters and reads:

With these two hearts separated by chance
May they be bound by unconditional love
Ties not to break in any circumstance
Lest the sun stop shining from above

May their hearts beat for each other alone
And cast out all outside thoughts
If love from another fails to be shown
The other must submit to a deadly cost

Pretty morbid if you ask me. I've never been in love or wanted to get revenge, it's just not my testimony. But if the alternative to not feeling reciprocated love is to take my own life, then I think I'll take my chances with waiting for the real thing. She also showed me how to properly use the Drunken Fools potion — I did get accidentally wasted a few times, but the question of whether it was really an 'accident' still goes unanswered. When I first experienced its effects, Loni told me once I sobered up that it makes you feel as if you're drunk. When — after two unsuccessful tries — I had the common sense not to sniff it, she explained that the scent alone can make one feel dizzy, euphoric, and make one lose control of their faculties. She said it's because it has ethanol — specifically targeting the neurotransmitters in the brain that sends signals to your body. Instead of having control of your body, you're being puppeteered by the potion, and are none the wiser to it. Sure, you're all giddy and happy and ignorant to reality — but this is the state when you're most vulnerable, and the easiest target. She showed me how to make it, if I ever need my own supply, and how to make it not so dangerous that I put someone through a coma. Two parts ethanol to block the signals in the brain. One part Liquid Love to flood the serotonin and dopamine. Three parts Child's Play — which is a yellow, grainy paste-like substance that lets you see from a kid's point of view — and a blow of a Bastet's lips. When all the ingredients are mixed together they make a dark blue liquid — but when a Bastet recites the chant and blows ever so gently on the mixture, we activate the potion so all the parts work together. The chant goes:

> *The fool that dares to block my path*
> *Shall lose their senses in helpless glee*
> *The drunken fool then suffers the wrath*
> *Of protector's need to be rightly free*
>
> *Joyous fun and drunken play*
> *Shall be all that you crave*
> *Dancing into the night 'til it becomes day*
> *Becoming your victim's slave*

When you do that, gold sparkles shine in the potion and illuminate the particles that'll target the senses. Or at least that's what's supposed to happen. It took me a few tries to get it right. I either spit in it a little bit, didn't blow hard enough, blew too hard and spread the potion everywhere, or my head just wasn't in it. To be honest, every single time my head wasn't really in it.

"You aave to believe it, J," Loni said, as I sat there defeated for the umpteenth time. "The only way to activate the potion is to center yuhself — remba that the person that you would use dis against has done somethin' to you, or someone else, that is getting in your way. This potion removes dem as an obstacle. Think of someone who is always gettin' in the way of you movin' forward, of advancin'."

When she said that, all I could think of was Ms. Boykin. I know she's got her own life, with circumstances I could never understand that led to who she is, but the woman has mercilessly made my life a living obstacle course. I think of all the bad grades she's given me. All the times she was short with me and cut me off. And it's not even that serious, but little things can build up until it makes a difference. And my dam is starting to crumble. When I leaned down to blow on the potion, I put my desire to be rid of her blocking me. I thought of being respected for my point of view, for having the space to comfortably say my peace, and to not be poked with microaggressions. When I opened my eyes, gold sparkles began to shine through the potion — glowing as it spread down to the bottom of the bowl. I smiled with satisfaction and looked at Loni, who smiled with an encouraging look. She made me bottle it in my own glass vial — me being the type-A person I am, I colour coded it with a blue label and gold letters. I can't take any chances of getting wasted on my own product because I didn't know what was what. Besides, it's not like I'm ever going to use it — it's more of a souvenir.

Nellie, when she has the time, has also helped me to properly control the manipulation of time — only Bastets know when the time flow has been interrupted. Even when a distant descendant with no powers experiences it, it feels like time has shifted and changed. Those times when the day seems like it's been moving really slow, or moving ridiculously fast, are usually telltale signs that a Bastet manipulated the flow of time. Our ability to have premonitions of the future and have visions of the past is our ability to see through the layers of conventional time — and with the ability to see comes the ability to navigate, and the freedom to move freely. Manipulating time has its limitations; speeding through time isn't really possible — you can slow it down and move at your own speed, but that isn't moving faster than everyone else. And seeing into the future still happens from where you are in the now; going into the future is another thing altogether. But slowing time to stop something from happening is one of our abilities. In conventional time there are 60 seconds in a minute, 60 minutes in an hour, 365 days in a year — you get the gist. But this is a man-made measurement to help us understand the concept of time; and the hitch with this is that it assumes time is linear. But as Loni explained, time is ongoing and recurring, and it's more like a cycle. When the dinosaurs went extinct, one would think that life and time would end there — but life regrew and here we stand today.

Nellie and I were at home and up late at night when she was teaching me, but it was the only free time we both had in a while. We moved Bastet lessons to the home office, pushing the desk and chair to the side to give us more room. A tall wooden bookshelf stood in the left corner, with the desk and desktop computer just in front of the window. A printed-burgundy rug covered most of the floor, with the parts not covered exposing the hardwood. A dark green loveseat pushed against the right wall holds printed cushions, with an ottoman in front of it. Candles are almost always lit in there, so it's warm and welcoming, and smells earthy and spicy. The sun would always set right as we were about to start and would warm up the space even more with a deeply-golden aura. I took my post in the loveseat, while Nellie would often sit on the edge of the desk to face me.

"When you manipulate time," Nellie explained, "you have to see it like a circle and not a line. It's helpful that clocks are often made in the shape of a circle — because seeing time move as you try to manipulate it tends to help control anything bad from happening. That eye you drew that winked at you was definitely someone helping you out; they must've known you would slow time, and given you a sign to help you control it. But if you lose control, you may end up causing something way worse than what you were trying to prevent."

"Like what?" I asked.

"Well, you understand the butterfly effect right? You make something happen and it causes something to happen somewhere else in the universe. And even though time is like a loop, it can still have consequences that make that loop more... complicated. Take the assassination of Malcolm X —"

"*We caused that?*"

"No — not explicitly. But one of us tried to stop it. She had a premonition that the other group of black Muslims were plotting to kill him and got herself in the room. She left a diary and it talked all about it — I know her great-niece, we met when I was on vacation in Atlanta and she let me read it when we got closer as friends. She sounded like one hell of a woman, and was at the forefront of a lot of the protests back then. From what she wrote, she slowed the flow of time and tried to take the gun from the shooter's hands — but she lost control of the timeline and ended up helping his aim."

I sat there wide-eyed, not believing my ears; that's one hell of a legacy to leave. I definitely don't want to accidentally wreak havoc, so getting a handle on my power has to be done sooner rather than later. To practice she gave me a pocket watch — she said it belonged to her grandmother, and she and mom had kept it ticking for all these years. It was gold with the chain; it was weathered and worn down from time, but it's still ticking.

"Look at the hands of the watch as it ticks," Nellie said. She sat on the edge of the desk to speak directly to me. "Try and drown out everything else and focus on the hands of the clock."

I did as she said and focused on the clock. I blocked everything in my periphery and kept my eyes on the hands as the seconds ticked by.

Nellie continues, her voice softening, "Now, if you can, try to zone in on the sound. Drown out everything else. Close your eyes if it helps you, but just focus on the ticking of the clock. That might help you to really close in on the speed of the time flow."

I listened to her words and tried to let that be the last thing from her I focused on. I stared at the hands for a moment longer, breathing deeply in and out, and then closed my eyes. I absentmindedly fingered my amulet, rubbing the curves of the pendant between my fingers. I've been doing that often — it gives me a boost because I can feel the power of protection seep into me when I do. The ticking of the clock immediately became sharper; and as I breathed deeper and slower, the ticking began to echo in my eardrums and created a thrum within my head. Suddenly that thrum went from a feeling in my ears to a visible force behind my eyes. A shiny blue tube, its surface glimmering with millions of tiny lines, and see-through so I can see the other side of the tube, shoots from my ear through my head to my other ear. It filled the darkness behind my eyelids and filled my vision. I flew my eyes wide open, my breath accelerated in fear, and I looked at Nellie and saw her looking back at me with an expectant look. And that same shiny tube running through the room. Its glowing surface had cast an eerie blue light on the room, the space not close enough in shadow. It looked like it was moving — slowly, so slow I barely noticed it at first, but then as I looked closer I realized that it was *us* that was moving. Moving along the surface of the tube as it turned; its surface, iridescent from tiny lines, was shifting every which way at different speeds. Lines turned clockwise as the others turned counter-clockwise, while others ran perpendicular and others parallel. It was a dizzying juggling of time, and it was going on while Nellie looked at me, waiting for me.

"You see it?" she said more than asked. I nodded, my mouth agape from shock, and my eyes wide — as I refused to blink lest this phenomenon disappear. I slowly stood up and walked closer to Nellie, my eyes never leaving this glowing blue tube. Nellie then went to the window, looked outside before she closed the blinds. I ran my hands along the curves and felt that same thrum that vibrated in my ears on my palm.

"Now you see it — now try and control it."

"What am I supposed to do?" I asked. "I never saw this when I did it the first time, and it was an accident. Where do I even begin?"

"You see it moving, right?"

"Yeah. But isn't it us that's moving?"

"Yeah, but the lines are moving too. Those lines represent the seconds, minutes, and hours that have passed and are yet to come. You see how they're all moving in different directions? That's because time isn't going in one direction. It's going forwards, backwards, and turning in on itself — and we're just along for the ride. I want you to look closely and try to pinpoint where we are."

"But we're the ones that are moving, how am I supposed to do that?" I asked helplessly.

"Just try, Mama. Look at the timeline, and try and find the lines that move at our speed. It'll be hard, but just focus on the vibrations of the time flow."

I looked at her unconvinced, but looked back to the time flow. It made my eyes cross with all of those lines moving in different directions, but I focused on one line at a time and followed it for a few moments, and then moved on to the next one. Then I found one that was moving diagonally, curving towards me along the surface and moving at the same speed as us. I counted in my head — one, two, three, four — and found it moving in time with the seconds. The other lines moved faster, and some moved much slower, but this line moved with us — and followed us as we moved along the flow of time. I reached out towards the line, palm outstretched, and hovered above it. Nothing happened, and I looked to Nellie — *what do I do now?* She looked back at me with a look that said '*go on*,' and I looked back to the line and tried to focus. I thought back to what happened that day during lunch period — and how I reached out my hand reflexively to stop Michael from falling. I remembered that urgency sparked within me and pinpointed it, and harnessed that feeling until it pooled in the center of my palm. Then, imagining my hand like a gun, I shot a golden light towards the line and it pierced the line like a laser. It slowed until it looked like it was just about to stop, and for a moment I thought it was completely stagnant. But I leaned in closer and saw it was moving at a snail's pace; barely enough for me to notice. I laughed in disbelief, excited I was able to pull this off. I looked up to Nellie with a stupid grin on my face, expecting to see a grin of pride on hers, only to see her looking at me with that same expectant look on her face.

"Nellie, I did it!" I exclaimed. She continued to look at me with that expectant look, not registering my words. I stood up confused, wondering why she wasn't excited and still expecting me to do more.

"Nellie," I called. She didn't respond. I leaned towards her, my head cocked to the side in confusion; until I slowly began to realize why she wasn't registering my words. It was because she hadn't heard them. Yet.

Her eyes started to blink, moving in slow-motion, while I blinked three-times the speed as her. I thought she wouldn't be affected by me interrupting the flow, and that she'd be moving at normal speed like me — but she moved along with the flow of time, as I controlled its speed with the palm of my hand. The thrum that was pulsing in my ears and vision became more of a deep echo, delayed by the flow of time. I looked back to the line and saw its connection to my hand with that golden ray. As I moved my hand away, the golden ray disappeared. When I placed it back over again, it reappeared; connecting the time flow to my hand like a magnet. Okay, so I got a handle on the time flow. Now how do I make everything go back to normal? I looked to the chair I was sitting in and reached for the gold watch — the hands of the watch were lethargically moving at the same speed as Nellie. The seconds sludged along instead of ticking its swift tune, letting me focus on the hands better. I turned towards the time flow and extended my hand, reaching into the tube and placed the pocket watch in the time flow. The moving lines that were unaffected tickled my arm, moving through and around it like an invisible speed bump. I watched as the hands of the pocket watch and timeline moved slowly — the echo of the vibration deepened as I focused, until the vibration echoed within me. Then, with all my focus laser-sharp, I winked. The golden ray that was shooting from my hand lit up the entire line; it shot around the surface of the time flow, curving around until it met back up at the point it began. Then the entire room was flooded with golden light, and the line resumed its regular speed. Nellie, who looked like someone pressed pause on her, moved like I hit the play button.

She started to talk as if no time had passed. "And try your best to —" She stopped, her brows furrowed in confusion as she looked at me. She cocked her head to the side while her eyes were asking me a silent question.

"Something's... off," she said.

"I would think so," I replied with a smile. Her eyes settled in realization, and she returned my smile as it widened with pride.

"Now *that's* what I'm talkin' about."

Soon November came, and applications for post-secondary are fast approaching. I still haven't made the decision on which college I want to go to yet. I've narrowed it down to one program at both Ryerson and York University, but I don't know if I want to commit to being a history major or devoting my life to social and environmental justice. History is dear to my heart — it's one of the things that my mom and I shared. Our love of history — the ups and downs and twists and turns — are among the many ways we bonded. And history is also a big part of who I am as a person in general. There are so many nuances to being a black girl, and a lot of it has to do with the history of my people, and the world. To deny history would be to deny myself— and I might be a bit melodramatic, but even if I don't look at that aspect, history is something that can't be forgotten. Or else we won't know what to do to ensure the bad parts of history aren't repeated. At the same time though, I have become so passionate about righting the wrongs from history that environmental and social justice seems like the right fit. You can't go through life without knowing the history of it, but to make a better future you have to combat the consequences of that history — and that comes from knowing the ways to proactively rectify it. I've been going over my options over and over in my mind, and while I'm doing that I'm making myself feel guilty because I'm taking so long with an option that I'm lucky to have. Not everyone in my family got the chance to finish high school let alone go to school. Nellie is the first one in my family to get a degree — and one in nursing, no doubt. My mom went to a local college that has classes in those copy-and-paste-looking office buildings — she got a diploma in marketing and worked at a family-owned construction company until she died. She made herbs and remedies on the side for people in the neighbourhood, and the extra cash usually went towards groceries or my allowance money. Mom told me that my grandmother never finished high school; she got pregnant when she was 14 and had to drop out to raise Nellie. Instead, she taught herself to sew, and worked as a seamstress. She also babysat other kids for working mothers in the town and worked at the grocery store on the weekends. Nellie told me that they also had a mango tree in the backyard — it grew only Julie mangoes which, in my humble opinion, are the only ones that matter. It grew so many mangoes she'd have baskets full of them every few days. She would sell them for $2 each, or make juice out of them and sell bottles for $5. She was a real entrepreneur and hustled to make sure Nellie and Mom had a roof over their heads, clothes on their backs, and food always in their bellies.

Nellie told me that Grandma Belle wished she could go back to school. She would always look over the fence at the schoolgirls, headed to school in their uniforms, and pray for the day she could go back. Nellie, being as caring then as she is now, would teach Belle what she learned at school when she got home. Nellie would teach her math and science, and Mom would help her with her reading, writing, and vocabulary. When she was dying, Nellie said she kept crying because she would never get the chance to go back to school. It was her dying wish to get her diploma, but that wish died with her. So going to school is a big deal for us, and the fact that I'm struggling with the chance of going to not one but two schools makes me feel guilty — because so many don't get that chance. I have to decide soon because this isn't just about me. It's about making them proud.

It's Thursday, and the itching for the weekend is palpable as I pass students in the hallway. Last week I did my checkup with Dr. Aida, and he said my ankle has healed enough that I can come off my crutches. My ribs are still healing, so he said to take it easy and continue to take my medication every day until the bottle is finished. Every once in a while I'll feel the ache of my broken ribs; if I bend down to tie my shoes, or reach up to put my books in my locker, or even pulling my hair up into a bun — but as the days have been going by the pain has lessened. I haven't seen Ricky Brass or the other two boys that were with him since they attacked me. Blanco's boys still hang out on the same street corner, messing around as usual, but I've yet to see my attackers. And what's more, they don't antagonize Michael and I anymore. We speed up on our bikes when we pass them like always, but they just look at us and let us pass — not jeering, no jesting, just a simple nod acknowledging us and going about their business. This morning it happened for the third time, and Michael looked back at me with a confused look on his face.

"So they respect us all of a sudden?" he asked sarcastically. "That's the third time this week they haven't messed with us — if they keep doin' it I might get cocky and cruise by without even looking at them."

"Don't do that," I warned. "They're still Blanco's boys. If we don't at least acknowledge them, then we're gonna be in deep shit."

"Still," he said, "it's crazy they're leaving us alone all of a sudden. I wonder what changed."

I shrugged along with him, but I didn't have to wonder. Michael doesn't know about my late-night escapade that winded me up at Blanco's house — if he did, he'd explode. Not to mention I'd be assaulted with questions faster than I'd be able to come up with lies to answer them. Blanco must've told his boys to leave us alone after that night; I see them still messing around with other kids from my school that pass by, but they leave us alone. He must've said something — and Blanco doesn't seem like the type to be challenged.

I head towards art class and see Michael talking to Taylor at the door, her leaning on the door frame and looking up at him sweetly. He's got a dopey smile plastered on his face, and his eyes couldn't scream '*I'm in love with you*' any louder if he wanted to. His arm is above her head and holds him up as he leans towards her, and she giggles from something he says and grabs his hand, threading her fingers between his. I take out my phone and sneak a picture. I'm going to save it for their future wedding, just to prove to everyone that they've always been so cavity-level sweet. I walk up to them with a smug smile on my face — when Michael sees me the smile slips from his face and turns to one of embarrassment. He abruptly stands up and clears his throat, fidgeting with the straps of his backpack; Taylor kisses her teeth and grabs his hand, again threading her fingers between his and smiling up at him. He smiles back at her and sinks into his dopey love.

"You guys are so cute — you should have a Netflix special," I say sarcastically, but smiling wide from their pda.

"Yeah, are you gonna be our agent?" Taylor asks.

"Oh yeah, girl," I reply. "Hollywood *wishes* they could get on my level. Ellen's been begging me to get y'all on the show, but she'll have to give me a little more to work with, you know what I'm sayin'?"

She smacks me on the shoulder and we laugh, as Michael rolls his eyes with a small smile on his face.

"Aight, let's head in," Michael says. He turns to Taylor and says sweetly, "See you later, baby."

"See you," she replies, pecking him on the lips. She squeezes my shoulder and mouths a goodbye, as she walks to go to her English class upstairs. We walk into the class and head to the table closest to the post that Ms. Cortez usually stands by, dropping our bags on the floor and relaxing into our seats.

"You guys are so cute," I revel. "You've gotten so close so quickly, it's crazy when you could barely say two words to her, what, two months ago?"

"I know right," he marvels. "You were the girl I was closest to, and now it's Taylor."

"Yeah," I reply. A pang hits me in the chest, slightly hurt by this. I really like Taylor, but I have noticed that Michael and I aren't hanging out as much as we used to anymore. He's been busy with his relationship with Taylor and tutoring kids at the middle school three times a week, and I've been busy with Bastet lessons and helping Loni out at the diner — but he doesn't know how busy I am with the former because he doesn't even know about it. The spare time we both happen to have we spend together, but he always talks about Taylor and how close they're getting, and I'm distracted with thoughts of these newfound powers I'm possessing and wishing I could tell him. Even though he could never begin to comprehend this hidden world, I just know he'd know exactly what to say — he's my best friend and he knows me better than I know the back of my hand. But it's starting to feel like we're becoming distant — and if anything, I need Michael. I need my best friend. I don't want us to drift apart; I want us to grow old and grey together, looking back on our lives and our childhood and youthful memories. I don't want that to change.

Ms. Cortez walks in and interrupts my thoughts. I tell myself to get it together. Get these thoughts out of my head, I need to stop overthinking and focus. Michael smiles, and I look to see him texting Taylor. The dude just saw her two minutes ago and he's already talking to her again — aren't they going to give each other a break? I tap him on the shoulder, pointing to Ms. Cortez as she gets herself together at the front. He sits up and slides his phone in his back pocket, turning to the front to focus. Ms. Cortez fumbles as she tries to put her big bag down while taking off her denim jacket while also trying to keep things from falling out of her bag. Flustered as always, I can always count on Ms. Cortez to entertain me. Finally done struggling, she stands up breathless — tightening the scrunchie on her low bun and smoothing her oversized white shirt.

"Okay," she says, clapping her hands together. "That wasn't difficult at all." The class chuckles at her joke, as she shrugs her shoulders.

She continues, "Now that I've got myself sorted, I'll hand back your sketches from last class. I'm really impressed with your work guys, I'm starting to see your improvement." She pulls out a folder from her bag and begins handing out assignments back to us. When in front of Anthony Giuseppe, she exhales with exasperation, looking at him with a smirk.

"You never fail to disappoint me, Anthony," she says sarcastically. "You might want to find another muse besides the naked female body — y'know, to challenge yourself."

"Nah, Ms. C," he replies with gusto. "That's my signature! I'd be disappointing my loyal audience if I didn't give them what they wanted."

"Mmmmmm," she hums disapprovingly, shaking her head. "Well if you want to showcase the beauty of the female form — maybe look into different mediums to use. If this is your signature, as you so claim, then get creative."

He looks at her speechless, and she smirks and pats him on the shoulder. Michael and I snicker, shaking our heads at Anthony's juvenileness. She makes her away around the table and loops over to our side. For this assignment, I sketched a black girl with an afro, except the curls were made of a bunch of words to describe her. The assignment was just about shading really, but I added something extra just because I felt like it. She comes up to me and looks at me with a smile, handing my paper back to me.

"I loved this one, good work," she says, winking at me. I smile as she walks to hand Michael his assignment. I turn the sketch over to see a 93% circled in red, and underneath her lazy cursive. *Excellent shading, I can tell you listened. I love the words in the hair — you really personalized the piece!* I smile, pleased by my grade, and turn to pay attention to her next instruction. She tosses the folder on the floor by her bag and turns to us, sliding her hands in the back pockets of her baggy jeans.

"Alright, on to the next one," she says excitedly. "For this next assignment, I want you to use whatever materials you can find and create whatever piece you want — the catch is, none of the materials can be used in this classroom. That includes the things in your pencil cases!"

The class hums in curiosity; some groaning and others leaning forward in interest. She paces in front of us, looking at each one of us as she continues, "I want you guys to get creative! Go to the art stores — even the dollar store if you have to — but find things that can help you make whatever it is you're creating. It could be a portrait, it could be graffiti, it could even be a photo — but use things that you wouldn't normally use to create your piece. Surprise me." With that, she goes to the side room and we're left to our own devices. Chatter fills the room as students talk to their friends about what they're going to make, while some just scroll through their phones. Ms. Cortez is pretty lenient with how we spend class time; as long as we get the assignment done within an acceptable time, she could care less.

"What are you thinking of making?" Michael asks, pulling a notebook out of his backpack.

"I don't know," I admit. "I love the freedom we get with her projects, but when I don't know what to make I kinda wish she'd just tell us what to do."

"I feel you," he sympathizes. "Even for that last assignment I was strugglin', man."

"It was just a shading assignment. You could've drawn a flower and she probably would've accepted it."

"I didn't want to do something basic though. I tried drawin' the formula for special relativity in big block letters, and then shading it with tiny versions of the formula within it."

"Damn," I say. "That uh… that sounds hard."

"It was so hard!" I laugh as he shakes his head, his face fallen with defeat.

"Aw, it's okay," I mock. "Art just isn't your thing," I grab his face and squeeze his cheeks together, teasing in a baby voice, "and that's totally okay."

He kisses his teeth, pushing my hands away as I throw my head back in laughter. He looks at me deadpan which makes me laugh harder, and my throat makes that scratchy sound all black people make when they're laughing really hard. That's a trigger for him because he bursts out laughing with me, pushing me as he moves side to side from laughing. I stomp my foot as my laughing becomes silent, instead I struggle to breathe as I catch my breath. Ms. Cortez comes out from the supply room, finding the source of the loud laughter.

"That's a lot of laughing I'm hearing," she calls to us. "I hope it's helping you create *your assignment*."

We settle ourselves, stifling our laughter as best as we can. "Sorry, Ms. Cortez," Michael says. "We're working, we promise."

"Mmmmmmm," she hums, shaking her head amused before going back to her task. We get the last of our giggles out before trying to get serious.

"What are you thinking of doing?" I ask him.

"I think I might want to do something about my parents — I've been thinking about them a lot lately."

"Because of the anniversary?" I ask. He nods solemnly, and I squeeze his shoulder. The anniversary of his parents' death is coming up next week; Michael's handled their deaths marvelously, but he always gets more melancholy around this time of year. The day they died it was oddly cold, and it was snowing — but it was raining earlier in the day, so ice was all over the roads. When that drunk driver ran into them, the ice caught under the wheels — even if he was sober, it would've been impossible to stop that semi from crashing into them. On the day of the anniversary of their death, Michael and I always take the bus to the Lakeshore just before the sun sets. He would write a letter to each of them — about things that happened to him over the past year that he wishes they could be here to see — and reads it out while we stand at the edge of the lake. Then he would put it on one of Ms. Dell's biscuits which, she hates to admit, are hard as a rock. But Michael's dad, God bless him, always ate them no matter how tough they were. He loved his mother and would've done anything to please her. And Michael is the same — except he usually sneaks the biscuit into his pocket when she's not looking and feeds it to the stray dogs that roam the alleyways. He keeps a couple though close to the anniversary; they're the perfect thing to float the letters on the water, and it's a little inside joke between him and his dad. The lake would carry the letter with the tide, and we'd stay and smoke a joint until we couldn't see it anymore. By the time it's gone, the sun is usually completely set and we're both higher than the sky. Luckily Nellie knows of our experiments with weed, and would let Michael sleep on my bedroom floor. Ms. Dell would have smelled the weed on him as soon as he walked in the house, and she wouldn't care that it was the day his parents died — she would've given him an earful until he goes deaf.

"Let me know if you want my help," I say. He smiles at me appreciatively, trying his best not to choke up.

"Thanks, J," he says. I smile back and turn to take a notebook out of my backpack, not wanting to make him more emotional. I flip through the filled pages and land on a freshly lined page. I write in the header Art Assignment - Nov 16th, 2020. I tap my pen on the page as I will something to come to me. This is probably the vaguest Ms. Cortez has been with an assignment. Even if I'm better with art compared to Michael, he always knows what he's going to do as soon as he hears about a project — even now, he's hunched over his page and rapidly writing what he's going to do. And I'm just drawing a blank. I stare at the page, hoping a vision will materialize and fill the page so I don't have to. I sit there for a few minutes until I think about my applications for college. It's still making me anxious that I don't know which school I want to go to. Applications officially close next Friday, and I have to tailor different essays for each application and I haven't even begun them yet. Having to choose between history and justice seems impossible, but it has to be done.

Wait a minute. I jump back slightly, looking at the page now as a clean slate and not a daunting task as an idea pops into my head. Choosing between history and justice isn't just something that I have to do to choose which school I want to go to — it's what all of us have to do when we decide what kind of person we want to be. I hunch forward and start drawing a scale of justice, jotting notes down in the margins. People have to choose whether history is important when fighting for justice — can we make things better and forget the ugliness of the past? Or do we need to remember to ensure that history doesn't repeat itself, and we get real justice for the injustices caused by history? I've heard so many arguments about this and never connected it to how I now have to choose one or the other for my next academic career.

I lazily shade the body of the scale, drawing an arrow to the side and writing *Fill scale* with words - parts of history and historical events of justice. I draw the strings to hold up either side of the scale, drawing a triangle with the bottom bowed in. Then I sketch the outline of a woman off to the side holding the scale in her hand. I know that a woman holds the scale, but I don't actually know what it's supposed to mean — I open up Google to see what the woman represents in the scales of justice. The first result explains that she represents the measure of a case's support or opposition. She's the moral force in judicial systems and has a blindfold, a balance, and a sword. The blindfold is the impartiality to the case, the sword represents the finality of justice, and the scales themselves represent the weighing of evidence. I keep reading, and see that the scale dates all the way back to ancient Egypt — what a coincidence, so do my ancestors. I wonder what I can do with that information. If I'm writing a bunch of words inside the actual scale, who am I going to put to hold the scale? And am I going to have all the other elements in there too?

My phone screen lights up, and I look to see a notification from the

news app: Jailing of famous sitcom actress Leila Windam for three months
— is this justice or a joke? Interested in the article, I open the app and read.

> Windam gave the school over $3M in donations over
> the course of two years. The majority of these donations
> coming before Windam's daughter was enrolled at the
> school, and during the time her daughter would be
> applying for post-secondary schooling. This sentence
> comes after the recent sentencing of Tameka Burns, a
> Detroit mother who was sentenced to seven years in prison
> for putting the incorrect address on the school forms that
> her son was attending. Burns lives in a different district
> from the school she was sending her son to, and put the
> address of her cousin so her son could attend — the local
> school her son would have attended is among one of the
> highest in the city for low attendance and low graduation
> rates. "I wanted my son to go to a good school," Burns
> said, as she was interviewed on the court steps before the
> verdict was announced. "There are no opportunities for
> the kids in my neighbourhood — they need a good school
> to open doors for them, and the only thing stopping my
> son from having a better life is 'cause I'm five minutes
> away from the district? That ain't right." Tameka's son will
> go into the foster care system while Burns serves the rest
> of her sentence — she may receive probation if she shows
> good behaviour. This has everyone questioning whether
> the punishment matches the crime; given Burn's offence
> received much harsher punishment and is argued, by some,
> to be less an offence and more of a mother protecting her
> child. But can the same be said for Windam? Or is this
> another case of showman's justice? The school has still yet
> to comment on the severity of Windam's actions.

I look at the article speechless, at a loss for words by the stupidity of
this sentencing — for the actress and Tameka Burns. How could they each
get such different verdicts? Neither of their 'crimes' match the punishment
they were given — that's not fair. All Tameka Burns did was write a
different address on the school forms; it wasn't even a random address, it

was a family member's address. As long as it's family, I don't see what the problem is. Windam bribed the school with millions of dollars so that her daughter could go to that school — taking a spot from other kids who earned that spot. I sit back in disbelief, my eyes passing over my sketch on the page. I know exactly what I'm going to do.

I write on the bottom of the page materials I'll need for the project:

- Clay
- A printed photo of Canada's founding fathers
- String
- Fabric
- Printed news headlines

I sit back satisfied, excited to get started on this project. This might just be my most creative project yet, and I really hope it turns out the way I envision it. I look to Michael who's still doodling on his page; I lean over to peek at his sketch, but he catches me out of the corner of his eyes. He leans his shoulder over and covers the page with his arm — I look at him with wide eyes, questioning what the problem is.

"No peeking," he says.

"Oh, come on," I protest.

"Uh-uh," he replies curtly. "I'm keeping this a secret 'til I've got everything together. I don't want it gettin' messed up and then you're wondering what happened. You'll see it when it's done."

I look at him annoyed, with a face that says *'Really?'* while his face responds with a look that says *'Yeah, deal with it.'* I roll my eyes but relent, letting him get back in his zone. With my idea all planned out, all that's left is to actually get started. But I can't do that right now, so I have to find something to pass the time. I push back my chair and stretch my legs, sighing with relief. I turn to see Ms. Cortez through the window of the supply room, hunched over a book and leaning on her hand. I get up and walk to the supply room, standing in the doorway. Funny enough there is no door, just empty hinges and an open space where a door should be. The supply room is small, with a window on the left side so everyone can see in. It's like a bright, colourful mural of all the students' past work. Paint covers the walls, floor, tables, and chair in different colours, and dim light casts some of the darker colours in shadow. Ms. Cortez is deep into her book, not even noticing me there. Her mouth moves as she silently reads the words, and nibbles on her fingernail. I knock on the door frame and she looks up. Seeing it's me she smiles and straightens her back.

"Hey, Jamila. What's up?"

"Nothing much, just finished planning my project so I don't know what to do now."

"Wow, you've got a plan already?" she asks happily. "I can't wait to see it. I'm just reading this book, and it's such a good read. It talks about the intersectionality of feminism, and provides advice on what we can do to be more aware and accepting of different perspectives."

"Oh that sounds so interesting," I say, walking beside her. "I feel like that's a discussion that we need to be having more of — not just women of colour but all women, and men too. If I even hint that my female experience is different — and, God forbid, worse — then I ain't getting a word in."

"Tell me about it," she sympathizes. "Being a Latina and not being born in this country, I see things differently. And growing up in Cuba definitely made me go through things others never did, and just saying that can be so offensive to people. Because it highlights our differences, which some men and women don't want to be reminded of."

"Yeah — because doing that would mean admitting things are worse for other people."

"Tell me about it," she exclaims. "And even within my own country there are so many nuances — I'm a brown Cuban, but there are so many black Cubans that I know go through things even worse than I do. Everybody knows that, but no one is willing to talk about it because of why it is that way — because of slavery. That's within our own country; imagine what it's like in this country with a bunch more ethnicities for people to get 'confused' about."

"I don't have to imagine," I say sarcastically. She smirks, looking at me with a sympathetic face.

"Well," she says, "if you ever need an ear to vent to, you can always count on your art teacher. I may not understand everything, but I can try."

I smile in gratitude, and she smiles back. She finicks with her bun again, tightening it as she balances her book on her knee. She puts her book on the table and stands up, resting her hands on her hips. "Well, if you need something to do... you can help me clean up here."

"Clean up?" I ask cautiously. She chuckles, walking behind me and gently pushing me forward. I reluctantly step forward — of course I had to go and make myself free. Now I have to help clean.

"No matter how many times I clean this place up, you guys always find a way to mess it up again. And I think it's best to keep your hands busy, so," she points to a messy pile of paintbrushes dramatically, "have fun."

I grimace but comply, shuffling forward to get to work. She chuckles and sits back down, picking up her book and leaning on her hand. I grab a clean mason jar in a tub underneath the table and head to the sink to the right of the room. I fill half of it with lukewarm water while I look around — usually, there's a shelf with cleaning supplies but it's constantly moving as we kids find new places for things. I spot some rubbing alcohol on a wall shelf to my left, and reach for it while trying to keep the jar underneath the tap. After the bottle is in my hands, I turn off the tap and fill the rest of the jar with alcohol. I lightly shake the jar so the water and alcohol swirl together, and head back to the table to put the paintbrushes in to soak. When that's done, I look if there's anything else I can do. I notice my foot kicking debris on the floor, so I grab a broom from the right corner and start sweeping the floor. I sweep up pencil shavings, dust bunnies, and dried paint. I grab the dustpan and sweep it all in, bending over and making sure I get everything before dumping it in the trash can. With that done, I start organizing the tables so all the supplies are in alphabetical order. Brushes here, pastels there, paper up top — what can I say, I'm type-A.

"Would you look at that," Ms. Cortez says sarcastically, feigning a look of surprise. "Look at the amazing things that happen when you guys clean up after yourselves — you know where everything is and you can actually *see* the floor!"

"Who's *we?*" I ask incredulously. "I did this all by myself, don't give those other yutes my credit."

She laughs heartily — slapping her knee and throwing her head back. Her booming laugh causes me to laugh, and we do that for a few seconds until my stomach hurts. Ms. Cortez reminds me of Nellie when she does that, and it makes me more fond of her. Some of my classmates look into the room as our loud laughter grabs their attention. Even Michael looks up from his hunched position and smiles as he sees us laughing.

"Oh man," I say breathlessly, "Oh I needed that. It's been a minute since I've had a really good laugh."

"Oh yeah? Teenage angst boggin' you down?"

I laugh half-heartedly, "Yeah, something like that." She looks at me inquisitively, squinting her eyes as she thinks.

"You wanna talk about that something?"

Oh man, she doesn't even know how much I want to. "It's complicated," I say.

"Yeah. Life often is — but talking about it helps. Taking your time and processing it bit by bit could help." I nod, thinking about a way I can explain everything I'm feeling without giving anything away.

"Well, I just learned something about my family that's… huge. It makes me rethink everything I knew about myself and the world, and I've had to do a total reset on what I thought I knew — which was really nothing." She nods, listening attentively, and letting me get everything out.

I continue, "And as I'm learning all of these things, I'm in a perpetual state of anxiety. I have to learn all these new things that totally contradict everything I know and value and… it's all so much."

"I can only imagine," she says empathetically. She leans forward and looks at me kindly, continuing, "Learning new things can be so anxiety-inducing because you have to go outside of your comfort zone and be in an unfamiliar place. That was what it was like for me when I moved here — I was six and barely spoke any English. And I can imagine that was what it was like for your mom and aunt — things are different here than they are on the islands. And whatever it is that you're learning about your past is probably poking holes in your safety bubble, right?"

"Yeah," I scoff, "you have no idea." She smiles softly, while I think about it more. She realizes there's more, and encouragingly prods me with caring eyes.

"I just don't want everything to implode because I can't handle all this new stuff I have to process."

"I don't think that'll happen," she says matter-of-factly.

"Really? Why's that?"

"Remember when I was your substitute teacher for your art class in elementary school? I was an assistant teacher doing my placement hours for school, and I filled in for your art teacher for two weeks while he was on vacation."

"Oh yeah," I say with a smile. "I totally forgot about that — I keep forgetting I met you earlier than just last year. You let us write on the pavement with chalk and the principal got mad and called it '*introductory-level graffiti.*'"

She laughs, nodding as she remembers the principal and his face that effortlessly resembled a tomato. "Yeah, well that was a few months after your mother had passed."

I lean back, looking at her in realization. "Yeah, it was. How did you know that?"

"A couple of the permanent teachers were talking about it in the lounge during your recess. They were talking about this black girl who suddenly lost her mother, and how they're worried it was taking a toll on her performance. They spoke so fondly of you, and it wasn't long before I figured out you were the kid they were talking about."

She gets up from her seat and comes to stand in front of me, looking at me with a smile. "You were so quiet, and I remembered thinking to myself '*This girl conveys so much sadness, and she isn't even 10.*' You didn't have to say anything but I could feel the sadness just rolling off you. I knew you didn't really talk, but I've never seen someone so young express emotions so openly without having to say a word. No one else seemed to see it — but I could. When you drew, it was like everything you were feeling came out through your hand. Even a sunflower I asked you guys to draw and you drew yours differently from the other kids."

"What can I say, I've got raw talent," I joke.

"Funny," she says, "but true. Well, I kept watching you because I wanted to make sure you were okay. And then one day you came to class and you were *bald*. I was so shocked I had to keep myself from staring!"

I laugh, as I remember the stares from the other kids at school. "Yeah, a lot of people didn't get that memo."

"Yeah, well after that day you were talking. Better than that, you were engaging with your other classmates, you were smiling. You even threw a couple of jokes, and girl, you are *funny*."

"Ah, well I try my best," I fake humility, laughing an aunty-laugh and making Ms. Cortez laugh in reply.

"Well, you're pretty good at that too. And after seeing you engaging again and being a part of things, I just became so proud. I didn't know you all too well, but I've seen your emotions go from utter sadness to happiness, transitioning from darkness to light. You did that at such a young age which made me smile because it was inspiring. *You* are so inspiring."

My heart swells as her words hit, and my eyes prick as tears threaten to spill over. "Ms. Cortez you gas me up too much — lots of kids lose their parents, it's not that big a deal."

"Don't try to be humble, Jamila," she says. "You could've done a bunch of things after losing your mom — you could've cried all the time, gotten angry and took it out on others. Hell, you could've pushed it down to not feel the pain anymore until you forgot it altogether. But you *felt it* — you felt the fullness of your pain and then, bit by bit, you brought yourself from that pain into a place where you could feel other things again. To feel happy and childlike joy. Some grown-ups can't even do that. But you did. And that is a big deal."

She walks up to me and lifts my chin so I look at her — something Nellie would do. I lose the fight to hold back my tears and they spill from my eyes, while she looks at me firmly and with a smirking smile.

"I thought this was supposed to be an art class," I say thickly. "Not a therapy session."

"Consider me multifaceted." I laugh wetly as she chuckles, cocking her head to the side.

"But if anything that's supposed to remind you how mature you are — even when you're in it and feeling all the things, you're going to be able to come out on the other side. I've seen it — everyone around you has seen it — and there's not a doubt in my mind that you'll be okay. Changes are hard, but if anything this is just a test — and from what I've heard, you're pretty good at those."

"The best," I joke.

"Well then consider this a test from life itself. You have to study, which means learning all of these new things, and before you know it you'll be prepared for that test. Imploding is the last thing I think will happen; you may be shaken from the inside, but you won't crumble. I think you'll keep yourself together and rebuild yourself from the inside."

"You sure believe in me a lot," I say softly.

"Yeah — and I think you should believe in you too."

I look at her speechless, not knowing how to respond to that. No one has ever called me out by my name before — but does this count if it's for my benefit? She reaches for me and squeezes my shoulder, looking into my face with a caring one of her own.

"No one is going to help you by believing in you better than you believe in yourself. You won't grow that way, and growth is a good thing. Don't see it as something scary, see it as a journey with new horizons. And never forget that people are going on this journey with you — but you have to pilot the ship to get there safely. No one else is going to be able to

293

do that for you. Only you are going to be able to get yourself to a place beyond where you are — and that starts with believing in you." She points to my chest and looks into my eyes to make sure I hear what she's saying.

"I got you," I say.

"Yeah?"

"Yeah."

"Good," she says with a smile. "I can only imagine the places you'll go when you dare to believe that you can get yourself there."

I smile warmly, seeing the faith she has in me is melting the icy anxiety within me. She pats me on the shoulder and looks at her watch, then heads out to the classroom to make an announcement. I look at the clock on the wall and realize that class is almost over, and head back to my seat to pack up my things.

"Okay class," Ms. Cortez announces loudly. "The bell's about to go off so let me just remind you real quick that this assignment is due in three weeks — really guys, I want to be wowed. Go outside of your comfort zone. Yes, I know, you'll have to stay off your phones for a while, but surely you'll survive."

The murmur of our chuckles fills her pause before she continues, "Also, I won't be here next class, so consider it a free period." That gets a rounding cheer from the class.

"I still expect you to work on the assignment," she yells over our cheers, but to no avail. She chuckles and shakes her head, waving her hand in defeat. The bell finally rings and we all jump up for lunch.

Mr. Min owns a convenience store, but he somehow has access to everything you would possibly need — regardless of the event or the occasion. Forget just snacks and drinks and household items; you need supplies to renovate? The man's got it for you. Fabric to start sewing? Fabricland doesn't have anything on him. Art supplies? The man's got the stuff to satisfy Picasso's wet dream. Luckily for me, I happened to need some things in small quantities, and Mr. Min is just the guy for that. I bike down the road and reach the convenience store, lifting one leg from the pedal and coasting on the other until I reach the door. Mr. Min doesn't have a bike rack, or anywhere for me to put my bike, but he's nice to let me ride it in — as long as I don't make a mess. I lift the bike onto the step and as I'm about to roll it in, Reggie comes from the side with a mop and a bucket. And a less than happy expression.

"Whoa, whoa, whoa," he says upset. "The hell you think you're doin'? You can't come rolling in God knows what from outside after I *just* mopped these floors."

"Well look at you," I say, feigning surprise. "For a second there I thought you were actually being responsible enough to care what happens to this place."

"Don't flatter yourself, sweetheart," he counters, shooting me a lazy smile. My heart skips a beat — it's impossible to deny how fine this man is, despite my best efforts. He continues, "If my dad saw the floor still dirty after he told me to clean it, I wouldn't hear the end of it."

"Well I can't leave my bike out here by itself, so what do you propose I do?"

He sighs, looking at me with an annoyed expression. I shoot him a look, cocking my hip and resting my hand on top. His eyes begin to soften with a small smile threatening to creep in from the corner of his lips, amused by my sassiness — he can't be that annoyed if I could make him cave that easily.

"Just give me the bike," he relents. "I'll keep it by the cash register until you're finished."

"That's still bringing the bike into the store, genius. Doesn't that defeat the purpose of this scintillating conversation — thereby making it pointless."

"It is so annoying when you talk like that," he says monotone. I walk in, move past him and turn to face him again. "You talk like a geriatric teacher with a midlife crisis."

"What can I say — I'm wise beyond my years," I say, shrugging with an annoying smile. He shakes his head, but that smile finally takes over his face. He tries to hide it, but it's too late. He mimes lifting the bike — with one hand, wow — and points to it with a flourish.

"Unlike you, I actually exercise, so I'll lift it and put it by where I haven't cleaned yet."

"Ah," I say. "I see your thought process."

"Right," he says, rolling his eyes and walking away. I chuckle and look around the store — I seem to have a knack for never knowing where things are when I need them, so I'll need Reggie's further assistance.

"Actually," I say probingly. He turns around with an impatient expression, and I lift my hand up in apology. "I actually need some things, and I'm not exactly sure where they'd be."

"What do you need?" he asks, dropping the bike and leaning it against the counter. The veins in his arm pop out as he does so, and my throat catches as the butterflies flitter away in my stomach.

"Uh," I stammer, making him smile. "I, uh, need some clay."

"Some clay?" he says more than asks.

"Yes," I say firmly, trying my best to hold it together. "For my art project."

"Ah," he says, with a flattering smile on his face. "Anything else?"

"Yes," I reply, clearing my throat. He smiles again as he looks at me, a look I'm not used to seeing in his eyes. Attraction.

I continue, "I also need some strings and fabrics. Preferably black, if you have it."

He looks at me for a moment, silently and with that same look in his eyes, before turning and heading for an aisle. He glances behind him, and I move forward in a start as I realize he expects me to follow him. Towards the back of the third aisle are some household items and maintenance supplies — including, surprisingly, small containers of clay.

"It's a wonder your dad has literally everything in this tiny store."

"Yeah, he's a man of wonder and mystery," he says monotone. I smile and chuckle, which actually makes him smile sheepishly. Weird.

"How much do you need?"

"Not much," I reply. "I just need to make a scale."

"A scale? For like, weighing yourself?"

"No," I reply with a laugh. "Like the scales of justice. I'm making something for art class and I need the clay for the scale."

"And you expect to make a scale with what exactly? I know you're smart, but I didn't exactly take you for an artsy type."

"I'm a woman of many talents," I reply sagely. He smiles and chuckles under his breath, and to my surprise I find myself getting tingly. C'mon girl — he's a flirt who would charm the shoes off a thief, get yourself together.

"Well one container should do you good — and we have some twine and ribbon, if that'll do for the string."

"Yeah," I say softly. "That works." He nods and reaches over to the opposite shelf, grabbing beige twine and a carton of clay for me.

"Okay, and fabric. We only have cotton right now, unless you want to buy some nice napkins and cut those up."

"No, no, the black cotton will do. Thank you," I say kindly.

"No problem, sweetheart," he replies.

Unable to resist, I reply, "It's Jamila. Not sweetheart — just *Jamila*."

"Mmhmm," he hums, backing away with a smile. I roll my eyes, but my stomach still flutters with butterflies. Girl pull yourself together — he's just a flirt, not a knight in shining armour. And even if he was, that stereotype is an ancient form of patriarchy that's meant to strengthen the damsel-in-distress archetype and I am no damsel. I'm a Bastet for crying out loud; back up and tell those butterflies to chill out.

I resist the urge to grab a candy bar, knowing that Loni will feed me with something when I get to the diner. I walk to the cash register and pay for my art supplies.

"Thank you," I say as he hands me the bag.

"No problem, Jamila," he says obnoxiously, making me roll my eyes. He chuckles as he grabs my bike easily with one hand and carries it out the door. Plopping it on the ground, he turns to me and motions to the bike with a flourish. I look at him deadpan as I lift my leg over the seat, rolling my eyes as I try to conceal my smile.

"Don't be a stranger, sweetheart," he says over his shoulder.

"I told you, it's —"

"Yeah, yeah, yeah," he says, waving me off. I scoff annoyed and pedal down the sidewalk, biking back towards Loni's. I mutter under my breath — wondering how this guy can stand straight with all the air blowing up his head — until I finally reach the diner. I lock my bike to the rack and head in, waving quickly to Ray and going through the back doors.

"Hey, baby girl," Loni says, her hands deep in a vat of batter and moving at lightning speed. "I'm a little busy. Do me a favour — go downstairs an' start readin' some of di books I put down on di table, an' I'll come fetch yuh when I can. Just do some readin' for today, we'll give di otha stuff a rest."

I nod and let her get back to work, looking to make sure no one else sees as I head for the closet. I close the door behind me and turn on the single light bulb. I lift the hatch to the steps below and make my way down; my steps are sure and quick, as I'm now used to coming down here more regularly, and the lights flicker on to welcome me.

I make my way to the far side of the room and plop my backpack and convenience store bag on the table. I pull out the container of clay and string, and head to the sink and fill a bowl with water. I pull out my notebook and open it to the page with the crude sketch of my project idea. I pull out my phone and search for an image of a scale of justice for reference, and set it aside at my work station. For the next hour, I work on moulding the clay into a believable scale. I have a pretty good skill of being able to redo an image just by looking at it, and I guess the same goes for moulding clay. My hands press and form the shape and, on a whim, take a toothpick from the potion pantry and draw cracks in the mould. A scale of justice, for the argument of my assignment, wouldn't be solid and would — in fact — have cracks in its foundation. Wow, I think to myself, chuckling — I amaze myself.

I finish the base and begin forming the actual scales, two hollow dishes, and string them to the top of the pedestal. For the person holding the scales, I'll use one of Michael's old 'action figures' that he left in my room a while ago, and tape a photo of the founding fathers to the head. I pull out a stack of printed headlines from my backpack and start cutting out the headlines. I printed off as many that were contradictory to each other — the claim of the Indigenous population given proper reparations while another highlights how many communities have birth defects from too much lead in their water. One claim says the major cities have a rising GDP, while another touts an unsustainable and expensive real estate market. I cut these up and tape them all over the base and upwards towards the top of the pedestal. Making room for the cracks to show through, as it covers the entirety of the base. Satisfied with my work for now, I grab the books stacked on the table and head to a spot by the wall to the left.

The one great thing I like about being a Bastet is that I come from a line of badass women. And I get to learn about them from these books Loni's been having me read, and I am a sucker for a good history book. Something tells me I'm just reading books today so that I can take a break from all the physical power practice — a much-needed break if you ask me. After grabbing a Vanilla Bean milkshake and some plantain chips to snack on, I sit on the floor — leaning against a soft part of the wall beside one of the larger bookshelves. The afternoon rush is in full effect, so Loni, Ray, and Dionne — one of the diners' new hires — are upstairs holding down the fort. Luckily I was able to sneak away without having to buss the tables; Loni definitely needs the help, but for the work I've been doing lately, a girl's gotta get paid.

I flip open a thick evergreen book to the first page, seeing very crude drawings of women in the shape of a circle. They're wearing very little clothing, only covering their chest and private areas — and coloured in black ink that still holds its colour, even though it looks like this drawing is centuries old. Some of the pages look like they've been chopped short on the edges, so clearly this book was put together over a period of time and used all of these different pages to tell the story. The page feels delicate as if it'll rip in my hands with one wrong move, so I slowly and carefully flip to the next page. The backside of the page has three women: one in the top corner, one in the middle, and the other at the bottom of the page. There's also a group of people beside each woman. The woman at the top has her hands up in the air, with little stars trailing from her hands to a circle drawn around a group of people. Underneath her are symbols in a language I don't understand, but I think this drawing shows our ability to protect ourselves and others. The second woman leans forward through a doorway, with a hand cupped to her ear — she listens to another figure, in front of other figures, that are outlined in red. The sun is drawn just above her, while the moon is drawn on the other side of the figures; this must be our power of talking to the afterlife. I take a sip of my milkshake, greeting my tongue with the taste and savouring it as long as I can. There's no chance I'm going up there for another — and get pulled into working the night rush? I'm good down here.

The woman at the bottom lays on her side asleep, with small circles trailing upwards to an infinity symbol. In one of the circles of the symbol is a pile of what looks like dirt, and in the other circle that same pile with a newly emerged plant growing from below. This has to be our ability to see into the future — and it connects to the drawing on the next page, which shows our power of controlling the time flow. A rod with several lines drawn every which way is behind another woman, with her hands stretched on either side of her over the rod — it's outlined in blue, with little stars drawn just above its surface. Below this drawing are bowls, bottles, and jars, and below that another woman; transforming into a panther. Showing the Road to Homo Sapien again, but Bastet's edition. A woman goes from a standing position to a bent position, and then is no longer a woman and, instead, a ferocious black panther with bared sharp teeth. I stare at this panther — its colour shiny with the dark ink — and wonder how this power felt. How did my ancestors feel when they went from their human form to this ferocious beast? I flip to the next page, and it's riddled with drawings. The same symbols I don't understand occupy the top of the page, but underneath that is more writing in different languages;

translations of the original text. How many women translated this after losing their languages? How many hands touched these pages? How did Loni come to have it? I skim down the page, noticing French, Dutch, German, and finally English.

We are the protectors of those defenseless — who cannot fight for themselves and would perish without us. We bring justice to those who are wronged, avenging them and punishing their oppressors.

Damn, that's some heavy-duty stuff.

Let the power of protection overtake you — and the wisdom of our Bast ancestor to guide you. This transformation will give you the strength of 50 men and the speed of 1,000 horses. You will scare men who are fearless, and protect the defenseless. You are strength and softness; remember your duality, lest you eternally perish to your animal form.

Well, that's not appealing. Lest I eternally perish to my animal form? So what Loni was saying before — of Bastet women not being able to transform back to their human form and staying a panther forever — wasn't just some sick initiation joke. This is real, and apparently it's been happening since before our ancestors were stolen into slavery. I still can't believe we were able to do that — to turn into a fierce beast. But from everything I'm able to do, I shouldn't be surprised that one more superhuman ability would be added to the list. I look to the right page and see a list of names written closely together. About the first 30 are smudge out, but after the 45th name, I begin to see them clearly. Fula Ncata. Shurei Kinta. Ashley Smith, formerly Leona Akana. I stop at that name, immediately intrigued by the two names side by side. This must've been one of the first of our ancestors to be enslaved and given a slave name. All the names are written in black ink but are underlined with a deep red colour that looks less inky and more like a dye. As I continue to read further down the page, I see more 'formerly' preceding their birth names. Beside these names are dates, and I can only make out the earliest date being 1672. Everything before that is smudged ink that gives nothing away. As I read further down the list and flip to the next page, the dates get further and further apart. One name has a date that says 1925, but the next date after that jumps to 1977. When I come to the last date of 2001, freshly inked compared to its predecessors, I stare at the name that sits beside it. Nyla Mason — lazily scrawled in cursive handwriting. This list of names must be a list of all the Bastet women that's ever been recorded. I'm sure that there must've been more, surely not all of their names could be recorded in the contents of this book, but this is still a pretty extensive list. It has the names of the women and the dates that they must've revealed their identity — or maybe when they were born, or when they died — I don't know. But this is the first piece of evidence that shows me how many of us there were — not just a sprinkling of humans with powers here and there. No, rather a nation of women capable of magnificent things. And I'm a part of it.

I look at the list again and find Nellie's name at the top of the second page — Nellie Freeman, 1996. Nellie was born in 1975, so this must've been when she revealed her identity to Loni — I recognize her handwriting anywhere, it was Loni that wrote Nellie's name. Just below Nellie's name is my mother's — Keba Freeman, 1996. My breath hitches in my throat as I drag my fingertips along her name; dried down and textured on the paper, I trace the lines of what's left of my mother in these pages. I miss her so much. Sometimes, I think of going to the Realm of Duality just so I can see her. To talk to her again, and hold her hands as she caresses my fingers, just like she used to. But even I know that's not a good idea — it's not healthy to hold on to something that's gone, even if you can get it again. It would be toxic for me to keep using the Realm as a crutch; my mother's watching over me, but she's doing so from her grave. There's no beating around the bush. She's not coming back, regardless of whether I have the power to go to her when I please. I have to be able to go on without falling back to needing her all the time. I have to be strong and do this without the comfort of safety in her arms. I grab my backpack from where it was laying on the floor and fish in my bag for a pen — finding a nice one, I write below Nyla Mason's name. Jamila Freeman, 2020. I nod, satisfied. Saying I'm a Bastet is one thing, but putting my name among the dozens of names that came before me is another. It's the silent reveal of myself, my true self, and is more of an acceptance of myself than just going through the motions and saying it. I look at my name again, and the date I wrote down; then, I start to notice my name beginning to fade. Odd, I think, as it loses its colour — I write over the fading ink again and press down on the pen so that it stays. But as soon as I lift my pen, my name begins fading again. I furrow my eyebrows as I look at the page in confusion — why is my name disappearing? Is this some weird spell-book hiccup where only a certain person can write in here? But the number is still there — still stark and dark as ever — so why is my name disappearing into the page? I decide to come back to this oddity later, surely it's not that pressing.

I turn back to the first page and look at the first dozen names. I try to make them out, but they must've been written in pencil or some other writing instrument. No matter how hard I squint, I can't seem to distinguish their names, or the dates of their identity revealed. The earliest one I can make out is Leona Akana. Turned Ashley Smith, identity revealed 1702. She would've been a slave around this time — and, if she was in Jamaica, then it would have been long before slavery was abolished. She did not live long enough to see her freedom. To think of the life she had to live: of servitude, constant hiding, and fear — makes my stomach rest uneasy. To think of the strife she lived with to no longer have her name, to even write her slave name down in a book that's for and by us, makes my hair stand on end. To think that she had to sit with the hope of something better — with the knowledge that she would never see it — makes my heart break from the blow. It can be easy to look back into history and see definitively when something began and something ended — but she was living in it, and she had no idea when the suffering would end. For all I know it could've been endless for her, and that is true hopelessness. I stare at her name and drag my fingertips along the underline of her name; this woman is one of the eldest ancestors I can trace myself back to. The link between my past and my present, and learning about her could dictate my future. Words cannot express how grateful I am for her sacrifice — not to die for me. No, to live for me without actually living. That's a sacrifice that taxes the soul in a way that hits deeper and whose aim is truer. I absentmindedly trace the underline as I stare at her name and my eyes losing focus as I slip into space. My vision gets more and more out of focus, until shapes lose their distinction. I try to bring myself back to reality — which everyone does when they've stared into space for a time — but I can't seem to. I will myself to come out of that state, but I'm stuck — no longer aimlessly staring into space, I'm stuck in the ether. Then suddenly, red pools in from the corners of my eyes and seeps towards the center of my vision — flooding my eyesight and turning the basement into a horror movie. I start to panic and hyperventilate because whatever is happening is not normal. And that I am fully confident in saying despite all the crazy stuff that's been happening lately. Last time I checked, my visits to the Realm of Duality never started out this way and even then, I wasn't really aware of my body in the physical world. For all intents and purposes, when I was in the Realm, I was *in it*. Everything I saw, smelt and felt there was like I was really there, and I had no consciousness of my body in the real world. But I can feel my body here, and I can't move. I have no control of my motor functions, and I can barely see anything. I'm stuck in an immobile, blind shell, and I don't know how to regain control of myself.

The pool of red gets darker, and thicker, until everything turns black. I breathe faster as I panic — I can't even call upstairs for help. No one is supposed to know I'm down here let alone this place exists, and I can't even control my voice. But then the darkness begins to clear away, and shapes start to reform. I try and calm my breathing as I slowly regain some of my vision — pinpricks shoot through my arms as I regain feeling in my body, and I tepidly move my limbs to take back control. I blink my eyes as the red film pulls back from my eyes, and breathe deeply to bring more air into my lungs. I look around to bring myself back to a state of calm, trying to point out things I can see to ground me, but I don't recognize any of the things around me. I'm not in the basement any more.

The cool air of the basement is replaced with hot muggy air, and the chirping of crickets and people's chatter replaces the quiet I was just enjoying. It's dark, most likely the middle of the night, and deep in the heart of a forest. The dirt ground is soft, and the rocks I'm leaning against hard on my back. I sit on the edge of a camp, with a fire pit in the middle and a bunch of people milling around to finish their tasks. Makeshift tents pepper the surrounding of the firepit — an area with a table and overturned baskets sit to the far left, which must be a dining area. Black people, with the darkest skin I've ever seen, quickly walk around the camp. Some preparing food for a meal, others sewing clothing and armour while others forge weapons, and some just walk to their respective duties that I cannot see. The men wear white and cream-coloured pants rolled up their calves, with string pulled across their chests to hold knives and small pouches. The women wear pants or coverings that look like skirts, and thin fabric that stretches from one shoulder across their chests to cover their breasts. The noise of their conversations fill my ears, as I recognize their thick Jamaican accents. But these are different — they seem more rustic and thick with another accent. Jamaican accents nowadays are more enunciated, but it changes from place to place — especially in the country or for older people that've been in Jamaica for a long time. I look up to see tall trees shooting up to the sky, their leaves almost covering the starry night and the glowing moon. I look past the camp to the hilly plains; mounds of dips and hills extending far beyond where I can see, and making the trees around us staggering on the uneven ground.

I stand up, trying to figure out where I am and how I got here. This must be a vision, or a visit to the Realm or something, but this transition is different from every other time that I've visited. It's scary and debilitating, and it's throwing me for a loop — I need to get it together to process what's happening, but I'm feeling dizzy with confusion. I nervously finger my pendant as I try to catch my bearings. I shuffle forward while looking at the people, who all wear very little clothing and whose sweat glistens on their skin. I don't blame them — my armpits are pricking with sweat as we speak, and my edges are curling up from the humidity. I catch sight of a man on the far side of the fire, sitting on a stool with his back hunched over his task. He whittles away at a long staff, sharpening the end to a deadly weapon. He sits a ways back from the rest of the camp, even though several other people are making weapons on the other side of the camp, closer to the fire. He looks forlorn, melancholy, and his movements get sharper as he whittles. I watch him as he looks at the staff with intense eyes, and realize I recognize this man. It's the man from my first vision to the past, the one stooped down watching the slaves hack away at the sugar cane. He wanted to go in and save them right then, but his friend came from behind and stopped him. I remember him looking upset that he couldn't do anything at that moment, and it looks like this is fairly recent after that. He couldn't see me the last time, and he probably won't be able to see me this time, but he's a familiar face. I walk towards him, skirting the treeline and being as quiet as I can. I pass behind some men standing over a stone slab, moving around figurines and talking with authority, and some women weaving baskets and clothing, before coming close to the man. I look at his head for a second, watching him in his solitude, and take a step forward.

"I wouldn't do that," a deep voice says. I whirl around to find a woman standing among the trees, looking at me intensely. "Quao doesn't tek kindly to people comin' up behind him."

She walks closer to me, and I can see her more clearly as the light from the fire pulls the shadows away. She wears a skirt covering and a one-shoulder strap across her chest. Strings criss-cross across her chest and hold daggers, small vials, and a shotgun strapped across her back. Her hair is wrapped in a white cotton scarf, and accentuates her sharp cheekbones and strong nose. Her scars that are in the shape of crescents arch from her cheekbones over her eyebrows, not taking away from her beauty. Her almond-shaped eyes are dark — almost black — and her upper lip glistens, just as the rest of her body does. Muscles extend over her entire body — her shoulders, arms, and legs rippling and sinewy — and her hands are taut from a life of work. She looks at me stone-faced, but with a hint that a smirk is always on her face when she's around close company.

"You're her," I say. "The woman that was talking to that guy."

"I'm assumin' *'that guy'* is the one whittlin' away at that staff like a sad puppy dog?" She walks up beside me and looks at Quao, resting her hands on her hips. "Doesn't get his way an' he mopes like a baby, gettin' on me damn nerves. He betta cut it out before I lick him pon di head."

I look at her wide-eyed, wondering what the hell is going on. They couldn't see me in the last vision, so why can she see me now? She turns her head and looks at me amused, raising her eyebrow at my rude staring. I quickly look away, embarrassed, but look back to her. She cuts her eye and looks back to Quao, shaking her head.

"He'll be alright. He'll get ova it eventually." She looks and turns to face me, cocking her head to the side. "You on di otha hand need an explanation, right?"

"That would be nice," I say meekly. She smirks, nodding her head and turning back to the trees. She walks into the forest wordlessly, and with no one else here to fill in the blanks I quickly follow her. She walks fast — I thought commuters walked fast, but they don't have anything on her. I rush to keep up with her and pick up my stride, struggling to not trip over the uneven terrain while she walks with light and sure steps.

"You must be wonderin' what's goin' on," she says. "I can only imagine how confused you must be."

"Oh no, everything's fine and dandy," I say sarcastically. She stops and looks at me with raised eyebrows.

"Sorry," I say quietly. She smirks a little before walking again. I guess she's got a sense of humour.

"Well, I figured out that you're a Bastet soon as I saw yuh. Me know everybody in dis camp, and seein' a girl in weird lookin' clothes, actin' like she naave nuh sense, caught my eye pretty quick."

"Where are we? Who are you?" She looks at me with surprise, and a happy look in her eyes.

"Well look at you," she says surprised. "Finally askin' the right questions." We finally come to a more open clearing; not that big, but big enough to give each of us enough breathing room. I look around to the trees — the bark textured and dark, with green leaves extending to the sky and bush peppering the dirt on the ground. Small fruits grow here and there, and the scent thickens the humidity in the air.

"We're in Jamaica, aren't we?"

She nods, crossing her arms and looking at me intently. "During the first Maroon war," she says. The first war? That wasn't too long before slavery was abolished here. I wonder if she got to see that day — she looks to be in her mid-30s and has lived this long. Maybe she lived long enough to see her own freedom. Or maybe her life ends shortly after this.

"Why am I here?" I ask.

"Well, chances are you gotta hold of di Bastet Tree, and brought yuhself eere."

"What's that? And how did I do that?" I ask.

"Issa book with a list of names of Bastets, with di year they committed to recordin' their identity." So I was right about the number. I do a mental dust-off of the shoulder, but quickly getting serious.

She continues, "That list has the most names recorded of any Bastet eva, and it's the greatest threat to our people."

"Why?"

She walks toward me, gliding gracefully on the ground while looking fierce with strength. "If you could get yuh hands on a book that had a list of Bastets, and a time period around the time they were alive, don't yuh think it would be pretty valuable?"

"You'd know the names of Bastets in the present day," I realize, "and could hunt them down." She nods, as it clicks in my brain.

"Not tuh mention be able to track otha Bastets down that are descended from di people on di list — even if they're not on it an' don't aave nuh powers yet. It'd be like sendin' us to di firing squad without even tellin' us what we're in for."

I shake my head in disbelief. I didn't even think of the risks of putting names on a list when there's literally a supremacist cult hunting us, and that would be the perfect source for them.

"That list must've been kept a secret for centuries — and I can't imagine many women knew about it. That would only widen the risk of being found out." She looks at me with a look that's hard to place, sort of a mixture of inquisitiveness and pride.

"What?" I ask.

"Nothin'," she says. "You're jus' so well-spoken. Mek me feel good inside."

"Yeah?"

"Yeah," she says, sighing deeply with a whisper of a smile. "Because that means we did something right."

I don't know what she means by that, but I give her a small smile anyways. She doesn't smile back, but I do see a slight smirk — something tells me that's the best I'll get with her.

"You didn't answer my other question," I say.

She looks at me with a raised eyebrow, asking, "An' what was that?"

"Who are you?"

She slowly blinks and nods, and looks at me expressionlessly for a second. She walks closer to me and looks me in the eye — she's a little bit taller than me, but most of the height is probably coming from the headwrap. I start to backup reflexively, slightly intimidated by her power, but I make myself stay where I am and straighten my back. She must appreciate that, because her smirk deepens and her eyes flash with respect.

"I don't think you're meant tuh know dat yet."

"What?" I ask incredulously. "I'm in a strange place, surrounded by people I don't know and you're the one person I can sort of rely on — but I still don't know you, but you expect me to listen to you blindly?"

"Yes."

"Tuh," I exclaim. I turn away and put my hands on my hips, shaking my head annoyed. I angrily wipe the sweat off my forehead and pull my shirt away from my torso as the fabric sticks to me. Crickets chirp louder now that we're deeper in the forest, and the earthy scent of dirt and animals swell into my nostrils. She grabs my arm, shocking me — this is the first time she's touched me, and her grip is firm but caring. She brings me towards her again and looks at me intensely — that must be her go-to look.

"All yuh need tuh know is that I'm here tuh help yuh. I'm your ancestor, and the fact that I can see you means you must'a called me. Whether you did that by accident or on purpose me nuh know, but if I didn't need to tell you somethin', den we wouldn't be talkin' right now."

"But how would I have called you?" I ask exasperatedly. "One second I was reading up on our history and the next I'm paralyzed and brought to the plains of Jamaica? I have no idea what I did."

"You were reading the list of names, right?" I nod confused as she continues, "Those names are written in di book, but there's a protection spell that was cast on it years ago dat mek it suh you caah see dem. To mek dem visible, we seep our blood on di page. All names are underlined in blood — you probably didn't realize it 'cause it's dried down by now, but all'a us dat wrote our names in the Bastet Tree did so. We commit to di risk by underlinin' our names in our blood and makin' it permanent, and tracin' that bloodline brought you directly to me."

I stare at her wide-eyed, horrified, and disgusted. "I was touching *your blood*?" She kisses her teeth and snarls her upper lip, chastising me without saying a word.

"Oh relax, it ain't gonna kill yuh. That's not important. The point is dat doin' dat summoned me, an' our ancestors must'a known dat yuh needed tuh speak to me."

"But how would you know what to say to me? You didn't even know I was coming."

"Yes, I did." She raises her chin while looking into the night — not looking at me but talking to me. "You came to me in a dream last night — I couldn't see yuh face, but I could see one of my descendants in trouble. One'a our ancestors warned me of di trouble dat would come to you, an' that you needed guidance."

"So you know about the Toubab that attacked me in the hospital?" She doesn't answer right away, her eyebrows briefly furrowing for a moment.

"What's a *hospeetal*?" I pause, I guess hospitals weren't really a thing during the slave era. They were lucky to know someone who could fix a toothache let alone a doctor.

"Never mind," I say with a smile. She slightly shrugs, letting it go.

"Best tuh leave it dat way, let di unknown be di unknown. But that's not what I saw — what the ancestors warned me about is yet tuh 'appen to you. You need to know that the worst is yet to come, so I need you tuh listen carefully." Her tone gets more serious. Sensing a grave warning in her voice, I hold my breath as my nerves instinctively jump.

"You are goin' tuh be attacked many times — by enemies for different reasons. They are goin' tuh violate you, an' use your own power against you. Your power as a woman and as a Bastet. Some will succeed. Some will fail. You aave to mek sure that no matter what you keep yuh head together."

My heart starts beating fast as I begin to panic. I've already been sexually assaulted by Ricky Brass and attacked by a Toubab in a public hospital. Both times I got away, but barely. And I barely held it together then — how am I supposed to keep it together if this is going to keep happening?

"I know that Toubabs are constantly hunting us — I almost got taken by one — and women get assaulted all the time —"

"No," she interrupts firmly. "I'm not talking about some likkle one-two grabbin' from a man. You're goin' tuh be violated in di worst ways — they will try to torture you. Rape you. Kill you. An' you aave to keep yuhself calm and together when it happens. Your powers are di one thing that'll help yuh when you're attacked, an' you aave to start treatin' them more like a weapon. You're not a likkle girl anymore — you're a woman, an' you aave to start protectin' yuhself. Because no one else will."

I look at her speechless; my mouth gaping as I try to find words, but failing to get anything out. I rapidly shake my head in denial, my eyes frozen wide, and my heart racing. I start hyperventilating again, and tears start springing into my eyes. She sees my episode and walks toward me, firmly grabbing me by the shoulders and giving me one hard shake.

"Stop the foolishness," she says, her voice emboldened with stone. My heart immediately stops, then resumes its regularly scheduled programming — something in her voice just triggered every angry reprimand I ever got as a child, and her exasperation has never been more familiar.

"Gettin' all scared and freakin' out like it's goin' tuh help yuh. Dis is life — people are selfish and will suck you dry until you don't serve dem any purpose. Di only thing you can do is leave a likkle bit fah you and those who caah fight fah demselves. You know dis wasn't goin' tuh be easy. This isn't somethin' you can try an' work yuh way around. You aave never been thru anythin' like dis. You cannot predict anythin' dat's goin' tuh 'appen, but you caah jus' shut down because of dat either! You aave a life tuh live, a job to do, an' breakin' down because yuh scared isn't the flip side of di coin. You caah just tek di easy way out wit' fear. You're a Bastet! You guide people in life an' in death. You protec' people from sickness an' death, avenge people who were wronged, and tek down those who brought dem pain. *You can change time.* Men aave been pillagin', rapin', and murderin' for years to mek riches for their life on earth in vain — tryin' to cheat death wit' wealth an' powa when all dis time we been securin' it in ways dey could neva imagine. An' you wanna panic because they're gonna try an' hurt yuh?"

"Yes," I say weekly. She leans back and looks at me, her eyes softening a little bit.

"They can *try*," she says softly. "But they'll fail."

"And what if they don't?" I ask with fear.

309

"You aave to believe dat they'll fail — if you don't, then you're already dead."

My nerves spike on the inside, but I try my best to keep my cool on the outside. But this is a Bastet I'm talking to — one of the OG's, and she could see me fronting from a mile away.

"You're still scared," she says.

"Oh yeah," I scoff. "I'm not like you or the other Bastets. From everything I've heard and read, you guys did the damn thing."

"Women," she corrects. "Don't insult me by callin' us by dem weaklings dat dey like to call men."

I smile, as my heart warms with the hint of a kindred feminist spirit. "Sorry," I say. She smirks in reply. I think she's feeling that heart-warming feeling too.

I continue, "You fought slavers, rapists, and your own people, and still managed to not have our lineage snuffed out. I can't even handle the idea of getting attacked without freaking out."

"I neva said yuh have to be fearless," she says matter-of-factly. "You really think I went thru all I went thru and didn't feel scared?" She scoffs and shakes her head, walking a ways away and shifting her feet. With her back turned to me she looks up, her body settling from its straight-as-an-arrow stature to one weary with fatigue. Her taut muscles loosen as her shoulders sag, and her feet seem to sink into the dirt as the weight of her duty presses further down.

"I was terrified," she says wearily. "I still am. But I do it anyway." She turns and looks at me — despite the sinking of her body, she looks at me with a conviction that pierces right through me, and my body sensing her power from here.

"I fight for my freedom, an' fah di people who followed me to fight for theirs. Being a Bastet doesn't mean being fearless. It jus' means doin' what all'a dem people told you dat yuh couldn't do even when you're scared inside. That's real courage — not that fake nonsense the Toubabs try to sell. Yuh jus' aave tuh mek di choice to act *despite* di fear — and trust your enemies will fail."

"I know I have to — I just... I just don't think I can."

"You must," she replies. "You want tuh live, don't you?" I nod and shrug as if the answer is obvious, before she continues, "Then yuh aave no choice but to act thru to fear. You caah say yuh can't if it's really 'cause yuh won't."

We look at each other silently for a minute, while I let her wisdom sink in. This woman, this powerful force that I'm descended from, is cutting down my fear and insecurities with a razor-sharp blade. For every outcry of my fear of failure, she matches with a booming one of her own that dissects that fear into a pitiful, self-debilitating, sales pitch. *'Don't try to sell me that shit'* she's telling me — because you know damn well it isn't true. I know it isn't. But the security of using failure as a deterrent is appealing. But that's only keeping me from processing the fear of failure and seeing it for what it is — a bitch. And I ain't no bitch.

"Thank you," I say authentically. "This is definitely not the way I'd imagine to get advice, but who better to give it to me than a bad-ass ancestor who's seen it all, right?"

"That's right," she says with a smirk. I'm starting to like that smirk of hers; she definitely reminds me of the women I love. Or is it them that remind me of her? This whole time-loophole thing is sending me in circles.

"And I've gotta give you props —"

"Eh? Gimme what?"

"Props," I say with a laugh. "It's giving you respect when you deserve it."

"Oh," she says surprised, a content look on her face.

"Yeah — but I really do have to give you props. I don't know anyone that can beat around the bush like you can, and still have me thinking I wasn't the one with the unanswered questions."

"Whatcha talkin' about?"

"You still haven't told me who you are."

She scoffs with a smirk, shaking her head amused while she looks at me. She walks toward me and stands close in front of me, looking at me with an expression that I can't seem to figure out.

"You saw my name — you traced my blood to get here."

I shudder, still disgusted by it. "Don't remind me. And I may know your name, but who is Leona Akana?"

She looks at me — expressionless and, for several moments, without a word.

"Nice try," she says finally. But only two words, and they suck.

Suddenly, her head shoots to her right, looking for something in the trees. I look too, waiting to see a person or animal coming through the foliage, but hear and see nothing. But she can — she stares into the trees with intensity, her muscles now taut from anticipation. The distant chatter of the camp is the only thing I can hear — even her breathing is quiet, which makes me try and lower my breathing too. Then I hear a rustling in the trees, distant but definitely headed this way. She lowers her stance and grabs my arm firmly, tiptoeing to the right with the delicacy of a ballet dancer. I follow her but with less grace, stumbling behind her as fear rises within me. It's just a rustling in the trees, it could be anything really, but her demeanor tells me that whatever is on the other side of that noise is no friend to us. We creep into the bushes and hide, breathing low and slow and anticipating the mystery visitor's arrival. The sound of rustling now becomes visible, as leaves in the distance get pushed aside by whatever is coming. It's tall and seems to be coming from more than one spot — people. A group of them. Could this be the officers and slavers coming to capture and kill them? The heat that was thick in the air weighs heavier on me, and my armpits sting as sweat springs from my underarms, and my stomach flutters with butterflies. Suddenly shouting booms from the camp behind us, and we shoot our heads into the trees as we hear fearful shouts and the slapping of running feet. Men shouting to each other, while the women shush crying children. Leona shoots up and then looks to the rustling in the trees. I shoot up too and come slightly behind her — but with the rustling in front of us and the shouting behind us, there's no safe place to be when you're in the in-between. The rustling gets closer to us, as the leaves get dashed away and we begin to see figures of men slashing away with machetes. I start hyperventilating as I hear their breathing — so close I can hear their grunts as they slash closer towards their prey. Leona steps forward, her fists clenched by her side and her back taut. I grab her arm to stop her — she looks at me, seeing that I'm scared and worried. Her face softens as she looks at me, and gives me a look in her eyes to console me. *'It's going to be okay,'* she says. I nod as I understand her silent message — and even though I'm still terrified, I stand up taller in preparation for whatever is coming. Then she pokes my forehead with her finger, and an invisible force knocks my head back.

CHAPTER ELEVEN

I jolt up from where I sit, drenched in sweat, and my heartbeat racing. She must've cut the connection to the Realm of Duality, and sent me back to the physical world. I didn't even see it coming — she's *good*. I feel the book in my hands, open on the page showing the Bastet Tree. My pencil case hangs out of my backpack that's strewn by my feet, and the milkshake sits pathetically beside me; the bubbles and frothiness dissolved away. I must've been in the Realm for a while. I wipe the sweat off my forehead as I try to catch my breath, and fan myself with my shirt to dry off the sweat on my body. I wonder if I'll get used to these visits enough that it doesn't affect me so much physically. I'd like to not be sweating buckets in the middle of school if there's an unexpected visit to the Realm — maybe Loni and Nellie can help me control my senses so I ease the transition back from the spiritual world to the physical one. I look around me to catch my bearings, grounding myself in the diner basement. Over to the right is the indoor garden, with the sink to the right of it and a small desk to the left. Further to the left is the bookshelf with books filling its shelves from top to bottom, and a long table beside that with even more books atop its surface. Beside me is a table with bowls, vials and bottles, and above me hangs the potion pantry on the wall. I'm in the diner basement. I'm safe. Just breathe.

I look back at the list, my name still disappeared from the page. No wonder it kept vanishing away — how would I have known I had to cut myself and bleed onto the page? I think I'll just leave it for now. I'm still a little apprehensive to take on the risk, so it can wait until I've processed everything a little better. I turn the pages back to the first initial page of names, and find the name that I was tracing. Leona Akana — she wouldn't tell me who she was, but I know her name. I can put a name to the face in my mind — the fierce woman that guided me in the Realm, without even knowing who I was. I'm just as much a stranger to her as she is to me, but I needed help and she didn't hesitate in giving it to me. At least as much as she could without giving too much away or freaking me out. We just met but she seems like a kindred spirit; she barely smiled and intimidated the hell out of me, but I like her. She is basically my great-grandmother times I don't even know how many generations, but I feel like if she lived in the present day we'd definitely kiki at a coffee shop or something.

I shake my head and close the book — this can go back on the shelf for now. I slowly push myself up to stand, slowly putting more weight on my legs to test if I can hold myself up. Shaking the static out of my legs, I shuffle to the bookshelf and reach up to the fourth shelf to slide the book back into place. As the book hits the back of the shelf wall, a book to my right slides out on the shelf directly in front of my face. I inch back confused — that book must be too big to fall out of place. I move closer towards it and pick it up. It's small and worn away from time, its cover a canvas-looking material and the pages rough in texture. I push it back into its spot, and then the book I had just put away slides forward above me. I look at it with a start, looking back to the small book in front of me and then back up to the first book. What the hell? I keep my hand on the book in front of me and reach up on my tip-toes, using my left hand to push the first book back into place. It hits the back of the shelf, and my arm shoots back as the book in front of me shoots forward and flies across the room. It slams into the wall and falls onto the table, opening to a page somewhere in the middle of the book. I hold my hand in shock and look wide-eyed at the book — if there's a duppy in here, I don't want any beef. I may be able to guide the dead but I haven't done it yet, and I don't really want to invite spirits around me just yet. I walk slowly towards the book and stop a ways away from the table, peering from my spot to see what's on the page.

It looks like a diary entry — written in an old-school cursive, with a date etched on the top-right corner. I look back to the bookshelf, the first book is tucked away in its place and doesn't look like it'll jump out at me any time soon. I turn back and walk up to the table, grabbing a stool and sitting down. I tentatively reach for the book and tap it once before pulling my hand away — nope, no response. No spinning blades or gnashing teeth to chomp on my hand. It's just a book. I reach for it again and actually pick it up this time, holding it open to the page it fell on.

1720

Me and Quao found land in Blue Mountains. Perfect
to keep an eye out for slavers, and a good place to hunt
for food and get water. The people are tired — many
have gone back to the plantations, some have run away.
I threatened the ones that left — if they tell the white
devils anything, I will find a way to wish they had neva
left. They will not ruin our escape because they were
too scared to leave slavery. The ones that have stayed are
complainin', and drivin' me mad. All they can talk about
is how tired they are, how long the walks are, and the
little food and water. More food will be comin', I saw it
in a vision last night. Plants will grow in this place, and
the goats and chicken we stole with us will make more
offspring and give us food. They just have to wait. There
are bigger things to worry about. The future came to me
in the same dream last night — slavers will come and find
us, with the Toubabs disguised as soldiers. They will bring
the most powerful of their guns, machetes and knives, and
will kill us before they try to recapture us. The Toubabs
are so deep in the army, the leading officer does not even
know that it is a Bastet he is fighting. But I know the
Toubabs that are hunting me, and I will be ready.

This must be Leona's writing — she said herself the man with her was
Quao, so this has to be when they first discovered the land where they'd set
up camp. The trees we walked further into were so thick and close together,
which explains how their land was perfect to protect them against slavers
and the army. It can't just be a coincidence that her diary would jump out
and reveal itself to me. This book somehow found me — I brought myself
to Leona, and Leona somehow brought herself to me. Through her life,
her stories, her experiences. This diary is her life. And I'm able to see all
of it. I flip through the pages quickly — the first few pages are torn out
and stuck into the spine of the book, and the pages are different from the
pages of the actual book. They look older and more worn down, and the
writing is barely visible, smudged away by poor maintenance and time.
How did Loni get this? She must've been smuggling more than just guns

and weapons back in the day; these must've taken years to find, and even longer to hide. I wonder if she knows about the blood dripped on the pages — did she visit the ancestors too? Did she speak to them while they were still alive in their own time, and learn all that she knows? Does she know who Leona Akana was?

The lights above start twinkling — once, twice fast, and three times slow. I rush to put the diary in my backpack before Nellie comes down — I don't know why I feel the need to hide it, but something in me is telling me that what just happened is not ordinary. Even for us. I stuff it between my books and zip the bag closed as she opens the hatch door and light pours onto the steps. I clean up the other books I was reading and dash them on one of the tables as she comes down the steps. I lean against the edge of the table and pretend to be reading a book — Ways to Prevent Defecating during Childbirth. Ew. I look up as if I was deeply reading, and smile as nonchalantly as I can.

"Hey," I say, a little too enthusiastically. She looks at me with her brows furrowed, probably thinking I'm crazy.

"Hey," she says slowly, putting her bag on the table with a smirk. She points to the book with an amused look on her face. "Having fun with preventing fecal matter?"

"Oh yeah, y'know, you can never be too careful. It's fascinating, really, to see how extensive it is."

"I bet," she says sarcastically. She looks at me deadpan as she takes the book and flips it around. "And I can only imagine how much more interesting it is to read about it *upside down*."

I... am such an idiot. She chuckles and shakes her head, as she begins to put the books I was reading back on the shelf.

"How was your shift?"

"Long," she replies, her fatigue evident in her voice. "Did you eat all the dinner I made for you last night?"

"Yeah, and I just bought food at school for lunch." She nods and gives me a weak smile, sliding her arm across my shoulder. I grab my bag and the dishes my snack was on and we head upstairs. I slowly lift the hatch and check to make sure the coast is all clear, and then walk up the steps as quietly as I can — which isn't very quiet at all. Once Nellie's beside me, I look down into the basement below and see the lights dim as I close the hatch door. We quickly exit the closet with the door closed behind us, when Ray rounds the corner with a big box of frozen patties in his hand.

He looks at us, the closet door, and then back at us, with a confused look on his face.

"Did y'all just come out of that closet?" My heart jumps in panic, but quick as a whip I'll have to come up with a lie that'll make sense.

"Yeah," I say with a laugh. "I study in that closet when the evening rush brings all the noise — being in that small space really helps me focus. Nellie was just grabbing me to go home." He nods as if it makes complete sense and shrugs, waddling under the weight of the patty box and his extended gut. Nellie steps forward and looks at me with a cocked eyebrow — looking impressed and worried at the same time.

"You seemed to have no trouble concocting that lie," she says.

I shrug and respond, "What can I say? Practice makes progress." She smirks and closes her eyes, shaking her head as she walks towards the diner floor. Loni raises her head from the dumplings she's making, throwing Nellie a quick head nod. She has flour dusted on her forearms and the front of her apron, with the net loosely atop her hair. Her thick arms move as she continues to form dumplings, standing in front of the fan that oscillates lazily beside her. Ray opens the oven and quickly piles patties onto baking sheets laid atop the three shelves.

"How was di study session?" she asks me. She might've overheard my lie I tried to sell Ray, and I'm assuming she's not asking about school.

"Good," I say nonchalantly. She nods knowingly and gives me a small smile, while Ray bends back up and closes the oven — going back to the floor to attend to the customers. Nellie tussles with her bag by the front counter, most likely looking for her car keys which she always seems to lose within the depths of her bottomless bag. She looks like she'll be preoccupied for a few moments, so I walk closer to Loni. I need to know if she knows about the diary — about Leona Akana and her magic book — but I can't give anything away that may worry her if she doesn't. If it's not normal to have books jump out at you, then I don't want to add more worrying around my already worrisome situation.

"Hey Loni," I say casually, lowering my voice, "are all those books down there about our history, potions and spells and stuff?"

"Well, yeah," she replies. "What else would dey be about?"

"I don't know. I mean, I know that most of them were written by our ancestors with all the knowledge they acquired over the years. But were any of those books about their actual lives? Of themselves, with their own stories, fears and emotions?"

"Well a couple of di books used stories to describe somethin'. Like an example of what not to do or why we use a potion or spell for a certain reason. Our stories were the only way we could keep ourselves alive — an' for so long we couldn't even write anythin' down. An' even if we did, those of us dat were enslaved couldn't undastan it after a while because the slavers and Toubabs made us forget our language."

"Yeah, I know that. I can only imagine how much of our history is permanently lost because we've lost our languages and stories." Okay, time to throw the gold breadcrumb here. "But was there ever a personal book that a Bastet was able to keep hidden long enough for it to be salvaged? Like a diary or something?"

"A diary?" she asks confused.

"Yeah," I reply quickly. "Just something for me to look at to remind me that these were real women. Real people, y'know? I'm learning about all the amazing things we're able to do, but just seeing how they actually handled all of it could remind me that I'm not the only one who was in the dark about all this."

That wasn't a complete lie — it's not the reason I'm asking, but it is something that's in the back of my mind. Loni nods as she understands what I'm saying, grabbing the bowl with all the dumplings and walking towards the stove.

"I see what you're sayin'. Well, all those books had stories eere an' there, but there was neva any sort of diary that a Bastet had. They were just stories about us as a whole, not individually. An' if there eva was somethin' about one Bastet specifically, it was usually told by anotha Bastet that knew them later on."

"Are you sure?"

"Last time I checked," she replies. She quickly drops the dumplings into a bubbling oil vat, and they begin to get brown quickly as oil spits into the air. "They were only ever stories told from anotha perspective — from otha Bastets or women that knew about our world — an' they're more about helpin' new Bastets undastan their powas an' abilities."

"Huh," I reply, giving a casual shrug. If Loni is telling the truth — and for all I know she could be lying, she has been doing that for years to protect our people — then she must not know about Leona's diary. When I flipped through the pages, they all had similar handwriting. It couldn't just have been a book of our stories; it was a collection of *her* stories. My visit to the Realm connected me directly to her, and I've brought that connection back into the physical realm — and this book is the proof. I don't know if I should tell Loni just yet about this — if she didn't know about this book, then the fact that I do must be intentional. I'm meant to learn Leona's story, for whatever reason, and it's for my eyes only. I'll keep it to myself for now — just for now.

"Okay, well I'll see you tomorrow." I peck her on the cheek and she waves me away with a small smile. I smile back as I grab my backpack and walk through the swinging doors. I narrowly miss getting hit in the face with a tray as Ray walks past with three full plates to a table. I walk up to Nellie and lean on the counter — she finally finds her keys, after who knows how long. She pulls them out of her bag and lifts them into the air. She throws me a dopey smile and an expression that says 'Aha!'. I chuckle and shake my head. There are times where Nellie is hopelessly dorky, and I live for every moment of it.

"When we get home, can we talk about how to ease my transition in the Realm better?" I whisper.

"Is it becoming more overwhelming?" she asks.

"Well, it's just that every time I come back into the physical world I'm all sweaty, my heart's racing, my stomach's upset —"

"Yeah, well that's what happens when your brain snaps from one plane of consciousness to another."

"Okay, well are there any tips, or breathing exercises, or something you could give me to help me calm myself down?"

She looks at me with a small smile and a sweet and knowing look in her eyes. "Sure," she says, sliding her arm across my shoulder and pulling me into a side hug.

We make our way to the door as it opens, a customer walking in at the perfect time. While it's open I look for our car in the lot, and see a sleek black car parked across the street. The same black car from the other day. I stop in my tracks as my blood runs cold, grabbing Nellie's arm with a vice-like grip. She looks at me confused, and a worried look on her face.

"What, Mama?" she asks.

"That car," I say shakily. "That car was outside my school the day after I escaped from the hospital."

She looks to where I'm looking, her eyes darting as she tries to find what I see, and finally spots the car — its windows are tinted and has the same shiny sheen as the other car. It's sleek and low to the ground and looks like a fairly new model. I don't know much about cars, but I just know that this is the same one. She raises her eyebrow as she continues to look at the car, but nothing happens — no one comes out, the windows aren't rolled down. Nothing. But there is someone in the car — I know there is. Fear rises in my stomach as my nerves stand at attention, and my breathing gets shallow. Nellie realizes I'm panicking and looks at me — she moves in front of me and raises her hand slightly — moving it up and down, breathing in and out slowly trying to get me to mimic her. I breathe in slowly but shakily through my nose, and exhale just as shakily through my mouth. We do that for a minute, as customers seated nearby give us intrigued glances. *What are these two women doing breathing like that in the middle of a diner?* That's probably the thought running through their heads, along with, *Oh no, here are the crazy people to ruin my meal.* I nod quickly to let her know I've calmed down, but get more uneasy when I look at the car again. She nods and holds my hand, pushing open the door with her other hand. As soon as we're both outside, the window to the driver's side of the car rolls down but we can't see who sits in the seat. But they can see us. Nellie stops dead in her tracks and stares at the car — she realizes that this isn't just some ordinary car, and now she's on the defensive. This makes me worried. The door opens, and a long leg swathed in black steps onto the street. She grabs my arm and pulls me to the left, and I now see our car parked in the closest spot to the door. A packing truck drives from the main street onto the side street and briefly blocks us from seeing the person getting out of the car — it also blocks them from seeing us, giving us an out. Nellie opens the car quickly and we plop in, throwing our bags on the backseat. She starts the car aggressively, all the while her face is stoic and calm.

"Recline your seat," she commands. I do so quickly, my heart racing in fear. She puts her arm on the back of my seat and looks behind her, quickly backing out of the parking spot. She drives forward, not stopping for a couple walking from the street to the diner — they raise their arms in annoyance as she speeds left. Now onto the street to head home, the mystery leg that was hidden by the truck has been revealed — and becomes a person. I press myself against the seat, hoping somehow it'll hide me further even though it does nothing, and look up through the window as we drive by the car. Standing there, looking into our car, is Churchill — dressed in a black suit and tie, hair combed to perfection, and Ray-Ban glasses perched on his nose. He looks into our car as we drive by, and even though it's only for a split second he sees us, it feels like forever. I feel his stare through his glasses — even though I'm reclined as far back as my seat can go, I know he can see me. Nellie stares straight ahead, unblinking, and speeds down the road towards home.

Nellie opens the door and walks in the house, dropping her bags on the couch and heading straight to the home library. I try to follow, quickly taking off my shoes and struggling to get my backpack off my back as I shuffle to the room.

"Nellie, what's going on?" I yell. She rustles in the room, looking for something and not answering me. I walk to the office and see her bent over the desk, looking in the drawers for something.

"Nellie," I repeat. "Tell me what's going on."

"We have to move," she mutters to herself. "If we get the next flight out we might be able to get away without them finding us again…"

"Nellie what are you talking about? What flight? What do you mean?" She continues to ignore me, her mouth moving slightly as she mutters silently to herself. She goes to the bookshelf and rifles through the third shelf until she finds what she's looking for — our passports. Then, she places her hands underneath the shelf and slides it out, her arms taut as she balances all the books on top of it. With the space now exposed, a small, blue-ish grey door is revealed, with a silver keypad in the center. A safe.

"What are you doing?" I ask. She keys a code into the PIN pad — 1767 — and the screen goes green, beeping a short high-pitched shrill before the door slowly opens. Inside are bundles of cash — and not just in Canadian dollars, in other currencies too. One's I've seen before and others I don't immediately recognize. She pulls out a wad of cash, at least $5,000 or so, and pulls out other currencies that are probably around the same amount. She stuffs them in the crook of her armpit as she reaches into the safe again — she pulls out a stack with passports and IDs, all with our faces on it but with different names. She opens two of the passports to show our faces — one of them has her face but says Vanessa Wilkenson, and the other has my face on it and says Kyra Wilkenson. The other passports are different. One looks American and the other from a European country — not Canadian — but they also have our faces on them. The IDs in her hand are a Canadian health card and an American driver's licence; my face is on both, with the names Natasha Leon on one and Kelly Prince on the other.

Why does she have so many IDs with our faces on them, but with different names? What is this, Mission Impossible? What the hell is going on? She sorts through them in her hands and turns to the table, throwing them on top of the cash. She bobs her finger in the air and looks here and there, her thoughts whirling through her head as she tries to collect them. I stare at her — am I invisible? Is she deaf? I have questions that need answers, and she can't just leave me in the dark without shedding a little light.

"NELLIE!" She abruptly turns to me, a shocked look on her face.

"What *the hell* is going on? Why do you have so many IDs with our faces on it but with different names? Why do you have stacks of cash like you're running a drug operation or some shit? *What the hell is happening?*"

"We're getting away." I look at her, taken aback from her abrupt honesty, and silence. She takes an exasperated breath, dropping what's in her hand on the table and massaging her forehead. She leans against the table and crosses her arms.

"We both saw Churchill at the diner today, and for all we know he was probably in the car at your school. He knows where you are and all the places to find you, which means you're at risk. Not to mention Michael and Loni — anyone close to us isn't safe from the Toubabs, whether they're a Bastet or not, and Loni's been under the radar for years. We can't jeopardize her cover, she's worked too hard to keep her freedom and anonymity. We have to leave the city and get to a safe house."

"A safe house? We have money for something like that?"

"Bastets have been buying cheap property around the world for decades, places no one would ever buy, and fixing them up on the inside discreetly so our people could stay there. They're everywhere, so we could have safe houses at locations closest to us if the need arises. And the need is definitely here." She picks up the cash in one hand and the IDs in the other.

"These will get us to safety," she continues. "We can't escape with our real names, but these fakes are good enough to get past modern technology — and it'll give us a little shield from the Toubabs while they continue their search. They're never going to stop looking for us, but it'll be a little harder to find us when we have different identities to hide behind."

"Wait, slow down," I say wearily. "You make it seem like we're going into the witness protection program. We're leaving Toronto? When? And for how long?"

"Right away, Jamila. It won't be long before the Toubabs find our house, and our protection spell can only do so much — if they want to bring an entire army, they can. Maybe they will. They're so deep in law enforcement — here and everywhere — so no one would question them. We need to get out while we still have a chance, and we'll probably be gone for a while."

"How long is a while?" I ask warily.

"As long as we need until they lose our trail. And you've lived here for your entire life, so we'll probably have to stay away for just as long."

I widen my eyes as what she's saying sinks in. "You're talking about moving away permanently. Nellie, we can't do that! My whole life is here — I have school, Michael, colleges I want to go to. We can't just up and leave with no explanation. What about all my assignments and exams? Teachers aren't going to take a sudden escape as a reasonable excuse for why I couldn't get my work done. And Michael! He's my friend, Nellie — I've already had to keep so much from him, and now I have to just leave and never come back? And I can't tell him why? This is insane!"

"No, this is survival," she replies seriously. She walks towards me and continues, "This isn't just a story from those books anymore, J. The villains may have been just characters in a story in those pages, but our villains have faces — those faces have seen yours, and they won't stop until they see your face again enslaved for them."

"This is your life now. I had hoped you'd never live to see the day where they'd find you, but they have — and they're not going to stop until they have you in their grasp. And they will do anything to take you. They've gotten so much power over the years that they have the resources and forces to do it, and will use it to the fullness of their ability if it means they can get you. They'll kill people just to get to you, ruining lives just so they can have you — this is no longer a game. It's a race, and we have to make sure we stay at least three steps ahead because it's not just one thing hunting you anymore. You'll be running from a threat behind you, meanwhile, the same threat is coming from different directions that you weren't even expecting."

She continues, "Even if you're keeping an eye out for Toubabs, there's the police, politicians, and people from all different places that are secretly hunting you and you won't even know it. No, it's not safe here for us anymore — the only chance we have to get you safe and living life somewhat normally again is somewhere far away from here."

My eyes get hot as they well with tears, as I realize that I'm truly no longer in control. I thought I had a hold on some semblance of control on my life, but now it's truly free from my grasp.

"But what about Michael?" I ask pathetically. Her eyes soften as she looks at me, my face trembling as tears silently roll down my face. She grabs my neck with both of her hands and gently massages the nape of my neck — lifting the nappy strands of hair out of my bun and puffing them up into a small tumbleweed of hair.

"Michael will be safer if he's nowhere near you. I know you love him — I do too — but he can't know about this world. About us. Just being around you now puts him at risk. If he should know about all this and the Toubabs find him, they'll kill him on the spot. They have no sympathy for allies."

"But I can't just leave him," I say thickly. "He's my best friend. My person. I have to tell him why I'm leaving — we've been there for each other through everything, and he needs an explanation. I owe him that much."

She nods reluctantly. "Okay, but you can't tell him about any of this; you can't even tell him the real reason we're leaving. Leave out as much of the details as you can — but if you must, tell him that some distant relatives need our help and we have to go see them. We don't know how long we'll be gone — our 'relatives' don't have the Internet, and we don't have an international phone plan, so you won't be able to keep in touch very well. When we leave, you cannot contact him. You can send a letter every once in a while but you can't put a return address, and you can't say where you are — and I will send it. If you don't know where you're even sending it from, the less risk there'll be. And the letter will just be to let him know that you're safe, and you love and miss him."

"Well, at least that last part will be true," I say sarcastically. She gives me a weak smile but looks at me sadly. She pats my cheek and turns back to the table, grabbing the cash and the rest of the IDs and putting them in a small bag. She goes behind the desk and turns on the computer, the blue light illuminating her face. I stand there with crossed arms, my bones hollow and weak — I'm going to be on the run for who knows how long, and I won't be able to talk to anyone or tell anyone anything. I'll have to leave Michael, my best friend and the one person I can tell anything, and I don't even know if I'll ever see him again. I angrily wipe my tears away and sniffle my nose, then join Nellie behind the table and lean on it with my forearms. She looks at flights leaving Toronto, with several tabs open on different travel websites. She clicks from the current tab — showing flights from Toronto to New Orleans — to another tab showing flights from the city to Jamaica. And they are really cheap.

"Whoa," I marvel. "$300 for two tickets to Jamaica? Why are plane tickets so cheap?"

"Well, with everything that has happened with the pandemic," she replies, "flights are getting cheaper to get people to travel. So many are staying where they are, even though vaccines have been distributed for months, and the flight companies have to make money somehow — hence, cheap flights."

She continues on that tab and looks for two economy seats for us, and clicks the departure date as November 23rd, 2020, with no return date. That's next week.

"Nel, are we really leaving?" I ask.

She responds, "We have to leave soon, and a week is better than no time at all to prepare."

I nod solemnly, and she turns back to the screen to finish buying the tickets. A week will at least give me time to take everything in — our home, our community, our people. Things I may never see again, and never thought I'd have to commit to memory lest I forget forever.

She finishes the order, paying the fee for each of us to have a check-in bag, and pulls up a PDF of the tickets to print off. Sending an email would leave an electronic trail so it's better to have a printed copy than to have a trail for the Toubabs to pick up on. She leaves the room and heads down the hallway to her room — I go to the door and lean on the frame, waiting for her as she disappears into her room. She comes back out with a long leather pouch, where she puts the cash, our IDs, and our plane tickets in.

"We'll start packing the essentials tomorrow, and leave first thing that morning. We have an early flight so you'll have to go to sleep early the night before."

I nod emotionless, the hollowness in my bones blocking any emotion from resonating within. She cocks her head and looks at me empathetically, and exhaling deeply. She feels for me, but this is how it has to be. I want to live, and there are contingencies. Whether I like it or not.

"Why don't you finish your homework and get ready for bed — you've had a long day."

"I already finished my homework before going down to the basement," I say.

"Okay, well go get cleaned up and we can watch TV — or maybe read together for a bit, like we used to."

"That sounds nice," I say, giving her a small smile. She smiles back, and I walk towards the bathroom. Once inside, I close the door behind me and look up at the skylight — the last glow of sun disappears, and the glow of warmth sets its gaze from the room. Tears silently well in my eyes, and my bones settle with misery as the tears roll down my face. This isn't fair — I don't want to live my life on the run. I want to build a life in the place I've always known. I don't want to have to leave those that I love without an explanation as to why. I want to create memories with these people that I can remember fondly when I'm old and grey. I want *to live* to be old and grey. I don't know if I'll live that long to experience it.

I softly wipe the tears from my face as I take off my clothes, grabbing my shower cap off the door hook, and stepping into the shower. I turn on the water and step back, waiting for the delay as the water flows from the pipes to the showerhead. One spurt, two spurts, water. It's hot, but not hot enough. I want it burn-my-skin-off hot. I turn it hotter and stand underneath the water as the heat beats into my skin. I wash my face slowly, massaging my skin with tender fingers as the hot water soothes the tension in my muscles. I soap up and rinse myself off — going slowly and delicately, giving myself a mini DIY spa session. Finished bathing, I turn off the water and step out of the shower to grab my towel. I pat myself dry and wrap myself before turning to the counter to do my skincare routine. When I'm done, I open the door and realize Nellie's room door is open and she's sitting on her bed reading a book. She's hunched over and biting a hangnail — one of her bad habits. I smile as I watch her read — we both love getting immersed in a good book, but unfortunately neither of us have really had the time to escape to other worlds for fun. Lately, it's been more out of sheer necessity. Seeing her now, relaxed and at ease, eases me too. I smile as I watch her silently, but her intuition is heightened and she looks up to see me watching her. She smirks and goes back to reading, and I chuckle as I walk to my room.

I moisturize and get my comfiest pyjamas, slipping them on and feeling bliss as fleece slides over my skin. I walk through the Novelfall, looking at all the titles to see if there's one I've yet to read. *Tiger's Curse* — read it. *The Coldest Winter Ever* — read it. *Harry Potter and the Sorcerer of* — ha! Read that enough for a lifetime. *The Water Dancer*. I cock my head as I look at the cover — I haven't read that one yet. I untie the strings from its spine and extract the book, finding a bookmark on my desk. I stand there looking at the Novelfall for a moment and suddenly feel sad; if we run away, I may never see this again. No — I definitely won't. I could maybe make another one wherever we wind up, but it won't be the same. This Novelfall is the first one — my mother and Nellie helped me make it. Together we made this special little space and it wouldn't be the same if I try to replicate it. I walk forward and walk through the books one more time, grazing my fingertips along the strings, causing the books to sway in the air. I exhale low and slow, watching them sway for a while longer before heading to Nellie's room.

I enter to see her still hunched over and reading, one leg bent and on the bed with the other hovering above the ground. She sees me and closes her book, then gets up from her bed.

"Want some tea or hot chocolate?"

"Ooooo some hot chocolate," I say.

"*With Baileys*," we both say. We laugh as she goes to the kitchen, and I make myself comfortable. I grab a few decorative pillows and her fuzzy blanket thrown over her ottoman and make a seat on the floor. By the time I'm a chapter in the book Nellie returns with two steaming mugs, setting them down on the floor. She jumps into bed and lays on her stomach, her elbows on the edge of the bed while my back leans against it.

"What's your poison?" she asks.

"The Water Dancer," I reply. She nods and smiles, picking up her book and jumping back into her story. I open my book and start reading as well — this is what life should be. But now it's just going to be moments — glimpses into serenity — amidst a tumultuous flurry of uncertainty. I have to savour these moments as much as I can when they happen because I don't know how long they'll last, or when they'll happen again.

Time is funny — when you want it to speed up, it seems to move at a snail's pace. The hours get longer, and the days seem to drag on, and the day you're waiting for to come seems like it's taking a lifetime to reach. When you want it to slow down — like now for instance — the days seem to move at warp speed. Everything moves past you in a haze, while you stay where you are. Life moves on while you try to hold on to it in vain, and what seemed like an endless amount of time will be an ever-approaching end before you know it. That's how the past few days have been for me. It's been four days, but it seems like the hours are moving at double-time. Nellie took me to the hospital and we got a new Coronavirus vaccine shot — we should be good for another six months before we have to get another in Jamaica. She was able to forge a record with our fake IDs — so Kyra and Vanessa Wilkenson, Natasha and Lauren Leon, and Kelly and Tasha Prince have had two vaccinations. Without it, we'd get flagged and brought to a facility for quarantine, and we can't end up in the system. Even with fakes, the Toubabs will have the technology to search us through facial recognition. Nellie and I have been packing up the house — she's packed away all our photos and the newer furniture, and dropped them off at a storage facility. She paid in cash, and will mail in the cash with her storage locker number written on the envelope so there won't be any trail leading back to us. I've been packing up what we'll be bringing with us — essential clothes, toiletries, some books with spells, potions and our Bastet history, and the leather pouch. We have a duffel bag and one suitcase each — everything else went into storage or got sold. I didn't realize how attached I was to everything until it came down to having to get rid of them. I donated the books to the library, but I had to keep some; the ones my mother wrote in. Those are too precious. I put most of them along with the photos in storage, but I still have to take down the books hanging in the Novelfall. I don't know why I've been hesitant to take them down — maybe because it's been around for as long as I can remember. Maybe because it was something my mother and I did together, and I don't want to put an end to it. Whatever the reason, I'm going to have to overcome it eventually.

As we've been preparing to leave, I've been getting more and more distant at school. I'm not raising my hand in class anymore, I'm quiet and have been keeping more to myself — I have a lot to think about after all. But it's starting to look a lot like when my mother passed, and a lot of my teachers have noticed and have been asking questions. My biology teacher even pulled me aside after class to ask if I was okay. How do I explain that I'm depressed from having to go on the run from a colonial hunting clan that wants to use me for my powers and then kill me? I just said I was fine. Even Michael and Taylor have noticed that I've been acting out of character — they try to include me in conversations, but even when I try to get involved my mind starts to wander. I'm so worried about forgetting them and savouring their memories that it is getting in the way of making new ones while I'm still here. They're still happy and in love as ever, so after including me in their conversation, they'll just go back to talking to each other. I hate to say it, but seeing how easily Michael's getting on without me — while I'm still here — makes me feel worse about all of this. I don't want him to be miserable with sadness or anything, but is it wrong to want him to be a little more upset about us drifting? He doesn't know that he may never see me again — this could just be the normal drifting between friends that happens when you're in your first relationship. Except it's not. I just want him to miss me. I want someone to be upset over losing me.

It's Friday afternoon — my last day at this school. Our flight is on Sunday, and after that I have no idea what my days will look like. I just finished my last period and will soon head to my locker. Kids rush out of the room, excited to escape chemistry, but I stay back a little longer. I look at the desks as I walk through the aisle, grazing my fingertips atop the wood — Mr. Sorella is quickly packing up his things in his briefcase when he notices me dawdling. He is always kind to me, kind to everyone, but that just gives everyone more of a reason to walk all over him. He was one of the first to notice my change in behaviour this week — he politely asked if I was alright, and when I said I was fine he didn't press me any further. He didn't want to upset me, but just that simple ask made me so grateful.

"Everything alright, Ms. Freeman?" he asks politely.

"I'm good, Mr. Sorella," I say with a small smile. "Thanks for asking." I really mean it — so much. He smiles kindly and nods, closing his briefcase and waving once as he leaves the room. I sigh and look at the whiteboard, the calculations still on the board. I hear a small sigh and look to my left, seeing that same strange boy from a couple weeks before. I only saw him that once, and here he is again — at his spot by the heater, leaning against it with crossed arms and a smug look on his face.

"You'd think the man would get a clue," he says sarcastically. "If anyone cared about these calculations they might actually treat him with some respect instead of like a doormat."

"Some people are kind just for the sake of being so," I say, looking at a mug on his desk that reads *Best Teacher Ever* and smiling. He scoffs haughtily, leaning further back against the window.

"And look where that's gotten him, being the butt of everyone's jokes and getting walked all over."

"Maybe," I reply, turning to him. "And maybe, in the end, they'll look back and wish they'd told him just how great he was to them. People remember you for what you did and who you are — and that's going to only be good things when it comes down to it."

He stops smirking and looks at me wide-eyed, a look of pure shock on his face.

"W-w-wait," he says, "you heard me?"

"Well, of course I heard you," I say sarcastically, "you're not exactly being quiet."

"Y-y-yeah, b-but," he stammers and straightens up, walking towards me with his eyes saucer-wide. "B-b-but I thought you were just talking to yourself, y'know? I didn't think you were actually responding to me or anything."

"Well, I was," I say, backing away and giving him a side-eye. He gasps and leans back, reaching his hand out to me and shaking it in the air as the words he's trying to use taking its time to come to him.

"You can really hear me, and see me." He grabs his head and fists his hair, backing away in shock but then coming right on back. "This is crazy," he mutters, "no one has ever been able to see me before!"

"What are you talking about?" I ask confused. "You're right here in front of me, how would I not be able to see you?"

"That's just the thing — only you can see me. No one else has been able to see me before. I've tried everything, but no one has been able to. Until now."

I look at him with a worried look, and slowly start to back away. "Um, well that sucks — but I should really get going. I don't want to keep my friend waiting."

"W-w-wait!" He reaches for me, trying to grab my shoulder. I look at him with disgust and fear, but he misses me — actually, he doesn't miss me, but his hand isn't touching my shoulder. It just passes right through. I look at his hand in shock, then back at him, then back at his hand, then back at him. He looks back at me with a relieved and excited look, his head nodding fast and closely resembling an excited child.

"Wait, do that again." He obeys and reaches for me, but his hand passes through me again — my body unbothered by his touch. I do feel something, but not the normal contact of his hand that I should feel — more like a hum inside me that kind of aches. It feels numb and yet aches at the same time, and it pulses there for a while before disappearing. I look at his hand again with shock, and this time I reach for it, and my hand passes right through. I take a step back — now it's my turn to look at him wide-eyed.

"What are you?"

"My name's Jeremy — and you must not get out enough, but I'm *a guy.*"

"Yeah, *I know* you're a guy," I stutter, "but what *are* you?"

"What? My hand going through you and you being the only person to see me didn't give it away?"

I just look at him, breathing shallowly as I process what he's saying. "But ghosts don't exist. *Ghosts aren't real.*"

"And yet here you are, looking at me and talking to me." He walks past me, "And here I am — and have been for years. Alone." He turns back to me, a smirk on his face but a melancholy look in his eyes.

"But not anymore."

CHAPTER TWELVE

We both look at each other for a moment in silence; both of us shell shocked, but for different reasons. He has finally found someone he could talk to, and I find a ghost. *A ghost!* I don't know why I thought this last week in the city would go by uneventfully, but I was just never expecting to discover that I could talk to ghosts. I thought my ability to speak to the afterlife just happened when I was in the Realm of Duality — but I guess ghosts don't discriminate on time or place.

"You have no idea how long I've waited for someone to be able to see me," he says. "I've seen you around the school with that guy you're always hanging out with, but you've never been able to see me before now. But you're different now — I don't know what it is, but every time I see you I can feel that you're different."

"Yeah, well, I've changed a lot recently," I say monotone. I look at him and circle around him, looking him up and down. He looks so real, so physical and whole in front of me. He's wearing a green zip-up hoodie and a grey t-shirt. Dark blue jeans and scuffed up runners — even the dirt on the tips of his shoes look real. I end up in front of him again, looking at him with wonder and a little bit of fear.

"I can't believe — I just… I can't —"

"I'm guessing you aren't getting top grades for public speaking," he says sardonically, fisting his pants pockets and smiling smugly. I cut my eyes and look at him — man, for a ghost who hasn't spoken to anyone in a long time, you'd think this dude would be a little more polite.

"And I'm guessing you've had time to perfect it, huh? But without anyone to actually hear you, it's hard for anyone to vouch for you."

"Oooooooooooo, burn," he says with a humourless laugh. "I'd call the fire department, but they wouldn't actually be able to hear me."

"Thank God for that," I say, causing him to smile. "How are you here? What are you still doing here? Shouldn't you be going into the light or something? Resting in peace and all that?"

"You think I wouldn't have already done that if I could?" he asks. "No kid, dead or alive, wants to be at Brimmer Hall for longer than they have to — but I don't think I have a choice. I've been stuck here ever since I died."

I'm about to ask him when that was when a voice behind me calls, "Ms. Freeman?" I whirl around to see Mr. Carlyle, leaning on the door frame. "Are you alright?"

"Yeah, I'm fine," I say quickly. I turn back to Jeremy with a worried look, who looks at me and shrugs.

"He can't see me, remember?" I exhale relieved and look back to Mr. Carlyle, who looks at me strangely.

"Were you... talking to someone?"

"No, no," I stutter, "no, I was just talking to myself. I was studying for my quiz on Monday and I got a little excited." I let out a short laugh and he chuckles, shaking his head.

"Why does that not surprise me?" he asks rhetorically with a chuckle. "Well you're going to have to take the fun elsewhere — I need this room for detention."

"Oh okay, I'll leave right now." I tighten my bag straps on my shoulder and scuttle out of the room, nodding a goodbye to him. Jeremy follows me, looking at Mr. Carlyle with a pompous grin and walking past him haughtily.

"Man, I must be getting better at this lying thing," I mutter under my breath.

"I beg to differ," says Jeremy. I look at him and scowl, and turn right. He follows me, walking with a loose gait and a silly smile on his face. He walks past kids passing us in the hallway — looking at them with a goofy grin and swinging his arms like he's putting on a show.

"Excuse me," he says mockingly, stepping away from one passing kid. "Pardon me," he continues, mock-bowing to another and feigning apology.

"What are you doing?" I ask annoyed. "They can't even see you."

"You gotta find fun ways to pass the time when time doesn't affect you anymore, Freeman," he says, stopping mid-hallway for a kid to pass through him. The kid sneezes, and his friend blesses him as they continue walking. Jeremy snickers with a smug grin, continuing his showman walk.

"Why are you following me? Don't you have something better to do?"

"Like what? Haunt my foes and possess people? Nah, that's not really my vibe. I'm more of a make-things-levitate-to-drive-the-teacher-crazy kinda guy."

"Yeah, I got that vibe," I say. We arrive at my locker and I open it — he stands just behind me and a kid walks our way. He walks right through Jeremy and for a second Jeremy disappears, like someone disturbed his reflection in the water. The kid sneezes in the air and shivers, goosebumps immediately appearing on his arm.

"Sorry," the kid says to me.

I look at him strangely, replying, "Don't worry about it." He looks away with a confused look on his face, shrugging once before walking away. I look at Jeremy, who just shrugs and smirks, leaning against the locker. I point at his shoulder, confusion settling further and further.

"Okay, how is it that you can lean against things but then you can't touch people?"

"Listen man, I would *love* to talk your ear off about the logistics of this whole ghost thing, but if I knew how it worked I would've figured out how to *stop* being a ghost a long time ago and just skip to the whole rest in peace bit."

He's got a point there. I begin to empty my locker, putting all my books into my bag and carefully taking the pictures off the inside of the door.

"Okay, well how come you're still here — it sounds like you've been here a while, why haven't you tried to leave?"

"Dude, are you deaf? Or, are you dumb?" I look at him with raised eyebrows, and he returns my look with a grin. "Hey, being around a bunch of kids lets you learn all the new trends and slang, what can I say?" Huh, I guess there's no better way to keep up with the times than shadow a bunch of teenagers for who knows how long. The smile slightly slips off his face, as his body language gets more serious.

"I've been trying," he says. "Ever since I died I've been in this school, and I can't leave. I've tried everything, but every time I try to go through the front doors I just end up on the second floor hallway."

"Why?"

"That's where I was shot." I look at him shocked — his face empty of emotion. He looks at me and shrugs, leaning his head on the locker.

"I think you've figured out I have a unique sense of humour — turns out some kids didn't take to it, and they just so happened to be a part of Blanco's boys. Who knew they'd be so sensitive about their fade — but I guess there's only so many times a guy will take jokes about his hairline."

"I'm sorry," I say. He shrugs again, looking at the ground and shuffling his feet.

"It's whatever," he says nonchalantly.

"How old were you?"

"15." Wow, he was younger than me. "My birthday was just the week before — who knew that would've been my last?" he asks rhetorically.

"Have you been here for long?"

"Time works funny when you're dead," he says. "Time will pass for a long time but it feels like I've only been here a day or two — but luckily, this is a school. You can't go anywhere without seeing the date posted up somewhere — so from what I can see, I've been here for about 16 years."

"*16 years?*" He looks at me with a smile, nodding once.

"04 was a good year." I look at him wide-eyed. This poor kid has been stuck in this school for 16 years, without any glimpse of the outside except through the kids here.

"So what was 15-year-old Jeremy like?" I ask, in an attempt to lighten the mood. Luckily this guy doesn't seem to like to dwell on things, so it works.

"Total gamer," he says with a smile. "I was at every new video game release — I used to camp out just so I could be the first in line and everything. I loved to skate too. Man, I wish I could take one of these kids' boards and tear up the stairwell. No need to worry about breaking my neck when I'm already dead."

"Sounds like the good end of the deal," I say with a small smile. He chuckles, but a faraway look in his eyes doesn't allow the humour to reach them.

"I wasn't ready to die," he says, "but it is what it is, right? Now I think not being ready for my life to end is why I'm stuck here, and I can't figure out how to leave. Being stuck in Brimmer Hall? Might as well be hell." He's right. He's had to watch people come and go and hasn't been able to do the same. For 16 years? That is hell.

"Maybe you have unfinished business?"

"Unfinished business? I'm a *teenager*, my life ahead of me was unfinished business."

"Okay, alright, no need to get snippy."

"I'm a ghost, Freeman. You're lucky I'm not possessing you." He pauses and then smiles, with a snobby grin on his face. "Maybe that's my ticket out of here — possessing your body wouldn't be the most terrible thing in the world."

"Ew," I say, turning away and putting the rest of my things in my bag. He clicks his tongue and winks, leaning against the locker again and chuckling.

"You know you're kinda into it."

"You're agonizingly annoying," I say.

"Wouldn't you take that over excruciatingly dull?"

"Oh, I'm Jeremy," I imitate, lowering my voice to mock Jeremy. "I think life is only enjoyable when it's at the expense of others and I enjoy sullen forms of humour that take its material from a four-year-old diary."

"Actually, I take most of my inspiration from a college freshman's memoir, but I'd understand why you'd get them confused." He smirks and I smirk along with him — he's a pain in the ass, but not often can people match my cynicism. It's refreshing. Even if he is dead.

"You sure are taking a lot of books home with you," he says, as I continue to empty my locker into my backpack. "I've seen you and your friend around and all you talk about is homework, but are you seriously gonna do that much work? If I were alive, I wouldn't spend the weekend doing all that work."

"Yeah, I bet being a hermit and gaming all week was pique vitality for you. Unlike you, I actually like learning new things. Maybe that would've helped you when you were alive — maybe you'd take the hint that you're not funny when you crack a joke and all you get is crickets."

"Or a bullet," he says sardonically. I lean back shocked as he looks at me with a smirk. He really does have a weird sense of humour — morose and grim. I guess 16 years in purgatory will make you find the funny in anything.

"J!" Michael yells. I turn around and see him and Taylor walking hand-in-hand towards me. "You talking to yourself?" he asks amused, with one eyebrow cocked.

"Does that sound like something I would do?" I ask jokingly.

"Honestly? Probably," he says. I roll my eyes and he laughs, and Taylor chuckles along with him. Jeremy sees them holding hands and raises his eyebrows, with an amused look on his face.

"He's dating her? She's *hot*. I thought you guys were together. Even you seem like a stretch for this guy — this dude's a total square."

I whisper under my breath, "Shut up, grandpa. It's not 2004 anymore." He looks at me annoyed, and I discreetly cut my eyes.

"Damn," Michael says, pointing at my now empty locker and nodding his head at my now full backpack. "You Marie Kondo-ing your locker?"

"Yeah, you know, thought I'd clean out my locker before the winter break — might as well get it over with."

He shrugs, looking to Taylor with a smile. "I'll see you later baby, I promised J we'd binge watch that new show together."

"Okay, see you," she replies, kissing him sweetly. She smiles and walks away, throwing me a quick smile and a wave before walking to the front doors. I watch her a little while longer as she walks away — this may be the last time I see Taylor, and for all my minor jealousies I have of her time overcoming mine with Michael, I know that I'll miss her.

"Aight, you ready?" Michael asks.

"Yeah," I say slowly, glancing at Jeremy. I close my locker and take the lock — leaving my hand on there for a second longer before turning away. We walk down the hallway, but Jeremy is following me — Michael is oblivious to it all, but Jeremy's smug look is annoying the hell out of me.

"It's so nice to make new friends. I mean, I never thought I'd set the bar for friendship so low until you were able to see me, but when you're dead I guess you'll take what you can get," Jeremy says.

"Oh, hold on a sec," I say to Michael, stopping and grabbing my phone out of my pocket. I pretend to answer a call and say, "Hello? Oh, hey Jeremy."

"Jeremy?" Michael and Jeremy ask — Michael jokingly coy and Jeremy confused. I wave Michael away as he shakes his shoulders with a goofy grin.

"Hey I'm glad you called, so we could finally find a time to talk," I say, looking at Jeremy pointedly. He nods and smiles as realization hits, and yet still looking annoyingly smug.

"Listen," I say into the phone, "I'm glad that you finally found someone to talk to, but I don't really have time to… make new friends."

"Dude," Jeremy says, coming up beside me, "you are the first person I've held a conversation with in 16 years — like it or not, we're glued at the hip until you help me get the hell out of here."

"I can't help you," I say. Michael looks at me with a raised eyebrow as my voice rises — I chuckle and wave it off, and he shrugs as we approach the doors.

"You have to help me," he says. He keeps the same chill look on his face, but his voice betrays him; a small intonation of desperation rises in his voice. I look at him with surprise, and feel empathy towards him. There's no doubt that he needs my help, and I probably could help him. But I'm leaving in two days — even if I could, I wouldn't have enough time to learn how.

"I'm sorry, but I can't. I won't… be around to help you."

"What are you talking about? Nerds like you don't miss a single day of school — come Monday morning I'll be waiting by your locker."

"You can wait, but I won't show up. I won't be here Monday."

"At school?" Michael and I finally arrive at the doors — he pushes them open and walks to the bikes, but I hold back a second and look directly at Jeremy.

"No," I whisper. "In the country." He looks at me confused, and I return his look with an apologetic one of my own. I step through the doors and they slam shut behind me. I look back and see Jeremy come right up to the doors, looking at me through the glass — and in that second the cool-guy facade falls away, and I can see him for what he really is. A scared 15-year-old boy.

I meet Michael at the bikes and throw my bag into the basket, and the whole bike bouncing down in protest. I grimace as Michael chuckles, buckling his helmet onto his head. It's chilly today, so I zip up my jacket as I'm shivering and wish I hadn't put on ankle socks. We pull back from the bike rack and bike towards home.

"You wanna drop your stuff off at your house and then come over at mine?" Michael asks.

"Yeah, sure," I respond emphatically. Seeing as this might be the last time we can hang out, just the two of us, I don't want to waste a second. I'll even be happy to hear Ms. Dell nagging us. "You got any popcorn?"

"Nah, but I got Sweet Chili Heat Doritos for you, and a couple of island sodas."

"Okay, I want popcorn though — can we stop by Min's and get some extra-buttery popcorn?"

"Yeah, sure," he yells as he pulls ahead of me, swerving aside to avoid a huge pothole. A car honks behind us and we steer closer to the sidewalk, Michael actually hopping on the sidewalk to the chagrin of an older Italian woman with her grocery cart. He looks behind him with a mischievous grin and I grimace playfully as we speed past her and her admonitions. The cool November breeze is settling in, and brings goosebumps to my skin, even underneath my jacket. Michael's shirt billows behind him in the breeze, as he rises from his seat and cycles with straight legs. He must be freezing — that shirt doesn't look very thick, and Michael's a pretty skinny guy. I can just hear Ms. Dell's voice now — *you ah go catch yuh death, Michael Smith!* The sun didn't grace us with her appearance today, and instead, it's overcast with grey clouds crowding the sky. There's no chance of rain today, but the gloominess of the day seems to match my emotions. We swerve and criss-cross as we bike down the street, turn down this street, and bike down the main road. Min's Convenience comes into view and we slow down a bit, knowing that Blanco's boys will be nearby. They still haven't bothered us since Blanco drove me home that night, but just because a threat seems to be gone doesn't mean you trust without taking a few cautionary measures first.

We hear them before we see them — Future's latest track booming through a car speaker is a dead giveaway. They're all crowded around a black Escalade, talking to someone who leans out the driver's side seat. They look like they're talking about something serious, so hopefully we can ride by without any issues. Michael slows down for me to come up beside him, offering me a buffer, and we watch with cautious eyes as we coast towards the store. Some of them holding cups that they're drinking out of or holding with their fingertips, while some smoking a blunt or cigarette, while others are simply talking to the person in the car. One of them looks at a girl walking by, kissing his lips at her — to her great disgust — then we finally catch his eye. He looks at both of us and bumps a shoulder beside him, causing the man to look to see what he's calling him for. When the man turns around we realize it's Ricky Brass, whose face turns cold and defensive as soon as he sees us. The others slowly turn their heads to watch us as they see Ricky's eyes never leaving us, but we continue to coast by without any of them coming over. Then the person in the driver's seat stands up to see what they're all looking at — we see Blanco, and he sees us. And he smiles.

He nods once at me with a small smile, acknowledging us and letting us pass freely. Michael nods once before turning to me, his eyes wide in disbelief. I shrug in disbelief too, but I know that this isn't just a happy accident — Blanco's making sure we're not bothered, and I'm grateful to him for that. I don't know why he's being so kind to me — to us — but ever since that night, I can see that he's not made of stone. Michael speeds up a little, the ego setting in as he sees his future is clear of Blanco's boys and I follow, throwing Blanco another nod in gratitude. He winks and goes back to his seat, looking at Ricky Brass pointedly as he walks past him — Ricky straightens up and fixes his face, turning back to Blanco to talk whatever business they had.

We come up towards Min's front doors, and see Reggie smoking a joint as he leans on the wall.

"Look who it is," he jokes with a flattering smile, "prom king and queen."

"Oh, didn't J tell you?" Michael asks rhetorically. "Prom queen is outdated — its societal implications suggest women are prizes for the masses to enjoy, and she vehemently rejects it."

"I know you're joking," he says, "but I don't understand half of what you just said."

"He's basically saying that it's sexist and outdated," I reply. "And he's not wrong — I do think it's ridiculous."

"You say that now," Reggie says, taking a long drag of his joint, "but when you hear your name get called, I bet all that would go out the window and you might actually start acting like a real girl."

"Ha," I say humorlessly, causing him to chuckle. "Can you actually be a decent human being and watch our bikes for a second?"

"Yeah, sure," he says smiling. We lean our bikes on the wall, and head inside before Reggie stops me — lightly touching my arm. He looks at me with a dazzling smile, making butterflies flutter in my stomach.

"Just so you know, I think you'd be a great prom queen."

"Didn't you hear?" I ask coyly. "I don't believe in making women into a prize, and purposely drown out all mentions of patriarchal misogyny."

"Okay," he says. "You can discount it, but you definitely deserve to be put on a pedestal."

I look at him surprised, and he just smiles deeper as he leans back onto the wall. I open my mouth to say something but without any idea of how to respond to that, I just stumble into the store. I berate myself silently in my head as I hear him chuckle behind me. God, he's so hot — if I didn't have to leave and never come back, I might actually... what? Who am I kidding? Even with superhuman powers, when it comes to men I'm a complete coward.

A sensor dings as I walk through the doors, but Mr. Min is bent over restocking the lottery tickets so he doesn't see me. The local news plays on a TV above the register, and an older Italian man walks past me — not even bothering to wait to use his scratch-off. Michael's at the back of the store, looking for energy drinks in the fridge, and I head to the third aisle to get some extra-buttery popcorn. Passing the chips, dips, and foreign snacks, I finally find a small box of extra-buttery popcorn. And it's marked down! It's my lucky day. I grab the box and feel around in my pockets to see if I have enough change as I make my way to the cash register. Mr. Min cashes out a customer in front of me with only two things: a pack of Altoids and a pack of cigarettes. A bit counter-intuitive if you ask me, but it's not my business. He's nicely dressed in a crisp black suit and nice shoes — definitely wealthy enough to afford to shop at one of the pricier drugstores, but Min has a way of bringing in all kinds of people. I pull out a few nickels and a loonie from my pocket, but unfortunately, I'm still $1.25 short. I'll have to use my card, and I hate using it for such a small transaction. Not to mention, Nellie doesn't want me using my card for the rest of our time here — we don't need any more of a trail for them to find us before we can even leave. Michael walks towards me, and I smile widely at him — he slows down as he looks at me with a side-eye.

"What?" he asks.

"Could you be the best friend in the world and buy this for me?"

"Dude, I already got Doritos for you at home," he says annoyed.

"Yeah, but best friends go above and beyond for each other — and in this case, that would be to buy me the popcorn too." I flash him a big smile and slowly give him the popcorn. He just side-eyes me and cuts his eye, but he takes the popcorn anyways and I consider that a win. I chuckle and squeeze his arm, annoying him more but making him chuckle too. Mr. Min sees us goofing around and greets us.

"Michael," he says in his Korean accent. "You getting taller every day, my boy. Keep growing and you'll go right through my roof!" He chuckles a hearty laugh, causing us to smile in reply. "And Jamila my dear, you getting prettier every day — the boys will come knocking on your door soon, yeah?"

I chuckle and shake my head, waving my hands as he laughs louder. He bags up the customer's things in front of us — but the customer turns to look at us. He's wearing glasses so I don't recognize him at first, but then he takes them off and looks at me with those cold blue eyes that I prayed

I'd never see again. My blood runs cold and the coins fall out of my hand as I go numb. Michael looks at me confused, bending down to pick up the coins before handing them to me. He looks at the man to see why I'm riled up, before his face sparks in realization.

"Dr. Churchill," he says surprised. "What are you doing here?"

"Hello, son," he replies politely. "Just buying the essentials, as a man does. Hopefully, that's alright with you." He tries to joke, but his voice just makes it seem more unsettling. Even Michael's half-laugh shows he's not totally comfortable with him. I know I'm not — I'm surprised I haven't run away by now. He looks at me again, not giving anything away but inside I can feel his energy change — it was always cold, but now it's more dangerous. He's been looking for me, and here I am in his lap.

"Ms. Freeman," he says to me. "You look well. Your injuries have healed very well, and quite quickly I see. I take it your recovery went well." I stand there silently, frozen from shock. Michael looks at me and discreetly taps me — I open my mouth to speak, but nothing comes out. Michael comes to my rescue and answers for me.

"Yeah, she recovered pretty well," he says. I exhale shakily, as I try to catch my bearings. Churchill smiles, grabbing his bag from Mr. Min and nodding a thank you. He turns back towards us and addresses me.

"I'm glad all things considered; however, I'm concerned that you still have not taken the test concerning your scans. Wouldn't you prefer to have peace of mind?"

"Dr. Aida said I should be fine," I say, finally finding my voice. "And I haven't shown any signs that would point to there being a mental disorder."

"The scans themselves surely were enough of a sign," he says, feigning concern. "The last thing you'd want is to go about life without properly preparing for any threats to your health."

I look at him pointedly, as I sense an underlying threat to his words. This gives me more strength somehow, and the fear I had quickly slips away. I walk up closer to him, putting on a fake smile but showing the true emotion in my eyes.

"Thanks for your concern — but I'm aware of every threat against me, and I'll be ready for all of them."

He raises an eyebrow, but the rest of his face remains the same. It's creepy how immobile and empty he is.

"Well, I sincerely hope so, Ms. Freeman." He looks to Michael and nods to him once, "You two have a good evening." He walks mechanically out of the store, and I finally let out a decent breath. I breathe slowly to try and bring my heart rate down, and try to smile with Mr. Min as we step up to the counter.

"What was that?" Michael asks me with a cocked eyebrow.

"What do you mean?" I ask.

"Don't play with me," he says. "That wasn't just about your scans — there was some tension there. What was that all about?" I take in a breath as he reaches to pay, taking a moment to think of a lie. Luckily, with getting so much practice over the past few weeks, one comes to me almost instantly.

"He came to my room before visiting hours were over my last night at the hospital — he was pushing for me to get the scans, but Nellie wasn't there with me."

"He was talking to you without a guardian there?" he asks surprised.

"Yeah," I reply, raising my voice to really sell the outrageousness of the story. "He was just being so pushy, he was obsessed with me getting that scan, and it just made me uncomfortable."

"Tuh, I don't blame you," he says. "That guy's vibe gave me the creeps when I was there with you. Super pompous energy — like you'd be stupid to not follow his directives." Mr. Min bags up our things and hands it to Michael. We smile a thank you and wave goodbye, and I savour the last of Mr. Min's sweet smile before turning to leave.

"Don't get me wrong," he continues, "he is a doctor, and you should be following the doctor's advice most of the time —"

"Except my actual doctor said that it wasn't necessary," I counter. Michael nods and shrugs, agreeing with me. "Dr. Aida was definitely confused by the scans — I mean, we all were — but he didn't try to push a test on me. The way he talked to me…" I think about my actual altercation with Churchill, and I shudder inside as disgust rises in my throat. "It was so domineering, I had to get out of there." That part wasn't a lie.

Michael looks at me as he senses discomfort in my voice, and his eyes soften. He silently stretches out his arm and puts his hand on my head. I chuckle and smirk as he tries to cheer me up; he pouts at me and blinks his eyes quickly, succeeding. Reggie looks up from his phone and sees us, looking at us with a confused side-eye. We laugh and grab our bikes, as Reggie cocks his eyebrow at us.

"Thanks, man," Michael says.

"Yeah, thanks Reggie," I say, swinging my leg over my seat.

"Hey prom queen," he says to me and I turn to look at him as he shoots me a sweet smile. "Don't be a stranger, sweetheart."

My smile fades as his words bring me sadness. I don't know why it was those words that broke me, but the fact that I will be a stranger to him, and everyone I know, come Monday makes me melancholy. I turn and roll forward, as I get lost in my thoughts. This entire week I've been anticipating the moment that it would all come crashing down on me — the weight of the harrowing fact that I will never see any of these people again. And it's Reggie's words, a simple statement from the boy next door, that crushes my chest with its weight.

I bike slowly as the weight thickens the very blood in my veins when Michael looks at me over his shoulder. He slows down and lowers down onto his seat, with a concerned look on his face.

"Hey, you okay? Listen, don't pay any mind to that Churchill guy — he's a creep and a half, and he's not worth your time."

"No, no it's not that," I say, before thinking better of it. "Well, it's not *only* that — it's just… this feeling."

"What kind of feeling?" he asks.

"It's hard to explain," I say. And it really is. Even if he knew everything about what is happening in my life, I'd have no idea where to even begin explaining how I feel.

"Sometimes I get a feeling like that too," he says. I look at him, his face somber as a memory comes to him that reflects in his eyes. "It's one of those things that feels deeper than words, but no words could even begin to describe how it feels."

"Yeah," I say. "Exactly."

"Well, why don't you try with the feeling? Where do you feel it?" I think about it as we slowly pedal, feeling the weight in my body and feeling it in my heart.

"It's in my chest," I say. He nods silently, giving me the space to continue. "It's like a weight is crushing down on me. And it's so heavy it starts to spread through my entire body and my whole body feels like it's getting weighed down."

"Why do you feel this way?"

"Well… it's a bunch of things really." I try to think of ways to explain it to him — but now that we're actually talking about it, which I haven't been able to do with Michael much lately, I have no desire to hold back on my feelings.

I continue, "It's this feeling of being obligated to do something, and feeling like if I don't do it then I'm disappointing my loved ones and wasting my potential. But at the same time, I feel like I'm not even meant to do this thing — but I don't know if that's because I'm not actually able to do it or just because I'm scared. And then there's this... power. It wants me to not do this thing I think I can't do, and is doing everything in its power to make sure I don't do it. This only makes me more scared, which makes me think I can't actually do it, which makes me feel more..."

"Heavy." I look at him and sigh, finally feeling heard.

"Yes," I exhale. "Exactly. And I don't want the power to win... but I also don't want to just do this thing to spite them. I want to do it because *I want to*, and because I feel ready."

He nods, looking off into the distance as we continue to pedal slowly. I look at him, waiting for him to say something, but he continues to look into space as he collects his thoughts. I look at him now, with nothing stopping me from taking all of him in, and I get even more heavy — I'm really going to miss him. There's no one like Michael that knows exactly what to say, regardless of the situation, regardless of whether he understands it or not. He just sees a situation for what it is, and can go at it from a bunch of angles until he finds a solution. Like a calculation, he tries a bunch of different ways until he finds the answer — a mathematician through and through. But he never makes it a life or death situation — no matter what the problem is, it can be solved. And it's this thinking that makes him so light-hearted, so jovial, so Michael. I'll never find a friend like Michael, and it's this fact that squeezes tighter on my heart.

"I don't know what this thing is that you feel obligated to do," he says. "But I've had this feeling before."

"You have?" I ask. We pass Mr. and Mrs. James, talking in front of their stores, and wave to them quickly as we pedal around the corner.

"Yeah. When my parents died, my nana wanted me to be in STEM more than anything. Whether it was math, science, she didn't care — she just wanted me to follow in my father's footsteps. And I love math more than anything, but when she pushed me to do it, it made me hate it. Remember those workbooks that taught the different subjects?"

"Yeah," I reply. "I used to love doing the English ones."

"Yeah, well, she'd make me do those workbooks on the weekends when I just wanted to hang out. And it was fun for a while, and I was definitely good at it, but she pushed me so much that it made me not like it anymore. It wasn't even about me at that point, it was about my dad. I was just another shot for her to get what she had with her son — and I'm not bitter with her for it, but I felt like I was just a clone for her to live out her dreams through me."

"Do you still feel that way?"

"Sometimes. I feel those same things you do — feeling like I'm not right to do it, and feeling like if I don't I'll disappoint Nana and my parents. But then I think about why I feel like I'm not right to do it — I realize that not being able to do it is not the reason, because I can do math better than my father could when he was my age. And then I ask myself if it's because I'm scared — and honestly, yeah. Yeah, I am a bit scared — but only because I don't want to disappoint the people I love."

He looks at me seriously and continues, "But as long as I try, then I wouldn't be disappointing them."

I nod as I think about his words. I've been scared of losing reality ever since finding out that I'm a Bastet, and resisted my powers every step of the way. But it was only when I started to actually try to accept them that I felt less scared. He's right — I just have to try.

"And what about the powers that be?" I ask. "The ones hell-bent against you succeeding and feeding those fears?"

"What could be worse than society?" he asks. "I'm a black kid who dares to dream that he can be one of the greats — along Newton, Hilbert, and Einstein. I could make the next great mathematical equation that changes the whole world. I could help find life on another planet. I could do all of those things. Just thinking that dares to say that I'm not what *they* say I am — a criminal or delinquent or something. And if I don't see black men like me doing the things that I want to do, that just feeds the insecurity that I couldn't do it. But I think of it this way: there's going to be a little black kid just like me, somewhere in the world, who loves what he does. But it's not what a black boy is 'supposed' to do, so he's scared to do it. Instead, it would be easier to be what everyone says he is, to do what they say he should do because someone like him *shouldn't* be good at stuff like that. But if he should see me doing what he's actually passionate about, then maybe he'll believe that he can do it. So screw the powers that be — I need to do this for me and that little black boy who's too scared to try. And all it takes is me trying."

"Prove the man wrong," I joke, but he shakes his head.

"If you're thinking about 'them', then it's still not about you. I don't wanna try to prove them wrong, I want to prove myself right."

That hits me hard; I've chosen to accept who I am because if I don't I could die. That's the fact, plain and simple. But I see all of my ancestors in the books I've been reading — their power despite their circumstances, and their persistence in the face of adversity — and I still wonder if I'm worthy to have my name written alongside theirs. I still fear my power and doubt that I'll be able to make it to that level. But am I even thinking of myself and my capabilities? Or am I still thinking of the Toubabs, who want to use me and my powers? Am I holding myself back from fully embracing my powers and harnessing them because I'm scared of what they can do if placed in the wrong hands? Am I thinking about the Toubabs motives and mistaking my own hands as the wrong ones?

"What is this really about, J? You can tell me, you can trust me."

"I know I can, Michael. But it's too hard to explain, you wouldn't understand."

"How do you know?" he asks. "You seemed to agree with everything I was saying before, so why would now be any different? Maybe if you tell me what's wrong, I could try to understand."

"I can't Michael," I say, as I'm getting exhausted from his probing. "There are just some things that you wouldn't understand, and there are some parallels between our situations — but mine is more of a life or death sort of thing."

"You make it sound like mine isn't valid," he says offended. He stops pedaling and stands, and I come to a stop.

"No, no, that's not what I'm saying at all." I struggle to turn my bike around to face him. "Listen, I want to tell you but I just can't."

"Why?" he asks defensively. "You make it seem like someone's stopping you from telling me — but it's just you, and I'm your best friend. You can tell me anything, you know that. I told you about my situation, why can't you tell me yours?"

"It's not that I don't want to tell you Michael — I'm glad you told me your story, okay? I'm your friend, and you know you can confide in me, but I'm just not ready to tell you my story yet."

"And you think I was ready to tell you mine? I told you so I could help you process your situation — but I'm still trying to come to terms with it too, J. Guys don't get the chance to feel these things — no matter how much progress we've made, I don't get to talk about my feelings. But

I told you, and you're not willing to ignore all the 'shoulds' and tell me. Your friend." He scoffs, cutting his eyes. "Some friend. I unload all my heavy shit and you can't even tell me yours?"

"This isn't show and tell, Michael," I say hotly. "Just because you tell me your story doesn't mean I'm ready to tell you mine!"

"I'm not saying it's show and tell — I'm saying it's trust! How can we be friends if you won't even trust me?"

"I do trust you; even when I feel like I'm losing you. You haven't been much of a friend to me lately either, Michael!" He fixes his face and looks at me, and I cross my arms.

"What are you talking about?"

"I've been going through my own thing for weeks, Michael. For weeks. But you've been preoccupied to notice. You're only just picking up on it now because Taylor's not here."

"Taylor? What does Taylor have to do with anything?"

"You two are attached at the hip," I say sardonically. He scoffs and rolls his eyes. "I've barely seen you in a month. I used to see you every day and now it's more like a couple times a week, and even then Taylor's always there. I like Taylor, I do, but we had our own thing going — and it's okay for that to just be the two of us. At least every once in a while!"

"Seriously, J?" he asks rhetorically. "You're gonna make this about me and my girlfriend?"

"Can you seriously tell me that you've been much of a friend to me lately? You're so focused on your relationship with Taylor it seems like you forgot about me."

"I have a girlfriend, Jamila. I can't give you every second of my time, because I'm trying to spend some time with Taylor so I can get to know her. I've been crazy about her for years, and you know this!"

"Oh, I know this?" I ask hotly. "Seems like it's driven you so crazy all you see is her — and now I'm just invisible. Unlike you, I don't have a boyfriend to go to when you're not around, Michael. You're my friend, the closest thing to a brother I have, and there's no one else that could even come close to the relationship we have."

"Well, maybe that's your problem, J." I lean back and furrow my brows as I feel a jab from his words.

"So I have a problem now?"

"You make it seem like I'm your heaven and earth — well maybe that's your problem. You're so attached to me you don't even have any other friends."

"Oh, like you do?"

"Yeah, actually I do. *Taylor.* She's not just my girlfriend, J, she's my friend. We've bonded as we've been dating, not just because we're into each other but because we actually like each other. Maybe if you stop intimidating everyone that comes your way, you could actually get some people to stick around."

A sharp pain rips through my heart, and I inhale sharply. His eyes waver a bit as he sees he has hurt me, but he stands firm and sets his face tauter.

"You stuck around," I counter weakly.

"Yeah," he says quietly, "well, you're not making it easy." He sits down on his seat and looks at me coldly. "I'll drop off your mom's books later, but I'll just watch the show by myself."

I inhale shakily as he rolls forward, and he pedals past me. Tears spring into my eyes and sting as they roll down my cheeks, as I hear his bike crunch on the pavement. I can't believe this is happening — this is one of the last times I'm going to ever see Michael, and it ends in a fight. All I've wanted to do since going through my journey learning my powers is to tell Michael — because I know I could confide in him. Even if he could never comprehend the full extent of my powers, he'd be able to understand how I feel. He always has. But if I should tell him, then he'd have to know about the Toubabs — and Michael is already a conspiracy theorist in the making. He gets paranoid over everything, and even if he is able to keep my world a secret, he'd constantly be looking over his shoulder. And no matter how much I want to keep him as a friend, I don't want to subject him to a life of turmoil if that's what it takes. I turn around, hoping he's still there, but he's long gone now. I sniffle my nose and use my sleeve to wipe the snot running from my nose.

I turn and bike down a side street, and head to take a shortcut through the park. That same feeling of heaviness returns to my bones, as my heart squeezes from the pain. Silent tears roll down my face and blur my vision, and I angrily wipe them away as I pedal home. Being a Bastet comes with a price. I've lost everything I've ever known. My reality, my sense of safety, even my closest friend. I don't get the luxury of safety, or to settle down in a place I can call home, or to have friends I can confide in. Not anymore, anyway.

I feel more and more uneasy as I pedal through the park, as memories from my assault settle in my bones into a familiar feeling of dread. The chain on my back wheel starts to lock up — something that happens when your bike is a decade old — and I kiss my teeth in frustration. I abruptly stop, dirt and gravel flying underneath my wheels as I brake, and I bend down to fiddle with the chain. I aggressively pull and prod until my finger jams between the spoke and the chain, ripping a cut into my skin. I hiss and pull my hand away, sucking my finger to alleviate the pain. Then, a chill shoots through my body, and goosebumps shoot up through my skin. I stop immediately, feeling a presence around me — and it's not amiable.

I slowly stand up, scanning from left to right as that chill brings a shiver to my spine. I grab my pendant, squeezing hard to feel the power — but my efforts are futile. I feel anything but protected. I can feel where the presence is — and as I slowly turn to the right, I feel my bones start to hollow with pain, and know that whatever, or whoever, has joined me is soon to be discovered. Just as I'm about to fully turn around, my skin spikes — I whirl around, and a rag is clamped down onto my mouth. I thrash as the strong scent of chemicals enter my mouth and my nose. Arms clamp onto me as I thrash, and strong muscles clench as they try to hold me down. I kick in the air and try to push my body away — but this person is strong, and he only squeezes tighter onto me as he presses the rag harder onto my face. I feel my body getting heavier as the drugs work its sick magic, and dark spots pepper my vision. I try to fight it, but soon fall victim to the darkness.

CHAPTER THIRTEEN

A burning in my nostrils is the first thing I feel as I come to consciousness — followed by the putrid smell of cigarettes and the skunk of weed. I try to will my eyes open, but the throbbing pain from the overpowering scent is the second thing I feel, and makes just opening my eyelids an arduous task. I try to open them again — chapped and crusty, they slowly crack open — and look up to a bubbly ceiling. A ceiling fan lazily spins to the left, and the light casts a yellowish glow. I start to hyperventilate as I remember that I was drugged; I was on my way home, and someone drugged me while I was in the park. I don't know where I am, I don't know the time, or even what day it is. I try to slow my breathing and gather myself, taking inventory of my body. I try to move my fingers and luckily feel them flutter, and feel the wiggle of my toes as I test my feet. I'm laying down, and I'm on top of something soft — a blanket, maybe? I look at the ceiling to try and focus on one space to calm me down, and then I realize that I recognize this ceiling.

I slowly turn my head to see a table to my left below a window, where the sun breaks through and shines the last of its light in the room for the day. I look down to see a beige carpet littered with cigarette and joint butts and weed bottles, and immediately smell the musty carpet. I look farther up and see a big flat screen TV on a TV stand, with an iPhone charging and resting on the top shelf. I hyperventilate as I realize exactly where I am — the room from my first vision, and I know exactly what's going to happen next. I try to lift myself, but the drugs have muscle — and I immediately feel my body weighted down as I try to exert myself, and I pant from the effort as I relax. I look to my right to the wall that the bed is pushed against, and faintly notice a pillow beneath my head. I hear footsteps outside the room and freeze — the door is open, and I can't get up to close it, so my heartbeat accelerates as the footsteps move from the hallway to the door. Ricky Brass appears in the doorway and leans on the door frame, smoking a cigarette and looking at me. I lean further into the bed, staring at him as my breath gets shallow.

He takes a long drag on his cigarette and looks at me with an intense look in his eyes — like he's eyeing down his prey. He's wearing a wife beater and jeans that sag low on his hips. It's hot in here, and as soon as I notice this I feel the fabric of my shirt stick to my underarms. The sun glints on his gold chain, but he remains unmoving, except to lift his arm to take another drag of his cigarette. I return his stare with one of my own — I try to appear defiant, but inside my heart is pounding and I'm not sure whether my face is betraying me.

He takes a short drag and walks forward, extinguishing the lit cigarette in an ashtray on the windowsill. He leans on the edge of the table, lifts his chin and looks down at me wordlessly.

"Well, aren't you going to say good morning?" I ask, testing my tongue; luckily it's sharp as ever. His nostrils flare and he pushes himself off the edge of the table.

"You've got some mouth, you know that?" he asks rhetorically. "Thinkin' you can just talk to me however you like without me settin' it straight."

"Oh yeah? Didn't think you'd be able to do that with those teeth of yours."

I feel the punch before I see it — my face shoots to the right, shocking me. Then I feel my jaw jump with pain, and the metallic taste of blood wells in my mouth. His brass knuckles are on, and now I see why he was given such an infamous name — he's strong, and the punch would hurt regardless, but the brass knuckles only amplified it. I try to lift my hand to block him, but my body hasn't caught up. I look at him wide-eyed as his nostrils flare to twice their size, and a dangerous anger in his eyes.

"You think you can do whatever you want," he says venomously. "You say shit like there ain't gonna be consequences — but I'm Ricky Brass. Nobody messes with me and gets away with it, and it's about time you learned that."

"Just because I refuse to take your shit doesn't mean I'm messing with you," I say matter-of-factly. "You think that you can just insult people without owning up to your actions, and you've gotten away with it long enough."

He inhales sharply and punches me again — blood shoots from my mouth and spatters onto the wall as my head whips to the right, and I feel like one of my teeth is about to dislodge. I look back at him with a steely stare and spit the blood onto the bed. His nostrils flare and his mouth tenses.

"You think you're the shit — that you can go on doin' whatever you want. You forget that you're just a negro, bitch — and it's time you finally learn yo' lesson."

He punches me again and reaches his arm back, again and again, to lay punch after punch onto me. Assaulting me with his brass knuckles, his strength doesn't wane as he punches me. I try to muster my hands to block my face, but the drug delay my movements and I take every punch.

"See how you feel after this, bitch," he mutters as my mouth pools with blood. "Unpretty you and see if you can act uppity," he says. I spit as two teeth crack from my gums. I finally block his punches, but my hands soon feel his punches as he continues his rage. Finally he slows and stops to catch his breath. I slump my arms down and my head lolls to the side, as cuts on my face burn afresh and my jaw and nose throb intensely. I've never felt a pain like this before; but I manage to feel numb to it as the waves of pain roll through me. I manage to block the pain as conviction shoots to the forefront. I manage to loll my head and look at him — my face messy with blood, but my eyes razor-sharp.

"You're a narcissistic, egotistical, sexist excuse of a man," I say with a thick tongue. "You can't stand the idea that I'm bold enough to stand up for myself, and because I won't put up with your shit I'm disrespectful? Tuh!"

He reaches to punch me again, but the fire within me ignites and fuels my strength. I shoot my arm up and stop his punch, grabbing his fist and looking him dead in the eye. His face contorts in surprise, but the anger quickly returns.

"You're a paper man that hides behind bravado and a gun, and you think that'll be enough. But I have a stronger foundation; I actually believe in myself, and in my right to deserve human decency — and that scares you. Because you have to scare people into giving you what I know I deserve."

His face drops, losing all anger and emotion, as he returns my stare. He pulls his arm back and stands straight, looking down at me with empty eyes — which scares me more than the anger. It makes his actions unpredictable.

He wordlessly reaches to the nightstand and opens the drawer, pulling out a rag and a gun. My heart stops and my body freezes as he continues to look at me. He turns off the safety on the gun and aims — point-blank and deadly. I look into his eyes as fear rises within me, and dread fills my soul. His mouth tenses as he continues to look at me, still aiming the gun at my head. This is it. I'm going to die by the hands of a heartless killer, and no one will know where I am. I don't get to say goodbye to my Nellie, Loni, or Michael, I don't get a dying wish. Except to not feel any pain, and to go quickly.

His face gets frustrated as his hand shakes, the gun bobbing slightly in the air. A calming feeling starts to flow through me, and I begin to wonder why I'm suddenly feeling more at ease. I look at his hand on the gun, so I can be prepared when he pulls the trigger — then I see his finger isn't on the trigger, and instead rests on the side of the gun. Suddenly, he drops his arm and exhales annoyed; slouching slightly and shaking his head with closed eyes. My heart jumps and beats at double time, and I sigh heavily as I try to catch the breath I was holding. He opens his eyes and looks at me again for a moment, and I look at him with eyes filled with fear — because for all my talk, I'm still terrified when it comes down to him being able to take my life. He takes the rag in his hand and clamps it down onto my mouth — wide-eyed I inhale sharply in shock, which only allows the drug to make its way in freely. I feel myself get groggy, and my head slouches against the pillow as the drug begins to work.

He drops the rag on the floor and leans on the bed, lifting his leg to kneel over me. My head still slouches against the pillow, but I'm able to look at him with drugged eyes. His nostrils flare and his mouth tenses as he stares at me — then, wordlessly, he begins to unbutton his jeans and pull them down. I look at him, confused as to what's happening, but when he's down to his briefs I realize with dread. Still wordless, he starts to unbutton my pants, and wiggle them down my hips. I try to push him away, but the drug is settling in my blood and my arms weighing down with stone. I try to say something, but I can't open my mouth — all I can manage is a garbled scream that fails to pass my lips. By the time my pants are at my ankles, my field of vision begins to go dark. I try to fight it — but the drug is strong, and in the face of fear I am weak. The last thing I feel is the air from the fan hitting my legs, and the jolt of my body as my underwear gets ripped apart. And then it all turns to black.

I feel consciousness return to me, and I slowly savour the last few moments of darkness before trying to open my eyes. A pounding in the center of my forehead pulses and shoots outward, and my jaw throbs with pain. Even breathing in through my nostrils hurts, and I try to breathe through my mouth to abate nausea. I will myself to slowly open my eyes, and try to raise my arm to shield my eyes from the light overhead. It's taking a monumental amount of effort, and my arm feels like stone, but I'm able to lift it and thump it over my face to cover my eyes. Everything is blurry, but I'm able to make out the room. The blurry shape of the TV, and the table, and the sky outside as the day turns to dusk. I try to move, and immediately stop as I feel a sharp and throbbing pain from below my pelvis. I gasp in pain and curl into the fetal position, cradling my pelvis and bobbing back and forth.

It happened just how I visioned it. Nellie and Loni were right — I was seeing something in the future, and now it's come to pass. I don't remember anything, I was unconscious during all of it, but the pain below my pelvis cannot be ignored. The burning pain that feels like it's pushing against me. I never used to dream about when I would be intimate for the first time — I just always knew that I wanted to experience my first time with someone I could trust, who would genuinely care for my well-being and my pleasure. I never thought it would happen like this, that there would be no intimacy whatsoever — and my heart starts to break as the crippling fact that my hope was stolen from me becomes all too clear.

I hear someone moving around on the other side of the wall — hearing a drawer close and keys jangle. Heavy footsteps are muffled by a carpet, and they shuffle to-and-fro. I look at my shirt as the sight of blood catches my eye, and I see my entire neckline and the top half of my shirt stained with my blood. I move my hand to my face and feel the crusted blood that dried overnight under my nostrils and on the sides of my mouth. The metallic taste of blood and morning breath fills my mouth and the stench wafts into my nose — how long have I been here for? I hear a door open and footsteps walk into the hallway. The door is open so I can see Ricky pulling up his pants and buttoning them — they still manage to sag below his butt, and even more so when he puts his wallet in his back pocket. He stops for a moment and sees me looking at him, then keeps walking forward. My breath is shallow and my heart heavy, and I feel numb. I lie there motionless, still curled into a ball. He returns with a bomber jacket on and a black baseball hat, and looks at me with a vacant look in his eyes.

He walks in and wordlessly goes to the window, pushing hard against it and shutting it closed. He pulls a blind down and the room gets dark, and the shadow he casts is even darker. He turns around and is lighting another cigarette. It ignites, and he pulls in a drag as he walks over to the bed. I try and back away, ignoring the shooting pain, and move closer to the wall. He sits on the edge of the bed and smokes his cigarette, and the smoke blowing in my face. I hate the smell of cigarette smoke, and it only makes me more nauseous. I try to breathe through my mouth discreetly — silently praying that my stomach can hold out a little longer. It grumbles as it gets more unsettled, but I can't remember the last time I've eaten — and with no idea what the time is, the chance of actually emptying my stomach is unlikely.

"You were aight," he says, void of emotion.

"You're disgusting," I say, my voice breaking. "You —"

"Chose not to pop your skull, so watch your mouth 'fore I change my mind," he replies, his voice monotone. He's calm as he smokes his cigarette — his breaths smooth and slow as if he didn't just kidnap, drug, and violate me. His calmness makes me uneasy and angry all at the same time.

"Oh, and I should thank you? *You violated me.*"

"Bitch, shut the hell up," he says, still eerily calm. "I had the right mind to take you out, but I was decent enough to let you live. You been carryin' on for too long, thinkin' that you can just say whateva the hell you wanna say and people ain't gonna set you straight."

"Decent enough? You think kidnapping me and violating me did me a service? You're delusional. I didn't deserve to be punished for defending myself — and even then, what you did wasn't punishment. It's assault. I don't care what you think I deserve, but I know I don't deserve this."

"It's betta than killin' yo ass."

"It's rape. No matter how you swing it, it's a crime — and it's wrong."

He looks at me silently and takes another drag from his cigarette. He nods slightly and checks his watch, and gets up wordlessly. He closes the door behind him, and a click of a lock slides into place. I exhale woefully as I curl tighter into myself — dread fills and overwhelms me as hopelessness overtakes my conviction. Tears burn my eyes and I wail in grief. I hear the front door close, and let out my wail into an anguished cry. I feel completely and utterly alone — where were my protective powers when I needed them the most? I was able to fend off the Toubab just fine; why couldn't I prevent this from happening? And I saw it coming too, I knew it would happen. Why didn't I do more? I feel so weak. So hopeless.

I look at the window through tear-filled eyes, and my heart sinks further in despair. I have no idea how to get out of here. The blinds allow a little bit of light to pass through as the sun begins to rise — I thought it was dusk, but it's *dawn*. I've been here for an *entire night*? That means it's Saturday. I sniffle and try to push myself, pushing through the pain as I sit up on the bed. My heart fills with dread that weighs down my body, but I have to get out of here. I only have one more day here in the city, and I have to get to Nellie and Loni so they can help me. I don't know how, but surely there's a spell they can cast, or a potion I can take, that'll make me forget this. Make me stop feeling this pain. I have to get out of here — if I miss that flight, the Toubabs will be even closer to finding us. To finding me. Ricky Brass is a spineless narcissist — but he doesn't even come close to the danger I'll be in, and the pain I'll experience if the Toubabs find me.

I push myself up, hissing in pain, and hobble to the door. The lock — rare to find in most Toronto apartments — needs a key to open, which Ricky Brass took with him. I lean on the doorknob as I look at the room; the only other way out is the window. I walk to the window and pull the blinds up, and see the ground. Six stories below. I groan in frustration; even if I try to make that jump I'd sprain my ankle, which is only just recovering from the last time Ricky attacked me. I look around me, hoping to find something, anything, to help me get out of here. I lean on the windowsill and cradle my head in the palm of my hand — my head is pounding, and the rest of my body isn't doing too hot either. I slide my hand around my head, trying to massage the tension away, when my hand bumps on some bobby pins. Those aren't helping my headache either, I should just take them out. I immediately stop, my eyes wide.

Light bulb.

I pull out three of the bobby pins — two new black ones — and look at them like they're holy grail. This might just be my ticket out of here. I hobble down and ease myself down onto my knees in front of the door. I bend one bobby pin until it's completely straight, then bend the tip of one end until it's perpendicular to the rest of the pin. I take another and bend it so there's more space between the two sides — I leave the other one just in case. I stick the pin that I straightened into the bottom of the lock and push slightly against it, and put the other pin at the top. I pull it back and forth, angling up as I pull the pin out and back down in a sort of small arc when I push it back in. I keep slightly pushing on the straightened pin while I jimmy the other. I feel the pins of the lock grate against the bobby pin, and bite my lip as I begin to sweat from the exertion. Finally, I feel a click, and exhale the breath I didn't realize I was holding.

I turn the knob in disbelief, and the door opens. I hoot in excitement, moving the door back and forth in exaltation, then hiss in pain as I realize my body is not in the condition to be celebrating so much right now. Okay, I need to get out of here — the next hurdle is getting to the elevator and getting home. I know Ricky Brass lives in Mississauga — in the infamous building that was modeled after Marilyn Monroe's legs — so it's a long way home. But I will get there somehow. I look down at my blood-stained shirt, and just realize that I don't have any pants on. He wouldn't have put them back on me after finishing, but for some reason, he put my underwear back on — I don't know why. I can't imagine the guilt was eating away at him, so why would he do that? That seems pretty decent of him.

I see my pants on the floor and hobble over. Lifting my leg into my pants is a job and a half, and it takes me several seconds just to get my legs in each one. I finally zip up but leave it unbuttoned so my pelvis can catch a break. I hobble faster to the door as the sweet feeling of freedom gets closer and closer, and — remembering where Ricky turned when he left — turn left. I see the living room, if you could even call it that, and the kitchen separated by a wall behind some couches. And the front door straight ahead. The stench of cigarettes is stronger out here, and looking at the state of the living room I can see why. Except for a few couches and a table, there's no furniture, and the carpet stinks with the smell of old cigarettes and alcohol. There is, of course, a shiny flat-screen TV on the wall immediately to my left, with several video game consoles littered on the floor and two big systems with a myriad of wires. A window grants me a view of the other side of the apartment building, with splatters of grease and old-age all over the glass.

I hobble to the front door, and my heart leaps in my chest as I'm excited to get out of here. But then it sinks as the grating of the lock slides open, and the door opens to bring me face to face with Ricky and three of Blanco's boys. He's smiling and laughing at something his boys must've said, but his face drops and he freezes in his tracks when he sees me standing there. His boys look over his shoulder, asking him what's holding him up. One of them is really short, and the other two are tall. One of the tall guys is really skinny, and his ears stick out, while the other looks to be average but with really bad acne. He's eating from a big bag of chips and has dust all over his fingers and the sides of his mouth. When they see me, standing there like a deer-in-the-headlights, in my blood-stained shirt and my hair frizzy and wild, they look at him with a questioning stare.

"Ay yo Ricky," says the short one in a high-pitched voice, with a faint patois accent. "What's this girl doin' here? Blanco's been tellin' us not to mess with her, man."

"Shut up, negro," he says to him, hissing at him over his shoulder. His friend falls back, but the other two chime in.

"Seriously bruh, what's she doin' here?" asks the tall, skinny one.

"And why's she covered in blood?" the other asks loudly. Ricky shushes them and pushes them all inside, slamming the door behind him. He eyes me down with his cobra-stare, and I shrink backwards. The other three look at the two of us confused, and one of them actually looks sympathetic.

"Please," I plea to them, "you have to help me. He attacked me and brought me here, and he —" Ricky reaches me in two mighty steps and smacks me hard across the face, and I fall to the ground.

"Shut up, bitch," he hisses venomously, as I palm the side of my face that stings.

"What did you do?" the shorter guy asks cautiously in his high-pitched voice, looking at Ricky with a fearful look.

"Taught this bitch who's the boss 'round here," he says to him. "Nobody talks shit to me and gets away with it, Shortstop. Nobody."

"Except you're not the boss," he says matter-of-factly, "Blanco is."

Ricky cocks his eyebrow and looks at him, his nostrils flaring and mouth tensed. The short guy — Shortstop, I guess — must realize where he overstepped, as his face falls in fear.

"I mean," he stutters, "I mean, Blanco had said to not go near this girl, right? And he's the bossman, is all I'm sayin'."

"And I'm his right-hand man," Ricky says deeply. "And nobody should be steppin' to Blanco's right-hand man without proper respect. And she," he yells, pointing at me as I look up at him from the floor. He continues, "she didn't come correct."

"So you jumped her?" asks the one with acne.

"Yeah, and made sure she knew who the man was." The skinny tall one's face changes as he realizes what Ricky means, and he shakes his head as the truth reveals itself.

"Nah, man," says the short one. "Why'd you go and do that?"

"Are you deaf? Or, are you dumb?" Ricky asks him. "Didn't you hear what I just said?"

"Yeah, but messin' with the girl is only gonna get us in trouble, man. And she's not legal yet, man. Blanco ain't gon' be too happy if you get yo'self locked up."

"Which is why we're gonna cut all the loose ends," Ricky says. The three guys look at him warily, as Ricky looks down at me with his jaw set. I start to back away, crawling along the rough carpet, as he walks towards me. Suddenly he grabs my ankle and pulls me toward him and comes behind me, clenching my head between the crook of his arm and squeezing hard on my neck. I start gasping for air, thrashing around to find something to get me out of his grip, but he pulls me in tighter. The three guys look down at him dumbfounded, frozen in their places.

"Ay, what are you doin' man?" Shortstop yells.

"Getting rid of loose ends," he says, his voice strained as he squeezes tighter on my neck. I try to get out from under him, but that only makes him squeeze tighter. The skinny tall one starts to look apprehensive and bounces from leg to leg, while the one snacking on chips just stands there frozen, holding a chip in mid-air.

"Nah man," Shortstop says. "I ain't gonna be a part of this. I'm not gonna be an accomplice to murder!"

He kisses his teeth and heads for the front door, slamming it behind him. I try to yell while the door's open but Ricky sees me, and pushes harder onto my windpipe. The two tall guys still stand there, not sure what to do, and I look at them with pleading eyes. But they're not here to help me — they're not even here to help him. They're just cogs in a machine that tells them how to work.

I grab Ricky's wrist, my final attempt to get him off me — but he's determined to get rid of me. Dark spots begin to bubble in my vision as I feel myself losing consciousness again.

"That's what you get for tryin' me, bitch," he whispers in my ear. Now that makes me mad.

I feel that power surge within me — the same one that shot from my arm when Churchill tried to drug me, and my heart leaps with excitement that I might get away this time. But then a hollow ache starts to pit in the center of my chest, and quickly extends outward. The pain thrums hollow in my bones, then starts to feel like it's banging against my bones from within itself. I yell in pain, shocking Ricky enough for him to loosen his grip on my neck. I take a sharp inhale of air to reinflate my lungs, but then yell out again as that hollow pain bangs from within every part of my body. I collapse to the ground and claw the carpet, groaning in pain as my bones shift and change from within me. I have no idea what's happening — this isn't what happened last time — and Ricky and the two guys are clueless too. They look at me wide-eyed, Ricky's brows furrowed in confusion as he backs away from me.

"What the hell's wrong with you?" he asks confused.

"Whatchu do, Ricky?" the hungry one asks, his voice deep and slurred.

"What'd it look like, dumbass? I was chokin' her out — but she shouldn't be screamin' like this."

I continue wailing as the pain becomes unbearable, and my nails claw the carpet. My fingers change, and black fur sprouts from underneath. My bones move as they get thicker and shorter, and sharp claws shoot out from the ends. I feel the palms of my hands become rougher and tougher, and my arms fill with a strength I didn't have before. My back hunches as my body transforms — my legs get shorter and bend as they turn into hind legs, and my chest and stomach shrink into itself then elongate. My skin burns as fur sprouts all over from underneath the layer, and my face burns as my eyes change from small to wide, slanted ones. I groan in pain as my nose juts out wider into a wet snout, and my lips rip wider as sharp teeth jut out from my mouth. Whiskers extend from the sides of my mouth as I feel my ears move on their own volition. My vision turns black for a second and I close my eyes as I prepare to lose consciousness again — but then I open my eyes, and everything's crystal clear. My vision is sharpened, and my nose twitches as smells I didn't notice before floods my nostrils. The putrid smell of B.O., old food, and garbage floods my senses, and I fear I'll throw up right then and there. I feel like I'm sitting up, but when I look up at Ricky and the other two guys I feel closer to the ground — and they look down at me with fearful, disbelieving wide eyes. I exclaim, but instead of my voice, I hear the growl of an animal. Of a panther.

My ears twitch as I hear Ricky and Blanco's boys shout out in disbelief. The tall skinny one yells and jumps back onto the couch, his face comical and — in any other situation — would make me laugh. The one snacking on chips drops the bag and points at me, and starts hollering as his eyes get wider and wider. Ricky jumps back and falls to the floor, leaning against the wall with wide eyes and mouth agape. I pant heavily as the pain dissipates, but still echoes throughout my body.

"What the hell!" yells the skinny guy. He hoots and hollers in disbelief, stammering and bouncing back on the couch. His eyes get wider and wider, and I wonder if they'll pop out of his head.

"Oh! Oh! What the hell just happened?" yells the other. He hoots and backs away from me, walking to and fro.

Ricky remains speechless and continues to stare at me, breathless. I look at the window and see a faint reflection in the glass — and instead of seeing my human form, I see a black panther staring back at me. With stark yellow eyes, and a glistening pink nose that twitches as I breathe heavily. *Holy crap.* I shout out and a warbled growl escapes from my mouth; I stumble across the floor as I try to catch my bearings, scaring Blanco's boys. They scream and jump back on the couch. I bump into the TV stand and knock the video game system over. I scurry away in a frenzy and bump into the wall, falling to the floor and struggling to get my feet underneath me again. Growls continue to escape from my mouth as I try to get myself upright, and the sound scares me — making me growl and whine even more. I struggle to find my footing with my furry paws, but find traction on the carpet eventually and jump back. They jump away from me, the hungry one falling to the floor and scooting away, while the skinny one continues to hoot and bounce in his seat with wide eyes. I shake my head as I try to get rid of the pounding pain, and blink my eyes to adjust to my new vision. I look down to my arms, which are now powerful legs that hold up my strong, slender, velvety shoulders. I did it — I turned into a black panther like my ancestors used to. Bastets haven't been able to transform for generations, and Loni thought that this power had been lost forever — but I can do it.

I look back at Ricky, whose eyes are wide and filled with shock. All of a sudden I'm laser-focused — the events of the past few hours unfolding before me like a scene then and there, and my steps find sureness as I walk towards him. My chest flares with heat as power ignites within me. My purpose is all too clear. My ancestors could avenge entire villages. They could cast down their foes and bring justice to those who were wronged. I'm the only one that can avenge myself — no one else is here to help me or do it for me — and now I feel powerful enough to do so. Ricky's nostrils flare as he pushes himself further against the wall, his legs shuffling every which way as he tries to get further away from me. But I have him cornered, and I don't intend to let that happen.

"Get away from me," he says, his voice breaking. "Get the hell away from me freak!"

I growl in reply, a sound rumbling from my vocal folds, which only scares him more. For all the intimidation he tries to pull, and all the bravado he mimics, it's all fake. It's all fluff. When backed up against the wall, with life uncertain beyond this moment, he shows the first sign of true humanity that he's probably ever shown in a very long time. I'm still very confused, and very afraid, but that's on the backburner for now. Because right now all I see is him — and that's all I need.

I get right up in his face, showing a big, toothy grin and breathing heavily. My breath wafts into his face, and he turns his head as he pushes his head harder into the wall. This time his nostrils flare out of fear, and there's nothing he can do to hide it. I can't say anything — or at least I don't think I can — so I just stare at him. He violated me and abused me in the worst possible way; he can justify it until he's blue in the face, but he and I both know that what he did was unjust. And as I stare into his eyes, I show him that. I don't know how I did it, but I somehow connect to him through his eyes and I can show him everything he did to me — but from my point of view. It's like there's an invisible link between us, connecting our minds and our eyes, and I show him everything in a vision.

His face goes slack as he sees through my eyes, and like a movie, it plays out in front of our eyes. Every time he cornered Michael and I on our way to school, when he leered at me and came to my house to intimidate me, when he cornered me at Loni's and tried to assault me the first time, to yesterday when he kidnapped and violated me. I show him everything, no holding back. I show him all of my anguish, all of my hope that is now lost, and I know — even without any vocality between us — that he can feel all of it. His face eases and falls as I stare into his eyes, and a flash of guilt crosses his face. This link must not just be one way, because in his understanding of my pain, I now understand his guilt — and his reason for why he did it. He's a weak man, and has been for most of his life, and I'm one of the things that makes him feel weaker. That makes him feel like less of a man. And he thought that hurting me would 'put me in my place' — that it would make him feel stronger. Braver. More of a man. And seeing this now, feeling his inadequacy, I actually understand. And that infuriates me. After all the pain he put me through and the fear I felt because of him, I don't want to forgive him. I don't want to see his side, because there shouldn't be two sides when one causes you misery and anguish. He has changed my life forever from one single act of desire that he didn't care to control, and he has the nerve to show humanity now? I bare my teeth and growl low, crouching lower to the ground and clawing the carpet as the tension threatens to explode. But his face reminds me of the feeling I felt not too long ago, and my compassion stops me. I silently groan in frustration because, with even all the power in the world, it's no match for my empathy.

I back away from him, my teeth still bared but my claws retracting back into my paw. His eyes settle as he notices me backing away, and his breathing slows. The other two guys are still screaming and hooting in fear and disbelief, and when I look at them they hoot even louder. I shake my head, trying to shake this feeling out of me, and feel that same hollowness return again. But I welcome it because anything is better than having a piece of Ricky Brass inside my soul. The hollowness begins to thrum from within my bones and rack my whole body, and I growl ferociously as the pain becomes overbearing once again. I collapse to the ground and my powerful heart beats double time as I try to handle the pain. My bones start painfully changing again, and I feel my body returning to normal. The fur on my body recedes within my skin, and I look down to see my melanated skin rise back up. My stomach shrinks and my breasts reappear, and my legs elongate and reveal the brown legs I've looked down at for the past 17 years. I pant as the pain throbs in my body, and the low feline pant changes to my human pant as I try to catch my breath. I look up as I slow my heart rate, seeing the two tall guys still, and their eyes getting wider once again.

"Yo," yells the skinny one. "Yo! What the hell is goin' on, man?"

"I need to stop drinkin' Lean in the mawnin', man," says the hungry one, as he shakes his head and a pained look crosses his face.

I tilt my head and look at Ricky, who looks at me with a frozen look of shock on his face — but he's still, calm even, as he leans against the wall. I look at him as I push myself up to sit, and we exchange a look. We just sit there for a moment, silently. He just saw my experience, in a way that he could've never imagined or will ever be able to explain. And I saw a side of Ricky that made me actually understand him — which I never thought would happen either. I push myself to stand, contorting my face as I push through the pain that still thrums fresh. I'm surprised to find that I'm in the blood-stained clothes I had on before I transformed. The sun begins to rise, and I assume it's close to 7:00 a.m. I look at the two guys, who look back at me with the same wide eyes, and then back to Ricky. He sits there, staring up at me with fear and understanding — an understanding that this is over. I walk past him and head for the door, opening it and closing it calmly behind me. No one gets up to stop me.

I hobble down the hallway and head for the elevator, my foot dragging on the dingy red carpet. I push the elevator button and I feel a shock run through my finger — but with all the pain still throbbing throughout my body, I don't even flinch. The doors open and I head in; it's a very nice elevator to match the building, and am welcomed by soft elevator music and cool air conditioning. I push the button for the lobby and lean back on the wall, closing my eyes. The doors go down two floors before stopping on the fourth floor, and the doors open to an older Greek woman. She sees me and she stops with wide eyes — I smile at her politely, which must be a stark contrast to my blood-stained face and teeth. She slowly walks in, side-eying me and clutching her purse.

"Lobby?" I ask politely.

"Uh, yes, yes," she says, with a slight accent. I smile and push the button to close the doors, and stand with a wide stance as I watch the light signal the passing floors. I see her looking at me out of the corner of my eye, and struggle to conceal a smile. I don't know how I'm able to find a sense of humour amidst everything that just happened, but I'll take a laugh over pain.

We finally reach the first floor — I reach my arm out to allow her to leave first, but she politely shakes her head and motions for me to go ahead. I smile and walk out, heading for the front door — the short guy that was in the apartment stands by the front door smoking a cigarette, and is talking to someone on the phone. He sees me and his mouth falls open, and he drops his cigarette as the person on the other end of the phone calls his name. I smile politely, showing him my bloody grin, and nonchalantly walk through the front doors. I carefully maneuver myself down the stairs, still feeling pain below my pelvis and a throbbing in my bones, while looking from left to right. How the hell do I get home?

I pat my pants pockets and — by some sheer luck of fate, or the grace of God, or one of my ancestors looking out for me — I find my phone. With just enough battery life to call an Uber. I call an Uber and head for the shade of a big tree to the right of the building to wait until it arrives.

Five minutes later I see a car with the matching licence plate and hail it down. The driver looks like he's seen a ghost, and eyes me warily as I ease myself slowly onto the backseat. I pant from the exertion it took, and look at the driver — who looks back at me with a cocked eyebrow through the rearview mirror.

"Uh, are you Jamila?" he asks slowly.

"Yes. Yes, that's me." He nods slowly and puts the car in drive, still eyeing me warily.

"Okay, well let's get you to where you're headed." He looks at me over his shoulder with a wary look and asks, "Could you, um, try not to get blood on my seat? I just got her cleaned."

"I'll try my best," I say. He gives me a worried smile before turning around and driving me home. I look at my phone and check my notifications — 47 missed calls and 35 texts. Mostly from Nellie. Some from Loni. Some from Michael, and one from Taylor. I sift through them, but can't find the energy to type back — they'll see me soon enough. They must be worried sick — and I can only imagine the flurry of emotions Nellie is going to lay on me when I walk through the front door. That woman can go from happy to sad to upset in a matter of seconds — it's truly astounding — but I really don't have the energy for that right now. I just want to be home, in my bed, before it's no longer mine and instead belongs to some pre-teen on the other side of town. My heart wells with sadness as I remember that I only have one more day left in Toronto; come tomorrow I'll be on a plane to Jamaica and I probably won't ever come back.

I look out the window at the passing roads, buildings, and trees that are losing the last of their leaves as the winter chill makes its introduction. I'm just realizing I didn't even notice how cold it was, but I guess with all the pain I'm feeling it doesn't even register. I start to get groggy as discernible figures become a blur, and fall asleep in the back seat.

I wake up with a start as the driver parks the car — I look out the window with groggy eyes and recognize Ms. Dell's porch swing, and when I look through the windshield I see we're parked in the driveway of my house.

"We're here," the driver says, glancing at me warily. The front door opens and Nellie comes out, in sweats and her hair frazzled. Ms. Dell comes out behind her, with Michael not too far behind. I look at the clock on the dashboard and see that it's 7:55 a.m. The driver looks at me with an expectant look. This random girl with blood all over hops into his Uber in the wee hours of the morning, he's probably just waiting for me to get out of his car so he can breathe normally.

"Thank you," I say quietly. "No one's more deserving of five stars and a tip — thanks for being so kind."

He looks at me surprised and shoots me a genuine smile — and I return it, but with less flattery to work with, his face contorts with unease. I open the door and hold onto the top edge as I push myself up without crying out in pain, and turn to face my home. I quickly rate the driver on my phone and give him the biggest tip I can afford, because he truly does deserve it. It's the least I can do for scaring him and getting blood all over his car. Nellie looks tired — her face is ravaged with fatigue, and her eyes are red and bleary, from crying or staying up all night. Ms. Dell gasps and covers her mouth when she sees me, and Michael stands there frozen in shock as he looks me up and down. The driver backs out of the driveway and honks once in farewell. I turn to face them again, at a loss of what to say. I grab the edge of my pants and put one leg behind the other, bowing in a curtsy with a showman's smile on my face. Nellie shakes her head and breaks down, jogging down the steps towards me.

She stops just in front of me and looks me up and down, her eyes filled with pain and sadness.

"What?" she stammers. "How... where... Oh!" She grabs me and locks me in a fierce bear hug, cradling my head with her hand and tucking her face in my neck. I hiss in pain as she squeezes too hard, and she immediately lets me go and looks at me wide-eyed.

"Just a little sore," I say quietly.

"Sorry," she says, her voice almost breaking. She puts her hand behind my back and cradles my arm, walking me slowly inside. We walk up the steps at a snail's pace, and Michael reaches out his hand to help me up. I look at him with surprise in my eyes, and he just returns my look with a somber one of his own. And Ms. Dell, a woman that never fails to state the obvious, is her regular self.

"Why the hell are you covered in blood?" she booms. I can't help but chuckle, which only makes her scoff at my audacity. We walk into the house, but Ms. Dell has no intention of letting up.

"You got your aunt worried sick, little girl. Pacing around the house all hours of the night, worried that you were dead in a ditch somewhere, and you're gonna *laugh*? Where the hell were you?"

"Alright, Nana," Michael interjects, as he closes the door behind us. "I think J is aware of how scared we were — can you stop yelling at her now?"

"Me? You're the one who was pacing along with Nellie — I ain't never seen someone wring the neck of their shirt worse than you, Michael."

"You were up all night?" I ask him, my eyebrows raised. He looks at me and nods, rubbing his head.

"Well, yeah," he says. "I couldn't sleep after Nellie told me you were missing."

"I still don't know why you didn't report it to the police," Ms. Dell says to Nellie. "An Amber Alert could'a gotten her home a lot quicker than the mawnin'. But you insisted —"

"I insisted that we didn't need to involve the police," she says loudly, rubbing the skin between her brows.

"Tuh!" Ms. Dell exclaims. "Well, it sure beats runnin' tracks in your carpet. While you two were worryin' yourselves to death, I went ahead and reported it."

Nellie shoots her head up and looks at Ms. Dell with a shocked look. "You did what?"

"I called the police," says Ms. Dell. "That girl could'a been dead, and we would'a never find out without the authorities. Thank God he brought her home before that could happen — but getting the police involved made the most sense, baby girl."

"Ms. Dell, I was very clear that I didn't want to involve the authorities," Nellie says, restraining her anger. "I appreciate what you did, but I didn't want people I don't know looking for my niece."

"Why not?" Ms. Dell asks incredulously.

Because then there would be a record, which would create a trail for the Toubabs to find me. I understand this right away — because even though the police are meant to serve and protect, there's not much they can do when an old-age cult is after me. They might've even infiltrated the Toronto Police; Nellie said they've already inserted themselves in politics and major bodies of authority. What could hold more power than a body of power with a gun?

"It's hard to explain," Nellie says exasperatedly.

"Well there's no need," I say loudly, causing everyone to look at me as if they're seeing me for the first time. "I'm here, that's all that matters. Now we can get back to normal."

"Normal?" Michael asks incredulously. He looks at me wide-eyed, shaking his head in disbelief. "Jamila, we were worried sick. You didn't answer any of our texts, our calls, nothing — for almost *twelve hours!* We thought you were dead!"

"I know," I say calmly, walking towards him with a reassuring smile on my face. "But I'm not — I'm okay. See?" I jump from foot to foot, kicking my heels in the air and landing with a ta-da pose. "A little scraped up but I'm alright — nothing a couple of bandaids and a Tylenol can't fix."

"You call this okay?" he asks, pointing at my blood-stained face and shirt. "You look like an extra from Pulp Fiction! How can you act like any of this is okay?"

"I'm not saying that I wasn't hurt, but the point is that I'm okay now."

"No!" he shouts incredulously. "No, that is not the point! Who hurt you? You're covered in blood, so whoever did it had a reason. You are the last person I'd ever expect to get beat up, and I'm sorry but I'm having a little trouble being okay with you not explaining."

"Michael," I say exasperatedly. "Who else has been grillin' me for the past few months? Grillin' us? And who was it that put me in the hospital not too long ago?"

His face goes slack and his eyes get glassy. "Ricky Brass?" he asks. I nod somberly, and Ms. Dell tsks as she shakes her head.

"What happened?" Michael asks, his voice breaking. I hesitate, as emotion causes my voice to catch in my throat. Nellie takes my arm and turns me to face her, her eyebrow cocked and her face barely concealing anger.

"What happened, J?" she asks. I look at her deadpan, but tears well in my eyes as the events of the past day cause the pain in my body to throb afresh.

"He picked up where he left off," I say robotically. "You know, finished what he had started — but luckily it didn't end with me dead."

"Oh my God!" Michael says, closing his eyes and covering his face — walking briskly into the kitchen and out the side door into the alleyway. Ms. Dell's face pains as she collapses onto the couch, and Nellie's mouth tenses as her eyes quickly well with tears. Mine gets more cloudy as tears quickly fall down my face, and she silently pulls me in for a hug — causing me to sob uncontrollably. We both stand there for a while, crying aloud

— Ms. Dell gets up after a while and grabs our shoulders, putting her forehead on mine and mouthing her lips in prayer. I don't register what she's saying over my sobs but it doesn't matter, she's praying for me and that's all that matters.

Nellie lets me go slightly and looks at me; her face is wet with tears, and looks more haggard. I can only imagine how mine looks. She silently wipes the tears off my face and palms my cheek.

"I'm so sorry, Mama," she says.

"No," I say thickly. "I'm sorry. I made you worried sick over me, and I couldn't even defend myself —"

"No," Ms. Dell says loudly, causing me and Nellie to look at her with a start. "Don't do that. Don't go blaming yourself, baby girl. Men like that just take, take, take, and will justify it 'til the day they see the devil — then ask what they did wrong." She grabs my face and makes me look at her full-on, looking deeply into my eyes.

"You can't blame yourself for being scared," she says sharply. "Fear can be like a vice grip — no matter how prepared you are, or how strong you are, it'll freeze you if the fear is bad enough. So don't go beating yourself up, okay? You got out — and that's more than enough, baby girl."

I continue crying — I want to believe her, to believe it was enough, but Ms. Dell doesn't know what I can do. What I could've done. My ancestors had to deal with much worse and still brought their enemies to their knees. Sure, I may have done that towards the end, but what about when Ricky was actually kidnapping me and drugged me? When he was forcing himself on me? Where was my strength then? Where were my ancestors? They're supposed to be there to help me, to protect me, to guide me. Where were they when I needed help? Where were they when I needed protection? When I changed into the black panther, who was there to guide me? No one.

I turn to Nellie and look at her — *'we need to talk,'* I tell her with my eyes. Her face registers what I'm saying and she slightly nods — *'we'll talk about this later,'* she silently replies.

"I should go check on Michael," Ms. Dell says.

"No," I stop her, "I'll go."

I head for the side door and see Michael sitting on his doorstep, head bowed and hands rubbing the back of his head. I open the door, and the creak of the hinges causes him to look up abruptly.

"Hey," I say.

"Hey," he replies. I sit down on my doorstep and spread out my legs, hunching and looking at him silently for a moment.

"You okay?" I ask.

He scoffs, giving me an incredulous but small smile. "You're asking me that? Shouldn't that be my job?"

"What can I say, I'm a Virgo," I reply haughtily. He chuckles, shaking his head. His smile falls as we get somber again, and I tap his foot with mine.

"Really though, are you okay?"

"Jamila, I'm anything but," he says somberly. He looks at me stone-faced, but before long his eyebrows quiver and his eyes soften. "I was eating myself up inside for *hours*, worried that you could be dead. And that our last conversation would've been... the one we had."

"Yeah. Believe it or not, that crossed my mind when... everything happened."

"Yeah?"

"Yeah. I was scared I was going to die, too," I reply. My breath hitches and my eyes well with tears, again, as I look at him. "I was so scared, Michael."

His mouth quivers and he comes to my side, putting his arm around me and pulling me in for a hug. I rest my head on his shoulder and he rests his head atop mine.

"I was so scared."

"I know. I know."

"But even though I was scared, all I could think about was how I didn't leave things the way that I wanted to."

"With our fight?" he asks.

I hesitate for a moment, as I recall everything I've had to hide from him, but decide to leave it at that. "With everything," I reply.

"I know," he says again. "After I rode off, I immediately regretted what I said. I even rode back to talk to you again, but you weren't there. I mean, I'm not gonna lie, I'm still kind of butthurt over you not telling me your stuff. But when Nellie said you were missing, and you didn't come home, all I could think was that I would give anything for you to be home again. And even if you still wouldn't tell me about your baggage, all I cared about was having you back."

His voice wobbles as he starts to sob, and I look up at him and I'm surprised to see him crying openly. Even when his parents passed I never really saw him cry — he was always very somber about his parents passing, and would feel the pain openly, but I still never saw him cry. This is a first for me, and it's shocking. This time I'm the one to console him, and I grab his head in my arms and rock him to and fro. His body jolts as his sobs overtake him, and I cry silently as we share this moment of shared pain.

"It's okay, Michael," I reply thickly. "It's okay. It's in the past, okay?"

He nods but stays there for a few moments as I cradle him closely. After a few minutes, he sits back up and sniffles his nose, wiping the snot running down with the sleeve of his sweater. I just realize as I see his sweater how cold I am, and I start to shiver in my dinky little shirt.

"Oh," he says, "let's get you something warm." We stand up and head into the house, and I reach to click the kettle on, but see steam already rising from the spout. We walk back into the living room and see Ms. Dell and Nellie sitting and drinking tea on the couch. Nellie looks back at me, relieved to have me in her sights again.

"You okay, sweetie?" Nellie asks Michael. He nods, stuffing his hands in his front pockets.

"Yeah, I'm good now," he replies. We look at each other with a small smile. Nellie smiles and rises from her seat, and her eyebrows furrow as she sees the goosebumps on my arm.

"You cold, Mama?"

"Yeah, I'm just noticing it now," I reply. "I'm just gonna take a nice hot shower."

"Wait, let me have a look at you first — let me see if I can tape up some of those cuts."

"Okay," I reply, turning to Michael and giving him one more good hug.

He pulls away and rubs the top of my head, making me chuckle. "See you later," he says. A pang rings through my heart — because there may not be a later since we're still leaving tomorrow, but I fake a smile anyways. I wave to him and Ms. Dell as Nellie lets them through the front door, closing it behind them and locking it.

"You gave me one hell of a scare," she says, turning to me with a pained look. "You're really trying to give me grey hairs, huh?"

"What can I say — I live to entertain," I reply jokingly. She lets out a single chuckle, before walking to me and pulling me in softly for a warm hug. She rocks me side to side slowly, making me lethargic and drunk with peace. That's not any magical powers at play — no, that's just Nellie.

She pulls away and looks me up and down, putting one finger under my chin and turning my face left and right slowly so she can assess my injuries.

"Have a seat at the kitchen table, Mama," she says. She heads for the bathroom and I obey. By the time I sit, she returns with the first aid kit she keeps underneath the bathroom sink. She opens it, pulling out some bandages, cotton balls, and filling a small glass with water at the kitchen sink.

She sits down and grabs a damp white cloth, gently wiping my face clean of the caked-on blood. When she's satisfied that all the dried blood is gone, she drops the cloth on the table — it's not white anymore. She tsks as she looks at my face, cleaning the open cuts on my face with the water-soaked cotton ball. It hurts a little as she cleans deeper into the wound, and she looks at me apologetically but continues. This goes on for about 10 minutes before she covers up my cuts with bandages, sitting back and giving me the okay to get up. I stand and head for the bathroom, craving a nice hot shower. I rip my clothes off me at lightning speed, but stop as I see myself in the mirror. My face looks haunting — dark circles under my eyes make me look like a zombie, and bandages all over my face don't help either. A deep cut on my nose is covered with a bandage larger than the others, and I touch it lightly — I have a complicated relationship with my nose, but I hope it doesn't leave an ugly scar. I'll never complain about my nose again, but the last thing I want is for it to look worse.

I hop in the shower and crank the handle to boiling-hot, and sigh as the water slowly turns from ice cold to skin-melting hot. I turn backwards with my eyes closed, soaking it all in. The hot water soothes the ache in my bones, and I remember why my bones ache — getting beat up within an inch of my life, surprisingly, wasn't the highlight of the past twelve hours. I transformed into the black panther of my ancestors — and that shit hurt. I slowly soap up my body as I marvel at it. I still can't quite believe it happened, but even though I'm amazed, I'm also afraid. Our ancestors have done everything to keep our powers a secret, and what do I do when I first transform into a panther? I show Blanco's boys. Of all the people to discover my abilities, it had to be them? It had to be Ricky Brass? To be fair, I don't think there was anything I could've done to prevent it — I think it might've been a defensive response to almost dying. When Ricky Brass was forcing himself onto me, I was drugged with obviously a stronger drug than the one that Churchill partially injected into me — at least then I reacted quick enough to escape before I passed out. But with Ricky's drug, I was paralyzed, and couldn't do anything to defend myself at the moment — but I also wasn't dying. Maybe that was why I transformed, as a self-defense mechanism.

I finish washing off and turn off the shower, towelling myself dry and leaning on the sink. I look up into the mirror at myself — at this girl who is supposed to be able to do amazing things. And for all my doubts, all my insecurities, I actually in this moment believe it. The scars on my face embolden me, as they're a sign of the forces I'm able to stand up against. The circles under my eyes give me strength as they remind me of how hard I can push myself against the forces against me. And they are powerful forces. But so am I.

I moisturize my face and head for my room, but stop in shock as I see it almost empty. In her fear and worry, Nellie must've tried to keep herself busy, and she clearly was — she took out everything except for my mattress and a suitcase. And the Novelfall. This looks nothing like my room — my safe place — and my throat feels thick as reality settles in once again. I kneel on the floor and lay down my suitcase, opening it and finding my fuzzy pyjamas almost immediately. I slip them on and stand the suitcase back up, hanging my towel on the handle to air dry. I hear two female voices coming from the front of the house, and immediately recognize Loni's deep voice. As I walk to the living room, I look at Nellie's room and the home office as I pass them. Their doors are open so I can see the rooms, almost completely bare, and the home office holds nothing except a table and our documents on top.

My feet make the floorboards creak as I head for the kitchen, and Nellie and Loni look up at me as I appear in the entrance. Loni's large purse rests on the table, and she has a teacup in front of her as Nellie continues to nurse hers.

"Hi, baby girl," Loni says, easing herself up and pulling me in for a bear hug.

"Ah, ah," I warn. "Still a little sore."

She eases her grip but still hugs me, pulling back and grabbing my head in her hands. A caring look is on her face as she assesses mine.

"Men are a species I will neva understand," she says seriously. I laugh heartily — for the first time in a while — and Nellie chuckles.

"Who you telling?" I ask rhetorically with a smile. She smiles back, her eyes still somber.

"I'm glad you got out," she says. "I travelled to di Realm of Duality an' asked our ancestors to protect you, but I know dat you had a hand in gettin' yuhself out of there."

"Yeah, not gonna lie, the ancestors protection took a little time," I reply sardonically.

"Well, dey came thru eventually," she replies. "I know dis is really hard for you, but do yuh think you could tell us exactly what 'appened? Maybe we can see what we can do to help yuh. And Nellie said you had somethin' else to tell us."

"Yes," I say seriously. "I do." I grab a chair and sit down in front of them, both of them looking at me expectantly.

"Michael and I had a fight last night, and I ended up taking a shortcut through the park after he left."

"Yes, Micheal told me," Nellie says. "He regretted it so much J. He was eating himself up about it and berating himself over and over while we were waiting for you to come home."

"I know. I forgave him though, we're good now. But we were both upset so we went our separate ways. When I was in the park one of the chains on my back wheel got caught, and I bent over to fix it when I felt a presence behind me."

"Ricky Brass," Loni says.

"Yeah. It felt ominous, like it wasn't a friendly presence, so I knew something was wrong. But he was too quick. He put a rag over my mouth and drugged me, and when I woke up I was in his apartment."

Nellie inhales sharply through her nose, as Loni nods as she listens along.

I continue, "Well, he was pissed — going on about me not respecting him and me being too cocky and everything. I, being the person I am, defended myself — and, well, he didn't like that. He beat me senseless, but I didn't stop defending myself. I told him that he was afraid of me, and he's just a paper man that could never have the strength I have."

"You said that to the man that was beating you up?" Nellie asks incredulously. I shrug in reply, and Loni shakes her head.

"It stopped him for a second, but then he grabbed a gun and pointed it at me." My voice catches in my throat, and Nellie grabs my hand and rubs the curve between my thumb and forefinger.

"I was so scared," I continue, struggling to keep myself from crying as I tell the story. Loni and Nellie nod along sympathetically, and I take a deep breath to continue. "I had never stared down the barrel of a gun before, and I thought that it was really over for me then and there. But he didn't pull the trigger. I don't know why, but he didn't kill me. But he still thought I needed to be punished — which was when he drugged me again. And then..."

"And den your premonition came tuh pass," Loni finishes for me. I nod somberly, biting my lip to keep the sobs in.

"The drug had me paralyzed, and I passed out just as he forced himself onto me. When I woke up my clothes were off and there was an ache below my pelvis, so I figured out pretty quickly what happened when I was unconscious."

"Where was he when you woke up?" Nellie asks.

"He was in the next room, getting ready to leave. He said his usual spiel before he left — of how I deserved it, and how I'm lucky he spared my life."

"He'll be lucky if I spare his," Nellie says firmly. Loni raises her hand cautiously, calming Nellie down.

"What happened after he left?" Nellie asks. "Is that when you escaped?"

"No," I reply. "He had locked the door to the room I was in before he left, and I had to use my bobby pins to pick the lock — but he came back. With three of Blanco's boys. He slapped me to the ground, and tried to suffocate me when I asked the other three for help. One of them didn't want to stay so he left —"

"Didn't want to be an accomplice for murder," Nellie says, and I nod in agreement.

"The other two just stood there and watched while Ricky was strangling me. I was so scared and all I could think about was getting some air — and then I felt that feeling in my chest when I pushed Churchill away in the hospital room."

"Your protective abilities," Loni says with a grin. "They're getting stronger — comin' out when you need tuh defend yuhself."

"But it wasn't my protective abilities," I reply, Nellie and Loni looking at me quizzically. "Not the same ones from the hospital, at least."

"What do you mean?" Nellie asks softly. I hesitate for a moment, looking at both of them as they wait for me to speak.

"I started to transform... into a black panther."

Loni's eyebrows raise as she looks at me, and Nellie releases my hand as she sits back — looking at me wide-eyed.

"A black panther?" they ask simultaneously.

"Yes."

"You're sure?" Nellie asks.

"Uh, yeah, I'm pretty sure. 17 years in a human body, I'm pretty sure I'd know the difference when I looked down and saw *paws* instead of *hands*."

"Good Lawd," Loni says, frozen with wide eyes and brows raising the roof. She stands up and crosses her arms, one hand sticking out in the air as she tries to bring words to her mouth.

"This is... this is amazing," she mumbles. "No one's been able to transform into di black panther for generations. I thought dat that ability had been lost durin' slavery —" She looks at me, her eyes wide with wonder. "But you can do it. You can do it!"

"Apparently," I reply.

"What did it feel like?" Nellie asks.

"How long did it take?" asks Loni.

"Did it hurt?" Nellie asks.

"How long were you in your feline form?" Loni asks.

"Whoa, whoa, whoa," I interrupt, waving my hands in the air to stop them. "One question at a time." Nellie looks at me sheepishly, and Loni raises her hand in apology as she sits back down. They both lean over the table towards me, like two excited children.

I answer, "It felt like my bones were being ripped apart and put back together, and it hurt like hell. The transformation was pretty quick and it did not last very long — but it lasted long enough to scare the living crap out of Ricky and Blanco's boys."

"They saw you?" Nellie asks.

"Well, yeah, they were still in the room when Ricky was strangling me, and I was between them and the door when I transformed so they couldn't get out."

"Did they see you change into di panther an' change back?" Loni asks worried.

"They saw everything," I reply apologetically. She closes her eyes and exhales, and Nellie looks at her with a worried look.

"Okay, okay," Loni says, "we'll worry about dat later. But first we aave to get thru dis new ability of yours. You realize what dis means, right? You're di first Bastet in generations to be able to transform into a black panther. You've brought a powa back from the brink of extinction, an' it gives you a fightin' chance to protec' yuhself and othas too."

"But that also means I have more of a target on my back," I reply. "The Toubabs are already hunting me, and that was before I could transform into a panther. Isn't that going to make me more of a... luxury now?"

"That's what I was just thinking," Nellie says, looking at me with wary eyes. We look to Loni, who stares at a space on the table — deep in thought, and humming along as they bounce around in her brain.

"Hmm," she mutters to herself. "Mmhmm. You're gonna aave to be more cautious on di road — jus' because you're leavin' this behind doesn't mean dey won't be able tuh find you. If dem boys saw you, word will get around — and as soon as the Toubabs figure out dat you can transform into a black panther, they'll put all their resources into findin' you."

"Isn't there something you guys can do to keep them from talking?" I ask them.

Nellie stares off into the distance and a small smile creeps onto her face. "There is something we could do," she says, looking at Loni. Loni looks at her with a blank stare, before smiling as they exchange a silent message. I look between them, confused and waiting to be filled in.

"Uh, hello? Anyone care to fill in the confused teenager here?" Nellie looks at me, and smiles as Loni chuckles.

"Ricky tried to pull some nonsense back in the day when your mother and I were in school, and he was just starting out on the streets so he had all of this fake bravado that was just bullying. Your mother and I paid him a little visit in the Realm of Duality, and made sure he knew not to mess with us."

"You visited him in the Realm? How? He's not a Bastet, how would you have been able to connect with him there?"

"The Realm isn't just for us an' our ancestors, baby girl," Loni says. "Rememba how I told you dat Bast used to guide spirits to di afterlife? Well think of di Realm like a station where all souls can go — no matter if you're dead or alive, a Bastet or a normal human. We can connec' to everyone in the Realm of Duality, an' for people still alive it's like visitin' dem in a dream. That's why people always be talkin' about their dreams an' how they had a premonition or déjà vu or somethin' — that may have actually been one of us communicatin' with dem in their dreams, but in a way dat dey could undastan without losin' their minds."

"So you and mom visited Ricky in a dream and communicated with him?" I ask Nellie.

"No, just me," she replies. "It was our first time trying something like that, and your mother had to watch me to make sure I didn't stray too far in the spiritual side of the Realm."

"Well, what did you say? How does that even work?"

"Well, Ricky was messing with us at school and insinuating that he was gonna make us his 'girls'."

"Ew," I say.

"Yeah, that was what we thought back then too. And he was just being a bully — to everyone really, but especially to the girls in school. But he always came for your mother and me — I didn't think he liked that we were doing well in school and that we genuinely liked it, and he was struggling so much. And one day he cornered us after school and tried to scare us; so we decided to visit him in a dream and compel him to leave us be."

"Ha," Loni hoots. "Dis girl cornered Ricky in the dream and scared dat boy senseless!"

"Really?" I ask laughing, Nellie nodding with an amused smile.

"This girl had dat boy cryin' a river of tears, he was so scared. Pushed him against di wall an' threw him around like he was a rag doll! Boy was tryin' to crawl away and she jus' dragged his ass back."

"You could do all that in the dream?"

"Well, it's the Realm, J, and we have connections to the spiritual realm that has no limitations. He didn't feel anything when he woke up — except fear, of course."

Loni hoots, veins popping in her neck as she laughs uproariously. "She told him dat if he eva scare dem again, she'd mek sure dat she visits him in every single dream he'll aave. Ha! Dat boy didn't botha dem fah di rest of di year, I'll tell yuh dat. He even got all quiet when he walked in di diner — lookin' like he'd seen a ghost." Loni hoots and slaps her thigh as she recounts the memory, and I begin laughing too.

Nellie laughs along, saying, "Yeah, well, men like Ricky need a special kind of motivation to listen when they refuse to do so civilly. And I can teach you how to… convince him to not bother you again without drifting too far in the Realm."

"I don't know if I can face him again," I reply quietly. "Even if it's in his dreams. That's the last place I want to be."

"Well, baby girl, if he's done all'a dis already, chances are you were already in his dreams," Loni says. A lump forms in my throat as I think about Ricky Brass dreaming about me, and I start to get queasy.

"Well, I guess that's better than him telling somebody and the Toubabs finding out about it. But how do I control transforming? I didn't even know it was going to happen, and you said it yourself that sometimes our ancestors couldn't transform back."

"Well it's been a while since one'a us has been able to do this," Loni says. "I could start lookin' in my books to see if I can find anythin', but it'll tek me a while. There hasn't been anythin' about the feline transformation for hundreds of years — I might not even have any books that have information to help us."

"But what if I transform in the middle of the day on a busy street, or end up hurting somebody? I need to be able to control when and where it happens, and bring myself back."

"I know, Mama," Nellie says. "We're going to do as much digging as we can, but for now, just try to keep yourself calm. If this happened because Ricky tried to suffocate you, then Loni's right, it probably comes out as a self-defense reflex. All you can do is make sure you're calm, and to relax if you feel threatened."

"I'm literally being hunted by a cult and was just attacked by a gangster," I tell her, stone-faced.

"I never said it was going to be easy," she counters. I sigh and close my eyes, rubbing the skin between my eyebrows.

"What if Loni doesn't find anything in time? We're leaving tomorrow, and you said we can't contact anyone in the city."

"That's why I'll be comin' wit' you," Loni says.

"What?" Nellie and I ask.

"Jamila's right — I probably won't find anything in time, but if I'm wit' you then I can help you to control your transformation."

"But you can't come with us," Nellie says. "We're escaping to *protect you* — if you come with us, it defeats the purpose. And what about the diner? Who's going to cook the food and mind the diner?"

"Ray's been handling the diner on his own fah years — an' I just hired two new chefs who cook my food almost as good as me. They'll be able to hold down the fort until I get back."

"But aren't you afraid that the Toubabs will find you once you're back in Jamaica?" I ask.

"It's about time I stop runnin' away from those white devils anyway. I have nothin' to fear with my powers to protec' me and God by my side."

"Loni, I can't let you do this," Nellie says.

"Too late, I already bought di plane ticket," she says. Nellie looks at her wide-eyed and Loni just gets up, grabbing their teacups and placing them in the sink.

"You're not going to change your mind, are you?" I ask her.

"When aave you *ever* known me to change my mind?" I look at Nellie who looks exasperated, shaking her head in disbelief. Loni looks at both of us with a set face and amused eyes — there's no changing her mind when she's set in her ways, so there's no point in trying.

"I can't believe you're risking yourself for me," I say. "You've been safe for years, and you're just going to give that all up?"

She cocks her head and looks at me confused. "You're sayin' that like protectin' you isn't important. Baby girl, I am old an' grey, and I've lived a long life of hiding — I'm ready to come out of the shadows an' actually start *livin'* again. An' this is as good a time as any." I smile at her gratefully, and she smiles back warmly. I look to Nellie who looks between the two of us, leaning on her hand.

"Okay," she says. "Okay. I wasn't prepared for this but I guess it is what it is. What time is your flight?"

"The same time as yours," Loni replies. "I took a look at you buyin' your plane tickets in your dreams and bought a seat on di same plane."

"You snooped through my dreams?" Nellie asks incredulously.

"Oh hush, it's not like I was lookin' at anythin' else. In an' out, quick as a whip."

Nellie shakes her head and chuckles once, standing up and shrugging. "Well, then that makes it easier — at least we'll all be in one place and can protect ourselves better. I'm assuming you have some fakes on hand."

"Yes. You can call me Claudette Winston," she replies.

"Nice to meet you, Ms. Claudette," I reply, standing up and reaching my hand out for a handshake. Loni smacks it away playfully and rolls her eyes. I push my chair in when the whoop of a siren sounds outside. We all look at the door, and Loni and Nellie's faces become more serious. Nellie and I exchange a look as we see red and blue lights oscillate through the window. Three quick knocks on the door, and we stand there for a moment before Nellie moves and answers the door. I move to follow her, but Loni reaches her arm to stop me — she cocks her head towards the wall, and I hide behind it as she meets Nellie at the door.

"Good evening, ma'am," says a male voice. "We received a call late last night about a missing child, said to be your niece? We're just here to follow up on the case."

"Oh yes, that would've been Ms. Dell who called."

"And that is," he takes a second to flip through a stack of papers on a clipboard before continuing, "your next-door neighbour?"

"Yes, that's right. She was with me when I was looking for my niece and called it in without my knowledge, but she's home now."

"I see. Still, it's procedure to follow-up on all calls of missing persons. I just need to enter the premises and ensure everything is going smoothly. May I see the child, ma'am?"

"Officer I assure you, there's no need — she did give us a scare last night, but God bless her she got home safely and saved me from having a heart attack," Nellie says with a laugh. It didn't work in evading the subject, and the officer continues to press.

"And that is all well and good ma'am, but she is still a minor and we need to ensure the child is safe and being taken care of."

"Who betta to take care of her than her parental guardian?" Loni interjects, code switching to speak proper English. I peek around the wall to take a look at the officer — he's about average height, with a furry moustache above his lip and a stocky figure. Another officer stands just behind him, and stands there silently with his hands on his hips. They look nice, but I don't come out of hiding — I know better.

"Ma'am, it's just precaution. I want to close this case and allow you ladies to go about your day and enjoy the rest of the weekend — so could you work with us here? It won't take long, we just need to make sure she's alright and she's healthy and taken care of."

Nellie looks at him silently, and even from here I can see her jaw setting as she tries to keep her cool. She silently waves her arm and stands to the side, letting them in. He nods once and saunters in, the other officer following behind him. He tips his hat to Loni, but does so in a way that seems ominous to me. I lean further back, but still trying to peer around the wall. The first officer looks around as he makes his way to the center of the living room, before turning to Nellie.

"I apologize if I was rude," Nellie says, sounding less than apologetic. "I assure you I mean no ill intent. I'm not trying to obstruct in any way, I just wanted to let you know that my niece is safe now and there's no need to worry or blow this out of proportion."

"I appreciate that, ma'am," the officer replies. "But the fact that she is just now safe implies that there was a point in time that she wasn't safe. If there's any viable reason that your next-door neighbour would call in and report a missing person, it is our duty to see to it that your niece is fully assessed, so we can see exactly what we're dealing with."

"Well, she was roughed up a bit last night by some guys that work the block," Nellie says. "But luckily she made it home — but I don't want to press any charges, the last thing I want is to put more of a target on her. These men out here see that as an offense, and the last thing I want is for my niece to be put in more danger. You understand?"

"I understand you don't want to rock the boat, ma'am. But your niece is a minor — if her safety was jeopardized while in your care, we have to ensure that all efforts are taken to prevent this from happening again."

"These boys don't care at all for your laws," Loni says. "Boys and girls have been tormented by the lot of them for years under your noses, so what makes you think that this time would be any different?"

"I understand where you're coming from, Ms. Washington," he says. "But it is situations like this that will allow us to work on properly protecting everyone in the community. You understand, Ms. Freeman, that you alone won't be able to save your niece from being in danger." Nellie looks at him with her eyebrow slightly raised, her face stoic. Loni's face clouds, and she stands straighter as her eyes sharpen.

"Is there a problem?" the officer asks. She cuts her eye at him and looks back to the first officer.

"No, just a little confused," she replies.

"And why's that?" the officer asks, turning away and walking towards the kitchen. As he gets closer, that sick feeling gets worse in my stomach. I hold my breath and inch myself as close as I can to the corner. I can hear his footsteps creak on the floor as he gets closer, but he stops before coming in.

"I wasn't aware you knew our names," Nellie says.

"Yes, it was in the report," he says. "You and your niece's names were recorded in the file, and they're on record until the case is closed."

"I understand that, but that doesn't explain why you know Loni's name."

My stomach sinks as the room gets quiet. I hear the first officer chuckle, and hear him walk back the way he came.

"You're right," he says. "That doesn't explain it." His voice gets dark, and my stomach is completely upset as it rises with unease.

"You mean telling me how you know my name?" Loni asks.

"Well, Ms. Washington, I can't do that without providing my reason for being here."

"Have you not done that already?" Nellie asks.

"In a manner of speaking," he replies. I peer around the wall again, and see him turned towards the left wall as Nellie and Loni look at him with distrusting eyes. The second officer now has his hands on the front of his belt, giving me a clear vision of the gun and baton stowed in his belt.

"How do you mean?" Nellie asks.

He gently rubs his pinky finger, which holds a rustic gold ring. There's an emblem on the top surface, and I squint my eyes to make it out as recognition piques my interest.

"We've come to see your niece, and assess her condition to see what exactly we're working with," he replies. He turns and looks at them with a blank expression. "The better understanding we have of her abilities, the more we'll be able to control and harness them."

My stomach sinks to the floor and my digestive system threatens to stop working. My heart rate jumps and I smack my hand over my mouth to keep my sharp breaths from being heard. Nellie and Loni both inhale sharply and step back, their posture now straighter and stronger. The second officer grabs a taser from the left side of his belt and walks towards them. Nellie moves in front of Loni and looks him dead in his eye. She reaches for her pocket and pulls out a vial with a dark sludgy liquid inside and gold flecks throughout. The Drunken Fools potion. She begins to chant:

> *"The fool that dares to block my path*
> *Shall lose their senses in helpless glee*
> *The drunken fool then suffers the wrath*
> *Of protector's need to be rightly free".*

She uncorks the vial, ready to throw it at the second officer, but the first officer spots her. He pulls out his gun and cocks it, releasing the safety and firing right at Nellie.

"NO!" I yell, jumping out from behind the wall. The officer shoots his head towards me, just as the bullet rips through the gun. I reach my hand towards Nellie, and feel a pulse ring through my ears. I focus on the pulse and let it match the beating of my heart, and feel a power emanating from the center of my palm. The air gets thicker as time slows, and Nellie,

Loni, and the two officers move at the speed of a sloth. The energy from my palm becomes visible as I move a single line on the timeline that appears. It glows as it runs through the room, starting from the wall near the kitchen and passing Nellie to go through the far wall near the foyer closet. The bullet the first officer fired now moves slowly, and I can see it in mid-air as it heads straight for Nellie. I gingerly reach for it and grab it — not feeling anything, I move it towards the wall, and move Nellie and Loni further apart so that the bullet is nowhere near them. I look at the glowing timeline and the line connected to my palm, ready to disconnect it, before thinking better of it. I head towards the first officer and move his arms farther back, and put the back of the gun just in front of his face. If the shock from the bullet not hitting Nellie doesn't surprise him, then getting hit in the face by a rebounding gun will.

I head towards the second officer and bend his arm, turning the taser towards his chest, and back up to stand behind Loni. I look at the one line that's moving in accordance with the beating of my heart, that strings a connection from the timeline to my palm, and wink. Time goes back like a flash as a pulsing energy reverberates through the room. Loni and Nellie stumble as they fall further away from each other, and the bullet hits the foyer wall. Volts of electricity shoot from the taser into the second officer's chest, and he jolts before falling unconscious to the floor. The gun smacks into the first officer's face, and he jumps back into the wall grabbing his face. He looks at us wild-eyed, looking between Nellie and Loni and the bullet hole that missed both of them, before setting his eyes on me. He does a double-take, confused to see me here after not being here before, and for a few more moments he tries to combobulate himself. He reaches for his gun again, and in fear that he'll hit them this time, I will myself to find some sort of protection. I begin to feel that hollow ache throbbing in my chest, and knowing this time what it means, I encourage it to surge through me quickly. Even knowing how painful it is, I'm not ready for it. I slam to the ground as my bones drastically change, more pain racking my body as my bones shift and my muscles contort as I transform into a panther. It's worse than the first time, which was only earlier this morning so I'm still feeling the ache from that transformation. Add it to this new, sharper pain, and I struggle to breathe through it. Finally, my bones stop shifting, and the fur rises all over my body. My senses are heightened as I smell things with ease and my vision sharpens with clarity. I pant heavily as I try to push through the pain, and slowly push myself up on my legs.

The first officer's eyes get wider, which I didn't think was possible, and his face goes slack in shock. Nellie and Loni are also looking at me shocked, but stand closer to me knowing that they'll be safe. I turn back to the first officer and stand over him in one mighty leap. I look down at him and bare my teeth, a deep growl rumbling from my vocal folds. He trembles and reaches for a taser on his belt, but I bite his hand and forcefully shake his hand. The taser drops from his hand, and I feel a clean break between my teeth as his wrist breaks. He screams out loud and grabs his wrist, pushing himself against the wall and trembling. I growl in his face, getting closer and breathing directly on him — he closes his eyes and turns his face away, and I stare at him for a moment longer. Figuring he's adequately scared, I start to back up, looking at him the entire time and my teeth still bared. He tries to push himself up while he's still holding his wrist, but he struggles as he keeps sliding on the floor. Out of the corner of my eye, I see someone standing to my left — thinking it's another Toubab, I whip my head towards the person and growl loudly, baring ferocious teeth and a powerful noise escaping my vocal folds. But it's not another Toubab. Far from it. Just a very scared Michael.

I stop, and my breath catches in my throat as he stares at me. Frozen in shock with eyes wide, he looks down at me as I look back at him. What is he doing here? Did he come through the back door? I didn't even hear him come in. My nerves jump as I panic, and I begin to transform back into my human form. His eyes get wider and his mouth drops as the fur makes may for my brown skin to emerge, and my bones shift back into my human skeleton.

"Wha... wha," he stammers, as he breathes shallowly.

"Michael," I say, struggling to push myself and breathing as normally as I can through the pain. "Michael, I can explain."

"Wha... how... I..."

"Michael, sweetie," Nellie says, walking towards him slowly. "Don't freak out." Loni takes the vial from her and quickly walks to the first officer. She mumbles the spell quickly underneath her breath as she grabs a fist of his hair and sticks the vial under his nose. He struggles for a second as she recites the spell, but soon gold sparkles shine in his eyes and he relaxes into a drunken stupor. She drags him to lie beside the second officer, and he stares whimsically at the ceiling.

"How... how were you just — and then you were — and they're... they're..."

"They're Toubabs," Loni says calmly, standing beside him.

"They're police officers," he exclaims, his voice breaking.

"No, they're Toubabs disguised as policemen," Nellie says. "They came here looking for Jamila, and were going to hurt us."

"Why would they do that?" he asks, with a side-eye.

"Because we're Bastets, and they're hunting us for our powers," Nellie says.

"Bas-what?"

"Bastets," Loni replies matter-of-factly. "A long line of women that can do powerful things — and the Toubabs are an old cult that has been hunting us for centuries and using us for our powers."

"Powerful things?"

"Magical things," Loni replies. "Defying space an' time an' protectin' people from sickness an' death. An' the Toubabs are di people who hunt us to mek us do dat fah dem, an' who kill us when we refuse."

He furrows his eyebrows and shakes his head, grabbing his head as he starts to pace. Nellie raises her hands to calm him down, but he's not paying attention to her.

"This is insane. This is insane. None of this makes any sense — this isn't supposed to be *possible*."

"But it is," I reply. "I didn't think so either at first, but it's true."

"But it *can't* be. *Magical powers?* You can't be serious. Humans aren't supposed to be able to do magical things. We breathe, we work, we have a little fun, and then we die."

"Lord," Loni mutters. "No wonder you two are friends."

"And who is this cult that you're talking about?" Michael continues. "And why would police officers be involved in a cult that hunts people with magical powers?"

"Who better?" Nellie asks. Michael looks at her bewildered, shaking his head and continuing to pace.

"And how would any of that explain how you can turn into a black panther?" he asks incredulously. "*A black panther!* I've known you since we were little, and I've never seen you turn into a black panther — that's not exactly something you can hide so easily!"

He chuckles humourlessly, looking at the ceiling for an answer with a dry grin on his face. He mumbles, "I'm losing my mind. That's what's happening. I pull an all-nighter and I start seeing things — why couldn't this be a bad trip from an edible or something?"

"Michael," I say, walking towards him. "I know, it's crazy —"

"That's the only thing that makes sense — that this is crazy! I have to be dreaming..."

"But you're not, Michael." He looks at me with his brows furrowed together, hoping that I'll give him another answer. "Everything you saw really happened. Everything Loni and Nellie are telling you is true."

He looks at me silently for a moment, breathing shallowly as I wait for him to respond.

"You're... a Bastet?"

"Yes."

"And you have magical powers?"

"A few."

"A few," he scoffs. "I'm guessing one of them is turning into a panther."

"That's right."

He nods slightly, his eyes glancing at Nellie and Loni behind me. "And you can all do that?"

"No," Loni replies. "Bastets don't all have the same powers."

"Why?" he asks.

"Think of it like genetics," Nellie says. "You inherit certain traits from your mother and father, and after a while the Bastet genes get drowned out by other dominant genes."

"Okay," he says. "Okay." He nods as he tries to make sense of it in his head, when his eye catches on the two policemen behind us. I look back at them, and see the first officer still in his stupor and the other still unconscious. Michael looks at me warily, and takes a deep breath.

"Okay, I need you to tell me everything."

I look at Nellie and Loni, who exchange a silent look for a few moments. They weigh the options, deciding whether it's worth the risk before, finally, Loni gives me a short nod. I turn back to Michael, who looks at me with an inquisitive look.

"Okay."

CHAPTER FOURTEEN

———— ∞ ————

Michael sits in his seat, staring at the ground — we sit in chairs on the other side of the table as we wait for him to process everything. A glass of water sits in front of him but remains untouched. His eyes are wide and unblinking as the gears shift in his brain at full-speed, and Nellie and I look at each other as we worry about whether we should've told Michael everything. Did I just break Michael?

"Michael, are you okay?" I ask.

"I'm… I'm, uh… I'm processing."

"Okay," I say warily. "How do you feel?" He takes a sharp inhale of air and looks just above our heads as he tries to come up with an answer.

"Um… overwhelmed. Shaken. Flabbergasted. I don't really know if there's a word to describe how I'm feeling right now." He takes a shaky inhale of breath, looking at us with a timid smile. We smile back encouragingly, even though I'm secretly hoping he's not freaking out on the inside right now.

"And I'm still trying to… wrap my head around the fact that there are two men unconscious in your living room and that's, what, not insane?"

We turn to the living room, seeing the two men still soundly unconscious and ignorant about what's going on. I look at him sheepishly as Nellie shrugs her shoulders — he closes his eyes, shaking his head as he tries to process it all.

"So you come from a long line of women that have powers?" he asks.

"Yes," we say.

"And that includes talking to the dead, stopping time, and… turning into a panther?"

"Well," Nellie says, "if we're being specific —"

"Yes," Michael says. "Yes, please be specific."

"Okay, well we don't just speak to the dead — if we practice, we can talk to our ancestors, to people who have died who aren't at rest, and even people who are still alive."

"And how does that work exactly?" he asks, leaning forward with inquisitive eyes.

"Well, it's kind of like visiting them in a dream," Nellie responds. "There's this place that we can go to that is sort of an in-between place — not limbo exactly, just a place where we can connect with the spirit world and the physical world at the same time. We can travel there because our brains can detect different planes of existence that most people can't see — but it is possible. But their brain would have to be in a hyperactive state for us to connect to them — hence, the dreaming."

"Is that why Jamila has so much activity in her visual and auditory cortices?" he asks.

"Yes," I say excitedly. He nods with a smile as he begins to understand, a classic student willing to learn, and my nerves settle a little. "From how Nel and Loni explained it, our brains are basically wired to see and hear things on a plane that no one else can see. But if the rest of your brain is resting, the back of your brain gets a chance to explore the planes of existence — because there is more than just one."

Nellie interjects, "The back of your brain is firing up because the rest of your brain took the spotlight during the day — when you're resting, the visual cortex finally has a chance to let loose. And that allows you to see and hear things that seem to make no sense, but really you're just seeing things on a different plane. A lot of the time you are just dreaming random stuff, but sometimes you're opening your mind up to a plane of existence that exists along with this one — just not as visible."

"Even people who have hyperactivity in these cortices — like your project that was dealing with schizophrenia — can see these things," I say. "But people call it craziness because most people aren't able to see or hear what they can see. What we can see. I guess the best way to think of it is that we can see planes of reality and connect to forms of consciousness because of genetic traits that make hyperactivity permanent — so we're constantly seeing planes of existence so it becomes more than just one reality."

"Fascinating," he says, his voice whimsical. "It's crazy that I picked that as the topic for my assignment and — and you're the perfect example.

You and your ancestors harnessed this, they didn't try to suppress it with herbs or medicines —"

"No, quite di opposite," Loni says. "We strengthen it with potions an' herbs to make the connection stronga, and strengthenin' our sight of the other realms of dis world."

He lets out a short laugh, sitting back in his chair and looking mesmerized. "A-and you're able to control the flow of time."

"Yeah, it's really cool," I say, getting more and more excited. "The first time I did it I had no idea what was happening, but when Nellie explained it to me it started to make a little more sense."

"Really? Was I there when you did it?"

"Yeah — it was when you fell over in the cafeteria," I say with a laugh. His face goes slack in shock, his eyes slowly widening as recognition clicks.

"Oh my God. It all makes sense now! I thought I was going crazy — I could've sworn that I was going to fall flat on my face, but then all of a sudden I'm safely on my ass and holding my tray? With nothing spilled on the floor?"

I shrug with a smile, and he lets out a bewildered chuckle. "This is amazing. Do you know how long scientists have been trying to make sense of the concept of time?"

"And they didn't even scratch the surface," I say with a laugh, leaning forward.

"You have to tell me how you do it," he says excitedly. Just as I'm about to settle into it, Nellie raises her hand.

"Okay, as much as I would love to satisfy your need for knowledge, I'm going to have to cut this short."

"But Nellie —"

"No buts, Mama. You have to finish packing — we're still leaving tomorrow, that hasn't changed."

"Leaving?" Michael asks, confused. "Where are you going?" My breath hitches in my throat as I realize I haven't dropped that bomb yet — and I'm going to have to leave him with all of this information and never see him again.

"We're leavin', baby," Loni says, leaning forward over the table. "We're leavin' di country."

"What? Why?"

"Those Toubabs we told you about," I say. "They found us. They found me."

"That cult that's been hunting your ancestors for centuries?" I nod silently, and Nellie hums in confirmation. "Well, for how long?"

"I... I don't know how long."

"What do you mean you don't know?" he asks. "You're coming back, right?"

I hesitate for a moment, and his face drops. "You're coming back, right?"

I struggle to come up with air, as the confrontation I thought would never happen plays out, but Nellie saves me.

"Dumplin', you have to understand — this isn't just a hate group. This is a hunting party. If they find us, and catch us, they'll use us for our abilities. They'll make us do terrible things for them, and torture us if we try to resist. And if they don't do that, they'll just kill us."

"These people think we're a disease," Loni says. "A sickness on dis earth — an' would rather kill us off than tuh let us live our lives in peace. Dey started when witchcraft was given di death penalty, an' sought to kill us off when dey discovered our abilities. Dat thinking nuh change, even as di years done passed, an' dey aave more money and resources in dis modern age to hunt us unda di radar. The only reason they would let us live is if we do things for dem."

"What kind of things?" he asks.

"Things that are too terrible to even speak of, sweetie," Nellie says.

"But you can get help," he says, his face getting more and more upset. "We can call the police, contact the government, something!"

"Baby, di Toubabs been around long'a than dey tek dis country from di Natives. Dey probably in the police an' govament already."

"Think about it, Michael," I say. "How many police officers have you seen that are racist? Homophobic? Xenophobic? How many politicians? How many leaders of countries? Is it really that hard to believe that an organization that's been around since the dawn of colonialism would be a part of our governing bodies?"

Nellie adds, "It was the governing bodies that let these things happen in the first place — countries have been built on it, and made it so they survived off it. To not do that would cause their systems to crumble, and they could never have that."

"But... but are you ever going to come back?" Michael looks at us with a sadness in his eyes, and my heart breaks as I have to say the hardest thing I never thought I'd ever have to say.

"Probably not," I say, my voice catching in my throat. He looks at me with a pained expression, shaking his head in disbelief.

"We have to hide, Michael," Nellie says. "These Toubabs are no joke — not even the people around us are safe."

"That means you, baby," Loni says.

"But it's not like I'll say anything," he says, his voice emotional. "I'll keep it a secret. I promise!"

"Oh baby, we know you'd try. But you're not the best at keeping secrets."

"I know, I know," he says, raising his arms in admonition. "But I promise I'll keep this one — I mean, it's *your lives* on the line. I would never say anything. Ever. I swear."

"Even if you won't say anything, jus' bein' around us would put you at risk, my dear." Loni stands up and goes to Michael's side, holding his face in her hands and turning his face up to hers. "You're an obstacle — an' Toubabs dispose of obstacles so absolutely nothin' is in di way."

"We don't want you to get hurt," I say. He looks at me and leans back in his chair again, a defeated look on his face.

"Well, I don't want you to get hurt either. You're my best friend — but now I'm never going to see you again? When were you going to tell me? You were just gonna — what — up and leave? With no goodbye and no explanation?"

"Michael, I wanted to tell you," I say tiredly. "I've wanted to tell you everything from the moment I found out about all this stuff — it's been driving me crazy not being able to tell you. But I can't put your life at risk — you're my best friend, and I'd rather you alive. Even if it means that I may never see you again." He looks at me for a moment, silently nodding with a pained expression.

"What time do you leave?"

"Our flight is at 6 a.m.," Nellie says. He shoots his head to her, his face surprised and disappointed.

"So soon?" he asks. Loni nods sympathetically, and he looks up at her. "You're going too?" he asks.

"The Toubabs been huntin' me for years, dear. I, more than anyone, know how to evade dem. I left Jamaica when I was only a little bit olda than you, an' I had to leave everythin' behind. An' I'm tired of runnin'."

"But won't they find you if you go back?"

"Maybe. Maybe not. One thing's for certain — these two will aave a betta chance of evadin' the Toubabs if I'm there to help dem. They can't do dis alone for long."

"But you won't be able to stay for long either," Nellie says. "How long do you expect to stay in Jamaica? You can't just leave the diner behind on such short notice."

"Dey can manage a few weeks without me," Loni says nonchalantly, coming back over to our side of the table.

"Meh," Michael says, making us chuckle. "Maybe Ray could, but I doubt that for the customers. They're gonna miss your cooking."

"The cooks I hired will suit just fine — your safety is more important." She places her hand on my cheek and looks at me fondly, and I smile warmly in thanks. A small smile lifts on Michael's face but it's shaded by sad eyes.

Loni continues, "I'll go wit' you, stay for three weeks, an' come back. Quick an' easy."

"Tuh," Nellie scoffs. "All of this is anything *but* quick and easy." We nod silently, sitting there for a moment as it all sinks in. Loni gets up and grabs the Drunken Fools potion, making her way to the Toubab that involuntarily tased himself and wafting the vial underneath his nose as she mutters the spell under her breath.

"I just can't believe you're leaving," Michael says, "and never coming back." He looks at me with somber eyes, and mine begin to tear as I feel his emotion. I get up wordlessly and grab him in a bear hug — he stands up and doesn't hesitate to hug me back, and we rock each other side to side as I silently cry. As I pull back, I see that he's crying too — and I'm still not used to it, so I'm a little taken aback.

"Nellie said I can still send you letters — but I can't let you know where I am, so you won't be able to send me anything back."

"Actually, Michael," Nellie says, getting up to stand in front of us. "I know someone who works at a post office not too far from the airport — I'll call and see if I can set something up so you can send letters to a PO box or something. That sound alright?"

"I guess it'll have to do," he says quietly. She gives him an empathetic smile and pulls her phone from her back pocket, going to the hallway to make a call.

"There's another way you two can keep in touch," Loni says, making her way back to us.

"Really?" I ask hopefully. "How?"

"Visit him in the Realm of Duality."

Of course. Why didn't I think of that before? Nellie did it to Ricky Brass back in the day, and from what I've heard, they seemed to have a pretty interactive conversation. I could keep up with Michael's life and we could still communicate with each other in our dreams. I smile at him hopefully, and he smiles back.

"You'll have to practice though," Loni continues. "You've never contacted a human in di Realm before, an' you don't want to mess wit' di human mind — theirs doesn't snap back as easily as ours can."

"Yeah, don't turn me into a vegetable because you want to tell me how your day went," Michael jokes. I let out a short laugh, not really feeling it. His smile slips off his face as the gravity of all of this settles back in, and we just look at each other for a moment. There hasn't been a week that Michael and I haven't talked — even if he went to summer camp, or I was working a lot of shifts at the library during the summer, we always found a way to talk to each other. Now we'll have to try to not talk to each other, to prevent a trail that could lead the Toubabs to me, and we may never see each other again. Even if I do end up coming back to Toronto, it may be when we're both much older — time would pass and our friendship along with it.

Nellie comes back into the room, ending her call with the person on the other line. "Okay," she says. "My friend figured out a way to get your letters to us; instead of writing Jamila's name, write Malai J. on the envelope."

"Why Malai?" Loni asks, Michael joining her with an inquisitive look.

"It's an anagram," I reply, Nellie smiling in confirmation. "When you rearrange the letters you get Jamila."

"Huh," Michael marvels, giving a short laugh.

Nellie continues, "If you write that name on the envelope, my friend will know it's for us — but you can't write too often, sweetie. We don't know if the Toubabs already know about you, and they might be watching you if they do. And even with the anagram and no return address, it might tip them off that you're writing letters to another country when you've never done it before. It's best to keep it minimal — no more than 1 every few months, alright?"

"Every few months?" he asks surprised.

"Under the radar, remember?" He nods, his expression a little defeated. "I'll write down the PO box number for you — do not lose this, you understand? Don't let anyone see it and do not misplace it — keep it in a safe place that only you have access to."

"Yes, ma'am," he says. She nods, giving him a warm smile. She sighs and looks at me, a soft look in her eyes; I'm not exactly sure what. Sadness, empathy, fatigue, I'm not entirely sure. Maybe a combination of the three — I wouldn't put it past her to be a jumble of emotions right now. I, myself, am a mess, and I'm wondering how I'm keeping it together. Somehow I've managed to suppress the fact that I was kidnapped and violated in the last 24 hours, enduring physical, mental and sexual violence, while also manifesting another power that's been lost in our lineage for centuries. And using it twice in one day! I have to give myself props for standing upright and not breaking into tears; but I can't deny the fact that Nellie's in the same boat with me. While I was going through all of that, she was probably terrified that I was going through it while at the same time praying that I wasn't. And praying that I was safe. And to find out that her worst fears were confirmed true, must be the most soul-crushing feeling. When she saw me in the driveway she looked like she'd seen a ghost — and probably thought I was, assuming she thought the Toubabs had gotten me, which wouldn't be a stretch considering who's currently on our living room floor.

Suddenly, I remember the other thing I wanted to tell Nellie — in retrospect, it's not as important as everything else that's going on, but it's still strange enough to warrant mentioning.

"Oh... by the way," I say. "There's one other thing I have to tell you." Nellie turns to me, and Loni cocks her eyebrow.

"More eventful than you turning into a panther?" Loni asks.

"A bit." Nellie turns to me fully, giving me her undivided attention.

"Friday, when school was over, I met someone new..."

"Okay..." Nellie says slowly.

"I had seen him in my chemistry class recently, but he always caught my eye because he was always in the same spot by the heaters. But he never spoke up in class, and no one really paid attention to him. I finally said something to him, when he was being snarky, and..."

"And?"

"And it turns out only I can see him."

"How is that possible?" Michael asks.

"Because apparently only I can see ghosts."

Michael, Loni, and Nellie all look at me wordlessly — all with confused and shocked expressions. A few moments of silence pass by, until their questions finally reach the tip of their tongues.

"Wait, what?" Loni asks.

"Okay... okay..." Nellie stammers. Michael just raises his finger in the air with his mouth opening and closing, struggling to form a question.

"I saw a ghost," I repeat. "His name's Jeremy, he's 15 — or at least he was before he died — and he's been stuck at the school since 2004."

"What a minute!" Michael yells, waving his hands in the air. We look at him, waiting for him to speak. "You saw a ghost?" Loni and I exhale exasperatedly, as Nellie massages the wrinkle between her brows.

"Yes, I think we've covered that, sweetie," Nellie says, then turns to me. "How long have you been seeing him for?"

"Only since I started practicing my powers a few months ago — I saw him once before, but never thought much of it. Turns out he was shot by some other kids and has been stuck at the school ever since. He can't go past the front doors, and hasn't figured out how to get out. And no one else can see him, so he hasn't been able to get any help either."

"Well, no," Loni says. "Most people aren't able to see people after dey passed. But he's been trapped in di building for 16 years? That's long, 'specially for someone dat was as young as him. He must aave something holdin' him back from passin' on."

"Wait," Michael interrupts again. Loni sighs exasperatedly, but Michael's got a question, and he won't rest until it's answered.

He continues, "Are you saying ghosts are real? Because that would go against pretty much everything I believe to be true."

"Which is what's been happening since we've told you everything," Nellie notes.

"True," he admits. "But ghosts? That would mean that all those ghost stories and myths and stuff are true."

"I don't know about all the ghost stories, but Jeremy is definitely real — in a manner of speaking, I guess."

"Oh, so you're on a first-name basis?" Nellie asks.

"Yeah," I reply. "After I figured out that he wasn't alive and I was somehow the only one who could see him, he showed me a little of his biting personality. The guy's a jerk, and it's not hard to understand why someone got annoyed with his antics while he was alive."

"People don't suddenly become different once they die," Nellie says.

"They are who they were — and if this boy's stuck in the same place he was in before he died, I can only imagine how cynical he is of 'life after death'."

"How so?" Michael asks.

"Because being stuck in the same place with no one to listen to you or anyone to talk to — and no way of moving forward — is no kind of life," Nellie says. "It's purgatory."

"He seemed so sad," I say, thinking back to our conversation. "He asked me for my help, but I said no because we're leaving tomorrow. Even when he was being sarcastic I could see the pain in his eyes. The desperation."

"I bet," Michael says, and I look up at him with a questioning look. He continues, "You're his one ticket out of there, his one chance of finally seeing something else, and there's nothing that you can do."

"Yeah," I admit. "I wish I could help him."

"You haven't gotten to that point yet, Mama," Nellie says. "It took me years before I could confidently guide spirits from the physical world to the spiritual. If the human mind was delicate while they were alive, imagine how fragile it would be when they're dead."

"But I feel terrible leaving him there, knowing how long he's been trapped there. Alone." A thought pops in my head and my face changes, and seeing this, Nellie's face becomes cautionary. "Maybe you could help him."

"No, Mama," Nellie says. "We're leaving tomorrow, we can't risk staying another day."

"So let's go today," I say.

"What?" Loni asks incredulously. "It's a Saturday, baby — the school isn't open."

"Actually," Michael interrupts, "the principal is always there on Saturdays to prepare for that meeting the teachers have every Monday morning, and sometimes I see a couple of teachers there getting the classrooms ready."

"You see," I say happily. "We could just drop by, do a quick one-two spirit cross over, and then be on our merry way."

"Jamila, baby, don't yuh think it'd be a little bit strange if we were at the school on a Saturday?"

"No," I say, holding my finger up and running to my room to grab something. I jog back, holding my art project in my hand. "Not if I'm dropping off an assignment."

"What is that?" Loni asks.

"It's a project for my art class." Michael does a double-take, looking closer at it.

"Is that my Batman action figure?"

"Maybe," I reply, slowly. He looks at me with a blank expression and I cave. "Okay, it is, but it's your fault for leaving it in my room for so long."

He kisses his teeth, and I hold up the scale for Nellie to see. I continue, "If I drop this off, it'll be the perfect cover. It's the last project I have that needs to be graded anyway, and I might as well drop it off before we leave — seeing as we're not coming back."

Nellie thinks, pondering whether or not it's worth the risk, then relents. "Alright, fine." I smile widely, but she points her finger in the air. "10 minutes. That's all he'll get — and if he decides to test my patience, he'll see it's a losing battle."

"Okay, okay," I agree. "Thank you, thank you, thank you!"

"Yeah, yeah, yeah," she says, concealing a smile.

"I'll come wit' you," Loni says. "We'll get it over wit' quicker if both of us are helpin' him. An' I need to grab my bags from the dina anyway."

"Okay," Nellie says. "We'll stop by the diner on our way back."

"Can I come too?" Michael asks. We turn to him with looks of surprise.

"Really?" I ask.

"Yeah," he replies with a smile. "The first proven sign of life after death and you think I'm missing it?"

We laugh and nod, and he mouths a *'yes'* in joy. Nellie turns and looks to the men lying unconscious on the floor. She exhales wearily, slightly shaking her head.

"Now what are we going to do with them?"

Now *that's* an excellent question. We stare at them for a moment, trying to come up with a solution to our Toubab problem. It's noon now — it's the middle of the day in broad daylight, and people are going to notice if we're hauling limp bodies out of our house. It's not like they're invisible. Then, light bulb.

"There's that alley down by the ramp to the highway — we can slow the time flow to get them in the car and drop them there."

Loni and Nellie look to each other, and Nellie's eyes widen with excitement. "You see, this is why you're the smarty-pants in the family."

I chuckle as we head to the living room, Michael following behind us with curious eyes.

"If we join hands, we'll all be connected and we'll be able to see the flow of time for what it is — only we will be able to move freely without the confines of time slowing us down."

I grab Nellie's hand, and she grabs Loni's — I close my eyes and focus on the beating of my heart. Letting that reverberate through my eardrums, I feel the thrum behind my eyes, and I open them to see the time flow shining through the room. They cast an eerie blue light over the Toubabs' faces, but it's only visible to us.

I look at Michael who stands just behind me, and he looks at me with an expectant look. "Now we'll connect to the time flow and slow it, but only we can move normally through time."

"Is it something you can see?" he asks.

"Yeah," I reply. "It's right here in front of us."

"I can't see it," he says, looking blankly across the living room for something he won't find.

"No, sweetie," Loni says. "The time flow isn't visible to people without our powas. An' when we get the Toubabs in di car and come back, it'll be as if nothing's changed for you."

He nods slowly, and we turn around to face the time flow again. I look to Loni and we both position our hands over the same timeline — with her hand beside mine, we shoot our power towards the timeline, and it begins to slow. A pulse shoots through the room and the timeline begins to barely inch forward. I look behind me to see Michael standing almost still, his movements incredibly slow — he starts to blink his eyes, and I count an entire minute in my head before his eyelids make it halfway to his pupil.

"Okay," Nellie says. "Let's get this done. Loni, you open the door and get the trunk lid open. J and I will carry them to the car."

I scowl as I reluctantly bend down, my body going through the time flow but the other timelines remaining undisturbed. I grab the taller Toubab by his shoulders as Nellie positions herself by his feet. She bends down and grabs his thighs, and we both lift — his dead weight is incredibly heavy, and I try to breathe normally as we inch towards the door. We walk past Michael who's still blinking in slow motion, and walk through the door. Loni looks around at the neighbouring houses as she stands by the car, and we waddle towards the trunk. We plop him into the trunk and the car slightly bounces. I then go beside Nellie and grab a leg to help push him in — but he's tall, and his head roughly smacks against the back of the seats. We grimace and hold our breaths for a few seconds, but he doesn't rouse from his slumber. We exhale with relief and continue to push him in, folding him at the waist so his feet bend and he's fully in the back. We head back in and grab the other Toubab, and this one is even heavier than the first.

"C'mon girls," Loni shouts, "use your core. Lift wit' yuh legs!"

I cut my eyes at her as we walk past her, and she chuckles annoyingly. We put him in feet first, then his head follows, but I lose my grip and his head thuds against the back bumper. His eyes flutter for a second, and I back away wide-eyed, but they shut again. Nellie looks at me with a pointed look and I grimace in apology. Finally, he rests on top of his companion and we manage to close the lid down to lock.

We make our way back inside and join hands in front of the time flow. Loni and I put our hands beside each other again, and focus our power above the timeline — a watch rests around Loni's wrist, and as I close my eyes, I allow the ticking of the hands to be the only thing that matters. Then I feel that power that connected us to the timeline return to my hand, and time resumes. We turn to Michael, who's blinking normally and looking at us patiently — his face is slowly looking confused, and he raises his eyebrow amusingly.

"Can I help you?" he asks. We laugh and shake our heads, and his face falls as he sees the floor empty.

"Whoa — where did they..." We smile and wait, and his face changes as it clicks.

"Oh," he says with a meek laugh. I pat him on the shoulder and head to my room. Seeing as it's basically empty, except for the Novelfall that still remains, I find my art project pretty quickly. I grab it and rush back, meeting everyone at the car. Nellie and Loni sit in the front seats while Michael and I squeeze into the back. He looks cautiously to the trunk at the sleeping Toubabs, and I rest a wary eye on them too.

"You sure they won't wake up?" I ask them.

"Not with the dose of potion I gave him," Loni replies. "An' after I gave the otha a dose of the potion too, dey should be out for hours."

I nod, but my nerves are still shaky. I cast a wary eye on them as Nellie backs out of the driveway, and we head for the highway.

Michael and I drop the Toubabs near the dumpsters, looking to make sure no one is walking by to see. A rat scurries past amidst the garbage littered, and we jog back to the car. Nellie backs out and heads for the school — by now it's the middle of the afternoon, and the wind is blowing ferociously outside. The sun is shining, but the air is frigid to the bone. My bones ache as it settles, and I grimace in pain.

"You okay?" Michael asks me. Loni looks behind to see what the issue is, but I weakly wave them off.

"I'm fine," I say. "Just the aches and pains — the trials of an assault victim."

"Assault survivor," Loni corrects. I smile warmly, and she smiles back with kind eyes. She turns back to face forward, and Michael looks at me with a sad look.

"Don't look at me like that," I say, chirpily. "I could still bike circles around you, even in this state."

"I don't doubt it," he agrees. Usually, he'd fire back with a sarcastic reply, but he must be too sympathetic to bother. I squeeze his hand and look at him, showing him gratitude and giving the assurance that it'll all be okay in that one look — even though I'm not entirely sure if I truly believe it myself.

We pull up at the school and park at the front, opening the doors before the car even gets in park. We look around as we make our way up the steps, and Michael heads around the back.

"The front doors are locked, but the back doors near the student parking lot is always open."

"How do you know this, Michael?" Loni asks.

"I spent a lot of weekends at school solving equations when J was at her summer job," he says. "I got... pretty close with the janitor."

"Bobby?" I ask.

"Yeah," he says with a smile. "He's a great guy."

We arrive at the back doors and see a wooden block propping the door open. We make our way inside, and Loni and Nellie look to us for direction.

"Art department?" Nellie asks.

"Follow me," I reply. We head down the hallway and turn left, making our way to the double doors. The light's on and the doors are open, and neo-soul music plays faintly from a speaker. We come to a stop, Michael and I looking at each other in questioning. We slowly make our way to the doors, when suddenly, Ms. Cortez comes out. We jump back, startling each other — she grabs her collarbone in shock, as the other hand holds a dirty handkerchief covered in paint.

"Jamila!" she exclaims. She sees Michael and says, "You scared me!"

"Sorry, Ms. Cortez," we say sheepishly.

"What — do you have a habit of scaring the life out of your teachers?"

"No, no, no," I say with a laugh. "We're sorry, I just came by to drop off my art assignment."

"Oh," she says breathily, toweling her hands. I now see her hands stained with paint, as well as her baggy jeans and the sleeves of her blue button-up shirt.

"Well, why couldn't you just wait 'til next week? That's when the assignment is due — surely you could've just waited until then."

"Well, uh, I just wanted to drop it off now just in case — I don't want to get a late mark or anything."

"Well, are you not going to class that day?"

"No," I reply, my nerves spiking. "I'm actually going to be... gone for a while."

"Really?" she asks surprised. "How come?"

"Uh..." I stammer, struggling to come up with an excuse.

Nellie comes up behind me, a sweet smile plastered on her face. "We have some family troubles abroad — it's pretty sudden, but we have to leave as soon as possible."

"Oh, I see," she says, understanding, a polite smile crossing her face. "Well, I hope everything's alright."

"We hope so," Nellie says, her voice high and sweet. "But we won't know 'til we get there, y'know?"

"Yes, of course," she replies. "I don't believe we've met — you must be Jamila's aunt."

"Yes," Nellie replies, reaching out to shake Ms. Cortez's hand. "That's me. Nice to meet you."

"It's nice to meet you too," Ms. Cortez replies kindly. "I'm so glad we finally met — your niece is very talented."

"Oh really?" Nellie asks, looking at me with a smile and raised eyebrows.

"Oh yeah, she's got a great set of hands. Technically, her projects follow the guidelines to the letter, but I always look forward to the message she delivers. No project is the same, and it's amazing to see such depth and... transparency in her work."

"You really think so?" I ask. She looks at me with a kind smile and smirking eyes — making me smile in response.

"There isn't a time where you've failed to make me enjoy your work, Jamila. Not to mention, I think you're pretty cool too."

I smile deeply as she smiles back, throwing me a wink.

"And how about me?" Michael asks, his eyes childlike and sparkling. Ms. Cortez hesitates, but that sweet smile slides back on her face quickly.

"Michael, you and Jamila never fail to entertain, and I love the effort you put into your assignments. I can see it, I truly do. Just a little tweaking on your technique and you should be off to the races."

Michael's smile fades a little, but he nods to brush it off. I try to hide a smirk but fail, and Michael cuts his eye at me as he sees.

"Well, since you're already here," Ms. Cortez says, "let's see it."

I lift my scales of justice and lay it in the palm of my hand to face her. She cocks her head to the side and her brow furrows as she takes it in for the first time.

"Huh," she says. Her eyes scan the base of the scale and the action figure, and the remainder of the scale.

"What's your message?" she asks. "Your inspiration?"

"The partiality of justice," I reply. "I saw a headline about that case where an actress bribed a school to get her daughter in and she ended up getting a slap on the wrist."

"Oh yes, I saw that. She got, what, only three months in jail?"

"Yeah, compared to a black woman from a low-income community that got seven years in prison for just putting a different address on the forms — so her son could go to a better school."

"I remember reading about that case," Michael says. "It's mind-blowing that two cases that are in the same vein got treated so differently."

"It's not really that mind-blowing," Ms. Cortez counters. "Especially if it's been happening for years."

"Yeah," I say with a smile. "Yeah, exactly." She smiles back smirkingly, making me like her even more.

I continue, "Well, I wanted to portray the scales of justice as an unstable foundation — when you look at how stark the differences are in the 'justice' people are given, you can see there are cracks in the foundation. And this so-called 'justice' is what the founding fathers, and all leaders that govern this country and other Western countries, try to feed us. But it's not gonna keep — it'll only spoil if we allow it to pervade our lives for much longer. And the blindfold is basically how society is blind when it wants to be, and then chooses to be 'impartial' when it suits itself."

She nods as I speak, listening along and glancing at the scales every now and then. When I'm finished talking, she rests her fingers on her lip and looks at the scales again.

"Well, you definitely followed the assignment to the letter," she says. "And I do like your literal portrayal of a weak foundation — that's nice."

"Thank you," I say.

"I do think, however, that saying the onus is solely on the founding fathers isn't completely accurate. You could argue that they enabled this form of 'justice' as you so call it, but it only continues to exist because we allow it to."

"Okay," I say. "That's true. I guess I didn't think to focus on that because, really, the hand that discerns the impartiality and transparency of justice is the hand that rules most of our society — and I thought the founding fathers would be a pretty recognizable representation of that."

"I see, I see," she says, slowly smiling. "Well, okay, this is a great submission, Jamila. I'm very happy with your take on this assignment. Seeing as you won't be here tomorrow, I'll just tell you now that you get an 89%. I can't give you a perfect grade every time — people will start to think that I have a favourite." She winks and I smile with a chuckle, taking my scale with a pleased look on her face. She smiles at Michael and Nellie and waves goodbye, looking at the scales as she walks back inside.

"Okay," Nellie says, "let's find Casper."

"Jeremy," I correct.

"Oh, you know what I mean," she says, waving me off. We turn and head back the way we came, and I lead them up the stairs and towards my classroom. The door is closed and the lights are off, but I test the handle and the door opens. I turn on the lights and look around, hoping to see Jeremy, but the room is empty.

"Is he here?" Michael asks hopefully.

"No," I reply disappointedly. "He's not here."

"Why isn't he here?" he asks. "Isn't this where you saw him? He's trapped in here, right?"

"Yeah, but he's not trapped to this room; he can move around the whole school, so he's probably somewhere else."

"Let's head back downstairs," Nellie says. "Maybe he's in the gym or cafeteria or something."

We follow her down the stairs and head towards the front for the cafeteria. We pass my locker when I hear a young, juvenile voice behind me.

"Sup, Freeman?" Jeremy shouts. I whip around wide-eyed — he's leaning against my locker, his hands in his pockets, and a smug smirk on his face. "What's wrong? You look like you've seen a ghost."

"You're here," I marvel.

"It's not like I'm going anywhere," he says snarkily. I shoot him a side-eye and roll my eyes, turning to Nellie and Loni.

"Can you see him?" I ask.

"Yes," Nellie says.

"Sort of," Loni replies. "I'm not too well-practiced wit' seein' the deceased, but I can get by off dey energies. And I can hear him."

"Well, he looks like how Jamila described him," Loni continues. "And just as lippy."

Jeremy's face falls slack, looking to me in disbelief. "They can see me?" I nod, and he looks back to them wide-eyed. He whoops loudly and jumps, shooting his fists in the air in a Rocky pose.

"It's about damn time! Oh God, you have no idea how happy I am to see you guys. I thought I was never going to see you again."

"I thought so too," I reply. "But I told them about you, and they agreed to help me in helping you." Jeremy smiles — a genuine and grateful smile — and for the first time, I actually take a liking to him.

"Is he here?" Michael asks, oblivious to what's going on.

"Yeah," I reply. "He's grateful that we're here and was jumping for joy, which I didn't really think was on brand for him."

"Freeman, when you haven't been able to talk to or be seen by anyone for 16 years, you loosen the reins on 'shoulds'," he replies. "Wait, how come they can see me too?"

"They're like me," I reply. "We're Bastets."

"Bas-*what*?"

"It's a long story," I reply. Nellie steps forward, her smirking smile on her face.

"The gist of it is that we can see you, and we can try to see what's holding you here and help you cross over."

"Cross over," he says with a smug smirk, waving his fingers in a spooky gesture. "To the great beyond?"

"To a place better than here," I reply sharply. "Certainly being at rest is better than being stuck in the halls of Brimmer High for another 16 years."

"Hmm," he hums, seemingly agreeing with me. He looks at Michael and points, saying, "And he can't see me?"

"No, he's not like us." Michael's eyebrows raise as he realizes I'm referring to him, and I wave him off to assure him it's all okay. "Only us three can see you — but he's never believed in ghosts before —"

"And he wanted to see if all the stories were true," Jeremy finishes. He walks towards Michael, looking him up and down — Michael, still unable to see him, just looks at us expectantly.

"Guess I can't blame the guy for wanting to finally see his first ghost," Jeremy says sardonically. "But he's outta luck — I'm not up to performing parlour tricks today."

I notice the sharp tone of his voice, and ask, "Are you alright?"

"You mean besides knowing the existential ironies of my existence? Oh, just the typical blues." He looks at me blankly, then walks past us going down the hallway. I start to follow him — with Nellie, Loni, and Michael following behind me.

He continues, "When I was alive I was a loner — I didn't want to talk to people, and they didn't want to talk to me. I preferred it that way; it meant I didn't have to deal with people's excuses and stupidities. Guess I got it from my parents — they sort of developed a knack for it before they finally divorced."

We continue to follow him as he walks — Michael looks at us confused, waiting to be filled in, and Nellie looks at me with a cocked eyebrow. I'm just as confused as they are; I didn't think ghosts *spoke* let alone had lengthy monologues.

He continues, "People didn't see me in school. They didn't bother trying. But it gave me complete freedom to see them. The popular kids, the jocks, the nerds, they were all the same — scared teenagers who didn't have a clue what they were doing, and thought following everyone else was the best way to get by. I was invisible, and people show their truest selves when they think no one's watching. But the one thing that kept me going was that I'd get out of here — finally do something that would actually mean something, and not be surrounded by people who care only about themselves and what's *normal*."

He turns around suddenly, looking at me with an amused face but upset eyes.

Then, he continues, "And what do I get when I die? An endless existence of watching and listening to people, unable to go anywhere else or escape, unable to be seen or heard, and with no one to talk to. Now that's some rock hard irony right there."

I look at him silently, unable to come up with a response to his monologue. But Nellie fills in for me.

"Surely you've had plenty of time to analyze the realities of your existence," she walks up to him, looking into his face. He leans back, startled, but captivated nonetheless. She continues, "But now it's time to stop analyzing and do something about it. Or would you rather wallow in an endless cynical rut?"

Jeremy stares at her for a moment, with a little fear in his eyes — I can't blame him, Nellie's directness can be daunting and intimidating at first. Especially for those who've never had a confrontation with their demons before.

"No," he replies meekly.

"Good," Nellie replies. She turns around with a small smirk on her face and throws me a wink. I smile back, grateful to have this force of a woman in my life.

"What about you," Jeremy says, pointing towards Loni, "you can see energies, but not me?"

"She can see energies and auras," Nellie says, answering for her.

"I see what I need to see," Loni says. She's looking in Jeremy's direction, but not directly at his face. "I can see your pain — what you felt when you died an' the one you're experiencin' right now. You have a young energy, so I'd know that you died young without Jamila tellin' me, and an aura about yuh that tells me dat you were defiant in your past life."

"Ooooo," Jeremy jokes. "Does it look like a kaleidoscope? Or is it just a blob of black?"

"Could you be any more annoying?" I ask exasperatedly.

"Oh definitely," he says with a smirk. I roll my eyes and stand beside Michael, who looks at me with a cocked eyebrow.

"He's being a smart ass?"

"You have no idea," I reply.

"Well, no wonder you're clashing," he says. I look at him questioningly, and he continues, "Like-minded people never get along." I move to hit him but he jumps back, standing safely behind Loni and chuckling.

"He's got a point," Jeremy says, and I cut my eyes at him. "He's starting to grow on me."

"Well, then maybe he can help you cross over," I reply, tight-lipped.

"Alright, alright," he says, holding his hands in the air in surrender. "No need to get your panties in a wad, I'll wave the white flag. So, how are you Bastets gonna jailbreak me outta here?"

"Well, we first need to know how you died," Nellie replies. "The circumstances and any events that led up to your demise."

"Classic comedians' plight," he replies, shrugging as he leans back on the locker, stuffing his hands in his pockets. "Wisecracked to the wrong people with a vanilla sense of humour — and they took my life for it."

"Were they also students?" she asks.

"Yeah," he replies. "Seniors. I thought I was invisible, but when you bag on a guy's hairline, they suddenly begin to notice you. Can I help it if my sense of humour is niche?"

"I would say more mind-numbingly pathetic," I reply monotone.

"Meh, it's all semantics." He jokes but his eyes get cloudy, and his face loses its lustre. "Anyways, regardless of how you spin it, they didn't take it too well. I was in detention so I was at school later than everyone else — in your chemistry class, actually. Even after 16 years, they haven't changed where the 'delinquents' are kept after-hours."

I come closer and lean on the locker, looking at him as I listen. He looks at me, but not with his normal smug look. He's trying his best to make this seem nonchalant, but inside he's filled with sadness.

"Anyway… they cornered me after basically everyone was gone. I knew that some of the kids were starting to hang around with Blanco's boys, but I had no idea they'd already been initiated. Imagine my surprise when Deandre — that was his name — imagine how shocked I was when he pulled a gun out from his pants."

"Was it just this one boy?" Nellie asks. "Or were there others?"

"There were three of them — Deandre, Elijah, and this guy named Richard, but everyone called him Shortstop. He was really just a bystander, it didn't look like he even wanted to be there."

I look at him wide-eyed, and he looks at me confused. "Shortstop?" I ask.

"Yeah," he replies slowly. "You know him?" Nellie and Loni both look to me with questioning looks.

"Yeah," I reply. "He's still a part of Blanco's boys. He... stood by when they harassed me."

Nellie's face changes as she realizes I'm referencing to my attack last night, and Jeremy — still not fully clued in — just slowly nods.

"Well, I guess some things haven't changed," he says. "Anyway, the three of them jumped me outside of the classroom and dragged me inside — Mr. Sorella and the other kids had already left, and the rest of the floor was empty. They beat me up by the heaters, kicking and punching the life out of me, until finally... Deandre pulled the gun out."

"I'm sorry that happened to you," Nellie says.

"It all happened so quickly. I don't really remember what happened in the last few seconds — I think I might've been wisecracking —"

"As per customary-Jeremy fashion," I joke. He chuckles low once, but settles back into the memory.

"I didn't die right away," he says, his voice thick. We're silent as he stands there — even Michael, who must feel the gravity of the situation in the air.

Jeremy continues, "They stood over me for a while, just laughing at me while I was gasping for air and trying to apply pressure." He places his hand over a spot in the middle of his chest, just below his heart, and holds it there as if the blood is still pooling from the wound.

"When they left, I was still alive — but I was so weak, I couldn't get up. I couldn't even call for help — I was just gargling as the blood was rushing into my lungs. It felt like my lungs were on fire, and I thought I was going to die alone. But help came. Or at least he tried."

"Someone found you before you died?" I ask.

"Yeah," he replies with a small smile. "Mr. Sorella." I raise my eyebrows in surprise, and he smiles deeper. "For all the crap I gave that guy, he was always good to me; even near death. He heard the gunshots and rushed back to the room — he called 911 and tried to save me, but I had already lost too much blood. Even then, it was almost impossible to survive a shot to the heart at such close range for long — the ambulance would've never made it in time." My eyes begin to tear, and Loni sighs deeply.

"I'm so sorry," I say. He shrugs nonchalantly, standing up a little straighter.

"It's not your fault," he says quietly. "It's not like you pulled the trigger."

"No, but I almost didn't come back," I reply. "I almost left you... to die again."

His face wavers for a second, but he collects himself. "Well, good thing you came back then," he says. "Besides, it was a long time ago — it's not a big deal."

"You don't believe dat," Loni says. He looks at her and she walks up towards him — she looks him up and down, analyzing every part of him. "Your energy is practically pulsin' wit' pain." She lifts her hands — he leans back, apprehensive, but she just hovers them above his body, with eyes closed.

"It's everywhere," she says. "Like it's etched into yuh bones itself — an' it tells a story. The story of your death, an' the parts of yuh life where you felt dead inside."

She looks directly into his face, and he looks back at her startled. "You can try tuh lie," she says, "but di energy speaks di truth. An' you're hurtin', child."

At this, Jeremy's eyes begin to tear, and his nonchalant facade begins to crumble. His lip quivers, and he begins to look his actual age. Loni's face goes soft and she gives him a kind smile, her eyes reading his pain.

"Let's see if we can help yuh, yeah?" He nods obediently, quickly wiping away his tears like a little child. Loni smiles wider and turns, and I smile with her — glad we were able to reign him in. But the good feeling doesn't last for long.

"Hello, Ms. Freeman," says a familiar voice down the hall. I whip around, seeing the sun cast its light on his tall frame, casting Churchill in shadow.

CHAPTER FIFTEEN

It's like a vacuum sucking all the air from my lungs, and my body freezes as I'm rooted in place. I look at Churchill wide-eyed in shock, while he stands in front of the doors at the other end of the hallway. He's wearing his signature black suit — no overcoat to protect him from the chill outside, just a jet-black suit and shiny black shoes. He takes off his dark sunglasses and gingerly wipes them with a cloth, then tucks them in a pocket inside his blazer. Nellie and Loni quickly come beside me, and Michael — recognizing Churchill — stands behind us, putting his hand on my shoulder for support.

"Pleasure to see you again," he says. His voice is low and normal — but like a calm before the storm, his appearance is like ominous dark clouds, looming over us. I slowly reach for my amulet, rubbing my thumb along the curves. With eagle eyes, his eyes zero in on my neck — I freeze, but still holding the amulet in my hand for strength.

"We wish we could say the same," Nellie says, her voice cold and sharp.

"Ah," he says, as if he's just seeing her. "Ms. Freeman — I hope you don't mind me calling you Nellie, just to minimize confusion."

"I'd rather you keep my name out yo' mouth," she says, her fists clenching and posture straightening.

"Hmm," he hums, nodding clinically.

I'm still frozen, and unable to breathe. I start trembling as fear overtakes my body; Loni realizes and grabs my hand, squeezing tightly. Jeremy looks at us in confusion, to Churchill, and back to us.

"What's wrong with you guys?" he asks. "Who's that?"

I breathe shakily, managing to squeeze a word out. "Churchill," I say.

"Okay, so why are you guys acting like you're in a game of Mortal Kombat?"

"He's a bad guy," I say, my voice low and limp.

"What do you mean?" I look at him. My eyes are filled with fear, and my entire body trembles like a leaf in the wind — his face falls as he sees my state, and his brows furrow in apprehension.

"He's a bad guy," I repeat. He slowly looks to Churchill, giving him the once over, before looking back at me. He nods once and turns to face Churchill before suddenly disappearing.

"I'm disappointed Ms. Freeman," Churchill says, looking at me as he begins to walk forward. "I thought a young woman with a mind such as yours would be smart. Be logical. Working with us would be the least painful option — and, with proper cooperation, could potentially provide you with some benefits." He stops, puts his hands in his pockets, and looks at me disappointed — almost remorseful.

"But you're no different from the rest of your kind. You're erratic, and overly emotional. It's a shame — you could've provided real value to us. But you've insisted on being difficult."

"Difficult?" I ask incredulously, eyes widening in anger. I step forward, and Nellie tries to stop me, but I break past her arms.

"You attacked me," I continue. "You disguised yourself as a doctor, as someone that I should be able to trust, and tried to drug me to use me. For what, I don't even know. I don't know what your cult does nowadays; all the stories I've heard of what you used to do to us —"

"Ah, the stories," he says with a humourless laugh. "Your kind always did have a knack for the theatrics."

"Well, just because our history is filled with drama, it doesn't make it any less true," Nellie says.

"But the omission of the truth straddles the same lines that form the foundation of a lie, doesn't it, Ms. Freeman? I've seen some of your storybooks — the ones my associates and predecessors have accumulated and collected over the years —"

"Collected? Or stole?" Loni chimes in, her voice laced with venom.

"It all comes down to perception. Doesn't it, Ms. Washington?" Loni inhales sharply, and my nerves spike. "Yes, you've been quite the tale in our agency, Ms. Washington. Tales of the elusive woman that has evaded our resources, and lived under our noses for over 40 years. I would be remiss to not give you credit where it's due — you truly are a force to be reckoned with."

"You have yet to see the lengths my wrath will go," she says, her voice sharp and even intimidating me.

"Yes," Churchill says with a small smile. "I have no doubt about that. But I also don't doubt the omission of truth that I'm sure you, and the rest of your kind, have been committing for so long. And criminally so, might I add. Are you curious as to the truth I'm referring to, Ms. Freeman?"

"Not particularly, no," I say, my voice hard despite the trembling that racks my bones.

Churchill ignores me, saying, "The truth your kind omits lies in the motives that drive our organization. You've painted us as this unjust, predatory force —"

"Because you are," I yell, emotion firing my spirit.

"I disagree, Ms. Freeman," he says calmly, angering me even more. "That would imply that our motives are displaced — which I strongly disagree to be true. We are an organization that was founded on the bases of equality, free will, and the protection of all. Our predecessors travelled the seas with these very theologies giving fire to their spirit — these are what provided the groundwork for the establishment of our countries, and what gives us direction as we navigate the development of our societies. Your kind threatens those ideals."

"In what way?" I reply hotly.

"Your kind possess... capabilities that defy the moralities of human evolution. Beyond the merits of human capability lies your kind — a most abhorrent obstacle. You pose a threat to the very ideals that we uphold — how are we as a society to be equal when there are people out there that have abilities that grant you things beyond your imagination? How are we as humans to have free will when your spells can control our actions, how we think, how we treat others, and how we defend ourselves? Your spells and potions can make men drunk with lust and debilitate the very facets that make them men. And how are we, as protectors of society's goodness, to fulfill our obligations with your kind having ulterior obligations to yourselves?"

"We don't have ulterior motives," I say. "We're not some other species that are deliberately trying to control people; we are *human*, just like anyone else. We're trying to survive in this world as best as we can, a world that has done everything to exterminate us, but more than anything — we're trying to *live*."

"Aren't we all, Ms. Freeman?" he asks with an emotionless smile.

"But does your desire to survive justify your actions, and how they affect humankind? That is the question we pose, and what we subsequently answer with our actions. And the answer is no, your actions do not justify your will to survive. Which leaves us with the only logical conclusion — to extinguish the options of survival."

"You're insane," Michael says behind me, his voice troubled and upset.

"No, young man. I'm logical," Churchill says. He tsks and says, "I'm disappointed in you as well — a young man of your countenance, I would've expected you to not involve yourself in such risky extracurriculars. Their association puts you at risk — and makes you too much of a risk for our organization. We can't allow you to be aware of this group of people; the potential of spreading misinformation would cause hysteria, and threaten the stability of our society."

Michael shrinks, his face growing weary with worry. "You can't scare me into compliance — I would never betray their confidence to begin with, but you're not the end-all-be-all of my free will. You're a tyrant in a suit."

"I am a champion of the truth," he replies. "One told from all perspectives, and with a bird's eye view."

"Well, if there was ever a bird, you'd fit the bill," Loni says hotly. Churchill looks at her with a cocked eyebrow, slightly confused as to what she means. I laugh to myself. For all his education and intellect, he's useless when it comes to the colloquialisms of the chameleon class.

"Um," Jeremy says. We look at him as he reappears in front of us, looking between Churchill and us in confusion. "There's clearly something I'm missing here, and I'd really hate to break up what seems like a necessary conversation, or whatever, but you came here to help me cross over... is that still happening, or..."

I look back to Churchill, who just looks at me with expectant eyes and an emotionless expression.

"Well, you can take your ideals and shove it where the sun don't shine," I say, with a kind smile.

"Hmm," he hums, his eyebrows furrowing perplexedly. "You continue to disappoint me, Ms. Freeman. You leave me no choice — actions must be taken to ensure the safety of the general population."

At that, the front doors open behind him. Men in dark clothing begin to swarm in, with guns poised in their hands. Their clunky boots barely make a noise on the linoleum floor, and they move with ease amidst the bulletproof vests, thick jacket and cargo pants they wear. They poise guns at the ready in our direction, red laser pinpointing our location. They stand behind Churchill, at least a dozen of them, awaiting his command. A noise behind us makes us turn, to see even more men in black pouring in from the back door leading to the student parking lot. Michael begins to breathe rapidly, and I also start to hyperventilate. These men move as if they're dancing, gracefully moving along the floor like a swan on a lake, with a stillness that brings a chill down my spine.

"Holy crap," Jeremy says.

"No, no, no, no," Michael wails. "No, I don't want to die!"

"Hell," Jeremy says, with worry in his eyes. "I'm dead and even I want to get out of here. I thought you were just a nerd — what the hell are you involved in?"

"You see, Ms. Freeman," Churchill says. "Your efforts are futile, and our forces are boundless. Please, for the sake of your young friend, come with us willingly. We can discuss the terms of your work with us, and see if it can be mutually beneficial."

"You must be out of your mind," Nellie says with a chuckle. "You don't want her to work with you, you want her to work for you — it's slavery by another name, but slavery all the same."

"You misunderstand, miss. Our methods have evolved over the years. Traditional methods, if any should be taken, occur rarely — only in the event of absolute disobedience, but Jamila is a smart girl. I'm sure she would see reason."

"Oh, she sees reason all right. Reason is on our side, and she's not going anywhere with you."

Churchill exhales slowly, shaking his head in disappointment. "I was hoping it wouldn't have to come to this, but you've left me with no choice. We will have to take you by force."

"Like hell you will," Loni says. She comes in front of us and stares him down, muttering a chant underneath her breath. Churchill must recognize what she's doing, and makes a gentle motion with his hand.

"Gentlemen," he signals. A click plays through their horde as they take off the safety, aiming to kill. Michael whimpers and grabs my hand, and I squeeze back tightly as my eyes begin to tear. They fire, both sides at once, and my heart stops. I feel that heartbeat pulse through me, and a gleam of light flashes across the insides of my eyelids. It's dark for a moment, and silent — I'm not sure if this is death or me dissociating from the here and now. I slowly open my eyes, not sure what I'll see, and come face to face with a bullet poised frozen in the air in front of my face. I jump back in shock, but the bullet doesn't move. I look to see all the other bullets frozen in the air, with the men in black and Churchill frozen in place. Sparks fly from the gun nozzles as their effect delays with the flow of time. Loni and Nellie are also frozen, and their assigned bullets have yet to find their destination. The clock on the wall above the lockers is silent, as the second hand rests still. The time flow runs through the hallway, running from the back of the hallway near the student parking lot, all the way through the front doors and out onto the street.

"What... the hell?" I whirl around, surprised to hear Michael's voice. He looks around us in confusion — at Nellie and Loni posed in defensive positions, and at the bullets moving through the air like it's honey. He waves his hand in front of Nellie's face, but she remains unmoving and unblinking. He turns and sees me looking at him. He looks at me with confused eyes, and I return his stare with a perplexed one of my own.

"How..." I stutter. "How are you... moving?"

"I don't know," he says dazed. He looks at the bullets, face slack with shock as he takes in a superpower in action — stopping bullets in mid-air. Suddenly, he looks down at our joined hands, raising it in the air to look at it like holy grail.

"Maybe..." I realize what he's getting at, and the idea alights like a light bulb in my brain.

"I stopped the flow of time... and you can see what I see." I look at him, eyes wide with wonder. "Is that it?"

"That must be it," he says. "Your fight or flight response must've triggered you to stop the time flow — but I thought only you, Loni and Nellie could move freely. I didn't know you could make a normal human see what you can see."

"I didn't know that either," I say.

"Uh, me either," says Jeremy. I look at him in surprise, as he looks at me with a comically confused expression. "Okay, seeing a ghost is one thing. But *this*?" He motions around him, his arms erratic. "*What the hell is this?* Why is everyone frozen? Why are there *bullets* in mid-air? People aren't able to do this. You're not normal — this is not normal — this is... this is abnormal."

"Yeah," I admit. "Yeah, I can't argue with you there."

"Oh my God," Michael says. His eyes are wide and mouth agape, as he looks… directly at Jeremy. Jeremy does a double-take, staring back at Michael with equally wide eyes.

"Wait, wait, wait," Jeremy stammers. "Can you see me too?"

Michael just nods wordlessly, his mouth still wide open and eyes amazed. Jeremy looks at me in confusion, his mouth opening and closing.

"But… but he couldn't see me before. I was invisible to him like everyone else — how did… how come he can see me now?"

I raise our joined hands in reply, and Jeremy's face slowly realizes that I'm the independent variable. Michael slowly walks forward, looking Jeremy up and down like a scientist analyzing a specimen.

"You're *here*. You're *real*." Michael's eyes flitter as he tries to make sense of what he's seeing, and afraid I'll mess up the time flow, I creep up behind him — making sure he's still holding my hand. "You look so normal," he continues. "Like, I wouldn't be able to tell you're a ghost — oh, I'm sorry."

"Don't worry about it," Jeremy says with a smirk. "Besides, it's true."

Michael chuckles once, still mystified by what he's seeing. His eyes catch the light from the time flow, and he zeroes in on it — the shiny blue light casts its glow on his face as he peers down at it. He bends down to get a closer look, looking over the surface of the time flow.

"How are you doing all this?" he asks. "I mean, I know that your powers let you do it, but *how* do you do it?"

"By connecting to the here and now," I reply. I hover my hand over a timeline, and a ray of golden light snaps from my palm to the timeline. His eyes widen in amazement, showing a kid-like wonder that makes me smile.

"Time doesn't work on a linear pattern; it goes in different directions, all at the same time. It's a flow of time, but more of a cycle than a straight line. We're able to tap into the timeline that's this time, here and now, and manipulate it."

"And because you're the one manipulating it, you're able to not be affected by it?"

"Yeah," I reply. "Since I'm basically changing the speed of the time flow for this timeline, it's as if it has to start from a new reference point — and when it makes its cycle around the time flow, it returns to me."

"Oh," he says in realization. "You're point zero."

"Yes, exactly!"

He nods, looking at the time flow all the while. The timeline I'm affecting is barely moving, and I pull my hand away to stand back up.

Michael stands up too, all the while holding my hand so he doesn't miss anything.

"So how do you think you're making me see all of this?" Michael asks.

"Your guess is as good as mine," I reply. "It must have something to do with my brain and yours — my brain can experience this all the time because the back of my brain is turned up to 100% all the time —"

"And you stopped the time flow for the first time when you panicked when you saw me falling," he fills in. "Your stress response must stimulate your abilities, which come out the more active your visual and auditory cortices are without even having to try."

"Which means I also have the ability to —"

"Stimulate the visual and auditory cortices of regular people." We look at each other amazed — working out the problem like two classic honours students — as the puzzle pieces of my powers begin to fall into place. Then Michael's eyes blink, as he finally takes note of the bullets nearing us.

"Um, b-b-bullets."

"Yeah, I know Michael," I reply. I walk forward, dragging him behind me like a rag doll. I start to move the bullets out of the way — moving one headed for Nellie's nose to fly past her ear, and another aimed at Loni's heart to go through the crook of her arm. I continue to move the bullets out of the way, and Michael joins in — moving the bullets that were shot behind us. Jeremy walks towards one of the shooters, peering into his face. He goes to Churchill and peers into his face, giving him the once over.

"This dude's a total stiff," he says. "Very unlikeable — classic snob. Hmm." He walks back towards us, stuffing his hands back in his pockets and leaning on the lockers again.

"Aren't you going to help us?" I ask annoyed.

"Freeman, I'm dead. My hand would just go through those bullets."

"Maybe in normal time — but maybe slowing it down gives you a loophole."

He looks at me for a moment, a smug look on his face, but he walks forward anyway. He sticks his hand out towards the bullet, a small smirk on his face — his hand reach the bullet and bumps it out of place. He looks at the bullet in shock, his eyes wide with confusion. He looks at his hand, flipping it over and then back to his palm. He reaches for the bullet again, pinching his fingers, and he's able to move it.

He looks at me wide-eyed, his face shaking. "This is... this is..." His eyes begin to tear, as he stares at his hand in disbelief.

"Jeremy? Are you okay?"

"Yeah, no… I'm fine. That's just the first time I've been able to actually touch something, like, for real, in 16 years. Kind of a weird thing to get emotional over, huh?"

"No," I reply softly, giving him a kind smile. "No, it's not weird at all. It makes absolute sense."

He smirks and bows his head, trying to hide his emotion. He breathes in deeply and silently begins to help us move the bullets safely out of the way. After what seems like a few minutes, all the bullets are safely out of our way and heading to different locations.

"Okay," Michael says. "Now what?"

"We have to get out of here," I reply.

"But you and I are the only ones moving freely," Michael says. "Nellie and Loni are still frozen — and how are we going to get Jeremy out of here?"

I look to Jeremy, who returns mine with an expression; one that is desperate, and longing to get out. I turn to Nellie and Loni, who are still sluggishly slow. I grab Nellie's hand with my free hand, and feel a connection between us like a coiled rope pulled taut. She blinks and shoots into movement, looking around herself in confusion before turning to me in realization.

"Thank God for your reflexes," she says breathily. I chuckle, and she grabs the side of my face; looking at me with loving eyes. But there's not much time for the moment to last — she reaches for Loni's hand, and she too snaps into movement, quick as a whip.

"C'mon then," she says. "Let's not dawdle around, waitin' for dem tuh aave another true aim."

She starts walking down the hallway towards the student parking lot, leaning left and right, ducking down and sideways, to avoid the bullets, walking at a pace brisker than I've ever seen her walk.

"What about me?" Jeremy asks, walking quickly beside us. "I still can't get through the doors."

"Jeremy," Loni says, "I've just met you, but somethin' tells me dat di only thing keepin' you from walkin' thru dem doors is you."

"What?" Jeremy asks confused. We come up to Churchill's men, being careful to not touch or move any of them — we tiptoe around them like a living game of Operator. Their faces are concealed behind masks to cover their mouths, and only their eyes are fully visible. Some of them look hard, their faces wrinkled in angry expressions, concealed by their gears — but some of them look cold, clinical, and void of even anger. Like Churchill.

"You been here for 16 years," Loni continues. She moves through the men nimbly, with the sure step of a gymnast. "You've been harbourin' feelings of resentment and jealousy towards di people dat made you feel invisible — so much so dat you haven't even been payin' attention to what you need to be doing, which is to let go."

"That's not true," Jeremy says defensively.

"Child, you died in 2004. The kids dat hurt an' ignored you back then are grown adults now. I can't speak for the boys dat killed yuh, but the other kids you spoke about — di ones dat you say neva bothered to see yuh — those kids are people who aave learned from their mistakes. Whether they're sorry for payin' you no mind or not, the fact is that dey aave their whole lives to learn from their actions. You don't, my dear."

Jeremy looks at Loni, his boyish nature making another appearance.

"You aave been feelin' all di pain an' hurt as if it's fresh, child," she says softly. "The point of restin' in peace involves actually *restin'* in your *peace*. Your energy is rife, child — all I see is pain an' hurt flowin' thru you. How do you expect to cross over if you're not willin' to leave di pain behind?"

Jeremy looks at her, as if for the first time he's hearing the truth, and looks at the door. He sighs wearily, shaking his head slightly.

"But I'm so angry. I died too soon. Too young. And I didn't even get to live the life I wanted to." Loni stands beside him, looking at the sun now peeking through the cold clouds.

"Well, I'm sorry to tell you, sweetie, but you're neva gonna get dat life back. It's gone — but di life waitin' for you isn't. Not yet. You can't stay here for anotha 16 years. You don't aave to be di boy you once were. Your pain and resentment are literally locking you within its walls, an' you're letting it happen. Until you stop lettin' it aave powa ova you, you're gonna stay stuck in here. It's time, Jeremy. It's time to let go."

"Will I cross over as soon as I get through the doors?"

"You aave to much pain you been carryin' wit' you — we still aave to bring you to the Realm of Duality to properly cross you over. First thing is to get you thru di doors."

Loni opens the door, waving her hand to usher him out. He looks at her for a moment, and I notice his fingertips rubbing together in fear. He slowly steps forward, slightly hunching inward in preparation for I don't know what. He reaches the doorway and stops, breathing deeply as he braces for the disappointment, and takes a step forward going outside. He keeps walking for a few steps, not realizing that he's outside — he suddenly straightens and freezes in place. He looks slowly from left to right before his head slowly cocks back, his eyes closed as he breathes in freedom.

"Right, now that's sorted," Loni calls out, walking briskly forward. Michael and I jog behind her to catch up, still holding hands, and Nellie makes sure the door is closed behind us. She reaches her hand out and mutters a spell underneath her breath, and a gold light glows from her palm and settles onto the door handles. I look up to see birds that were flying in a v-shape in the air, their wings frozen mid-upstroke.

"C'mon, y'all," Nellie says, opening the car and plopping into the driver's seat. She has a thought and gets up — jogging to the passenger door to aggressively slam her hip into it while pulling the handle, getting the creaky door open. I turn around to look for Jeremy, he's still standing in front of the doors, looking mystified. Emotions overtake his face as he stands there limp, and the snarky sarcasm is replaced with mature peace.

"C'mon, Jeremy," I call. He blinks as if just noticing us here and straightens with a start, making his way to the car. Michael opens the door and slides in, and I sit in the middle. Jeremy slides in, and I reach through him to close the door. Nellie puts her arm behind Loni's seat and looks through the back windshield. As soon as Loni closes the door, Nellie takes off like a light, and Michael and I brace ourselves from the sharp movement of the car reversing.

"Jamila," Nellie says. "Do your thing."

I nod and close my eyes, placing my hand out in mid-air, trying my best to steady my heart despite the bumping car. The pain below my pelvis pulses, reminding me my body is not in top shape, and I grimace as I try to ignore the pain. I zone out almost instantly, now being well-practiced in tuning into only my heartbeat. I feel my heartbeat pulsing in my brain, forming into a light behind my eyes, and I see the time flow — feeling the connection between my hand and the timeline, seeing the golden light between my hand and the timeline, I clench my fist. The golden light shoots around the time flow and behind my eyelids, and the timeline returns to normal. I look outside at the birds in the sky, back to flying to their destination.

"Is time normal again?" Michael asks. I release his hand, and nod.

"Yes," I reply.

Nellie speeds down the path and out onto the street — we look out the window to see Churchill and his men running out through the front door. They shoot at us; a bullet rips through the trunk, and we scream and dunk our heads. Another bullet rips through the front windshield, barely missing Nellie's head. She looks at the hole wide-eyed, but floors it. We pass the stop sign, and I figure it's safe enough to look through the back windshield. Churchill's men mill around, but Churchill stands in the middle of the road — still, and staring at us as we drive away. Even from here I can feel his domineering presence, and turn back around willing the lump in my throat to disappear.

I turn to Jeremy, who still looks to be in a daze. "Are you alright?"

"Yeah, I'm okay. I'm... I'm better than okay." He looks at me, a disbelieving smile on his face amidst relief. "I'm out. I'm finally out."

"Yes you are," I say with a smile.

"Hopefully not for long," Nellie says. "It's time to put you to rest."

We hop out of the car as Loni opens the door to the diner. It's busier than ever, with church-goers attending to their hungry bellies — lively commotion fills the space. Ray waves at us as he navigates the counter, and I take a good look at him, keeping him in my memories. Families laugh in their booths while snacking on their meals and drinking their shakes, cups of Milo, and teas. Old School music plays through a speaker hanging up on the wall, connected to a sound system that stands where the jukebox used to be.

"Hey," Michael says. "Where's the juke?"

"Poor thing sang its last hurrah," Loni says. "Ray was able to get a good deal on a sound system down at di store, an' the new cooks found all the old songs an' albums that we played in di jukebox on this music website. We don't undastan a lick of dis new streamin' business, but bless their hearts dey got it all sorted out for us."

Jeremy looks around him in awe, taking a look at life 16 years after his passing, as we head to the back. The new cooks Loni hired wave to us, then return their hands to work. We discreetly make our way to the back closet, Nellie and Loni being the only ones maneuvering through the tiny space. Michael's face turns surprised as he sees Loni descend into the basement below, and I chuckle as we follow. Jeremy — all the while — is mesmerized, taking in everything while he can.

The lights illuminate as we enter the space — Michael's dumbfounded and frozen, and his face makes me laugh. Jeremy is equally as mesmerized, but walks around the basement, admiring the books, potions, and aura of the abode.

"Right," Loni says, grabbing a few bags and placing them by the stairs, "let's get started, yes? Jeremy," she calls, and with that, he looks at her.

"You guys really aren't average women, huh?"

"What would ever give you that impression?" Nellie asks with a smirk — he smirks back, but not smugly. He must be taking a liking to her — I didn't think that was possible for him.

"This place is amazing," Michael says. "I can't believe this was underneath the diner the whole time."

"Oh, believe it, sweetie," Loni says with a deep chuckle. "Dis dina is protected wit' di strongest spell I eva cast — imbued wit' all di strength I could muster."

"So you put your foot in it," I joke. She rolls her eyes and chuckles.

"Yes, in a way," she smiles, looking up with fond eyes, "dis dina here has been good to me; protected me for years from dem Toubabs. It's my home." She turns to Jeremy behind her, walking up to him. "An' hopefully we can send you to a new home."

He takes his hands out of his pockets, his fingers rubbing together in anticipation, and he nods.

"Michael, baby, why don't you preoccupy yuhself wit' some of di books ova there suh," Loni says. "Just don't touch anythin' else — if you're anythin' like dis one," she gestures to me, "you'll make a mess." I give her a look, and she cocks her eyebrow to challenge me. I won't — she's not wrong.

"Come sit, child," Loni says. Jeremy obeys and sits in the middle of the floor. Loni grabs a box from the potion pantry and a teapot. She pours water in and pulls tea leaves from the small box. Putting them in a steeper in the teapot, she ignites a fire below the teapot. Michael's eyes widen and he tries to move in for a closer look, but Loni swats him away. She mutters a spell underneath her breath, and a dull golden light glows from her palm above the teapot. She pours the now steaming tea into three teacups, bringing them and the teapot on a platter over to us. She sets the platter down in front of Jeremy, and she and Nellie sit across from him cross-legged. He copies them, looking at them anxiously.

"It's going to be okay, Jeremy," Nellie says, clueing in to his energy.

He lets out a nervous chuckle, and looks at me warily. I sit down beside him, giving him a supportive smile.

"So is this the part where we sit in a circle of candles," he jokes nervously, "room shaking, speaking in tongues, all that jazz?"

"Your guess is as good as mine," I say. "I've never done this before, I'm just here to watch — and to be here for you."

He nods, smiling gratefully. Loni hands two teacups to me and Nellie, taking one for herself. They drink it slowly, then tip the teacup to finish the whole thing — I follow suit, but my face screwing from the taste.

"You couldn't sweeten it or something?" I ask.

"We aave to mek sure our connection is strong here," she replies. "Sorry sweetie, no shuga."

I pout but finish the tea, and Loni opens the teapot and scrapes the leaves into a tiny wooden bowl. She strikes a match and lights the surface on fire, and waits for it to smoke up. She wafts the bowl near where Jeremy's nose would be.

"Breathe in," she commands. He looks at her warily but obeys, breathing in deeply. Suddenly his face relaxes, and his eyes slowly close. Loni grabs Nellie's hand, and Nellie grabs mine.

"Close your eyes," Loni says. I do, and Loni begins to chant:

> *The restless soul that walks dis earth*
> *I now command to depart*
> *As your body feeds di dirt*
> *Allow peace to enter thine heart*
>
> *Join us in di Realm between worlds*
> *Cast aside your earthly strife*
> *Let thine worries an' troubles unfurl*
> *As you enter di spirit life*

For a second my vision goes black, but then I'm in a bedroom — but not mine. It's messy, with clothes all over the floor and the blanket scrunched up on the bed. Posters hang everywhere on the walls, a CD player atop a dresser, and wires connected to a video game system and an old-looking TV. Nellie and Loni are with me, looking around, and Jeremy sits on the bed with his eyes still closed. Loni takes notice of Jeremy — now being able to see him — and her face softens as she gets a look at him for the first time.

"Hello, dear," Loni says to Jeremy. He looks up at her in surprise, his eyes widening.

"You can see me?" he asks. She smiles and puts her hand on his shoulder, lightly squeezing. His face crumbles a bit, and he slumps under her touch.

"Yes, dear," she replies. "I can see you."

He sighs in relief with a smile, and begins to look around the room — he doesn't recognize where he is at first, none of us do, but then his eyes widen in realization.

"Oh my God," he says, standing up slowly. "How did... how did we get here?"

"Jeremy, where are we?" I ask.

He doesn't answer at first, emotion overtaking him, but then he responds, "This was my room." He looks around in awe, slightly shaking his head in disbelief.

"Why are we here?"

"The Realm of Duality appears to people in different ways," Loni says. "When a person is unable to cross over, the Realm becomes di place that was the most impactful to them. The place that sits deep in their hearts."

"Your home must've been the most important to you," Nellie says.

"Important," he says, tasting the word around in his mouth. "I wouldn't say that — home was sort of a touchy subject."

"Did you not feel at home here?" I ask.

"I probably felt more at home here than anywhere else," he replies. "But that doesn't mean it was all good."

He walks to the door and reaches for the doorknob; he opens the door slowly, and walks into the hallway. We follow him down the hallway as he makes his way to the living room — the walls hold framed pictures of him with an older man and woman that must be his parents. There's a picture with Jeremy and his parents with another boy. He's very handsome — must be six or seven years older than him — and smiles a sparkling smile. They're all smiling, except for his father — he remains unsmiling.

We come up to the living room, and the kitchen beside it — it's colourful, with dark brown furniture and a vibrant rug on the floor. The smell of jasmine permeates the air, with the smoke from an incense stick trailing upwards along the painted red walls. The man and woman from the pictures are here; the man working on a nightstand and the woman in the kitchen cooking a meal.

"Mom," Jeremy says breathily. "Dad."

"These were your parents?" I ask.

"Yeah," he replies.

"No child," Loni says. "Even after you've passed, they don't stop bein' yuh parents."

He nods somberly, walking up to his mother in the kitchen. They can't see us since this is just a memory — frozen in Jeremy's mind in a place where time cannot reach them. She has a kind smile, and is kneading away at marinating curry chicken in a bowl. She's tiny, but looks warm — and Jeremy looks at her fondly.

"My mom was the sweetest person ever. Even when I was acting like a dumb teenager, she would always be kind. People can be nice any day of the week, but she was kind; she cared deeply, not just surface level."

"She sounds like a great woman," Nellie says. He nods, then looks at his father.

"My dad, on the other hand, cared more about us continuing his legacy than us and our feelings."

"Us?" I ask. He hesitates, bowing his head.

"My brother and I," he replies. He confirms my suspicions about the other boy in the photos, and the look on his face implies something terrible happened.

"Did he die too?" I ask.

He nods somberly, his fingertips brushing together rapidly as he tries to conceal his sadness.

"He was the model child," he says. "Our parents loved him, all his teachers and the kids at school loved him; even if he pissed me off, I couldn't deny that I loved him too. Vijan — that was his name — he was just like Mom, kind and caring to everybody; but he was fun. He was social. Everyone in school liked him. He got good grades and wanted to be somebody, and got into all the good schools. He was five years older than me, so by the time I got to high school, there was already a reputation preceding me. I resented it because I never compared to my brother, and it started to make me resent him too."

He walks over to his father, and continues, "My parents were angry with me — said I was jealous of my Vijan. Maybe I was. More than anything, though, I was upset that I had a mold set for me before I even got a chance to decide how I wanted to fit in the world. There were all these expectations for how I should act, and I was nothing like how people expected me to be — and it made me mad when people got disappointed with me being who I am. Me."

Jeremy sits down beside his dad, leaning his arms on his knees. "One night, Vijan was back from school for a break, and the entire family was in this huge fight. Dad was yelling at me for being jealous of Vijan, I was yelling at him for not accepting me for me, Dad was yelling at Mom for being weak — for giving me a Western name, saying it's the reason I'm the way I am — and Mom and Vijan were trying to conserve the peace. That was what they did best, but Dad and I weren't having it. We were releasing all the pent up emotions we'd been harbouring for the sake of Mom and Vijan — and I blew up at Vijan in my anger. I said some pretty terrible things, things I still regret, and I knew I hurt him. I could see it on his face."

Jeremy starts to cry, his snarky demeanour now hiding behind a young boy's whimpering and cries. "He left to go for a drive," he says. "He had just bought a car he had been saving for years to get, and he drove away to clear his head. It was late, probably almost 1 a.m. in the morning, and Mom didn't want him out that late. But I didn't care — I was angry, and wasn't thinking straight. I just needed someone to be mad at. But it was raining and the roads were wet. And there was a trucker driving a semi — he was drinking. He tried to tell us in the courts that usually he could handle it, but his excuse was worthless. He rammed into my brother at 80 km/hr, and my brother died before the ambulances even got there."

"Oh my gosh," I say, covering my mouth with my hand.

"He was going places," Jeremy cries, now losing all control of his emotions. "He could've been somebody — he could've had a wife and a family, and lived a good life. But he died before that could happen; if it weren't for our fight, he never would've left. If it weren't for me, he would still be here!"

"Don't," Loni warns. "Don't go blamin' yuhself."

"How can't I?" he asks incredulously, looking up at her with tear-filled eyes. "Vijan never did anything to me except be a good big brother — whatever I resented about him setting an expectation for me didn't even have anything to do with him. It was all me; me and my insecurities. But I took it out on him — blamed him as if he was the reason for my loneliness and insecurity. I drove him away — I drove him away until he died."

"Listen here," Loni says, kneeling in front of him. "Your brother sounded like a good boy, an' it's a shame dat he died. But you *are not* di reason he died — it was di drunk driver dat took his life, Jeremy. Not you."

"But he never would've left if it weren't for me," Jeremy whimpers. "You don't understand how much it ruined our family — how heartbroken my parents were. My mother couldn't sleep. She couldn't eat. All she did was cry and walk around the house — and if she wasn't doing that she was cooking, cleaning, or doing something to keep her busy. And my dad got even angrier than before; all he did was blame me for something or complain about the way my mom did things. It ruined our family. I ruined our family."

"You had a teenage outburst," Nellie says, "that ended tragically. But the way it ended is not your fault. Your brother left to calm himself down — because he knew that what you were saying wasn't true. Because deep down he knew that you loved him, Jeremy. That you *love him*."

"There are ways dis universe works dat will neva seem fair, my child," Loni says. "But blamin' yuhself doesn't preserve his memory. It doesn't make you a betta person — it only harbours di pain, an' keeps you from restin'."

She grabs his hand and squeezes, rubbing the skin between his thumb and forefinger.

"Your brother is waitin' for you on di otha side — waitin' for you to finally stop beatin' yuhself up an' rest in peace. That was all he ever wanted for you when you were alive. That doesn't change wit' death."

"But what if he hates me?" Jeremy asks weakly.

"He doesn't," Nellie says, her voice catching in her throat. "He's your brother. He loves you. And he's waiting for you."

He looks at her as tears roll down his face — hunched over and clutching Loni's hand. My eyes begin to tear, and I walk over to him and sit on the arm of the couch. He looks up at me, and I look down with a teary smile.

"I think everyone in the real world has heard all of your jokes and quips," I joke. He chuckles wetly, wiping his nose with his sleeve. "I'm sure your brother would love to hear some of your jokes."

"He always was a great audience," Jeremy jokes, looking at me with a grateful smile. I've never helped someone transition over to rest in peace — I have no idea where to even begin — but I've gotten a feel for Jeremy.

I've got an idea for what speaks to him — and a little humour may have killed him, but it'll also help him.

"You're a snarky, sarcastic piece of work," I say. Loni kisses her teeth and Nellie looks at me incredulously. "But you've grown on me."

"Like a tumour," he says.

"No," I laugh. "More like a fond memory. You may be annoying, but I'll always think of you fondly. And I know you think you're responsible for his death, but you need to let it go, dude. You are not the reason for all the pain that's been caused — and you weren't a mistake or hindrance. You were a breath of fresh air that not everyone bothered to take in. Not even yourself. But I think it's time; let it go, and let you be you without apology."

He nods, looking into space as he thinks. Loni stands up and pulls him up as well, walking him towards the front door.

"You've spent enough time trapped in your own cage in di real world," Loni says. She opens the door, and a light shines in — not quite gold, not quite white, not quite like any colour I've ever seen before. The best way I could describe it is warmth; visible warmth and peace before my eyes. Suddenly, a figure appears in the light — a tall man standing on the other side. He walks forward, and the light pulls from his smiling face. Jeremy's eyes widen and he runs forward, launching forward to hug his brother.

"Oh my God," Jeremy says. "Vijan, Oh my God."

Vijan laughs, a deep hearty laugh booming from his chest. "Hey, little bro," he says, rocking him side to side. "Good to see you." Jeremy pulls away and Vijan is smiling, but suddenly smacks him up the backside of his head.

"What took you so long?" Vijan asks. "You seriously telling me you needed 16 years to get here? Dude, you're always late!"

"How was I supposed to know I would be stuck in that school for that long?" Jeremy asks incredulously. "You know I thought all this stuff didn't exist — I thought I'd just cease to exist. Imagine my surprise when I'm stuck in limbo for over a decade."

"Only you would get stuck in school; the one place you disliked the most," Vijan jokes. Jeremy rolls his eyes, but Vijan laughs and throws his arm around his neck.

"I've been waiting for you man," Vijan says. "I've been watching you stuck for 16 years, just waiting for you to move on. Life after death... it's so freeing. It's impossible to describe the feeling without experiencing it

— and it's nothing like we've ever felt. I wanted to help you man, to bring you to rest with me, but you had to get here on your own. But you kept beating yourself over my death — even though it wasn't your fault, man. I wish you had stopped blaming yourself and making yourself suffer — you could've laid yourself to rest a long time ago."

"Well," Jeremy says wetly, "I'm here now."

"And I couldn't be happier," Vijan says. He sees us standing there and gives us a grateful smile.

"Thank you," he says, then looks directly at me. "Thank you for helping my brother."

"Of course," I say. He smiles wider, a charming smile, and I impulsively smile back. I walk up to Jeremy, knowing this is the last I'll see him for, hopefully, a very long time.

"It was nice knowing you," I say. My lip quivers, and he gives me a look.

"C'mon, Freeman," he says. "You seriously gonna give me the waterworks? I didn't think that was your style."

"I'm fluid," I say wetly. He laughs, then goes quiet — we look at each other silently, then he reaches down to hug me. No smokescreen, no snarky facade — he hugs me deeply, and I sink into his embrace.

"Thank you," he says. "I wouldn't be here without you, and I can't thank you enough."

"You don't have to thank me," I say.

"Us either," Loni says, with Nellie smiling in agreement. "This is your time, child. We bid you rest, an' a life of peace in the hereafter."

He smiles and goes in to hug her — she chuckles her hearty chuckle and hugs him, patting his back. He stands up and turns to Nellie; she cocks her eyebrow and smirks at him.

"And here I thought you weren't into hugs," she jokes.

"I'm fluid," he jokes, and I smile. He hugs her, and she rocks him side to side. He stands up and looks at his parents behind us; his mother still peacefully cooking, and his father busy with his work.

"What about them?" Jeremy asks. "I never found out what happened after they divorced, and that was 14 years ago."

"That's not our problem anymore, bro," Vijan says — Jeremy turns to him, with a boyish look on his face. Vijan continues, "They're adults; what they choose to do with their lives is their business. We can't make ourselves fret over their choices — whether because of us or not."

"But I need to know what happened to them after their divorce — I only found out through gossip the teachers were spreading in their lounge. I have no idea how their lives have turned out since then."

Vijan puts his hands on Jeremy's shoulders, looking at him with a kind smile. "Dad remarried, and has two daughters with a woman who's just like mom. She's nice, and he's good to her. Mom went back to school, and she's teaching lessons to students back in her village. She's happy — she's making her own money, lives with her sister and her family, and she prays for us often. But she believes that we're at rest. And now, that's true for the both of us."

"How do you know all this?" Jeremy asks.

"I can't waste my breath spoiling all the surprises, now can I?" Vijan asks joyfully. "Why don't you come and see for yourself?"

Jeremy smiles warily at first, but soon joins his brother's side. Vijan throws his arm over his shoulder, and Jeremy throws all his inhibitions away. They walk towards the open door, the warm light welcoming them in. Jeremy stops just at the doorway and breathes in deeply, and it's almost as if all his pain that was held in his body releases — dissolving away in the light. He turns around, and his face has a peace that I've yet to see on anyone — that I'm surprised to see on his. It brings a glow to his face that shines from within him, and he's more beautiful than anything I've ever seen. He smiles at me gratefully, and I place my hand over my heart, smiling back. He gives one last smirk and a wave to Loni and Nellie, before Vijan throws his arm once again over Jeremy's shoulder, and they walk into the after.

CHAPTER SIXTEEN

My vision goes black for a second before I open my eyes abruptly, inhaling sharply. I open my eyes to the diner basement, and Michael looks down at us with crossed arms and a worried expression. His face eases as he sees me open my eyes, and he exhales a breath he'd been holding in for, I'm assuming, a very long time.

"Oh thank God," he says. "I was worried you were going into a coma."

"No, my child," Loni says with a chuckle. "Very slim chance of dat 'appenin'."

"Jeremy's gone?" Michael asks. "He's crossed over? After we left the school, I couldn't see him anymore."

"Yeah," I reply. "He's gone. He's resting in peace with his brother."

"His brother?" I nod, with a sad smile on my face. He nods, smiling also — glad that Jeremy can now be at peace.

"Well," Loni says, "now dat that's sorted, I'll jus' grab my things an' we'll get outta here." She starts going to-and-fro the shelves and tables, packing books and vials in a brown leather satchel.

"What a day," Michael says breathily. "I've never been assaulted with so much new information at once like this; not even information, an *entire world* within this one that I never knew existed. This is *a lot*."

"You're telling me?" I ask rhetorically. "Just this morning I was escaping my assaulter, but that seems like a lifetime ago."

"Oh my goodness," Nellie exclaims. "I'm so sorry, Mama. Can you believe I actually forgot about that?"

"I don't blame you," I reply. "I almost did too. But the pain is still there, so it's kind of hard to forget."

Nellie looks at me with sympathy, and I wave my hand to let it be. But she grabs my hand and rubs the skin between my thumb and forefinger.

"I'm so sorry that happened to you, Mama. If I had known where you were, entire armies couldn't stop me from saving you."

"I know Nel," I reply, pulling her in for a hug. "It's not like you could've known — even I didn't know where I was 'til I woke up, or what had happened afterwards. There's no point in harping on the could've-beens. But if you can teach me that little 'dream-visiting' trick of yours, I'll secure myself some much-needed justice."

"That sounds like a plan," Nellie says with a smile.

"Alright," Loni says, now laden with three bags strewn around her, "let's get out of here."

Michael chuckles, walking over to help Loni with a heavy paisley bag. "Here, let me grab one."

"And me," I add in, grabbing the green canvas satchel.

"Oh, thank you," she breathes, giving us a kind smile. We walk back up the stairs — Michael stays on the step for a moment, looking at the basement below and breathing it in, before the lights dim and cast the space in darkness. We quietly make our way out of the closet and close the hatch door below. Ray comes out of the cooler and sees us, a confused look on his face.

"Were you all in there?" he asks. "That's kind of a tight fit, ain't it?"

"Oh, we were just messing around, Ray," Nellie says with a smile. She puts her hand on his shoulder, giving him a sweet smile. "But we have to get going now. I'm glad I got to see you before we leave. See you around."

"Aight, Nel," he says, with a perplexed smile. "I'll be seein' you."

Loni squeezes his shoulder and they smile at each other, and he and Michael give each other the nod. I go up to him and he smiles at me — his broad face stretches even farther as his smile overtakes him, and he looks down at me with that jovial nature that I've come to associate with him. For all the talking he does, I'm really going to miss this man. I reach in for a hug, tucking my face into his meaty neck, pressing against his extended belly.

"See you around, Ray," I say. He chuckles, patting me on the back.

"Man, you women are *emotional today*, huh? I'll see you later, baby girl."

He chuckles and shakes his head, grabbing a tub of ice cream to bring to the freezer underneath the front counter. I follow slowly behind him — looking at his shuffling walk as he pushes through the swinging door, greeting the new slew of customers. Nellie is waiting at the door, with Loni and Michael already by the car. Michael is putting her bags in the trunk while Loni is looking at her diner, with an indescribable look on her face. I walk towards her slowly, looking at the people in their booths eating as I walk by. I look at my after-school spot — this homey little diner in the heart of my city. Its vibrant walls and vibrant people bringing life to the spot, giving me breath to last when I leave. I close my eyes and listen to the voice of Buju Banton through the speakers, his gritty voice making my soul sway. Nellie puts her hand on my shoulder and I open my eyes — she looks at me with a knowing smile, gently guiding me to the door.

"C'mon, Mama," she says. "It's time to go."

I nod reluctantly and walk with her to the car — Loni sits in the front seat and I join Michael in the back. Nellie takes a deep breath, looking at the diner for a few moments before she starts the car and pulls out of the parking lot.

We sit in silence as we drive down the road that we've always driven down; but with a melancholy undertone. The apartment buildings that once looked like a slum to me, run-down and stacked close together, now look like beautiful blocks of Jenga. I look at the businesses I've come to recognize as we drive by, burning it into my brain so that I never forget them. The beauty salon and barbershop, now closed for the weekend — a shame, I'd like to see them one last time.

We turn on our street and come into our driveway — Ms. Dell's porch swing is empty, but a light is on in the kitchen. We open the doors and help Loni bring the bags into the house, taking our shoes off at the door and dropping them by the door. We all stand there, just looking at each other, and then, for no reason at all, Nellie starts laughing. Michael and I look at her confused, and Loni gives her a raised eyebrow. Nellie starts chuckling low, then hunching over in uproarious laughter.

"Am I missing something?" Michael asks.

"I'm with you there," I say, looking at Nellie with her face screwed in laughter.

"Oh," she says, trying to speak through laughs, "Oh, I just have to laugh. This whole day — Ha! It's been a roller coaster! This morning I thought you were dead in a ditch somewhere. But no, oh no, that's not it at all — you were just assaulted, kidnapped and violated. And not only did you come back to me violated and beaten within an inch of your life, you almost got killed for the second time within 24 hours by the cult that's been hunting us since birth. Ha!"

"Nellie," Loni says slowly, as Nellie continues to laugh. "Are you alright?"

"Oh! Oh, but that's not even it," Nellie says wide-eyed, eyes teary as she continues to laugh. "Then we discovered that Jamila's uncovered another power amidst all of this, which brought us right back into the Toubabs hands, and they almost captured us! Am I missing anything?"

We're silent for a moment, but then I add in, "Well, now Michael knows everything about us — which was the very thing you were trying to avoid."

She hoots in laughter — and despite the seriousness of the situation, I start laughing too. Loni chuckles at our silly laughter, and Michael joins along with us. We laugh for quite a while — at the ridiculousness of the day, the sheer audacity of it. Finally, we start to settle down, and scatter.

"Loni," Nellie says. "You can sleep on the air mattress with Jamila. I'll sleep on a fluffy blanket on the floor."

"Oh, Nel, I couldn't ask you tuh do dat," Loni objects.

"No, Loni, I insist. Don't worry about it, I'll survive on the floor for one night." Loni smiles and squeezes Nellie's hand in gratitude and Nellie smiles, shaking Loni away.

Suddenly, we hear Ms. Dell's voice near the kitchen door, calling Michael from the alleyway.

"Michael, is that you?" she asks.

"Yeah, Nana," he yells back, looking at me with a worried grimace. I return it, sympathetic for the earful he's about to receive. "Could you come with me? She yells at me less when there's company around."

"Sure," I say laughing. We walk through the kitchen side-door, and Ms. Dell's already standing in their doorway with her hands bent on her hips. Oh, he's in deep trouble.

"Michael Jermaine Smith," she exclaims. I have to hide my laugh behind my hand, and Michael notices and cuts his eye at me. She continues, "Where have you been? You've been gone all day without tellin' me where you going. You vex me, child!"

Oh, he really is in trouble — Ms. Dell's accent rarely comes out, and only slips into her Patois when she's mad. And she's *mad*.

"I know, Nana, I'm sorry."

"Sorry can't buy soldier lorry," she replies instantaneously. "I've been callin' and textin' you all day — and you know I don't like to use that smartphone you made me get. Kept saying I'd reach you faster and you didn't even pick up or answer any of the texts!"

"Okay, Nana, I'm sorry! But I'm here now, okay? What's so life-and-death that you needed to tell me?"

"That we have company," she says. From behind her a tall figure emerges from the kitchen, and walks down the hall towards us. As the overhead light passes over his face, my stomach sinks to the floor and Michael's face goes slack. Churchill gives us a mechanically polite smile and stands behind Ms. Dell — his stature looming over Ms. Dell, making her seem so small compared to him.

"Hello, children," he says. He speaks politely, but I know his choice of words is no coincidence. "Glad to see you've gotten home safely."

"Nana," Michael says tensely, "what is he doing here?"

"Oh, Mr. Churchill here is from the school board," she replies. "He came by to tell me that you won an award for Mathematical excellence! He said you're among the top students in the country, and you won a scholarship for the school of your choice. I'm so proud of you baby!"

"He's from the school board?" he asks. "And he came by on a weekend? I don't think that's customary."

"Well," Churchill interjects, "a young man with your accomplishment warrants exception, Mr. Smith." He smiles at us; his robotic, unnatural smile.

"Surely you could've called," I say tightly. "Or sent an email. I see no reason to come to his home on a weekend."

"Jamila," Ms. Dell scolds. "That's not the way you talk to adults."

"Oh, it's quite alright, Ms. Smith," Churchill says. "But, Ms. Freeman, your friend here is quite an exceptional young man. His intelligence and proficiency in mathematics will take him far in life. If he takes the right routes, and goes in the right direction, he could lead a successful career and a happy life. I just came to let his grandmother know of his opportunities — he has a lot of potential, and it would be a shame to not take advantage of his options."

"How do you mean?" he asks. Churchill looks at him, the smile still on his face but with cold eyes.

"Well, I just mean the risks of making a mistake going the wrong path," he replies. "Following the wrong people. It could have drastic repercussions on your future. On your life. I just came by to remind your grandmother that that doesn't have to be the case — you have options, a life waiting for you. And I truly hope you take advantage of it while it's here — because it may not be around forever. Not to mention, young men of your demographic rarely make it in this field; from what I understand, your parents were quite the mathematicians as well."

"Oh, his mother and father were so smart," Ms. Dell says with a smile. "And my Michael is just like them."

"I can imagine," he says with a smile. "Well, I'm sure your grandmother would love to see you follow in your parents' footsteps. Hopefully not their entire life — but again, that all depends on you."

The air leaves my lungs, and Michael's hands start shaking. Ms. Dell looks at Churchill curiously as Churchill fixes his jacket, and steps into the alleyway. He's about to say something, but then stops when he sees something behind me. I look behind me to see Nellie and Loni, standing firm, with equally firm faces.

"Well, I must be off," he says. "But I do hope you take my advice into consideration, Michael." He looks at me, a polite look on his face but expression void in his eyes.

"And I hope to see you again, Ms. Freeman. Your talents have not evaded us, and I truly hope they can be put to good use."

"Her talents will be her business," Nellie says firmly, "and hers alone."

"Well, only time will tell."

He looks at Nellie silently, and Nellie just returns his look with an unmoving one of her own. Churchill finally relents and nods his head to Ms. Dell in farewell, walking down the alleyway and into the street. My breath finally returns to me, although shaky, and Michael stares at the spot where Churchill was.

"Oh my God," he mutters. He repeats, "Shit, shit, shit —"

"Michael Jermaine Smith," Ms. Dell scolds. "We do not use that kind of language in this house!"

"I'm not in the house," he says absentmindedly. Ms. Dell cocks her eyebrow at his audacity, but he's too freaked out to care.

"Jamila, that was a threat," he says shakily. "He came to my house, he knows where I live!"

"I know, Oh my God, I know," I reply, freaking out.

"What if he tries to hurt me?" he asks. "He basically threatened to end my future — hell, he threatened to end my life! He knew about my parents, he was with Nana alone. Nana, Jamila! He could've hurt her!"

"Ay, ay, ay, what are you on about?" Ms. Dell asks.

"That man," Nellie says, "is not someone to be trusted."

"He seemed like a good man to me," she replies.

"Many of those types of men do," Loni says, walking into the alleyway to Ms. Dell's side. "But it's jus' a mask to hide the ugliness underneath. He's one of them, Dell."

"One of those Toubab men that are hunting you?" Ms. Dell asks, as Loni nods to confirm. Nellie, Michael, and I look at each other in bewilderment then to Loni and Ms. Dell.

"Wait a minute," Michael says, waving his hands in the air. "You knew about all this?"

"Well, yes," Ms. Dell says nonchalantly. "Loni and I have been friends for over 30 years — I was bound to find out eventually."

"It's damn near impossible to keep anythin' from dis one," Loni says with a chuckle.

"Even though you tried," Ms. Dell says with a laugh. "You failed miserably."

Ms. Dell and Loni laugh, while we just continue to look at them in astonishment. Michael puts his hands on his hips, looking at Ms. Dell, as he imitates her.

"Let me get this straight," he says. "You knew about this the whole time? About Bastets and Toubabs and their whole world?"

"Yes, Michael," she says exasperatedly. "Honestly, with your smart brain, I think you'd keep up faster."

"But you told me not to say anything to anyone," I say to Loni. "And Ms. Dell's known this entire time? Did she know that I was a Bastet?"

"Have you started getting powers?" Ms. Dell asks me. "I knew Loni, Nellie and your mother were Bastets, but I didn't know you were too. But it makes sense — genetics, after all."

"Wait, you knew that Keba and I were Bastets this whole time?" Nellie asks incredulously.

"Well, of course, dear," she replies. "You think I'd be living next to women with superhuman powers and I wouldn't know about it? Loni was smart enough to tell me."

"After I made sure she wouldn't tell anyone else," Loni explains. "She's got a tongue that fixes for gossip — I would've neva told her our secret without knowin' dat she wouldn't betray us."

"You knew all this time," Michael mutters, *"and you didn't tell me?* I'm your grandson! And Jamila's my best friend."

"Yes, and even she didn't tell you," Ms. Dell says, flicking his mouth. "One thing you inherited from me is your flapping lips — you can't keep a secret to save your life, child."

"Why does everybody keep saying that?" he asks sheepishly.

"Because it's true," we all exclaim. He rolls his eyes and waves us off, crossing his arms and pouting.

"Michael's right," Loni says. "Churchill came here to threaten Michael — an' you too, Dell. Churchill is one of di most dangerous men among di Toubabs. He was jus' a boy when he started huntin' Bastets — didn't even aave facial hair yet. But from then until now, he's the same wretched tyrant. There've been years of whispers from di grapevine mentionin' him — wherever Churchill was, death or ruin followed. He came here to set Michael straight — to scare him into bein' quiet, or to face di consequences."

"What consequences?" Michael asks warily.

"Jus' because you're not a Bastet doesn't mean you're not a threat to dem," Loni says. "Anyone besides dem and Bastets knowin' about dis world, about our powas, is one too many."

"It's like a breach of security," Nellie says. "One unstable cog in the system could lead to the whole system collapsing, even if the cog is unaware of the role they play in this."

"What role would that be?"

"Upholdin' their idea of a stable society," Loni responds. "Upstanding citizens dat work, pay their taxes, provide for their families, participate in dis society — without question or objection to their involvement in it. To know about dis world would be to question if di way dis society works is effective, an' if it's even worth it."

"You find out about us, then it leads to you finding out about them, and then their veil of ambiguity falls," Nellie says. "If enough people knew about them, there would be riots in the streets — they're in *everything*. The police, the army, the government, our financial systems — they act as if they're facilitating a society of free will and democracy, but narcissism runs rampant through that cult and parades itself as benevolence. That goes against the morals of modern society they claim to have built, but they figure if no one knows about their real involvement, they can keep on keeping on."

"Jus' you knowin' puts a target on yuh back," Loni says. "They've paid people off with hush money and bribes fah years to keep dem quiet

Bastet's Legacy

— even then, dey always keep an eye on our allies, or people who've jus' figured it out. If they still think about talkin', di Toubabs ruin dem. Dey get dem fired from their jobs, stage affairs to end their marriages, even stage their deaths."

"But I thought you were safe from the Toubabs, Loni," Ms. Dell says. "You said you escaped, you said you were safe."

"Safety is relative for us," I say.

"Well," Ms. Dell says worrisomely, "what are we going to do? If they know that Michael and I know, and where we live, then we're not safe either."

"No," Loni says. "You're in danger now."

"I don't wanna die," Michael says fearfully.

"You're not going to die," I say firmly.

"No, sweetie," Loni replies. "You're coming with us."

We all look at her surprised, and Ms. Dell raises her eyebrow.

"Come with you where? Where are you going?" she asks incredulously. Loni cocks her head, motioning for us to move this conversation inside. We congregate in the kitchen, as we fill Ms. Dell in.

"We're goin' to Jamaica," Loni says.

"Jamaica?" Ms. Dell repeats.

"Yes, Jamaica. That's what me ah say," Loni replies.

"When are you going?"

"Tomorrow."

"*Tomorrow?*"

"Yes, Dell! Stop repeatin' me, man!"

"Sorry, sorry," she apologizes. "Why are you going to Jamaica tomorrow?"

"They've found us, Ms. Dell," Nellie replies. "They already tried to take Jamila when she was in the hospital — they're after her, and we have to lay low. We have to leave the country, and stay away until it's safe to come back, which may be never."

"So you were jus' goin' to leave without tellin' me goodbye?" she asks incredulously.

"Dell, we can't have anyone knowin' our plans," Loni explains. "If we didn't have to tell you we were leavin', then you wouldn't aave known where we were goin'. But now dat you're on Churchill's radar, you aave to come wit' us."

"But won't they be in more danger if they're with us?" I ask.

"They're in danger regardless," Nellie replies. "But at least with us, we can protect them."

"To Jamaica?" Ms. Dell asks. "I can't come with you to Jamaica — and *tomorrow*? No, no, no, that's too short notice. I have a prayer meeting at the church on Wednesday, and I have to organize the food bank for this Friday —"

"Ms. Dell," I interject, "I'm sure there are other deaconesses that can take over for you."

"No, baby girl, I'm the head deaconess. Without me that place would fall apart. Not to mention Michael's still in school — winter break isn't for another three weeks, and he can't just leave school on a whim, with no explanation."

"You don't aave a choice," Loni replies. "You eitha come wit' us an' stay alive, or stay behind an' be at di mercy of di Toubabs. And dey not merciful, Dell."

Ms. Dell shakes her head, inhaling deeply. "I can't just drop everything on a whim and leave. How long will we be gone for? What do I even bring? Where will we be staying? Is it nice enough to bring my church dresses, or just casual wear? And is there even a church nearby? Oh, Loni, I have to attend Sunday service —"

"For cryin' out loud, Dell! Even Jamila didn't ask all of these questions, an' she's di one in more danger. Jus' tell people you're goin' on a much-needed vacation an' aren't sure when you'll be comin' back. You can tell Michael's teachers dat he'll submit his assignments through email — but you aave to use an anonymous email for dat, okay Michael?"

"Wait, wait, wait," he says, chuckling nervously as he shakes his head. "I'm still trying to process the fact that now we're leaving. This morning I thought I was never going to see you guys again because you had to go into hiding, and now we're going into hiding too?"

"You won't have to hide out for very long," Nellie reassures. "Just a few weeks to get Churchill and the other Toubabs off your back. When you come back, they'll still be watching you, but they'll be too preoccupied trying to find us. You'll feign curiosity, mention how weird it is that we left without saying goodbye, and how you have no idea where we could've gone. I know you can lie, so you'll do it like your life depends on it — because it does. I should have enough points left to get you a ticket, and we'll get you on a separate flight before ours to avoid suspicion."

"Getting a plane ticket on such short notice is going to be expensive," Ms. Dell complains.

"Well, consider dis payback for damagin' my car in '95," Loni says with a smirk. "Put me out $700 — dat should cover it, don't yuh think?" Ms. Dell kisses her teeth, but smiles anyway.

"Wait, so this is happening," Michael says anxiously. "We're leaving tomorrow."

"Yeah," Nellie replies. "We leave tomorrow."

I make sure the air mattress is properly filled up, closing the plug quickly so no air escapes. The sun had set about a few hours ago, with only two hours left in the day. The chill in the air got worse as the day turned into night, so we all put on sweats to keep warm. Nellie's wearing her signature U of T sweater with sweatpants, and I'm wearing a thick grey sweater with matching pants. Loni wraps her cardigan tighter, and drinks a cup of tea, and Michael and Ms. Dell went to their house to get their affairs in order. Nellie came in not too long ago from next door, and Loni just finished helping tape up the last of the boxes. Nellie was able to get a free ticket for Michael with her points, and he and Ms. Dell will be on a flight leaving 45 minutes before us — that is, of course, if everything goes according to schedule, which never happens nowadays. We're going to drive our car to Ray's and take separate Ubers from there, and use wireless headphones to keep in touch at the airport. Michael is anxious — and I don't blame him — while Ms. Dell is just complaining about how inconvenient all of this is. Mind you, I completely understand — who would think they'd have to uproot their lives, and then ask the same of their neighbours because they happened to be aware of something that they shouldn't be? But with Ms. Dell's particular brand of eccentricity, even I'm getting annoyed by her complaints at this point. After all, she can come back home after a few weeks and not have to worry all that much of her life being in danger — I, on the other hand, will be on the run for the rest of my life. This cult, this hindrance, decided that they have the right to dictate what happens with my life, and now I'm running from them. I will always be running from them. The distress rises within me, until it feels like I can't breathe. I need to get some space — I need to be alone.

"I'm going to finish packing up my room," I say to Loni. She nods and I head to my room. I slowly open the door to my almost empty room — the hardwood floor that I haven't seen in years shines in greeting, and all my furniture is sold or stored away. The only thing left is a suitcase and the Novelfall. I look at it fondly, grazing my fingertips along the books, making them sway while suspended in the air. I look up at the different coloured ribbons: ruby red, emerald green, sapphire blue, and royal purple, and their tacks in the ceiling. These books got me through a lot, and allowed me to escape into another world — who would've thought I'd need that escape now more than ever?

I reach up to *A Wrinkle in Time*, standing on my tiptoes to pull the tack from the ceiling — it's just out of my grasp, and for some reason, I start to cry. I claw for the tack, coming short a few inches, and my frustration makes me growl. The pain in my ribs resurface — whether it's phantom pain or real pain, I don't know — and my pelvis aches as I stretch beyond my capabilities. Hot tears blur my vision as I jump up once, but failing once again. I bow my head in defeat, trying my best to not hyperventilate. I don't know why I'm crying over a little height difference; of all the things to be crying about today, this should not be it. But maybe the events of today are catching up to me; the crack in my foundation, a silly piece of long ribbon. I look up at the ruby red ribbon, as it sways unbothered in the air.

"Kiss my ass," I say.

Suddenly a slender arm reaches past my face and pulls the tack from the ceiling with ease. I turn and see Michael looking at me, a smirk on his face.

"Now there's no need to be cussing out inanimate objects," he jokes. I chuckle, sniffling my nose and wiping away my tears.

"It was being a pesky bugger," I say. He looks at me with that expressionless face, nodding as if he understands.

"Well, why don't I take them down, and you pack them away?"

"Sounds like a plan," I reply with a small smile. He smiles back, and hands me the book. I look at it as he starts pulling the other books down, caressing my hand on the hardcover. I love this book, and memories of my mother and I reading it come back with fondness. Michael sees me staring at the book, and stacks the books he's pulled down in his hands.

"A Wrinkle in Time," he says. I nod silently, and he asks, "Your mom read that to you a lot, right?"

"Yeah," I reply. "It was one of our favourites — it made me fall in love with space travel and travelling through time. Other books that did the same thing made it interesting, but I never related to the main character. I never saw myself in them. When my mom read it to me, for the first time I saw myself — I saw an anxious, insecure girl, and I related. It's never the broken people that get to do great things, and for the first time, I believed they could. That I could."

Michael looks at me with kind eyes, and I try to brush off my monologue. "Yeah," I say. "It's one of my favourites."

"Well I never actually read it," I look at him wide-eyed, and he holds his hand up to stop me, "but it sounds like a great book. Maybe I'll read it sometime."

"Here," I say, giving it to him, "you can have it. Read it on the plane to pass the time — God knows I've read it enough times to last me a lifetime."

"You sure?" he asks.

"Yeah," I reply. "Just be careful with it."

"Of course," he replies with a smile. He hands me the books in his hand and I put them in a box. We get a good routine going for a minute or two — he takes the books down and wraps the ribbon around them, and I get them packed in the box — but there's a tension in the air that's impossible to deny.

"I'm scared," he says.

"I know," I reply. "Me too." We look at each other for a moment, I can see the childlike fear in his eyes, and I'm sure he can see it in mine.

"The Toubabs could find us in Jamaica," he says. "Churchill did mention having a lot of resources — and they must, if they've been hunting you guys for years and haven't let up."

"I was thinking the same thing. We could very well be walking into a trap and not even know it."

"Can't you see into the future?" he asks. "See if there will be Toubabs waiting for us?"

"I haven't been able to make a premonition happen on impulse yet. It just happens when it happens, I haven't been able to control it." His face falls in defeat. We stand there in silence, looking at the last few books hanging from their ribbons.

"Do you ever wonder," Michael starts, "if you'll ever get to live a normal life?"

"What do you mean?"

"Well, ever since you found out that you were a Bastet, you've had to perpetually live on the edge. These people are hunting you, and you have to constantly be looking over your shoulder, or wait for the ball to drop. I can only imagine how different life must seem to you — is there any point where it feels like you can rest?"

At first, I'm taken aback — although Loni and Nellie have been checking in with me, no one has really asked me something like this. It's expected that I have to deal with this, because of who I am — but Michael's question makes me see that just because I have to, doesn't mean I should.

"No," I reply truthfully. "It feels like I'm always trying to catch my breath. There are times when I forget about all this, but then I remember. And sometimes I can handle it — I go with the flow, and I feel like I can come out on the other side. But then I get this crippling doubt that I have no idea what I'm doing; which I don't, but I feel so low. So helpless. It's like a jolt — going from blissful forgetfulness to remembering that… that I'm not truly free."

"I've been thinking about that all day," Michael says.

"Really?" I ask. "Even during the bullet-infested chase at the school?"

He chuckles, replying, "Yeah, even then. I was just thinking to myself how stressed you must have been this entire time — I've been in my world with Taylor, thinking everything was fine. Meanwhile, your entire world is falling apart."

"That reminds me," I say. "What are you going to do about Taylor? You can't just leave for weeks without telling her."

"Isn't that what you were going to do?" he asks with a smirk. I grimace sheepishly, chuckling.

"Yeah, yeah it was. But I have to go into hiding for mine and your safety — you're coming back. You can go back to a normal life. Might as well make sure you have a girlfriend to come back to."

"I don't think life will ever be normal again," he says. "Just because I won't be on the run like you doesn't mean I'll forget everything you guys have told me. I can't go back to life as if nothing's changed — because *everything* has changed. Besides, don't you think telling her would put her at risk?"

"Not necessarily. She doesn't know about all of this. Just tell her you're going on vacation and you'll be back in time for the holidays."

"But will I be? We bought the tickets but didn't click a return date — I don't know when I'm coming back."

"Maybe not, but the fact is that you are coming back. There's no need to end something that you've been dreaming about for years; girls don't like to be ghosted."

He laughs, nodding his head. He looks handsome when he smiles. Michael is like a brother to me, but I can recognize beauty when I see it — he's grown into his face well over the years. He may still be a scrawny, lanky beanpole, but he's a handsome one.

"Okay, I'm going to call her," he says. I nod, and he heads into the hallway to make the call. I finish putting the books in the box, and they fit perfectly inside for me to close it. I caress the covers one last time, before closing the box and taping it up. I label Books on top, and bring it into the living room. I pass Michael who's now on the phone with Taylor, and drop the box off at the front door.

"Oh great," Nellie says, now settled on her blanket on the floor. "I'll leave those in the car when we drop it off at Ray's."

"Okay," I say.

"Your alarm set for 4:15?"

"Yeah, and another alarm set for 4:20 just in case." She smiles and chuckles.

"That's my girl." I smile, and Michael comes into the living room.

"Okay, all clear with Taylor," he says.

"Oh good, she understood?"

"Yeah," he replies with a smile. "I told her that I won't have good cell service, but I'll try to email her from my uncle's email when the Internet works. She said that's okay, and she can't wait for me to come back."

"Aw," I coo, making him roll his eyes. "You guys are like a cavity."

"Why would you say that?" Loni asks incredulously. Nellie chuckles, and Michael and I smile.

"She means that they're sweet," Nellie says. Loni's face changes as she understands, and we laugh at her naivety. "Now Michael, when you get to the airport, act as normal as possible. The Toubabs are watching us and you, so they might be on our tails when we get to the airport. They might have spies in the airport, so don't talk to anyone unnecessarily. Even if an employee wants to help you with your bags, insist that you can help yourself. They may drug you or notify the others of where you are."

"You really think they'll be waiting for us?" I ask.

"Toubabs are everywhere, Mama. If they have word that we're planning on leaving, they'll have infiltrated every point in the airport already. It's best to be cautious — so when you and Ms. Dell are going to your gate Michael, err on the side of caution."

"Alright, I will," he says. "I'll meet you guys at your car at 4:45."

"Sounds like a plan," I say. He gives me a quick side hug, rubbing my head with a devious smile, and walks through the kitchen door.

"Alright, Mama," Nellie says. "Try to get some sleep, you need your rest for tomorrow. We won't have any time to make breakfast so we'll have to grab something at the airport when we get through security."

"Are you sure those fakes will work? What about Loni?"

"Don't worry dear," Loni says. "I've got enough fakes for a dozen people — they work jus' fine."

"And the guy who got these for us has a good reputation," Nellie says. "Don't worry, they'll work." I nod, slipping under the covers beside Loni. Nellie turns off the light switch, and the room becomes shrouded in darkness. After a while, my eyes adjust to the darkness, and the little light the streetlights provide allow me to vaguely see shapes in the dark.

I close my eyes and take a deep breath, trying my best to relax and slow my breathing. Loni breathes deeper and slower, as she's drifting off slowly. Careful to not take too much space, I curl over to the side to make room for Loni — it's uncomfortable, and for a while, I can't seem to fall asleep.

"Can't fall asleep?" Nellie asks quietly.

"No," I reply defeatedly. "Too nervous."

She doesn't respond; she's silent, and for a minute I think she's fallen asleep too, until she says something.

"I know that all of this isn't easy for you," she says. "You're young — this is the last thing you should be worried about right now. You should be worried about tests, and college applications, and boys. But you have to take on all this responsibility, with no guarantee you'll ever get to relax."

"It's okay," I respond reflexively.

"No, Mama, it's not okay. It's anything but. Despite that, I want you to know that I'm proud of you."

"Really?" I ask. "I thought I would have driven you and Loni mad by now; I feel like I've done nothing but complain."

"Oh, there's definitely been plenty of that," she laughs. "But you've been *trying*. And look at what it's gotten you — already you've got such a handle on your powers with the time flow, and you've taken well to the potions and spells Loni has taught you."

"Well, I haven't had a chance to practice any of them yet, but I do like them. Feels like I'm in wizard school or something."

She laughs, saying, "I figured you'd think that. Even when you're not enjoying yourself though, you manage to push through. You try to deal with it until it doesn't become hard anymore. You remind me of your mother in that way."

"Yeah?"

"Oh yeah. Sometimes I just look at you and I catch myself almost saying her name."

"But I look nothing like her."

"Oh that's not true," she says. "You have her smile, and her laugh. Every time I hear you laugh, I swear it's like Keba's laughing through you. And you have so much of her spirit in you. That fire and grit you have when you're passionate about something is all her. A lot of things are learned, but many things are inherited, Mama. And with our kind, the Bastets, it's two sides of the same coin."

I think about what she's saying; there are times where people that knew my mother say I remind them of her. It always catches me off guard, because people aren't just seeing her when they see me. They see my mother's legacy, and how it survives through me.

"Can I confess something?" I ask.

"Of course, Mama."

I hesitate for a moment, before confessing, "I've thought less about Mom over these past few weeks than I've ever not thought about her since she died."

"Really?" Nellie asks surprised.

"Yeah. I still think about her — when I feel overwhelmed or insecure about mastering my powers. But even when I do think about her, I don't get that crippling sadness that I used to feel. And I stopped having the jungle dreams."

"Well, of course," Nellie says quietly. "Now you know what it means — there's no reason for you to have them anymore when they've taught the lesson it needed you to learn."

"I know," I say, slowly leading up to something. "I guess now that I don't have them anymore... I'm kind of sad. I had them for so long — and I knew it was because of the loss I was feeling from losing Mom. It was the one thing I had left of her, the one thing that stopped me from knowing all of this and maintaining some sort of normalcy — even though it was because of my sadness. And I miss it."

"Well," Nellie says. "You know that you can talk to her, you have the gift of being able to see her in the Realm. I was never able to do that, and to this day, I still carry that pain with me. Of not being able to say goodbye."

"Well, maybe you can now," I say. I hear her turn her head towards me, and see her faintly looking at me in the darkness. "You were beside yourself with grief — maybe that's what was stopping you from seeing her."

"I blamed myself," she says. "Still do sometimes."

"Yeah, but Nel, you know it wasn't your fault, right? You're a nurse, you're trained in the medical profession. You trusted the procedure because it had been done hundreds of times before without casualties."

"Yes, but she knew something was wrong," she says thickly. "She knew something bad was going to happen. But I don't have the powers of premonition. I didn't see it coming."

"It's not your fault that you weren't able to see," I say.

"But it was my fault that I didn't choose to listen."

I'm at a loss of what to say; Nellie's a grown woman, and Jamaican women are stuck in their ways. Even if that way leads to a self-deprecating life. Nellie's always been strong — a tiny woman with enough power in her punch to rival that of ten men. But even she has regrets. Even she has insecurities.

"There's no point in humming and hawing over the could've-beens," I say. "And I know Mom wouldn't blame you for her passing — and that's the truth, Nel. She's with the rest of her ancestors, watching over us and protecting us from what she can. Surely she wouldn't be able to do that if she was holding a grudge over you. So maybe you should stop beating yourself up over it, because I know she doesn't hold anything against you."

Nellie looks up at the ceiling and a small, sad smile rises on her face. She looks at me with a sad, yet playful expression.

"Oh, look at you giving me the pep talk," she jokes. "When did you become so wise?"

"I've always been this way," I say. "A wise, old, sage, in an adolescent's body."

She chuckles, turning her head back to look at the ceiling.

"Yes. That you are. Thank you, Mama."

"Anytime."

I close my eyes, with a smile on my face. I don't know what will happen tomorrow, or the tomorrows after that. Who knows what will be waiting for us when we get to Jamaica? My breathing slows, and my thoughts dissolve in the darkness, and the worries and questions in the air blow away as I fall deeper into slumber.

We arrive at the airport at 5:03 in the morning — the darkness has its hold on the sky, and the frigid cold sinks its teeth into my bones. I woke up wired and ready to go — despite falling asleep, my anxiety woke me up before the alarm went off. We ended up calling a cab, to make sure no electronic trail could lead the Toubabs to track us to the airport. Ray was less than happy that we arrived at his house so early, but he was going to get up soon anyway to open up the diner. We parked the car in his garage and called the taxis from there. I hugged him extra tight, getting lost in his fat as he hugged me back, and burned the image of his chubby smile in my brain. The ride was quick and quiet, Loni and Nellie too lost in their thoughts, and me too anxious, for us to bother speaking. We pay the tired driver and tip him handsomely — happy with his bonus, he hops out of the car and helps us with our bags. I pull the baseball hat lower down on my head and zip up my jacket as I grab a cart. Michael and Ms. Dell left in their cab well before we did, so they should already be past airport security and waiting at their gate. Once we're through airport security, the plan is for me to call Michael with my wireless headphones and communicate the next steps. The cab driver kindly loads our bags onto the cart and bids us farewell. Nellie shivers in her thick hoodie, not enough to protect her in the cold, and bounces lightly on her toes. Loni's wearing diva-sized sunglasses and a colourful turban, and I look at her comical outfit.

"Really, Loni? Did you have to wear sunglasses? *It's not even light out.*"

"And? It'll be a better disguise than dat ratty hat you got on top of yuh head."

"Alright, alright ladies," Nellie says. "Settle down. Let's focus on getting ourselves on the plane."

I sheepishly walk to the cart, while Loni walks haughtily forward. I start pushing, struggling to catch up to Nellie and Loni ahead of me. We walk into Terminal 1, and head to the Caribbean Airlines section. The airport is relatively empty, with off-season upon us, and many people still not choosing to fly from the recent pandemic. To our left is a wall of glass from floor to ceiling, separating the drop-off zone from the deserted terminal entrance. Shops of convenience stores, a Tim Hortons, a currency exchange kiosk, and other businesses stand to our left as we walk further in. A businessman talks on the phone as he walks by, and I briefly catch a heated conversation about stocks that have plummeted in the oil sector. A mother with her child and stroller approaches — the mother tries to calm down her crying son who walks beside her, evidently not happy about having to walk. A pilot with his flight attendant companion walks by; the woman smiling coyly as the pilot flirts shamelessly with her. We walk towards a kiosk and pull out the pouch with our fake IDs. Nellie takes a deep breath and starts to check us in. Luckily, everything's going smoothly — we pay for our luggage, print off our tickets, and our baggage tags. Loni keeps her big paisley bag as a carry-on, while I have my backpack and Nellie her large tote bag. Nellie moves to put the baggage tags on our luggage, but is struggling with the tape. A station agent notices her struggling and makes her way over to us.

She smiles kindly and reaches to take the baggage tags. "Can I help you with that?"

"Oh," Nellie says surprised. "There's no need, I can do it."

"Oh, it's not a bother at all, I know these stickers can be pesky. Besides," she says with a smile, "I have nothing else to do so early in the morning."

"Oh, well sure, thank you." The employee takes the baggage tags from Nellie's hand, deftly removing the stickers and taping the tag around the luggage handles. I pull my hat further down and keep my eye on her. She seems uninvolved enough — surely she's not a Toubab.

"There," she says standing up. "Now let's get them onto the luggage drop-off."

"Oh, I can handle that, thank you so much," Nellie says kindly, ending their exchange. We walk towards the moving ramp and haul our bags on. After they disappear behind the clear curtains, we head for airport security. I unzip my jacket as I feel warm, and my hands start to fidget.

Nellie notices right away. "Stop fidgeting," she says. "It'll only draw attention." I fix myself, sticking my hands in my pockets as we approach airport security. I duck underneath the lane separators while Nellie and Loni quickly zig-zag through the empty spaces. I reach the first lane, standing a ways back from the last person in line — Nellie and Loni catch up to me by the time there are only five people in front of us.

"Little girl," Loni says, huffing slightly. "You move too fast, man."

"Sorry," I say chuckling.

"Okay," Nellie says quietly, "here are your ticket and your passport — remember, your name is Kyra Wilkenson and I'm Vanessa Wilkenson. Loni's name is now Claudette Winston, and she's your great aunt. We're going to Jamaica for a funeral and intend to stay for family reasons — there's no need to say more than that. The more details you try to give, the more red flags they'll see. Keep to that story, and stay calm."

"Okay," I say. Even though she said to stay calm, I'm still anxious. A few airport security guards stand to the side, ushering flyers to available stations, and my armpits get pinpricks of sweat. I reach the front of the line, and look discreetly at the guard right in front of me. He looks disinterested and distant, probably wanting to be anywhere other than here — he looks at his watch several times in the span of just a few minutes, confirming my suspicions. When he ushers me to a station to the right, I do my best polite smile, but I can feel my face shaking. *C'mon girl, pull yourself together. You'll be fine. Well, actually, there's no guarantee you'll be fine — for all you know, you could be walking into a trap before you even get on the plane — but still,* chill out.

I put my backpack, phone, jacket, and hat in a tub — I reach to take my amulet off, reluctant to part with it, but knowing it will only be for a minute or two. The man in front of me walks through the metal detector with a shuffle, rubbing his face in fatigue as he waits for his bin to pass through screening. The guard at the screening station sticks his hand out, and I hand him my ticket and passport. I look at him as innocently as I can, even though inside I'm freaking out. I smooth my air down into the low bun, trying my best not to fidget. He looks at the photo on the passport, then at me, and nods, putting the ticket in the passport and handing them back to me. The guard motions me forward, and I walk towards him — I hold my breath as I walk through the metal detector, hunching slightly in. But he just nods, and I look back and see a green light at the top of the detector — I'm in the clear.

Nellie and Loni following behind me, going through screening quickly. We grab our bags and I put on my jacket and hat. Loni struggles to carry her paisley bag so I take it from her, giving her my backpack to carry. She smiles at me gratefully, and we head down the escalator towards the gates.

"Okay, we're at gate 52," Nellie says. "Michael and Ms. Dell should be at gate 61, and they should be close to boarding if they're not already on the plane."

"Okay, I'll call him when we get to our gate," I say.

"Good," she says, "but first let's get something to eat."

Grateful for the satisfaction of a full belly, I quicken my steps in search of a good place to eat. Loni chuckles as I look around, until I set my eyes on a small bistro shop; with sandwiches, salads, and soups listed on their menu. I make a beeline for the cash register, my stomach growling for me to hurry up. A small Polynesian woman sees me approaching, and greets me with a kind smile.

"Hello," she says, "welcome to Gaito's Bistro. What can I get for you?" Nellie and Loni come up behind me, looking at the menu with food on display.

"I," I drag out, skimming over the menu as quickly as I can, "will get a prosciutto and mozzarella sandwich, with an apple juice."

"Great," the cashier says, "and can I get a name for the order?"

I respond reflexively, "Jamila." I feel Nellie sharply pinch the skin on my elbow, and I realize my mistake. "Oh, sorry! No, I was thinking about someone else. The name's Kyra, sorry."

"No worries," the cashier responds with a laugh. As she taps the order on her screen, I look at Nellie. She glances pointedly at me, and then at a security camera on the wall above us. I have to be more careful — the Toubabs could be listening in, and that slip could've really ended us.

"Alright," the cashier says, "and what can I get for you ladies?"

Nellie and Loni make their orders — a turkey sandwich for Nellie and a spicy chicken burrito for Loni — and Nellie reaches into her tote bag for a wad of cash. Nellie took out the money from the safe in our office, and we left our bank cards in our wallets in the glove compartment of our car. It's cash only from now on.

After the cashier takes our orders, we sit down at one of the tables. I plop Loni's bag on the floor, but she kisses her teeth and puts it on a chair.

"Don't put my bag on the floor, child," she protests. "Didn't yuh motha ever tell yuh not to put yuh bags on di floor?"

"Yeah," I say with a smirk, "so that I don't lose money. It's just an old wives' tale, Loni, it's not real."

She guffaws, occupying herself with rearranging the contents in her bag. She takes her glasses off and places them in an inside pocket of the bag. The cashier brings our sandwiches on a tray, and we thank her with smiles. I open the wrapping and dive in, barely taking a second to breathe. Nellie and Loni nurse their sandwiches, looking at me with side-eyes as I wolf down my sandwich. They're still on their second half and I've finished mine and halfway my bottle of juice. Loni looks at me with a smirk and a raised eyebrow, and I happily drink away.

I feel my phone vibrate in my pocket, and see Michael's name pop up on the screen. I reach for my backpack beside Loni and put my earphones in my ears before answering the call.

"Hey," I say quietly.

"Hey," Michael says, his voice tinny in the earbuds. "Did you guys get through?"

"Yeah, we're just grabbing something to eat before heading to the gate." Nellie looks at me, mouthing *Michael* with a questioning look. I nod in reply, and she nods back.

I continue, "Where are you guys now?"

"We're just about to board. Nana complained that she should be one of the first to board since she's elderly."

I laugh, saying, "She's doing the most?"

"The absolute most," he says laughing. "She even tried to get one of those carts to drive us to the gate — I had to remind her that we're not actually going on vacation. I think she's trying to act like it is — maybe she thinks it's better than seeing it for what it really is."

"Let her be," I say. "As long as she doesn't say anything about us, then she can keep on thinking whatever if it'll keep her calm."

"How are you feeling?" Michael asks.

"Uh, nervous," I say. "I went through the metal detector feeling like I was going on death row."

Michael laughs. "Yeah, you should've seen me at the front counter checking in — my pit stains were as big as saucers."

"Ew," I laugh. I feel my bladder calling, and look for the nearest bathroom. "Hey, I gotta go, nature's calling. Talk to Nellie."

I hand the earphones to Nellie and she starts talking to Michael, telling him what to do when he lands in Jamaica. I walk to the nearest bathroom, just down the hall. Once inside, I pass a woman touching up her makeup in the mirror, and head for the nearest stall. Pee drippings on the seat and toilet paper clumped up in the toilet make me stop, and I cover my mouth as I walk to the next stall. Clean enough to pass the test, I pull down my pants and squat over the seat. I sigh with relief as I empty my bladder

— flushing and heading to the sink to wash my hands, smiling at the woman who's still fixing up herself. She's pretty; green eyes, shiny blonde hair to her shoulders, and dark red lipstick. She looks to be about in her late 30s, but who really knows when you have makeup on? She's wearing a nice black suit with black high heels — she puts her tiny makeup bag back in her purse, an expensive-looking one with a faint snakeskin print. She stands tall and straight, with her shoulders back but with a grace that you just develop with age. She looks like a boss — props to her.

"Vacation?" she asks.

"Yes," I reply, "and to visit some family."

"Oh, somewhere warm I hope," she says with a smile.

I smile back, saying, "Thankfully, yes."

"Lucky you! Get to escape this cold weather — I have to go to dreary old England."

"That doesn't sound too bad," I say, drying my hands. "England is beautiful; great food, diverse cultures, lots of tourist spots."

"Yes," she says, "but I'm going for work — and unfortunately, that doesn't leave you a lot of time to sightsee. Not to mention London is constantly raining and cold, regardless of the season, so no sunshine and blue skies for me."

"Oh man," I say sympathetically. "Well, maybe this'll be different. You could see something new you haven't seen before."

"Or meet someone new," she says coyly.

"Well," I joke, "with that lipstick I don't doubt that." She laughs heartily, throwing her head back so I can see her straight teeth.

"You're funny," she says. "I can only imagine all the boys must be after you."

"Ha," I laugh sarcastically. "You can say that — but I'd much rather they just leave me alone."

"I know what you mean," she says, rolling her eyes. But really, she doesn't. I'm not talking about adolescent boys — but how would she know that I'm talking about a cult of Toubabs literally chasing me?

"Well," she says, "sometimes the one that's really chasing you is the one who really wants to stick around. Someone wouldn't waste all that time if they didn't want some of your time."

"Oh, I don't doubt that," I reply quietly. "But my time is mine, and I'd rather use it for myself and not anyone else."

She looks at me with an expressionless look, shrugging and saying,

"Okay. Well, don't let them chase too long — you're a pretty girl, and I can tell you're smart and talented. Whoever's been chasing you would be lucky to have you."

"Thanks," I say with a smile. We walk out of the bathroom then turn to each other.

"Well, I'm this way," she says, pointing behind me.

"I'm that way," I say, pointing behind her.

"Well it was nice to meet you," she says, reaching to shake my hand. "I hope you don't mind — with everything that's changed, I'm not sure who still shakes hands these days."

"I don't mind," I say, shaking her hand. She has a solid grip, with soft, warm hands.

"I'm sorry, I didn't get your name," she says.

"My name is J... Kyra."

"Your name is Jkyra?"

"No," I say laughing, "no, just Kyra."

"Well, nice to meet you Kyra, my name's Atalanta." I look at her surprised, and she holds her hand up with a smile. "I know, it's different. What can I say, my mother was obsessed with Greek mythology."

"I am too," I say excitedly.

"You look like the type," she says with a smile. "You two have that in common." She moves to leave, but hesitates. It looks like she wants to say something else.

"What?" I ask.

"Oh, it's nothing," she says nonchalantly. "I just, I don't know, you don't seem like a Kyra to me."

"Really?" I ask, my heart rate quickening.

"Yeah, I don't know," she says shrugging. "That name just... doesn't do you justice." She smiles sweetly, and I smile back — she rests her hand on my arm. "Have a good flight," she says.

"You too," I say. She smiles and walks to her gate, a sure and confident walk. A man looks at her as she walks past him, taken with her beauty. I hope to have that grace one day — but for now, I just need to worry about staying alive and safe. I head back to the bistro, and see Loni and Nellie chatting.

"There you are," Nellie says. "You were in there for a while, I was about to send help."

I chuckle, grabbing Loni's bag. "No, no need for that," I say. "I was just talking with a woman in the bathroom."

"Who?" Loni asks.

"Just some businesswoman fixing up her makeup, we were just talking about random stuff."

"J, you can't just be talking to strangers right now," Nellie says. "Especially when we're not around. The Toubabs could be posing as anybody."

"No, she was nice," I counter. "It was really nothing, just small talk about her work trip and boy stuff."

"She could just be getting a feel for you, J — stalling, waiting for someone to move in," Nellie says, looking around discreetly. Loni puts her glasses back on, and moves to put the tray back on the front counter.

"Come," Loni says, "let's go to di gate. We'll be boardin' soon anyways. You aave tuh be more careful, baby girl."

"I'm sorry," I say quietly. "I didn't think it was a big deal. She didn't seem like a threat to me."

"Neither did Churchill at first," Loni says. At that, I shut up, and we quietly walk towards gate 52. I see more people lined up at the security checkpoint as we walk past, and the sun slowly peeking over the horizon through the glass window to our left.

"Michael's plane took off shortly after you left," Nellie says, giving me my earphones back. "They'll be waiting for us by the exit — if our flight's on time, we should get there 45 minutes after they land. If anything happens, and we don't get there within an hour and a half, I gave him directions to a restaurant that a family friend works at. He'll give them a meal and put them up for a night until we can get there."

"Do you think something will happen before we get there?" I ask. Nellie looks at me hesitantly, not answering right away.

"I don't know, Mama. Hopefully not."

That doesn't put me at ease, but Nellie's not one to be dishonest. My shoes squeak on the shiny floor, and the cold of the airport starts to settle in my skin. The loudspeaker sounds, calling for so-and-so to make it to their gate to make their flight, and a baby crying in the distance blares in my ears. Everything seems more heightened, and I don't know if it's because I'm tired, nervous, or what. I try to not focus on all of these different sounds assaulting my senses, and focus on the sky. The glass reflects dozens of planes waiting for passengers, with employees hauling carts with luggage to-and-fro. A gate opens its doors to let out a slew of passengers, and next to that gate is gate 52.

I find three empty seats next to each other and plop down, closing my eyes and cocking my head to rest on the seat.

"We're almost there," Loni says, sitting beside me. I look at the screen behind the station agent — another three minutes to boarding time. Nellie chooses to sit across from us, leaning forward and resting her arms on her knees. I pointedly look at Loni as I put her bag on the seat beside me, and she purses her lips exaggeratedly in reply. We sit there quietly — Loni and I looking at Nellie, and Nellie looking at us. We all exchange silent looks — in them lie our inquiry of the unknown, the uncertainty of our futures, the unreliability of our safety. And our fear. I know we all feel fear. Even though Loni has been doing this for years, and Nellie's solid as a rock, this is scary.

"You know the silver lining with all of this?" I ask.

"What's that?" Nellie asks.

"I'm finally getting to visit Jamaica," I say with a small smile. "See the beaches, go to the market, maybe even see Grandma's grave."

"Yeah," Nellie says with a small smile. "That would be nice. I've always wanted to bring you back home, but life caught up and one thing led to another, and before I knew it, there was barely any money and even less time."

"I know," I say. "And even though it's not the most ideal motives, I'm glad that I'll get to finally see it for myself."

"I'm glad I'll finally get tuh aave KFC," Loni says. "*Di good one.*"

We laugh, and Nellie's face turns reminiscent. "I can't wait for the festival," she says. "And fried fish on the beach. And the beach, oh! I miss the beach."

"You don't know dis," Loni says to me, "but your aunty was just as good a swimma as she was a runna. She was like a fish, she was so good; she practically lived in the water."

"Really?" I ask Nellie, and she nods with a small smile. "Well, why did you stop swimming? There's a community pool right by your hospital, you could've used it on your lunch break or something."

"Oh, I never took to community pools," she says with a grimace. "The chlorine always irritated my skin, and I just never trusted if they were clean. A salt water ocean is different from a small pool that dozens of people have been in."

I hum, agreeing with her, and thinking about what I can't wait for in Jamaica. "I want to try sugar cane," I say. Loni laughs, and I smile. "Mom used to tell me how she'd snack on it on her walk home, and it was better than any candy snack here in Canada."

"She was right," Nellie says. "If Mama was lucky enough, she'd get some sweet sugar cane to sell with some other things by the big tree in front of our house, and we'd sneak a cane and share it on our way to and from school."

"What kind of things?"

"Oh everything," Nellie says with a smile. "Mangoes, sugar cane, spices and herbs, anything she could get her hands on. She'd get them super cheap from the market or a friend and mark up the price — it was better than paying a pretty penny on the bus to the market in the city."

"Well, the way Mom described it, it sounds delicious," I say. "That's what I'm looking forward to."

"That's all?" Loni asks jokingly.

"No, that's not it," I reply cheekily. "But, it's the first thing that comes to mind. I want to try all the food, go to as many beaches as much as I can —"

"I'm so happy that you want to take in as much as you can," Nellie interrupts, "but remember that we're not going for fun. We're hiding out, J. We have to stay low, not draw too much attention to ourselves. If there's time for the fun stuff, then we will definitely do it — but I just don't want you thinking that it'll be a guarantee."

"Yeah," I say quietly. "I know." Nellie nods, giving me a sympathetic look for a second, but then it goes away.

The station agent calls for the first class flyers and preferred flyers to board — preparing myself for our section, I get my boarding pass and passport ready in my hand, and slide my backpack strap over my shoulder. After a few minutes, he calls for families and passengers with wheelchairs to board; knowing we're next, we stand up and wait. It's taking a while, as mothers and fathers trying to wrangle their children, and employees taking care of the elderly passengers. All the passengers are getting a mask before entering the plane, and their boarding passes are being scanned to make sure they have the most recent Coronavirus vaccine. Finally, our zone gets called, and we merge in line. One passenger is taking a while as his vaccine barcode isn't registering in the system — he finally lifts his sleeve and shows the deep divot below his shoulder, and the station agent thanks him and lets him through.

We finally reach the counter — Nellie and Loni go first, and I follow behind them. I hand the station agent my passport, with the ticket tucked into the spine. He looks at my passport, then to me, and scans the barcode on my ticket. The scanner beeps and the light turns green — he smiles and hands me my ticket, motioning to the door.

"Enjoy your flight," he says.

"Thank you," I say, exhaling in relief. I fix the strap on my shoulder and balance my weight as I carry Loni's bag in my left hand. We walk down the ramp and shuffle as we come closer to the plane door. Flight attendants with trained smiles welcome us into the plane, and we make our way to our seats. Once towards the back of the plane, we find our seats. Luckily, Nellie and I were able to get seats together, but Loni's two rows ahead of us on the other side. I put her paisley bag in the overhead compartment before bidding her farewell, and shuffle into my window seat. I put my backpack under the seat in front of me, and Nellie does the same with her tote bag as she sits beside me. An older man with furry eyebrows sits beside Nellie — we say hello, and he nods emphatically in response. I sigh deeply, leaning my head on the seat. Nellie looks at me, a small knowing smile on her lips.

"We're almost there," she says. "Four more hours 'til sunshine and blue skies and reggae music."

"Yeah," I say. "Then what?"

She takes a deep breath, shaking her head. "I don't know, Mama. I guess we'll have to find out."

I nod slightly before looking out the window. I'd much rather occupy my time with the burgeoning sun. I put my phone on airplane mode and connect to my music streaming app. Neo-soul plays through my earphones as I stick them in my ears, and I lean my head on the window. The flight attendants go through their routine, demonstrating the safety exits and procedures in case of a crash, and after another ten minutes, the passengers are settled and the pilot closes the door. I look outside to the ground — airport employees back away from the plane, and head to another to load luggage underneath. Their bright orange vests are sharp against the dark pavement, and the yellow stripes glow as the sunlight glints against them. I look to the terminal through the window, and the people waiting for their planes are now like tiny dolls. A figure walks to the glass and looks at the planes, his hands in his pockets. I look longer, and my stomach immediately sinks. This tall figure, dressed in black, is still. And familiar. I sit up, unable to look away, as I try to squint to see if this figure is who I think it is. The figure just stands there, unmoving — and I know, from a place deep within my soul, that this figure is looking at me. The plane starts to pull away, and I stare longer as my stomach twists into a knot, until he disappears from my sight. I sit in my seat sick to my stomach, clutching the armrests with a vice-like grip.

"Hey, you okay?" Nellie asks.

"Yeah," I say shakily. "Just thought I saw something. It's probably nothing."

She nods and closes her eyes, leaning her head back. I shakily reach for my seat belt and buckle myself up — I tighten it in my unease, but loosen it to take the pressure off my unsettled stomach. The plane makes it to an empty lane, and quickly accelerates. I jolt back from the force, and struggle to breathe as the plane shakes violently. My stomach sinks as the plane lifts in the air, that brief feeling of weightlessness making my heart stop. We make a higher incline until the plane straightens out, but my grip remains tight on the armrest, as fear keeps its grip on my heart.

CPSIA information can be obtained
at www.ICGtesting.com
Printed in the USA
BVHW041348190720
583720BV00006B/29

9 781532 099601